Erastus Ranney Ellis

Biographical Sketches of Richard Ellis

The First Settler of Ashfield, Mass., and His Descendants

Erastus Ranney Ellis

Biographical Sketches of Richard Ellis
The First Settler of Ashfield, Mass., and His Descendants

ISBN/EAN: 9783337014964

Printed in Europe, USA, Canada, Australia, Japan

Cover: Foto ©Raphael Reischuk / pixelio.de

More available books at **www.hansebooks.com**

DEA. DIMICK ELLIS.
(72)

Biographical Sketches

—OF—

RICHARD ELLIS

THE FIRST SETTLER OF ASHFIELD, MASS.,

—AND—

His Descendants.

COMPILED AND ARRANGED BY

E. R. ELLIS, M. D.
(751.)

"A people who have no interest in the achievements of remote ancestors are not likely to accomplish anything worthy of the recollection of their descendants."—MACAULEY.

"There is a tendency, even in this democratic America, to trace our conspicuous men back to a noble ancestry, but a sound mind, in a sound body, is all that modern civilization demands, and these, inherited from honored parents with early lessons of frugality, virtue and manliness, are really worth more than any patent of nobility."—GEN. W. T. SHERMAN.

———————

DETROIT, MICH:

WM. GRAHAM PRINTING CO.

1888.

PREFACE.

There is a saying that the "first shall be last, and the last first." If this saying has any relation to the making of books it means that the first few pages of a book are often the last to be written and printed; so with these two pages, which enables the writer, in concluding his work, to make a few remarks thereon.

Some four years ago, for reasons which are stated on page 115, he began tracing out the descendants of Richard Ellis, of Ashfield, Massachusetts, his first ancestor in this country. It was supposed, at that time, that this work could be accomplished in a few months, and the printing of the same, which would probably be limited to a hundred pages, or thereabouts, be completed in a year at most. The unexpected delay has arisen from the tardiness of many in responding to inquiries, the greatly extended nature of the work over what was expected at the outset, and the necessary occupation of the writer in his daily pursuit.

As but five hundred copies of the book are printed, and as these are expected to go only to relatives and those who may have a personal interest therein, the writer will not make any extended apology for inflicting upon mankind another book, of which they are now greatly overrun.

It is proper in this connection to mention a few of those to whom the reader and writer are under special obligations for information furnished, and without which the work would have been far more imperfect than it now is. Of these Rev. Wm. L.

Chaffin, pastor of the Unitarian church of Easton, Massachusetts, George G. Withington, Esq., clerk of Easton, the clerk of Sunderland, Massachusetts, Messrs. Henry S. Ranney, Frederick G. Howes and George Bassett, of Ashfield, and Hugh B. Miller, of Colerain, Massachusetts, deserve special mention.

In the printing and binding of the book (as less than one hundred copies were subscribed for) considerable advance payment was necessary, which, to the amount of nearly one thousand dollars, has been most kindly and generously advanced by Messrs. George W. Ellis, of Philadelphia; Wilbur D. Ellis and Dr. John Ellis, of New York City, without which the work could not have been undertaken.

The writer has had a personal meeting with but few of the more distant relatives mentioned in this volume, but through extended correspondence with them he has come to have a greater seeming nearness of the ties of relationship and a very kindly feeling withal, which with the satisfaction he hopes they may derive from his work, will serve as compensation for his labor.

In conclusion, he desires to convey his thanks to all those who have aided him, and also express the hope that, as other generations come, successors may be found who will take up his work and follow it down through succeeding generations.

While family traits and traditions are of no general interest, they should be of value to those who are more directly involved, especially if attended with a constant, unwearied effort and aspiration to improve upon the moral, physical and intellectual heritage of their progenitors.

E. R. E.

DETROIT, MICH., May, 1888.

Richard Ellis,

OF ASHFIELD,* MASS.

ICHARD ELLIS, the subject of this sketch,.was, according to his own account, born in Dublin, Ireland, August 16th, 1704. His father was a native of Wales, England, and his mother may have been a Welsh or Irish woman.

Richard said that his father was an officer in one of the many armed forces which at that time were numerous throughout the British dominions. Just at what time his father went to Ireland does not appear from any record which is now accessible.

Richard's youth was spent in Dublin, and he mentioned having traveled in other portions of Ireland. This unhappy country then, as now, was the scene of much disorder. The strife was mostly between Catholics and Protestants, or those in favor of or against whoever happened to occupy the throne. Richard said that it was a common occurence, seemingly enjoyed as a pastime, for the officers of the army to order, in the morning, before breakfast, a squad of prisoners "drawn in quarters," hanged or shot. Such scenes were made public spectacles, and were said to give the officers a relish for their meals.

When Richard was thirteen years of age, his father having died, his mother undertook to send him to Virginia where he had an uncle with whom she expected he would find a home. With this view she paid for him a cabin

---

* See Note 1 of the *Appendix*, where will be found a historical sketch of Ashfield from its first settlement, including some items never before published.

passage to this country, but the captain of the vessel vio-
lated his trust, and landing at a sea-port in Massachusetts,
he, in accordance with a custom then somewhat prevalent,
sold the boy, or his services, until he became of age,
ostensibly to pay for his passage.*

Richard said that he became a member of the family of
a miller who was a very stern man, and often harsh with
his own children, consisting of several daughters, yet to
him he always showed the utmost consideration and kindness.† Of his mistress he always spoke highly, especially
of her efforts for his mental and moral improvement. He
had made some progress in education in Dublin, but of
this he said nothing, thinking thereby that his new
teacher would give him more attention. On several
occasions he excited her surprise by pronouncing difficult
words in advance of her instructions.

After Richard attained his majority, he went to Easton,
Bristol county, Mass., where in 1728 he married Jane
Phillips, daughter of Capt. John Phillips, and sister of Thos.
Phillips, who afterwards was the second settler in Ashfield. Richard lived in Easton until about 1740, when
he removed to Deerfield in the same State. Six of his
children were born in Easton, and one or more in Deerfield. Altogether he had nine children, but one—Benjamin
—died at two months of age.

Richard's father-in-law, Capt. John Phillips of Easton,
was one of the soldiers in the expedition against Quebec
in 1690, and consequently was among those who became
entitled to "rights" of land mentioned in another part of
this work. This fact probably was what led Richard
and family, and his brother-in-law, Thomas Phillips, to
settle in Ashfield, (then called Huntstown,) which he,
Richard, did about 1745. (Richard's son John, born in
Deerfield, 1742, said his father removed to Ashfield when
he was three years of age.) Ashfield was then a wil-

---

* For a slightly different version of this, see *Appendix*, Note 2.

† See *Appendix*, Note 3.

derness and Richard was the *first settler.** The locality where he selected his "right" and made his home is about one and one-half miles north-east of what is now known as Ashfield Plain, and is in the north-east part of the township. At this point two roads cross at right angles, and Richard's house and farm was on the south-east corner where, forty years ago, Hiram Belding, Esq.,† lived, and where Mr. Leonard D. Lanfair now resides. Richard's house was about six rods south easterly from Mr. Lanfair's home. One-half mile, or less, west of this point is Bellow's Hill, and eighty rods north, Bear river runs from west to east. Opposite Richard's house on the north side of the road, and about forty rods east, is an ancient burying ground where lie the earthly remains of Richard Ellis and wife and several of their descendants.

Of the scenes and incidents among the pioneers of this rough and rugged country, much has come down by tradition to the present time. The country was mountainous, being on the eastern slope of the Hoosac range. The roads consisted mostly of trails and cow-paths; the snows were deep and the winters most rigorous. Added to all the other obstacles which the early settlers had to encounter, was the greatest of all, the danger from the tomahawk and scalping-knife of the Indians. On one occasion Richard was alarmed by the Indians while in his sugar-bush, and, it is said, he made quick time to a place of safety with his five-pail kettle on his back.

Richard related that, not unfrequently, messengers would ride swiftly through the country giving warning to the inhabitants that the Indians were coming down upon them. At such times the women and children would be quickly placed on pack-horses and started for the old fort at Deerfield, some ten or twelve miles easterly from the Ellis settlement. Then the men and boys would

* There is some evidence that Richard began his settlement in Ashfield one or two years earlier than this date, while his family was yet in Deerfield. See *Appendix*, Note 1.

† Hiram Belding was the father of "Belding Brothers," the most extensive manufacturers of sewing silk in this country. See *Appendix*.

rally with their guns and drive back the savage foes. These Indians were from New York and Canada, and were very jealous of the encroachments of the white man. The old Fort at Deerfield was constructed in early times, as a defense against the Indians, and did good service for more than a century.

Few of this generation can realize the privations and dangers encountered by the heroic men and women who pushed their way into these wilderness regions. Nearly all the conveniences of modern life were unknown among them. Simple and rude were all their implements. Going to church, to town, to mill, or on a neighborhood visit, was either on foot or horseback. Sometimes, in the spring of the year, from backwardness of the season, provisions became exhausted, and some of the inhabitants were obliged, it was said, to subsist for a time on the buds and tender leaves of basswood trees until crops could be grown. Not all even had salt for such a repast as this, and those who had were regarded as quite fortunate. But in spite of all their privations, they grew up a most vigorous race of men and women, whose posterity have gone out and made a creditable mark on all the institutions of this country; and the wealth of character developed by these sturdy men and women, has been a rich inheritance for their children. No privations or obstacles seemed to daunt them, and in some ways unnecessary exposures were sought and encouraged as evidences of manly strength and in the belief that their systems were improved thereby. It is related that with some it was a lifetime custom, even in mid-winter, to jump out of bed in the morning, and without dressing, rush out to the wood pile, kick off the snow, and gather wood and kindling for the morning fire. They fancied that by such means their constitutions were invigorated; and certain it is that many of them lived to a great age.*

---

* The subject of this sketch was a good example of the sturdy race from which he sprung. Plutarch, a Roman historian of the first century, says "The ancient Britons were so habitually regular and temperate that they only began to grow old at one hundred and twenty years."

Richard Ellis was a true and loyal subject of the King of England, and in 1754 when war broke out between England and France and extended to this country, and known as the "French and Indian War," Richard was for about three years an officer in the commissary department of the English or Colonial service in New England and New York. Richard Ellis, it is said, was a man of strong will and remarkable memory; his physical vigor and mental powers were retained in a high degree up to the last years of his life. His grandson, Dimick Ellis, who was born in Ashfield in 1776, was familiar with Richard during the last twenty years of his life, and from him the writer (his grandson) obtained most of the items for this sketch. About the year 1764, Richard kept a country store and ashery in the north-east part of Colerain, a town about 15 miles in a north-easterly direction from Ashfield. His ledger or book of accounts covering the period from 1764 to about 1777, together with some correspondence had with him and others before and during the great Revolution, are now in possession of his great grandson, Mr. Lewis Ellis, of Belding, Mich. These books are quite a curiosity at this late day and give one quite an insight into what constituted articles of consumption in those times.* In them are found the names of nearly two hundred persons who were residents at that time, of Colerain and adjoining towns. Rum and tobacco were articles then, as now, of too frequent use, judging from the charges in these books. It is probable that this mercantile experience of Richard's was not a financial success, which may be accounted for from the fact that, according to his books, the largest part of pay for his goods he took in *ashes*, which he converted into pot and pearlash in his ashery.

It also appears that Richard engaged in the milling business, in company with Mr. Chileab Smith, Sr., who was the third settler in Ashfield. Their mill was the first

* For specimens of these accounts, see *Appendix*.

one built in that section, and was located on Bear river, about one hundred rods north of Richard's house, and about twenty rods east of the bridge on the roadway running north toward "Baptist Corners," as the neighborhood where Mr. Smith lived was called. This grist mill was a very primitive structure, as were all similar mills in those times. The grinding stones were run by water power, but the bolting and elevating was done by hand or manual labor.

In later years this mill came into the ownership of Richard's son Lieut. John Ellis and one of the Smiths, son of Chileab Smith,* who conducted it for a number of years. It would seem that the milling business was hereditary among Richard Ellis' descendants. Besides Lieut. John, Richard's youngest son Caleb, who settled at Ellisburg, Jefferson County, New York, about 1795, built mills there.

Also Richard's grandsons (sons of Reuben), Benjamin and Richard, and Benjamin's sons, Stephen, Moses and Benjamin Jr., were millers nearly all their lives. The latter built and operated grist and saw-mills, in New York, Pennsylvania, Ohio and Indiana, as do several of their descendants down to the present time.

About the year 1760 Richard's wife, Jane Phillips, died, and some twelve years afterwards he married Mary, widow of John Henry† of Deerfield, a town adjoining Colerain where he then lived, and had his store and ashery. Some years later, probably during the period of the Revolution, Richard returned to Ashfield, where he spent the remainder of his days with his son John and grandsons Benjamin, Richard and David Ellis (sons of Reuben), and grand-daughter Jemima Smith Annable, wife of Lieut. Edward Annable of Ashfield.

That Richard Ellis' father was Welsh admits of no doubt, for besides Richard's own statement to that effect most of his descendants resemble that people and some

---

* This was Chileab Smith, Jr., who was born in 1742, and died in Ashfield, in 1843.
† For an account of Mrs. Henry and her family, see *Appendix*, Note 4.

of them show marked peculiarities of the Welsh race down to the sixth generation.* This is not surprising, for it is well known that peculiarities or traits of character are often very enduring. Strongly develoved traits in a father will often show through many generations.

This is seen well illustrated in the Jews, who although scattered through different countries and subject to many adverse influences retain their early marks of character and features to the present day.

Of Richard Ellis' religious proclivities the writer knows little more than that he was an ardent Protestant, and it is fair to surmise that the ideas of religious liberty which brought the pilgrims to this country fully impressed him as a youth and extended to his manhood as well as through his entire life. Among the first settlers in Ashfield and even in the same neighborhood where Richard made a settlement, the Baptists were the first to organize their church and erect a meeting house, and from that time to the present that denomination has held a leading part in the religious sentiment of that part of the town of Ashfield. Three-fourths of a mile north of Richard's house was located the meeting house of this sect, and from that time to this that locality has been known as "Baptist Corners." The first minister located there was Rev. Ebenezer Smith, who married, in 1756, Remember, the second daughter of Richard Ellis.

Richard died Oct. 7, 1797, in his 94th year, at the house of his grandson Richard, the fourth son of Reuben Ellis. This Richard was born 1760 in Ashfield, and soon after his grandfather's death moved to the northern part of Pennsylvania, where he engaged in milling and founded the town of Ellisburg, Potter Co., where he died in 1841. His daughter Lucretia, who was born in 1806, and who is now the wife of Rev. John Stipp, a Presbyterian minister of Scio, Oregon, gives the following account of the last days of Richard Ellis, the subject of this sketch. The letter is dated Scio, May 26, 1884:

*The writer of this sketch was once asked "how long he had been over," by a Welshman, who said that he strongly resembled Ellises in Wales whom he knew.

"I do not know how old my great grandfather was when he came to live with my father in Ashfield, but I have heard my father say that he was very spry and at 80 years of age could jump upon a horse from the ground as easily as a boy. He always appeared well; the night before he died he called my father, at least father thought so, but when he went to him he said he had not called him. The second time likewise he thought he heard him call, but was again mistaken but at the third time my great grandfather said. 'Well, go to bed, child, it is a token of my death, I have not called you?' He died in the morning about nine o'clock apparently without pain."

[For an account of the Ellises of the old country, as well as some in this country not related to Richard Ellis, see *Appendix*.]

Jane* Phillips.

JANE PHILLIPS, who married Richard Ellis in Easton, Mass., in 1728, was born July 1, 1709. Her parents were Capt. John Phillips and Elizabeth Drake, his wife, and her grandparents (on her father's side), were Richard and Elizabeth (Packer) Phillips of Weymouth, near Boston, and Richard was a son of Nicholas Phillips.

Jane Phillips' sister and brothers were as follows : Experience, born 1699; Samuel, 1702; Joshua, 1704; Caleb, 1707; Thomas, 1712; Richard, 1713.

It does not appear whether Jane Phillips was born in Easton or Weymouth, but more probably the latter place.

It is said that she was a good woman and devoted to her family. She died in Ashfield about 1760. The Phillips family, of which she was a member, were numerous and influential in Easton and in Ashfield. For a more full account of them see *Appendix*.

* In the town records of Easton and of Capt. Phillips' family, this name is written Jane, Jean and Joan.

GENEALOGICAL RECORD

OF

𝕽𝖎𝖈𝖍𝖆𝖗𝖉 𝖆𝖓𝖉 𝕵𝖆𝖓𝖊 𝕰𝖑𝖑𝖎𝖘

AND THEIR DESCENDANTS.

Following this Record there will be Personal Sketches of every one mentioned herein, so far as the same can be obtained. The numbers at the head of each name in the Record refer to the same number and person in the Sketches.

FIRST GENERATION.

(1.) RICHARD ELLIS................Born, 1704; Died, 1797

(2.) JANE PHILLIPS.... ... . " 1709; " *1760

Married in Easton, Mass., in 1728.

SECOND GENERATION.

CHILDREN OF RICHARD AND JANE ELLIS.

4.	REUBEN ELLIS			Born,	1728;	Died,	1786
6.	BENJAMIN	"		"	1730;	"	1730
7.	MARY	"		"	1732;	"	....
9.	REMEMBER	"		"	1735;	"	1795
11.	JANE	"		"	1737;	"	1832
13.	MATTHEW	"		"	1739;	"	....
15.	JOHN	"		"	1742;	"	1827
17.	HANNAH	"		"	1750;	"	1839
19.	CALEB	"		"	1754;	"	1813

The first six of these children were born in Easton. The record is found in the handwriting of Mrs. Ellis' father (Capt. John Phillips), who was town clerk. He adds to the above the following : "John Ellis, son of Richard Ellis of Huntstown, born of his wife Jean in Deerfield." Hannah was probably born in Huntstown, (afterwards Ashfield,) as her parents resided there at that time. Caleb may have been born there, or elsewhere, as it was about this time that the French and Indian war began, when all the settlers left Huntstown, and went to the older settlements east and south for three years. See *Appendix*, Note 1.

---

* Names or dates with this mark (*) may not be *exactly*, but are very nearly, correct.

THIRD GENERATION.

(4) **REUBEN ELLIS**.......... .. ..Born, 1728; Died, 1786
(5) **MEHITABLE SCOTT**............ .Born, 1722; Died, 1804
Married in Sunderland, Mass., in 1749.

THEIR CHILDREN.

21. MARTHA	ELLIS		Born,	1750;	Died,	1832
22. BENJAMIN	"		"	1751;	"	1834
25. REUBEN	"		"	1752;	"	183-
26. JONATHAN	"		"	1754;	"	1812
28. SUBMIT	"		"	1756;	"	1834
29. RICHARD	"		"	1760;	"	1841
32. DAVID	"		"	1763;	"	1843

The first two of the above children were born in Sunderland, and the others in Ashfield.

(7) **MARY ELLIS**............... ......Born, 1732.
No report from her or her descendants, if she had any.

(9) **REMEMBER ELLIS**..............Born, 1735; Died, 1795
(10) **Rev. EBENEZER SMITH**...... " 1734; " 1824
Married in Deerfield, in 1756.

THEIR CHILDREN—All born in Ashfield.

34. IRENE	SMITH		Born,	1757;	Died,	1834
36. PRESERVED	"		"	1759;	"	1834
38. JEMIMA	"		"	1761;	"	1835
40. RHODA	"		"	1762;	"	1837
42. EBENEZER, jr.	"		"	1766;	"	1855
44. OBED	"		"	1770;	"	1828
46. RICHARD	"		"	1774;	"	1800

(11) **JANE ELLIS**.... ....Born, 1737; Died, 1832
(12) **JOHN PHILLIPS**.................. 1734; " 1805
Married in Easton, Mass., about 1759.

THEIR CHILDREN—All born in Easton.

47. JOHN	PHILLIPS, JR.		Born,	1761;	Died,	1841
49. MOLLY	"		"	1763;	"	1831
51. ENOS	"		"	1765;	"	....
53. PERCIS (a son)	"		"	1767;	"	1829
55. HANNAH	"		"	1770;	"	1856
57. MARCY	"		"	1773;	"	1832
59. PHEBE	"		"	1777;	"	1863
61. SALLY	"		"	1780;	"	1862

(13) **MATTHEW ELLIS**.... .... Born, 1739.
No report from him or his descendants, if he had any.

(15) JOHN ELLIS ... ...Born, 1742; Died, 1827
(16) MOLLY DIMICK .... " 1738; " 1827
Married in Ashfield, in 1763.
THEIR CHILDREN—All born in Ashfield.

63.	Hannah Ellis.. ....Born,	1764;	Died,	1839
65.	Dimick " .... "	1766;	"	1773
66.	Jane " .... "	1769;	"	1812
68.	John, Jr. " .... "	1771;	"	1848
70.	Edward " .... "	1773;	"	1801
72.	Dimick " .... "	1776;	"	1857
75.	Sylvia " .... "	1779;	" *1831

(17) HANNAH ELLIS ....Born, 1750; Died, 1839
(18) JAMES FULTON.. .... " 1749; " 1834
Married in Ashfield or Colerain, Mass.
THEIR CHILDREN—All born in Colerain.

77.	Robert Fulton...........................Born,	1773;	Died,	....
79.	James, Jr. " .... "	1775;	"	1838
80.	Caleb " .... "	1777;	"	1863
81.	David " .... "	1779;	"	....
83.	Lucretia " .... "	1782;	"	1843
85.	Daniel " .... "	1784;	"	*1865
87.	Elijah " .... "	1788;	"	1829
89.	Nathan " .... "	1790;	"	1844
91.	Jesse " .... "	1792;	"	1834
95.	Sarah " .... "	1797;	"	1872

19 CALEB ELLIS....................Born, 1754; Died, 1813
(20) MARY CROUCH................. . " 1757 " 1813
Married about 1779.

THEIR CHILDREN—Born, some in Central New York and some at Ellisburg, Jefferson
County, N. Y.

97.	Daniel Ellis.... ....:......Born,	1780;	Died,	1862
99.	Hannah " ....♦...... "	1782;	"	....
101.	John " .... "	1784;	"	1847
105.	Jane " .... "	1786;	"	1849
108.	Thomas " ..,. .... "	1788;	"	1877
111.	Squire " .... "	1790;	"	1813
112.	James " .... "	1792;	"	1823
115.	Robert " .... "	1794;	"	1863
118.	Polly " .... "	1796;	"	young
118.	Sally " .... "	1798;	"	"
118.	Betsey " ... . "	1800;	"	"

* Names or dates with this mark (*) may not be exactly, but are very nearly, correct.

FOURTH GENERATION.

(22) BENJAMIN ELLIS..... ....Born, 1751; Died, 1834
(23) RUTH PIKE........................ " ... ; "

Married in Ashfield, March 15, 1774.

OF THEIR CHILDREN—Stephen and Lurenca were born in Ashfield, the others
probably in Deerfield.

119. STEPHEN	ELLIS ....Born,	1775;	Died,	183–
121. LURENCA	"	"	1777;	"	1853
123. MOSES	"	"	1780;	"	1849
125. DANIEL	"	"	... ;	"	1812
126. BENJAMIN	" Jr............................	"	1784;	"	1859
128. REUBEN	"	"	1786;	"	1845
130. MEHITABLE	"	"	....;	"	....
132. CHELOMETH	"	"	....;	"	....

---

(26) JONATHAN ELLIS................Born, 1754; Died, 1812
(27) LOIS ALLIS........................ " ... ; " 1840

Married in Ashfield, March, 1799.

In this family there were eight children: Jonathan, Elijah, Reuben and a daughter died
in infancy.

134. SUBMIT	ELLIS.........................Born,	1803;	Died,	1877
136. ABEL WEST	"	"	1806;	"	1877
138. JOHN ALLIS	"	"	1809;	Living
140. BOADISEA,	"	"	1811;	"	1849

---

(29) RICHARD ELLIS.................Born. 1760; Died, 1841
(30) EUNICE CHILSON.............. " 1763; " 1791

Married in Ashfield, Dec. 12, 1780.

THEIR CHILDREN—Were as follows- all born in Ashfield.

143. HANFORD ELLIS...	.......................Born,	1781;	Died,	1782
144. LYDIA	"	"	1783;	"	1819
146. ASAPH	"	"	1785;	"	....
148. HANNAH	"	"	1787;	"	1810
150. LUCINDA	"	"	1789;	",	....
152. CONSIDER	"	"	1791;	"	....

(29) RICHARD ELLIS, the above—second wife.

(31) CHLOE CHILSON.......... ... .Born, 1767;   "   1819

Married Feb. 19, 1792. She was a sister of Eunice, Richard's first wife.

OF THEIR CHILDREN—Some were born in Ashfield, some in Southern New York, and others in the northern part of Pennsylvania, as follows:

154.	JOHN	ELLIS		Born,	1792;	Died,	1862
156.	EUNICE	"		"	1794;	"	....
158.	RICHARD	"	JR....	"	1795;	"	1827
160.	DAVID	"		"	1797;	"	1857
162.	POLLY	"		"	1799;	"	1799
"	BENJAMIN	"		"	1800;	"	1800
"	THOMAS J	"		"	1801;	"	1802
163.	POLLY	"		"	1803;	"	....
	MEHITABLE	"		"	1805;	"	1805
165.	LUCRETIA	"		"	1806;	†Living
168.	HARRY	"		"	1809;	"	1885
170.	ELIZABETH	"		"	1811;	"	....
172.	REUBEN	"		"	1813.	"	....

---

(32) DAVID ELLIS...................Born, 1763; Died, 1843

(33) SARAH WASHBURN.... .. .. " 1764;   " 1848

Married in Ashfield, July 8, 1784.

THEIR CHILDREN—As follows—were all born in Ashfield.

174.	MELINDA	ELLIS		Born,	1785;	Died,	1862
176.	WILLIAM	"		"	1787;	"	1873
178.	SARAH	"		"	1790;	"	1853
180.	DAVID	"	JR.	"	1793;	"	1866
182.	REBECCA	"		"	1799;	"	...

---

(63) HANNAH ELLIS............... ..Born, 1764; Died, 1839

(64) APOLLOS WILLIAMS........... " 1768;   " 1848

Married probably in Ashfield, 1789.

THEIR CHILDREN.

184.	RHODA	WILLIAMS.		Born,	1790;	Died,	1875
186.	HANNAH	"		"	1793;	"	1871
188.	DANIEL	"		"	1795;	"	*1813
190.	APOLLOS	"	JR.	"	1797;	"	1866
192.	JOHN	"		"	1799;	"	1825
194.	ALPHEUS	"		"	1801;	"	1877
196.	EDWARD	"		"	1804;	"	1847

* Names or dates with this mark (*) may not be exactly, but are very nearly, correct.

† Living at this date—1885.

(66) JANE ELLIS ... .Born, 1769; Died, 1812
(67) SAMUEL LINCOLN .... " ....; " 1812

Married in Ashfield, 1788.

THEIR CHILDREN—Some born in Ashfield, and others in Central New York.
[So little is known of this family that the order of their birth cannot be given correctly.]

198. PHEBE LINCOLN.
199. POLLY "
200. HANNAH "
201. MARILLA " .... Born, 1805; Died, 1883
202. BETSEY "
203. THOMAS "
204. ANNA "
205. BENJAMIN " .... Born, 1812; Died, 1858

---

(68) JOHN ELLIS, Jr .... Born, 1771; Died, 1848
(69) ABILENA PHILLIPS .... " ....; " 1854

Married in Ashfield, Dec. 30, 1795.

THEIR CHILDREN—All born in Niles, Cayuga County, N. Y.

206. VESPASIAN ELLIS... .... Born, 1797; Died, 1818
207. SYLVIA " .... " 1798; " 1858
209. AZEL " .... " 1799; " ....
211. HARRIET " .... " 1801; " 1801
212. TAMER " .... " 1802; " ....
214. HIRAM " .... " 1804; " ....
216. ELISHA " .... " 1805; †Living
218. RICHARD " .... " 1806; " 1853
220. PITTS " .... " 1808; " ...
222. JOHN J. " .... " 1810; †Living
224. CHARLES " ... . " 1811; " 1812
225. BENJAMIN " .... " 1813; " ....
227. EBENEZER " .... " 1815; †Living
229. RUTH " .... " 1818; "
231. ANTHONY W. " .... " 1820; "

---

(70) EDWARD ELLIS .... Born, 1773; Died, 1801
(71) AMANDA FLOWER. .. .. " ...; " 187-

Married in Ashfield, June 14, 1798.

THEIR CHILDREN—Born in Sempronius (now Moravia), N. Y.

233. CYRUS ELLIS .... Born, 1799; †Living
235. EDWARD D. " .... " 1801; Died, 1848

†Living at this date—1885.

(72) DIMICK ELLIS............... ....Born, 1776; Died, 1857
(73) POLLY ANNABLE................. " 1774; " 1826

Married in Ashfield, Dec. 11, 1799.

THEIR CHILDREN—All born in Ashfield.

237. DESIAH ELLIS....................... ....Born, 1803; Died, 1880
239. RICHARD " .... " 1805; " 1878
241. LEWIS " .... ". 1811; †Living
243. JOHN " .... " 1815; "

(75) SYLVIA ELLIS...... .... .Born, 1779; Died, 1829
(76) ASHER BELDING............... .. " 1777; " ....

Married in Ashfield, where all their children were born.

245. EBENEZER BELDING..... ....Born, ...; Died, ...
246. ARETUS " .. .. " ....; " *1840
247. JANE " .... " ....; " 1870
249. VOLNEY " .... " 1814; †Living
251. THOMAS " .... " ....; " *1880
253. CHANDLER " .... " ....; " 1884

(97) DANIEL ELLIS....................Born, 1780; Died, 1862
(98) CHRISTINE G. SALISBURY... " 1780; " *1832

Married in 1802, in Adams, Jefferson Co., N. Y.

THEIR CHILDREN—Born in Adams, Jefferson Co., N. Y.

260. ELIZABETH ELLIS........... ....Born, 1804; Died, 1873
264. MARIA " .... " 1807; " ....
266. LORENZO D. " ... . " 1805; " 1875
268. CATHARINE " .... " 1813; " 1830
270. GROAT N. " .... " 1815; " 1870
272. MARCUS A. " .... " 1817; " 1879
273. ALBERT " .... " 1820; " 1859

(99) HANNAH ELLIS................Born, 1782, Died, ...
(100) COMFORT CHAPMAN......... " ....; " ....

Married in ———.

THEIR CHILDREN—Were born in ———.

276. SIDNEY CHAPMAN................. ....Born, ...; Died, ...
278. DARIUS " . ... " ....; " ....
280. JOHN " .... " ....; " ....
282. SQUIRE " .... " ....; " ....
284. ELISHA " .... " ....: " ....

* Names or dates with this mark (*) may not be exactly, but are very nearly, correct.

† Living at this date—1885.

(101) JOHN ELLIS ....Born, 1784, Died, 1847
(102) MARY STILWELL .... " .... " ....
Married in ———, 181—
THEIR CHILDREN—Born in ———.

286. CALEB ELLIS ....Born, ...; Died, ...
288. SQUIRE " .... " ....; " ....

(101) JOHN ELLIS—Second wife.
(103) BETSEY SMITH ....Born, ...; Died, 1837
Married in ———, about ———
THEIR CHILDREN—Born in ———.

290. MARY ELLIS ....Born, ... ; Died,
292. DANIEL " .... " ....; "
294. ROGER " .... " ....; ..
296. HANNAH " .... " ....; "

(101) JOHN ELLIS—Third wife.
(104) KATE DURAN ....Born, ...; Died, ...
Married in ———, about ———.
ONE CHILD—Born in ——.

298. EDWARD ELLIS ....Born, ...; Died, ...

(105) JANE ELLIS ....Born, 1786; Died, 1849
(106) AMASA SHELDON .... " ....; " 1845
Married in 1808, in Ellisburg, N. Y.
THEIR CHILDREN—Born in Ellisburg.

300. PARLEY SHELDON ....Born, 1810; Died, 1862
302. WILLIAM " .... " 1812; " 1870
304. PHILO " ... . " 1813; " 1873
305. ROBERT " .... " 1815; " 1880
307. AMOS " .... " 1817; " ....
308. AMASA " .... " 1820; " ....

(108) THOMAS ELLIS ....Born, 1788; Died, 1869
(109) HANNAH SALISBURY .... " 1793; " 1867
Married in 1812, in Ellisburg, N. Y.
THEIR CHILDREN—Born in Belleville, N. Y.

310. RICHARD ELLIS ....Born, 1813; Died, ...
312. RUSSELL " ... . " 1815; " 1850
314. SARAH " ... . " 1816; " ....
316. DAVID " .... " 1818; " 1884
318. CALEB " .... " 1821; " ....
320. MARY " .... " 1823; " ....
322. VIAL (a son) " .... " 1827; " 1849
324. JANE " .... " 1829; " 1878
326. HANNAH " .... " 1832; " 1860
328. PHEBE " .... " 1834; " 1875

(112) JAMES ELLIS .. .. Born, 1792; Died, 1823
(113) RACHEL WEISER .... " ....; " *1858

Married in Ellisburg, N. Y., about 1815.

THEIR CHILDREN—All Born in Ellisburg.

330.	MARY ANN	ELLIS	Born,	1816;	Died, ...
332.	THOMAS	" .... , ..	"	1817;	" 1876
334.	JOHN W.	"	"	1818;	" ....
336.	ISAAC	"	"	1822;	" ....

---

(115) ROBERT ELLIS .... Born, 1794; Died, 1863
(116) MARY WEISER .... " 1798; " *1879

Married in Ellisburg, N. Y., 1816.

THEIR CHILDREN—All born in Ellisburg.

340.	LYMAN	ELLIS...	Born,	1817;	Living.
342.	JANE	"	"	1818;	Died,*1855
344.	MARY	"	"	1819;	" ...
346.	CHARLOTTE	"	"	1821;	" ....
348.	JAMES	"	"	1822;	" 1871
350.	ROBERT	"	"	1824;	" 1884
352.	GAD	"	"	1826;	" 1862
354.	HARMON	"	"	1828;	" ....
356.	RACHEL	"	"	1830;	Living.
358.	CATHARINE	"	"	1831;	Died, ...
360.	FRANKLIN	"	"	1834;	" ....

FIFTH GENERATION.

Descendants of Benjamin Sr. (22), Reuben (4), and Richard Ellis, of Ashfield, Mass.

(119) STEPHEN ELLIS .... Born, 1775; Died, 1838
(120) SUSANAH COBURN .. .. " ....; " 1819

Married at or near Sempronius, N. Y., about 1800.

THEIR CHILDREN—Born in Sempronius.

362.	PRUDENCE	ELLIS...	Born,	....;	Died, ...
364.	MEHITABLE	"	"	....;	" ....
366.	GRATEFUL	"	"	... ;	" ....
368.	JONATHAN	"	"	....;	" ....
370.	ABIGAIL	"	"	....;	" ....
372.	LESTER	"	"	....;	" ....
374.	LOIS	"	"	....;	" ...

* Names or dates with this mark (*) may not be exactly, but are very nearly, correct.

(121) LURENCA ELLIS..... ....Born, 1777; Died, 1853
(122) JOHN PHELPS..... .. .. " . ..; " ....
Married probably in or near Moravia, N. Y.
THEIR CHILDREN—Born at or near Moravia.

376. JOHN PHELPS, JR.... ....Born,*1818; Died, ...

---

(123) MOSES ELLIS....................Born, 1780; Died, 1849
(124) ELIZABETH JUDD... ... . " 1782; " 1841
Married in Cayuga Co., N. Y., Oct. 14, 1804.
THEIR CHILDREN—Born in Cayuga County, except the last one.

380. LAURA ELLIS......... ....Born, 1806; Died, ...
382. MARY JUDD " .... " 1808; " ....
384. LEWIS " .... " 1811; " ....
386. ELIZA ANN " .... " 1813; " 1842
388. HESTER ANN" .... " 1816; " ....
390. ANNIE S. " .... " 1822; " 1849

---

(126) BENJAMIN ELLIS, Jr....... ...Born, 1784; Died, 1859
(127) ABIGAIL HOWARD .... " 1793; " 1883
Married in Sempronius, N. Y., Feb. 23, 1809.
THEIR CHILDREN—Born in Sempronius or near there.

392. RHODA ELLIS...................... ....Born, 1813; Died, 1833
393. MYRON " .... " 1817; " 1858
395. LEWIS R. " .... " 1822; " ....
397. AMANDA M. " .... " 1826; " ....
399. NATHAN H. " .... " 1834; " ....

---

(128) REUBEN ELLIS ....Born, 1786; Died, 1845
(129) ELIZABETH KING.............. " 1793; " 1876
Married in Cayuga Co., N. Y., about 1812.
THEIR CHILDREN—Born some in Cayuga Co., some in Orleans Co., and
the younger in Clymer, Chautauqua Co., N. Y.

401. OLIVET ELLIS...................... ... Born, 1812; Died, ...
403. HENRY K. " .... " 1813; " 18—
405. EUNICE " .... " 1815; " 1816
406. FANNY " .... " 1816; " 1817
407. DANIEL " .... " 1817; " ....

---

* Names or dates with this mark (*) may not be exactly, but are very nearly, correct.

409.	EDMUND ELLIS....		Born,	1819;	Died,	1857
411.	LOIS E.	"	"	1821;	"	....
413.	LYDIA E.	"	"	1823;	"	1862
415.	EDWIN M.	"	"	1825;	"	....
417.	ELIZABETH	"	"	1828;	"	1852
418.	REUBEN E.	" ....·	"	1832;	"	....
420.	ALFRED O.	"	"	1835;	"	....

---

(130) MEHITABLE ELLIS............ ....Born,*1788; Died, ...

(131) LAWRENCE KEMP............ ... " ....; " ....

Married probably in or near Sempronius (now Moravia), N. Y.

No report of their children.

---

(132) CHELOMETH ELLIS...........Born,*1790; Died, ...

(133) WALTER AVERY..............,...... " ....; " ....

Married probably in or near Sempronius, Cayuga Co., N. Y.

No report of their children.

Descendants of Jonathan (26), Reuben (4), and Richard Ellis, of Ashfield.

(134) SUBMIT·ELLIS....................Born, 1803; Died, 1877

(135) NATHANIEL HAVENS........ " 1800; " 1874

Married in Moravia, N. Y., Sept. 9, 1819.

THEIR CHILDREN—Born in Moravia.

426.	GEORGE	HAVENS.. ....Born,	1821;	Died,	1855
428	LOIS	" .... "	1824;	"	....
430.	SARAH ANN	" ... . "	1826;	"	....
432.	MIRANDA JANE	" .... "	1831;	"	....
434.	SUSAN	" .... ·· "	1834;	"	1885
436.	NATHANIEL	" JR .... "	1838;	"	...
438.	LYMAN	" .... "	1842;	"	....
440.	JOHN WEST	" .... "	1845;	"	....
442.	SUBMIT	" .... "	1848;	"	....

* Names or dates with this mark (*) may not be exactly, but are very nearly, correct.

(136) ABEL WEST ELLIS............Born, 1806; Died, 1877

(137) MARGARET NORTON......... " 1806; " 1866

Married ―――― 1832, in Alleghany Co., N. Y.

THEIR CHILDREN—The first born in Alleghany Co., and the others in Ripley,
Chautauqua Co., N, Y.

444. VAN R.   ELLIS..........................Born, 1833; Died, 1877
446. JOHN S.   "   ....   " 1835; " 1835
447. CYRUS   "   ....   " 1837; " ....
449. AMARILLA "   ....   " 1839; " 1858
451. SARAH J.   "   ....   " 1841; " 1884
453. MARY ANN "   ....   " 1843; " ....

---

(138) JOHN ALLIS ELLIS ....Born, 1809; Died, ...

(139 ELIZA ANN FAIRCHILD...... " 1813; "

Married March 20, 1833 in ――――.

THEIR CHILDREN—Born in Conneaut, Ohio.

455. WILLIAM AVERY ELLIS....... .... Born, 1833; Died, ...
457. ORSON HENRY   "   ....   " 1835; " ...
459. MARY JANE   "   ....   " 1837; " 1865
461. JOHN DEMETRIUS   "   ....   " 1842; " ....
463. JULIA FRANCES   "   ... ...   " 1845; " ....
465. SARAH ALICE   "   ....   " 1850; " ....

---

(140) BOADISEA ELLIS....., ...Born, 1811; Died, 1851

(141) WILLIAM W. KING.... .... " 1799;   Living

Married in 1839 in Moravia, N. Y.

Of their five Children two died in infancy.

467. WILLIAM R. KING.......................... Born, 1841; Died, 1871
468. CHARLES D.   "   ....   " 1843; " ...
469. EMILY D.   "   ....   ". 1848; " ....

**Descendants of Richard (29), Reuben (4), and Richard
Ellis, of Ashfield.**

(144) LYDIA ELLIS............ ....Born, 1783; Died, ...

(145) DANIEL H. BACON .... " ....; " *1855

Married ――――.

THEIR CHILDREN—Born in Delmar, Tioga Co., Pa.

470. OLIVER   BACON.......................... Born, ...; Died, ...
      LEWIS   "   .... " ....; " ....

DANIEL	BACON...........................	Born, ...	; Died,	....
NANCY	"	"	....;	" ....
EUNICE	"	"	....;	" ....
HANNAH	"	"	....;	" ....
CHLOE	"	"	... ;	" ....

---

(146) ASAPH ELLIS................ Born, 1785; Died, ...

(147) AMANDA SPENCER.......... " ....; "

Married ——.

THEIR CHILDREN—Born in Clearfield Co., Pa.

482. CHARLES	ELLIS...........................	Born,	....; Died,	...
RICHARD	"	"	....;	" ....
HORACE	"	"	....;	" ....
CHAUNCY	"	"	....;	" ....
PLINY	"	"	....;	" ....
HANNAH	"	"	....;	" ....

---

(150) LUCINDA ELLIS................ Born, 1789; Died, 1842

(151) DAVID HENRY................... " ....; "

Married ——

THEIR CHILDREN—Born near Wellsboro, Pa.

495. WILLIAM	HENRY........................	Born, ...	; Died, 1882
CHARLES	"	"	... ;	" ....
DAVID	"	"	..;	" ....
LOVICA	"	'	....;	" ....
MARY	"	"	...;	" 1871
LYDIA	"	"	....;	" ....
MARGARET	"	"	....;	" ....

---

(152) CONSIDER ELLIS............ Born, 1791; Died,*1866

(153) MARY LOVELL .... " ..; " ....

Married in or near Delmar, Pa.

THEIR CHILDREN.

500. GEORGE	ELLIS...........................	Born,	....; Died,	...
JOHN	"	"	....;	" ....
PRUDENCE	"	"	....;	" ....

(154) JOHN ELLIS .... Born, 1794; Died, 1862
(155) ELIZABETH FAULKNER..... " .... " 1837

Married in ———.

THEIR CHILDREN—Ten in number, but names of five not known. Born, some in
Lycoming Co., Pa., and in Ellicottville, Cattaraugus Co., N. Y.

506.	RALPH ELLIS.............. .... Born, 1829;				....
508.	JOHN " .... " ......; Died, 1847
509.	WILLIAM " .... " ...; " ....
511.	LUCINDA " .... " ....; " ....
513.	MARGARET " .... " ....; " ....

---

(156) EUNICE ELLIS.................. Born, 1794; Died, 1874
(157) REUBEN HERRINGTON...... " 1791; " 1862

Married in Tompkins Co., N. Y., about 1813.

THEIR CHILDREN—Born in Tioga Co., Penn.

514.	JACOB HERRINGTON......................Born, 1815; Died, ...
515.	SARAH ANN " .... " 1817; " ....
516.	NANCY " .... " 1819; " 1843
517.	CHARLES " .... " 1821; " ...
518.	GEO. W. " .... " 1823; " ....
519.	DEROY " .... " 1825; " ....
520.	HARRIET E. " .... " 1830; " ....
521.	HORACE P. " .... " 1837; " ....

---

(158) RICHARD ELLIS, Jr...........Born. 1795; Died, 1827
(159 PATIENCE HERRINGTON . " 1802; " 1855

Married Feb. 3d, 1818, in ———.

THEIR CHILDREN- Born in or near Delmar, Pa.

522.	AMASA ELLIS... ....Born, 1819; Died, ...
524.	CONSIDER " .... " 1821; " ....
526.	SAM'L GILBERT " .... " 1822; " 1850
528.	JOHN M. " .... " 1825; " ...

---

(160) DAVID ELLIS............ ....Born, 1797; Died, 1857
(161) ORILLA DIMICK................. " 1801; " 1867

Married Jan. 13th, 1819, in ———.

THEIR CHILDREN—Born in Shippen, Tioga Co., Penn.

530.	THANKFUL ELLIS......................Born, 1820; Died, ...
532.	CHLOE " .... " 1822; " ....
534.	CHESTER " .... " 1823; " ....

536. JEFFERSON ELLIS... ....Born, 1826; Died, 1877
538. MARIA   "   ....   "   1828; "   1864
540. HARRY   "   ....   "   1831; "   ....
542. CRETIA ANN   "   ....   "   1836; "   ....
544. BAKER D.   "   ....   "   1838; "   ....
546. SEYMOUR   "   ....   "   1846; "   ....

---

(163) POLLY ELLIS....................Born, 1803; Died, . .
(164) PAUL N. DIMICK............... "   ....;   "
         Married in ——, about ——
         ONE CHILD—Born in —.
548. ....

---

(165) LUCRETIA ELLIS..............Born, 1806;   Living
(166) Rev. BENJAMIN AVERY.... "   .... Died, *1846
        Married in or near Delmar, Pa.
    THEIR CHILDREN—Three or four in number, but names not known.
549. ....

---

(165) LUCRETIA ELLIS AVERY.—Second husband.
(167) Rev. JOHN STIPP.............. .Born, ... ; Died, ...
         Married ——.
         ONE CHILD—Born in ——.
550. ....

---

(168) HARRY ELLIS... ....Born, 1809; Died, 1885
(169) BETSEY SEELEY............... "   ....;   "   1885
        Married ——, 183., in Ellisburg, Penn.
    THEIR CHILDREN—All born in Ellisburg.
552. ADOLPHUS C. ELLIS........................Born, ...; Died, . . .
554. WILLIAM   "   ....   "   ... ;   "   ....
556. RICHARD   "   ....   "   1840; . "   ....
558. ORSON   "   .. ..   "   ....;   "   ....
560. MARION   "   ....   "   ....;   "   ....
561. AMASA   "   ....   "   ....;   "   ....
562. GENETT   "   ....   "   ....;   "   ....
563. ELLA   "   ....   "   ...;   "   ....

---

(170) ELIZABETH ELLIS............Born, 1811; Died, ...
(171) W. M. CHAFFEE..... .... "   . ..;   "
         Married ——.
        THEIR CHILDREN—
564. ....

(172) REUBEN ELLIS................ ....Born, 1813; Died, ...

(173) —— SEELEY...................... " ....; "

ONE CHILD—

566. ....

Descendants of David Sr. (32), Reuben (4), and Richard Ellis, of Ashfield.

(174) MELINDA ELLIS............ ... ..Born, 1785; Died, 1862

(175) JOHN WING....... .... " ....; " 1857

Married in Ashfield, Mass., about ——.

ONE CHILD.—Born in Erie, Pa.

568. HAMILTON WING..................... ....Born, ...; Died, ...

---

(176) WILLIAM ELLIS ....Born, 1787; Died, 1873

(177) RHODA FLOWER.......... ..... " 1789; " 1864

Married in Ashfield, Mass., about 1808.

THEIR CHILDREN—Born, the first five in Ashfield, the others in Springfield, Erie Co., Pa.

570. WILLIAM ELLIS, Jr....................		Born, 1810;	Died, 1865
572. CHARLES P. "	....	"	1812;	"	1881
574. GEORGE "	... .	"	1814;	"	1814
575. HARRIET "	....	"	1815;	"	1858
577. LUCRETIA "	....	"	1817;	"	....
579. SAMUEL "	....	"	1821;	"	....
581. JAMES F. "	....	"	1824;	"	1849
583. MARY L. "	....	"	1828;	"	....
585. JOSEPH "	....	"	1831;	"	....
587. RUMINA "	....	"	1834;	"	....

---

(178) SARAH ELLIS...... ....Born, 1791; Died, 1851

(179) Capt. JAMES FLOWER........ " 1781; " 1832

Married in Ashfield, July 5th, 1810.

THEIR CHILDREN—Born in Wesleyville, Erie Co., Penn.

589. ELBRIDGE G. FLOWER......................		Born, 1811;	Died, 1832
590. SALLY H. "	....	"	1813;	"	1885
591. DAVID E. "	....	"	1816;	"	....
592. WILLIAM S. "	....	"	1821;	"	....
593. CLARISSA A. "	....	"	1823;	"	....
594. MELINDA J. "	....	"	1825;	"	....
595. LYDIA W. "	... .	"	1828;	"	...
596. PHINEAS D. "	....	"	1830;	"	....
597. JAMES G. "	....	"	1832;	"	....

180. DAVID ELLIS, Jr. ....Born, 1793; Died, 1866
(181) RUMINA FLOWER .... " 1795; " 1872

Married in Ashfield, about 1814.

THEIR CHILDREN.—Born, the first three in Ashfield, and the others in Springfield, Pa.

598. Louisa	Ellis	....	Born, 1815;	Died,	....
600. Melinda	"	.... "	1817;	"	....
601. George	"	.... "	1818;	"	....
603. Marshall	"	.... "	1820;	"	...
605. Leonard	"	.... "	1823;	"	....
607. Peter	"	.... "	1824;	"	....
609. Sarah	"	.... "	1827;	"	....
611. Orman F.	"	.... "	1829;	"	1870
John	"	.... "	1832;	"	1835

(182) REBECCA ELLIS ....Born, 1799; Died, ...
(183) JONATHAN TAYLOR .... " ...; " ....

Married ———.

THEIR CHILDREN.—All born in Chillicothe, Ohio.

613. Phebe Taylor	....	Born,	....;	Died,	....
614. Sarah	"	.... "	....;	"	...
615. Mary	"	.... "	....;	"	....

Descendants of John Ellis, Jr., of Niles, N. Y., (68), John Sr. of Ashfield, (15), and Richard Ellis.

(207) SYLVIA ELLIS ....Born, 1798; Died, 1837
(208) JOHN SPRAGUE .... " 1793; " 1875

Married in Sempronius, Cayuga Co., N. Y, in 1816.

THEIR CHILDREN—Born in Perrysburg, N. Y.

616. Almerin Sprague	....	Born, 1818;	Died,*1853
617. Delilah	"	.... "	1824;	"	....
618. Lodoska	"	.... "	1827;	"	....
619. Corliska	"	.... "	1831;	"	1852
620. Ebenezer	"	.... "	1833;	"	....

(209) AZEL ELLIS .... .Born, 1799; Died, 1863
(210) MARY HAGERMAN .... " 1796; " 1859

Married probably in Cayuga Co., N. Y.

621. Edward Ellis	....	Born, 1831;	Died, 1857
622. Phebe	"	.... "	....;	"	1860
623. Lydia	"	.... "	....;	"	....

(212) TAMER ELLIS.....................Born, 1802; Died, 1855
(213) MATTHEW VANDERBILT... "   1805;   "   1877

Married May 8th, 1827, in ———.

THEIR CHILDREN—Born in Niles, N. Y.

624.	ABILENA VANDERBILT			Born, 1828;	Died,	....
625.	ANDREW	"		" 1832;	"	....
626	HANNAH	"		" 1838;	"	....

---

(214) HIRAM ELLIS.....................Born, 1804; Died, 1874
(215) POLLY FLOWERS.............. "   ....;   "

Married in Cayuga Co., N. Y.

THEIR CHILDREN.

627.	ELISHA ELLIS			Born, ...;	Died,	...
629.	———	"		" ....;	"	....

---

(216) ELISHA ELLIS.....................Born, 1805;   Living.
(217) HANNAH BRADLEY........... "   1811;   "

Married at Farmersville, Ind., in 182–.

THEIR CHILDREN—Born in Farmersville, Ind.

630.	NANCY ELLIS			Born, ...;	Died,	....
632.	ELIZABETH	"		" ....;	"	....
634.	ABILENA	"		" ....;	"	....
636.	ANN	"		" 1838;	"	
638.	JNO. DAVID	"		" 1842;	"	

---

(218) RICHARD ELLIS.....................Born, 1806; Died, 1853
(219) MARY P. SELOVER... .. .... "   1810;   "   1884

Married Nov. 6th, 1827, in Niles, N. Y.

THEIR CHILDREN.—The two first born in Niles, N. Y., and the others in Jackson, Hardin Co., Ohio.

640.	ISAAC N.	ELLIS		Born, 1829;	Died,	...
642.	CATHERINE	"		" 1833;	"	....
644.	MARY ANN	"		" 1837;	"	......
646.	WILLIAM M.	"		" 1845;	"	....
648.	RICHARD S.	"		" ....;	"	1854
649.	SYLVIA JANE	"		" ....;	"	1877
650.	JOHN			" ....;	"	1852

(220) PITTS ELLIS............... .. ...Born, 1808; Died, 1876
(221) LUCIA M. BALCOM............. `"` 1814; Living.

Married in Perrysburg, Cattaraugus Co., N. Y., Feb. 23d, 1832.

THEIR CHILDREN.—Born in Waukesha Co., Wis.

651. EDWARD ELVASTUS ELLIS....... .... Born, 1838; Died, 1839
652. HELEN M. `"` .... `"` 1842; `"` ....
653. LODOSKA S. `"` .... `"` 1845; `"` ....
655. PITTS B. `"` .... `"` 1851; `"` ....
657. ANNIE A. `"` .... `"` 1854; `"` ....

---

(222) JOHN J. ELLIS....... ....Born, 1810; Living.
(223) CATHERINE SELOVER....... `"` 1813; `"`

Married at Niles, N. Y., in 183-.

THEIR CHILDREN.—All born in Niles.

659. JOHN R. ELLIS.........................Born, 1839; Died, ...
661. MARTHA `"` .... `"` 1844; `"` ....
663. J. MYRON `"` .... `"` 1845; `"` ....
665. W. SELOVER `"` .... `"` 1852; `"` ....
667. NEWTON S. `"` .... `"` 1855; `"` ....

---

(225) BENJAMIN ELLIS...............Born,*1813; Died, 1881
(226) JEMIMA VANDERBILT........ `"` 1816; `"` 1883

Married at Niles, N. Y., Dec. 1st, 1839.

THEIR CHILDREN.—The first four born in Niles, N. Y., and the others in Marseilles, Ohio.

669. WILLIAM N. ELLIS..... ....Born, 1840; Died, 1863
671. JOHN H. `"` .... `"` 1843; `"` ....
673. MARSHALL `"` .... `"` 1846; `"` 1847
675. CLARENCE L. `"` ....,................... `"` 1848; `"` ....
677. MARY E. `"` .... `"` 1851; `"` ....
679. ABILENA `"` .... `"` 1853; `"` 1853
681. CURTIS MILO `"` .... `"` 1856; `"` 1856
683. MELINDA LOUISA `"` .... `"` 1861; `"` ....

* Names or dates with this mark (*) may not be exactly, but are very nearly, correct.

(227) EBENEZER ELLIS............Born, 1815;   Living.
(228) THEODOCIA PHILLIPS........ "   18..;   "

Married in Farmersville, Ind., 183-.

THEIR CHILDREN.

685.	JULIA	ELLIS	Born,	....;	Died,	....
687.	SOPHRONIA	"	"	....;	"	....
689.	EDWIN	"	"	1848;	"	....
691.	HARRIET	"	"	....;	"	....
693.	PITTS	"	"	1852;	"	...
695.	MARY	"	"	....;	"	1879

---

(229) RUTH ELLIS.... ....Born, 1818;   Living.
(230) GEORGE HALL.......... .... "   ....;   "   ....

Married in Niles, Cayuga Co., N. Y.

No report from this family or their children, if they had any. They are said to reside in Richland, Kalamazoo Co., Mich.

---

(231) ANTHONY ELLIS.............. Born, 1820;   Living.
(232) HANNAH VAN ETTEN........ "   ..;   "

Married Oct. 12th, 1843, in Niles, N. Y.

THEIR CHILDREN—Born in Niles.

708.	ELIAS	ELLIS	Born,	1844;	Died,	....
710.	ISAAC NEWTON	"	"	1846;	"	....
712.	ARTHUR DAY	"	"	1859;	"	1861
713.	DELLA JANE	"	"	1864;	"	....

Descendants of Edward Ellis of Niles, N. Y., (70), John Sr of Ashfield, (15), and Richard Ellis.

(233) CYRUS ELLIS................... Born, 1799;   Living.
(234) CLARISSA BIRCH.............. "   1800; Died, 1885

Married March 31st, 1825, in Niles, N. Y.

THIER CHILDREN.—All born in Niles (now Moravia), N. Y.

715.	EDWARD D.	ELLIS	Born,	1826;	Died,	1864
717.	POLLY	"	"	1828;	"	....
719.	MINERVA	"	"	1829;	"	1872
721.	CLARISSA	"	"	1832;	"	....
723.	HIRAM	"	"	1834;	"	....
725.	CYRUS	" Jr	"	1836;	"	1863
727.	BIRCH	"	"	1838;	"	....
729.	HENRY F.	"	"	1843;	"	1863
731.	MILES M.	"	"	1846;	"	....

(235) EDWARD D. ELLIS ... . Born, 1801; Died, 1848
(236) LEONORA M. CHAPMAN...... " 1805; " 1870

Married at Monroe, Mich., Feb. 2d, 1830.

THEIR CHILDREN.—All born in Monroe except the youngest, who was born in Detroit.

733. MARY MINERVA ELLIS...	Born,	1831;	Died,	1884
735. AMELIA	"	....	"	1833;	"	....
736. EDWARD CHARLES	"	....	"	1835;	"	....
737. JOHN C. C.	"	....	"	1837;	"	....
739. ELIZABETH T.	"	....	"	1841;	"	1868
740. BENJAMIN F.	"	....	"	1844;	"	...

**Descendants of Dimick Ellis (72), John Sr., (15), and Richard
all of Ashfield.**

(237) DESIAH ELLIS.................... Born, 1803; Died, 1880
(238) TIBERIUS BELDING......... .... " 1800; " *1870

Married in Ashfield, Mass., April 10th, 1828.

THEIR CHILDREN.—The first six born in Ashfield, and the others in Belding, Mich.

741. ANNABEL BELDING......................	Born,	1829;	Died,	....
742. FRANCIS	"	....	"	1830;	"	1876
743. EDWARD	"	....	"	1832;	"	1863
744. PRISCILLA	"	....	"	1834,	"	....
745. TIBERIUS	"	Jr.	"	1838;	"	...
746. WAITE	"	....	"	1840;	"	...
747. ELLEN	"	....	"	1845;	"	....
748. JOHN	"	....	"	1849;	"	...

---

(239) RICHARD ELLIS................. Born, 1805; Died, 1878
(240) HANNAH RANNEY............ " 1805; Living.

Married in Ashfield, Nov. "Thanksgiving Day," 1827.

THEIR CHILDREN —Born in Pittstown, Rensselaer Co., N. Y.

749. CHARLES DIMICK ELLIS.....................	Born,	1829;	Living.
751. ERASTUS RANNEY	"	....	"	1832;	"

---

(241) LEWIS ELLIS................... .. Born, 1811; Living.
(242) LOUISA WILSON. .... " 1812; "

Married in Ashfield, Oct. 22nd, 1834.

THEIR CHILDREN.—The first two born in Ashfield, and the others in Belding, Mich.
[Five others of their children, all sons, died in infancy.]

754. GEORGE B. ELLIS	Born,	1837;	Died,	1851
755. GEORGE W.	"	....	"	1851;	
757. MARY L.	"	....	"	1855;	

(243) **Dr. JOHN ELLIS**... ... ...Born, 1815,   Living.
(244) **MARY E. COIT**................... "   1817; Died, 1850

Married in Norwich, Mass., 1843.

THEIR CHILDREN.—Delia born in Grand Rapids, Mich., died in infancy.
The others born in Detroit.

759. ALFRED ELLIS...........................Born, 1847; Died, 1848
760. WILBUR D. " .... "   1848;

243) **Dr. JOHN ELLIS.**—Second Wife.
(245) **SARAH M. LEONARD**......... Born, 1828;   Living.

Married in Troy, Mich., Oct. —, 1851.

THEIR CHILDREN.—Born in Detroit, and both died in infancy.

762. LILLY   ELLIS........................Born, 1852; Died, 1852
763. EDWARD DELL " .... "   1855;   "   1855

Descendants of Daniel Ellis of Ellisburg, N. Y., (97), Caleb, (19), and Richard of Ashfield.

(260) **ELIZABETH ELLIS**............Born, 1804; Died, 1873
(261) **GEORGE PADDOCK**.. .... "   ....;   "   ....

Married in Ellisburg, Jefferson Co., N. Y.

THEIR CHILDREN.—Born in ——.

764. HENRY A. PADDOCK. ....Born, ...; Died, ...
765. MARIA   "   .... "   ....;   "   ....

---

(264) **MARIA ELLIS**...................Born, 1807; Died, 1863
(265) **ELISHA SALISBURY.** ...."   1807;   "   ....

Married in Ellisburg, N. Y., in ——.

THEIR CHILDREN.

766. MARTHA SALISBURY......... ... .Born, ...; Died, ...
767. ABIRAM   "   .... "   ....;   "   ....

---

(266) **LORENZO D. ELLIS**........ ...Born, 1805; Died, 1875
(267) **MEHITABLE B. MARTIN**. ... " *1815 ;   "   1866

Married in Cobwell, Canada in 1836.

THEIR CHILDREN—Born in Canada and New York.

768. CHRISTINA E. ELLIS............... ....Born, 1837; Died, ...
770. CARRIE M.   "   .... "   1839;   "   ....
772. MYRA   "   .. .. "   1842;   "   ....
774. OLIVER L. D. "   .... "   1845;   "   ...

(270) NICHOLAS GROAT ELLIS....Born, 1815; Died, 1871
(271) ZILPHA B. CASE .... " 1818; " ....

Married in Blenheim, Canada West, Feb. 20, 1844.

THEIR CHILDREN—Born in Canada and in Ellisburg, N. Y.

776. HENRY G. ELLIS........................ .. Born, 1845; Died, ...
778. GEORGE W. " .... " 1847; " ....
780. MARGARET J. " .... " 1849; " 1857
781. EDWARD D. " .... " 1851; " ...
783. LEWIS M. " .... " 1856; " 1885

---

(273) Rev. ALBERT A. ELLIS.......Born, 1820; Died, 1859
(274) ELECTA A. BARNEY.......... " 1822; " 1854

Married in Ellisburg, N. Y., Sept. 22nd, 1844.

THEIR CHILDREN.—Born some in New York and others in Michigan.
(Helen C., Alice C., and Eva C. died in infancy.)

785. EDWARD S. ELLIS........................ Born, 1847; Died, ...
787. MARY L. " .... " 1848; " 1885
789. CHARLES S. " .... " 1852; " ....

(273) Rev. ALBERT A. ELLIS—Second wife.
(275) MARY S. GREGORY.......... ..Born, 1821; Died, 1856

Married June 28th, 1855, in Plymouth, Mich.

ONE CHILD.—Born in Brooklyn, Mich.

791. MARY E. G. ELLIS..... .... Born, 1856; Died, ...

**Descendants of Thomas Ellis (108), of Ellisburg, N. Y.,
Caleb (19) and Richard, of Ashfield.**

(310) RICHARD ELLIS ....Born, 1813; Living
(311) EMILY A. CLARK............ ... " 1821; " 1849

Married in 1842 at Copenhagen, N. Y.

ONE CHILD—Born in Rodman, Jefferson Co., N. Y.

794. THEODORE C. ELLIS....................... Born, 1845; Died, .. .

---

(312) RUSSELL ELLIS........ .... Born, 1815; Died, 1850
(313) MARTHA COOK.................. " 1817; " *1878

Married in Pulaski, N. Y. in 1835.

ONE CHILD.—Born in ——.

796. HIRAM ELLIS........................... Born, 1837; Died, ...

(314) SARAH ELLIS............ ....Born, 1816; Died. ...
(315) DAVID FULTON.................... "   ....; "

Married in Belleville, Jefferson Co., N. Y. in 1836.

THEIR CHILDREN.—All born in Belleville.

800. JAMES   FULTON ....Born, ...; Died, ...
801. THOMAS   "   .... "   ....; "   ....
802. DAVID   "   Jr.. .... "   ....; "
803. CHARLES N. "   .... "   1855; "

------

(316) DAVID ELLIS.............. ....Born, 1818; Died, 1884
(317) PAMELIA CLARK............... "   ....; " 1865

Married in Belleville, N. Y.

ONE DAUGHTER.—Born in Belleville.

805. HANNAH ELLIS.... ....Born, 1862; Died, ...

(Two other daughters died in infancy.)

------

(318) CALEB ELLIS........ ....Born, 1820; Died, ...
(319) MARIA LOUISA BARKER..... "   ....; " 1858

Married in Ellisburg, N. Y., Jan. 17, 1843.

THEIR CHILDREN—All born in Ellisburg.

808. MARTHA ANN ELLIS......................Born, 1844; Died, ...
810. VIAL F.   "   .... "   1848; " 1864
811. RUSSELL   "   .... "   1852; "   ....
813. HENRY D.   "   .... "   1854; "   ....

(318) CALEB ELLIS....................Born, 1820; Died, ...
(319)* CHRISTINA E. ELLIS (2d wife).. "   1837; "

Married at Ellisburg, N. Y., Oct. 11, 1860.

THEIR CHILDREN—All Born in Ellisburg.

815. FLORENCE E. ELLIS ....'.... ......Born, 1863; Died, ...
817. GEO. EDWIN   "   .... "   1864; "
819. ALBERT F.   "   .... "   1869; "

* Daughter of Lorenzo D. Ellis. See No. 768, page 38.

(320) MARY ELLIS.................... ....Born, 1823; Died, ...
(321) LEONARD O. BARKER......... "   ....;   "   ....

Married in Ellisburg, N. Y., in 1843.

THEIR CHILDREN.—Born in Young, Onondaga Co., N. Y.

821.	FANNIE	BARKER......................	Born,	....;	Died,	....
822.	ADDIE	"	....	"	....;	"	....
823.	HANNAH JANE	"	....	"	....;	"	....
824.	MARY ADELAIDE	"	....	"	....;	"	....
825.	SARAH LOUISA	"	....	"	....;	"	....
826.	THURSTON GARNER	"	....	"	....;	"	....
827.	HERBERT EUGENE	"	....	"	....;	"	1873

---

(328) PHEBE ELLIS.................... Born, 1834; Died, 1875
(329) JOHN CHAMBERLAIN......... "   ... ;   "   1870

Married in ——, 1868, in Belleville, N. Y.

ONE SON.—Born in Belleville.

828. JOHN CHAMBERLAIN, JR...................... Born, 1869; Died, ...

(328) PHEBE ELLIS-CHAMBERLAIN—
GATES WHITE—Second husband... Born. ...:; Died, ...

Married in——, 1872.

TWO CHILDREN.—Born at Pulaski, N. Y.

829. GEORGE WHITE............................ Born, 1873; Died, ...
830. ELLIS   "   ....   "   1875;   "   ....

Descendants of James Ellis, (112), of Ellisburg, N. Y., Caleb, (19), and Richard, of Ashfield, Mass.

(332) THOMAS ELLIS,.................... Born, 1817; Died, 1876
(333) CYNTHIA SHERMAN,.......... "   1826;   "   ....

Married in Ellisburg, N. Y.

THEIR CHILDREN—

831.	POLLY	ELLIS	Born,	....;	Died,	....
832.	JAMES	"	....	"	....;	"	....
833.	WILLIAM	"	....	"	....;	"	....
834.	ADELBERT	"	....	"	....;	"	....
835.	LEVI	"	....	"	....;	"	....
836.	THOMAS,	"	JR......................... .	"	....;	"	....

(334) JOHN W. ELLIS................Born, 1818; Died, ...
(335) MARY FULLER............ ...   "   1825;   "

Married in Ellisburg, N. Y.

THEIR CHILDREN.—All born in Ellisburg.

837. RODERICK D. ELLIS................ ... .Born, 1843; Died, ...
838. HELEN   "   ....   "   1847;   " 1853
839. MARTHA   "   ....   "   1850;   "   ....
840. FRED   "   ....   "   1856;   "   ....

---

(336) ISAAC ELLIS...................Born, 1822; Died, ...
(337) MARGARET BEAMER..........   "   1830;   "

Married in———.

THEIR CHILDREN.—

841. ELLEN   ELLIS.......... ....Born, 1850; Died, ...
842. ALEXANDER " ....   "   1852;   "   ....
843. BENJAMIN " ....   "   1855;   "   ....
844. FRANK   " ....   "   1862;   "   ....

**Descendants of Robert Ellis (115), of Ellisburg, N. Y., Caleb
(19), and Richard, of Ashfield.**

(340) LYMAN ELLIS........ .... .Born, 1817; Died, ...
(341) MALVINA ZUFELT..............   "   1829;   "   ....

Married in Ellisburg, N. Y., 1848.

THEIR CHILDREN—All born in Ellisburg.

845. DETTE L. ELLIS.........................Born, 1850; Died, ...
846. FANNIE   " ....   "   1852;   "   ....
847. ARNITA   " .. ..   "   1856;   "   ....

---

(350) ROBERT ELLIS, Jr......... ....Born, 1824; Died, 1884
(351) BETSEY CHRISMAN............   "   1835;   "   ....

Married in Ellisburg, N. Y., in 1853.

THEIR CHILDREN.—All born in Ellisburg.

848. GAD   ELLIS...................... ....Born, 1854; Died, ...
849. CHARLES " ....   "   1857;   "   ....
850. WILLIAM " ....   "   1860;   "   ....
851. BYRON   " ....   "   1861;   "   ....

SIXTH GENERATION.

Descendants of Stephen Ellis (119), of Fayette Co., Ind., Benjamin (22), Reuben (4), and Richard, of Ashfield.

(362) PRUDENCE ELLIS ....Born, 1799; Died, 1871

(363) CHARLES T. HARRIS. .... " 1799; " 1877

Married in Cayuga Co., N. Y., May 11, 1817.

THEIR CHILDREN.—The first two born near North Bend, Ohio; the others in Fayette and Henry counties, Ind.

860	SUSAN	HARRIS.............	Born, 1818;	Died,	....
861.	MARY ANN	"	"	1820;	" 1821
862.	CHARLES W.	"	"	1822;	" 1831
863.	STEPHEN	"	"	1824;	" ....
864.	DORR K.	"	"	1827;	" 1828
865.	LESTER E.	"	"	1829;	" 1864
866.	LUCETTA D.	"	"	1831;	" ....
867.	ELIZA	"	"	1835;	" 1873

---

(364) MEHITABLE ELLIS........ .... Born, 1800; Died, 1874

(365) LEWIS ROBINSON........ .... " 1791; " 1843

Married near North Bend, Ohio, May 20, 1821.

THEIR CHILDREN.—Born some at North Bend, and the others in Fayette Co., Ind.

868.	MARY	ROBINSON.	Born, 1822;	Died,	....
869.	ELIAS	"	"	1825;	" ...
870.	RACHEL M.	"	"	1827;	" ...
871.	MINERVA	"	"	1829;	" 1873
872.	MARTILLA	" '	"	1834;	" 1863
873.	EUNICE	"	"	1838;	" 1860
874.	ERASTUS	"	"	1841;	" ....

---

(366) GRATEFUL ELLIS.... ....Born, 1803; Died, 1883

(367) CASPER TRASK................ " 1801; " 1873

Married in Fayette Co., Ind., Dec. 2d, 1821.
THEIR CHILDREN.

875.	MOULTON S. TRASK ....Born, 1823;	Died,	....
876.	CLARISSA	"	"	1825;	" ....
877.	LETTITIA S.	"	"	1827;	" ....
878.	HOWELL H.	" , ...	"	1829;	" ....
879.	LOIS	"	"	1832;	" ....
880.	EDWARD E.	"	"	1834;	" 1840
881.	HENRY V.	"	"	1837;	" ....
882.	AMELIA A.	" '	"	1840;	" ....
883.	DeETTE E.	"	"	1844;	" ....
884.	RUBIE S.	"	"	1846;	" ....

(368) JONATHAN ELLIS.... ....Born, 1805; Died, 1876
(369) CHARLOTTE JEFFREY...... "   ....;   "   ....

Married in Fayette Co., Ind., in 1829.

THEIR CHILDREN.—Born in Fayette Co.

885. Louisa   Ellis............................Born, ...; Died, ...
886. Alvah   "   .... "   ....; "   ....
887. William A."   .... "   ....; "   ....
888. Mary   "   .... "   ....; "   ....
889. Diantha J. "   .... "   ...; "   ....
890. Sarah Ann ''   .... "   ....; "   ....
891. John A.   "   .... "   ....; "   ....

---

(370) ABIGAIL ELLIS...................Born, 1806; Died, 1849
(371) JOSHUA WIGHTMAN.......... "   ... ;   "   ....

Married in Fayette Co., Ind.

THEIR CHILDREN.—

892. John   Wightman....... ....Born, ...; Died,*1864
893. Austin   "   .... "   ....; "   ....
894. Minor   "   .... "   ....; "   ....

---

(372) LESTER ELLIS.... ....Born, 1811; Died, 1868
(373) SALLY T. TROWBRIDGE..... "   1807; "   1879

Married in Fayette Co., Ind.

THEIR CHILDREN—All born in Fayette Co.

895. Diantha J.   Ellis.....................Born, 1833; Died, ...
896. Chester Coburn "   .... "   1839; "   1864
897. Polly   "   .... "   '1843; "   ....

---

(374) LOIS ELLIS..................... ..Born, 1813; Died, 1842
(375) JOHN JEFFREY.. .... "   ....; "   ....

Married in 1835, in Fayette Co., Ind.

THEIR CHILDREN.—Born in Fayette Co.

898. Jane Jeffrey.......... ....Born, ...; Died, ...

* Names or dates with this mark (*) may not be exactly, but are very nearly, correct.

**Descendants of Moses Ellis, (123), of Fayette Co., Ind.,
Benjamin, (22), Reuben, (4), and Richard,
of Ashfield.**

(380) **LAURA ELLIS**.....................Born, 1806; Died, 1881
(381) **JOSIAH SUTTON**............... "   1799;   "   1879
Married March 11, 1828, near Connersville, Fayette Co., Ind,
THEIR CHILDREN.—Born in Fayette Co.

899. Elsie   Sutton........................Born, 1828; Died, ...
900. Hester Ann "   .... "   1835;   "   ....

---

(382) **MARY JUDD ELLIS**..............Born, 1808; Died, ...
(383) **SUTHERLAND GARD**.......... "   ....;   "   ....
Married about 1830 in Fayette Co., Ind.
THEIR CHILDREN.—Born ——

901. Lucetta Gard.... ....Born, ... ; Died, 1850
902. Samantha   "   .... "   ....;   "   ....
903. Adeline   "   .... "   ....;   "   ....
904. Harriet   "   .... "   ....;   "   ....
905. Henry   "   .... "   ....;   "   ....

(382) **MARY JUDD ELLIS GARD.**
JAMES JAMES—Second husband.
Married ——.
THEIR CHILDREN.—Born ——.

906. Laura James...............................Born, ...; Died,*1860
907. Moses   "   .... "   ....;   "   ....

---

(384) **LEWIS ELLIS**.....................Born, 1811; Died, ...
(385) **SAMANTHA THOMAS**......... "   1811;   "   ....
Married in Fayette Co., Ind, Dec. 30th, 1832.
THEIR CHILDREN.—Born in Fayette Co.

908. Caroline   Ellis..........................Born, 1833; Died, ..
909. Lucy   "   .... "   1835;   "   ....
910. Oliver H. "   .... "   1836;   "   1837
911. Elvin   "   .... "   1838;   "   1839
912. Jasper D. "   .... "   1839;   "   1850
913. Emma   "   .... "   1841;   "   1841
914. Minor   "   .... "   1842;   "   1863

915. MELVIN ELLIS	....	Born,	1843;	Died,	....
916. NANCY	"	....	"	1845;	"	1870
917. ADELINE	"	....	"	1846;	"	1861
918. ANGELINE	"	....	"	1846;	"	1858
919. MARY	"	....	"	1848;	"	1848
920. ELIZA	"	....	"	1850;	"	....
921. ELLEN	"	....	"	1852;	"	....
922. EDWIN W.	"	....	"	1852;	"	....
923. HEWITT	"	....	"	1854;	"	....

(386) ELIZA ANN ELLIS..............Born, 1813; Died, 1842

(387) WILLIAM COLE................ " ....; " ....

Married 1834.

THEIR CHILDREN.

924. ANGELINE COLE	....	Born,	....;	Died,	....
925. LEWIS	"	....	"	....;	"	1863

(388) HESTER ANN ELLIS..........Born, 1816; Died, ...

(389) PHILANDER THOMAS........ " 1811; " 1865

Married in Fayette Co., Ind., in 1835.

THEIR CHILDREN.—Born in Fayette and Madison Counties, Ind.

926. LEROY THOMAS	....	Born,	1836;	Died,	....
927. MARY	"	....	"	1839;	"	...
928. ANN	"	....	"	1841;	"	....
929. LEWIS	"	....	"	1844;	"	1863
930. OLIVER H.	"	....	"	1849;	"	...
931. AVERY C.	"	....	"	1852;	"	....
932. IRVIN	"	....	"	1855;	"	....
933. MARSHAL	"	....	"	1856;	"	....

(390) ANNIE S. ELLIS..................Born, 1822; Died, 1849

(391) JONATHAN WARD............. " ....; " ....

Married in ——.

THEIR CHILDREN—Born in ——.

934. ELLEN WARD	....	Born,	1845;	Died,	....
935. EDWIN	"	....	"	1847;	"	1878

All errors and deficiencies in this part of the book will be corrected in the next section, under "Personal Sketches," so far as possible.

Descendants of Benjamin Ellis Jr. (126), of Groton, Cayuga
Co., N. Y., Benjamin Sr. (22), Reuben (4), and Richard,
of Ashfield.

(393) MYRON ELLIS....................Born, 1817; Died, 1858
(394) ——— CURTIS.................. "   ....;   "   ....

Married ———.

THEIR CHILDREN.—Born in Groton, N. Y.

936. AUGUSTUS ELLIS...........................Born, ...; Died, ...
937. BENJAMIN   "   ....   "   ....;   "   ....
938. CASSIUS   "   ....   "   ....;   "   ....
939. LYCURGUS   "   ....   "   ....;   "   1864

(393) MYRON ELLIS—Second wife.
NANCY DUNKS.

Married ———.

THEIR CHILDREN.—Born in Groton, N. Y.

940. RHODA   ELLIS...............................Born, ...; Died, ...
941. MARTHA   "   ....   "   ....;   "   ....
942. HELEN   "   ....   "   ....;   "   ....

---

(395) LEWIS R. ELLIS.................Born, 1822; Died ....
(396) ELIZABETH YALE.... ....   "   . ..;   "   ....

Married in Homer, N. Y.

THEIR CHILDREN.—Born———.

943. ALIDA ELLIS...............................Born, ...; Died, ...
944. ALBERT "   ....   "   ....;   "   ....

---

(397) AMANDA M. ELLIS............Born, 1826; Died, ...
(398) FILANDER H. ROBINSON.... "   1821;   "   ....

Married May 13th, 1849, in Groton, N. Y..

THEIR CHILDREN.—Born in Groton, Cayuga Co., N. Y.

945. EDMUND E. ROBINSON ....Born, 1851; Died, ...
946. LAVENE   "   ....   "   1856;   "   1861

---

(399) NATHAN H. ELLIS.............Born, 1834; Died, ...
(400) SARAH BOLLES............... "   1833; Died, ...

Married in Utica, N. Y., 1867.

ONE CHILD.—Daughter. Born in Groton, N. Y.

947. EDNA ELLIS ....Born, 1868; Died ....

Descendants of Reuben Ellis (128), of Chautauqua Co.,
N. Y., Benjamin Sr. (22), Reuben (4), and Richard
of Ashfield.

(401) OLIVET ELLIS..................Born, 1812; Died, ...
(402) ALMIRA POWERS..... .... "   ....; "   ....

Married March 3, 1839, in Clymer, Chautauqua Co., N. Y.

THEIR CHILDREN.—Born in Panama, N. Y.

948, Adelaide R. Ellis........................Born, 1840; Died, ...
949, Eveline C.   "   .... "   1845; "   ....

---

(403) HENRY K. ELLIS. ....Born, 1813; Died, 1853
(404) ELIZA ACKER................... "   ....; "   ....

Married Sept. 16th, 1837, in Clymer, N. Y.

THEIR CHILDREN—Born ———.

950, Henry R. Ellis.... ....Born, ...; Died, ...

---

(407) DANIEL ELLIS..................Born, 1817; Died, ...
(408) PHILINDA ADAMS.... .... "   ....; "   ....

Married April 19th, 1843, in Fredonia, N. Y.

THEIR CHILDREN.—Born in Panama, Chautauqua County, N. Y.

952, Francis Ellis... ....,........Born, ...; Died, ...
953, Newton "   .... "   ....; "   ....

---

(409) EDMUND ELLIS..................Born, 1819; Died, 1857
(410) ROXANA FAY............... ... "   ....; "   ....

Married Sept. 18th, 1842, in Chaut. Co., N. Y.

THEIR CHILDREN.—Born in Chautauqua County, N. Y.

954, Hollis Fay   Ellis........ ....Born, 1843; Died, ...
955, Henry Reuben   "   .... "   1846; "   ....
956, Lucien Elijah   "   .. .. "   1850; "   ....
957, Charles Edmund "   .... "   1853; "   ....
958, Lillie Phebe   "   .... "   1856; "   ....

(411) **LOIS E. ELLIS**........ ....Born, 1821; Died, 1881
(412) **WILLIAM R. DAVIS**............. ". ....; " ....
Married Aug. 27th, 1849, in Chautauqua Co., N. Y.

THEIR CHILDREN.—The first two born in Panama, N. Y., the last two in Wisconsin.

959. CATHARINE DAVIS.................. ....Born, ...; Died, ...
    ADELIA   " .... " ....; " ....
    JOAN   " .... " ....; " ....
    WILLIAM   " .... " ....; " ....

---

(413) **LYDIA E. ELLIS**.................Born, 1824; Died, 1862
(414) **HORATIO R. PALMER**......... " 1826; " 1864
Married Jan. 15th, 1851, in Chautauqua Co., N. Y.
THEIR CHILDREN.—Born in N. Y. and Wisconsin.

960. ALMARIAN S. PALMER.......................Born, 1852; Died, 1881
961. EMELINE B.   " .... " 1854; " ....
962. ALFRED S.   " .... " 1859; " 1863

---

(415) **EDWIN M. ELLIS**............ ...Born, 1825; Died, ...
(416) **DIANA GREEN**.................. " 1828; " ....
Married Sept. 16, 1846. (Now live at Lovell's Station, Erie Co., Pa.)
THEIR CHILDREN.—Born in Panama. N. Y.

963. ORLY J. ELLIS...........................Born, 1847; Died, ...
964. HENRY H.   " .... " 1849; " 1864
965. EDITH A.   " .... " 1852; " ....
966. CLARA A.   " .... " 1858; " ....
967. FRANCES E. " .... " 1861; " ....
968. REUBEN N. " ... . " 1867; " ....

---

(418) **REUBEN ERASTUS ELLIS** .. Born, 1832, Died, ...
(419) **HELEN FREEMAN**............. " 1833; Died, ...
Married Sept. 24th, 1854, in Portland, Chautauqua Co., N. Y.
THEIR CHILDREN.—The first two born in Nekimi, Winnebago Co., Wis., and the others in Portland, N. Y.

970. IDA E.   ELLIS..................... ....Born, 1856; Died, ...
971. EDMOND   " .... " 1857; " 1858
972. GEORGE ELMER " .... " 1864; " ....
973. WILLIE ALTON " .... " 1869; " ....

(420) ALFRED O. ELLIS............Born, 1835; Died, 1885
(421) HELEN M. SKIDMORE........ "   .. ; "   ....

Married 1858, in Portland, N. Y.

THEIR CHILDREN.—All born in Portland, N. Y.

974. PORTER ZERAH ELLIS......................Born, 1858; Died, ...
975. LORA BELLE   "   ....   "   1866; "   ....
976. CARRIE DELL   "   ....   "   1868; "   ....
977. JAMES EDMOND   "   ....   "   1870; "   ....
978. MINNIE MAY   "   ....   "   1872; "   ....
979. FRED. ARDEN   "   ....   "   1874; "   ....
980. ALGIA FRANK   "   ....   "   1877; "   ....

**Descendants of Abel West Ellis (136), of Ripley, Chautau-
qua Co., N. Y., Jonathan (26), Reuben (4),
and Richard, of Ashfield.**

(447) CYRUS ELLIS....................Born, 1837; Died, ...
(448) JENNIE S. HAYES............. "   1856; "   ....

Married Dec. 16, 1874, at Painesville, Ohio.

THEIR CHILDREN.—Born in Ripley, N. Y.

981. FRED HAYES ELLIS......................Born, 1876; Died, ...
982. EMMA MAUDE " ....   "   1878; "   ....

---

(451) SARAH J. ELLIS...... ....Born, 1841; Died, 1884
(452) GEORGE D. WILLOBEE....... "   1837; "   ....

Married Oct. 17, 1867, in Ripley, N. Y.

THEIR CHILDREN.—All Born at Cedar Run, Grand Traverse Co., Mich.

983. ABEL M   WILLOBEE.....................Born, 1869; Died, ...
984. CHARLES H.   "   ....   "   1871; "   1884
985. MARY D.   "   ....   "   1873; "   ....
     LOIS ALICE   "   ....   "   1878; "   ....
     SOLOMON R.   "   ....   "   1882; "   ....

---

(453) MARY ANN ELLIS.............Born, 1843; Died, ...
(454) DANIEL BUCHNER .. ..   "   1842; "

Married Jan. 19, 1875, in Westfield, Chautauqua Co., N. Y.

ONE CHILD—Born in Crowland, Ontario, Canada.

986. NELLIE MARGARET BUCHNER................ Born, 1877; Died, ...

Descendants of John Allis Ellis (138), of Conneaut, Ohio, Jonathan (26), Reuben (4), and Richard, of Ashfield.

(455) WILLIAM AVERY ELLIS .....Born, 1833; Died, ...
(456) MARIA HOLMES.......... ...... '' 1836; '' ....

Married in Saybrook, Ohio, Dec. 24, 1856.

THEIR CHILDREN.—Born in Conneaut and Ashtabula, Ohio.

987. HATTIE MANELLA ELLIS..... ....Born, 1857; Died, ...
988. FANNIE FLORENCE ''   .... '' 1861; '' ...
989. MINNIE MARIA   '' .... '' 1866; '' ....
990. WILLIAM WALTER '' .... '' 1872; '' ....
991. AMY F.   '' .... '' 1875; '' ....

(457) ORSON HENRY ELLIS .... Born, 1835; Died, ...
(458) ELIZABETH WOODARD....... '' 1835; '' ....

Married July 6, 1858, in Harrison, Illinois.

THEIR CHILDREN.—Born in Apple River, Ill.

992. JENNIE ELLIS................ ....Born, ...; Died, ...
993. JOHN FRANK '' .... '' ....; '' ...

(461) JOHN DEMETRIUS ELLIS...Born, 1842; Died, ...
(462) MARY JANE BRUCE........... '' 1843; '' 1875

Married in Conneaut, Ohio, Dec. 23, 1863.

THEIR CHILDREN—Born at Conneaut.

995. BRUCE L. ELLIS.. .   ...Born, 1865; Died, 1866
996. MARY L.   '' .... '' 1868; '' ....
997. EDITH   '' .... '' 1870; '' ....
998. BERTHA   '' .... '' 1872; '' ....
999. JOHN A.   '' .... '' 1874; '' ....

(463) JULIA FRANCES ELLIS......Born, 1845; Died, ...
(464) WM. BRADLEY COLE.......... '' ....; '' ....

Married in Erie Co., Penn., Jan. 10, 1864; now live in Jackson, Tenn.

THEIR CHILDREN.—Born in Erie, Penn.

1000. WALTER COLE........ ....Born, ...; Died, ...
1001. CARL   '' .... '' ....; '' ....
1002. ARCHIE   '' .... '' ....; '' ....

(465) SARAH ALICE ELLIS..........Born, 1850; Died, ...
(466) JOHN H. HART .... '' ....; '' ....

Married in Conneaut, Ohio; now live in Central City, Neb.

THEIR CHILDREN.—Born in ——

1003. BURT HART..... ....Born, ...; Died, ...
1004. JENNIE VEVE '' .... '' ....;'' ....
1005. PEARL   '' .... '' ....; '' ....
1006. GRACIE   '' .... '' ....;'' ....

**Descendants of Rev. Consider Ellis (152), of Ellisburg, Pa.,
Richard (29), Reuben (4), and Richard, of Ashfield.**

(500) GEORGE ELLIS...........Born, 1823; Died, ...
REBECCA RICE...............Born, ...; Died, ...

Married in ——

THEIR CHILDREN– Born in Alleghany Co., N. Y.

1007. WARREN ELLIS ....Born, ...; Died, ...
1008. RALPH " ... . " ....; " ....
1009. JOHN " .... " ....; " ....
1010. ELI " .... " ....; " ....
1011. JANE " .... ". ... ; " ....
1012. RUTH " .... " ....; " ....
1013. PRUDENCE " .... " ....; " ....
1014. FANNIE " .... " ....; " ....

**Descendants of Rev. John Ellis (154), of Ellicottville, N. Y.,
Richard (29), Reuben (4), and Richard, of Ashfield.**

(506) RALPH ELLIS.........Born, 1829; Died, ...
(507) CAROLINE W. EVERTS...... " 1838; " ....

Married in Benicia, California, in 1858.

THEIR CHILDREN—Born in California.

1015. WILSON R. ELLIS.......................Born, 1859; Died, ...
1016. CARRIE C. " .... " 1861; " ....
1017. FRANK E. " .... " 1864; " ....
1018. HENRY F. " .... " 1866; " ....
1019. MAGGIE M. " .... " 1874; " ....

(509) WILLIAM F. ELLIS............Born, 1815; Died, 1845
(510) MATILDA BERDINE........... " 1818; " 1845

Married in 1835,

THEIR CHILDREN.—Born in ——

1020. ELIZABETH ELLIS.......................Born, 1837; Died, ...
1021. FRED " .... " 1840; " ....

(511) LUCINDA ELLIS...... ....Born, 1820; Died, 1881
(512) PETER BERDINE.............. " 1816; " 1881

Married in 1840.

THEIR CHILDREN.—Born in Wisconsin and Iowa.

1022. HELEN BERDINE ....Born, 1841; Died. ....
1023. HATTIE " .... " 1842; " ....
1024. HENRY " .... " 1848; " ....
1025. RALPH " .... " 1849; " ....
1026. CLARA " .... " 1859; " ....
1027. CARRIE " .... " 1859; " . ..
1028. OLLIE " .... " 1862; " ....

Descendants of Elder Richard Ellis* (158), of Tioga Co., Pa., Richard (29), Reuben (4), and Richard, of Ashfield.

(522) AMASA ELLIS......... ....Born, 1819; Died, ...
(523) MARTHA SCHOONOVER...... '' 1831; '' ....

Married Sept. 29th, 1849.

THEIR CHILDREN.—All born in Allegany Co., N. Y., but now live in Westfield, Tioga Co., Pa.

1029. MARY E. ELLIS...........................Born, 1850; Died, ...
1030. DELOS   '' .... '' 1853; '' ....
1031. JAMES D. '' .... '' 1856; '' ....
1032. FRANK   '' .... '' 1857; '' 1864
1033. CHARLES '' ....:... '' 1862; '' ....

---

(524) CONSIDER ELLIS... ....Born, 1821; Died, ...
(525) MARGARET FORTNER....... '' 1820; '' ....

Married in 1845, in Allegany County, N. Y,

THEIR CHILDREN.—Born in Belmont, Allegany Co., N. Y.

1034. JOSEPHINE ELLIS.................... ..... Born, 1846; Died, ...
1035. DELPHINE   '' .... '' 1848; '' ....
1036. LILLIAN   '' ... . '' 1850; '' 1864

---

(526) SAMUEL G. ELLIS...............Born, 1822; Died, 1850
(527) ROSETTA CANFIELD......... '' ....; '' ....

Married in 1844 in Tompkins Co., N. Y.

THEIR CHILDREN—Born in ———

1037. ELIZA JANE ELLIS .... Born. 1845; Died, ...
1038. FRANCES   '' .... '' 1847; '' ....

---

(528) JOHN M. ELLIS............. .... Born, 1825; Died. ....
(529) ELIZA FORTNER.... .... '' 1827; '' ....

Married Feb. 25, 1852, at Ellisburg, Pa.
THEIR CHILDREN.—Born in ———

1040. ROSETTA H. ELLIS......................Born, 1853; Died, 1881
1041. MAGGIE E.   '' .... '' 1857; '' ....

* He was an unordained Baptist minister.

Descendants of David Ellis (160,) of Tioga Co., Pa., Richard (29), Reuben (4), and Richard, of Ashfield.

(530) THANKFUL ELLIS .... Born, 1820; Died, ...
(531) CHARLTON PHILLIPS .... " 1815; "

Married in Shippen, Tioga Co., Pa., 1838.

THEIR CHILDREN.—Born in Westfield.

1043. SYLVESTER D. PHILLIPS	....	Born, 1840;	Died,	....
1044. RACHEL	"	" 1842;	"	. ..
1045. ALICE	"	" 1844;	"	....
1046. ELLIS	"	" 1847;	"	....
1047. WILLIAM	"	" 1849;	"	....
1048. DELVIN	"	" 1851;	"	1879
1049. CLARENCE	"	" 1855;	"	...
1050. CLARA	"	" 1855;	"	....
1051. EMMA	"	" 1859;	"	....
1052. EVA	"	" 1862;	"	1863
1053. CHARLES	"	" 1869;	"	....

---

(532) CHLOE ELLIS .... Born, 1822; Died, ...
(533) JOB REXFORD .... " 1817; " 1880

Married March 3, 1844, in Big Meadows, Tioga Co., Pa.

THEIR CHILDREN.—Born in Big Meadows.

1054. PERRY EMERSON REXFORD	... .	Born, 1845;	Died,	....
1055. NANCY ORILLA	"	" 1848;	"	....
1056. HENRY GILBERT	"	" 1852;	"	1853
1057. STELLA	"	" 1860;	"	....

---

(534) CHESTER ELLIS .... Born, 1823; Died, ...
(535) CHLOE BLUE .... " 1827; " ....

Married in Wellsboro, Tioga Co., Pa., Sept. 25, 1848.

THEIR CHILDREN.—Born in Shippen, Wellsboro and Westfield, Pa.

1058. LAWRENCE A. ELLIS	....	Born, 1849;	Died,	....
1059. SEYMOUR D.	"	" 1851;	"	...
1060. SIMON W.	"	" 1857;	"	....
1061. IDA LUCRETIA	"	" 1858;	"	1862
1062. NELLIE J.	"	" 1861;	"	1863
1063. MYRA O.	"	" 1866;	"	....
1064. ANNIE B.	"	" 1869;	"	....

(536) JEFFERSON ELLIS.... ....Born, 1826; Died, 1877
(537) LORENA CHAPEL............... " ....; " ....

Married June 16, 1850 in Shippen, Tioga Co., Pa.

THEIR CHILDREN—Born in Tioga Co., Pa., and Marquette Co., Wis.

1065. SARAH ELLIS............................Born, ...; Died, ..
1066. ELLA   "   ....   "   ....;   "   ....
1067. JOHN   "   ....   "   ....;   "   ....

---

(538) MARIA ELLIS.......... ....Born, 1828; Died, ...
(539) JOHN J. MILLER............... " ....; " ....

Married Feb. 15, 1849, in Knoxville, Tioga Co., Pa.

THEIR CHILDREN.—Born in Potter and Tioga Cos., Pa.

1068. KATIE MILLER............................ Born ....; Died, ...
1069. NETTIE MILLER...................... .... " ....; " ...

---

(540) HARRY ELLIS..... .... Born, 1831; Died, ...
(541) SUSAN SCHUSLER.............. " 1836; "

Married Nov. 29, 1857, in Mansfield, Tioga Co , Pa.

THEIR CHILDREN.—Born in Mansfield.

1070. EMMA ELLIS... .... Born, 1860; Died, ...
1071. MINNIE " ....   " 1862; " 1865
1072. FRED D. " ....   " 1864; " ....

---

(542) CRETIA ANN ELLIS...........Born, 1836; Died. ....
(543) WILLIAM ANESLEY........... " ....; " 1881

Married Jan. 1, 1855.

THEIR CHILDREN.—Born in Potter Co., Pa.

1073. MARY ANESLEY.... .. ..Born, ...; Died, ...
1074. CARRIE   "   ....   "   ....;   "   ...
1075. HENRY   "   ....   "   ....;   "   ....

Descendants of Harry Ellis (168), of Ellisburg, Pa., Richard (29,) Reuben (4,) and Richard, of Ashfield.

(552) ADOLPHUS C. ELLIS...... .....Born, ...; Died, ...

(553) MARY HILL............ .... `" ....;   " ....`

Married in ——

THEIR CHILDREN.—Born in ——

1077. GENETT ELLIS.............. ....Born, ...; Died, ...
1078. MARY   `"` .... `" ....;   " ....`
1079. ELLA   `"` .... `" ... ;   " ...`

---

(554) WILLIAM ELLIS .. ..Born, ...; Died, ...

(555) ANNA DONALDSON.... .. ... `" ....;   "`

Married in ——

THEIR CHILDREN—Born in ——

1080. LETTIE ELLIS............ ....Born, ...; Died, ...
1081. HARRY   `"` .... `" ....;   " ...`
1082. WILLIAM `" JR`.............. .... `" ....;   " ....`

---

(556) RICHARD ELLIS................Born, 1840; Died, ...

(557) MAGGIE LOCKE................ `" 1846;   " ....`

Married at Ellisburg, Potter Co., Pa., Jan. 1, 1861.

ONE CHILD—Born in Ellisburg.

1084. NORA ELLIS ....Born, 1870; Died, ...

---

(561) AMASA ELLIS.... . ...Born, ...; Died, ...

ALLIE DONALDSON........... `" ....;   " ....`

Married in Ellisburg, Pa.

THEIR CHILDREN—Born near Ellisburg.

1087. ELIZABETH ELLIS........................Born, ... ; Died, ...
1088. MARY   `"` .... `" ..;   " ....`
1089. DONALDSON `"` .... `" ....   " ....`

---

(563) ELLA ELLIS.................... Born, 1851; Died, ...

JOHN SIMONS..... .... `" 1853;   "`

Married at Ellisburg, Pa., March 14, 1876,

ONE CHILD—Born in Ellisburg.

1090. KATIE SIMONS...........................Born, 1878; Died, ...

Descendants of Reuben Ellis (172), of Ellisburg, Pa., Richard (29), Reuben (4), and Richard of Ashfield.

(566) ALVIRA ELLIS....................Born, 1833; Died, ...

(567) CHARLES COATS...............   "   ... ;   "   ....

Married in Ellisburg, Pa., Jan. 31, 1850.

THEIR CHILDREN.—Born in Ellisburg.

1092. FRANCES E. COATS........................Born,	1851;	Died,	....
1093. CATHARINE E. " .... "	1853;	"	....
1094. HARRIET A. " .... "	1855;	"	....
1095. REUBEN E. " .... "	1860;	"	....
1096. WILLIAM H, " ... . "	1866;	"	...

Descendants of William Ellis, Sr. (176), of Springfield, Erie Co., Pa., David, Sr. (32), Reuben (4), and Richard, of Ashfield.

(570) WILLIAM ELLIS, Jr...............Born, 1810; Died, 1865

(571) SARAH GEER.....................   "   1818;   "   ....

Married Nov. 12th, 1840, in Springfield, Pa.

THEIR CHILDREN.- Born in Springfield.

1097. DAVID ELLIS.................. ....Born,	1841;	Died,	1870
1098. JESSE " .... "	1843;	"	....
1099. RHODA " .... "	1847;	"	1855
1100. MARTHA " .... "	1851;	"	....

---

(572) CHARLES P. ELLIS.......... .Born, 1812; Died, 1881

(573) SARAH HARRIS...... .... " 1816;   "   ...

Married in Springfield, Pa., Dec. 15th, 1839.

THEIR CHILDREN—Born in La Grange, Wis.

1101. PRISCILLA RUMINA ELLIS..... ....Born,	1845;	Died,	....
1102. JAMES ALFRED " .... "	1852;	"	....
1103. CHARLES ELLIOTT " .... "	1859;	"	....

(575) HARRIET ELLIS.... ....Born, 1815; Died, 1858

(576) AMOS SMITH ....   "   1815;   "   1851

Married Dec. 24th, 1835, in Springfield, Pa.

THEIR CHILDREN.—Born in Springfield.

1104. CYRUS E. SMITH... ....Born,	1839;	Died,	....
1105. CORDELIA L. " .... "	1841;	"	...
1106. JOHN B. " .... "	1844;	"	...
1107. WILLIAM E. " .... "	1847;	"	...

(579) SAMUEL ELLIS................Born, 1821; Died, ...
(580) AMANDA ADAMS. .... " ....; " 1850
Married in La Grange, Wis., in 1849.
THEIR CHILDREN.—Born in ——.
1108. WILLIAM EDWIN ELLIS...................Born, 1850; Died, ...

(579) SAMUEL ELLIS................Born, 1821; Died, ...
HARRIET FRENCH (Second wife) " ....; " ....
Married Sept. 17th, 1854.
THEIR CHILDREN.—Born in Palmyra and Eau Claire, Wis.
1109. CORA L. ELLIS....... ....Born, 1856; Died, ...
1110. FRANK E. " .... " 1858; " ....
1111. HARRY S. " .... " 1871; " ....

(583) MARY L. ELLIS........... ......Born, 1828; Died, ...
(584) JONATHAN MORRELL........ " 1824; " 1882
Married Aug. 12th, 1847, in Springfield, Pa.
THEIR CHILDREN.—Born in Springfield.
1112. CHARLES P. MORRELL.....................Born, 1848; Died, 1853
1113. JAMES E.   "   .... " 1851; " 1853
1114. MARCUS L.   "   .... " 1856; " ....
1115. FRANK W.   "   .... " 1861; " ....
1116. HARRIET R.   "   .... " 1865; " 1882

(585) JOSEPH ELLIS........ ....Born, 1831; Died, ...
(586) MARTHA WEED............... " 1842; " ....
Married Feb. 26th, 1863, in Springfield, Pa.
THEIR CHILDREN.—Born in Springfield.
1117. NEVADA A. ELLIS............. ....Born, 1865; Died, ...
1118. CARL   "   .... " 1868; " 1868
1119. GEORGE W.   "   .... " 1869; " ...
1120. CHARLES   "   .... " 1871; " 1872
1121. RALPH G.   "   .... " 1874; " ....

(587) RUMINA ELLIS................Born, 1835; Died, ...
(588) JOHN POTTER................ " 1830; " 1859
Married in 1856, in Springfield, Pa.
ONE CHILD.—Born in Eyota, Minn.
1122. GILBERT ELLIS POTTER...................Born, 1858; Died, ...

Descendants of David Ellis, Jr. (180), of Springfield, Erie Co., Pa., David, Sr. (32), Reuben (4), and Richard, of Ashfield.

(598) LOUISA ELLIS ....Born, 1815; Died, ...
(599) ROBERT PATTERSON........ " 1810; " 1868
Married in 1837, in Springfield, Erie Co., Pa.
THEIR CHILDREN.—Born in Springfield.
1123. WILLIAM S. PATTERSON....................Born, 1837; Died, 1878
1124. JOSEPH ELLIS " .... " 1841; " ....

(601) DR. GEORGE ELLIS...........Born, 1818; Died, ...
(602) EUNICE LYON.................. " ...; " 1861
Married in Springfield, Pa.
THEIR CHILDREN.—Born in Springfield.
1125. ORRA M. ELLIS. . . ..Born, 1848; Died, ...
1126. LOUELIA E. " .... " 1858; " ....

(603) MARSHAL ELLIS .. ..Born, 1820; Died, ...
(604) MARTHA JANE WILSON..... " ...; " 1886
Married in Springfield, Pa.
THEIR CHILDREN.—Born in Springfield.
1127. LILLIAN MAY ELLIS........,..............Born, 1860; Died, 1865
1128. HARRY W. " .... " 1868; " ....

(605) LEONARD ELLIS............. Born, 1822; Died, ...
(606) RHODA A. TAYLOR........... " 1826; " 1879
Married March 5th, 1854, in Spring Borough, Crawford Co., Pa.
THEIR CHILDREN.—Born in Springfield.
1129. ELVA C. ELLIS.....................Born, 1855; Died, ...
1130. DORA S. " .... " 1858; " ....
1131. MINA P. " .... " 1864; " ....
1132. FRED T. " .... " 1865; " ....

(607) PETER ELLIS..... .. .. Born, 1824; Died, ...
(608) VIOLETTA DAVENPORT..... " 1826; " ....
Married Feb. 11th, 1845, in Springfield, Pa.
THEIR CHILDREN.—Born in Springfield.
1133. LOUISA F. ELLIS............. .... Born, 1846; Died, 1850
1134. MARTHA R. " .... " 1847; " 1850
1135. GEO. WILBUR " .... " 1852; " ....
1136. HAZEN W. " .... " 1854; " ....
1137. ORMAN F. " .... " 1858; " ....

(609) SARAH ELLIS........... ....Born, 1827; Died, ...
(610) AARON WILSON............. ....   "   ....;   "

Married in Springfield, Pa.

THEIR CHILDREN—Born in Springfield.

1138. L. Estella Wilson.......................Born, 1854; Died, 1863
1139. Ellis R.   "   ....   "   1856;   "   1863
1140. Clara L.   "   ....   "   1866;   "   ....

---

(611) ORMAN F. ELLIS...............Born, 1829; Died, 1870
(612) MARTHA E. NELSON.........   "   1840;   "   ....

Married in Springfield, Pa., Sept. 23d, 1863.

THEIR CHILDREN.—Born in Springfield.

1141. Frank H.   Ellis.......................Born, 1865; Died, ...
1142. Charles Mark "   ....   "   1869;   "   ....

Descendants of Azel Ellis (209), of Niles, Cayuga Co., N. Y., John, Jr. (68), John, Sr. (15), and Richard, of Ashfield.

(622) PHEBE ELLIS...................Born, 1833; Died, 1863
JOHN WINSLOW...............   "   ....;   "   1863

Married March 3d, 1855, in Marseilles, Ohio.

ONE CHILD.—Born in Marseilles.

1143. Harriet Winslow.......................Born, 1857; Died, ...

---

(623) LYDIA ELLIS.....................Born, 1841; Died, ...
JOHN H. TERRY...............   "   1838;   "

Married 1865, in Marseilles, Ohio.

THEIR CHILDREN.—Born in Canon City, Colorado.

1144. William L. Terry.......................Born, 1866; Died, ...
1145. Nellie   "   ....   "   1872;   "   ....
1146. Joe   "   ....   "   1874;   "   ....

Descendants of Hiram Ellis (214), of Niles, N. Y., John Jr. (68), John, Sr. (15), and Richard.

(627) REV. ELISHA ELLIS..........Born, 1837; Died, ...
(628) LOVINA WELDON..............   "   1837;   "   ....

Married 1856, in Caton, Steuben Co., N. Y.

THEIR CHILDREN.—Born in Corning and Caton, N. Y.

1147. Edwin Ellis.............................Born, 1858; Died, ...
1148. Egbert   "   ....   "   1866;   "   ....
1149. Clark   "   ....   "   1874;   "   ....

(629) HANNAH ELLIS.................Born, 1834; Died, 1873
    WILLIAM COLE...... .... " 1836; " 1864
    Married in 1856, in Caton, Steuben Co., N. Y.
        THEIR CHILDREN.—Born in Caton.
1150. Clovy Cole........................... . Born, 1858; Died, ...
1151. Edwin " .... " 1860; " ....
1152. Ella   " .... " 1862; " ....

Descendants of Elisha Ellis (216), of Farmersville, Posey Co., Indiana, John Jr. (68), John Sr. (15), and Richard.

(630) NANCY ELLIS....................Born, 1829; Died, 1852
    H. W. HOLLEMAN.............. " 1826; " 1852
    Married in Farmersville, Ind., in 1848.
      THEIR CHILDREN.—Born in Farmersville.
1154. Elizabeth Holleman.... ....Born, 1849; Died, ...
1153. Elisha   " ... . " 1850; " 1858

---

(636) ANN ELLIS........................Born, 1836; Died, ...
(637) SIDNEY ALLYN... .... " 1832; " 1884
    Married in Farmersville, Ind., in 1854.
    THEIR CHILDREN.—Born in Farmersville.
1155. Hannah Allyn..................... ....Born, 1855; Died, ...
1156. Thena   " .... " 1857; " ....
1157. Elisha   " .... " 1858; " ....
1158. Bijah   " .... " 1864; " 1868
1159. Indiana " .... " 1867; " ....

---

(638) JOHN DAVID ELLIS...........Born, 1839; Died, ...
(639) HARRIET RUSSELL.......... " 1846; " ....
    Married in Farmersville, Ind., in 1862.
    THEIR CHILDREN.—Born in Farmersville.
1160. Elisha Ellis.................... ....Born, 1863; Died, ...
1161. Samuel " .... " 1863; " 1863
1162. Grant   " .... " 1865; " ....
1163. John   " .... " 1870; " ....
1164. Jay   " .... " 1872; " ....
1165. Birchard " .... " 1876; " ....

**Descendants of Richard Ellis (218), of Niles, Cayuga Co.,
N. Y., John, Jr. (68), John, Sr. (15), and Richard,
of Ashfield.**

(642) CATHARINE ELLIS............Born, 1833; Died, ...
(643) DR. C. J. RODIG................ "   ... ;   "   1864

Married in Toledo, Ohio, in 1854.

THEIR CHILDREN.—Born, the first in Toledo and the second in Wyandotte Co., Ohio.

1166. JOHANNA RODIG.......................Born, 1858; Died, ...
1167. LENA   "   .... "   1860;   "   ....

(642) CATHARINE ELLIS............Born, 1833; Died, ...
RICHARD WILLARD (Second Husband) "   ....;   "

Married in 1866, in Marseilles, Ohio.

THIER CHILDREN.—Born in Marseilles, Ohio, and Nebraska.

1168. INES WILLARD.........................Born, 1866; Died, ...
1169. CLARA   "   .... "   1868;   "   ....
1170. MARION   "   .... "   1872;   "   ....
1171. CLYDE   "   .... "   1875;   "   ....

---

(644) MARY ANN ELLIS.......... ...Born, 1837; Died, ...
(645) SAMUEL PHILLIPS............ "   1835;   "

Married Oct. 11th, 1857, in Marseilles, Ohio.

THEIR CHILDREN.—Born in Marseilles.

1172. JOHN W. PHILLIPS.......................Born, 1858; Died, ...
1173. EVA O.   "   .... "   1860;   "   ....
1174. HARLAN P.   "   .... "   1862;   "   1862
1175. MARY A.   "   .... "   1863;   "   1871
1176. JAMES E.   "   .... "   1865;   "   ....
1177. SELOVER K. "   .... "   1868;   "   1872
1178. CHARLES N. "   .... "   1870;   "   ....
1179. JENNIE O.   "   .... "   1872;   "   ....
1180. OTTO F.   "   .... "   1875;   "   ....
1181. ANNIE   "   .... "   1880;   "   ...

---

(646) WILLIAM M. ELLIS............Born, 1845; Died, ...
(647) MARGARET A. KEYES .. ... "   1843;   "   ....

Married Jan. 6th, 1869, in Niles, N. Y.

THEIR CHILDREN.—Born, the first in Niles and the others in Kenton, Ohio.

1182. SUSAN VIOLA   ELLIS ....Born, 1870; Died, ..
1183. EVA MINNIE MAY " .... "   1871;   "   ....
1184. LENA ADELA   "   .... "   1872;   "   ....
1185. ESSIE AMAND   "   .... "   1874;   "   1875
1186. KATE EDNA   "   .... "   1877;   "   ....
1187. EUGENE F. MEAD "   .... "   1879;   "   ....

(649) SYLVIA JANE ELLIS......... Born, 1835; Died, 1876
JOHN KISHLER................. ' ....; " ...
Married Nov. 7th, 1852.
THEIR CHILDREN.—Born in ——.

1188. PORTER S. KISHLER ... .Born, 1855; Died, ...
1189. CHARLES " .... " 1857; " ....
1190. ANNIE " .... " 1859; " ....
1191. MARY " ... . " 1866; " ....
1192. JENNIE " .... " 1868; " ....

Descendants of Hon. Pitts Ellis (220), of Genesee, Waukesha Co., Wis., John Jr. (68), John Sr. (15), and Richard, of Ashfield.

(653) LODOSKY S. ELLIS.............Born, 1845; Died, ...
(654) ALEX. R. BENZIE.............. " 1837; " ....
Married in Genesee, Waukesha Co., Wis., Aug. 2, 1866.
THEIR CHILDREN.—Born in Burns, Lacrosse Co., Wis.

1193. MINNIE L. BENZIE......................Born, 1867; Died, ...
1194. GEORGE N. " .... " 1868; " ...
1195. IDA MAY " .... " 1874; " ...
1196. CHARLES ELLIS " .... " 1878; " 1879
1197. DOTTIE LORINDA " .... " 1880; " ....
1198. HAROLD ALEX. " .... " 1883; " ....

(655) PITTS B. ELLIS.... . ...Born, 1851; Died, ...
(656) NELLIE DOANE................. " ....; " ....
Married in Waukesha, Wis., Sept. 1875.
ONE CHILD—Born in Bangor, Lacrosse Co., Wis.

1199. RICHARD CLAUD ELLIS....................Born, 1882; Died, ...

Descendants of Benjamin Ellis (225), of Niles, N. Y., John Jr. (68), John Sr. (15), and Richard, of Ashfield.

(671) JOHN H. ELLIS.................Born, 1843; Died, ...
(672) JANE McCLEARY............... " ....; " ....
Married in Marseilles, Ohio.
THEIR CHILDREN.—Born in Marseilles.

1200. JOHN ELLIS..............................Born, ...; Died, ...
1201. ELNORA " .... " ....; " ....

(677) MARY E. ELLIS............ ....Born, 1851; Died, ...
(678) VINCENT LONG............... " 1848; " ...

Married in Marseilles, Ohio. 1870.
THEIR CHILDREN.—Born in Marseilles.

1202 A. VILLROY LONG. ....Born, 1873; Died, ...
1203. SYLVESTER H. " .... " 1877; " ....
1204 CHARLES R " .... " 1883; " ....

Descendants of Ebenezer Ellis (227), of Farmersville, Posey Co., Ind., John Jr. (68), John Sr. (15), and Richard, of Ashfield.

(685) JULIA ELLIS.................Born, 1840; Died, ...
(686) JOHN H. MOCKETT........... " 1840; " ....

Married in Genesee, Wis., March 14, 1860.
THEIR CHILDREN.—Born in Genesee and Stark, Wis.

1205. JOHN H. MOCKETT, JR.... ....Born, 1860; Died, ...
1206. EDWIN R. " .... " 1863; " ....
1207. FREDERICK E. " .... " 1867; " ....
1208. EBENEZER E " .... " 1870; " ....

(687) SOPHRONIA ELLIS............Born, 1842; Died, ...
(688) RICHARD H. MOCKETT..... " 1838; " ....

Married in Genesee, Wis., April 24th, 1861.
THEIR CHILDREN.—Born in Genesee, Wis.

1209. ROBERT SQUIRE MOCKETT..................Born, 1863; Died, ...
1210. EDITH THEODOCIA " .... " 1866; " ....

(689) EDWIN ELLIS.................Born, 1844, Died, ...
(690) ELIZA J. MOCKETT.......... " 1848; " 1872

Married in Stark, Vernon Co., Wis.
ONE CHILD.—Born in Janesville, Wis.

1211. WILLIE EBENEZER ELLIS........... ....Born, 1870; Died, ...

(691) HARRIET ELLIS ....Born, 1847; Died, ...
(692) ANDREW DEAN............... " 1847, "

Married at Stark, Richland Co., Wis., Jan. 1st, 1869.
THEIR CHILDREN.—Born in Wisconsin and Nebraska.

1212. MABEL DEAN...........................Born, 1869; Died, ...
1213. NELLIE MAUD " .... " 1872, " ....
1214. ASA " .... " 1875; " ....
1215. ELLIS " .... " 1877; " ....
1216. MARY " .... " 1880; " ....

(693) PITTS ELLIS.............. .....Born, 1852; Died, ...
(694) OLIVE L. ROSE...... .... " ....; " ....

Married July 7th, 1880, in Scranton, Iowa.

THEIR CHILDREN.—Born in Denver, Colorado.

1217. RAYMOND EDWIN ELLIS ....Born, 1881; Died, ...
1218. MARION HAROLD " .... " 1883; " ....

---

(695) MARY ELLIS.............. .. ..Born, 1854; Died, 1879
(696) FRANK CLARK........ .... " 1845; " 1880

Married in Cuming Co., Neb., April 14th, 1876.

THEIR CHILDREN.—Born in Cuming Co., Neb.

1219. CLARA E. CLARK........................Born, 1877; Died, ...
1220. SAMUEL " .... " 1879; " 1880

Descendants of Cyrus Ellis (233), of Niles, Cayuga Co., N. Y., Edward (70), John, Sr. (15), and Richard, of Ashfield.

(715) EDWARD D. ELLIS.............Born, 1826; Died, 1865
(716) MARY CAMP..................... " ....; " ....

Married in Moravia, N. Y., Dec., 1850.

THEIR CHILDREN—Born in Moravia and Omro, Wis.

1221. CAMP ELLIS ....Born, 1851; Died, ...
1222. MARY " .... " 1858; " ....

---

(717) POLLY ELLIS......................Born, 1828; Died, ...
(718) THOMAS W. BAKER........... " 1808; " 1877

Married in Niles, N. Y., October 11th, 1854.

THEIR CHILDREN.—Born in Manitowoc, Wis.

1223. CLARA BAKER...........................Born, 1855; Died, ...
1224. EMMA " .... " 1856; " ....
1225. ELLIS " .... " 1863; " ....

---

(719) MINERVA ELLIS.................Born, 1829; Died, 1872
(720) EDWARD H. DEUEL.... .. .... " 1819; " ....

Married in Niles, N. Y., Feb. 5th, 1852.

ONE CHILD.—Born in Niles.

1226. MARY JANE DEUEL .. ..Born, 1853; Died, ...

(723) HIRAM ELLIS....................Born, 1834; Died, ...
(724) MARGARET VAN ETTEN.... " 1839; " ...

Married in Niles, N. Y., July 7th, 1859.

THEIR CHILDREN.—Born in Niles.

1227. LEVI L. ELLIS.......................Born, 1860; Died, ...
1228. HENRY " .... " 1863; " ....

---

(727) BIRCH ELLIS....................Born, 1838; Died, ...
(728) GERTRUDE SELOVER........ " 1837; " 1871

Married in Niles, N. Y., Nov. 7th, 1866.

ONE CHILD.—Born in Niles.

1230. GERTIE S. ELLIS.........................Born, 1871; Died, ...

---

(731) MILES M. ELLIS........... ......Born, 1846; Died, ...
(732) ELLEN M. CLEVELAND........ " 1846; " ...

Married in Sempronius, N. Y., Feb. 23rd, 1870.

THEIR CHILDREN.—Born in Niles, N. Y.

1231. ARTHUR C. ELLIS.................... ....Born, 1872; Died, ...
1232. FRED. A. " .... " 1875; " ....
1233. CYRUS H. " .... " 1876; " ....
1234. HERBERT L. " .... " 1880; " ....

**Descendants of Edward D. Ellis, (235), of Monroe, Mich.,
Edward (70), John, Sr. (15), of Ashfield, and
Richard Ellis.**

(737) JOHN C. C. ELLIS...............Born, 1837; Died, ...
(738) LUCY JANE WHITAKER...... " 1844; " ....

Married in Lansing, Mich., Dec. 24th 1863.

THEIR CHILDREN.—Born in Chicago, Ill.

1236. HARRIET A. ELLIS..................... Born, 1864; Died, ...
1237. ADA L. " .... " 1866; " ....
1238. LEWIS T. " .... " 1869; " ....

Descendants of Richard Ellis (239), of Belding, Ionia Co.,
Mich., Dimick (72), John, Sr. (15), and Richard Ellis,
all of Ashfield.

(749) CHARLES DIMICK ELLIS....Born, 1829; Died, ...
(750) ELIZA A. LOCKWOOD......... " 1842; " ....

Married in Grand Rapids, Mich., April 30th, 1862.

THEIR CHILDREN.—Born in Belding, Ionia County, Michigan.

1240. MAY LOUISA ELLIS........................Born, 1863; Died, ...
1241. WM. ERASTUS " .... " 1867; " ....

(751) DR. ERASTUS R. ELLIS........Born, 1832; Died, ...
(752) M. MINERVA ELLIS*........... " 1831; " 1884

Married in Belding, Mich., April 22nd, 1857.

THEIR CHILDREN.—Born, the first in Owosso, the three next in Grand Rapids, and the
last in Detroit, Mich.

1242. ELIZABETH B. ELLIS ....Born, 1858; Died, ...
1243. HELEN M. " .... " 1860; " ....
1244. JESSIE R. " .... " 1863; " ....
1245. EDWARD D. " ... . " 1867; " ....
1246. ANNA BELLE " .... " 1873; " 1874

*Daughter of Edward D. Ellis, of Monroe, Mich. See No. 733, page 37.

Descendants of Lewis Ellis (241), of Belding, Mich., Dimick
(72), John, Sr. (15), and Richard Ellis, all of Ashfield.

(757) MARY L. ELLIS ....Born, 1854; Died, ...
(758) FRED. E. RANNEY............. " 1853; ". ....

Married in Belding, Mich., 1875.

THEIR CHILDREN.—Born in Belding, Mich.

1247. ELLIS W. RANNEY.......................Born, 1878; Died, ...
1248. CARRIE L. " .... " 1880; " ....
1249. HATTIE B. " .... " 1883; " ....

From page 43 up to this point are included the sixth generation of Richard Ellis' descendants, except those of his son Caleb. The latter being much younger than the others it is
thought best to omit them from this part of the book, but their names will be given, so far as
can be ascertained in connection with their parents, under the next section of Personal
Sketches.

PERSONAL SKETCHES

OF

Richard and Jane Ellis

AND THEIR DESCENDANTS.

In this section will be found sketches of every descendant of Richard Ellis, so far as the same can be obtained. The numbers at the head of each name in the Sketches refer to the same number and person in the Record.

Where names or dates in the Record differ from those in the Sketches, the latter may be taken as correct.

FIRST GENERATION.

(1.) **RICHARD ELLIS.** (For sketch see pages 9 to 16.)

(2.) **JANE PHILLIPS.** (For sketch see page 16. For a more full account of the Phillipses see *Appendix*.

SECOND GENERATION.

Children of Richard and Jane Ellis and their wives and husbands.

(4.) **REUBEN ELLIS,** was born in Easton, Bristol Co., (formerly Plymouth Co.) Mass., Nov. 5th, 1728.

When about 11 years of age his parents moved to Deerfield, Franklin Co., (then Hampshire Co.) Mass. While his father's family were in Deerfield, his father made a location in Ashfield (at that time called Huntstown) and removed his family there about 1745. It is probable that Reuben remained in Ashfield with his father until near his majority. According to the records of the town of Sunderland, which is the first town south of Deerfield, Reuben Ellis was married to Mehitable Scott, June 4th, 1749. There in Sunderland they lived for about three years where their two eldest children, Martha and Benjamin, were born, as shown by the records of Sunderland.

About 1751 Reuben removed to Ashfield, as on the records of that town are found the names and dates of birth of all his children except the first two, his third child, Reuben, Jr., being born in Ashfield, Feb. 12th, 1752, and his youngest David in 1763. About this time Reuben purchased of his father, Richard Ellis, a lot of land known as No. 56 of the 50 acre "Rights" as the land was then divided. The deed was dated Dec. 25th, 1751. This probably is a part of the farm where Reuben lived and raised his family, and where after his death his youngest son, David Ellis, lived until 1818, when he sold out to Mr. Jesse Ranney and removed to Springfield, Erie Co., Penn.

Reuben Ellis was a man of worth and highly respected. In the French and Indian War from 1754 to 1757 he was an ensign in the Colonial service and was in several engagements. On one occasion, himself and several companions took captive a squad of French soldiers. Two of the guns taken were retained by Reuben and were in the possession of his sons, Benjamin and Jonathan, 60 years afterwards. They were old fashioned guns, but would carry a ball with great accuracy over a mile. When the Revolutionary war for American independence was opened he was too old for military service, but records in possession of his descendants show that he contributed liberally to the support of the cause. His three sons, Benjamin, Richard and David were soldiers in the Revolutionary army. He died April 21st, 1786, in the 58th year of his age. A stone in the Ellis neighborhood burying-ground* opposite where his father made the first settlement, marks his grave.

Reuben's residence was built upon the rise of ground about 60 to 80 rods south-west of the large house which

---

*This burying-ground was nearly opposite where Richard Ellis made the first settlement in this town. (See page 11.) It was in the Ellis neighborhood and will be mentioned in this work as the "Ellis' burying-ground." In after years it was known as the Belding burying-ground from Mr. John Belding having long resided where Richard Ellis first settled. The Beldings have all left Ashfield, but the members of the extensive silk-manufacturing firm of "Belding Brothers" (grandsons of John) were raised on this farm and as they occasionally visit Ashfield, this burying-ground is kept in order mainly at their expense.

now stands on that farm near the main roadway. This house like all houses in those early times, was built of logs. The remains of the cellar and the stone chimney were visible as late as 1840, when the writer, a small boy, visited that locality. It is said that up to the present time some relics of the old orchard, which was near the house, are to be seen.

Reuben's farm was considered one of the best in this part of Ashfield, and he displayed good judgment in erecting his house on a pleasant elevation of ground. Its healthfulness was evident from the vigor and longevity of his wife and children.

His farm comprised much more than the original 50 acre Right which he purchased of his father. In 1818 Mr. Jesse Ranney, father of Mrs. Hannah Ranney Ellis (240), purchased this farm of David Ellis (32). About 1790, David Ellis and his brother Jonathan (26) built the large two story square house which yet stands on the northerly roadway from Conway to Ashfield Plain. It is said that the brick used in the construction of the chimney, arches, oven and fire places, would be sufficient to build an entire house on the modern plan.

Here Mr. Ranney raised his family of ten children. He died in 1857. His son, Charles Ranney, succeeded to the farm, which he sold to Mr. John Mann, about 1860. Mr. Mann now owns and resides on this farm.

(5.) **MEHITABLE SCOTT**, wife of Reuben Ellis, was born in Sunderland, May 3rd, 1722, and died in Ashfield, Dec. 2nd, 1804, in the 83d year of her age. Her parents, Richard and Elizabeth Scott, were among the early settlers in Sunderland. She was said to have been a good and christian woman. It is probable that both she and her husband Reuben were members of the Baptist church. She was burried beside her husband in the Ellis neighborhood burying ground. Sketches of their children and families may be found from Nos. 21 to 32.

(6.) **BENJAMIN ELLIS,** second child of Richard Ellis, was born in Easton, Mass., Sept. 26th, 1730, and died Nov. 17th of the same year.

(7.) **MARY ELLIS,** third child of Richard Ellis, was born in Easton, March 28th, 1732. Of her descendants the writer gets no trace. It is most likely that she married in the eastern part of Mass., and was but little known to the Ashfield relatives. That she lived to mature years, is quite evident from a letter written in 1850 by Aaron Smith of Stockton, Chautauqua Co., N. Y., whose grandmother was Remember Ellis, (9) a daughter of Richard. Aaron Smith was born in Ashfield in 1792. and in the letter above referred to says: "Richard Ellis had eight children, four of whom John, Jane, Hannah and Remember I have seen."

(9.) **REMEMBER ELLIS SMITH,** fourth child of Richard was born in Easton, May 1st, 1735. She was about ten years of age when her father settled with his family in Ashfield, where she lived the rest of her life. July 1st, 1756, she was married to Elder Ebenezer Smith, a son of Mr. Chileab Smith, Sr., the third settler in Ashfield. The following account of their marriage, found in the records of the Smith family, has been sent to the writer. "There being no minister or magistrate at Ashfield at the time, on the wedding day the groom took the bride behind him on horseback and guided by marked trees rode from Ashfield to Deerfield to have the ceremony performed. His father Chileab Smith went before them on another horse with his gun to guard them from the Indians. She was reported in the family as a person of uncommon worth."

She died at Ashfield, Sept. 15, 1795, aged 60 years. She had seven children. Her husband

(10.) **ELDER EBENEZER SMITH,** was born in South Hadley, Mass., Oct. 4th, 1734, and died in Stockton, N. Y., July 6th, 1824. He was a Baptist minister, began to preach when 19 years of age, and was ordained Aug. 20th, 1761.

When a young man he served in the army in the French and Indian War, and assisted in building a fort around his father's house, which was a resort of the neighborhood against the Indians for about three years. After the death of Remember Ellis, his first wife, in 1795, Elder Smith married Lucy Shepardson, June 15th, 1796. She died Oct. 5th, 1808, aged 68 years. Jan. 5th, 1809, he married Esther Harvey, and she died Oct. 14th, 1814, aged 78.

Elder Smith was a pure and noble man and was held in high esteem by all who knew him, and he was extensively known throughout New England and New York. Elder Supply Chase, of Detroit, Mich., a Baptist minister now over 86 years of age, says: "Elder Ebenezer Smith's is one of the sanctified names in the Baptist denomination." Both he and his father, Chileab Smith, were pioneers in the Baptist faith in western Mass. The persecution they suffered on account of their religious belief was almost incredible. This extended over a course of about ten years and required them to make repeated journeys to the General Court at Boston for redress of their grievances. Their orchards were torn up and lands sold to pay tithes for the support of other churches than their own. Warrants for their arrest on fictitious charges were issued, but in each instance they were completely vindicated. A year before his death Elder Smith wrote quite a full account of his ministry and trials, extracts from which may be found in the *Appendix*.

Elder Ebenezer Smith was a son of Chileab Smith, Sr., who was born in South Hadley, Mass., in 1708, and he, Chileab, was a son of Preserved Smith, who was born in 1679, who was a son of Preserved Smith, born Jan. 27th, 1637, and the latter was a son of Rev. Henry Smith, of Wethersfield, Conn., who emigrated from England in 1636. In crossing the ocean they encountered such violent storms that all hopes of their reaching land was lost. However they were providentially preserved, and having a son born on the voyage, they gave him the name of Preserved, which has been a frequent name in the Smith family in every generation since.

Mr. Chileab Smith, Sr., was a very positive character, and the most noted man in Ashfield's history. On account of a schism in the church at Weathersfield, Conn., a large portion of the congregation removed to Hadley, Mass. Years afterwards another schism took place at Hadley, when Chileab moved to Ashfield in 1750—then called Huntstown. At the age of 80 years he was ordained a Baptist minister by his sons Elders Ebenezer and Enos Smith. At the age of 85 he married his second wife. He died in Ashfield in 1800, aged 92 years. His first wife, and mother of his children, was Sarah Moody. One of his sons, Chileab, Jr., was born in Hadley in 1742, and died in Ashfield in 1843, aged 100 years and seven months.

Elder Ebenezer Smith was a minister of the gospel 72 years, and preached 10,920 sermons, and rode one horse over 25,000 miles. He preached in Ashfield nearly 40 years. When 76 years of age he made a visit to Cayuga County, N. Y., where several of his children had settled. He made the trip on horseback and was gone 120 days, and preached as many sermons as he was days gone. At Throopsville, Cayuga Co., N. Y., he preached to the settlers there in the hollow of a large buttonwood tree* which held an audience of 32 persons. From this as a beginning the Baptist church there was founded.

His last sermon in Ashfield was "delivered May 22, 1815, before a large assembly." He was then in his 81st year. The sermon was printed and reads like a good, old-fashioned, strictly orthodox discourse. The next year he removed to Stockton, Chautauqua Co., N. Y., where his son Ebenezer, Jr., had settled in 1815. Every Sabbath thereafter, until his death, he rode his horse to the place of worship. He died at the house of his son Ebenezer, Jr., July 6th, 1824, aged 89

---

*I was at the tree in 1813. There was a door on one side.
—[Letter from Aaron Smith, 1850.

years, 9 months, and two days, in the full vigor of his mental powers, and as full of honors as of years. While he deplored his lack of educational privileges in his youth, he knew the advantages of early education and his eldest son, Preserved, and youngest son, Richard, went to Brown University, where they graduated. He raised seven children, and a year before his death estimated his posterity then living at 100 souls. Personally Elder Smith was about five feet eight inches tall, thick set and dark complexioned. For an account of his children and their descendants, see Nos. 34 to 46. For a more full account of the Smiths of Ashfield, see *Appendix*.

(11.) **JANE ELLIS PHILLIPS**, third daughter of Richard Ellis, was born in Easton, Nov. 11th, 1737. She probably was married in Easton, as all her eight children were born there. In after years several of her children settled in Windham Co., Vermont. After the death of her husband, in 1805, she lived in Newfane, Vt., many years. At the time of her death she was living with her son, John Phillips, Jr., in Marlboro, Vt., which is about 25 miles north of Ashfield, Mass. One of her grandsons, James Charter, of Williamsville, Vt., now 77 years of age, writes "I was well acquainted with her. She was a very devoted Christian of the Baptist denomination." She lived to the age of 95 years. She was very smart and could walk a mile up to a week of her death. She was of medium height and weight, light complexion and blue eyes. For an account of her children see Nos. 47 to 61. Her husband

(12.) **JOHN PHILLIPS**, was born in Easton, May 21st, 1734. He died Feb. 14th, 1805. He was a son of Samuel Phillips, who was born in Easton in 1702, and a grandson of Capt. John Phillips of Easton. Whether he died in Easton or in Vermont does not appear. For a more full account of the Phillipses of Ashfield and Easton, see *Appendix*.

(13). **MATTHEW ELLIS**, sixth child of Richard Ellis, was born in Easton, Dec. 19th, 1739. He was but two or three years of age when his father moved to Deerfield and but seven or eight when he settled in Ashfield. From no account which the writer can obtain does it appear with certainty what became of Matthew or where he settled. It is known that after the death of his mother in Ashfield (then Huntstown) his father removed to Colerain, in the same county, about 15 miles north-easterly from Ashfield. He took with him his two youngest children, Hannah and Caleb. That Matthew also went with them, or was there for a time, is evident from a charge found in his father's account book, under the date of Nov., 1768, in acct. with "William Clark, the First: * To stoneing your well 15 shillings. To Matthew one day at ye well 6 shillings and sixpence."

It is probable that Matthew Ellis was not married at this time, although he was 28 years of age, for no trace of him or his descendants are found in Colerain. Circulars of inquiry have been quite extensively sent throughout the States, from which the following response has been received from Indiana. Whether the writer is one of the descendants of Matthew Ellis of Ashfield, has not as yet been decided but it seems probable that such is the case. Further inquiry will be made, the result of which will have to be deferred to the *Appendix*, as it is too late for this part of the book:

JACKSON, Tipton Co., Ind., Dec. 16th, 1885.

Dear Sir:—I have before me a circular handed to my son, W. D. Ellis, making inquiries about the descendants of Richard Ellis, of Ashfield, Mass. My father's name was Eliphalet and his father was Matthew Ellis, who was, I think a son of Richard Ellis of Ashfield. My father Eliphalet was born in 1787, and settled in Indiana, about the year 1822, and died in 1844. I have heard him speak of Ellisburg, and of his brothers Enos, Seth and Levi, and sisters Ann and Sarah, but I do not know where they lived. His children were George, born 1815, Ann, 1817, William, 1819, Enos, 1821, David, 1823, Matthew, 1830, Reuben (myself) 1834, Levi, 1836, and Sally, 1838.

My father, Eliphalet Ellis, was in the war of 1812, and was in the battle of Sackett's Harbor. I think he was born in New York or Vermont. My older brothers are all dead and I have no knowledge of any more distant relatives. I will make inquiries and let you know if I learn anything further.

Yours &c., REUBEN ELLIS.

To Dr. E. R. Ellis, Detroit, Mich.

NOTE.—My aunt, Sarah Fulton Franklin [95], of Guilford, Vt., used to say that: "Levi Ellis and one they called 'Liph' Ellis [most likely Eliphalet,] were in the battle of Sackett's Harbor, Jefferson Co., N. Y. [May 29, 1813.] 'Liph' was then living in or near Carthage, Jefferson Co., N. Y."—*Letter from Robert Fulton, Green River, Vt., April, 1886.*

* "Richard Ellis lived near Mr. Clark's. My father bought the farm of Wm. Clark. I have been many times to the well spoken of. I was born here in 1812. My father, grandfather and great grandfather have lived here since the first settlement of the town. There are no Fultons or Ellises here now."—*Letter from Hugh B. Miller, Colerain, June, 1885.*

Jabez Franklin, of Guilford, Vt., now 90 years of age, who married Sarah Fulton, of Colerain, a grand-daughter of Richard Ellis, says that "some of the Ellises moved into Vermont, but he has lost the run of them." If these were related to Richard Ellis they must have been descendants of Matthew, as all the other Ellis families are accounted for.

(15). LIEUT. JOHN ELLIS, seventh child of Richard Ellis, was born in Deerfield, Mass., Jan. 23rd, 1742, and died in Ashfield, Aug. 17th, 1827, aged 85 years.

He said his father moved from Deerfield to Ashfield when he was three years old. July 19th, 1763 (records of Ashfield) he married Mary* Dimick. About this date he bought the farm 100 rods west of the corners where his father first settled. He built a log house about 15 rods west of where the present farmhouse now stands, in which all his family were raised. Remains of this log house were visible up to 40 years ago. About 1795 the present house was built, in which he resided until his death.† He was a man of quite large business capacity for his time. Besides farming he engaged in the milling business. On Bear river, which runs through the north part of his farm, he had a saw mill, and lower down the stream, about 20 rods below the roadway bridge, was the old grist mill erected by his father and the Smiths, which was later—about the time of the Revolutionary war—in his charge. He was one of the first to declare for the Independence of the Colonies and to take up arms in behalf of the cause. At this day we can hardly appreciate the moral heroism required of the Colonists to break away from and resort to arms against the mother country. At first many of the old and influential residents of Ashfield were opposed to the rebellion, as they called it. Families were divided and near and dear relatives opposed

*This name is also written Molly and Polly in various instances among the early generations.

†Mr. Charles Rogers now owns and resides on this farm. In the rear of the house stands an apple-tree ten feet and six inches in circumference, six feet above the ground. This tree, some years, produces 75 bushels of apples, and Mr. Lewis Ellis of Belding, Mich., who was born on this place in 1811, says that in the early years of his recollection it had been known to grow 150 bushels annually. It may be said that the hill-sides of that mountainous region were famous for growing fruit, principally apples.

each other in the early part of the conflict. Some of the most noted and outspoken tories in Ashfield had sons who had already gonè to the front in the patriot army, and had laid down their lives in its service.

Lieut. John Ellis was commissioned an officer in the war of the Revolution and did service during the whole conflict. He was in several engagements in Eastern New York about Saratoga and Lakes George and Champlain. From 1777 to 1780 he was, a portion of the time, detailed for home duty in raising recruits and provisions to carry on the war. In the *Appendix* will be found some interesting accounts left by him, bearing on this subject. He was said to have been a man of good judgment and large influence, which he exerted most judiciously in the support of the cause of independence. He understood and acted upon the highest principles of liberty. At various times irresponsible but over-zealous patriots proposed violence toward some of the leading tories. Lieut. Ellis condemned this vigorously and declared that every man's liberty was sacred so long as he committed no overt acts of hostility to the cause of independence. About 1800 he visited Central New York, where he bought tracts of land on which two of his sons settled. About this time there was quite an emigration from Ashfield, many of the residents seeking new homes in Cayuga and Onondaga Counties, N. Y. Among these were several of the Ellises, Annables, Bartletts, Phillipses and others from the Ellis neighborhood in Ashfield. Of these mention will be made in other parts of this work. Lieut. John Ellis in personal appearance was rather short in stature, thick set and of a hardy and vigorous constitution. He was a Methodist in religious belief and a class leader, so called, among the members. Headstones in the Ellis burying ground mark the graves of himself and wife. For sketches of his children, see Nos. 63 to 75.

(16). **MOLLY DIMICK,*** wife of Lieut. John Ellis, of Ashfield, was born in Barnstable, Mass., Dec. 6th, 1838, and died in Ashfield, Sept. 8th, 1827. At what time she came to Ashfield does not appear, but probably about a year before her marriage, for her brother-in-law, Samuel Annable, Jr., who married her older sister Desiah, settled in Ashfield about 1762. It is probable that Molly or Mary Dimick came at the same time. She was from "the Cape," as Barnstable Co. was called. Old letters from relatives there indicate that she had brothers, Edward, Charles, and Constant Dimick in or near Barnstable, and an older sister, who married an Agry, who lived in Hollowell, Maine. Mrs. Ellis was a very devoted mother, a respected and beloved neighbor, and a sincere Christian woman.

(17). **HANNAH ELLIS FULTON,** eighth child of Richard Ellis, was born Oct. 13th, 1750, and died in Guilford, Vt., in 1839. After the death of her mother in Ashfield her father removed to Colerain.† She went with him and her youngest brother Caleb. She was then about 15 years of age and was her father's housekeeper until her marriage in 1772 to James Fulton, of Colerain. They lived in the north-east part of the town, where they raised a family of ten children. She lived here until the death of her husband, when she went to her daughter, Sarah (95) in Guilford, Vt. She was rather short, weight 160 lbs., and of fair complexion. For an account of her children, see Nos. 77 to 95. Her huband,

(18). **JAMES FULTON,** was born May 24th, 1749, and died in Colerain, March 20th, 1834. He was a son of Robert Fulton, who was one of the first settlers of the town. In early times the Fultons were numerous and influential in Colerain. They lived in the north-east part of the town. In Richard Ellis' account book are found the names of William, John, Robert and Sarah Fulton,

---

*The name Dimick is found in old writings, Dimock, Dimmick and Dymock. Elder Thomas Dymock was early identified with the history of Barnstable. He died in 1658 leaving several children. He was probably the ancestor of all the Dimicks of the Cape. A further account of them will be found in the *Appendix.*

†This town probably received its name from Colerain, Antrim Co., in the extreme north of Ireland, from whence some of its earliest settlers emigrated.

residents there previous to the Revolution. James Fulton was a farmer, as were nearly all the residents of Colerain at that time and up to the present. He was tall and large, weight about 200 lbs., blue eyes, fair complexion, and curly hair, which he wore long done up in a cue, the Continental style.

(19.) CALEB ELLIS, ninth and youngest child of Richard Ellis, was born August 16th, 1754, and died in Ellisburg, Jefferson Co., N. Y., in March, 1813.

It is not probable that he was born in Ashfield, for at the time of his birth the settlers of that town had gone to the older settlements, to avoid the Indians during the period of the French and Indian war. However this may be, it is evident that he was with his father in Colerain early in life, and on the 24th of Jan., 1777, at which date his name is found in his father's books. He was then 22 years of age. He early joined the Revolutionary army, in which he served several campaigns. He was under Generals Gates and Ethan Allen at Lake Champlain, Ticonderoga, and when Burgoyne surrendered. He served through most of the Revolutionary war. About 1779 he married Mary Crouch and, it is said, lived for some time in Vermont. He next moved to Oneida Co., N.Y., near Litchfield, and in 1795 he settled permanently in Jefferson Co., N. Y., at a place which was named after him, Ellisburg. Here he purchased 500 acres of land and built a grist mill. This was his home until his death in 1813. He probably learned the milling business with his father. It is evident that he was a man of industry, courage, and perseverance, for it requires all these qualities to succeed in so wild and remote a region as Jefferson County was when he settled there. Here he raised his family of eleven children, and quite a number of his descendants now reside there and at Belleville, in the same county. (See Nos. 97 to 118).

(20.) MARY CROUCH, wife of Caleb Ellis of Ellisburg, N. Y., was born Aug. 4th, 1757. Where she was born or where married does not appear from any records found. She died in Ellisburg, N.Y., in April, 1813. She and her husband are said to have been members of the Methodist church.

THIRD GENERATION.

(21.) MARTHA ELLIS, first child of Reuben and Mehitable Ellis was born in Sunderland, Mass., in 1750. She
was a mute (deaf and dumb) and never married. After the
death of her parents in Ashfield she resided with her youngest brother David Ellis, and removed with him to Springfield, Erie Co., Penn., in 1818, where she died in 1832. She
was a very industrious, conscientious and Christian woman.

(22.) BENJAMIN ELLIS, second child of Reuben Ellis
of Ashfield, was born in Sunderland, May 7th, 1751.

March 15th, 1774, he married Ruth Pike in Ashfield,
where their two oldest children—Stephen and Lurenca—
were born ; the last named, born Jan. 10th, 1777. About
this time he joined the Revolutionary army and was a soldier several years.

His principal occupations were farming and milling. In
the early part of his married life he lived in Deerfield, Mass.,
where most of his eight children were born. In 1800 he
purchased a large farm in Sempronius,* Cayuga Co., N. Y.,
which he divided with his brother Jonathan, where they both
settled.

Benjamin soon after built a small grist mill at Montville,
near his farm, which he operated several years, and where
his sons Stephen, Moses and Benjamin, Jr., learned the milling business, which they followed long afterwards.

In 1818 Stephen and Moses Ellis removed to North Bend,
on the Ohio river, a few miles below Cincinnati, where they
rented a farm of General (afterwards President) Harrison,
and where they built a grist mill.

In 1825 Benjamin followed his sons to North Bend, and
in 1832 they all removed to Fayette Co., Indiana, where
Benjamin was Postmaster, at Plum Orchard in Fayette Co.,

---

*Sempronius at that time included several townships of land. This farm is in what is
now called Niles, and is about three miles north of Moravia.

up to the time of his death. About 1785 his wife Ruth died, and he married Lois Mann, who is said to have been of the family of which Hon. Horace Mann, once president of Antioch College, Ohio, was a member. He probably married Miss Mann in Deerfield, Mass., or thereabout. She was the mother of his three youngest children—Reuben, Mehitable and Chelometh. The date of her death is not given.

For his third wife Benjamin Ellis married Mrs. Zilpha Mills in 1822, in Sempronius. She was a widow with one daughter. After Benjamin's death in Indiana in 1835, she and her daughter removed to Illinois about 1837. Benjamin Ellis was said to have been a remarkably pure and upright man, of rare intelligence and excellent memory. For a sketch of his children see Nos. 119 to 132.

(23.) RUTH PIKE, first wife of Benjamin Ellis, was according to town records of Ashfield, married March 15th, 1774. When and where she was born is not recorded, so far as the writer knows. It is believed, that she died in Deerfield about 1784. She was the mother of Benjamin's five eldest children.

(25.) REUBEN ELLIS Jr., third child of Reuben and Mehitable Ellis, was born in Ashfield Feb. 12th, 1752. He was a mute, and never married. When his brother Richard moved from Ashfield to Tioga Co., in the southern part of New York, about 1798, Reuben went with him and afterwards to Tioga Co., Penn., where he died in 1832. He was a very industrious, upright and sincere Christian man. In 1820 the first Baptist Church in the western part of Tioga Co., Penn., was organized at Delmar, now called Shippen. Reuben Ellis was the oldest member. He was baptized June 20th, 1819. He was about 80 years of age at the time of his death.

(26.) JONATHAN ELLIS, fourth child of Reuben Ellis, was born in Ashfield, Aug. 25th, 1754. He died in Sempronius, Cayuga Co., N. Y., in 1812.

He lived at his father's home and with his brother David built, about 1795, the large house, which now stands on that farm in Ashfield. In March, 1799, being then about 45 years of age, he married and removed to Sempronius, N. Y., and settled on a farm with his brother Benjamin. He was a mute, but could make a sound which seemed like "daunt," and from this he was generally known by the name of "Daunt" Ellis. He was a great worker and it is said, was the most expert driver of cattle anywhere about. His oxen became so accustomed to him, that they obeyed him with the greatest precision. It is the tradition, which the writer has received from several of the older families who knew of him that, aside from the infirmity of hearing, "he was the smartest Ellis ever in Ashfield."

There were four mute children in Reuben Ellis' family, and Jonathan was the only one of them who married. He had eight children, four of whom grew to maturity, none of whom were mutes, and it is a gratification to be able to say that the calamity has not reappeared in any of the descendants. It is said, that on the birth of each child he made sounds to test the child's hearing capacity, and when he found it perfect in this respect, he manifested the greatest delight.

Mr. John Allis Ellis of Conneaut, Ohio, is the only one of this family of children now living. He was born in Sempronius in 1809. It is said, that he is almost an exact likeness of his father Jonathan, which fact gives additional interest to the very excellent likeness of him found on another page. (See No. 138). For sketches of Jonathan Ellis' children see Nos. 134 to 140.

(27.) **LOIS ALLIS**, wife of Jonathan Ellis, was much younger than her husband. She is said to have been a devoted wife and mother, and a most lovely woman. After the death of her husband, in 1812, she lived on the farm with her children for several years, when she married a Mr. Wells and had one son. Mr. S. V. R. Wells, the son, now resides in Westfield, Chautauqua Co., N. Y., with whom his mother lived at the time of her death in 1840.

(28.) **SUBMIT ELLIS,** fifth child of Reuben Ellis, was born in Ashfield, Mass., Oct. 28th, 1756. She was a mute and never married. She went with her brother Jonathan to Sempronius, lived with him and his children until his death in 1812.

She then went to her brother Richard in Pennsylvania, where she remained six or seven years, after which she returned to Jonathan's children in Sempronius, with whom she lived until about 1833, when she removed with her nephew Abel West Ellis (136) to Ripley, Chautauqua Co., where she died the following year. She was a very industrious woman, and became quite an expert in weaving, as nearly all cloths in those times were made in the family. She devised and wove many complicated and beautiful patterns for coverlids for beds, etc. Like all of this family of Reuben Ellis' children, she was a very pious, sincere and devout person. She was the fourth child in her father's family who was a mute, an almost unheard of affliction. The parents could not understand why they should be subjected to so great a misfortune, and naturally enough had felt somewhat rebellious. But when the fourth mute child was born, they agreed that it was for some good purpose of an All-wise Being that they were thus afflicted, and that it was their duty to be reconciled and submit. They accordingly named her Submit. Two other children were afterwards born, neither of whom were thus affected. In a Note, which will be found on page 88, is given some interesting particulars regarding these people.

(29.) **Dea. RICHARD ELLIS,** sixth child of Reuben, was born in Ashfield, Dec. 20th, 1760.

December 12th, 1780, he married Eunice Chilson, of Conway, the next town east of Ashfield. He lived in Ashfield a few years, and it is said, operated a woolen-mill. In 1788 to 1792 he lived in Shelburn, a town joining Ashfield

on the north, where he was engaged in milling. This mill
was on Deerfield river near the Charlemont line.*

In April, 1795, Richard Ellis leased of Mr. Levi Stone his
grist mill in the town of Kent, Litchfield Co., Conn., for one
year. Sometime after this he removed to Candor, Tioga
Co., N. Y., where he lived and kept a tavern for a dozen
years or more. In 1811 he went to Delmar, Tioga Co., Pa.,
when it was a wilderness, where he bought a large tract of
land and built two saw mills and two grist mills. He manufactured lumber on Pine Creek, which he rafted down that
stream and the Susquehanna river to the older settlements
east and south.

While at Delmar in 1819, he lost his second wife, Chloe
Ellis in an epidemic of fever, which swept over that part of
the country and proved fatal to nearly all who were attacked
with it. It was known ever afterwards as the "great sickness," and as to its cause was never fully accounted for.
Several years later he removed to Potter Co., (next county
west of Tioga), where he built a saw mill and grist mill at
a place named after him 'Ellisburg, where he died in May,
1841. He also built a hotel or tavern here to provide for
travelers, and the building is yet standing.

He was the father of 19 children, 15 of whom grew
to maturity and most of them to old age. Mrs. Lucretia
Stipp, of Scio, Oregon, wife of Elder John Stipp, a Baptist
minister, is the only one now living. (See No. 165).

Dea. Richard Ellis was a man of great industry and
enterprise. He was a Baptist, as were most of his children.
When the church was organized at Delmar, its members
were nearly all composed of these Ellises and their relatives.
Three of Richard's sons, John, Consider and Richard Jr.,

---

*Adjoining Richard Ellis on the north, lived Ebenezer Ellis, who was probably the father
of Dr. Edward Ellis of Meadville Pa. Dr. Ellis is now 82 years of age and writes that "his
father, Ebenezer, once had an interview with Richard Ellis of Ashfield (No. 1 of these sketches)
and that they could trace no relationship." About this time there were several Ellis families
in Goshen, the first town south of Ashfield, and also in Huntington, Hampshire Co. Dr. Ellis
of Meadville is a descendant of one of these. In Conway, next town east of Ashfield, lived
Barzillia Ellis in the latter part of the last century. He had a numerous posterity, most of
whom settled in Chautauqua Co., N. Y., 75 years ago or thereabouts. Dr. Samuel G. Ellis of
Syracuse, N. Y., and Dr. David E. Ellis of Belvidere, Ill., are descendants of Barzillia. The
latter was not a relative of Richard Ellis of Ashfield, unless through English ancestors.
Barzillia Ellis, Sr., died in Chautauqua County in 1825.

were ordained ministers of the Baptist denomination. Richard Ellis was a soldier in the Revolution for some time. He seemed to inherit from his grandfather, the first Richard, a trait which many of the Ellises since have had, that of becoming pioneers in new parts of the country. None of that name now live in Ashfield. The last to leave was Dea. Dimick Ellis, (72) who removed to Michigan in 1847. His children had all left some time before. The barren and inhospitable region of Ashfield and thereabouts made it absolutely necessary for all the surplus population to get out early in life.

When Richard Ellis settled in southern New York, that country was very wild. When he went to Tioga Co., Penn., that whole region was a vast wilderness, very difficult to reach. The woods were full of game and the streams abounded in trout and other fish. He settled on Marsh Creek, a branch of Pine Creek, at what is called Big Meadows. Ansonia, a station on a branch of the Blossburg & Tioga railroad, is located where Richard Ellis first settled in that county.

In three or four years after the death of his wife Chloe, Richard married a very worthy woman, a Mrs. Stanton, widow of Judge Stanton, and soon after removed to Ellisburg, Potter Co. After her death he married a widow Seeley, who was the mother of Betsey Seeley (No. 169) wife of Harry Ellis of Ellisburg, one of Richard's sons.

Richard lived here until his death, May 14th, 1841. Of him, Mrs. Chloe Rexford, (No. 532) one of his granddaughters, writes: "I recollect him well, his life was worthy of imitation, his neighbors found in him a wise counselor, his house, heart and hand were always open to the needy and unfortunate, he rejoiced with those who had joy, and sympathized with those in sorrow. It can truly be said, we have few like him now."

For sketch of his children see Nos. 143 to 172.

(30.) **EUNICE CHILSON,** first wife of Richard Ellis, was from Conway, Mass. She was born Feb. 11th, 1763, and died Nov. 27th, 1791. She lived in Shelburn at the time of her death, but she was buried in the Ellis ground in Ashfield, where a headstone now marks her grave. She was probably a Baptist. She had six children.

(31.) **CHLOE CHILSON,** second wife of Richard Ellis, was a sister of Eunice. Records of Ashfield, sent to the writer by Henry S. Ranney, Esq., who has been town clerk there for 40 years, give the following: "Richard Ellis and Chloe Chilson of Shelburn were married Feb. 19th, 1792." Richard had lived in Shelburn up to this time, when he may have removed to Ashfield. His wife, Chloe, was a Baptist and was one of the members who, with her husband, organized the first Baptist church in Delmar, Pa., in 1819. She had 13 children. She was born in 1767, probably in Conway, and died at her home in Big Meadows, Delmar township, Tioga Co., Penn., August 9th, 1819, with a malignant epidemic fever, which prevailed that season. One of her children and several other relatives died at the same time, with the same disease.

(32.) **Dea. DAVID ELLIS,** seventh and youngest child of Reuben Ellis, was born in Ashfield, Jan. 30th, 1763. When 16 years of age he was drafted into the service of the Revolutionary army in which he served several years. He was a faithful soldier, and as a young man was of more than ordinary intelligence and trustworthiness. On the 20th of May, 1794, he was appointed by Samuel Adams, then Governor of the commonwealth of Massachusetts, an ensign in the Fifth Regiment of militia for Hampshire county. (Hampshire then included Franklin Co., in which Ashfield is situated.) In Sept., 1795, Gov. Adams appointed him a lieutenant in the same regiment. July 8th, 1784, he married Sarah Washburn, and settled on the farm with his father. The latter died two years later, and his mother resided with him until her decease in 1804. David's brother Jonathan also lived with him until about the time of his marriage in

1799, and his eldest sister, Martha (21), remained with him during her whole life. She had the best of care, and was beloved by all who knew her.

David Ellis had five children, all of whom were born and reared on this farm—the old homestead where Reuben, his father, first settled in Ashfield in 1751.

In 1818 David with his sons William (176), and David, Jr. (180), sold out all their interests in Ashfield and removed to North Springfield, Erie Co., Penn. They made the journey with ox teams and were six weeks on the trip, the men walking most of the way. When they settled in their new home it was an unbroken wilderness of heavily timbered land. By dint of hard labor, energy and patience all the usual obstacles met with in a new country were gradually overcome, and they made homes where himself and wife passed the remainder of their days in comfort, and where many of their descendants now live. They first made a clearing and planted an orchard, some of the trees of which are yet standing to show the industry of the early pioneers. His daughter Sarah (178), who married Capt. James Flower in Ashfield, in 1810, removed with her husband to Wesleyville, Erie Co., soon after their marriage, and it is probable that this event was one of the reasons which induced her father and brothers to settle in the same section. David Ellis was an ardent Baptist and for many years a deacon in the church, and was noted for his Christian example. He lived as he believed God directed him to. Often he filled the pulpit in the absence of the pastor. He was a thorough Bible scholar, it being said of him that he could give the chapter and verse of any Bible quotation given him. His large family Bible, that was used daily in family worship, was brought with him from Ashfield, and is now in the care of his grand-daughter, Mrs. Louisa Ellis Patterson. (598.)

He always retained the old New England custom of rigidly observing the Sabbath from Saturday at sun-down to sun-down of the next day. His religious principles were carried into all the conduct of his life, and he was widely known for his integrity and reliability. An incident in confirmation of this was told by one of his grandsons (572), who settled in Wisconsin over 40 years ago. The latter desired to purchase a horse on credit of a man who had known his grandfather years before in Ashfield. He was informed that "if he was a descendant of Deacon David Ellis he could have the horse without other security than his word as to the terms of payment," thus proving that a good name is the best inheritance for children. He still liveth in memory, and his life on earth was one to the honor of his many descendants.

The old farm bought by Deacon Ellis was the home of his son William (176,) during his lifetime, and is now the home of his grandson, Joseph Ellis (585).

Dea. David Ellis died in North Springfield, in 1843. For sketch of his children see Nos. 174 to 182. This family of Ellises—Reuben's children—were mostly large, tall and with dark hair and complexion, which latter they most likely derived from their mother, who was a Scott (5). David Ellis' wife

(33.) SARAH WASHBURN, was born 1764. She was a daughter of Deacon Samuel Washburn, of Ashfield. The Washburns were a prominent family in Ashfield in those times and she was a woman of intelligence and refinement. Like her husband she was a radical Baptist. It is related that she often and expressly cautioned her children and grandchildren against the Universalists, a caution which not all observed, as some of the latter became in after years prominent members of that denomination. She died in Springfield in 1848, aged nearly 84 years.

Note to page 83.—In regard to these mute sons and daughters of Reuben Ellis of Ashfield—Martha (21), Reuben (25), Jonathan (26), and Submit (28),—there is a well-founded tradition worthy of further consideration. The generation which knew them in their early years has gone by, but some are yet living, who have heard these reports from their ancestors, and regard them as well founded. It is, that these persons all had, what was called among people in the neighborhood, "*Angels visits.*" It was claimed, that they had appearances to them of spiritual or angelic beings, who gave them instruction in the way they should live. At the time of these first occurrences they were young and possessed of all the vigor and gaiety of the average youth. They were favorites in society, attended most of the balls and parties, to which they usually had "free tickets". They could keep time to the music and go through all the changes of dancing in perfect order. All at once a great change came over them, they became devoutly pious, abjured all dancing and frivolity, and said, that "angels had appeared to them and instructed them how they should live to avoid sin and become upright and useful." They lived to old age, and all accounts agree that they never lost their religious principles or pious ardor. From central and western New York, Ohio and Michigan, the writer gets confirmation of these reports, which were traditional with many who had emigrated from that part of Ashfield 50 to 100 years ago, that these mutes "had angels visits, and all the people believed it."

Of Jonathan's (26) claim to these extraordinary visitations one instance is related, which convinced many of the people of their truthfulness. He said, that on a time when he was in the sugar-bush, sitting upon a log eating his lunch, he beheld an angel coming down to converse with him. The latter gave him some good instruction, and besides told him that across the Connecticut river, which was about 20 miles distant, there was a deaf and dumb man who wanted to see and talk with him. Jonathan went home full of enthusiasm and told the family of the occurrence, and began to make ready for the trip. His parents tried to convince him that it was folly and deception and to dissuade him from going, as he was a total stranger in the locality mentioned. He replied that the angel had offered to go with him and show him the way, and he must go. He dressed in his Sunday suit and started. In due time he returned and reported that he had found the man he went to see, and that he was *waiting* and *expecting* to see him and that he had had a pleasant interview, etc. As a memorable and convincing part of this occurrence it is stated as a fact, that during the time when Jonathan was under this angelic influence, he had his *speech* and *hearing*.

A relative now 75 years of age, who was born in Ashfield in 1811, and who lived there half his lifetime, and whose veracity none can question, informs the writer that several of those ancestors who knew Jonathan Ellis and his brother and sisters, told him of these occurrences, substantially as related above, and that they all believed them to be true.

All this was 100 years or more ago, long before modern spiritualism was heard of, and it is not surprising that the people in those times were much puzzled thereat and, without attempting to further investigate the phenomena, let it pass simply as "angels visits," a miracle or mystery beyond their ken. Of course phenomena such as above related are not in accordance with *Natural Laws*, and hence if susceptible of explanation at all, must be in accordance with *Spiritual Laws* or laws of mind, which it is no assumption to say, are as real as are those of a material character with which all are familiar. Probably the most profound investigator and voluminous writer in this department of learning which the world has ever known, is Swedenborg, who was born in 1688 and departed this life in 1772. It has occurred to the writer that probably one versed in his philosophy might give a reasonable explanation of such phenomena as above related. Accordingly he has submitted these proof-sheets to Rev. Mr. Frost of Detroit, Mich., a minister of the New Jerusalem Church (Swedenborgian), also to Rev. Elisha Ellis (627), of Westbury, N. Y., minister of the Christian Church, and to Elder John Stipp, of Scio, Oregon, whose wife, Lucretia (165), was a daughter of Richard Ellis (29), of Ellisburg, Pa. Elder Stipp is an aged minister of the Baptist Church. Each of these reverend gentlemen have been requested to give their views on the subject. If they respond, the same will be given at length in the *Appendix*. The phenomena mentioned are of a very interesting character and are well authenticated. It is presumed that with the light obtained from the Scriptures with that afforded by the revelations and investigations of these later times, an intelligent explanation of the same can now be given.

Children of Remember Ellis Smith, (9), and Elder Ebenezer Smith, (10), of Ashfield, and their husbands and wives. Grandchildren of Richard Ellis. From Nos. 34 to 46.

(34.) **IRENE SMITH ALDEN**, was born in Ashfield, July 4th, 1757, and died March 16, 1834. She married Isaac Alden, of Ashfield, who was a lineal descendant of John Alden and Priscilla Muggins, who came over in the Mayflower in 1620 and whose courtship has been immortalized by the poet Longfellow. The latter left a numerous posterity in Massachusetts. Several of them were residents of Ashfield in early times. One of these was John Alden, whose farm was on the north side of the road opposite Reuben Ellis' farm. This John Alden died about 1840, a very aged man. He was probably a brother of Isaac Alden, mentioned above.

Irene and Isaac Alden had nine childen, one daughter and eight sons. The daughter married Dr. John Rathburn.

(36.) Rev. **PRESERVED SMITH**, eldest son of Elder Ebenezer Smith, was born in Ashfield, June 25th, 1759. He died Aug. 15th, 1834, in Rowe, Franklin Co., Mass.

When 16 years of age, at the beginning of the Revolutionary war, he entered the army and served five campaigns as a soldier.　He was under Gen. Gates and present at the surrender of Burgoyne.

He was early imbued with a desire to obtain an education, and began preparation for college under the instruction of Rev. Mr. Hubbard, of Shelburn.　For some time he taught school in the winter and worked in the summer to procure means for study.　He entered college in Providence, Rhode Island, and graduated in 1786.　Soon after he commenced the study of theology with Rev. Mr. Emerson, of Conway, Mass.　In 1789 he settled in the ministry in Rowe, and in January the following year he was married to Miss Eunice Wells, the youngest daughter of Col. David Wells, of Shelburn.

Although his parents were the strictest Baptists, and he was reared under this influence, he began his ministry as a Congregationalist.　In 1804 he resigned his charge in Rowe and the next year settled in Mendon, Mass., where he preached to two societies or churches for several years. This double duty he found too great a tax on his energies and on a unanimous invitation from the church in Rowe he returned there in 1812.　About this time the Unitarian controversy began, and from his love of free inquiry and independent habit of thought he investigated the subject fully. The result was that he became openly a Unitarian, although he preferred the name purely of Christian to that of any sectarian designation.　He was a minister for forty-five years.

He had two children, Rev. Preserved, Jr., and Royal. The latter died early in life, about 1820.　The eldest, Preserved, Jr., was born in Rowe, Aug. 1st, 1789, and died in Greenfield, Mass., in 1881, aged 92 years.　Like his father he was a Unitarian minister and preached in Warwick, Franklin Co., nearly all his life.　He had his faculties unimpaired up to the time of his death.　He remembered well, and often related an interview which he had when ten years of age with his great-grandfather, Chileab Smith, Sr., who died in Ashfield in 1800, at 92 years of age—a remarkable event of two lives covering a period of 173 years.　He had three children: Preserved, Jr., who now resides in Dayton, Ohio; Fayette, who is a lawyer and judge in Cincinnati, O., and Eunice Wells Smith, who married Rev. J. F. Moors, a Unitarian minister who resides in Greenfield, Mass., where he has preached for twenty-five years.

(38.) JEMIMA SMITH ANNABLE, second daughter of Elder Ebenezer and Remember Ellis Smith, was born in Ashfield, March 18, 1761, and died in Marcellus, Onondaga Co., N. Y., Feb. 13th, 1835. She married Lieut. Edward Annable, of Ashfield, Nov. 24, 1782 and had a family of eleven children. She was a very pious woman, devoted to her family and of rare qualities of mind and heart. She had a good education for one of her times, and it was said was a natural mathematician and could solve problems in arithmetic and algebra mentally with more rapidity and ease than most persons could with figures. She was a great bible student and critic, and understood doctrinal points thoroughly. Her children were all born in Ashfield, except Fernando C., the youngest, who was born in Aurelius, Onondaga Co., N. Y., and he is the only one living at the present date.

(39.) LIEUT. EDWARD ANNABLE, husband of Jemima Smith was in his day one of the most noted men of Ashfield. He was born in Barnstable, Mass., June 22, 1753, and when nine years of age his father, Samuel Annable, Jr., settled in Ashfield. He was a large man and of commanding presence. At 18 years of age he entered the Revolutionary army and served seven years without a furlough.* He was at Bunker Hill, Saratoga, Brandywine, and at the winter encampment at Valley Forge. He commanded the company which relieved Gen. Anthony Wayne after the

*Lieut. Edward Annable's patriotism was of a high order and came from patriotic ancestors, although his father was at the opening of the Revolution a prominent tory. In Freeman's "History of Cape Cod" is found the following record: "In Barnstable, June 26th, 1776, Thomas Annable and 22 others issued an address to the citizens of the town of Barnstable urging them to aid the Independence of the Colonies. At a town-meeting held a short time before this, the tory element was in a majority and voted to do nothing to aid independence. Mr. Annable and the others protested in the following language: ' And we request that this Protest may be entered on the town book to let posterity know that there were a few in this town who dared to stand forth in favor of an injured and oppressed country, and that it is a matter of great grief to us that the Cause of Liberty is treated with such indignity by some of the inhabitants of the town of Barnstable.' "

surrender of Stony Point, May 31, 1779, and was with that
officer when it was recaptured July 15, 1779. He was one
of Andre's guard at his execution, and often dwelt on the
brave deportment of that unfortunate officer. He said that
when Col. Schamel told him to speak if he wished to say
anything, Andre raised the handkerchief from over his eyes
and said: "Gentlemen I wish you all to bear me witness that
I meet my fate like a brave man." His arms were tied so
slightly that with some difficulty he could raise the handkerchief from before his eyes.

Lieut. Annable married and settled in Ashfield. His
father was Samuel Annable, Jr., and his mother Desiah
Dimick, sister of Molly Dimick (16). Samuel, Jr., was born
in Barnstable, Mass., 1717, and died in Sempronius, N. Y.,
about 1806. His father, Samuel, Sr., was a descendant of
Anthony Annable and his wife Jane who came over in the
Anne* in 1623. Anthony Annable was a prominent man,
and much in public life. He died in Barnstable, 1674. He
had six children, one of whom, Samuel, born 1646, married
Mehitable Allyn in 1667, and died in 1678. He had four
children. His son John, born 1673, married Experience
Taylor in 1692 and had five children. Samuel, son of John,
born 1693, was the father of Samuel, Jr., of Ashfield and
grandfather of Lieut. Edward Annable.† A more full
account of the Annables will be found in the *Appendix*.

The children of Lieut. Edward Annable and his wife
Jemima, were Dimick, born Sept. 1st, 1783 (died in youth);
Mehitable, born Dec. 31st,1784; Annar, born June 29th, 1786;
Alcemena, born March 30th, 1788; Rhoda, born Jan. 5th,
1790; Desire, born Jan. 6th, 1793; Abby, born April 10th,
1795; Dimick, born Nov. 10th, 1798 (died in youth); Isabella
and Remember (twins,) born Aug. 28th, 1801; Fernando C,
born Dec. 24th, 1805. All born in Ashfield, except the last
who was born in Aurelius, Cayuga Co., N. Y.

---

*The Mayflower in 1620, Fortune in 1622, and Anne in 1623, were the ships which
brought the Pilgrims to this country.

†Edward Annable's brothers and sisters were Barnabas, David, Thomas, Mehitable,
Polly (73) and Bethia.

Mehitable Annable, born 1784, married Lucius Wheaton, and had a large family.

Annar Annable, born 1786, married Isaac Fish and had two children.

Alcemena Annable, born 1788, married Judge Smith, of Pompey Hill, N. Y. Two of her daughters married husbands named Ellis, but not descendants of Richard Ellis, of Ashfield; one of them, Robert Ellis, lives in Pompey, Onondaga Co., N. Y.

Rhoda Annable, born 1790, married John Fuller, a merchant of Sempronius, N. Y., Nov. 7th, 1808. She died Jan. 19th, 1883, aged 93 years, at the residence of her son-in-law, Judge Edwin Lawrence, of Ann Arbor, Mich. She was a women of great kindness and remarkable intelligence, and retained all her faculties up to a short time of her death. Mr. Fuller, her husband, died about 1825, and she remained a widow ever afterwards. Her children were, Edward L. Fuller, born in Sempronius, N. Y., 1810, died in San Francisco, Cal., 1851. Desiah Fuller, born 1813, married Anson Brown, and afterwards, Caleb N. Ormsby, who died many years ago, leaving two daughters who with their mother lived, up to a recent date, in Brooklyn, N. Y. Sibyl Fuller, born Jan. 28th, 1819, married Edwin Lawrence Nov. 21st, 1838. She died March 20th, 1872, at Ann Arbor, where she had lived from the early settlement of that town, and where her son, John F. Lawrence, a lawyer, now resides. Her husband, Judge Lawrence, died there in 1885. Mrs. Fuller and her children and their families were highly respected and influential people. She had resided with her daughters and Judge Lawrence, in Ann Arbor about 45 years. The writer met her first while a student at the University of Michigan over 30 years ago and occasionally since, the last time being a few weeks before her death. Her life was such as to leave a fond recollection by a large circle of relatives and friends.

Desire Annable, born 1793, married Rev. John S. Twiss and died in Union City, Mich. She had a son, Edward Twiss, M. D.

Abby Annable born 1795, married William Haines, became a widow early in life. She moved to Leslie, Mich., where she lived with a daughter who married Mr. Russell a merchant in that village. Her son, William Haines, is also a merchant in Leslie, and other of her children live thereabouts. The date of her death is not given.

Dimick Annable, born 1798, died in Newburg, N. Y., in early life. He left no children.

Remember Annable, born 1801, married Peter Weatherwax and lived in Phelps, Ontario Co., N. Y., many years. Isabella, her twin sister, died in infancy.

She died in Phelps, Ontario Co., N. Y., April 3rd, 1884, in her 83rd year. Her husband, Mr. Peter Weatherwax, died in 1876. She was buried in South Butler, Wayne Co., by the side of her husband. She had resided in Phelps about sixteen years.

Her last sickness was long and painful, much beyond the usual degree. Her youngest daughter, who was with her all her life writes: "I think that I am not overstating when I say she impressed all with a superior mind, noble in thought, generous, kind and obliging. There was a greatness in her whole character seldom met; her equal rarely found, her superior not often seen. Her self-control during the weeks of agony of her last sickness was marvelous, ever a pleasant word, a cheerfulness that was suprising with such intense suffering, her mind clear, thoughtful of and for others, occasionally she would say a word or two that showed that her mind wandered. At one time, soon after referring to what she had said, she remarked, 'I have many queer thoughts, but so far have managed not to express them.' This will give a slight idea of the power and greatness of her mind and the mastery she had over it. She was a true Christian woman and a member of the Christian church over 50 years."

She left six children: L. F. Weatherwax, Port Byron, N. Y.; D. Weatherwax, Northport, N. Y.; Mrs. C. W.

Sprague, Luther, Mich. (where her son William Sprague resides); Mrs. E. L. Bolles, Vineland, N. J.; Mrs. T. Finn, Scranton, Penn. and Miss Abbie L. Weatherwax, of Phelps.

Fernando C. Annable, born 1805, is the youngest child of Lieut. Edward Annable and Jemima Smith his wife. He was born in Aurelius, N. Y., soon after his parents had removed from Ashfield. He married Betsey Ranney, daughter of William Ranney of Ashfield, who married Betsey Alden, a daughter of John Alden who lived opposite Reuben Ellis' farm. William Ranney was a son of Thomas Ranney, a brother or cousin of George Ranney, father of Jessie and grand-father of Hannah Ranney (240).

Mrs. Betsey Annable died in 1881, aged 76 years. Her husband, Fernando C., now resides in Almena, Van Buren Co., Mich. They have one son, Edwin Ranney Annable, a lawyer in Paw Paw, Mich., and a daughter, Helen Annable, who married John Williams of Almena.

Mr. Fernando C. Annable has been a farmer most of his life. He now lives at Almena, Mich., in feeble bodily health, but active mental powers.

The writer is indebted to him for much valuable information in compiling this work.

(40.) **RHODA SMITH MERRILL**, was born in Ashfield, May 29th, 1762, and died Feb. 21st, 1837. She married Jesse Merrill and had three children, all daughters.

(42.) **EBENEZER SMITH, Jr.**, fifth child of Elder Ebenezer and Remember Ellis Smith, was born in Ashfield, April 1st, 1766, and died in Cassadaga, Chautauqua Co., N. Y., May 24th, 1855 aged 89 years.

He married Keziah Elmer, or Elmore, of Ashfield about 1791, and had seven children. She died in Cassadaga, March 17th, 1870, aged 93 years. The Elmers were one of the early families in the settlement of Ashfield. Mr. Wilson Elmer, a nephew of Keziah, died there in 1885 an aged man. For his second wife he married Mrs. Amanda Ranney Richmond, widow of Elijah Richmond, an enterprising citizen of Ashfield, who died about 1850. Mr. and Mrs. Elmer were married about 1875, and lived a short distance easterly from the old church at Baptist-corners, the Chileab Smith neighborhood. Mrs. Elmer died in 1884. She was a daughter of Jesse Ranney, who raised his family on the old farm of Reuben Ellis.

Ebenezer, Jr., moved with his family from Ashfield to Chautauqua Co., N. Y., in Oct. 1815. Several families from the Ellis neighborhood in Ashfield went with them, namely: Philip Phillips, Israel Smith and Daniel Whitmore. This was just about the close of the war of 1812 and the country was very new and the roads bad. They were over a month on the way from Ashfield. Mr. Smith purchased wild lands, made a clearing and built a log house. He was a farmer by occupation and a scholarly man. His knowledge of the Bible was very thorough, so much so that he was known as the " Concordance." There was not a passage of Scripture that he was not familiar with and could turn to readily. He was a Baptist, as were most of his descendants.

His children were Aaron, born 1792; Quartus, 1796; Fidelia, 1798; Gerry, 1803; Rebecca, 1808; Ebenezer and Keziah (twins,) 1813.

Of Aaron Smith, it was said that he was a great Bible student. He was a farmer, but gave considerable attention to the genealogy of the Smith family. He had recorded the names of over 11,000 of his kin. It was said of him that "he knew more and had forgotten fewer names and dates than any man of his times." He resided most of his life at Stockton, where he died Sept. 23d, 1876, aged 84 years. His children were Laurilla, born 1821, died 1825; Lucretia, born 1824, died 1825; Laura, 1826; Lucy, born 1828, married a Griffith, and died 1880; Pamelia, born 1830, died 1840; Cyrus, born 1831, died 1877; Milla, 1834; William, 1837; Caroline, 1839; Aaron, Jr., 1843. The last named lives at Burnhams, Chautauqua Co., N. Y.

Quartus Smith, born 1796, lived many years in Stockton, N. Y., and died in 1880. He married Pomilla Shepard. They had no children.

Fidelia Smith, born 1798, and died 1840. She married Elijah Wood, and had five children: Fidelia, who married Dr. Alonzo P. Phillips, of Fredonia, Chautauqua Co., N. Y. Ursula, who married James Rheem, and had three children —two dead and one now living, Mr. Charles Rheem, in Oshkosh, Wis. Mrs. Ursula Wood Rheem married for her second husband Albert G. Blakeslee, and they lived in Dequoin, Ill. Elijah married Jane McGregor. Livonia married a Goulding and afterwards Erastus Bowen. Her son, Charles L. Goulding, lives at Fredonia, N. Y.

Gerry Smith, born 1803, lived most of his life in Stockton, where he died July 16, 1882. He married Louisa Ellis, a daughter of Barzillia Ellis, Jr., of Chautauqua Co., N. Y. Their children are Hiram, William, Frank, Flora, and David.

Rebecca Smith, born 1808, married Freeman Richardson in 1830. In 1854 they removed to LaCrosse, Wis., where Mrs. R. now lives. Mr. Richardson died in 1868. Their children were : Melissa, died in 1876; Matilda, Jasper, Squire, and Florilla. The last-named married Wm. Gear, and now resides in LaCrosse and has three children, Elsie, Ella, and Edna Gear. Mrs. Rebecca Richardson now lives with her daughter, Mrs. Gear.

Ebenezer Smith, born in 1813, died in Chautauqua Co. in 1835, unmarried.

Keziah Smith, born 1813, twin-sister of the above, married Arunah Richardson, brother of Freeman Richardson. Their children were Eliza Ann, who married John Carpenter, and lives at Cassadaga, Chautauqua Co., N.Y. Lovina, married Albert Irons ; she lives at Cassadaga. Levant and Truman Richardson, live at Burnhams, N. Y.

(44.) **OBED SMITH**, sixth child of Elder Ebenezer and Remember Ellis Smith, was born in Ashfield, April 6th, 1770, and died in Stockton, N. Y., Oct. 17th, 1828. He married Rhoda Sears, of Ashfield. Their children were, Priscilla, Obed, Aretus, Keziah, Daniel, Irene and Preserved.

(46.) RICHARD SMITH, youngest child of Elder Ebenezer and Remember Ellis Smith, was born in Ashfield, June 20th, 1774, and died in Ashfield May 8th, 1800. He was a physician, and never married.

He was a graduate of Brown University at Providence, and was a very scholarly man. He was very proficient in astronomy and mathematics, and it is said once wrote an almanac.

All these families—children of Elder Ebenezer and Remember Ellis Smith—settled in Central and Western New York early in the present century, except Rev. Preserved Smith, their eldest son, who lived and died in Rowe, Mass.

Children of Jane Ellis Phillips, (11), and John Phillips, (12), of Marlboro, Vermont, and their wives and husbands. Grandchildren of Richard Ellis.
From Nos. 47 to 61.

(47.) JOHN PHILLIPS, Jr., eldest son of Jane Ellis and John Phillips, was born in Easton, Mass., Feb. 16th, 1761, and died Aug. 23rd, 1841. He lived many years in Marlboro, Vermont, where he died. His children were: Anna, Samuel, Cyrus, Ruth, John, Joseph, Polly, Sally and Linus, all of whom are now dead.

(49.) MOLLY PHILLIPS, second child of John and Jane Ellis Phillips, was born in Easton, Nov. 12th, 1763. Her name is written Polly in some of the records. No further account is given as to who she married or where lived.

(53.) PERCIS PHILLIPS, fourth child of John and Jane Ellis Phillips, was born in Easton, July 2nd, 1767. He died in April, 1829, in Vermont.

(55.) **HANNAH PHILLIPS**, born in Easton, March 14th, 1770, and died Jan. 13th, 1850. She is said to have married a Fulton.

(57.) **MARCY PHILLIPS**, sixth child of John and Jane Ellis Phillips, was born in Easton, Sept. 22nd, 1773. Her name in some of the records is given as Mary. She married Joseph Bryant. She died in Vermont, Feb. 21st, 1831.

(59.) **PHEBE PHILLIPS**, seventh child of Jane Ellis and John Phillips, was born in Easton, Mass., Feb. 4th, 1777, and died in Marlboro, Vt., Aug. 14th, 1863. On Sept. 5th, 1797, she was married by Rev. Mr. Lyman to James Charter of Marlboro. The latter was born in Hartford, Conn., in 1742, and died in Marlboro, April 22nd, 1821.

Their children were as follows: Philena Charter, born Oct. 1st, 1798, married Asa Worden Nov. 14th, 1819, and died Oct. 23rd, 1880.

Ruth Charter, born June 6th, 1800, and died March 6th, 1802.

Hannah Charter, born April 7th, 1803, married Orrison Bruce Feb. 21st, 1825, and died June 3rd, 1884.

John Charter, born Nov. 26th, 1805, married Hannah J. Yeaton Sept. 12th, 1830, and died Dec. 5th, 1881.

James Charter, Jr., born May 30th, 1809, married Mary B. Fillebrown April 2nd, 1829, in Boston, Mass. Mrs. Mary B. Charter was born in Orrington, Me., March 1st, 1813. She and her husband, James Charter, Jr., have resided many years in Williamsville, Windham Co., Vt. Mr. Charter has the old family bible of his mother and grandmother, Jane Ellis Phillips (11), and he has kindly sent me records of Mr. and Mrs. Phillips and their descendants, which were not to be found elsewhere. Mr. Charter is a farmer and an aged man.

His children are as follows: Mary Elizabeth Charter, married Elijah Morse, of New Fane, Vt.

James H. Charter, born 1832, married Mary A. Dutton, in E. Boston in 1853, and Esther L. Worden in 1870.

Charles M. Charter, born in Boston, 1837, married Rebecca Wyman in Boston, Mass.

Francis H. Charter, born in Boston, 1840, married Helen S. Gallager.

Anna Viola Charter, born in Vermont, 1844, married N. J. D. Leavett, in Somerville, Vt., in 1863.

Herbert F. Charter, born in Vermont, in 1848, died in Brewer, Me., 1864.

John F. Charter, born in E. Boston, 1852, died in Williamsville, Vt., in 1876.

After the death of Mr. Charter, Sr., in 1821, Mrs. Phebe Phillips Charter (59), married Mr. Joseph Bryant. They were married in Marlboro, Dec. 13th, 1831, by Rev. E. H. Newton.

Mrs. Phebe Charter Bryant was a very devoted Christian woman of the Baptist denomination.

(61.) **SALLY PHILLIPS**, youngest child of John and Jane Ellis Phillips, was born in Easton, Mass., May 2nd, 1780. She married Joshua Morse, and died May 17th, 1862.

Children of Lieut. John Ellis, (15), of Ashfield, and their husbands and wives. Grandchildren of Richard Ellis. From Nos. 63 to 75.

(63.) **HANNAH ELLIS WILLIAMS**, eldest child of Lieut. John Ellis, was born in Ashfield, May 1st, 1764. She died in Westport, Essex Co., N. Y., March 4th, 1839. About 1789 she married Apollos Williams of Ashfield, where they lived for some years, when they settled in Westport, which is on the western shore of Lake Champlain, where they lived many years. Her husband,

(64.) **APOLLOS WILLIAMS, Sr.**, was born June 8th, 1768. He was married in Ashfield where he lived some years before and after that event. He was a farmer. He died in Westport, in 1848.

Their children were: Rhoda, born 1790; Hannah, born 1793; Daniel, 1795; Apollos, Jr., 1797; John, 1799; Alpheus, 1801; and Edward, born 1804.

Rhoda Williams, born in Ashfield, Nov. 30th, 1790, died in Racine, Wis., Aug. 7th, 1874. She married Russell Phillips of Ashfield, Jan. 2nd, 1808. He died in Racine, April 15th, 1856. They lived in Ashfield, in one house, 21 years, where all of their children were born. They went to Wisconsin in 1849, to their son John's in Sun Prairie, near Madison, where they lived five years and then removed to Racine, where they both died. Mr. Russell Phillips was born in Ashfield, Mass., Aug. 31st, 1785. His father was Thomas Phillips, Jr., who was a son of Thomas, Sr., born 1712, the second settler in Ashfield, and the latter was a brother of Jane Phillips (2), who married Richard Ellis, the first settler in Ashfield. *See Appendix.*

The children of Russell and Rhoda Williams Phillips were eight in number as follows: Hannah, born 1811; Allen, born 1813; John, 1815; Monroe, 1817; Galusha, 1820; Mary, 1823; Sarah, 1825; Elizabeth A., 1832.

Hannah Phillips, born May 18th, 1811, married Calvin Flower, son of Phineas of Ashfield, Nov. 28th, 1833. She had five children—James N., born 1835, married, is a lawyer and lives in Chicago. Phineas A., born 1837, lives in Sun Prairie, Wis., and is a farmer. Ellen J., born 1839, died at 18 years of age in Wisconsin. George A., born 1841, died 1844. Edith C., born 1846, married Bradford Hancock, resides in Chicago and has two children.

Allen Phillips, was born in Ashfield, May 20th, 1813, married Louisa Cross of Ashfield, where he always lived and where he died.

John Phillips, born 1815 in Ashfield, married Ruth Grinnell, settled on a farm at Sun Prairie, Wis., where he died in 1877, leaving three children—Henry on the farm. Emma, who married Charles Vrooman, and resides at Green Bay, Wis., and Edna, who married H. W. Chenoweth and lives in Madison, Wis.

Monroe Phillips, born March 2nd, 1817, married Amanda Reed. They now reside at Davenport, Wis. They have three children—William and Ward who are farmers in Dakota, and Ella, who is at a musical institute in Warren, Ohio.

Galusha Phillips, fifth child of Rhoda and Russell Phillips, was born in Ashfield, April 27th, 1820. He married Stella B. Scranton, of Rochester, N. Y., Oct. 3rd, 1848. They reside in Rochester, and have no children. Mr. P. was in the hat cap and fur business there many years, but for twenty years past has been in the furniture trade. His wife is a woman of rare worth and intelligence, to whom the writer is indebted for most of the records of this branch of Phillipses. When a youth, Mr. Phillips lived about seven years on a farm with his mother's uncle Deacon Dimick Ellis (72), in Ashfield. At 14 years of age, he started out in the world to make his way alone, and it is much to his credit, that, in the midst of many discouragements, he has ever maintained an upright and honorable career worthy of imitation.

Mary Phillips, born 1823, married Simeon C. Yout, and they now reside in Racine, Wis. They have three children —Adelaide married a Mr. Petitt, he died in 1881. She lives in Racine and has one child. Amelia married Wm. Gillespie, they live in Englewood, a suburb of Chicago, she has one son. Nellie Yout married Harry Wright and lives in Racine. Louis Yout, unmarried, also lives in Racine. Mr. and Mrs. Yout lost two children, one of whom, their eldest, was killed in the war of the Rebellion at Chickamauga, Sept. 20th, 1863.

Sarah Phillips was born in Ashfield, May 12th, 1825. She married Charles Hill, who died in 1855, in Nashville. Tenn. She had one son who died in 1860, aged 12 years. Mrs. Hill had resided in Madison, Wis., for many years.

Elizabeth A. Phillips was the eighth and youngest child of Russell and Rhoda Phillips. She was born in Ashfield, Oct. 12th, 1832, and died in Madison, Wis., in 1873. She married Sidney Foote in 1857, and he died in 1877, in Jacksonville, Florida, where he had gone for his health. They left six daughters—Florence and Catherine Foote, teachers in public schools, in Madison, Wis. Martha, who lives in Rochester, N. Y., with her uncle Galusha Phillips. Ella, a teacher in Green Bay, Wis. Annie in Knoxville, Ill., and Ruth Foote, adopted by Mr. Smith in Winetka, near Chicago. Mr. Foote was a very bright man, a college graduate and a lawyer.

Hannah Williams, second child of Hannah Ellis and Apollos Williams, Sr., was born Jan. 25th, 1793 in Ashfield. She never married, but lived with her parents in Westport, N. Y., until their death, when she resided for a time with her brother Alpheus, in Coldwater, Mich., and afterwards with her brother Apollos, in Minnesota, where she died in 1871.

Daniel Williams, third child of Hannah and Apollos, was born 1795, and died when about 18 years of age. He died in Westport, from a wound accidently inflicted by a drunken man who was carelessly handling a gun at a general training, or muster.

Apollos, Jr., born Feb. 21st, 1797, died in Pleasant Valley, Minn., in 1866. He married Betsy Adams and had 11 children, whose names were: John P., born 1834; Alzina, 1837; Louisa, 1838; Ann, Lovinda, Lucy, Luther, Angeline, Augustus, Cynthia and Marian, all born in Westport. Augustus Williams lives at High Forest, Minn. His mother, who was born Feb. 11th, 1812, is still living; she has had 60 grand children, 44 of them now living.

Mr. and Mrs. Apollos Williams, Jr., moved to Pleasant Valley, Minn., in 1861 with their entire family of 11 children. Their son, John P. and his wife Irene, live there now. Their children are Cora, Roger, Ervin, Flora, Linn, Wendel and Warner. Alzina Williams married Wm. Toogood and their children are: Franklin, Albert, George, Mabel, Maud, Wright, Nellie and Wenn. Louisa Williams married Thomas Wallace and their children are: Jenny, Laura, Annie, Ella, Susie, Hugh and John. Lucy Williams married Dwight Toogood, and their children are: Effie, Nettie, Dory, Lyman and Merrit. Lorinda Williams married Isaac F. Johnson, and their children are: Alma, Clinton, Mattie, Rosa and Phillip. Ann Williams married John B. Dunham, and their children are: Ella, Minnie, Edith, Myrtle, Roy and Bertha.

Luther and Augustus Williams are unmarried, and live with their mother in Pleasant Valley.

Angeline Williams married Johnson Bentley, and their children are: Lewella, Nora, Edward, Irvin and Walter. They reside at Pleasant Valley. Cynthia Williams married Julius Whaler, and their children are: Blanch, Willie, Marcia and Irene. Marian Williams married Perry E. Babcock, and their children are: Ada, Harry and Nina, and two others dead, Etta and Bertha. In July, 1881, these families and Williams relatives had a reunion at Pleasant Valley,·at which 88 of them were present.

John Williams, born July 27th, 1799, married Sylvia McLane June 5th, 1823. He was accidently drowned in Lake Champlain, Nov. 23rd, 1825. He was on a vessel which was lost in a storm with all on board. He had one son, Daniel, born in Westport, March 9th, 1824, who now lives in Dexter, Minn., and is a thriving farmer and a man of uncommon intelligence and worth.

Mr. Daniel Williams married Miss Adelia Babcock, and they have 10 children and 11 grandchildren. Their children are: Martha Ann, born 1850; John Jay, 1851; Charles Henry, 1854; Clark Phineas, 1856; Sylvia Ursula, 1857; Melvin Daniel, 1859; Ira Rufus, 1861; Edward Perry, 1863; Alpheus Simeon, 1868; and Ida May, 1872. The first eight, born in Quincy, Mich., and the last two in Dexter, Minn. Mrs. Adelia B. Williams was born in New York, Nov. 6th, 1830.

Alpheus Williams, born Aug. 28th, 1801, married Sylvia M. Williams, widow of his brother John, Sept. 30th, 1827. He died near Coldwater, Mich., Oct. 10th, 1877. His widow is now living in Michigan. Their children's names are: George, born 1828; John, Henry, Edward, Monroe, died 1874, and Ann Eliza, 1840. Most of this family now live in and near Coldwater. Mrs. Sylvia M. Williams, the mother, was born May 21st, 1804, and now lives with her son Edward, four miles from Coldwater. George Williams has four children: Louella, Cora, Nellie and Sylvia. John Williams' children are: George, Lovina and Dan. Henry Williams, one child, Lena. Monroe Williams at his death left two children, Homer and Monroe. Ann Eliza Williams married a Bidleman, and has one son, Emmet Bidleman.

Edward Williams, youngest child of Hannah Ellis and Apollos Williams, was born Dec. 29th, 1804, and died in 1847. He married Ann R. Keith, and their children were: Harriet, born 1829; Albert K., 1834; Gulielma, 1842; Alborn and Hannah. The last two are dead. This family of children were born some in Vermont and some in Canada. Mrs. Ann R. K. Williams, the mother, was born June 25th, 1811, and died Aug. 20th, 1844. Albert K. Williams lives in Washington, D. C. Gulielma Williams married a Cooper, and they live in Winnebago, Minn.

The descendants of Hannah Ellis (63), and Apollos Williams, Sr., (64), are very numerous and have ever been highly respected and useful people. Apollos, Sr., and wife were Baptists and their good example and instruction has shown a good influence in the generation which has now passed, and will no doubt in those to come.

(65.) **DIMICK ELLIS,** second child of Lieut. John Ellis, was born in Ashfield, Oct. 23rd, 1766. He died Aug. 4th, 1773, according to records of his father's family. In the records of the town of Ashfield, his name is given as Edward Dimick Ellis, with date of death the same as above.

(66.) **JANE ELLIS LINCOLN**, third child of Lieut. John Ellis, was born in Ashfield, March 7th, 1779. She married Capt. Samuel Lincoln, in Ashfield, in 1788. They had nine children, some of whom were born in Ashfield, and others in central and western New York. Her husband,

(67.) **CAPT. SAMUEL LINCOLN** resided in Ashfield at the time of his marriage and for some time thereafter. He was a man of more than average energy and enterprise. About 1800 he moved with his family to central New York, where both himself and wife died about the same time in 1812. Upon this sad event this large family of children, most of whom were small, the youngest Benjamin, a baby of but a few months, were widely scattered. Mrs. Lincoln's brother Dimick Ellis (72), visited them and took two of the younger, Thomas and Anne to Ashfield, where they lived to maturity. The youngest Anne he carried in his arms most of the way, there being no roads then except for wagons and stages. Anne married a Mr. Haines and removed west. It is said that she had a daughter, Jane who lived in Cold-water, Mich.

Thomas Lincoln (203), was born Nov. 18th, 1808, in Byron, Genesee Co., N. Y. After the death of his parents in 1812, he lived with his uncle Dimick in Ashfield until 1825, when he went to New York. He married Miss Julia Rhodes, who was born in Sempronius, N. Y., Sept. 12th, 1812. They were married Sept. 21st, 1834, and settled in Springville, Erie Co., N. Y., where they and some of their children now reside. Mr. Lincoln is an architect and builder and has erected many of the finest buildings in Springville and surrounding country. In 1836 he moved to Monroe, Mich., where he built the first railroad bridge over the river Raisin. In 1840 he removed to Buffalo, N. Y., and in 1845 he returned to Springville, where he now lives, still actively engaged in his profession. Mr. Lincoln as an upright, public-spirited and honorable citizen in his town, has no superior, and enjoys the confidence of the entire com-

munity. Mrs. Lincoln is a very amiable woman, beloved
by all. She has been a member of the Presbyterian church
nearly 50 years. Their children are: Anna L., born 1835;
Marion T., 1838; Carlottie E., 1839; Helen M., 1843;
Americus C., 1845; Josephine J, 1847; Manly B., 1850;
Julia A., 1852.

Anna L. Lincoln, born 1835, married Dr. J. Swain of
Colden, Erie Co., N. Y. Marion T. Lincoln was a soldier
in the late war and was a prisoner at Saulsbury. He
married Miss Katie Gould of Greenville, Mich., where he
now resides. Helen M. Lincoln married a Mr. Eggert and
has a son, George T. Eggert. She afterwards married Mr.
Geo. W. Zink a prominent business man of Buffalo, and
they have a son, Geo. W., Jr. Americus C. Lincoln was a
soldier in the rebellion and was a prisoner at Andersonville.
Josephine Y. Lincoln married Wallace Popple of Collins,
Erie Co., N. Y. Their children are: Maud and Willie.
Julia Ada Lincoln married William Owen of Buffalo, and
their children are: Emily, Willie and Helen.

Hannah Lincoln (200), married Marvin Williams and
lived in Hinckley, Medina Co., Ohio, where she died about
1860, leaving one daughter Jane, who married George
Thayer of Cuyahoga Falls, Ohio. Their son, George
Thayer is said to be a druggist in Toledo, Ohio.

Phebe Lincoln (198), married Ira Butler, said to be a
cousin of Hon. Benj. F. Butler of Mass. They lived near
Medina, Ohio, the later years of their life. No further report
of them.

Of this family of Lincolns there was one (not in the list
on page 22,) named Dimick Lincoln. After his parents
death he lived for several years with Mr. Peleg Standish,
of Sempronius, N. Y., when he went away a young man,
as he said to visit the old world. No account of him has
since been found.

The youngest of the Lincoln children was Benjamin
(205.) He was a baby when his parents died. He was

reared by his sister Betsey, with whom he lived a time. Later in life he went to Ohio, at or near where his sister Marilla, Mrs. Prichard, lived. About the year 1849, he came to Otisco (now Belding), Mich., where his uncle Dimick Ellis (72) then lived, in his old age with his son Lewis (241.) Benjamin Lincoln at this time was a great sufferer from rheumatism, to such an extent that he was helpless. His uncle Dimick's children, Richard and Lewis Ellis, and daughter Mrs. Desiah Ellis Belding lived here. These were Benjamin's cousins, with whom he remained for about three years until his death. His disease took on the form of consumption, which proved fatal about 1853. He is remembered as a man of great patience and amiability of character, beloved by all.

Marilla Lincoln (201), was born Feb. 3rd, 1805. She married Sheldon C. Prichard Feb. 22nd, 1819. Mr. Prichard was born Aug. 1st, 1802. They lived in Moravia New York, a few years after their marriage, when they moved to Wauseon, Ohio, where Mr. Prichard died. Mrs. Prichard removed about 1875 to Prichardville, Barry Co., Mich., where she died Oct. 28th, 1883, at the home of her son Solomon Prichard. Mr. and Mrs. Prichard were members of the Presbyterian Church, and were highly respected and upright people. Their children were Alonzo, born 1824. He married a Worden, sister of Dr. S. T. Worden of Delta, Ohio. Alonzo Prichard now lives at Wauseon, Ohio. Charles born 1826, now lives at Prichardville, Mich. Julia born 1829, died in Ohio 1830. Hiram born 1830, now lives at Wauseon, Ohio.

Jane Prichard, born 1832, married Dr. S. T. Worden of Delta, Ohio. Helen Prichard, born 1835, married a man named Dando, is now a widow and lives in Prichardville, Mich. Solomon, born 1837, lives in Prichardville. George, born 1839, lives at Prichardville. Sarah, born 1842, married Isaac Weeks, lives in Prichardville. Mary, born in Liverpool, Ohio, Jan. 3rd, 1847, lived in Hillsdale, Mich. She married Dr. Chamberlin in 1863, and had one daughter

Myrtle Chamberlin.   Dr. Chamberlin died in 1875, and Mrs.
Chamberlin married Mr. Bernard in 1878.   Mrs. Bernard
lived in Jackson, Mich., several years and later in Hillsdale.
She died suddenly May 13th, 1885, greatly lamented by a
large circle of relatives and friends.   Her daughter now
lives in Hillsdale.   She is widely known as a highly cultivated and talented singer.

Polly Lincoln (199), married John Rose and they were
in Niles, Cayuga Co., N. Y., for a time about 1834.   No
further report from them.

Betsey Lincoln (202), probably married a Worden.
Where they lived was not known to the other relatives.   As
said above when Capt. Samuel and Jane Ellis Lincoln died
in 1812 their children were widely scattered, and some of
them became lost to each other as well as to their other more
distant relatives.   This was a matter of grief and sadness
in after life to the others, who felt a loneliness thereafter.

(68.) **JOHN ELLIS, Jr.**, fourth child of Lieut. John
Ellis, was born in Ashfield, Sept. 19th, 1771.   He lived with
his father until about the age of 19 when he enlisted in the
army and went with Gen. Anthony Wayne in a campaign
against the Indians in Ohio and Indiana from 1793 to 1795.
In a hard fought battle at Falling-Timbers, Ind., he was
severely wounded.   After his discharge he went down the
Ohio and Mississippi rivers to New Orleans, and thence by
vessel to New York, and from there home.   Soon after his
arrival in Ashfield he was married to Abilena Phillips of
that town, Dec. 30th, 1795.   They then settled in Sempronius (now Niles), N. Y., where they raised a large family of
15 children, all but two of whom grew to maturity, and
most of them to old age.   Four of them are yet living.

Elisha, born 1805, now living in Farmersville, Ind., John J.
born 1810, living near Auburn, N. Y.   Ebenezer, born
1815, living in Arkansas City, Kan., and Anthony Wayne
Ellis, born 1820, now lives in Niles on the old homestead.

John Ellis, Jr., was a Methodist in the early part of his life. He was quite a bible student and often an exhorter in the meetings. In the later years of his life he inclined to universalism. He was an honest, sincere and christian man. He died at Niles, N. Y., 1848. His wife,

(69.) ABILENA PHILLIPS, was born in Ashfield in 1776. She was a daughter of Vespasian Phillips, of Ashfield. She was a true and devoted wife and mother, and a good christian woman. After the death of her husband in 1848 she lived with her son Anthony W. Ellis in Niles, where. she died in 1854. She has a numerous posterity in New York, Ohio and several western states. For sketches of her children see Nos. 206 to 231.

(70.) EDWARD ELLIS, fifth child of Lieut. John Ellis, was born in Ashfield, March 20th, 1773. He worked on his father's farm during his youth. June 4th, 1798, he married Amanda Flower, of Ashfield, and very soon after removed to Sempronius, N. Y., where he settled on a farm which his father had purchased a short time before. They moved from Ashfield, with an ox team and were 14 days on the way. His wife took from Ashfield a young apple tree, which she planted in their front yard, and which yet bears fruit. Their oldest son Cyrus Ellis, who was born on this place in 1799, lived most of his life and died there in Nov., 1885. His father Edward, was a very ambitious and industrious man and died suddenly in 1801, it is said from overwork. At his death and burial so new was the country that no boards could be procured of which to make a coffin. The neighbors cut down trees, and. split out slabs of wood for this purpose, and to prevent the wolves from molesting the grave which was near the house, two loads of stone were placed over it. For sketch of his children see Nos. 233 to 235. His wife,

(71.) AMANDA FLOWER, was born in Ashfield, May 15th, 1780. She was a daughter of Bildad Flower, and granddaughter of Maj. Lamrock Flower, Sr., who lived and died on the farm opposite the home of Lieut. John Ellis.

Bildad Flower married Dorcas ——, and soon after entered the Revolutionary army as a soldier. After three years service he died and left a widow, and two young daughters. Ruth, born about 1777, married Jesse Ranney, of Ashfield, and Amanda, the subject of this sketch.

Amanda's mother, Dorcas Flower, after the death of her father, Bildad Flower, married Spencer Phillips, also a Revolutionary soldier, and they had a large family of children.

Amanda Flower Ellis, at the death of her husband had one son Cyrus (233), and another Edward D., who was born two months after his father's death. Mrs. Ellis was a small and frail woman, but had unusual resolution and endurance.

She took her two infant children and went to Ashfield. After a few months she resolved to go back to her new home in what was then "the west." (This was a very early manifestation of what has since become a general fact that eastern people who have once lived in the west cannot content themselves to remain long in the east again.) She left Cyrus with his uncle Dimick Ellis, and started back to Sempronius with her infant child Edward D. On the way she made the acquaintance of a young Presbyterian minister, Rev. Lyman Forbush, who was going into the same section of country. After a time they were married and settled permanently in Sempronius, where they remained the rest of their lives. Mr. and Mrs. Forbush raised a large family of children, mostly daughters. They were: Mindwell, born 1804, died 1854. She married William Potter, and lived in Hillsdale, Mich., many years. Lyman Jr., born 1807, died 1844. He married Emeline Huff. Minerva, born 1810, married George Davidson, and live in New York State. Dorcas, born 1812, died 1842. She married Otis Elwood. Thomas M., born 1815. Amanda, born 1818, married Thomas Van Arsdale, and now lives in or near Moravia, N.Y. Elizabeth, born 1822, died in 1844. She married Rev. Edwin R. Wade, a minister of the Christian Church, who now lives in McLean, Tompkins Co., N. Y. Huldah, born 1824, married Benj. Duryee, and she now lives in Niles, N. Y. Dorliska, born 1826, married Newton Brokaw, and lives in New York. Amanda Flower Ellis Forbush (71), lived in Niles, or Sempronius (see note page 80), over 70 years. There were but six families in the town when she and her first husband, Edward Ellis, settled there. Her second husband, Rev. Mr. Forbush, died there Aug. 7th, 1826, and she was a widow over 41 years. Left as she was by the death of her husband, with a large family of small children, the youngest but two years of age, few can realize the amount of courage needed to meet and overcome the obstacles and discouragements of her life. She died Nov. 14th, 1867, in her 88th year. She was a pure and noble woman, and retained her mental and physical powers in a high degree to the close of her life. She could count up children, grandchildren and great grandchildren, to the number of two hundred. Her memory will long be cherished.

(72.) **Dea. DIMICK ELLIS,** sixth child of Lieut. John Ellis and Molly Dimick his wife, was born in Ashfield, Nov. 26th, 1776. He was the youngest son of his father's family and remained on the homestead until his parents death in 1827, and for nearly 20 years afterwards, when he removed to Otisco, (now Belding), Ionia Co., Mich., where his three eldest children had settled some years before.

The homestead in Ashfield was a very hilly and rocky locality similar to nearly all the farms in that section. It would puzzle one who was accustomed to the broad and fertile fields of the Great West to understand how a moderate subsistence even could be obtained from most of the New England farms. That it was is evidence of great economy as well as thrift. All were required to labor, usually early and late. The principal "wealth" that was thus acquired consisted mainly in the vigorous physical and mental constitutions which nearly all acquired in a high degree.

When Dea. Ellis' father died in 1827, at 85 years of age, his surplus accumulations in property could not have been much, yet he made provision in his will for small legacies to each of his children, which his son Dimick paid in full according to old receipts found among his effects. The last of these was to his nephew, Benjamin Lincoln, (youngest child of his sister Jane, who married Capt. Samuel Lincoln of Byron, N. Y.,) which was dated Otisco, Nov. 22, 1852, about a year before Benjamin's death. These Lincoln children had become widely separated after the death of their parents in 1812, (see page 107) which accounts for the above mentioned delay.

December 11th, 1799, Dea. Ellis married Polly Annable. He had four children; Desiah, Richard, Lewis and John. (For sketch of whom see Nos. 237 to 243.)

Deacon Ellis was a Baptist in religious belief and always took an active part in religious matters. He was also a strictly temperate man and when the "Washingtonian movement," a temperance organization originated about 1825, he was one of the first in his town to advocate the cause. Previous to that time the use of ardent spirits was universal among all classes, in the churches and out. It required a great deal of courage to attempt interference with this ancient and popular custom of liquor drinking at that time, but Deacon Ellis always adhered to his temperance principles and was the means of converting many to his views, both by his upright and Christian example as well as the friendliness of all his ways. He was a prominent and highly respected man all his life, and represented his town in the State Assembly and Town Board for many years. From his father, and grandfather Richard, he learned much of the early history of those trying times, during and before the great Revolution. From him the writer (his grandson), derived most of the facts and incidents contained in the sketch of Richard Ellis, the first settler of Ashfield. (See page 9.) Dimick was about twenty-one years of age when his grandfather died, and he had lived in the same neighborhood and most of the time in the same family with him. He always felt a great interest in all his relatives, whether near or remote, and it was mainly in accordance with an expression of his, made nearly 35 years ago, that he would sometime trace them out and put the record in shape for future reference, that prompted the writer, at this late date, to begin the work. Although the task has proved to be many times greater than was supposed possible at the outset and quite perplexing from the slight data he had to begin with, yet the writer hopes in the end to make the work quite full and of interest to the many families included.

A year or two before his death Deacon Ellis wrote out some account of the early relatives, and their families, which he put in the keeping of his nephew, Mr. Cyrus Ellis (233,) of Niles, N. Y. All these interesting and valuable records were lost some years later in a fire which destroyed Cyrus' house and contents. The generation to which Deacon Ellis belonged has gone by. All their voices are hushed in a silence we cannot penetrate. They were a noble race of men and women, whose lifework was fully and well done. It is a pleasure to record their names, and a virtue in the present and coming generations, to respect and honor their memories and to imitate their example. "The memory of the just is blessed." The subject of this sketch was one of the purest and noblest of his time. He retained his physical and mental powers with increasing brightness until his last days, which he himself attributed mainly to his uniform sobriety, equanimity of temper and abstinence from those deadly poisons, alcohol and tobacco, and he used tea and coffee even but seldom. His life and energies were devoted to doing good to his fellow men by whom he was universally respected and beloved. His old age was happy, serene and beautiful, a joy to himself as well as to those around him.*

---

*It is worthy to note the influence which an upright, Christian and sober life has on men and women. All through these pages are recorded the names of many who have reached ages approaching one hundred years and still retaining a high degree of physical and mental vigor. This is especially true of the women, to whom fortunately custom forbids the habitual use of stimulants and narcotics. What a contrast is this with the malevolence and insanity caused by the use of alcohol and the filthiness of person, and ugliness of temper, often produced by tobacco. It is hoped that the present and future generations will appreciate the pure example of those noble ancestors, so far at least as to scrupulously avoid all unnatural stimulants and narcotics which are now producing such destructive effects upon our race. When this much is done it requires no great effort to live a useful and respectable life in the world.

He died at 82 years of age from an attack of inflammation of the lungs, brought on from exposure to cold, but his natural vigor of constitution might otherwise have served him for a dozen years. He was a large man and six feet high.

After the death of his first wife in 1826, Deacon Ellis married Mrs. Catherine Long Wilson, of Shelburn, Mass. She was a widow with six children: Samuel, Stephen, David, Dr. Milo, Mary who married Hiram Belding, Esq., and Louisa, who married Dimick's son, Lewis Ellis (241).

Mrs. Catherine Ellis died in Belding, Mich., about 1854, at an advanced age. Her son, Dr. Milo Wilson, died about 1875 in Shelburn Falls, Mass., where he had been a physician many years.

Her daugher Mary, who married Hiram Belding, Esq., lived in Belding, Mich., from whom that place was named. It is a thriving village in the township of Otisco, and but a few rods from where the Ellises settled in 1842 and '44, and where Lewis (241) and C. D. Ellis (749), son of Richard (239), and their families now reside.

The engraving in the front of the book is a very good likeness of Dea. Dimick Ellis when he was 78 years of age.

(73.) **POLLY ANNABLE**, first wife of Deacon Dimick Ellis and mother of his children, was born in Ashfield, 1774. She was a daughter of Samuel Annable, Jr., and Desiah Dimick, and a sister of Lieut. Edward Annable (39), all of Ashfield. She was a small woman and never of robust health, but a devoted wife and mother, and a sincere Christian. She died in 1826, quite early in life, considering the average longevity of most of those New England residents. She was greatly beloved by all her relatives and acquaintances. She left four children, the two younger of whom are Mr. Lewis Ellis (241), of Belding, Mich., who was born in Ashfield in 1811, and Dr. John Ellis (243), of New York City, born 1815.

(75.) **SYLVIA ELLIS**, youngest child of Lieut. John
Ellis, was born in Ashfield, June 26th, 1779. She married
Asher Belding in Ashfield, Oct., 1802, where all their chil-
dren were born. Their home was about one-half mile south
of the corner where Richard Ellis first located. She died
in Ashfield in the year 1829. Her children were: Aretus,
Jane, Edward, Ebenezer, Volney, Thomas and Chandler.
For sketches of these see Nos. 246 to 253. Her husband,

(76.) **ASHER BELDING**, was born in Ashfield, Jan.
20th, 1777. His father was Ebenezer Belding, Jr., and his
grandfather Deacon Ebenezer, Sr.,* both of ·whom lived in
Ashfield long before the Revolutionary War. It is probable that these Beldings came from Whately, which is
about 15 miles southeasterly from Ashfield. Asher Belding's parents were Ebenezer Belding, Jr., and his wife
Jenezer Ingram. Asher's brothers were, Ebenezer, born
Aug. 23rd, 1769. Abigail, born Sept. 2nd, 1771, and Nathaniel, born June 22nd, 1774. Mr. Asher Belding was a
man of considerable business capacity, which he exercised
in various pursuits and speculations, much like what the
more modern Yankee has become famous for. For many
years he was engaged in raising, buying, distilling and
dealing in peppermint oil and essences, in which he did a
prosperous business for those times—fifty to eighty years
ago. After the death of his first wife in 1829, he married a
Mrs. Sarah Allen in 1831; she was a widow with several
daughters, who married husbands named Sadler, Cutler,
and Combes. The two latter lived for a few years in
Otisco, Mich., early in the forties. Some years later
Mr. Asher Belding removed to Phelps, Ontario Co.,

---

*Another branch of Beldings was Mr. Samuel Belding. He was from Deerfield. He
purchased the farm where Richard Ellis made the first settlement in the town. Here he and
his wife Mary raised a large family of children, whose names were: Daniel, born 1754; John,
1756; Mary, 1758; Mercy, 1759; Esther, 1761; Samuel, 1762, died young; Asenath, 1764;
Louisa 1765; Samuel, 1767; Elizabeth, 1770, and Aaron, 1774. John Belding, born Dec. 17th,
1756, lived on the homestead until his death in 1839. He married Priscilla Waite, (probably a
daughter of Seth Waite, a prominent resident of that town), July 15th, 1784. Their children
were David, Tiberius (239), Hiram and others. Hiram Belding, born about 1805, married
Mary Wilson. They lived on the homestead of his father and grandfather until about 1853,
when they settled in Belding, Mich. Their children were David W., Milo M., Hiram H.,
Alvah N., Frank H. and Jennie. The latter died in Belding, Mich., about 1873. The five
sons compose the extensive silk manufacturing firm of Belding Bros. & Co. Their mills
are at Rockville, Conn., Northampton, Mass., Belding, Mich., San Francisco, Cal., and
Montreal, Canada. They are men of great enterprise and ability.

N. Y., where he died in 1852. It may be said that in the early part of the present century, trafficking in various oils and essences was a very common pursuit in that part of the country. About 1815 Ashfield had attained its largest population, so that there was quite a surplus of inhabitants, and hence a pressing necessity for all who could, to seek other and newer locations. And it is not far from truth to say that about the first and second generations in the present century of New England youths, when they attained to years approaching manhood, invariably supplied themselves with a pair of willow baskets or tin trunks, and with these well filled with oils, essences, pins, needles, thread, etc., suspended from their shoulders with a yoke, started out from the parental fireside to "see the world," and prospect for a situation in life. *Many thousands* of these young men, full of life and energy, and Yankee sagacity, thus equipped, perambulated New York and the western States. They were the pioneers in all the newer sections of the West, where most of them made for themselves a habitation and a name before they returned to the old homes in the east, unless, as was the case with many, to make a hasty visit to secure a wife from among the blooming damsels left behind, who proved themselves no less courageous and desirous to face the trials of pioneer life, than had their brothers and newly made husbands before them.* Indeed it is conceded that to the energy, enterprise and heroism of New England youth is attributed the rapid settlement, development and populating of several western States, and wherever this influence was felt, there was left for all time the impress for good, of New England's best genius, independence and love of justice and liberty. And it is only fair to say that this was but the natural outgrowth of principles which caused that band of exiles, the Pilgrims, to brave the ocean's storms in mid-winter and establish their homes on

* However widely separated they became there ever remained an attachment for the old home which time could not efface. Love for the scenes of their youth grew with the years and were ever fresh in their memories. Truly could they say :

We see it all—the pictures that our memories held so dear,
 The homestead in New England far away,
And the vision is so natural-like we almost seem to hear
 The voices that were hushed but yesterday.

New England's sterile shore, two hundred and sixty-five years ago. Their deeds should be praised and their memory honored by every descendant of New England, for all time to come.

Since the New England States have become so extensively engaged in manufacturing, within the last fifty years, this emigration to the West has been greatly reduced, and hundreds of enterprising and populous villages and cities have sprung up giving profitable employment to all the people therein. But Ashfield, not having any water-powers of importance on her streams, has never become a manufacturing town.

Children of Hannah Ellis Fulton (17), and James Fulton (18), of Colerain, Mass., and their wives and husbands. Grand Children of Richard Ellis. From Nos. 77 to 95.

(77.) ROBERT FULTON, eldest son of Hannah Ellis and James Fulton, was born in Colerain, Franklin Co., Mass., May 23rd, 1773. He settled in Thetford, Orange Co., Vermont, where he lived to old age. He had five sons and three daughters, named Henry, Stephen, Jesse, Elijah, Chapel, Minerva, and two others names not given, but one married a Burrows.

Henry and Stephen Fulton lived in Thetford, Elijah in Portland, Me., Jesse in Boston, Mass., and Chapel died in Thetford when about 21 years of age, soon after graduating at Dartmouth College.

(79.) JAMES FULTON, Jr., was born in Colerain, May 7th, 1775. In 1799 he married Miss Sally Choat, by whom he had nine children. Mr. Fulton settled in 1806 in Champion, Jefferson County, N. Y. He was a farmer. He was a soldier in the war of 1812, and was in the battle of Sackett's Harbor, May 29th, 1813. He died at Champion in 1838. His children were: Samuel, born 1801, died 1881; George, born 1803, died in 1879; Lucy, born 1805, died in 1861; Richard, born 1807, died in 1871; Hannah, born 1809, died in 1874; Jesse, born 1812; Nathan, born 1815, died 1874; Maria, born 1817, and Ellenor, born 1820. Mr. Jesse Fulton, born 1812, now lives in Watertown, Jefferson Co., N. Y. He is a farmer and has one daughter.

(80.) **CALEB FULTON** was born in Colerain, May 11th, 1777. He married Polly Barnes and settled in the town of Wilna, Jefferson Co., N. Y., in early times, where they both died at an advanced age. He was a soldier in the war of 1812 and was in the battle of Sackett's Harbor. Their children were: Simeon, Fanny, Mary, James, Sally married Becker; Lydia, Lury and Elisha, all farmers.

Simeon Fulton has no children.

Fanny Fulton married a Lanphear. She died about 1879. Her children are: Madeline, married a Thompson; Hiram, Nelson and Simeon Lanphear.

Mary Fulton married Samuel Keys, a farmer of Wilna. She died in 1883, leaving her husband and four children. George, Alfreda married a Palmer, Samuel Jr., and Caleb Keys.

James Fulton was married in 1843 to Caroline Nichols. He died in June 1868. They had five children, namely: John Caleb, born 1844, a lawyer in Carthage, Jeff. Co., N. Y. Francis, born 1846; Simeon B. (died in 1864). Mary N. married a Wilkinson. Larissa (died in 1871); Sally Fulton married Lewis A. Stacy, and had three children. Maryetta, Fanny and William L. Stacy. Her present husband is Jeremiah Becker. Elisha Fulton lives on the old farm of his father Caleb in Wilna. His children are Maria, Joseph and Sedate, twins, born in 1858, Jane and Clark.

Lury or Filury Fulton married a Gustin, and had Lorenzo, Byron died in the army in the early part of the late war, and Edwin Gustin. After Mr. Gustin's death she married Charles Hosford and had two children, one of whom, Mary Esther, married a Mr. Crowner.

John Caleb Fulton (son of James), born Aug., 1844, is a lawyer in Carthage, Jefferson Co., N. Y. In Nov., 1869, he married Mary L. Woodward of Philadelphia, Jefferson Co., N. Y., and they have five children : Carrie E., born Dec., 1870; Edwin W., born 1872, Mabel A., Nov., 1874, Beth L., and Herbert F., Dec., 1883.

(81.) **DAVID FULTON** was born in Colerain, Dec. 25th, 1779. He married Jennie Taggart and they settled in Jefferson Co., N. Y., at an early date, where they raised eleven children. Their names were Betsey, Hannah, Susan, Jane, Phebe, John, David, Jr., Sarah, Laura, Luke and Mary.

David Jr., married Sarah Ellis (314) eldest daughter of Thomas Ellis (108) of Ellisburg, N. Y. They were married about 1841, lived in Belleville, Jefferson Co., N. Y., and have four sons, James, Thomas, David and Charles N., all farmers.

(83.) **LUCRETIA FULTON** was born in Colerain, Mass., March 28, 1782. She married Abel Carpenter and settled in the town of Rutland, Jefferson Co., N. Y., where they both died. She had ten children. One of her sons, Elmer Carpenter, resides at East Houndsfield, Jefferson Co., N. Y.

(85.) **DANIEL FULTON** was born in Colerain, Mass., March 21st, 1784. He married Polly Wood and settled in Carthage, Jefferson Co., N. Y., in 1810, where he started in the business of cloth-dressing and wool-carding. In 1813 he removed to Watertown in the same county, and continued in the same business. In the same year he was engaged in the battle of Sackett's Harbor. In 1815 he removed to Champion, N. Y., (Jefferson Co.,) where he went to farming and where he remained until 1836, at which time he removed to a farm in Ohio. He died in 1875. His wife died in the year 1864. They had nine children whose names were Hiram, Anna, Elijah, Betsey, Robert, Ruel, Gaylord, Roxie, and another who died in infancy.

Hiram Fulton, born in Colerain, married Polly Jones. He was a farmer in Champion, where he died in 1876. His wife Polly died in 1879. They had four children, Clark, Elijah, Fred, and one who died young.

Anna Fulton (daughter of Daniel,) married Nat. Rounds in Champion, and moved to Ohio, where they raised a large family. She died about 1866.

Elijah Fulton (son of Daniel,) was born in Champion, N. Y., in 1811. When eleven years of age he began learning the clothiers trade with his uncle Nathan at Burrs Mills, N. Y., with whom he worked until he was 18 years old, when he went to Antwerp, Jefferson Co., N. Y., where he worked at his trade. In 1840 he married Betsy Heald. They had one daughter, Anna Elizabeth, who died in her 24th year. Mrs. Betsy Fulton died about 1855.

In 1865 Mr. Elijah Fulton married for his second wife Miss Lavina A. Ellis of Antwerp, a daughter of Joseph P. Ellis, a prominent resident of Antwerp, Jefferson Co., N. Y. Miss Ellis' grandfather was Luke Ellis, who lived at Wareham, Plymouth Co., Mass. Mr. Luke Ellis had two brothers, John and Seth, and one sister, Thankful. By his first wife, he had one son, James, who was lost at sea. His second wife was Elizabeth Collins, and they had ten children : Naomi, who lived and died unmarried in New Bedford, Mass. Mary, who married John Bennett, lived in Wareham, where her husband died. She had four children. She went to Iowa with her son, James Bennett, where she died. Eliza, the next child of Luke Ellis, married a Washburn, had three children, and lived in Mass. Lavina Ellis married Jedediah Hammond, moved to Philadelphia, Jefferson Co., N. Y. They had no children. Sarah, the next, married a Mr. Maxon, had four children, and lived in Fall River, Mass. Eunice Ellis married Mr. Stetson and had one child who was lost at sea. Deborah Ellis married Harvey Farrington, had two children Harvey Jr. and George, both in business in New York City.

Joseph P. Ellis, son of Luke and father of Mrs. Elijah Fulton, settled in Jefferson County, N. Y., and married Almira Steel and had eight children, five daughters and three sons. Mr. Ellis was a thrifty merchant and produce dealer extensively known in northwestern New York. He and his wife died in Antwerp some years ago. Their son J. D. Ellis, a very prominent man and at one time a member of the State Legislature, lives at Antwerp. Benj. R. Ellis a son of Luke had a family of 10 children. He and his wife died in Croghan, Lewis Co., N. Y. Charles F. Ellis, youngest son of Luke, was a physician. He died in Philadelphia, N. Y. early in life, unmarried. These Ellises, of whom Mrs. Elijah Fulton was one, were not among the descendants of Richard Ellis of Ashfield.

Betsy Fulton, next child of Daniel (85), was born in Watertown, N. Y., married a Rawson and moved to Lorain County, Ohio, where she raised a large family and where she now resides.

Robert Fulton was born in Champion, N. Y., went to Ohio, when young, married Lois Vaughn and had one child, a daughter, who died at about 18 years of age. They live in Pittsfield, Lorain County, Ohio. Ruel Fulton married Mary Humphrey and had two children, a son and a daughter. The latter, a very promising child, died at 12 years of age. The son, Delancy Fulton, is a Baptist minister. His mother lives with him and his father, Ruel, died soon after returning from the war of the rebellion in which he was a union soldier.

Gaylord Fulton, the youngest son of Daniel, had four children, Alice, Harry, Ella and Frank. He had the homestead of his father and was a successful farmer. He died about 1885. His wife and children live at the old home in Ohio.

Roxie Fulton, youngest child of Daniel, married Richard Peck. They live in Ohio and have two children, a son Horace, a farmer in Ohio and Marian, the daughter, who lives in New York City.

(87.) **ELIJAH FULTON** was born in Colerain, Feb. 2d, 1788. He married Phebe Bennett about 1810. He started a woolen mill at Carthage, N. Y. He also engaged in the same business in Plattsburg, N. Y. He died at Great Bend, Jefferson Co., N. Y., about 1829. His daughter Sylvia, lives in Iowa. He had five children.

(89.) **NATHAN FULTON** was born in Colerain, Apr. 25th, 1790. He married Philena Hastings and settled at Burr's Mills, Jefferson Co., N. Y., where he run a clothing mill. He removed to Iowa, where he died about 1844. He had seven children. He has a son Harry who lives at Keokuk, Iowa. About the year 1835 Nathan Fulton visited his mother and the old home of his birth in Colerain. The farm was owned by Mr. Aaron Franklin, but the house was vacant and dilapidated. His mother, then very aged, could not recollect him, although she could recite the names of all her children.

(91.) **JESSE FULTON** was born July 25th, 1792, in Colerain, where he always lived and where he died March 12th, 1834. He married Sophrona Franklin and had five children, Robert, born Oct. 4th, 1827, Aaron, born 1829.

Robert, born 1827, married Hannah E. Worden, a daughter of Asa and Philena Worden, (see (59) page 100) and great granddaughter of Jane Ellis Phillips (11.) Mr. Robert Fulton lives at Green River, Vt., and is a farmer. He has rendered invaluable aid in gathering records of his near and remote relatives for this work. It was mainly through him that a clue was found to the descendants of his grandmother's brother, Matthew Ellis, who settled in Vermont about the time of the Revolution, and whose sons, Seth and Noah Ellis, lived in Thetford, Vt. Mr. Fulton's wife Hannah was born Feb. 10th, 1836, and died Sept. 17th, 1881, leaving her husband and three children—Alice E., born 1857, Lizzie J., 1859, Hattie E., 1862, and Robert H., 1875, died in infancy. Lizzie J. Fulton was married March 20th, 1884, to Mr. H. C. L. Kellerman of Canton, Mo.

Mr. Robert Fulton married for his second wife, Miss Ellen Horn of Ohio.

(95.) **SARAH FULTON,** youngest child of Hannah Ellis and James Fulton, was born in Colerain April 28th, 1797. She married Jabez Franklin and lived many years in Guilford, Vt. Mr. Franklin is yet living (1886), aged over 90 years. Mrs. Franklin was a woman of uncommon talent and worth. After the death of her father, in 1834, her mother, Hannah Ellis Fulton (17), lived with her for about five years. The daughter related that often in the latter part of her mother's life (she died at 90 years of age) she would be startled at some unusual noise and exclaim "that the Indians were coming." She had a vivid recollection of the scenes in her youth, in Ashfield, when there were incursions of the savages. She was then about five or six years of age. (See pages 11 and 12). And when her other faculties had failed she recalled these with much alarm. She many times spoke of how the cattle bellowed when the dead were brought into the fort at Deerfield after the massacre at what was called Bloody Brook, when a detachment went out to gather fruit, and the Indians, lying in ambush, cut them off from their stacked arms and murdered all but one who jumped into the river and escaped. It is said that she was a woman of a "very mild and amiable disposition, while her husband (18) was of the sterner make of many of the early settlers."

Mrs. Sarah Fulton Franklin resided many years in Guilford, where she died in 1872. Her husband Jabez, aged 92, and son James H. Franklin, now live at Guilford Center, Vt. Their daughter Hannah died in early life.

Mr. Jabez Franklin although at the great age of 92 years possesses all his faculties in a high degree. He is a man of uncommon natural abilities, and although passing a quiet life in a country town, he has been noted from his youth up for strict sobriety, honesty and all the elements of a noble character.

Mr. James H. Franklin married Emma M. Franklin, and their two sons, Harry J. and Neil S. are the only grandchildren of Jabez and Sarah Fulton Franklin.

It will be seen that a large number of these Fultons, children of Richard Ellis' daughter Hannah (17), who married James Fulton of Colerain, Mass., settled in Jefferson County, N. Y. It is probable that their mother's brother, Caleb Ellis (19), having settled here about 1795, is what led these Fulton relatives to seek the same locality.

Later inquiries show that several of Matthew Ellis' (13) sons lived in the same county in New York for a time in the early part of the present century. Matthew, Caleb and Hannah, (children of Richard Ellis) lived *mostly* in Colerain, and knew but little of Ashfield, where their brothers, Reuben and John, always lived and where their father had made the first settlement in that town, and where he died in 1797, after his return from Colerain, where he had lived fifteen to twenty years.

Children of Caleb Ellis (19) of Ellisburg, Jefferson County, N. Y., and their wives and husbands. Grand Children of Richard Ellis of Ashfield. From 97 to 118.

(97.) **DANIEL ELLIS**, eldest son of Caleb and Mary Crouch Ellis of Ellisburg, N. Y., was born Aug. 23d, 1780. He was probably born in Vermont or possibly in Colerain, Mass., (which is near the Vermont line) where his father lived when a young man. Daniel was about 15 years of age when his parents settled in Ellisburg, and here he remained until his death in 1862.

Daniel Ellis was in the war of 1812 and was a captain in the service. In 1802 he married in Adams, Jefferson Co., N. Y., Mrs. Christina G. Salisbury. About 1829 he married his second wife, Miss Orpha Pratt, who was born in Marlboro, Vt. She was a Presbyterian, but soon after her marriage joined the Methodist church of which her husband was a member. She was a woman of great, good judgment, force of character, and rare intelligence and worth. She always took pride in her New England extraction, and manifested the greatest independence even in the last years of her life, and after she became blind from age. From her great kindness of heart she constantly sought to help and comfort all who were in need. She died Sept. 22d, 1883, aged 91 years, in full faith of a blessed immortality.

Daniel Ellis was a man of rare worth, intelligence and christian virtues. He was a farmer in Ellisburg all his life. His wife,

(98.) MRS. CHRISTINA G. SALISBURY, was the mother of his seven children. (See Nos. 260 to 273.) Her maiden name was Groat. By her first husband she had three children, one of whom, Edward Salisbury, died in Ellisburg about 1875. She died about 1825. She is remembered as a woman of great beauty and loveliness of character. Both herself and husband Daniel Ellis were active and prominent members of the Methodist church.

(99.) HANNAH ELLIS, eldest daughter of Caleb of Ellisburg, N. Y., was born April 3d, 1782. She married Comfort Chapman and had five children. (See Nos. 276 to 284, page 23.)

(101.) JOHN ELLIS, second son of Caleb, was born Feb. 3d, 1784. He was a farmer in Ellisburg, N. Y., where he died in 1847.

His first wife was Mary Stilwell, by whom he had two children—Caleb, born 1807, and Squire, born 1809.

John Ellis' second wife was Betsey Smith, by whom he had four children. (See Nos. 290 to 296.) She died in 1837.

John Ellis' third wife was Kate Duran by whom he had one son, Edward N. Ellis (298), who is a captain of a vessel on the lakes. She died in Ellisburg in 1884.

(105.) JANE ELLIS, second daughter of Caleb, was born February 6th, 1786. About 1808 she married Amasa Sheldon, in the town of Ellisburg, N. Y. She died in Ellisburg about 1849, and Mr. Sheldon in 1845. They had six children, all born in Ellisburg. (See Nos. 300 to 308, page 24.)

Parley Sheldon, born 1810, settled in Ohio. He was a wealthy farmer, had a large family, and died about 1862.

William Sheldon, born 1812, died about 1870, leaving four or five children.

Philo Sheldon was an invalid all his life. He died about 1873.

Robert Sheldon was a farmer and a very bright and successful business man. He died about 1880.

Amasa Sheldon, Jr., the youngest child of Jane Ellis and Amasa Sheldon, left home about 1850 to go " to sea," and has not been heard from since.

(108.) THOMAS ELLIS, third son of Caleb Ellis of Ellisburg, N. Y., was born June 19th, 1788. He was a soldier in the war of 1812. He was a farmer in Belleville, town of Ellisburg, all his life, where he died in 1869.

Thomas Ellis was a deeply religious man and an ardent Methodist, in which church he was a prominent and influential member, as well as a liberal supporter. He was a strictly temperance man all his life. He was a man of uncommon mental endowment and provided a liberal education for all his children. His wife,

(109.) HANNAH SALISBURY, was born in 1793. They were married in 1812 in Ellisburg, N. Y., in which town all their children were born. They had ten children. (See Nos. 310 to 328.)

(111.) SQUIRE ELLIS, sixth child of Caleb, was born June 6th, 1790. He was a miller with his father in Ellisburg. He died unmarried in 1813.

(112.) **JAMES ELLIS,** seventh child of Caleb, was born Aug. 12th, 1792. About 1815 he married Rachel Weiser of Ellisburg, where they raised a family of four children. (See Nos. 330 to 336.) Mr. Ellis was a farmer. He was a soldier in the war of 1812, and in the battles of Sackett's Harbor and Big Sandy Creek, Jefferson Co., N. Y. He died in Ellisburg, N. Y., in 1823. His wife,

(113.) **RACHEL WEISER,** was a daughter of Nicholas Weiser and Margaret Walrad, his wife. They were from the Mohawk valley in Montgomery Co., N. Y., but settled in Ellisburg early in the present century. Nicholas Weiser, was a soldier in the Revolutionary war, and famous as a scout, and was greatly feared by the Indians and tories. His father, Conrad Weiser, a man of learning and genius, came from Germany in 1711, and settled in New York. Mrs. Rachel Weiser Ellis, raised a family of four children, three of whom are now living. She died in Ellisburg, in 1858.

(115.) **ROBERT ELLIS,** eighth child of Caleb, was born March 24th, 1794. He married in 1816 and lived in Ellisburg, N. Y., where he raised a family of eleven children. (See Nos. 340 to 360.) He was a farmer. He was four years old when his father settled in Ellisburg, being the first settler in that town. They soon built a grist mill at what is now called Woodville, a small village in the town of Ellisburg. His father settled on what was called the south branch of Sandy Creek, but their grist mill was on the north branch of the same stream. Robert Ellis was a soldier in the war of 1812, and in engagements at Sackett's Harbor and Sandy Creek. He was an honest and upright man. He died in 1863. His wife,

(116.) **MARY WEISER,** was born in 1798, and died about 1879. She was a sister of Rachel Weiser (113.)

(118.) **POLLY, SALLY, AND BETSEY ELLIS,** were the three youngest children of Caleb and Mary Crouch Ellis of Ellisburg, N. Y. They were born—Polly, April 24th, 1796; Sally, March 14th, 1798, and Betsey, May 25th, 1800, and it is said all died in infancy or early life.

FOURTH GENERATION.

(119.) STEPHEN ELLIS, eldest son of Benjamin, Sr., was born in Ashfield, Feb. 21st, 1775. In his early youth his father moved to Deerfield, where Stephen probably married his wife Susanah Coburn, Jan. 1st, 1798. Early in the present century he removed to Sempronius, N. Y., where his father had settled about the year 1800. Here he raised his family of seven children.

Stephen Ellis, was a farmer and miller. It is said that he joined with his father in building a small grist mill at Montville, a little hamlet in Cayuga County, in or near Sempronius. The mill was built of logs, and was the first one in that section of country. In the year 1818, Stephen Ellis together with his brother Moses and their families removed to North Bend, Ohio, on the Ohio River, a few miles below Cincinnati, where they landed Aug. 2nd, 1818, and rented a farm from Gen. W. H. Harrison, "the hero of Tippecanoe," and afterwards president (in 1841) of the United States. Stephen and his brother lived here about eight years, during which time they built a grist mill. In the spring of 1825, they settled on farms in Fayette Co., Ind., near Connersville, where Stephen lived several years. He died in Yorktown, Ind., in 1838. Stephen Ellis was a man of industry, upright and honest in all his conduct. He was born one year earlier, and in the same neighborhood in Ashfield, as his father's cousin Dea. Dimick Ellis, whom he is said to have greatly resembled. (See likeness in the front of the book.) He was a member of the Christian church. For his second wife he married Mrs. Martha Huntington, who survived him a number of years. She had several children by a former husband, one of whom, Emily Huntington, lived some years ago at Putnam, Ill. The latter married Mr. John Langley, of Lafayette, Ind.

(120.) **SUSANAH COBURN**, born April 13th, 1777, wife of Stephen Ellis and mother of his children, was probably from Deerfield, Mass. In removing from Sempronius to North Bend, Ohio, they went across the country over 100 miles to Olean, Cattaraugus Co., N. Y., on the Allegany river, where with small boats and rafts they went down that river to Pittsburg, and thence on the Ohio river to North Bend, a few miles below Cincinnati. This must have been a difficult journey and attended with great fatigue. Within a year after their arrival Mrs. Ellis died. For account of her children, see Nos. 362 to 374.

(121.) **LURENCA ELLIS**, second child of Benjamin Ellis, Sr., was born in Ashfield, Mass., Jan. 10th, 1777. Where she married does not appear, but with her husband John Phelps and family she lived in Cayuga Co., N. Y., near Moravia, all her married life. She had ten children. She died Oct. 28th, 1853.

Lurenca Ellis' and John Phelps' children were : Alvah Phelps, born March 7th, 1799; Susanah, born May 22nd, 1802, died May 26th, 1870; Sinthia, born Oct, 25th, 1804, died Feb. 16th, 1832; Ruth, born Sept. 18th, 1806; Lucy born Aug. 27th, 1807, died Oct. 24th, 1830; John W., born Sept. 12th, 1811; David L., born April 4th, 1814; Benjamin E., born Oct. 13th, 1816, died Feb. 16th, 1840; Lurenca, born May 19th, 1819, died May 25th, 1842; and Ashie, born Sept. 18th, 1823, died Jan. 9th, 1824. John W. Phelps, born 1811, now lives on the homestead in Niles, near Moravia, N. Y., where he has raised his family.

(123.) **MOSES ELLIS**, was born Sept. 17th, 1780, probably in Deerfield, Mass. About the last of Nov., 1802, he left Mass. for Sempronius, N.Y., where his father bought a farm in 1800. He married Elizabeth Judd, Oct. 14th, 1804, and after her death, in 1841, he married Desire Harris, about 1844. She died in 1846.

In 1818 Moses Ellis and his family left Sempronius, Cayuga Co., and settled at North Bend, Ohio. In 1825 he removed to Plum Orchard, near Connersville, Ind., where he resided until his death January 16th, 1849. He was a member of the Christian church, well-educated, scholarly and an upright and honorable man, and enjoyed the confidence of the relatives in Ashfield, as is evidenced by an ancient receipt which the writer finds among old papers of his grandfather, in which on Nov. 27th, 1802, Moses Elllis was entrusted with a sum of money to be conveyed to Moses Bartlett, of Sempronius. It will be remembered that this was before the formation of express companies, and the only means of conveying money to distant parts in those times was by individuals of known integrity and capacity. It is probable that the above was the date at which Moses left Massachusetts, to settle in Sempronius, where his father had bought a farm two years before. His wife,

(124.) **ELIZABETH JUDD,** was born March 11th, 1782, and died near Connersville, Aug. 5th, 1841. She had six children, all of whom except the youngest were born in Cayuga Co., N. Y. (For sketches of these see Nos. 380 to 390.) She was a member of the Christian church.

(129.) **DANIEL ELLIS,** son of Benjamin, Sr., was probably born in Deerfield about 1782. He left Massachusetts early in the present century, and went to Sempronius, N. Y. At the outbreak of the war of 1812 he enlisted, and went with his company to the Niagara River, where they were stationed for a time. His next younger brother, Benjamin, Jr., was a member of the same company, and while the latter was on a furlough visiting the home in Sempronius, Daniel was taken sick and died. Mr. Joseph Lassell, of Moravia, N. Y., now 93 years of age, was in the same company and remembers Daniel well. Mr. Lassell was born in Buckland, Mass., next town north of Ashfield, and when 12 years of age settled in Moravia, N. Y., where he has ever since resided. He has a very clear recollection of all these Ellises who lived in that vicinity in the early part of the century.

It is not probable that Daniel Ellis was ever married. When he left Massachusetts for Sempronius the Ashfield relatives intrusted him with money to be paid to friends in Sempronius, and he faithfully complied with the trust.

(126.) BENJAMIN ELLIS, Jr., was born in Deerfield, Mass., Feb. 13th, 1784. He was a farmer and miller, and for many years an exhorter, or unlicensed minister, in the Methodist Church, of which he was a devoted member. He was a strictly sober and temperate man all his life, and a prominent member of the Sons of Temperance, a very numerous and popular order some years ago, for suppressing the evils of intemperance. He was a leading officer in this order, and when he wore the regalia peculiar to the same it gave him a very venerable appearance. He was a soldier in the war of 1812. He was widely known and universally respected as a pure and upright man beloved by all.

In an early day he purchased a farm three miles north of Moravia, N. Y., on which he raised his family. It was an altogether new country at that time, and deer, bears and wolves were numerous. No grain could be grown until the trees were cleared off and the ground broken up. In those times money was scarce, as well as all the comforts of life. An annual tax of forty cents on a farm was thought extravagant. Canals and railroads were then unknown and the settlers few in number. Great economy was necessary in those times to meet the simplest expenses.

He learned the milling business with his father at their little mill at Montville, near Moravia.

While a soldier on the frontier at Niagara River he was given a furlough to visit his family in Sempronius, or Niles, as it was afterwards called. In making the trip he walked on foot both ways. He died in Groton, Tompkins County, N. Y., May 11th, 1859. He had five children, three of whom survived him. (See Nos. 392 to 399.)

Benjamin Ellis, Jr.'s wife,

(127.) **ABIGAIL HOWARD**, was born in 178-. She married Mr. Ellis in Sempronius, Feb. 23d, 1809. They always lived in that town or vicinity. She died Feb. 5th, 1883, at the residence of her son, Nathan H. Ellis, in Ludlowville, Cayuga Co., N. Y., with whom she made her home after the death of her husband in 1859. She was a woman of superior education and talents, and of a remarkable memory. She retained her mental and physical powers in a high degree up to her last days, and she lived to be over 90 years of age.

Before her marriage she crossed the Catskill Mountains on horseback and rode 190 miles to meet her intended husband. It was in the month of February, and she often related that the weather was so mild that peach and other fruit trees were in bloom—a cheerful omen for a bride, which was fully realized in all her married life.

(128.) **REUBEN ELLIS**, fifth son of Benjamin, Sr., was born probably in Deerfield, Mass., April 7th, 1786. He died in Clymer, Chautauqua County, N. Y., Nov. 24th, 1845. He was a half-brother to the elder children. His mother was Lois Mann, the second wife of Benjamin Ellis, Sr. (See page 81.) When a youth he lived with his father in Sempronius, at which place he was married to Miss Elizabeth King, Feb. 6th, 1811, where five of their children were born.

About 1819 he removed to Murray, Orleans Co., N. Y., and from there to Clymer, Chautauqua Co., about 1830. He was a farmer and a Baptist in religious belief, and said to have been an honorable and upright man in all his ways. His wife,

(129.) **ELIZABETH KING**, was born April 3d, 1793. She died in Portland, Chautauqua Co., March 23d, 1876. She was a Baptist. She had twelve children. (See Nos. 401 to 420.)

(130.) **MEHITABLE ELLIS**, daughter of Benjamin Ellis, Sr., was born about 1788, probably in Deerfield. It is said that she married Lawrence Kemp, at or near Sempronius, N. Y. They soon after removed from there, and the writer has not been able to get any further trace of them or their descendants, if they had any.

(132.) **CHELOMETH ELLIS,** youngest child of Benjamin, Sr., was born about 1790, in Massachusetts. She married Walter Avery, Jr., in or near Sempronius, and had five children. She died in 1844. Her husband, Walter Avery, was born in 1787, and died in Erie County, Pa., in 1861.

The children of Walter and Chelometh Ellis Avery were : Fannie, Melvina, Lyman, Sarah, and Mary.

Fannie Avery, born May 15th, 1826, died Jan. 22nd, 1851. She married Zalmon Ames, and had three sons, Cyrenus C., Alfred O., and Francis M. Ames. They lived at Mina, Chautauqua County, N. Y.

Malvina Avery, born Dec. 27th, 1827, died April 25th, 1876. She married William Haven, and had four children: Martha, Etta, Ella and Walter Avery Haven. They lived in Chautauqua Co., N. Y.

Lyman Avery, born June 1st, 1830, died in 1863. He married Mary Haven, and had two daughters, Emma and Ida May. They lived at Findley's Lake, Chautauqua Co.

Sarah Avery, born April 29th, 1832, married Ransom Wood. She had three children: George, Elias, and Esther Wood. They now live at Spring Creek, Warren Co., Pa.

Mary Avery, born July 30th, 1834, died Oct. 24th, 1875. She married Zalmon Ames, and had seven children: Lydia M., Henry, Mary E., Fred C., Eva J., Warren M., and Hattie Jane Ames. They lived at Brownsdale, Mower Co., Minn.

Children of Jonathan Ellis (26), of Sempronius, N. Y., and
their husbands and wives, Grandchildren of Reuben
(4), and Great-grandchildren of Richard
Ellis. From Nos. 134 to 140.

(134.) **SUBMIT ELLIS**, eldest daughter of Jonathan
Ellis, was born in Sempronius, N. Y., April 19th, 1803. She
died in Bronson, Branch Co., Mich., Jan. 23rd, 1877.
September 9th, 1819, she married Nathaniel Havens, at
Moravia, N. Y., and had nine children. She had 46 grandchildren and 20 great-grandchildren. Two of her sons were
Union soldiers in the war of the Rebellion. Most of her
children were born in Cayuga Co., N. Y., but later in life
she and her husband lived in southern Michigan. Her
husband,

(135.) **NATHANIEL HAVENS**, was born in Sept.,
1800, and died at Liberty, Jackson Co., Mich., Nov. 6th, 1874.
He was a farmer, as were all his children. The names of the
latter were George, Lois, Sarah Ann, Miranda Jane, Susan,
Nathaniel Jr., Lyman, John West and Submit Havens.

George Havens, was born June 18th, 1821, married
Lorinda Jane Clifford, Nov. 12th, 1846, lived in Erie, Pa.,
and died Aug. 21st, 1855.

Lois Havens, born April 16th, 1814, married Hiram
Moses, June 23rd, 1846. They lived at Somerset Center,
Hillsdale Co., Mich.

Sarah Ann Havens, born April 28th, 1826, married
Nelson Gould, April 5th, 1840. They are farmers and live
at Byron Center, Kent Co., Mich. Mr. Gould was born in
Homer, Cortland Co., N. Y., April 28th, 1818. Their
children are John H., born in Somerset, Hillsdale Co.,
Mich., Apr. 3rd, 1842, enlisted as a Union soldier and died
in the army Nov. 10th, 1862. Amanda A., born in Somer-
set, Sept. 1st, 1843, died Jan. 27th, 1854; Lena A., born in
Somerset, Feb. 23rd, 1846; Cynthia E., born in Somerset,
Dec. 9th, 1848; George R., born in Darien, Walworth Co.,
Wis., Feb. 3rd, 1852; Endress N., born in Jamestown,
Ottawa Co., Mich., March 30th, 1854; Seymour W., born

in Jamestown, July 4th, 1857; Emmet F., born in Jamestown, Oct. 21st, 1859; Clarissa S., born in Somerset, March
23rd, 1863; Sarah E., born in Jamestown, Feb. 12th, 1866,
and James F. Gould, born in Jamestown, Oct. 1st, 1869.

John Havens, born Oct. 6th, 1828, died Feb. 16th, 1833.

Miranda Jane Havens, born Sept. 3rd, 1831, married
Benjamin F. Havens, May 3rd, 1855. They live at Addison, Lenawee Co., Mich.

Susan Havens, born Oct. 21st, 1834, married Alonzo C.
Heydon, March 15th, 1853. They lived in Erie, Pa., where
her son Emery Heydon now resides. She died June 12th,
1885.

Nathaniel Havens Jr., born May 28th, 1838, married
Tirza M. Swift, June 17th, 1860. They live on a farm six
miles from Bronson, Mich. They have had four children.
Orville W., died in infancy. Fred L., died in infancy.
Arthur J., born Feb. 24th, 1867, in Somerset, Mich. Burt
L., born Aug. 25th, 1873, in Bronson.

Lyman Havens, born Sept. 27th, 1842, married Mary L.
Pepper, April 8th, 1866. He married his second wife Mary
Beebe, Nov. 28th, 1868. He lives at Byron Center, Kent
Co., Mich. He enlisted in Company G., 18th Mich. In-
fantry, and was a prisoner in Cahawba prison six months.

John W. Havens, born Sept. 4th, 1845, married Amy
Rhoads, July 12th, 1868. He married his second wife,
Augusta Baldwin, Aug. 16th, 1874. He now resides at
Moscow, Hillsdale Co., Mich. He was a Union soldier in a
Mich. Battery, and served two years.

Submit Havens, born Aug. 15th, 1848, married James
Rhoads, July 12th, 1868. She lives at Liberty, Jackson
Co., Mich.

(136.) **ABEL WEST ELLIS,** son of Jonathan Ellis,
was born in Sempronius, about three miles north of Moravia,
N. Y., March 3rd, 1806. He died in Ripley, Chautauqua
Co., N. Y., May 14th, 1877. He was a farmer in Ripley,
where he settled in 1836. He lived for a time in Alleghany

Co., N. Y., where he married his wife. Mr. Ellis was over six feet tall, straight and well-proportioned, black hair and eyes and dark complexion. His wife,

(137.) **MARGARET NORTON,** was born in Alleghany Co., N. Y., July, 1806. She was married July 21st, 1832, in Alleghany Co., where her parents lived many years. She died in Ripley, Sept. 19th, 1866. She had six children. (See Nos. 444 to 453.)

(138) **JOHN ALLIS ELLIS,** son of Jonathan, was born in Sempronius, March 16th, 1809. His father died when he was about three years of age, but he was raised on the farm where his parents settled in 1800. When of age he made a visit to his uncle Richard Ellis, in Ellisburg, Pa., and in 1833, he visited his uncles David in Springfield, Pa., and Benjamin Sr., at Plum Orchard, (near Connersville) Ind. March 20th, 1833, he married Miss Eliza Ann Fairchild, in Ripley, Chautauqua Co., N. Y., to which place his elder brother and mother had removed some time before. He lived in Ripley, where his three eldest children were born, until about 1839, when he bought a farm near Conneaut, Ohio, where he has since resided and where he now lives at an advanced age.

Mr. Ellis is a scholarly man, of close observation and remarkable memory. From his ample correspondence the writer has learned much regarding the early members of the Ellis family, which could not be had elsewhere, and which has been of great value in compiling this work. In nearly every instance, statements from him founded on his recollection from personal observation or communicated to him by his ancestors, have been verified by statistics from various sources.

Mr. Ellis is a tall man over six feet high, and dark complexion. The likeness of him on opposite page was copied from a photograph, taken when he was 75 years of age. His wife was Eliza Ann Fairchild, of Batavia, N. Y.

(138.) JOHN ALLIS ELLIS,

OF CONNEAUT, OHIO.

[139.]

(139.) **ELIZA ANN FAIRCHILD**, was born in Batavia, N. Y., Feb. 8th, 1813. Her father was Henry, and her grandfather John Fairchild, of Columbia Co., N. Y., Mrs. Ellis had been an invalid, and a great sufferer from sciatic rheumatism for several years. She died in the spring of 1886. She had six children. (See Nos. 455 to 465.)

(140.) **BOADISEA ELLIS,* youngest child of Jonathan Ellis and his wife, Lois Allis, was born on the homestead in Niles or Sempronius (three miles north of Moravia), N. Y., July 25th, 1811. Early in life she married Mr. John Fritts and had two children, one of whom died young. The other, Mr. Alvin Fritts, born in Cayuga Co., in 1832, married Mary Gray in Concord, Mich., in 1849. Their children were: Avery, born 1852; Emma, born 1854; Charles, born 1856 and John Fritts, born 1860. At last accounts they lived at Albion, Mich., where Emma married a Mr. Aldrich. Towards the close of the war, Mr. Alvin Fritts enlisted and went to St. Louis, Mo., where he was attacked with fever and died. He was a man of superior ability, commanding in appearance, pleasing in his address and won for himself many friends.

Mr. John Fritts died about 1834, and in 1839, when twenty-eight years of age, his widow married Mr. Wm. W. King in Ripley, Chautauqua Co., N. Y., to which place she had removed just before. They soon after removed to Erie, Pa., for two years, thence to Concord, Jackson Co., Mich., where she died Sept. 4th, 1851. In her youth she joined the Methodist church, of which she was a member until after her marriage to Mr. King, when she joined the Baptist church.

Her friends remember her as true and kind hearted. The poor spoke of her as benevolent and her children love to think of her as the noble self-sacrificing mother who sought

---

* This name is found in history at an early date. About A. D., 10, Boadisea was Queen of Iceni, a province which is now comprised in several counties in the interior of England. She was a woman of great beauty and courage. She was defeated by the Romans, under Cæsar, in a battle in which over 80,000 of her subjects, which she commanded, were slain.

to shield them from sorrow and mitigate their cares. The church remembers her as a faithful, consistent member, ever loyal to her vows. Full of Christian charity she won for herself many friends.

"Who knew her, but to love her;
Who'l name her, but to praise."

(141.) **WM. W. KING,** was born in Pownal, Vt., March 30th, 1799. His parents died when he was young, and he was brought up by a brother of his mother. At nineteen years of age he went out into the world to make his way. At twenty four-years of age he joined the Baptist church, and has ever been noted for his strong religious convictions and Christian deportment. About 1853 he settled on a farm near Carson City, Montcalm Co., Mich. where he yet resides a hale and hearty old gentleman, at the unusual age of 87 years, widely known and respected. He lives with his only son now living, Mr. Charles D. King, on the homestead which he took up from the government in 1853.

The children of Mr. and Mrs. King were: William R., born 1841, died in 1871; Charles D., born 1843; James, born 1844, died 1845; Emily D., born 1848 and George, born 1850, died 1852.

William R. King married Melissa Richardson in Bloomer, Montcalm Co., Mich., in 1866. Their children were: Ina, born 1868 and Electa, born 1870.

Charles D. King was born in Erie Co., Pa. In early life he went with his father to Montcalm Co., Mich., when that section was a wilderness. His father bought a large farm near Carson City, where the father and son now reside. Mr. Charles D. King lives on the homestead. In 1867 he married Miss Jennie Smith, of Bushnell, Montcalm Co. They have one child, Ethel King, born 1881. Besides farming, Mr. King engages in various other business pursuits. He is a very enterprising and highly respected man.

Emily D. King was born in Concord, Mich. When three years of age her mother died. At the age of six years her father settled near Carson City, at a time when schools were few and not of the best, but with energy and perseverance she fitted herself at 18 years of age to become a teacher, which pursuit she followed nearly nine years, a portion of the time as teacher in the grammar department of the Union School in Carson City.

June 1st, 1874, she married Dr. Henry H. Cook, by whom she had two children: Henry H., Jr., and Ely Cook. The latter died in 1881.

Mrs. Cook resides in Mason, Mich. She is secretary of the Board of Education and also has a lucrative and responsible position in the office of county treasurer at Mason where she is highly respected.

Children of Dea. Richard Ellis (29), of Ellisburg, Pa., and their wives and husbands. Grandchildren of Reuben (4), and Great-grandchildren of Richard Ellis of Ashfield. From 143 to 172.

(143.) HANFORD ELLIS, first child of Richard, was born, probably in Ashfield, Nov. 7th, 1781. He died Nov. 6th, the following year.

(144.) LYDIA ELLIS, was born Feb. 1st, 1783, and died in Shippen, Tioga Co., Pa., Aug. 2nd, 1819. She married Col. Daniel H. Bacon in 1798 and had seven children. They were married in Candor, Tioga Co., N. Y., where they lived until 1815, when they removed to Delmar, Pa., and purchased a large tract of wild land, which Mr. Bacon and his sons cleared up and made for themselves homes.

Their children: Oliver, born 1801, died April 30th, 1882; Eunice, born 1803, died 1884; Nancy, born 1805, died 1872; Lewis, born 1807, died 1864; Hannah, born 1809; Chloe, born 1812; Daniel, born 1815, died 1865.

Oliver Bacon, born April 2nd, 1801, married Miss Catharine Houghton March 30th, 1823, and their children were: Chauncy, born Aug. 26th, 1825, married Electa Satterlee, of Delmar, died 1857. Eunice, born Jan. 15th, 1828, married in 1848 J. C. Barth, of Delmar. Simeon, born June 12th, 1830, married in 1868 to Frances Shelton, of Delmar. Pharez, born June 12th, 1834, married in 1883 to Lottie T. Green, of Williamsport, Pa. Eli, born July 5th, 1832, married in 1853 to Adaline May, of Charleston. Dr. Daniel, born May 21st, 1836, married in 1876 to Florence Green and lives in Wellsboro, Pa. Lydia, born May 19th, 1838, married in 1853 to G. F. Butler, of Delmar. Esther, born Oct. 26th, 1840, married in 1875 to James Van Degrift, of Delmar. Aspah, born Aug. 18th, 1843, married in 1867 to Neomi Brooks, of Madison Co., Ill. Oliver, Jr., born Nov. 14th, 1845, married in 1869 to Elsie M. Barth. She died in 1874 and Mr. Bacon married for his second wife, in 1882, Jennie Bunnell, of Greene, Chenango Co., N. Y. They now live in Wellsboro, Pa. Seth, born Oct. 14th, 1847, married in 1869 to Helen Barth, of Delmar, where they now live.

Mr. Oliver Bacon, Sr.'s wife, Catharine, lives with her son, Oliver, Jr., on the homestead at the advanced age of 82 years.

Eunice Bacon, born 1803, married in 1821 to William Dimick. She died in 1884.

Nancy Bacon, born 1805, married in 1825 to James Henry. She died in 1872.

Lewis Bacon, born 1807, married in 1844 to Filena Frost. He died in 1864.

Hannah Bacon, born 1809, married in 1830 to Calvin Newton.

Chloe Bacon, born 1812, married in 1838 to William Howe and live in Delmar.

Daniel Bacon, born 1815, married in 1838 to Louisa Atherton.

(146.) **ASAPH ELLIS**, third child of Richard, was born Sept. 8th, 1785, and settled in Clearfield Co., Pa., where he raised a family of eight children. Clearfield is about one hundred miles southwest of Ellisburg, Pa., where many of Asaph's relatives lived, and but little is known about himself and family. His wife was

(147.) **AMANDA SPENCER.** Their children were: Charles, Richard, Horace, Chauncy, Harriett, Pliny, Hannah and Orlando. If the writer obtains any definite information regarding them it will be given further on under No. 482.

(148.) **HANNAH ELLIS**, fourth child of Richard Ellis, of Ellisburg, Pa., was born probably in Shelburn, Mass., March 12th, 1787. She married Frederick Tanner, while her father lived in Candor, N. Y., and had one child. She died in New York at the age of 23 years.

(150.) **LUCINDA ELLIS**, was born April 3rd, 1789, and died in Wellsboro, Pa., in 1842. She married David Henry and lived near Wellsboro, where they raised seven children.

William Henry died in 1882.

Charles is a farmer, married and lives in Delmar.

David is married and lives in Wisconsin.

Lovica married Richard English and they live in Wellsboro, Pa.

Mary married a King. She died in 1871. Her sons, Hugh and Galusha King, are married and live in Westfield, Tioga Co., Pa.

Lydia lives in Wellsboro and her sister, Margaret Henry, died in Wellsboro in 1877.

(152.) **REV. CONSIDER ELLIS**, son of Richard Ellis, of Ellisburg, Pa., was born Nov. 6th, 1791, in Shelburn, Mass., and died in Ellisburg, Pa., 1866. He was a Baptist minister and also engaged in milling a portion of his time. He had three children, see No. 500. His wife,

(153.) **MARY LOVELL,** born 1804, married Mr. Ellis in Delmar, Pa., June 23rd, 1822. She now resides in Ellisburg with her daughter, Prudence, who married Samuel Rouse.

(154.) **REV. JOHN ELLIS,** son of Richard Ellis, of Ellisburg, Pa., was born Aug. 27th, 1792, in Shelburn, Mass. He was a Baptist minister. He married Elizabeth Faulkner, and had five children. See Nos. 506 to 513. About 1830 he left Pennsylvania, and settled with his family in the town of Great Valley, about two miles south of Ellicottville, Cattaraugus Co., N. Y., where he lived until his death, March 14th, 1862. At Great Valley, he had a good farm and grist mill, also a saw mill near the latter. Himself and family are said to have been very excellent people. His wife Elizabeth, died early in life, 1837.

(156.) **EUNICE ELLIS,** born May 3rd, 1794, and died at Big Meadows, Pa., 1874. She was a Baptist, and a truly noble and Christian woman. She married Mr. Reuben Herrington, about 1812, and settled at Big Meadows, where they always lived, and where Mr. Herrington died in 1862, age 71 years. They had twelve children: Richard, Jacob, Sarah Ann, Nancy died in 1843, Charles, Geo. W., Deroy, Elsie, Leonard P., Harriet E., Horace, and Benjamin Herrington.

Jacob Herrington, born 1815, married Katharine Ann Thompson, about 1840. They had four sons and one daughter. Mr. Herrington now lives in Sweden, Potter Co., Pa. He is an extensive farmer and lumberman. His wife died about 1870.

Sarah Ann, born 1817, married Chester Corsan, and had seven children. They live in Sweden, Pa., where they keep a hotel.

Charles, born 1821, married Sarah Jane Mathers. They had six children. They live in Wellsboro, Pa. He is a farmer and lumber merchant.

George W., born 1823, married Matilda Schoonover, and they have three daughters living in Ansonia, Pa. He was in the saw and grist-mill business, and more lately keeping a hotel.

Deroy, born 1825, married Maria Merrick, and had four children. They reside at Ansonia, Tioga Co., Pa. He is a farmer.

Harriet E., born 1830, married John Purvis, and they reside at Niles Valley, Tioga Co., Pa.

Horace P. Herrington, born 1837, married Elizabeth Holmes, and lives on the homestead at Ansonia, Pa. They have three children.

(158.) **ELD. RICHARD ELLIS, Jr.,** son of Richard, of Ellisburg, Pa., was born Dec. 6th, 1795, and died in Wellsboro, Tioga Co., Pa., 1827. He was a Baptist minister, but unordained. He had four children, all born in Delmar, Pa. (See Nos. 522 to 528.) His wife,

(159.) **PATIENCE HERRINGTON**, was born 1802, and married Mr. Ellis Feb. 3rd, 1818. She was a Baptist and a sincere Christian woman. She died at her home near Whitesville, Allegany Co., N. Y., in 1855.

She was a sister of Mr. Reuben Herrington, who married Eunice Ellis (156).

(160.) **DAVID ELLIS**, was born July 8th, 1797, and died at Big Meadows, Tioga Co., where he had resided nearly all his life. He was a mill-wright by trade, and for ten years a justice or magistrate and for six years a county commissioner. He was highly respected and a consistent and active Christian of the Baptist faith all his life. He died in 1857. His wife,

(161.) **ORILLA DIMICK**, was born in 1801 and died in Shippen, Pa., 1867. Jan. 13th, 1819 she married Mr. Ellis and they raised nine children, (see Nos. 530 to 546.) She was a Baptist. It is said that she was distantly related to the Dimicks of Ashfield and Barnstable, Mass.

(162.) **POLLY, MEHITABLE, BENJAMIN** - and **THOMAS J. ELLIS,** children of Richard Ellis, of Ellisburg, Pa., all died in infancy.

Polly was born Feb. 4th, 1799, died on the 28th of the same month. Benjamin, born March 8th, 1800, died the same month. Thomas J., born April 25th, 1801, died April 6th, 1802. Mehitable, born May 4th, 1805, died Sept. 4th, of the same year.

These four children were born in Candor, Tioga Co., N. Y., where their parents lived after their removal from Massachusetts, up to about 1811, when they settled in Tioga Co., Pa.

(163.) **POLLY ELLIS**, daughter of Richard Ellis, of Ellisburg, Pa., was born Aug. 12th, 1803, and died of a malignant fever in the autumn of 1819 at Big Meadows, Pa. She married Paul N. Dimick, who was born in 1799, and they had one child.

(165.) **LUCRETIA ELLIS**, was born July 15th, 1806, in Candor, Tioga Co., N. Y. In 1829, she married Elder Benjamin G. Avery, and they settled in Allegany, Cattaraugus Co., N. Y. They had six children. Richard B., born 1831; Thomas W., born 1833; Mary P., born 1835; William C., born 1837; Sarah L., born 1840; and James T., born 1843.

Richard B. Avery, was born June 8th, 1831, in Allegany N. Y. He was an officer in the Union army; first in the commissary department, and afterwards adjutant-general. He married a lady in Mississippi soon after the close of the war. They have two children, Hattie and Blanch. They now reside in Mississippi. Mr. Avery, is the inventor of the "Avery Hydro-Carbon fuel and illuminating gas process," which is said to be an invention of great merit.

Thomas W. Avery, born in Allegany, N. Y., June 13th, 1833, removed to Oregon with his mother and stepfather, where he died Dec. 8th, 1867. He was a member of the Oregon legislature the year before his death.

Mary P. Avery, born in Allegany, N. Y., April 30th, 1835, married Mr. C. M. Sawtelle, and removed to San Francisco, Cal., where she now resides with her family. She has four children living. She has studied and graduated in medicine, and is engaged in the practice, and is widely noted as a lecturer on medicine, physiology, and hygiene. She also publishes a paper called the Medico Literary Journal.

William C. Avery, was born in Mercer Co., Pa., Sept. 5th, 1837. He was married to Salome A. Larkin, Nov. 1867, by whom he had one son and three daughters, Mary, James, (drowned in Mill-Creek,) Minnie and Alice. Mr. Avery died in California, March 25th, 1875.

Sarah L. Avery, born in Mercer Co., Pa., Dec. 27th, 1840, died in Aug., 1845.

James T. Avery, was born in Vermillion Co., Ill., June 4th, 1843, and died in Clackamas Co., Oregon, June 24th, 1867. He was a school teacher.

Elder Benjamin G. Avery, husband of Lucretia Ellis, was a minister of the Old School Baptist denomination, and devoted his energies and life to the cause of his Master. In 1843, he moved with his family to Danville, Vermillion Co., Ill. In 1844 he went as a delegate to the Spoon River Association, about 200 miles from home, where he was taken sick with a fever in Sept. and died. He was a man of a pure life, and highly respected by all who knew him.

Mrs. Lucretia Ellis Avery, after the death of her first husband, married July 6th, 1846, Mr. John Stipp, a widower with four children. The next year Mr. Stipp with his children, his wife and four of her children, started by the overland route for Oregon, where they arrived Sept. 11th, 1848. They settled in Clackamas Co., when the whole territory was a wilderness, and wild animals and savage red men were all around them. It is almost beyond conception the courage required to undertake such a journey, as was this in those early days. For courage, resolution and faith in God such a migration was equal to that which actuated the Pilgrims of two centuries before.

Mrs. Lucretia Stipp, is a woman of uncommon intelligence and worth. To her the writer has been greatly indebted for many facts and items, regarding the early relatives who settled in Pennsylvania, many years ago. She is the only child of her fathers' family, (Richard Ellis of Ellisburg, Pa.) now living. She now resides at Scio, Oregon. Her second husband,

Elder John Stipp, was ordained in May, 1853, a minister of the Old School Baptist Church, (*not* Presbyterian as stated on page 15.) He was born in Berkley Co., West Virginia, Nov. 10th, 1806. He is devoted to his calling, and is still traveling over the country, preaching the gospel at his advanced age. Of their children, who went with them in their western journey, but one of his and one of his wife's are now living. They are most worthy people entitled to a reward of everlasting joy in the life to come.

(168.) **HARRY ELLIS,** was born March 11, 1809 and died at Ellisburg, Pa., Jan. 24th, 1885. Early in life with his father, Richard, they settled in what is now Ellisburg, Pa., when that country was a wilderness. He was a farmer and miller and a very industrious and worthy man. He was a Baptist in religious belief. For three or four years previous to his decease he was sick and helpless from age and infirmities. His children were eight in number, (see Nos. 552 to 563), several of whom resided at Ellisburg. His wife,

(169.) **BETSY SEELEY,** was a daughter of Mrs. Seeley, the last wife of Dea. Richard Ellis (29), of Ellisburg, Pa. At the time of Mrs. Ellis' marriage, May 1836, to Harry Ellis, she was the widow of Harry's brother, Reuben Ellis (172), by whom she had one daughter, Alvira Ellis (566), now the wife of Charles Coats, Esq., of Ellisburg. Mrs. Betsy Ellis was a very worthy woman and a Baptist in belief. She died at Ellisburg, Jan. 16th, 1885. Her brother, Lewis Seeley, now lives at Ellisburg.

"Uncle Harry and Aunt Betsy Ellis," as they were called by friends and neighbors, had lived in Ellisburg over fifty years, and most of the time in the house which Harry and his father built when they first settled in that town.

They were people of gentle manners and great kindness of heart, widely known and greatly beloved. They had been married nearly fifty years and died but eight days apart.

(170.) **ELIZABETH ELLIS,** born March 22nd, 1811, married Mr. W. M. Chafee and lived in Mercer Co., Pa., where both died some years ago. They had two children. Mr. John Chafee, of Wellsboro, Pa., is her grandson and Mrs. Seymour D. Ellis (1059), of the same place, a granddaughter.

(172.) **REUBEN ELLIS,** youngest child of Richard, and Chloe Ellis, of Ellisburg, Pa., was born in Delmar, Tioga Co., Pa., Feb. 15th, 1813. May 9th, 1832, he married Betsy Seeley and had one child, Alvira Ellis, (see 566). About this time Reuben went from home and no certain report of him has ever been had. It is believed that he died a year or two thereafter.

All these Ellises, of Tioga and Potter Counties, Pa., like their father Dea. Richard Ellis, were ardent and prominent Baptists. Three of them were ministers of that faith and all were noted for their upright lives and Christian example. The father of them, Richard, was born in Ashfield, Mass., at a time and near a part of the town (Baptist Corner) where the Baptist faith and influence greatly predominated. This religious faith still prevails with nearly all his descendants down to the present time. An account of Dea. Richard Ellis' and his children's effort to establish their church and promote the gospel in Pennsylvania, in the early part of the present century, will be found in the Appendix.

Children of Dea. David Ellis Sr., (32), of Springfield, Erie Co., Pa., and their wives and husbands, Grandchildren of Reuben (4), and Great-grandchildren of Richard of Ashfield. From 174 to 182.

(174.) **MELINDA ELLIS,** eldest child of Dea. David Ellis, and his wife Sarah Washburn (33), was born in Ashfield, March 22nd, 1785. She married Mr. John Wing, about 1810, and settled in Erie Co., Pa., soon after. Mr. Wing died in 1857, and his wife in 1862. They had one son

Mr. Hamilton Wing, who it is said lived in Chillicothe, Ohio.

(176.) WILLIAM ELLIS, second child of Dea. David Ellis, was born in Ashfield, March 28th, 1787. He lived on the farm with his father until June 1818, when with his family and parents he removed to Springfield, Pa. He was a Baptist in religious belief, and of unusual piety and devotion. He was a tall and very fine-looking man, and like his brother David Jr., was fond of music. They both, in early life, were in great demand at "musters," or general trainings, and were noted for their skill in martial music, when one played on the fife, and the other the drum. When he settled in Erie Co., Pa., the country was new, and he purchased a farm which he cleared up and made for himself and family a comfortable home. About 1810 he married Miss Rhoda Flower of Ashfield, and they had ten children five of whom were born in Ashfield, and the others in North Springfield, Pa. He died may 13th, 1873. His wife,

(177.) RHODA FLOWERS, was born in Ashfield, Sept. 27th, 1789. She was a daughter of Capt. Lamrock Flower Jr., and granddaughter of Maj. Lamrock Flower Sr. These Flowers lived directly opposite the residence of Lieut. John Ellis (15), and were among the early settlers in the town. Mr. Joshua Hall now lives on that farm where he has resided over thirty years, Mr. Bildad Flower, son of Maj. Lamrock Flower Sr., was a Revolutionary soldier and died in the service, leaving two infant daughters, Ruth, who married Jesse Ranney, and Amanda (71), who married Edward Ellis (70). Mr. Horace Flower who lived near Belding, Mich., several years previous to his death in 1874, was a brother of Mrs. Rhoda Flower Ellis (177). Horace's daughter Louisa married Volney Belding (249), and now lives at Reeds, Mo. Her brother W. H. Flower is a merchant in Muir, Mich. Mrs. Rhoda F. Ellis, was a Baptist and a true Christian woman, and highly respected by all her acquaintances. She died in Springfield, Pa., Aug. 26th,

1864. Her children were William Jr., Charles P., George, Harriet, Lucretia, Samuel, James F., Mary L., Joseph, and Rumina Ellis. See Nos. 570 to 587. Joseph Ellis now lives on the old farm.

(178.) **SARAH ELLIS,** third child of David. Sr., was born in Ashfield, Mass., July 18th, 1791. She was married in Ashfield, July 5th, 1810, to Capt. James Flower, of Conway, and soon after settled in Wesleyville, Erie County, Pa., where they raised nine children. She died Dec. 3rd, 1853. Her husband,

(179.) **CAPT. JAMES FLOWER,** was born in Conway, Mass., Feb. 21st, 1781. He was a soldier in the war of 1812. He died in Wesleyville, Pa., Feb. 24th, 1832. Their children, all born in Wesleyville, were:

Elbridge G., born Aug. 26th, 1811, died March 17, 1832.

Sally H., born Dec. 13th, 1813, married a Potter, and lived in Wesleyville, Pa.

David Ellis Flower, born March 6th, 1816, lives in Albion, Pa.

James M., born July 11th, 1818, died Aug. 3rd, 1819.

Dr. William S., born May 27th, 1821, is a physician and lives in Cochranton, Pa.

Dr. Clarissa Ann, born May 3rd, 1823, married Dr. Chauncy Fuller, of Fredonia, Chautauqua Co., N.Y., where she now lives and practices medicine. Her husband died in 1872.

Melinda Jane, born Dec. 9th, 1825, married Dr. Davenport, and lives in Wesleyville., Pa.

Lydia W., born April 18th, 1828, lives in Fredonia, N.Y.

Dr. Phineas D., born May 13th, 1830, married and lives in Albion, Pa., where he is a physician.

James G., born April 17th, 1832, married in Fredonia, and lives in Jamestown, Chautauqua Co., N. Y.

(180.) **DAVID ELLIS Jr.,** was born in Ashfield, Dec. 26th, 1793. In 1818 with his wife and three children, and his parents and brother William and his family, they removed to

Erie Co., Pa. The writer's mother, who was raised in Ashfield and is now 81 years of age, well remembers when these
people packed their worldly goods on wagons, and with ox
and horse teams wended their way over the hills of their
native town, to seek a new home in the then wilds of
western Pennsylvania. To part with them was a deep
sorrow to those who remained, but the universal desire of
mankind to better their condition, impelled these old and
respected residents to make the change. Others followed
their example, and in less than thirty years after, there
were no Ellises remaining in that town, in which their
ancestor Richard Ellis, was the first settler in 1745, and in
which, for just a century, no other name was more familiar. David Ellis Jr., died in Springfield, Pa., Feb. 21st,
1866. He was noted as an upright and honorable man.
His wife,

(181.) RUMINA FLOWER, was born in Ashfield, ——
1795, and died in Springfield, Pa., —— 1872. She was
a sister of Rhoda Flower (177), who married William
Ellis. Mrs. Ellis was a member of the Christian Church.
She had nine children, the three eldest born in Ashfield, the
others in Springfield, Erie Co., Pa. See Nos. 598 to 611.

(182.) REBECCA ELLIS, youngest child of David
Ellis Sr., was born in Ashfield, May 10th, 1799. She removed to Springfield, Pa., where she married Mr. Jonathan
Taylor, and settled in Chillicothe, Ohio, where their three
children, Phebe, Sarah and Mary Taylor were born.

**Children of John Ellis Jr. (68), of Niles, Cayuga Co., N. Y.,
and their wives and husbands. Grandchildren
of John Sr., and Great-grandchildren of
Richard Ellis of Ashfield.**

(207.) SYLVIA ELLIS, was born in Niles or Sempronius, Cayuga Co., N.Y., Oct 7th, 1798. In the spring of
1816, she was married in Sempronius to Mr. John Sprague,
and the next year moved to Perrysburg, Cattaraugus Co.,
N. Y. Mrs. Sprague died at Perrysburg, in Sept. 1837,

leaving five children.   Almerin, Delilah, Lodoska, Dorliska
and Ebenezer.

Almerin Sprague was born in 1818.   He was a farmer
and settled in Genesee, Waukesha Co., Wis.   He went to
California in 1853, where he died, leaving a wife and five
children at Genesee, Wis.

Delilah Sprague, born Aug., 1824, married for her second
husband George Harrington.   She is now a widow and has
five children.   She resides at Hayward, Wis.

Lodoska, born Feb. 16th, 1827, married a Mr. Sullivan.
She is now a widow, and lives with her only child a married
daughter in Chicago, Ill.

Dorliska, born March, 1831, married William Medbury,
about two years before her death which occurred in Feb.,
1852.

Ebenezer, born Oct. 25th, 1883, married and has six
children.   He is a traveling man and resides in St. Louis,
Mo.

John Sprague, husband of Sylvia Ellis, was born in
Luzerne, Warren Co., N. Y., June 20th, 1793.   He was a
farmer.   He died April 18th, 1875, at Cedar Falls, Dunn
Co., Wis.   His father Ebenezer Sprague, was born in 1769,
and died in 1877.   His mother Hannah Martin, was born in
1768, and died in 1875.   They were formerly Baptists, but
in their old age they became Universalists.   John and Sylvia
Ellis Sprague were formerly Baptists, but afterwards became Universalists.   Mr. Almerin Sprague, brother of John
Sprague, now lives at Brodhead, Wis., 86 years of age.

(209.) **AZEL ELLIS**, was born in Niles, N. Y., Nov.
25th, 1799.   At about 25 years of age he married Phebe
McGee, and she died about one year later.   October 30th,
1828, he married Mary Hagerman, who was born in New
Jersey, Oct. 23rd, 1795.   They had three children, Edward,
Phebe and Lydia.   About 1841, Mr. Azel Ellis and family
settled on a farm in Marseilles, Wyandot Co., Ohio, where
he died March 21st, 1863, and his wife Oct. 5th, 1859.   He

was a carpenter and builder, and an upright and honorable man. For a sketch of his children see Nos. 621 to 623.

(212.) **TAMER ELLIS,** daughter of John Ellis, of Niles, N. Y., was born Aug. 18th, 1802, in Niles. May 8th, 1827, she married Matthew Vanderbilt, of Sempronius, N. Y., and they had three children, Abilena, Andrew and Hannah. About 1840, Mr. Vanderbilt and family settled in Marseilles, Ohio, on a farm where Mrs. Vanderbilt died in 1855, and Mr. Vanderbilt in 1877. Of their children,

Abilena, born Dec. 18th, 1828, married Stewart S. Adams. They lived in Marseilles, Wyandot Co., Ohio.

Andrew, was born Nov. 22nd, 1832. Lives in Marseilles.

Hannah, was born July 29th, 1838. She married Mr. R. L. Willard, and they live in Marseilles.

(214.) **HIRAM ELLIS,** son of John and Abilena Phillips Ellis, was born in Niles, N. Y., Jan. 7th, 1804. He married Martha Flower in 1832, and they raised two children. Hannah and Elisha, both born in Niles, (see 627 and 629). Mr. Ellis was a thorough bible student, and of remarkable memory. He was radical in his opposition to the use of tobacco, (which he had used up to 45 years of age,) alcoholic liquors, and even tea and coffee. He was a man of great benevolence and generosity, and contributed largely to aid the afflicted and suffering. He was a farmer, and the last few years of his life lived in Caton, Steuben Co., N.Y., where he died in 1874. His wife died in 1864. Mrs. Ellis was a sister of Mrs. Wade, the mother of Rev. E. R. Wade, of McLean, N. Y. Elder Wade says of Mr. Hiram Ellis that " he was a God-fearing man, and as honest as sunlight."

(216.) **ELISHA ELLIS,** son of John Ellis, was born in Niles, Cayuga Co., N. Y., April 7th, 1805. When a youth of thirteen years he went with his uncle, Elisha Phillips, when the latter with his family removed to Mt. Vernon, Posey Co., Indiana, on the Ohio river, in the extreme south-western part of the State. They went down the Alleghany and Ohio rivers, on rafts and flat-boats with their household goods, and settled in what was then a very wild country. When Elisha reached manhood (1828), he married Miss Hannah Bradley, and purchased a new farm at Farmersville, Posey Co., two miles north of Mt. Vernon, where he raised his family, and where himself and wife now reside, at an advanced age of over 81 years. When he first saw Mt. Vernon, now the county seat of Posey Co., in 1818 it had but two log huts. Now it has a population of 6000. In his youth Mr. Ellis was a cooper and carpenter. When 21 years of age he visited his old home and parents in Niles, for the last time. In 1849, when the "gold-fever" broke out in California, he went there by way of the Mississippi river, Isthmus of Panama, which latter he crossed on foot, and sail vessel to San Francisco. The vessel was becalmed and they were 90 days out of sight of land, and were reduced to exceedingly low rations of water and food. He remained in California about one year. In 1827 he was appointed a captain in the State militia, and held the commission for five years, and is always addressed by acquaintances as the "Old Captain." He is widely known, and esteemed as an upright, honorable and Christian man of the Universalist faith.

(218.) **RICHARD ELLIS,** son of John, of Niles, N. Y., was born in that town June 16th, 1806. November 6th, 1827, he married Mary P. Selover of Niles, where they lived until about 1836, when with his family he settled on a farm in Jackson, Hardin Co., Ohio, where their three youngest children were born. In 1849 Mr. Ellis went to California, and on his way home he stopped at his brother Ebenezer's, who then lived at Farmersville, Ind., where he was taken sick and died. This was in 1853.

(219.) **MARY P. SELOVER,** wife of Richard Ellis, was born in Niles N. Y. She was the youngest daughter of Isaac Selover of Niles. After the death of her husband, she removed with her family to Marseilles, Ohio, where she died April 5th, 1884, aged 75 years.

(220.) **HON. PITTS ELLIS,** son of John, was born in the town of Murray, Genesee Co., N. Y., (where his parents lived for a time,) Feb. 29th, 1808. He received a good education for those times, and in early life was a mechanic. In after life he was a farmer, and dealer in cattle and produce. He was married in Perrysburg, N. Y., Feb. 23rd, 1832, to Miss Lucia M. Balcom, and they had five children, four of whom grew to maturity, and are now living. See Nos. 651 to 657. In 1841 he was one of the pioneers in the settlement of Wisconsin. He located at North Prairie, and afterwards at Genesee, Waukesha Co. He was the first justice of that town, also supervisor and register of deeds of the county, He was elected to the territorial legislature in 1845, and in 1846 to the constitutional convention, on which the territory was admitted as a state to the Union. He was again a member of the Legislature in 1850. He was a strong advocate of temperance, and the same may be said of all his brothers and sisters. He was an upright, honorable and Christian man. He died in Genesee, Wis., Feb. 1st, 1876. His wife,

(221.) **LUCIA M. BALCOM,** wife of Mr. Pitts Ellis, was born Feb. 22nd, 1814, in Gorham, Ontario Co., N.Y. She joined the Baptist church at 14 years of age, and has always been a member of a church since. Since the death of her husband she has lived in Milwaukee, with her daughter Anna, who married Lewis Barling. Mrs. Ellis' parents were Dr. Isaac Balcom and Anna Burr, his wife, who settled in Perrysburg, N. Y., in 1821. Mrs. Ellis and her husband, in later life were inclined toward the Universalist church in their religious belief.

(222.) **JOHN J. ELLIS,** son of John, of Niles, N. Y., was born in Murray, N. Y., March 14th, 1810. He married Catharine Selover, about 1838, and they have raised five children. See Nos. 659 to 667.

Mr. Elllis and his wife, reside in the town of Sennett, Cayuga Co., N, Y., about three miles from Auburn, where he has a home and a shop, in which he carries on the business of manufacturing wagons and carriages. He is quite a mechanical genius, and has invented several very useful implements. He is widely known and esteemed as an upright, honorable and Christian man, although not a church member. Mrs. Catharine Ellis, was born in Sempronius, July 1st, 1813.

(225.) **BENJAMIN ELLIS,** son of John, of Niles. N. Y., was born in Niles, June 11th, 1813.* He married Jemima Vanderbilt, at Niles, Dec, 1st, 1839, where their four eldest children were born. In 1850 he settled in Wyandot Co. Ohio, on a farm. He died March 18th, 1881, and his wife June 20th, 1883. They had eight children. See Nos. 669 to 683.

In 1856 Mr. Ellis left his farm, and engaged in the grocery business in Marseilles, until the war of the rebellion, when he sold out and enlisted in Co. D., 81st Ohio Infantry Volunteers. He served thirteen months when he was discharged for disability. He was in the battles of Pittsburg Landing, Shiloh and the siege of Corinth. After his discharge he was made First Lieut. of Co. G., 144 Reg. of Ohio National Guards. After the close of the war he engaged as carpenter and builder. He was a man of unusual intelligence, strictly sober and temperate, a great bible scholar, a member of the Methodist church, and an upright and highly respected man.

(227.) **EBENEZER ELLIS,** was born in Niles, June 18th, 1815. At 22 years of age he left New York, and settled in Farmersville, Ind., where he married Miss Theodocia Phillips, April 11th, 1839. They raised six children, all born in Farmersville. See Nos. 685 to 695. In 1859 he removed to Genesee, Wis. His wife and himself with their son Pitts, now reside in Arkansas City, Kansas.

(229.) **RUTH ELLIS,** youngest daughter of John Ellis, was born in Niles, N. Y., March 24th, 1818. She married

*This date is from the family bible of his parents in Niles. His children in Ohio, have records giving the date of his birth as 1810.

Mr. George Hall, and for several years they resided in Richland, Kalamazoo Co., Mich. Mr. Hall died there in 1872. Mrs. Hall still lives there with her children. The names of the latter were: Maria, Horace and Abilena.

(231.) ANTHONY W. ELLIS, youngest son of John, and Abilena Phillips Ellis, was born in Niles, N. Y., Jan. 6th, 1820, where he now resides on a farm. He has been a farmer all his life. October 12th, 1843, he married Miss Hannah Van Etten, in Niles, and they have raised three children. See Nos. 708 to 713.

In the old age of his parents Mr. Ellis lived with them, and from the old family bible, and other sources he has sent the writer family records, and much other information of value in compiling this book. Mr. Anthony W. Ellis was the youngest of his parents' large family (16 children) and they are all noted for being men and women of the strictest sobriety, morality, and sound religious principles, although not all of the so-called orthodox faith. He was named in honor of Gen. Anthony Wayne, under whom his father was a soldier, and for whom he had great admiration.

Children of Edward Ellis (70), of Niles, Cayuga Co., N. Y., and their wives. Grandchildren of Lieut. John (15), and Richard Ellis of Ashfield.

(232.) HANNAH VAN ETTEN, wife of Anthony W. Ellis, was born in Owasco, Cayuga Co., N. Y., Sept. 13th, 1826. Her parents were Anthony Van Etten and his wife Jane Cuykendall, who moved from Orange Co., N. Y., to Cayuga Co., about 1820.

(233.) CYRUS ELLIS, eldest son of Edward, was born at Niles, about three miles north of Moravia, Feb. 2d, 1799. When two years of age his father died and his mother (71) returned with him to Ashfield, where Cyrus remained most of the time with his grandfather, John (15), and his uncle Dimick Ellis until he became of age. He then went out to Sempronius or Niles, N. Y., where his mother, after her second marriage, to Rev. Mr. Forbush, was living on the homestead which Cyrus' father settled upon in 1798. Cyrus soon after purchased this farm of his mother and here he made his home for the remainder of his long and active life. March 31st, 1825, he married Miss Clarissa Birch, who was his faithful companion up to the time of her death in the autumn of 1885, a period of over sixty years. They raised a family of nine children, six sons and three daughters. See Nos. 715 to 731.

Mr. Cyrus Ellis was a man of very radical views. He was one of the earliest Abolitionists of this country and never omitted an opportunity to aid the fugitive slave who was trying to escape from the bondage of the southern master. When the great war of the slaveholders' Rebellion broke out in 1861 four of Mr. Ellis' sons enlisted in the Union army to aid in the preservation of the government.* Of these loyal and courageous young men who shouldered arms with the sanction and blessings of fond parents three gave up their lives a sacrifice on the altar of their country, a great bereavement to their loving parents but the latter, thus deeply stricken, did not diminish in the ardor of their patriotism. It was just such heroism as this of hundreds of thousands of noble sires and sons (and mothers and daughters too) which carried this government through the awful peril of the Great Rebellion and saved it from perishing off the earth. Their achievements demand the gratitude of posterity to the latest generations.

Mr. Ellis was all his life a most ardent advocate of temperance and opposed the liquor traffic in every form. He was a man of good mind and judgment and his advice and counsel was often sought by his neighbors to such

---

*Mr. Ellis himself, although over 60 years of age, such was his patriotism and desire to free the slave, sought to enlist as a soldier, and was quite indignant when it was intimated that his eye-sight or physical powers might be defective.

NOTE.—On the preceding page (160), through the printer's error a mistake was made in misplacing the No. (932) and name of Hannah Van Etten. She is the wife of Anthony W. Ellis, and was not one of the "Children of Edward Ellis, etc.," and her name should be above those three lines.

an extent that he was widely known and respected as the "sage" of his town. He was a small man of great nervous energy and activity and never allowed time to waste on his hands. The writer remembers his visiting western Michigan in the summer of 1848. He walked much of the way for the last 100 miles, not being railroads there at that time, visited four families of relatives near Belding, and was on his way home the same day of his arrival. He never "set around" but "made hay" whether the sun shone or not—traits which he probably derived mostly from his mother, (though it is stated as a fact that his father died at the early age of 28 years from overwork.) Unusual economy was one of Cyrus' leading traits. It is told that when a boy in Ashfield and working among the thorns and briars on the old farm of his grandfather he would often remove his shoes and roll up his pants to preserve them from wear and tear, not minding the injury inflicted on himself. He died Nov. 19th, 1885, in his 86th year, with all his faculties bright until near his end. His memory of the relatives and early events connected with this work has aided the writer greatly in his task. His knowledge of the olden times was both minute and extensive. His wife,

(234.) CLARISSA BIRCH, was born Jan. 30th, 1800, at Argyle, Washington County, N. Y. She died at the homestead Aug. 17th, 1885. The funeral discourses at the burial of both Mrs. Ellis and her husband were preached by Elder E. R. Wade of McLean, N. Y. Elder Wade for his first wife, married Miss Elizabeth Forbush, half sister of Cyrus Ellis, (see page 112.) He was intimately acquainted with Mr. and Mrs. Ellis nearly all his life and writes that he had for them the highest regard and esteem, and that this was the uniform opinion of all who knew them. Honesty, integrity and virtue were the guiding principles which ever actuated them. They have gone to the reward of the just, and their memory should be cherished forever.

The following is an extract from a letter of Elder Wade's written soon after the funeral of Mrs. Ellis :

"The Book says, 'the righteous shall be in everlasting remembrance.' If this be true, a word in remembrance of the noble mother who was consigned to the grave north of Moravia, last Wednesday, Aug. 19th, will not be out of place.

"In the year 1825, Cyrus Ellis and Clarissa Birch were married, and in a log house north of the hamlet afterwards called Pennyville began the work of creating a good farm and a nice home, from the domain of nature around them. How well they succeeded in their effort, the large farm and the princely residence will tell. For sixty years they have resided on the farm where they commenced married life.

"With them, 'Life was real, life was earnest,' and from early morn till dewy eve, work went on and the farm and the home are a monument of their joint labors, and of the children that came to them as the years rolled on. Not a dollar gained by speculation, but all by hard and honest toil.

"As the years were passing nine children came to them in the old log house, or in the new one, that burned near where the present residence now stands.

"Six sons and three daughters found a home with them as time rolled on. With all the care of farm, home, and children, she had time to aid and care for the sick, and to help the poor and needy.

"Her ear was quick to hear the cry of the sick or dying and all homes opened at her approach, as did the ward gate of the prison, at the tread of the God-fearing apostles.

"Her hand was light ; her presence sweet ; and her care was pleasant in the sick room. She always had time to do good in the home and abroad. Four of her sons enlisted and rallied at the call of country, and in defense of human freedom. Three of them did not return alive. With the grandeur of a Roman mother, she did not complain. She had laid them on the altar of her country. She could not visit the last resting places of her dead, where they were resting among the "Unknown Dead."

> And where the unknown in their silence are sleeping,
>   The feet of the angels are pressing the sod;
> And vespers of harmony 'round them are keeping,
>   While Martyrs of Freedom, have gone to their God.

"Mother Ellis, was a religious woman in the largest and broadest sense of the word. Her religion was not bigotry. She was at home among all Christians, and had in her heart the truth that all who loved God and humanity were children of one God, and members of one household, and were of one brotherhood. This she saw long before the great world of religionists saw or felt it. She was in her religious life the embodiment of the great truth voiced by Abraham Lincoln: 'With charity for all, and malice toward none,' and her life, and creed, were harmonious and not in conflict.

"She was as kind and sweet as the breezes that fan the fields, when reapers sing among the garnered grain. In the closing hour of life, when her sandals were already in the stream, once again she sang one of the old songs of triumph, that had lived in her heart, and her kind and loving spirit passed on to the great land, and home of the hereafter. Loved but not lost; gone on to the higher and better life.

"The funeral was held at her late residence and was attended by a crowd of old friends and neighbors.

"Cyrus Ellis, now 86 years of age and quite feeble, was able to sit up during all the exercises. All the remaining children, five in number, were present, and all reside within a distance of twelve miles.

"One by one the old residents on the hill where I was born are called home, and now but one remains in that vicinity.

"The Fathers, where are they? and the Prophets, do they live forever?   EDWIN R. WADE."

(235.) HON. EDWARD D. ELLIS, youngest son of Edward Ellis, of Niles, N. Y., was born in Niles, Oct. 7th, 1801, about two months after the death of his father. His early years were passed on the farm on which his parents settled when they removed from Ashfield in 1798. When a young man he was put to service with a tanner with a view of his learning that trade. This occupation soon proved distasteful to him and feeling a strong desire to become a printer, he sought and obtained a position in a printing office in Auburn, N. Y. He took to the business readily and in due time became proficient in it. When about twenty years of age he visited his grandparents and other relatives in Ashfield and from there went to Springfield and Boston, Mass., where he worked for a time as a journeyman printer. He returned by way of New York city, Poughkeepsie and Cooperstown to his home in Niles. During this trip and for several years before and after he kept a journal in which is recorded his doings for nearly every day with comments on all the principal events of those times. In this way he became a close observer and a ready writer on political and other topics. He anticipated, by several years, that famous saying of Horace Greeley, "Go West, young man" and purchased an outfit for a printing office and started for Michigan. He landed at Monroe, where he opened an office and began publishing the "Michigan Sentinel," in 1825. This was the first newspaper printed in the territory of Michigan, outside of Detroit. It commanded a large patronage for that time and brought Mr. Ellis into prominence as a political writer. The leading party about that time, or soon after, was the Democracy, often referred to in the present time as the "Jacksonian democracy," of which Gen. Andrew Jackson, (afterwards President,) was the leader. Mr. Ellis was an intelligent and enthusiastic supporter of his party and its successive leaders until the year 1847, when he broke loose from it on account of its secession proclivities and its support of slavery.

Mr. Ellis was several times elected a member of the territorial and state legislatures and also of the convenion which formed the constitution on which Michigan was admitted into the union of states. In the latter he proposed an original statute which was adopted and ever since retained in the organic law of the state (and since by several other states,) that money paid as fines for crimes and misdemeanors should be devoted to purchasing and sustaining public libraries in every town and city. Mr. Ellis was a ready debater and withal a man of large influence in the early history of the state of his adoption. About 1842, he sold his interests in Monroe and removed to Detroit, where he continued the printing business and publishing of the "American Vineyard," a paper which he started in the latter town. In the political campaign of 1847 and 1848, he took strong grounds in favor of Gen. Zachary Taylor, the hero of the Mexican war, for president, and it is said that he was the first publisher of a newspaper to propose Gen. Taylor's candidacy for that high office. His efforts in his cause attracted the attention of Gen. Taylor, and the latter wrote him in acknowledgment and appreciation of the same. Just before the meeting of the nominating convention which placed Gen. Taylor before the people as a candidate, Mr. Ellis was taken suddenly sick and died. A day or two before this sad event he overexerted himself at a fire and it was thought that some internal injury had been received which accounted for his sudden and unexpected demise, which was a great shock to his family and numerous friends.

Mr. Ellis had many friends among the older residents of Monroe and Detroit, who hold his memory in high regard to the present time. His paper, the "Sentinel," was changed in name to the "Commercial" and for the past 35 years has been published in Monroe by Mr. M. D. Hamilton and Son, and is one of the most enterprising journals in the state. A few years ago Mr. H. printed a series of articles found among the unpublished papers of Mr. Ellis, which attracted considerable attention from the people of Monroe and other parts of the state.

Among papers and letters sent the writer is found one from Hon. Wm. Woodbridge, one of the early Governors of Michigan, dated Jan. 31, 1849, and which contains the following: "I was long and intimately acquainted with the late Mr. Edward D. Ellis and no man regretted more sincerely I think than I did his sudden and unexpected death. To a mind stored with much and varied knowledge and of great native strength and energy he united a most amiable and generous heart. Strong in his friendships he was still more inflexibly firm in his principles. So far as my long acquaintance with him enabled me to judge I know of no man more confiding, I know of no man more *purely honest* than was he."

In all respects he was a man of strict sobriety, integrity and uprightness in all his conduct and his memory is held in high esteem by all who had the honor of his acquaintance. He was a small sized man, nervous temperament, with dark eyes and hair. He died in Detroit, May 15, 1848. For sketch of his children see Nos. 733 to 740. Feb. 2d, 1830, he married

(236.) **LEONORA MARY CHAPMAN**, in Monroe, Mich. She was born in Buffalo, N. Y., March 25, 1805, and was a daughter of Mr. Asa Chapman, an early resident of Buffalo. Mr. Chapman was a millwright and built a number of grist and saw mills in New York, and Ohio. When a young woman Miss Chapman and a younger sister went to Kentucky, where they became teachers in families. Public schools were then unknown in that section and nearly every family employed teachers. Miss Leonora was thus engaged for several years in the family of Gen. Gaines, a prominent citizen of Kentucky. Most of the people in that section were Roman Catholics in religious belief and these two young women embraced that faith, to which they ever afterwards adhered. The younger one, Permelia, took ecclesiastical "vows," and was made a Sister of Charity and Superior of St. Vincent's Academy, a school for young ladies at Morgansfield, Ky., at the head of which she remained during her life. She died about 1850. Another sister, Eliza, a strong Presbyterian, married Mr. Drake. She was soon left a widow and settled with her two children, a son and daughter, in Farmington, Mich., where she lived highly respected and died about 1860. Her son, Francis M. Drake, died at the same place about 1880, leaving a widow and eight children, three of whom have recently graduated at the University of Michigan, at Ann Arbor. Mrs. F. M. Drake and one daughter, Mrs. Imogene Brown, now live in Brighton, Mich., and Mrs. Dr. Avery, another daughter, in Pontiac.

Mrs. Leonora M. Ellis was a woman of superior education and culture. After the death of her husband in 1848, she resided with her children in Chicago and Detroit, the last few years with her eldest daughter, Minerva, in Detroit, where she died Aug. 26, 1870.

Children of Dea. Dimick Ellis (72), and their husband and wives. Grandchildren of Lieut. John (15), and great-grandchildren of Richard Ellis, all of Ashfield.

(237.) DESIAH ELLIS, eldest child and only daughter of Dea. Dimick Ellis was born in Ashfield, Mass., Aug. 19th, 1803. She lived with her parents at the old homestead until her marriage, April 10th, 1828, to Mr. Tiberius Belding, of Ashfield, where they made their home about 80 rods south from the corner where Richard Ellis made the first settlement in that town. Here six of their children were born. In the autumn of 1840 they removed to Michigan and settled in Otisco, the north-west corner town of Ionia Co. Their home was one and one-half miles west of what is now the flourishing village of Belding.

They were among the first settlers of that township, probably not over a dozen families preceding them. This whole region was then a wilderness and quite difficult ot access, no railroads being nearer than Detroit, which was 140 miles distant. But this was a beautiful country and settled almost wholly by intelligent and enterprising emigrants from Massachusetts and Central New York. The name of the town was given by settlers from Otisco, Onondago county, N. Y. They were a very hospitable people and any settler was known to and considered "a neighbor" of all the others who were not more than ten or twelve miles distant. The land was mostly open "plains" and was quite easily brought under cultivation. The willing soil yielded an abundance of the necessaries of subsistence and a more cheerful, contented and virtuous people than these settlers could nowhere be found. "Aunt Desiah," in a surpassing degree had the love and esteem of every one. Her house was always open and a kindly greeting was extended to all. Forty rods north was the district school-house which served also as the meeting-house for many years. Although neither herself or husband were church members, the "circuit" ministers of all denominations went straight to her home and always were welcomed by herself and husband. She never wearied in doing good to everybody and her memory should endure forever. She died at the homestead Dec. 25th, 1880. Her husband,

(238.) **TIBERIUS BELDING,** was born in Ashfield, Sept. 15th, 1800. He was a son of Mr. John Belding, who lived all his life on the farm where Richard Ellis settled in 1745. Tiberius was next oldest brother of Mr. Hiram Belding, who settled at Belding, Mich., (Otisco township), about 1854.

Mr. Tiberius Belding was a man of uncommon good sense, generous, upright, industrious and respected. It required all these traits with a noble ambition which he possessed to impel one, with a large family, to brave and overcome the privations of a new country such as was this in the Forties. He died in Otisco, Nov. 19th, 1870. Mr. and Mrs. Belding raised eight children to maturity. These were Annabel P., born 1829; Francis W., 1830; Edward E., 1832; Priscilla A., 1834; Tiberius, jr., 1838; Waite, 1840; Ellen M., 1845, and John D., 1849.

Annabel Polly Belding was born in Ashfield, June 8th, 1829. She married Charles F. Morse at Otisco, Feb. 4th, 1849. They had seven children, four of whom are now living; the others died in infancy. About 1870, Mr. and Mrs. Morse moved from Otisco to Milo, Lincoln Co., Kansas, where they settled on a farm. Mr. Morse died at Milo, July 12th, 1884. He was born in Homer, Courtland Co., N. Y., Nov. 9th, 1820. He and his brother, Hon. John L. Morse, were of the first settlers in Otisco about 1837. Mrs. Annable P. Morse resides in Milo, with her children. Her son, Charles Lee Morse, born 1851, married Phoebe Early of Simpson, Kansas, in 1885. Lewis Ellis Morse, born 1858, lives in Milo, Kansas, and has two children. Fred Morse born 1861, also lives in Kansas. Nellie Desiah Morse born 1864, is a school teacher near her mother's home in Kansas.

Francis W. Belding, born Oct. 28th, 1830, married Miss Julia Day, daughter of Daniel Day, Esq., of Otisco. He settled on a farm two miles west of Otisco Center, where his widow and children now live. He died March 6th, 1879, after a long and painful illness. He was a man of uncommon intelligence and industry and was held in high esteem by all who ever knew him. His children are Edward E., Ralph, Blanche, Grace and Pearl. They have an excellent farm and beautiful home.

Edward Ellis Belding was born in Ashfield, Dec. 2d, 1832. At the beginning of the Rebellion he enlisted in Company B, 16th Michigan Volunteers, and was in the seven days battle before Richmond in 1862. He died at Harrison's Landing, Va., July 15th, 1862, from sickness brought on by exposure and fatigue incident to the campaign after twelve months of active service. One of his comrades, now the Hon. A. B. Morse,* Chief Justice of the State of Michigan, wrote the following lines:

Lines on the Death of Edward E. Belding, Company B, 16th Michigan Volunteers.

Died at Harrison's Landing, Va., July 13th, 1862.

Another form has passed away
    Another heart is cold ;
Beneath the earth we laid to-day,
    A soldier true and bold.
And sadly have we, comrades all,
    Around his lonely grave,
With tears our silent tribute paid
    A noble soul and brave.

Among the first he left his home
    And friends at Duty's call,
His Country's honor to maintain,
    With her to stand or fall.
And twelve long months, through hardships dire,
    A soldier's armor wore—
The toilsome march, the wet bivouac
    He proudly, calmly bore.

Fatigue and cold, the burning heat
    His soul could never tire ;
No danger great, no duty chilled,
    That heart of patriot fire ;
And ever in the battle front
    On Gaines's bloody field,
His manly form the foremost was
    Among the last to yield.

*Allen Benton Morse was born in 1837 and was the first white male child born in Otisco He was the eldest son of Hon. John L. Morse, whose farm and house joined Mr. Tiberius Belding's on the south. He enlisted in the same company with Edward E. Belding, with whom he had been acquainted from his childhood. Young Morse was promoted to a lieutenantcy and adjutant and served through the war. After the close of the Rebellion he practiced law in Ionia, Mich., until the spring of 1885, when he was elected Chief Justice of Michigan over Chief Justice Cooley, one of the most noted public men in this State, by the astonishing majority of over 32,000 votes. Judge Morse has literary and judicial ability of a high order.

The fearful days and sleepless nights,
  That marked our "change of base,
The hurried march, the desperate fight
  Found Belding in his place.
And when fatigue brought on disease,
  And quick and fevered breath ;
He suffered pain without complaint
  And calmly waited Death.

Here, Edward, may thou sleep in peace,
  This noble oak beneath,
Where loving comrades made thy bed,
  And wove the laurel wreath.
May holly wave and wild rose bloom
  Above thy resting place,
As long as yonder noble stream
  Its silvered course shall trace.

And may no coward traitor's hand
  Disturb thy quiet grave ;
Oh, God of right and truth protect
  The bones of lifeless brave ;
In life thy soul they could not daunt,
  In death it soars above,
And dwells with heroes of the past,
  In realms of endless love.

At home, the ones that loved him well,
  Kind friends and parents dear,
Will sadly miss his cheerful face,
  And weep the bitter tear,
And mem'ry will thy worth engrave.
  In every comrade's mind,
Of one who dared to do and die,
  A faithful friend and kind.

                                   A. B. MORSE.

James River, Va., July 18th, 1862.

Priscilla A. Belding, second daughter of Tiberius and
Desiah Ellis Belding, was born at Ashfield, Sept. 28th,
1834. She married Aug. 9th, 1857, Mr. John D. Snyder
of Otisco, who lived for several years fifty rods north of
Mr. Tiberius Belding.   Soon after their marriage Mr.
Snyder and wife settled on a farm three miles north of
Ionia, where they raised their family of five children.
On March 27th, 1884, Mrs. Snyder and her two daughters

visited Ionia and in returning home in the evening the horse became frightened and ran away, throwing out the occupants. Mrs. Snyder, was instantly killed but her daughters escaped serious injury.

Tiberius Belding, Jr., was born at Ashfield, Sept. 2d, 1838. He married Miss Eliza King of Orleans, Mich., in 1862, and have one daughter, Bertha Desiah. Mr. Belding was a farmer three miles east of Greenville, Mich., for several years. About 1880, he removed to Groton, Brown county, Dakota, where he is extensively engaged in farming and hotel keeping.

Waite Belding was born in Ashfield, April 25th, 1840, and was six months old when his parents settled in Otisco. He has been an invalid most of his life and resides with his sisters, Ellen and Mrs. Snyder, previous to the death of the latter.

Ellen M. Belding was born in Otisco, July 7th, 1845. She married Mr. James Granger and they have three children, Frank, Carl and Glenn. They live on the homestead of Mrs. Granger's parents.

John Dimick Belding was born in Otisco, Nov. 18th, 1849. He married Miss Amelia Deitz, whose parents lived at Otisco corners, three-fourths of a mile south of the Belding home. They have one daughter, Grace, and live in or near Groton, Dakota.

All these children and grandchildren of Desiah Ellis and Tiberius Belding, Sr., were and are sober, upright, industrious and highly respected and hold in high regard the memory of their devoted parents.

(239.) **DEA. RICHARD ELLIS,** eldest son of Dimick and Polly Annable Ellis, was born in Ashfield, March 20th, 1805. He lived at home until his majority when he took a trip through Vermont and northern and central New York. He settled at Pittstown, Rensselaer Co., N. Y., about 1826, where he engaged in the coopering business. On "Thanksgiving Day," in November, 1827, he was married to Miss Hannah Ranney of Ashfield. They at once took up their home at Pittstown, two miles east of the town "corners," at what is now Boyntonville P. O., named in honor of Mr. Wm. Boynton, now a leading citizen there who was born about 1830. Dea. Ellis lived here until his removal to Michigan in 1844. He was largely engaged in coopering, employing many hands for several years manufacturing barrels for market at Troy, 15 miles distant. About 1840 he took a leading part in organizing the Christian church there and erecting a meeting-house. May 1st, 1844, he started with his family, wife and two children, for Otisco, Mich, where his sister, Desiah (237) had settled in 1840 and his brother Lewis (241) in 1842. They went up the Erie canal to Buffalo, by steamboat to Detroit and thence with ox teams to Otisco, 140 miles northwesterly from Detroit. They reached their new home after a journey of 21 days. The same trip can now be made in 24 hours. Dea. Ellis purchased about 200 acres of new land and began its improvement. His farm is on the north side of Flat River, a part of which is now in the thriving village of Belding.

In 1844 this was a wild country, with deer, bears and Indians numerous. Dea. Ellis was a man of delicate health all his life but with industry, perseverance and good management he made for himself and family a good home. Soon after locating in Otisco, he began the organization of a Christian church in connection with Rev. Wilson Mosher who, about that time, together with eight or ten families from Pittstown, had located there. This church was the principal one in that part of the town for many years and about 1870 a commodious church building was erected at Belding. Dea. Ellis took great interest in his church and was a most exemplary member thereof. For eighteen years he was a justice of the peace, in which official position he settled many difficulties with contentious parties, with seldom a lawsuit, and it is said that he never had a lawsuit of his own. He was a man of uncommon public spirit, always aiding every enterprise which tended to benefit his town and its people.

Dea. Ellis was reared in Ashfield, in the midst of strong Baptist influences and was from early years of decided religious inclinations, but his independence of thought led him to reject much of the Calvinistic doctrines of his early teachings. About 1835, he embraced the doctrines of the Christian denomination, to which he devotedly adhered the remainder of his life, and it is but truth to say that his was the leading spirit in that church both in Pittstown and Belding, in which his time, labor, counsel and money were ever freely given. In every relation of life his example was a model for others. No unjust act was ever attributed to him. He lived without an enemy and died regretted by all who knew him. He died March 26th, 1878. His wife,

(240.) HANNAH RANNEY, was born in Ashfield, Dec. 15th, 1805. She was the eldest daughter of Jesse and Ruth Flower Ranney, old residents of that town. When Hannah was 13 years of age, her father purchased the farm and home of David Ellis, Sr., (32) which is about one-half mile east of the corner, where old Richard (David's grandfather) made the first settlement in the town. In the beginning of the present century the Ranneys were numerous in Ashfield, they having come there from Connecticut about the close of the Revolutionary war. Mr. George Ranney (Hannah's grandfather) had a large family of children in Ashfield, and one of his grandsons, Henry S. Ranney, Esq., a cousin of Hannah, is now and has been for over 40 years, the town clerk. The latter has aided the writer greatly in procuring statistics and gathering items of interest, regarding the early history of the town, for this book. In the Appendix will be found much of this nature, with a sketch of the Ranneys from the time of their early settlement in America.

Mrs. Hannah Ranney Ellis now resides on the homestead with her eldest son Dimick, (749) where herself, husband and two sons located in 1844. She has in a high degree the vigorous constitution of her New England progenitors and withal an excellent memory which has greatly aided the writer, her youngest son, in compiling this book. She has for over 50 years been a consistent member of the Christian church.

(241.) **LEWIS ELLIS,** third child of Dea. Dimick Ellis, was born in Ashfield, Sept. 27th, 1811. He was brought up on the farm with his father and grandfather, John (15), on which he lived until his removal to Michigan, in 1842. He was a farmer and lived on the old homestead with his parents. October 22d, 1834, he was married to Miss Louisa Wilson of Ashfield. They have had eight children, all of whom, except the two youngest, Geo. W. (755) and Mary L. (757), died in infancy or early youth. The sterilty of the soil and frigidity of the climate of western Massachusetts, finally induced Mr. Ellis to seek a new location. About that time many New England people were emigrating to Michigan, and several from Ashfield had settled in Otisco, and in the opening of 1842 Mr. Ellis with his family, then consisting of his wife and two children, started for the latter place, where he purchased a large farm on the north side of Flat River, opposite the present village of Belding, and adjoining his brother Richard on the east. Here he made for himself and family an elegant home and is now in his old age surrounded with every comfort. When he located there the country was new and there were not more than a dozen families in the town. The nearest market was Grand Rapids, 30 miles distant. For ten or twelve years wheat and surplus grain was drawn by teams to that place for sale. Prices were low for their productions, and high for all they purchased, and money was scarce. But it may be said that the best of lumber was abundant and cheap. Six miles to the north were the great pine districts, which gave to this part of the State great advantages over central and even southern Michigan. For many years the best of pine lumber could be had for four dollars per thousand feet, payable in hay and coarse grains, so that about all the ready money which was required for building purposes was what was paid for nails and glass. Long after the latter sections had to depend upon rude logs for houses and barns the former was well supplied with comfortable and often elegant houses and other buildings, and Otisco has long stood in the front rank of Michigan towns for wealth, intelligence and general prosperity, and Belding is a thriving place and an important station on the Detroit, Lansing & Northern Railroad in the northeastern part of the town of Otisco.

Mr. Ellis although not a church member, is a Universalist so far as regards a belief in the elevation of man in this world and his final salvation in the next. He is a man of large influence and has always taken an active interest in the politics and general welfare of his town and county, but has never sought official position himself.

(242.) **LOUISA WILSON**, wife of Lewis Ellis of Otisco, (Belding P. O.) was born in Shelburn, Mass., Nov. 3rd, 1812. When about 17 years of age her widowed mother (see page 116) married Dea. Dimick Ellis and she removed to Ashfield. After Louisa's marriage to Mr. Lewis Ellis their parents lived with them in Ashfield and followed them to Belding in 1846, where they passed the remainder of their earthly days with them in the quiet contentment of a serene and happy old age. Mrs. Louisa W. Ellis is a Baptist in religious belief, and is a most devoted wife and mother, and grandmother too.

(243.) **DR. JOHN ELLIS,** youngest child of Dimick and Polly Annable Ellis, was born in Ashfield, Nov. 26th, 1815. During his youth he worked on the farm and attended the district school and later the academy at Shelburne Falls, and the Sanderson Academy on the "Plain," as Ashfield Center was called, about one and one-half miles from the Ellis home. He was always of a very studious turn of mind and early determined to study medicine and become a physician. He had a decided mechanical gift and learned dentistry, which he practiced during his studentship to obtain means to enable him to attend college. With this view he took a trip through some of the Southern States, returning from Central Alabama on horseback, stopping here and there for a time to work at his business. This was about 1840 to 1841. Before this, and on his return he attended medical college at Pittsfield, Mass., where he graduated in the fall of 1842. After this he attended the medical college at Albany, N. Y. Dr. Ellis began practice in Chesterfield, Mass., where he married Miss Mary Elizabeth Coit, his first wife. After about one year he removed to Grand Rapids, Mich. Here he remained about two years; and during this period he began to investigate the homeopathic method of treating diseases, and at its end he spent a winter in New York City, attending lectures and visiting physicians, and on his return to Michigan in the spring he settled in Detroit, and opened an office as a homeopathic physician in connection with Dr. P. M. Wheaton, who died of the cholera at Cincinnati in 1849 or 1850. He purchased books and medicines for the purpose of investigating homeopathy while in Grand Rapids and began their use. He was surprised and pleased at the results obtained. He located in Detroit in 1846, where he practiced until 1861, when he settled in New York City, where he now resides. He and Dr. Wheaton were the first homeopathic physicians in Detroit, and among the first in the State. He acquired a large patronage and held the confidence of the people in a very high degree. For professional knowledge and skill he was regarded by his patrons as without a superior.

Dr. Ellis in his early practice was a surgeon of rare skill. In 1845 he made the first successful operation of the kind then on record of tying both carotid arteries, at an interval of only about four days, in the neck of a man who was slowly bleeding to death from a gun-shot wound through the neck. He lectured six years in the Homeopathic Medical College in Cleveland, Ohio, just before the Rebellion, and was often called by the regular surgeon to assist him in difficult operations. He also was Professor of the

Theory and Practice of Medicine for two years in the New York Homeopathic Medical College. The beginning of his practice was before the discovery of chloroform and the unavoidable suffering consequent on surgical operations, and the infinitely more mild and satisfactory practice of medicine on the homeopathic principle gradually led him to mainly withdraw from the former in favor of the latter practice. For the last fifteen years he has almost wholly given his time to the oil business, but has written much upon medical and theological subjects. Although a medium sized man, a firm of hatters in Detroit said he had one of the largest heads in Michigan. His general culture and qualities of heart are no less ample. He is a man of few words, unusual modesty, quiet, gentle and amiable disposition, but in a discussion he is prepared to go to an exhaustive degree to sustain his point. Both in medicine and theology he is well informed and thoroughly grounded in his principles. He has been a religious man and for nearly 40 years a member of the New Jerusalem Church (commonly called Swedenborgian) to which he devotes a small portion of his time, labor and income in propagating its doctrines. At his own expense he has written, printed, and circulated gratuitously, to the clergy of the United States and Canada, over 60,000 copies of an "Address to the Clergy," of 24 pages; and an equal number of a work of 260 pages on "Skepticism and Divine Revelation," and also a pamphlet of 52 pages on the "Deterioration of the Puritan Stock." These three works have been sent to every clergyman of every denomination in the United States and Canada whose name could be obtained. One of his late publications is a work of over 700 pages condemning the use of fermented wine as a beverage, or for sacramental purposes, as being unsafe and unscriptural. A number of ministers attacked him for this, but good judges concede that he has the best of the argument. The silence of his opponents seems to confirm this, which shows prudence on their part even if they are not convinced, for Dr. Ellis when he is sure that he is right *never gives up* in anything he undertakes. His principles are *fixed*, and in religion, temperance and medicine, which so vitally affect mankind, he is *inflexible*.

Some years ago Dr. Ellis published a volume on the "Avoidable Causes of Disease" and another on "Family Homeopathy." These books have had a large sale and are works of a high order of merit.

While residing in Detroit, Dr. Ellis invested considerable money in lands, mines and stocks. The lands proved good investments, but the mines and stocks were a failure.

While engaged in practicing medicine in New York he took an interest in an oil refinery at Binghamton, N. Y.; and finally invented a new process of refining petroleum, and in connection with the President of the Company, he obtained two patents for the same; but the refinery, entrusted to the care of others, did not prove a financial success; but his son, Mr. W. D. Ellis, and Mr. T. M. Leonard, nephew of his wife, commenced selling the oils in New York. In 1874, in connection with his son and Mr. Leonard, he started a refinery in Brooklyn, with his improved process for refining oil for lubricating purposes; he attending to the manufacturing department of the business, while his son and nephew attended to the selling of the products. The business prospered and increased to such an extent that in 1881 they purchased a large tract of land at Edgewater, New Jersey, on the Hudson River, across from New York City and about opposite 117th street, where they constructed one of the finest oil refineries in the world. From small beginnings, about fifteen years ago, this business has grown to large proportions with demands for their oil, and depots for its sale, in every part of the globe. It is Dr. Ellis' characteristic to have whatever he produces *first quality*, and it is this, together with the strenuous efforts of his son and partner to push its sale far and wide, which has brought their "valvoline," for oiling machinery, into such extensive demand.

The likeness of Dr. Ellis, on opposite page, was copied from a photograph taken in 1865 when he was about 50 years of age. He is now in his seventy-second year, not robust but in the enjoyment of good health, resulting mainly, from the simplicity and strict sobriety of his life. He is said to resemble his grandfather, John (15), in mental and physical characteristics. Dr. Ellis has had five children, only one of whom, Wilbur D., is now living. For sketch of the latter see No. 760.

(243.) JOHN ELLIS, M. D.,

OF NEW YORK CITY.

[181]

—— In writing history, or biography it is not always considered safe to say too much of the living. The mutations of life, and changeableness of human character, are such as sometimes to most unexpectedly reverse our early opinions of men and women. But when they have closed their earthly career, and passed on to the other life, the situation is different. Their record is then made, it is unchangeable. With this view it has been the policy of the writer of these pages to say what he truthfully could of the latter, but with the former, those now living, treat with brevity and conciseness. If any departure from this course can be made, with absolute assurance of right, it is in reference to the one now under consideration. It is not often that we can say of any one that he contains all the perfections of the ideal man. But the writer voices the opinion of many others, as well as his own, in the expression that of all of the Ellises whom he has known, as well as of *all* men, he excels. Always calm, never impulsive, never spurred hither and thither by each desire that comes uppermost, but self-controlled, self-balanced, always self-reliant, and governed by the joint supremacy of the intellect and the will; never an act, or expression, without calm deliberation; firm in his convictions of truth and right, with the natural always subservient to the spiritual; living in the world, yet above it; theoretical, yet thoroughly practical; with an unfailing reliance on Divine Providence; presenting all the traits of a pure, noble, and Christian man in an exalted degree; he is, and has been from early manhood, an example worthy the imitation and reverence of men.

June 29, 1843, Dr. John Ellis married in Chesterfield, Mass., his first wife,

(244.) **MARY E. COIT.** She was born in Norwich, Hampshire Co., Mass, in 1817. She was the second daughter of Harvey and Nancy Stone Coit. Mr. Harvey Coit lived many years in Chesterfield, Mass., but in later years he removed to Columbus, Ohio. His sons, Messrs. Harvey Coit, jr., and George Coit, are now living in Columbus.

Mary E. Coit was a descendant of John Coit, who came from Wales in 1635. He was among the settlers at Salem, in 1638, at Gloucester, in 1644, and at New London, Conn., in 1650, where he died in 1659. His wife, Mary Jenness Coit, died in 1676 aged 80 years. One of their descendants was Dea. Joseph Coit, born 1673, married Martha Harris. One of their sons, Col. Samuel Coit, born in Plainfield, Conn., in 1708, married Sarah Spaulding. Their son, Benjamin, born 1731, married Abigail Billings and lived in Griswold, Conn. Their son, Rev. Joseph Coit, born 1763, married Experience Wheeler of Stonington, Conn., and they were the grandparents of Mrs. Mary Coit Ellis. Mrs. Ellis was a woman of unusual beauty, gentleness and loveliness of character. She died in Detroit, Oct. 15, 1850, aged 33 years. Of her three children but one, Mr. W. D. Ellis, (760) of New York city, is now living.

Mrs. Dr. Ellis was a cousin of Mrs. Aurelia Coit Caskey, wife of Hon. Samuel Caskey, an old and prominent resident of Detroit. Mrs. Caskey's father, John H. Coit, lived in Norwich, Hampshire Co., Mass. She has a genealogical record of the Coit family, published in 1874, from which, by her courtesy, the writer has procured the above statistics.

(245.) **SARAH MARIA LEONARD,** second wife of Dr. John Ellis, was born in Barker, Broome Co., N. Y., Aug. 14th, 1828. Her father, Joseph Leonard, Jr., was born in Chenango, N. Y., about 1791 and died in Port Huron, Mich., in 1874. Her mother, Margaret Hammar was born in Somerville, N. J., in 1794, and died in Ionia, Mich., in 1882, aged 88 years. Mrs. Ellis' parents settled in Troy, Oakland Co., Mich., in very early times, when Michigan was a territory. Their children were, Mary Ann, born 1818, married Ezekiel Crocker Leonard and they live in Edgewater, N. J. Their only son, Theodore, is a partner of Dr. John and W. D. Ellis in the oil business. Seth, born 1820, is a farmer and lives in Troy, Mich. Catherine, born 1822, married Alanson King, and they have lived in Ionia, Mich., for many years (Mr. King died early in 1887), Elizabeth, born 1824, married Hiram King and lived in Saginaw, Mich., several years where Mr. King died about 1880.

Dr. and Mrs. Ellis were married in Troy, Oakland Co., Mich., Oct. 30, 1851. A short time previous to his last marriage Dr. Ellis had built a large double brick four story residence at 41 and 43 Congress street, west, in Detroit, where he resided and carried on his medical business until his removal to New York in 1861.

In June, 1884, Dr. and Mrs. Ellis started on an eastern tour to the old world. They visited nearly every country of Europe, and Egypt and the Holy Land. They were gone just one year. A full account of their trip was published weekly in "*The Dawn*," a London publication, and sent to a large number of their friends in this country.

Mrs. Ellis is a very bright woman, well-educated, is a graduate in medicine and, several years ago, lectured in the Woman's Medical College in New York. She has aided her husband greatly in his literary, medical and business pursuits. Her two children died in infancy. The eldest, Lilly, was born Aug. 5th, 1852, and died Sept. 27th of the same year. Edward Dell Ellis, their second child, was born May 30th, 1855, and died Aug. 6th, 1855. Dr. and Mrs. Ellis own elegant apartments in "The Chelsea," a new apartment house, or block, ten stories high, at 222 West 23rd Street. This kind of a structure is a modern invention in which four or more complete residences are constructed on each story with one or more elevators, besides stairways, leading to the top. The owners of each residence form a joint association for its general management, and none are allowed to buy or rent therein unless acceptable to all the others. The upper stories of such a building are very cool, airy and sightly, and withal quite desirable apartments for those who wish to get above the din and dust and confusion of the over-crowded streets below. These buildings are about 130 feet high, fire-proof, and the light and ventilation of the upper stories, at least, all one could desire.

Children of Sylvia Ellis (75), and her husband, Asher Belding. Grandchildren of Lieut. John and great
grandchildren of Richard Ellis, all
of Ashfield, 246 to 253.

(246.) **ARETUS BELDING**, eldest child of Sylvia
and Asher Belding, was born in Ashfield in 1803. He
married Nancy Pine in Ypsilanti, Mich., where he died
in 1830, leaving no children.

(247.) **JANE BELDING** was born in Ashfield, in
1806. She married, Mr. John Shaw in Washtenaw Co.,
Mich., but they settled in Otisco, Mich., about 1838. Mr.
Shaw was a farmer, a Baptist in religious belief, an
Englishman by birth and a man of great good sense,
enterprise and wealth. His farm was one and one-half
miles north of Otisco Center, where his son, Asher, now
lives with his family. Mr. Shaw died about 1880, at
Greenville, Mich., to which place he had removed about
1865.

Mrs. Jane Shaw was a woman of great energy and
business talent and of the most upright character. She
was widely known and respected. She died in Greenville
in 1869. Her three children were, William, who lived in
Mapleton, Dakota, some years ago; Sylvia, who married
James Tallman, a thriving farmer, in Ordway, Dakota, and
Asher, who lives on the homestead in Otisco.

(——) **EDWARD BELDING**, second son of Sylvia and
Asher Belding, was born in Ashfield in 1810. He died at
10 years of age.

(248.) **EBENEZER BELDING** was born in Ashfield,
in 1811. It is said that he went "to sea" when about 24
years of age and was never heard from afterwards.

(249.) **VOLNEY BELDING**, was born 1814. Like most
of Ashfield youths he started out early to seek a new
location. In the spring of 1837, he settled in Otisco, one
mile north of the town corners or center, where he located
a farm of 160 acres of excellent land. Soon after he also
engaged in lumbering on "Lincoln creek," about 10 miles
further north, where he built the first saw mill in that part

of the State. About 1845, he built other mills three miles further up on Flat River, at what is now Gowan, a station on the Detroit, Lansing & Northern Railroad. All mills in those times were run by water power and the streams were dammed by hard labor and at great expense, and were subject to frequent "wash-outs" from floods. Mr. Belding's experience in this business was varied by all the ups and downs which could be conceived of. But he was a man of the most undaunted courage, perseverance, and hopefulness and ever held the respect and confidence of the people of all that section. In 1844 he returned to Ashfield, where he married Miss Louisa Flower, a daughter of Horace or Horatio Flower and niece of Rhoda (177) and Rumina Flower (181), who married William and David Ellis, Jr. She is a woman of rare intelligence and worth. Soon after their marriage they returned to Michigan, where Mr. Belding continued farming and lumbering nearly twenty years, when he removed to a farm at Saltville, Kansas. They have had eight children, six of whom are now living in Kansas and Missouri. These are Mary Jane, Edward E., Pauline E., Carrie L., Sylvia E. and John Asher Belding.

Mr. Volney Belding is in poor health and lately has been residing with his son at Flat Creek, Barry Co., Mo.

(251.) **THOMAS BELDING** was born in 1816. He went to Michigan with his brother, Volney, and located a farm just east and adjoining the latter. In 1846 he married Miss Emeline Weaver, a daughter of Mr. Aaron Weaver, a very aged resident at the present time, of Otisco. Mrs. Belding died a few years later leaving no children. At the breaking out of the gold-fever excitement in California, in 1850, Thomas went there and remained until 1872. He died in 1878, in Nevada, where he had a farm.

(253.) **CHANDLER BELDING,** youngest child of Asher and Sylvia Ellis Belding, was born in Ashfield in 1819. In 1850 he went to California and in 1872 to Nevada, where he had a ranch or farm with his brother Thomas. He died in 1883, leaving no children.

Children of Daniel Ellis (97), of Ellisburg, Jefferson Co.,
N. Y., and their husbands and wives. Grandchildren of Caleb (19), of Ellisburg, and
great grandchildren of Richard, of
Ashfield. From 260 to 273.

(260.) ELIZABETH ELLIS, eldest child of Daniel Ellis, was born in Adams, Jefferson Co., N. Y., 1804. She married Mr. Geo. Paddock and had two children, Henry A. and Maria, who are married and live in Prophetstown, Whiteside, Co., Illinois. The latter married a Mr. Nichols, and he died about 1860.

(264.) MARIA ELLIS, daughter of Daniel Ellis, was born in Adams, Jefferson Co., N. Y., June 11th, 1807, and died in 1863. She married Mr. Elisha Salisbury of Ellisburg. She had one daughter, Martha, and three sons, Abiram, Daniel and David. The latter are said to live in or near Midland, Mich.

(266.) LORENZO D. ELLIS, son of Daniel, was born in Adams, N. Y., Nov. 11th, 1805. He married a Mrs. Mehitable Brown Martin, a widow with one daughter, Julia Ann. She was one of a family of eleven children. Her parents lived at Chazy, Clinton Co., N. Y., and were Oliver and Ann Babcock Brown, and all were Methodists and highly respected people.

Mr. Ellis and Mrs. Martin were married at Alburgh, Vt., in 1836. Mrs. Ellis died in 1866, leaving four children, Christina E., Carrie M., Myra and Oliver L. D. Ellis. Christina, born 1837, married Mr. Caleb Ellis of Ellisburg, N. Y., (see 319). Carrie M. was born Oct. 22d, 1839, in Champlain, N. Y. She has never married, is a teacher at Brooklyn, Cal. Myra was born at Bangor, Franklin Co., N. Y., July 18th, 1842, educated at Union Academy, at Belleville, and in 1864 married Capt. Edwin Swan of Adams, N. Y. Capt. Swan was in the Union army and was a highly respected man. He died in 1865. Mrs. Swan afterwards married Mr. George Nichols of Water-town, N. Y. He is a druggist and has lived at Grand Rapids, Mich., for the past 15 years.

Oliver L. D. Ellis, youngest child of Lorenzo D., was born at Bangor, N. Y., June 20th, 1845. He enlisted in the Union army at 16 years of age and served through the Rebellion. He is married, has five children and lives in Kansas. His wife was Fannie Barker, daughter of Leonard O. Barker (320) of Young, N. Y.

Mr. Lorenzo D. Ellis was too old to join the army during the Rebellion, but he served some time in the hospital at Hampton, Va. He died in Manlius, Onondaga Co., and was buried in Adams, N. Y., in 1875. His wife died in March, 1866. She was a lovely, patient, hopeful and deeply religious woman.

(268.) CATHARINE ELLIS was born August 11th, 1813, and died in 1830.

(270.) NICHOLAS GROAT ELLIS, son of Daniel and Christine Groat Ellis, was born at Ellisburg, N. Y., May 2d, 1815. He married Miss Zilpha B. Case, who was born in Watertown, N. Y., Sept. 16th, 1818. They were married Feb. 20th, 1844. Their children were Henry G., born Feb. 26th, 1845 ; Geo. W., May 3d, 1847 ; Margaret J., Sept. 18th, 1849, died Sept. 4th, 1857 ; Edward D., Dec. 2d, 1851, and Lewis M., Oct. 13th, 1856, the last born at Ellisburg, N. Y., and the others in Canada West.

Henry G. Ellis married Clara V. Fuller in Wisconsin, in 1867.

Geo. W. Ellis married Alma Earl, at Bronson, Mich., in 1873, and have two children, Maggie Louisa and Lois Maria.

Edward D. Ellis married at Salt Lake City, Utah, in 1883.

Lewis M. Ellis married Louisa S. Doust, at Charlotte, Mich., in 1880. Their children were Bertha, Beulah and Paul. Mr. Lewis M. Ellis, with his family, settled at Mason, Mich., where he was secretary and general manager of the Mason carriage works. He was also an alderman of the village and a very prominent and highly respected man. He died Nov. 2d, 1885, much regretted, as he was young and gave great promise of further usefulness to his family and friends.

Mr. Nicholas Groat Ellis died in 1871.

(272.) **MARCUS A. ELLIS,** son of Daniel Ellis, of Ellisburg, was born Nov. 25th, 1817. He died in 1879, unmarried.

(273.) **REV. ALBERT A. ELLIS,** youngest child of Daniel Ellis of Ellisburg, N. Y., was born in Adams, (next town north of Ellisburg) April 6th, 1820. He joined the Baptist church and was ordained a minister of that denomination. He came to Michigan in early life and preached for a time at Brooklyn, Northville and Plymouth. He married Electa A. Barney, in Jefferson Co., and they had several children. Edward S., born 1847, is a lawyer and judge in Lisbon, Dakota, and also mayor of the town. He married Alice Kearney in 1876. Mary L., born 1848, married Mr. Frank Pratt of Painesville, Ohio. She died in 1885. Charles S. Ellis, born June 26th, 1852, married Maggie S. Leys, Feb. 14th, 1883. They live in Sarnia, Canada, where Mr. Ellis is a dry goods merchant.

Mrs. Electa A. Ellis was born Dec. 2d, 1822, married at Ellisburg, N. Y., Sept, 22d, 1844, and died in 1854.

Rev. Mr. Ellis, for his second wife, married Mrs. Mary S. G. Noyes, June 28th, 1855. She was born Aug. 29th, 1821. Her maiden name was Mary Sherwood Gregory ; born in Perington, Monroe Co., N. Y., and at the age of nine years removed with her parents to Plymouth, Mich. She first married Dr. Justin Noyes, who died, as did also two children by him, Emma and Mary Noyes.

Mrs. Mary S. G. Ellis, died in Brooklyn, Jackson Co., Mich., June 7th, 1856. Her parents were William S. and Lydia Gregory, of Plymouth, Mich. She was a woman of sincere piety and usefulness and was beloved by all. A sister of hers Mrs. Lyon, wife of Hon. T. T. Lyon, lives in South Haven, Mich., where Mr. Lyon is engaged largely in raising fruit and is a man of considerable note in this State. She left an infant child, Mary E. G. Ellis, born in Brooklyn, May 17th, 1856, who married Mr. Dewitt H. Moreland, at Plymouth, Jan. 30th, 1876. They now reside in Detroit, and have one daughter, Lois Claire Moreland, born May 7th, 1877.

Mr. Moreland is in the railroad business. He is general traveling agent for the St. Paul, Minneapolis & Manitoba Railroad. He was born and raised in Plymouth, Mich., in the same neighborhood with his wife. The latter, after the death of her mother in Brooklyn, Mich., was reared by her aunt, Mrs. T. T. Lyon, who then, and for many years after, lived at Plymouth.

Rev. Albert A. Ellis for his third wife married Mrs. Jane Brink Swift, of Northville, Mich. Her first husband was a brother of Dr. Swift, now and for many years a prominent physician of Northville. About a year after her marriage to Mr. Ellis the latter died. Afterward Mrs. Ellis was again married to Mr. Clark of Sarnia, Canada, where they both now reside. Mr. Clark is a wealthy and highly respected merchant there. Mrs. Clark is a woman of great refinement, unusual intelligence and amiability. Several of Mr. Ellis' children by his first wife were reared by her after the death of their father.

Rev. Mr. Ellis was a man of uncommon talent, both as a minister and business man. He dealt largely in pine and other lands and in 1859 visited Grand Rapids, Mich., on a business expedition. He was taken sick at his hotel, the old National, where the Morton House now stands, and suddenly died, in a day or two after. Rev. Mr. C. C. Miller, now of Oxford, Mich., and some other church and lodge friends of an order to which Mr. Ellis and they belonged were notified and sent the remains to his family in Northville. Rev. Supply Chase of this city, the oldest Baptist minister in this State, recollects Mr. Ellis and his last wife and speaks of them both in the highest terms of commendation.

Rev. Mr. Ellis' parents and grandparents were ardent Methodists in religious belief, as were all the Ellises in and about Ellisburg, N. Y., and he was reared in this belief, but what induced him to depart from the faith of his fathers and become a Baptist does not now appear. However, it may safely be attributed to that feeling of independence and desire to investigate, each for himself, which is an Ellis trait, and as he was a man of unusual intelligence, this assurance may be taken as positive.

Children of John Ellis (101), of Ellisburg, N. Y., and their
wives and husbands. Grandchildren of Caleb (19)
and great grandchildren of Richard, of
Ashfield. From 286 to 298.

(286.) **CALEB ELLIS**, eldest son of John, was born in Ellisburg, N. Y., Nov. 17th, 1806. He died several years ago, leaving three children: Melvin, who is a physician, Mary Etta, who married a Lockwood, and Arvilla, who married a Canwell and lived in Toledo, Ohio.

(288.) **SQUIRE ELLIS**, son of John of Ellisburg N. Y., was born March 1st, 1811. He married Theresa Washburn and had three children.

Elizabeth married Capt. William Gilbert and they live at Henderson Harbor, N. Y. He sails the schooner Wm. Gilbert.

Caroline married Augustus Sanford, a farmer, and they live in Ellisburg.

John H. Ellis, son of Squire, married Nancy Goodnough and they have two daughters: Libbie, who married Avery Otis, a farmer in Illinois, and Carrie, who married Mark Howard, a farmer in Ellisburg.

Mr. Squire Ellis died Dec. 17th, 1843, and Mrs. Theresa Ellis again married a Mr. William Cronk. They now live at Ellisburg and are over 75 years of age. They have four children, all married, Joseph, Silas, Julia and Owellen Cronk.

(290) **MARY ELLIS**, daughter of John (101), and Betsey Smith, his second wife, was born in Ellisburg, N. Y., Sept. 12th, 1822. Jan. 30th, 1844, she married Wm. McKinley and he died in 1847, leaving two sons, John and Frank, both married and living in or near Benton Harbor, Mich. Mrs. Mary Ellis McKinley was again married to Mr. Hiram Tubbs of Benton Harbor, where they now live. They have four children, Edgar, Everett, Ella and Hattie.

(292). **DANIEL ELLIS**, son of John (101), was born in Ellisburg, N. Y. Aug 23d, 1824. He married Laura Etta Woodruff. Mr. Ellis died leaving three children, all now living at Benton Harbor, Mich. Frederick, William and Mary, who married Thomas Winters.

(294.) **GEORGE ROGER ELLIS,** son of John (101), was born in Ellisburg, N. Y., Aug. 1st, 1830. He was married and had two sons. He was thrown from a horse and killed.

(296.) **HANNAH ELLIS,** daughter of John (101), was born in Ellisburg, N. Y., March 22d, 1833. She married George Fuller and now lives at Benton Harbor, Mich. They have three children : Adelbert, born 1852, Mary, 1856, and Maggie, 1862. The latter married Frank Ellis and they live at Ellisburg, N. Y. Adelbert Fuller is married and lives at Benton Harbor.

(298.) **CAPT. EDWARD N. ELLIS,** son of John (101), and his third wife, Kate Duran, was born in Ellisburg, N. Y., Oct. 21st, 1839. He is a sailor and has been on the lakes since he was ten years' old. He has commanded several boats and is now in the iron ore trade between Marquette, Mich., and Lake Erie ports.

Dec. 23d, 1865, he married Miss Ann Minor, a daughter of Capt. Wm. and Margaret Swarthout Minor. Capt. Ellis has one daughter, Mary Louisa, born Aug. 26th, 1875. His family reside at Ellisburg, N. Y.

Capt. Ellis' mother's (Kate Duran,) maiden name was Kate or Catharine Colon. Her first husband was William Duran, by whom she had four children : Capt. A W. Duran, Nancy, who married Capt. Hiram Emory and now live in Grand Traverse, Mich., Mary Duran, who married Nathan Farnam and lived in Ellisburg, N. Y., and Jane H., who married a Lafayette and live in Oswego, N. Y. Eight years after Mrs. Duran's marriage to Mr. John Ellis (101), she was again left a widow, with a family of young children. She was married to Mr. Ellis Jan. 20th, 1839. She was a woman of great courage, industry and perseverance, and was highly respected by all. She died at Ellisburg, N. Y., April 19th, 1884.

Children of Thomas Ellis (108), of Ellisburg, N. Y., and
their wives and husbands. Grandchildren of
Caleb (19), and great-grandchildren of
Richard Ellis. From 310 to 328.

(310.) **RICHARD ELLIS**, eldest son of Thomas, of Ellisburg, N. Y., was born Feb. 7th, 1813, in Woodville, Jefferson Co., N. Y. He graduated at Hamilton College, in 1834, and ever since has been engaged in teaching in academies. In 1842, he married Miss Emily A. Clark, a daughter of John Clark, a mechanic and farmer of Copenhagen, Lewis Co., N. Y. She died in 1849 at 27 years of age, leaving one son, Theodore C. Ellis.

In 1853, Mr. Ellis was again married in Cazenovia to Miss Elizabeth A. Barrett, a farmer's daughter. Her father, Amasa Barrett of Cazenovia, died in 1865. Her mother, Fanny Damon Barrett, died in 1875. She was a graduate of Oneida Conference Seminary and since her marriage to Mr. Ellis has been engaged in teaching with her husband. Mrs. Ellis was born in 1825. Mr. and Mrs. Ellis now reside at Cazenovia, Madison Co., N. Y., having partially retired from teaching. They have taught in the Belleville Academy, Hudson River Institute, and for the last twenty-three years in Cazenovia. They are members of the Methodist church.

Mr. Ellis' son, Theodore C., born in Rodman, Jefferson Co., N. Y., in 1845, is a lawyer, graduated at Marietta, Ohio, and now resides in Kansas.

(312.) **RUSSELL ELLIS**, second son of Thomas, was born in 1815, in Woodville, N. Y., (township of Ellisburg.) In 1835 he married Miss Martha A. Cook, of Pulaski, N. Y. Mrs. Ellis was born in 1817 and died in 1878. Mr. Ellis was a merchant and in 1850 went to California, and, in returning from San Francisco to Panama on a vessel, was taken sick and died on the passage. He had one son, Hiram Russell Ellis, born in Woodville, N. Y., in 1840. The latter now resides in Grand Rapids, Mich. He married Francis A. Pierce in Grand Rapids, July 6th,

1865, and have had eight children, Russell P., born 1867 ; Lola, 1869 ; Harry H., 1872 ; Frank H., 1875 ; Gertrude, 1877, died in 1881 ; Gilbert C., 1879 ; Edwin D., 1881 ; Geo. H., 1884.

Mr. Hiram R. Ellis was an officer in the Union army. He enlisted from Saugatuck, Allegan Co., Mich., August 19th, 1862, as Sergeant of Co. I, Fifth Michigan Cavalry. August 15th, 1864 he was appointed First Lieut., and Brevet Capt. of U. S. Vol. March 13th, 1865, for gallant and meritorious services during the war. He was mustered out June 5th, 1865.

(314.) **SARAH ELLIS**, eldest daughter of Thomas, was born in Ellisburg, N. Y., in 1816. She married David Fulton, Jr., in Belleville, N. Y., (Ellisburg township) Jan. 13th, 1841. Mr. Fulton was born in Ellisburg, in 1817, and was a son of David Fulton, Sr., (see 81, page 121) and a grandson of James and Hannah Ellis Fulton of Colerain, Mass. Mr. David Fulton, Jr., died in Belleville, Oct. 9th, 1886. He was a farmer. Mrs. Sarah Ellis Fulton lives on the homestead and has four sons : James, born 1843 ; Thomas, 1849 ; David, Jr., 1852, and Charles N., 1855.

James Fulton married Frances Grant of Belleville. They have two children.

Thomas Fulton married Abbie Evans of Belleville, where they now live.

David Fulton married Ella Young, of Young, N. Y., and they have one child.

(316.) **DAVID ELLIS**, son of Thomas, was born in 1818, in Belleville, N. Y. He married Miss Pamelia Clark in Belleville, September, 1841. Mrs. Ellis was born in 1820 and died in 1865, leaving one child, Hannah. Mr. David Ellis held the office of Sheriff of Jefferson County several terms, and was a very prominent man. He was a man of great physical strength, very sociable and of uncommon popularity. He died in 1884. Two of his children died in infancy. Hannah, born in 1861, is now living in Belleville.

(318.) **CALEB ELLIS**, son of Thomas, was born in Ellisburg, N. Y., in 1820. He married Maria Louisa Barker in Ellisburg, Jan. 17, 1843. Mrs. Ellis was born in 1820 and died in 1858, leaving four children: Martha Ann, Vial T., Russell and Henry D. Ellis. Martha Ann, born 1844, married Mr. Vernon Herrington, have four sons and all live in Walker Township, P. O. at Grand Rapids, Mich. Vial T. born May 19, 1848, died Oct. 29, 1864. Russell, born Jan. 12, 1852, married Miss Gertie A. Enos, Jan. 22, 1873. They have two children and reside at Grand Rapids, Mich. Henry D., born June 8th, 1854, is unmarried and lives at Ellisburg, N. Y.

Mrs. Maria L. Barker Ellis was a sister of Mr. Leonard O. Barker of Young, Onondaga Co., N. Y., who married Mary Ellis (320), a sister of Caleb Ellis, of Belleville, N. Y. Mr. Ellis was a teacher in early life but when his father became aged he took the farm and homestead, where he now resides.

Mr. Caleb Ellis' second wife is

(319.) **CHRISTINA E. ELLIS**, a daughter of Lorenzo D. Ellis (266). The latter is a cousin of Caleb. Mrs. Christina E. Ellis was born in Colwell's Manor, Canada, in 1837. She married Mr. Ellis, Oct. 11th, 1860, at Bangor, Franklin Co., N.Y., and they now live at Belleville. Mrs. Ellis was a school teacher for several years in Bangor and afterwards at Ellisburg previous to her marriage. She has three children, Florence E., Geo, Edwin, and Albert T. Ellis. Florence E., born May 19th, 1863, graduated at Union Academy at Belleville and has been a teacher. She joined the Methodist Church in early childhood, and is greatly devoted to that and the Sunday School work, and is a prominent member of the Chautauqua Circle, a literary society of rare purity and excellence. She is also much devoted to music and painting, and has spent considerable time in New York City studying art with noted teachers. Geo. Edwin, born Dec. 22nd, 1864, graduated at Union

Academy at the age of sixteen, then entered at Syracuse University, where he graduated at the age of twenty. He is now studying law at Syracuse. He gives promise of uncommon success and usefulness.

Albert T., born April 10th, 1869, lives at home, and is attending Belleville Academy.

Mr. Caleb Ellis is a farmer and lives in Ellisburg, where all his children were born. His wife, Mrs. Christina E. Ellis, is a woman of unusual intelligence and worth and has aided the writer greatly in this part of his work.

(320.) **MARY ELLIS**, second daughter of Thomas Ellis, was born in Ellisburg, N. Y., 1822. She married Leonard O. Barker in 1843, at Ellisburg. Afterwards they removed to Young, (Clay Township), Onondaga Co., N. Y., where they now live. They have had seven children.

Fannie Barker, the eldest, married Oliver L. D. Ellis, a son of Lorenzo D. Ellis (266), and they have five children. They reside in Kansas.

Addie Barker died in infancy.

Hannah Jane Barker is a graduate of Oswego Normal school and was a teacher. She married Charles McKissic, Jan. 20, 1866.

Mary A. Barker married Lee B. Hibbard of Centerville, N. Y., and they have two children.

Sarah L. Barker married Amos E. Freeman, of Young, N. Y., and they have one child.

Thurston G. Barker is a farmer, unmarried.

Herbert E. Barker died in his eighteenth year.

Mr. Leonard O. Barker is a farmer. Mrs. Barker is a woman of superior education and talent.

(322.) **VIAL ELLIS**, youngest son of Thomas Ellis, of Ellisburg, N. Y., was born in 1825. He graduated at Hamilton College, N. Y., at 21 years of age. He died about one year thereafter, prematurely closing a very promising life.

(324.) **JANE ELLIS**, daughter of Thomas Ellis, of Ellisburg, N. Y., was born in 1828. She married George Waterson of Missouri. They moved to San Francisco, Cal., where Mrs. W. died in 1878. She was a teacher of music and was very proficient in the art. She had no children. She experienced religion and joined the Methodist Church when a child, and was a woman of uncommon amiability, intelligence and worth.

(326.) **HANNAH ELLIS**, daughter of Thomas, was born at Ellisburg, N. Y., in 1831. She married Charles Rounds of Ellisburg, about 1857. She died in 1862, leaving no children. She was a person of very bright intellect, rare wit, and loving diposition. Her early death was greatly deplored by a large circle of relatives and acquaintances.

(328.) **PHEBE ELLIS**, youngest child of Thomas, was born in Ellisburg, N. Y., in 1833. She married John Chamberlain in 1868, in Belleville, and had one child, John Jr. Mr. Chamberlain died in 1869, and in 1872, Mrs. Chamberlain married Mr. Gates White of Pulaski, N. Y., and had two children. Mrs. White died in 1875. Her husband and three children live in Pulaski, Oswego Co., N. Y.

Children of James Ellis (112), of Ellisburg, N. Y., and their wives. Grandchildren of Caleb (19) and great-grandchildren of Richard of Ashfield. From 330 to 336.

(330.) **MARY ANN ELLIS**, eldest child of James, was born in Ellisburg, N. Y., in 1816. She is unmarried and lives in Ellisburg.

(332.) **THOMAS ELLIS**, son of James, was born in Ellisburg, N. Y., in 1817. He married Cynthia Sherman. They lived in Ellisburg where they had six children. Mr. Ellis died in 1876. His widow and children settled in Berrien Co., Mich. Their children are Polly, James, William, Adelbert, Levi and Thomas Jr.

(334.) **JOHN W. ELLIS,** son of James, was born in Ellisburg, N. Y., in 1818. He married Mary Fuller, who was born in 1825, and they have had four children. Roderick D. Ellis, born 1843, married Minerva Albro and they have three children, Helen, Edith, and John E. They live at Ellisburg. Helen Ellis, born 1847, died in 1853. Martha Ellis, born 1850, married M. M. Johnson, and their children are Laura, Ellis and Ernest Johnson. Fred. Ellis, born 1856, married Phebe Matthews in 1874. She died the following year and he married Sybil Matthews in 1877 and they have one son, Leon D., born 1879. Mr. John W. Ellis is a farmer in Ellisburg.

(336.) **ISAAC ELLIS,** youngest son of James, was born in Ellisburg, N. Y., in 1822. He married Margaret Beamer and they have four children : Ellen, born 1850; Alexander, 1852 ; Benjamin, 1855, and Frank, 1862.

Mr. Isaac Ellis is a farmer and lives at La Hogue, Iroquois Co., Illinois. His daughter, Ellen, married Henry Moore and they live in Unadilla, Otoe Co., Nebraska. Alexander married Hattie Crell and they reside in La Hogue. Benjamin married Kate Snyder and they live at Spring Bay, Woodford Co., Ill. Frank Ellis married Maggie Fuller and lives at Ellisburg, N. Y.

Benjamin Ellis married Kate Snyder in Spring Bay, Ill., July 23rd, 1876. He was born in Ellisburg, N. Y., July 27th, 1855. His wife was born in Spring Bay, Sept. 6th, 1856. Their children are : Alice L., born May 29th, 1877 ; Hannah A., Dec. 29th, 1879 ; Julia E., March 4th, 1884 and Mary, Sept. 18th, 1886.

(340.) **LYMAN ELLIS**, eldest son of Robert, was born in Ellisburg, N. Y., Dec. 17th, 1816. His wife was Malvina Zufelt, born 1829. They were married at Ellisburg in 1848, where they now reside. Their children are : Dette L., born 1850, Fannie, 1852, and Arnita, 1856. Mr. Ellis is a farmer.

(342.) **JANE ELLIS**, eldest daughter of Robert, was born in Ellisburg, N. Y., Feb. 18th, 1818. She died in 1855.

(344.) **MARY ELLIS**, daughter of Robert, was born in Ellisburg, N. Y., Nov. 10th, 1819.

(346.) **CHARLOTTE ELLIS**, daughter of Robert, was born in Ellisburg, N. Y., Jan. 29th, 1821.

(348.) **JAMES ELLIS**, son of Robert, was born at Ellisburg, N. Y., Oct. 22d, 1822. He died May 9th, 1871, at Black Lake, Muskegon Co., Mich. He was a farmer and never married.

(350.) **ROBERT ELLIS, JR.**, son of Robert, Sr., was born in Ellisburg, N. Y., April 25th, 1824. He married Betsey Chrisman in 1853, and had four children. His wife was born March 17th, 1835. In 1866 Mr. Ellis moved from Ellisburg to Grand Ledge, Mich., and in 1868 to Black Lake, Muskegon County, Michigan, where he died May 6th, 1884. He was a farmer. His children were : Gad, born Sept. 20th, 1854, married Samantha Evart ; Charles, July 2d, 1857 ; William, February 3d, 1860 ; Byron, Jan. 25th, 1681. Most of this family now live at Black Lake.

(352.) **GAD ELLIS**, son of Robert, was born in Ellisburg, N. Y., April 2d, 1826. He died in 1862.

(354.) **HARMON ELLIS**, son of Robert, was born in Ellisburg, N. Y., Dec. 10th, 1828.

(356.) **RACHEL ELLIS,** daughter of Robert, was born at Ellisburg, N. Y., July 16th, 1830. She married Joseph Hoyle and lived in Ellisburg until about 1877, when she removed to Stone Mound, Kansas. She has two children, Bertha and Ellsworth Hoyle. For her second husband, Mrs. Hoyle married Mr. David Smith, who is a farmer at Stone Mound, Kansas.

(358.) **CATHERINE ELLIS,** daughter of Robert, was born in Ellisburg, N. Y., Dec. 16th, 1831.

(360.) **FRANKLIN ELLIS,** son of Robert, was born, in Ellisburg, N. Y., Sept. 26th, 1834.

FIFTH GENERATION.

Children of Stephen Ellis (119), of Fayette Co., Ind., and their descendants. Grandchildren of Benjamin, Sr. (22). Great-grandchildren of Reuben (4), and great-great-grandchildren of Richard, of Ashfield. From Nos. 362 to 374.

(362.) **PRUDENCE ELLIS,** eldest daughter of Stephen and Susannah Coburn Ellis, was born in Sempronius, Cayuga Co., N. Y., April 13th, 1799. She married Charles T. Harris in Sempronius, May 11th, 1817. She removed to North Bend, Ohio about 1818. She died at Fairview, Randolph Co., Ind., Sept. 15th, 1871. She was a member of the Lutheran Church. Mr. Charles Thomas Harris, husband of Prudence Ellis, was born in Montreal, Canada, August 3rd, 1799, and died at Rochester, Fulton Co., Ind., March 22nd, 1877. His religious belief was Universalism. He was a gun-smith by trade. His parents were: Hopkins Harris, born March 4th, 1776, and Desiah Niles, born in 1784. Mr. Hopkins, Sr., was a blacksmith, and the later years of his life he was also pastor of the Campbellite Church at Freeport, Ind. He died in 1837 and his wife in 1846.

Mr. Charles T. and Prudence Ellis Harris had eight children: Susan, Mary Ann, Charles W., Stephen, Dorr K., Lester E., Leucetta D. and Eliza Harris.

Susan Harris, born March 18th, 1818, in North Bend, Ohio, married Mr. Reuben C. Niles, at Knightstown, Ind., Sept. 6th, 1833. Mr. Reuben C. Niles was born in Cayuga Co., N. Y., Sept. 17, 1812. His parents removed to Troy, Perry Co., Ind., in 1819. About the time of his marriage he removed to Charlottesville, Ind., where they now live. He is in the hardware trade.

(364.) **MEHITABLE ELLIS,** second child of Stephen Ellis, was born in Sempronius, N. Y., Nov. 21st, 1800. She was a member of the Baptist Church for a number of years before her death, which took place July 14th, 1874. She was married at North Bend, Ohio, May 20th, 1821 to

(365.) **LEWIS ROBINSON,** a farmer and shoemaker. He was born in New York, June 10th, 1791. He was a Baptist from his youth and was a sincere Christian man. He and his family lived many years on the same farm in Harrison township, Fayette Co., Ind., where he died May 13th, 1843. They were highly respected people, beloved by all. Their son Erastus Robinson now lives on the homestead. His mother had lived on the same farm over fifty years at the time of her death in 1874.

Mr. and Mrs. Robinson's children were: Mary, born 1822; Elias, 1825; Rachel N., 1827; Minerva, 1829, died 1873; Martilla, 1834, died 1863; Eunice, 1838, died 1860; Erastus, 1841.

Mary Robinson married Lorenzo Carver in 1838.

Elias Robinson married Sylvia Ward.

Rachel M. Robinson married Daniel T. Taylor Jan. 4th, 1846. Mr. Taylor was born in New York, Jan. 19th, 1823. He is a farmer and carpenter. Himself and wife are Baptists. They live at Harrisburg, Fayette Co., Ind. There children were: Elias R., born 1846; Alice, 1848, died

1851; Ellen, 1851, died 1870; Mary A, 1853, died 1874; Minerva, 1855, died 1872; Herbert L, 1859; Abbie, 1861, died 1884; Irvin, 1870, died 1871. Elias R. and Herbert L. Taylor live in Harrison township.

Minerva Robinson married Jonathan Ward. (See 390).

Martilla Robinson married Lemuel Leffingwell.

Eunice Robinson married Hiram Hiltabidle.

Erastus Robinson married Frances Smith and they live on the homestead of his parents in Harrison township, Fayette Co., Ind.

(366.) **GRATEFUL ELLIS,** third daughter of Stephen Ellis, was born at Sempronius, N. Y., Jan. 28th, 1803. She was a pure and noble woman. She was married Dec. 2nd, 1821 to Casper Trask, probably at North Bend, Ohio. Mr. Trask was born Jan. 20th, 1801. They lived several years in Fayette Co., Ind., afterwards in Freeport, Barry Co., Mich., where they died. Mr. and Mrs. Trask were Baptists. He died May 25th, 1873, and Mrs. Trask Feb. 7th, 1883. Mr. Trask's death was sad and untimely. He was in the field where his men were drawing stumps with a team hitched to one end of a long pole or timber and the other end made fast to the stump. The chain broke, allowing the pole to spring back striking him and breaking both of his lower limbs. He died soon after. His wife Grateful, was the last of Stephen Ellis' children.

Their children were: Moulton S., born 1823, is a farmer and lives near Dunkirk, N. Y.

Clarissa, born 1825, married Chester P. Dow, and lives at Irving, Barry Co., Mich.

Lettitia S., born 1827, married Edward L. Cook. They live at Putnam, Ill.

Howell H., born 1829, married in 1848 Mary L. Stafford, and they live in Grand Rapids, Mich. Mr. Howell H. Trask was a Union soldier, entered the service Oct. 10th, 1861, as Sergeant of Co. B., 13th Michigan Infantry. Was made Second Lieut. Jan. 20th, 1863, and First Lieut. April

25th, 1865. He was wounded at Chickamauga, Tenn., Sept. 19th, 1863, and again at Savannah, Ga., Dec. 12th, 1864.

Lois Trask, born 1832, married Jacob G. Drake.

Edward E. Trask, born 1834, died 1840.

Henry V. Trask, born 1837, married Jennie Stephenson in 1874. His first wife Mary M. Young, died in 1870. He married her in 1865. Mr. Henry V. Trask, lives at Salmanaca, N. Y. He is a Railroad engineer.

Amelia A. Trask, born 1840, married Joshua F. Norton.

De Etta E. Trask, born 1844, married Charles B. Lee in 1865, and Isaac N. Hubbard in 1872. Mr. Lee died in 1868. Mr. and Mrs. Hubbard live about two miles from Yankee Springs P. O., Barry Co., Mich.

Rubie S. Trask, born 1846, married Oliver L. Newton in 1872. They now live at Freeport, Barry Co., Mich.

(368.) **JONATHAN ELLIS,** son of Stephen Ellis, was born in Sempronius, N. Y., Oct. 14th, 1804. He married Charlotte Jeffery, in Fayette Co., Ind. in 1829, moved to Illinois in 1839, and died at Waynesville, Dewitt Co., Ill., in 1876.

Their children were: Louisa, now dead. Alvah who is a farmer at Wapella, Ill. William A., now dead, Mary dead. Diantha J., Sarah Ann and John A.

Diantha J., and John A. Ellis, live at Sedgewick City, Harvey Co., Kansas. Sarah Ann, married Jasper Buck, and they live at Waynesville, Ill.

(370.) **ABIGAIL ELLIS,** daughter of Stephen, was born in Sempronius, N. Y., Sept. 22nd, 1806. She married Joshua Wightman, in Fayette Co., Ind., and had three children. John, Austin and Minor.

Mr. Austin Wightman lives in Padua, McLean Co., Ill.

Mrs. Abigail Ellis Wightman was a member of the Christian Church.

(372.) **LESTER ELLIS,** son of Stephen, was born in Sempronius, N. Y., Sept. 2nd, 1811. He married Sally T.

Trowbridge, in Fayette Co., Ind., about 1832. Their children were: Diantha J., Chester Coburn, and Polly Ellis, all born in Fayette Co., Ind.

Mrs. Ellis was born 1807, and was a daughter of Levi and Abigail Trowbridge. She died in 1879, age 72 years and six months.

Mr. Lester Ellis died June 26th, 1868. Himself and wife were Baptists in religious belief.

Diantha J. Ellis, born 1833, married Robert W. Oldfield April 24th, 1856. They are farmers near Rome, Jeff. Co., Ill. Mr. Oldfield served three years a Union soldier against the great Rebellion. Of their children, Effie Jane was born 1857; Elbert, 1859; William T., 1860; Robert C., 1862; Lucius Ellis, 1866; Frank C., 1868.

Chester Coburn Ellis, born 1839, was a soldier and was killed by the rebels near Atlanta, Ga., Sept. 2nd, 1864. He was a remarkably bright and promising young man. His death was a great grief to his parents, he being their only son. Such is the fate of war.

Polly Ellis, born 1843, married John R. Cunningham, Jan. 29th, 1866. Their children are: Carrie May, Lester Ellis, Maude Bell, Silas Arthur, Theodore Berthold, Louie Bryson, and an infant. Mr. C. was three years a Union soldier. They live near Rome, Jeff. Co., Ill.

(374.) **LOIS ELLIS,** youngest child of Stephen Ellis, was born in Sempronius, Oct. 10th, 1814. She married John Jeffery, in Fayette Co., Ind., in 1835. She had one child, Jane, who married a Mr. Jones. Mrs. Jeffrey was a member of the Christian Church.

Children of Moses Ellis (123), of Fayette Co., Ind., and their
husbands and wives.   Grandchildren of Benjamin,
Sr. (22).   Great-grandchildren of Reuben (4),
and great-great-grandchildren of
Richard of Ashfield.
From 380 to 390.

(380.) LAURA ELLIS, eldest child of Moses Ellis,
was born in Sempronius, N. Y., in 1806. She was about
twelve years of age when her parents moved to North
Bend, Ohio, and about twenty-one when they all settled in
Fayette Co., Ind., near Connersville.   March 11th, 1828,
she married Josiah Sutton, a physician.   They lived in
Madison Co., Ind., where they both died.   They were
members of the Christian Church.   She was a very intelligent woman with a remarkable memory.   Mr. Sutton died
in 1879, aged 80 years.   His wife died in 1881.   They had
two children, Elsie and Hester Ann Sutton.

(382.) MARY JUDD ELLIS, second daughter of
Moses Ellis, was born in Sempronius, N. Y., 1808.   About
1830 she married Sutherland Gard, a farmer and miller.
He was born in 1809.   They were members of the
Christian Church.   Mr. Gard died in 1841, in or near
Connersville, Ind.   They had five children, Lucetta, born
1831, died 1850; Samantha, 1833; Harriet, 1835; Adeline,
1838; and Henry, 1840.

About 1843, Mrs. Mary J. Ellis Gard married for her
second husband Mr. James James, a farmer.   Mr. James
was born in North Carolina.   He was a member of the
Christian Church.   Mr. James and family moved to Illinois
in 1859.   He died in 1867, in Marion Co., Ill.   In 1882
Mrs. James went to Waterville, Minnesota, to live with a
daughter and 'died there in April, 1886.   Mr. and Mrs.
James had two children, Laura Ann, born 1844, died 1861;
and Moses 1847.

(384.) LEWIS ELLIS, only son of Moses Elllis, was
born in Sempronius, N. Y., April 11th, 1811.   Dec. 30th,
1832, he was married in Fayette Co., Ind., to Samantha
Thomas.   She was born in Tompkins Co., N. Y., Dec. 3rd,

1811. They both now reside on a farm near Connersville, Ind., and have had 16 children.

Caroline Ellis, their eldest, was born Nov. 11th, 1833. She married Charles R. Williams, Aug. 2nd, 1851. They have one daughter Hattie.

Lucy, born June 5th, 1835, married J. A. Leffingwell, Oct. 2nd, 1853.

Oliver B., born Aug. 2nd, 1836, died Aug. 24th, 1837.

Elvin, born March 17th, 1838, died July 29th, 1839.

Jasper D., born Nov. 15th, 1839, died Oct. 26th, 1850, killed by a horse running away.

Emma, born Jan. 29th, 1841, died April 7th, 1841.

Minor, born Jan. 25th, 1842, died Sept. 21st, 1863, of camp diarrhœa at New Orleans. He was a Union soldier.

Melvin, born Nov. 10th, 1843, married Harriet King, May 16th, 1866. She was a daughter of Benjamin King, born in Aug. 1843, and raised in Fayette Co., Ind. They have two children, Lewis, born June 1868, and Irene, born Sept., 1870. Mr. Ellis and wife are Baptists.

Nancy, born April 25th, 1845, died Feb. 22nd, 1870.

Adaline and Angeline, born Aug. 12th, 1846. The first died Oct. 1st, 1861, and the last Dec. 16th, 1858.

Mary, born Nov. 6th, 1848, died Nov. 20th, 1848.

Eliza, born April 10th, 1850, married John Payne, Jan. 7th, 1870. Mr. Payne was born in Fayette Co., Oct. 30th, 1842. He was a son of Thomas T. and Eleanor Rees Payne. Mr. and Mrs. John Payne have seven children, Wm. T., Edwin C., Lucia, Charles E., Daisy, Edna and Mamie.

Ellen, born Oct. 16th, 1852.

Edwin W., born Oct. 16th, 1852, married Ada S. Budd, Oct. 2nd, 1883. He lived with his father on the farm until 1880, when he began the study of medicine. Previous to this he had studied surveying and was elected county surveyor several terms. He graduated in medicine at the college in Indianapolis in 1882, and began practice at Connersville. In 1883 he settled at Falmouth, Fayette Co., Ind., where he took the practice of his preceptor, Dr. Jacob Redding, and where he now resides. His wife was a daughter of Samuel O. Budd, a prominent man of Muncie, Ind. Dr. and Mrs. Ellis have one child, Ivy, born Aug. 22nd, 1884.

Hewett T., born Aug. 29th, 1854, married Ida Zellar, Feb. 8th, 1882. She was born in Connersville, July 6th, 1857. They have one child, Zellar, born Jan. 9th, 1883. Mr. Ellis is in the livery business in Connersville.

(386.) ELIZA ANN ELLIS, daugher of Moses, was born in Sempronius, N. Y., in 1813. She married William Cole, in Fayette Co., Ind., 1834. Mr. Cole was a shoe-maker. Himself and wife were members of the Christian Church. They moved to Madison Co., Ind., where Mrs. Cole died in 1842. She had three children, Angeline, Lewis E. and Laura.

In 1844 Mr. Cole married Matilda Floyd, and removed to Mason Co., Ill., where he now lives.

(388.) HESTER ANN ELLIS, daughter of Moses Ellis, was born in Sempronius, N. Y., April 24th, 1816. In 1835 she married Philander Thomas in Fayette Co., Ind. Mr. Thomas was a farmer and a member of the Christian Church. He was born in Tompkins Co., N. Y., in 1811, and died in Feb., 1865, at Centralia, Ill., where his widow and several children now reside. They had eight children : Leroy, born 1836; Mary, 1839; Ann, 1841; Lewis, 1844, died 1863; Oliver H., 1849; Avery C., 1852; Irvin, 1855 and Marshall, 1856.

Oliver H. Thomas is a dentist and lives in Pendleton, Ind.

(390.) ANNIE S. ELLIS, youngest child of Moses Ellis, was born at North Bend, Ohio, in 1822. She married Jonathan Ward and had two children—Ellen and Edwin. Mr. Ward was a farmer and a Baptist. Mrs. Ward died in 1849. Mr. Ward married for his second wife Minerva Robinson, a daughter of Mehitable Ellis Robinson, (364). Mr. Ward was a Union soldier, a brave, noble and highly respected man.

Children of Benjamin Ellis, Jr. (126), of Groton, Cayuga Co.,
N. Y., and their wives and husbands. Grandchildren of Benjamin, Sr. (22). Great-grandchildren of Reuben, (4) and great-great-
grandchildren of Richard Ellis,
of Ashfield. From 392
to 399.

(**392.**) **RHODA ELLIS**, eldest daughter of Benjamin Ellis, Jr., was born in Sempronius, N. Y., Oct. 30th, 1813. She died July 9th, 1833. Unmarried.

(**392.**) **MYRON ELLIS**, eldest son of Benjamin Ellis, Jr., was born in Sempronius, Aug. 20th, 1817, and died in Groton, N. Y., Feb. 13th, 1858. He was a miller by trade and a lawyer by profession and practiced law the latter years of his life. He was a man of uncommon memory and intelligence. His first wife was a Miss Zurilda Curtis, by whom he had four children, Augustus, Benjamin E., Cassius M. and Lycurgus. Mrs. Ellis died in 1848, and Mr. Ellis married for his second wife Miss Nancy Dunks and four more children were born, Rhoda, Martha, Helen and Emma. After Mr. Ellis' death, his widow married a Mr. Hubart, and they now live in Locke, N. Y. About 1843 Mr. Myron Ellis and his first wife moved to the Fox River country in Illinois, where Mrs. Ellis died at Aurora. Soon after Mr. Ellis married his second wife, they returned to Groton, N. Y.; this was in 1851.

Of Mr. Ellis' children, Augustus Ellis went west many years ago, and no further report of him is given.

Benjamin Eber Ellis, was born in Owasco, Cayuga Co., N. Y., Nov. 21st, 1839. In 1859 he returned to Illinois, where he has since resided. He married Eliza J. Felts, at Carbondale, Illinois, May 20th, 1869. Mrs. Ellis was born Aug. 5th, 1850. She was a daughter of George W., and Rebecca Ellis Felts. (Rebecca Ellis was a daughter of Arthur Ellis, of Belleville, Ill. Her brothers and sisters were: Maria, Francis, Jane, Thomas, George, Albert and Edward. It does not appear that these Ellises are descendants of Richard Ellis of Ashfield, Mass.) Benjamin Eber Ellis and wife have four children: Emma, born 1872; Edgar, 1875; Albert, 1881; and Franklin, 1883.

Cassius M. Ellis, son of Myron, is a farmer at Red-House, Cattaraugus Co., N. Y. He was a Union soldier, and taken prisoner at Petersburg, Va., June 17th, 1864, and was conveyed to Andersonville, Ga., that infamous prison where thousands of Union soldiers were confined and starved to death. Here he found his brother Lycurgus Ellis who had arrived there two days previously. Mr. Cassius Ellis, after a few months escaped from Andersonville, and was in the swamps of South Carolina for thirty days. After over 200 miles travel he reached the blockade squadron off Charleston, and was transferred to New York City, where he was in hospital for some time.

Lycurgus Ellis was a Union soldier, and a prisoner at Andersonville, Ga., as stated above. He was stripped of his clothing, blankets and cooking utensils, and although at first in excellent health was quickly reduced by the starvation practiced on all Union prisoners. In the latter part of August he was attacked with fever, and died on Sept. 7th, 1864. He was a very bright and promising young man, ever true to virtue and honor, and was greatly beloved by all who knew him.

Of Mr. Myron Ellis' children, by his second wife Nancy Dunks, Rhoda married Charles Niles, and they live in Locke, Cayuga Co., N. Y. Helen married Mr. Maine, and they live at Cortland, N. Y.

(395.) **LEWIS R. ELLIS,** son of Benjamin, Jr., was born in Sempronius, June 5th, 1822. He learned the miller's trade with his father and is engaged in that business at North Rose, Wayne Co., N. Y., where he resides. In early life he was a Methodist minister, but gave up preaching several years ago. He married Elizabeth Yale of Homer, N. Y., and they have two children : Alida and Albert.

(397.) **AMANDA M. ELLIS,** daughter of Benjamin, Jr., was born in Sempronius, Aug. 11th, 1826. She married Mr. Filander H. Robinson May 13th, 1849. Mr. Robinson is a miller and resides in Groton, N. Y. He is proprietor

211

of the "Dew Drop Mills." He was born in Virgil, Cortland Co., N. Y., in 1821. They have had two children: Edmund E. and Nathan Lavere.

Edmund Ellis Robinson was born in Groton, Sept. 22nd, 1851. He is married and has three children. He resides at Ithaca, N. Y. He has been train dispatcher for the Lehigh Valley Railroad many years, and is also chief of the fire department of Ithaca. He married Alice Wyckoff at Moravia, N. Y., Oct. 3d, 1876. She was born at Springport, Cayuga Co., N. Y., May 17th, 1857. Their children are Winnifred, born 1879; Frederick, 1881; N. Lavere, 1883. All born in Ithaca.

Nathan Lavere Robinson was born in Groton, June 16th, 1856. He died June 23rd, 1861.

(399.) **NATHAN H. ELLIS**, youngest child of Benjamin Ellis of Groton, was born Oct. 9th, 1834. He is a miller, and run the mills at Ludlowville, Cayuga Co., for many years. He now owns and runs the "Old Red Mills" at Owego, N. Y., where he resides. He married Miss Sarah Bolles in Utica, N. Y., in 1867. She was born in Litchfield, Conn., in 1833. She was a daughter of John Bolles. Mr. and Mrs. Ellis have one daughter, Edna, born 1868.

Children of Reuben Ellis (128), of Chautauqua Co., N. Y., and their wives and husbands. Grandchildren of Benjamin Sr. (22.) Great-grandchildren of Reuben (4), and great-great-grandchildren of Richard Ellis, of Ashfield.
From Nos. 401 to 420.

(401.) **OLIVET ELLIS**, eldest son of Reuben, was born in Cayuga Co., N. Y., in 1812. March 3rd, 1839, he married Almira Powers, and they now live in Harmony township, (Panama P. O.), Chautauqua Co., N. Y. Mr. Ellis is a farmer. They have two children, Eveline C., born 1840, and Adelaide R., born 1845. The latter lives in Rochester, N. Y.

(403.) HENRY K. ELLIS, second son of Reuben, was born in Cayuga Co. in 1813. He married Eliza Acker in 1837. He was a farmer, and a Baptist. He died in Murray, Orleans Co., in 1853, leaving a son, Henry R., and four daughters.

(407.) DANIEL ELLIS, third son of Reuben, was born in Cayuga Co., N. Y., in 1817. April 19th, 1843, he married Philinda L. Adams and settled on a farm of 116 acres in Panama, Chautauqua Co., N. Y. They are Baptists in religious belief. They have two sons, the eldest, Francis A. Ellis, is on a farm of his own near Panama. Their son Newton D. Ellis has been an invalid all his life. Mr. Daniel Ellis is a deacon in the Baptist church and believes in living his religion every day in the year. When two years of age his parents moved from Cayuga Co. to Orleans Co., and when he was thirteen years of age they settled in Clymer, Chautauqua Co. Mrs. Philinda Ellis died March 7, 1887.

(409) EDMUND ELLIS, fourth son of Reuben, was born June 28th, 1819. He married Roxana Fay, Sept. 18th, 1842. They had five children. Mr. Ellis was a farmer in Portland, Chautauqua Co. He was a Baptist. He died Oct. 6th, 1857. His children were Hollis Fay, Henry Reuben, Lucien Elijah, Charles Edmund and Lillie Phebe.

Henry R. Ellis, born 1846, resides in Detroit, Mich. He is a physician.

Lucien E. Ellis, born 1850, lives in Detroit. He is a physician and surgeon of eminence. His home is on Welch avenue in the western part of Detroit.

Lillie Phebe Ellis, born 1856, now resides with her mother and brother Henry on Maybury avenue, Detroit. They are all very highly respected people.

Mr. Edmund Ellis died Oct. 6th, 1857, in Portland, N. Y.

(411.) LOIS E. ELLIS, daughter of Reuben, was born in 1821. She married William R. Davis and had four children, the first three born in Panama, N. Y., and the last in Wisconsin, near Winona, where they lived many years. Mrs. Davis died in 1881.

(413.) **LYDIA E. ELLIS** was born in 1824. She married Horatio R. Palmer Jan. 15th, 1851, and they lived in Chautauqua, N. Y., for a time, when they removed to Bradtville, Grant Co., Wisconsin, where Mrs. Palmer died in 1862 and Mr. Palmer in 1864. They had four children, Almarion S., Emeline B., Alfred S. and Martin. The last two died young.

Almarion S. Palmer, born 1852, married Lydia Luce in 1878 in Fennimore, Wis. They had one child.

Emeline B. Palmer, was born 1854, married Edson H. Hoyt Aug. 13th, 1876, at Clymer, Chautauqua Co., N. Y., where they now live on a farm. They have two children, Arthur H. and Effie Hoyt.

Mr. Horatio R. Palmer was a tanner and currier. He enlisted in the Union army in 1863 and died the next year of disease in the service.

(415.) **EDWIN M. ELLIS** was born in Orleans Co., N. Y., in 1825. He married Diana Green Sept. 16th, 1846, and they now reside at Lovell's Station, Erie Co., Pa. They have had six children, five of whom are now living. (See page 49.) Mr. Ellis is a mechanic. He is a Baptist.

(417.) **ELIZABETH ELLIS** married Willis Tullar, July 4th, 1849. Both died childless.

(418.) **REUBEN ERASTUS ELLIS**, son of Reuben, was born in Clymer, N. Y., May 15th, 1832. He married Helen Freeman Sept. 24th, 1854. Their children are, Ida E., George Elmer and Willie Alton Ellis. They all reside in Westfield, Chautauqua Co., N. Y.

(420.) **ALFRED O. ELLIS**, youngest child of Reuben, of Chautauqua Co., N. Y., was born Oct. 17th, 1835. He married Helen M. Skidmore in 1858. He was a resident of Portland, Chautauqua Co., N. Y., and was a mechanic and builder. He was accidentally killed on the railroad near Brocton, N. Y., in 1885. He was a prominent member of the Baptist church at West Portland, Chautauqua Co. He was a first-lieutenant in the 112th N. Y. Regiment, a brave soldier and an estimable citizen of genial manner and noble qualities. He had seven children. (See names on page 50.)

Children of Abel West Ellis (136), of Ripley, Chautauqua
Co., N. Y., and their wives and husbands. Grandchildren of Jonathan (26), great-grandchildren of Reuben (4), and
great-great-grandchildren of Richard Ellis, of Ashfield.
From 444 to 453.

(444.) VAN R. ELLIS, eldest son of Abel West Ellis,
was born in Allegany Co., N. Y., April 24, 1833. In 1836
his father settled in Ripley, Chautauqua Co. He died in
Memphis, Tenn., Dec. 19th, 1877. His widow, Mrs.
Laura Ellis, and two children were living in Memphis at last
accounts.

(447.) CYRUS ELLIS, son of Abel West Ellis, was
born Dec. 7th, 1837, in Ripley, Chautauqua Co., where he
now resides on a farm. He married Jennie S. Hayes, at
Painesville, Ohio, Dec. 16th, 1874. They have two children, Fred. H., born July 25th, 1876, and Emma Maude,
born June 15th, 1878.

(449.) AMARILLA ELLIS was born in Ripley, Feb.
5th, 1839. She died Dec. 20th, 1858, of brain fever, just as
she was about to graduate at the Westfield Academy.

(451.) SARAH J. ELLIS was born in Ripley, Sept.
28th, 1841. She married George D. Willobee in 1867.
They removed to Cedar Run, Grand Traverse Co., Mich.,
where she died April 19th, 1884, leaving five children.

(453.) MARY ANN ELLIS, youngest child of Abel
West Ellis, was born in Ripley, Oct. 15th, 1843. She married Daniel Buckner, in Westfield, Chautauqua Co., Jan.
19th, 1875, and has one daughter, Nellie M. They reside at
Crowland, Ontario, Canada.

Children of John Allis Ellis (138), of Conneaut, Ohio, and their wives and husbands. Grandchildren of Jonathan (26), great-grandchildren of Reuben (4), and great-great-grandchildren of Richard Ellis, of Ashfield. From 455 to 465.

(455.) WILLIAM AVERY ELLIS was born in Ripley, Chautauqua Co., N. Y., Dec. 22nd, 1833. He married Maria Holmes, Dec. 24th, 1856. She was a daughter of George and Maria Smith Holmes, who came from England just before the birth of their daughter Maria. They settled in Saybrook, near Ashtabula, Ohio. Mrs. Holmes died in 1866. Mr. Holmes still lives on the farm he purchased in 1837. Mr. Ellis settled in Ashtabula, where he carried on for twenty-two years a plow handle factory. In April, 1886, he disposed of this and went to Chattanooga, Tenn., where he purchased an interest in a furniture establishment and where he now resides.*

Mr. Ellis has five children, Hattie Manella, born 1857, was married in Ashtabula Nov. 22nd, 1883, to Henry Elias Smith, of Conneaut. They have one daughter, Florence Manella Smith, born April 3rd, 1885, and a son, William Ellis Smith, born Dec. 31st, 1886.

Fannie F., born 1861, is a teacher in the Union school in Ashtabula.

Minnie M., born 1866, is a teacher in Plymouth, Ohio.

William W. and Amy F. live with their parents.

(457.) ORSON H. ELLIS was born Nov. 8th, 1835. He married Elizabeth Woodward July 6th, 1856. He resides in Conneaut, Ohio. They have had two children, Jennie and John Frank Ellis. Jennie died several years ago.

(459.) MARY JANE ELLIS was born Dec. 31st, 1837, in Ripley, N. Y. She married Robert Stewart in 1862. She died May 8th, 1865.

---

*He writes under date of Dec. 21st, 1886, " that on the 6th inst., his father, John A. Ellis (138), of Conneaut, Ohio, walked to the post office, about one mile, and while there was stricken with apoplexy and died at once. That morning he was feeling more jocular and lively than usual." The latter is a peculiarity, often noticed in cases of the sudden departure of good people to the other life. It seems as if the heavens opened and the angels were waiting to receive and welcome their kind to the happy shores of eternity.

(461.) **JOHN D. ELLIS** was born Nov. 19th, 1842, in Conneaut, Ohio. He married Mary Jane Bruce Dec. 23rd, 1863, at Conneaut, Ohio. Her father was Alanson Bruce, of Springfield, Pa., and her mother Sarah Sargeant Bruce. Mr. Ellis' children are Mary, Loretta, Edith, Bertha and John Alanson. Mr. Ellis is a machinist and runs a steam pump of the railroad near Conneaut.

(463.) **JULIA FRANCES ELLIS** was born Oct. 19th, 1845. She married William B. Cole and they now live in Jackson, Tenn. They have one child living, Archie C. Cole, born 1875 in Erie, Pa.

(465.) **SARAH ALICE ELLIS**, youngest child of John A. Ellis, was born in Conneaut, Ohio, Feb. 17th, 1850. She married John H. Hart in Conneaut May 10th, 1871. They now live in Central City, Nebraska. Mr. Hart was born Aug. 5th, 1844, at North East, Erie Co., Pa. Their children are, Bertrand Ellis, born 1872, Genevieve 1874, Pearl M. 1877, and Grace Ellen 1880.

Children of Elder Asaph Chilson Ellis (146), of Clearfield Co., Pa., and their wives and husbands. Grandchildren of Dea. Richard Ellis, (29), of Ellisburg, Pa. Great-grandchildren of Reuben (4), and great-greatgrandchildren of Richard Ellis, of Ashfield. See No. 482, page 29.

(482.) **CHARLES ELLIS**, was born in Delmar, Tioga Co., Pa., Jan. 15th, 1815. He now lives at Stuart, Holt Co., Nebraska. He is a farmer and unmarried. He was the eldest son of Asaph Chilson Ellis (146.) The latter was named after his mother's father, Asaph Chilson, of Conway, Mass.

HORACE ELLIS, son of Asaph, was born at Delmar Nov. 24, 1817, and died in 1822.

RICHARD SPENCER ELLIS, son of Asaph, was born Sept. 17, 1821, at Delmar. He now resides at Mahaffey,

Clearfield Co., Pa. He married Julia Ann Avery, a daughter of Elder Benjamin G. Avery (see page 149,) in 1839. They have seven children. Horace A. born 1840. He was a Union soldier, was twice wounded and was one of thirty-seven to whom Congress gave a medal for· special bravery. He was a Methodist in religion. He died in Wisconsin unmarried.

Asaph A., born Aug. 11th, 1843, was a soldier all through the Rebellion. He married Hannah McCartney and had three children. He went to Wisconsin, where he died in 1870 of consumption contracted in the army. He was a Methodist.

Amanda was born in June, 1845, and is married to Samuel Markley and they live at Ostend, Clearfield Co., Pa. Mr. M. is a farmer, was a soldier, and is a Methodist. They have seven children.

John was born in June, 1847. He was a soldier and was killed at Fort Stevens in 1864.

Warren B. was born in May, 1849, is married and lives at Mahaffey, Pa.

Maria was born in March, 1851, married P. R. Miller, a farmer at Decker's Point, Indiana Co., Pa.

Deroy was born about 1860, lives with his parents.

CHAUNCY A. ELLIS was born Nov. 30th, 1821, at Delmar. He was a soldier, wounded, and draws a pension. He married Sarah Ann Bell, daughter of Maj. James R. Bell, and had seven children, of whom four are now living. They were Baptists. Mrs. Ellis died May 5th, 1886. She was born Dec. 1st, 1825. Mr. Ellis now lives with his son-in-law Samuel Stearns, at Purchase Line, Indiana Co., Pa.

The children of Chauncy A. Ellis were Louisa, born 1849, Orlando S. 1851, Rebecca A. 1852, Sarah Lucy 1855, died the same year. Hannah E. 1856, John C. 1858, died 1882. Emily A. 1860, died 1880. Mr. Ellis served nearly three years in the late war and was severely wounded, for which he receives a pension. He is a carpenter by trade. He is a member of the Baptist church.

MOSES E. ELLIS, son of Asaph, was born Dec. 6th, 1823, at Delmar, and died in 1845. He was a licensed Baptist minister, and a very bright and promising young man.

HARRIET AMANDA ELLIS, daughter of Asaph, was born March 5th, 1826, at Wellsboro, Pa., where her father was at that time living and teaching in the academy. She married Samuel Sunderlin Dec. 18th, 1843. Mr. S. was a grandson of Sergeant Samuel Sunderlin, of the Vermont Rangers in the Revolutionary war. They live at Meig's Mills, Clearfield Co. They have had thirteen children, all living but one. Mr. and Mrs. S. are Methodists and farmers.

LUCY ELIZA ELLIS was born Sept. 9th, 1828, at Wellsboro. She married Charles Kingsbury and lives in Stuart, Nebraska. They have five children. Mr. K. owns a large farm. They are Baptists.

ORLANDO AARON ELLIS, son of Asaph C., was born near Tioga village, Pa., Feb. 14th, 1831. When four years of age his parents moved to Allegany Co., N. Y., and about a year thereafter moved on a raft down the Allegany river to Sharpsburg, Pa., a few miles above Pittsburg. A few months later they settled in Bell Township, Clearfield Co., Pa. This was Nov. 5th, 1835. They settled on a farm of 500 acres of wild pine and hemlock land. Their nearest neighbor was one and a half miles away, and they passed through many hardships. The nearest store was sixteen miles distant, and the school house four miles off.

Mr. Ellis' mother, Amanda Spencer Ellis, was a graduate of a High school in Hartford, Conn., and took great pains to train and educate her children. The main occupation consisted in clearing the farm and making lumber, which was rafted down the Susquehanna river to market. The streams were well supplied with fish and the forests with bears, deer, panthers, turkeys and other game in abundance. In 1843 Mr. Asaph C. Ellis built a saw mill on the Susquehanna.

Mr. Asaph C. Ellis was a very enterprising man, just fitted for his day. Like many of the Ellises of those times he was ever pushing out into some new venture.

In April, 1844, Mrs. Amanda Ellis died, in the forty-seventh year of her age, leaving a large family. She was an ardent Christian woman of uncommon virtues and talent. It is said that she was never known to be angry. She was married to Mr. Ellis April 7th, 1813. In December, 1846, Mr. Asaph C. Ellis married Mrs. Elizabeth Fairbanks, of East Mahoning, Indiana Co., Pa. She was a daughter of Ezra Warner, of New Lebanon, N. Y. She was an estimable woman. She was a Baptist. Mr. Asaph C. Ellis died April 30th, 1853, aged about 70 years. He was a deacon in the Baptist church and held a license to preach. He was an active, earnest Christian, and a scholarly man and a justice over fourteen years. His last wife died in 1855.

Mr. Orlando A. Ellis was married Sept. 30th, 1855, to Louisa Lawrence, in Clearfield Co. She was 15 years of age and her husband 24 when they embarked on the ship of matrimony. They have had eight children.

Lucy Marie, born 1856, died 1857.

Ira Chauncy, born 1858. He is a wagon and carriage maker in Marion. He married Mary Cramer.

Julia Ann Ellis, born 1860, married John Barr and had four children.

Ida May Ellis, born 1862, died 1877.

Olmer Ripley Ellis, born 1866; is a wagon and carriage maker, working with his brother Ira, in Marion, Indiana Co., Pa.

Hattie Jane Ellis, born 1868. Is a graduate of the Dayton High school.

Charles Francis Ellis, born 1872. Will graduate at the above school in 1888.

Harry McGregor Ellis, born 1876; lives at home.

Mr. Orlando A. Ellis was a Union soldier in Co. A, 61st Regt. Pa. Vol. He enlisted in Aug. 1861. He served his country well and faithfully and was wounded three times. He was in the battles of Fair Oaks, Chantilly, Antietam, Williamsport, Fredericksburg, Gettysburg and the Wilderness. He lost his right arm from a gunshot wound. He has been a town constable for 14 years and deputy sheriff for six years in Indiana Co., and for one term assistant sergeant-at-arms of the house of representatives at Harrisburg, the State capital.

Mr. Ellis has been a member of the Methodist church 30 years. He now resides at Marion, (Brady P. O.), Indiana Co., Pa.

PLINY POWERS ELLIS, son of Asaph C., was born near Tioga, Pa., July 14th, 1833. He was a soldier, was severely wounded at the second battle of Bull Run, Va., and lay on the field eight days before being cared for. He was discharged but re-enlisted and wounded again. He draws a pension. He is married ; is a farmer in Bloomer, Chippewa Co., Wis.. Is a Universalist in religious belief.

HANNAH JULIA ELLIS was born July 13th, 1836, in Clearfield Co., Pa. She married Daniel W. Fairbanks, who enlisted, was taken prisoner and starved to death in a rebel prison. His widow married Dec. 10th, 1870, Samuel Barker, an engineer. They are Methodists. They live in Sykesville, Jefferson Co., Pa. They have one child, Richard E., now living.

URIAH SPENCER ELLIS, child of Asaph C. and Amanda Spencer Ellis, was born in Clearfield Co., Pa., Dec. 4th, 1839, and died in 1841.

ASAPH CHILSON ELLIS, Jr., was born in Clearfield Co., Pa., Sept. 7th, 1842. He died in July, 1851.

Children of Rev. Consider Ellis (152), of Ellisburg, Pa., and
their wives and husband. Grandchildren of Richard (29), great-grandchildren of Reuben
(4), and great-great-grandchildren of
Richard Ellis of Ashfield.

(500) GEORGE ELLIS, eldest son of Elder Consider
Ellis, and Mary Lovell Ellis, his wife, was born near Ellisburg, Pa., in 1823. In 1837 he removed with his parents to
the town of Great Valley, Cattaraugus Co., N. Y., where
his father engaged in farming and milling until 1844, when
they removed to Ellisburg, Pa., where his father died in
1866 and where his mother now lives at an advanced age.

Mr. Ellis married Rebecca Rice and they have had eight
children, (see page 52). They lived at Stone Dam, Allegany
Co., N. Y.

PRUDENCE ELLIS, daughter of Elder Consider Ellis,
was born in 1825. She married Samuel G. Rouse and they
now reside at Ellisburg, Pa. They have no children. Mr.
Rouse's mother (153), now 83 years, lives with Mr.

JOHN L. ELLIS, second son of Elder Consider Ellis,
was born near Ellisburg, Pa., March 19, 1833. He married
Mrs. Jane A. Wilson, of Leroy, Minn., in 1862. Her
maiden name was Needham. Her father, Horace C.
Needham, was a prominent man in Vermont. He died
when Mrs. Ellis was young. Mr. Ellis and family live at
Red Bird, Nebraska. He is a farmer. He has two sons,
Orson B., born April 5, 1863, in Osage, Mitchell Co., Iowa.
Fred H. was born in Osage, June 23, 1865. He married
Miss Ada S. France, of Runningwater, Dakota, in 1884.
They have one son, Clifford, born in Feb. 1885.

(506.) **RALPH ELLIS** was born at Tioga, Pa., in 1829. In 1853 he crossed the plains to California where he engaged for a time in mining. In 1855 he was treasurer and messenger for the banking house of Everts, Wilson & Co. In 1857 he was elected clerk of Sierra Co., Cal. In 1861 he settled in Napa valley and in 1865 was elected sheriff of Napa county; since the expiration of this term of office he has been engaged mostly in the wheat and milling trade. He is also editor and manager, in connection with his son, of the "Lodi Sentinel," the leading newspaper in the great San Joaquin valley.

Mr. Ellis married in Benicia, Cal., in 1858, Caroline W. Evarts, a daughter of Dr. T. C. Evarts from Indiana, who settled in California in 1856 where he died in 1865. Mrs. Ellis was born at Laporte, Ind., in 1838. Their children are, Wilson R., born 1859; Carrie C., 1861; Frank E., 1864; Henry F., 1866 and Maggie M., 1874.

Wilson R. Ellis married Alice Davis in California in 1884. They have one son, Ralph F., born in 1885. Mr. Ellis is manager of the "Sentinel."

Carrie C. Ellis married Prof. Freeman B. Mills in Aug., 1885.

(508.) **JOHN ELLIS**, son of Elder John Ellis of Ellicottville, N. Y., was born in Tioga, Pa., and died unmarried in Ellicottville, N. Y., Oct. 15, 1847.

(509.) **WILLIAM F. ELLIS**, son of Elder John Ellis, died leaving two children, Fred and Lizzie, both living in California. Fred Ellis is a mill owner and rancher and resides at Yountville, Napa Co.

William F. Ellis and wife both died the same night of cholera, in Cincinnati, Ohio, about 1852. Their children were then brought to Ellicottville, N. Y., and soon after their uncle, Ralph, took them to California.

Lizzie Ellis married D. H. Berdine, a printer, and publisher of "Once a Week," a temperance journal. They reside at Stockton, Cal. They have one child, Carrie E., born in Ohio in 1860.

William F. Ellis' wife was `Matilda Berdine.

(511.) LUCINDA ELLIS was born in Pa. in 1820. She married Peter Berdine in 1840. They removed to Wisconsin where both died in 1881, leaving seven children.'

(513.) MARGARET ELLIS, daughter of Rev. John Ellis, was born at Big Meadows, Tioga Co., Pa., about 1821. While on a visit to her brother, William, at Cincinnati, she took a fever and died there at about 25 years of age.

Of Elder John Ellis (154), and his family, Mr. Arunah Ward, a lawyer at Ellicottville, N. Y. writes: " The family were old friends of mine and were very nice, respectable people, and had a good farm and mill property when the father, John Ellis, died."

Children of Elder Richard Ellis (158), and their wives. Grandchildren of Richard (29), of Ellisburg, Pa. Great-grandchildren of Reuben (4), and great-great-grandchildren of Richard Ellis, of Ashfield, Mass. From 522 to 528.

(522.) AMASA ELLIS was born in Tioga Co., Pa. Feb. 18, 1819. He married Martha Schoonover Sept. 29, 1849. She was born in Tioga Co., July 29, 1831. When Mr. Ellis was about seven years of age his father died and he thereafter lived with his uncle, David Ellis (160). Mr. Ellis has been a farmer until recently, owing to ill health, he has bought a home in Westfield, Tioga Co., Pa. In his early married life Mr. Ellis lived in the town of Willing, near

Belmont, Allegany Co., N. Y., where all their children were born. Mr. Ellis is a Baptist and very active in the church and Sunday school service. His children are Mary E., Delos, James D., Frank and Charles.

Mary E. Ellis was born Oct. 10, 1850. She married E. A. Buck, January 1st, 1871. They have three children, Emmer, Annie and Lula. Dèlos Ellis, born Sept. 13, 1853, married Hattie Bush Oct. 10, 1882. All now live in Westfield, Pa.

(524.) CONSIDER ELLIS was born in Shippen, Tioga Co., Pa., Oct. 20, 1820. He married Margaret Fortner in 1845. She was born in Tompkins Co., N. Y., in 1820. Forty years ago Mr. Ellis settled in Belmont, N. Y., on a fine farm which he carried on in connection with wagon making, which trade he had learned in early life. He was a very prosperous man and his farm was noted as being one of the best in Allegany Co. He was a very generous and open-hearted man and highly respected by all his towns-people. He died suddenly Aug. 3rd, 1886, leaving his wife and two daughters, Mrs. Brown of Belmont and Mrs. Fowler of Rochester.

(526.) SAMUEL G. ELLIS was born in Tioga Co. Pa., in 1822. He married Rosetta Canfield about 1844. She was raised in Tompkins Co., N. Y. They had two daughters, Eliza-Jane and Frances. They moved to Canada in 1849 where Mr. Ellis died the next year. Mrs. Ellis afterwards married a Mr. Lincoln and lived in Washington, D. C., at last accounts.

(528.) JOHN M. ELLIS, youngest child of Elder Richard Ellis was born in Tioga Co., Pa., Nov. 6th, 1825. He married Eliza Fortner, Feb. 25, 1852, at Ellisburg, Pa. She was born in 1827 in Independence, Allegany Co., N. Y. They are farmers and now live at Waverly, Beamer Co., Iowa. They have two children, Rosetta H., born in Independence, N. Y., March 28, 1853, died June 1st, 1881. Maggie E., born in Franklin, Iowa, May 15, 1857; married A. V. Viner, Jan. 31, 1883. They have one child, Zada May Viner, born at Waverly, June 24, 1884.

Children of David Ellis (160), of Tioga, Pa., and their Hus-
bands and Wives, Grandchildren of Richard (39),
Great - Grandchildren of Reuben (4) and
Great-Great-Grandchildren of Richard
Ellis of Ashfield. From 530 to 544.

(530.) **THANKFUL ELLIS,** eldest daughter of David
Ellis, was born in Shippen, Tioga Co., Pa., in 1820. She
married Charlton Phillips, Aug. 11th, 1838, in Shippen. Mr.
Phillips was born Feb. 27th, 1815. After their marriage they
moved to Westfield, Tioga Co., Pa., where they have lived
ever since. Mr. Phillips is a merchant miller in Westfield.
Forty years ago Mr. Phillips bought a farm which he cleared
up and on which he yet resides. He built a saw mill and
grist mill, hotel, stores and houses. Mr. and Mrs. Phillips
are active members of the Methodist church. They have
had eleven children.

Sylvester D. Phillips, born 1840, went into the army at
the outbreak of the Rebellion. He was captain in the
Bucktails, a celebrated regiment of Pennsylvania volunteers.
He was promoted to major and remained in the service until
the close of the war. He was married Oct. 22nd, 1865, to
Villa Thompson. Capt. Phillips died Dec. 6, 1886, from
disease contracted in the army, a victim of the Rebellion.

Rachel Phillips, born in Westfield, Sept. 11, 1842,
married Rush C. Doty in Westfield. Mr. Doty died
March 17th, 1868, after which his widow married James
Richtmyer of Moravia, N. Y., where they now reside on a
farm.

Alice Phillips, born Oct. 13th, 1844, was a successful
teacher, and at the age of 24 married C. D. Spafford, of
Moravia, N. Y., a farmer. They have one son.

Ellis D. Phillips, born March 18th, 1847, married Jennie
Closson. They have two children. He is a miller in
Westfield, Pa.

William D. Phillips, born Feb. 14th, 1849, married Ella
Broughton, Aug. 17th, 1885.

Delvin D. Phillips, born May 22nd, 1851. He was an engineer at Williamsport. He was accidently killed Sept. 8th,

1879, and was to have been married on the day he was buried.

Clarence and Clara Phillips were born Aug. 29th, 1855. Clarence is a miller, unmarried. Clara married O. A. Tremain, of Westfield, and they have two children.

Emma Philips, born Feb. 15th, 1859, married William Pease, of Westfield, Sept. 19th, 1885.

Eva Phillips, born Aug. 14th, 1862, died Feb. 8th, the next year.

Charles N. Phillips was born March 28th, 1867. All these Phillips' are highly respected and prosperous people. The father, Mr. Charlton Phillips, is a man of uncommon energy, probity and intelligence. He is said to be a descendant of Capt. John Phillips of Eastern Massachusetts. (See page 16.)

(532.) CHLOE ELLIS was born April 18th, 1822. She married Job Rexford March 3d, 1844. Mr. Rexford was born Jan. 23d, 1819, in Cortland Co., N. Y., and came to Pine Creek, Tioga Co., and engaged in manufacturing lumber and rafting it down the Susquehanna River to market. About 1877 he settled at Harrison Valley, Potter Co., Pa., where he died Feb. 23d, 1880. Mrs. Rexford is a Presbyterian, and a very bright and intelligent woman. She sends the writer an account of a visit to her grandfather, Richard Ellis (29) at Ellisburg, Pa., when she was quite young. " My oldest brother, a young lady cousin from Wellsboro, and myself, drove our own team over the country. It was very cold and we were nearly three days on the road. Grandfather was very much pleased to see us. He showed us about his house, took us to the saw mill and the grist mill, showed us the process of grinding grain into flour or feed, the water wheels and the improvements he intended soon to make, then took us to his hotel, which at that time was leased to another party. This same building stands there now, but improved and built around with other buildings. He introduced us as his grandchildren, who had come to see him for the first time. He showed us through the building, and when in the bar-room ordered made good glasses of 'sling,' as he said he wanted to drink to the health of his grand-children the first time they came to see him. How times have changed in these fifty years! But he was a true and righteous Christian man."[*]

Mrs. Rexford's children are Perry Emerson, born Feb. 22d, 1845, married to Clara Sweetland June 26th, 1870. They are both Baptists. Mr. Rexford is a farmer at Harrison Valley.

Nancy Orilla, born May 31st, 1848, married Capt. Jason W. Stevens May 1st, 1870, who was a soldier all through the war. Capt. Stevens carries on an extensive mercantile business in Harrison Valley.

Henry Gilbert, born Feb. 24th, 1852, died Dec. 20th, 1853.

Stella, born Oct. 15th, 1860, married Dr. E. J. Shaw, Jan. 1st, 1879. He died Feb. 12th, 1881. All of Mr. and Mrs. Rexford's children were born in Tioga Co., Pa.

(534.) **CHESTER ELLIS,** son of David Ellis, was born in Tioga Co., Pa., April 22d, 1823. He married Miss Chloe Blue in Wellsboro, Tioga Co., Pa., Sept. 25th, 1848. Mrs. Ellis was born in Tioga Co., August 29th, 1827. Mr. Ellis is a millwright and is now in Las Vegas, New Mexico. His children were all born in Tioga Co., Pa. They are :

Lawrence A. Ellis, born March 14th, 1849. He is an architect and builder, and resides at Laurel, Maryland, where he has constructed several of the largest and finest buildings in that part of the state. He married, June 3d, 1875, Sarah Elizabeth Curley, who was born July 9th, 1853. They have had three children : James C., born 1876, died the same year ; George Frederick, born 1878, and Norman R., born 1880.

---

[*]Wonder is often expressed that ministers and religious people cannot *now* use ardent spirits with the safety that they did a few generations ago. This is attributed, by some to the present *impurity* of liquor but it is not so. for the more pure whisky is, the more dangerous it is The true reason is that formerly religious people used liquors with the conscientious, although mistaken, belief that they were useful. but that from religious motives, they must be constantly on their guard, and restrain themselves from intoxication *Now*, all men of intelligence know that their use is vile and sinful and that to tamper with them is to sport with the devil. and when they do the good influences of heaven and the angels are withdrawn from them. Without these restraints drunkenness and insanity soon result.

Seymour David Ellis was born March 25th, 1851, in Shippen, Pa. He is a carpenter. Mr. Ellis lives in Wellsboro, Tioga Co., Pa. He married Aggie Chafee, of Greenville, Mercer Co., Pa. She was born Dec. 18th, 1860.

Simon W. Ellis, born at Westfield, Pa., June 1st, 1857. He is a carpenter and resides at Wellsboro.

Myra O. Ellis, born at Westfield, May 10th, 1866. She married Lee English, and they reside at English Mills, Lycoming Co., Pa.

Annie B. Ellis, born Feb. 9th, 1869, lives with her mother at Wellsboro.

(536.) JEFFERSON ELLIS was born June 13th, 1826. He married Lorena Chapel June 16th, 1850, in Shippen Township. Mr. Ellis died about 1877 in Wisconsin.

His children were Sarah, Ella and John.

(538.) MARIA ELLIS was born May 11th, 1828. She married John J. Miller Feb. 15th, 1849. Mrs. Miller died Feb. 21st, 1864. Her children were Katie, born Nov. 11th, 1849; Lillian Mary, Feb. 7th, 1852 ; Nellie Alphoretta, June 21st, 1857; Henry Maurice, July 18th, 1862, died the next year ; and Maria Bell Miller, Feb. 13th, 1864, died the same year.

The Millers live in Williamsport, Pa., at present.

(540.) HARRY ELLIS, born in 1831, in Tioga Co. He married Susan Schusler, Nov. 29th, 1857. They live at Mansfield, Tioga Co., Pa., where Mr. Ellis is engaged in carpentry and selling wind mills. Himself and wife are ardent Baptists. Mr. E. has been prominent in the church over twenty years, and for nine years at the head of the Sunday school.

They have had three children : Emma, born Dec. 8th, 1860 : Minna, born Nov. 13, 1862, died April 17th, 1865 ; Fred D., born Dec. 6th, 1864.

(542.) CRETIA ANN ELLIS, born Feb. 7th, 1836, married William Annesley Jan. 1st, 1855. Mr. Annesley was born April 24th, 1833. He died Oct. 5th, 1880. They had three children : Mary, Carrie and Henry. They live at Pike Mills, Potter Co., Pa.

(544.) **BAKER D. ELLIS** was born April 20th, 1838. He married Bertha Fay, of Detroit, Mich., April 23d, 1882. She was born Dec, 12th, 1860. They live at Hector, Potter Co., Pa. Mr. Ellis' younger brother, Seymour, born 1846, died in 1848.

Children of Harry Ellis (168), of Ellisburg, Pa., and their Wives, Grandchildren of Richard (29), Great-Grandchildren of Reuben (4), and Great-Great-Grandchildren of Richard Ellis of Ashfield. From 552 to 563.

(552.) **ADOLPHUS C. ELLIS** was born in Ellisburg, Pa., in 1837. He married Mary Hill and they have three children: Nettie, born 1864; Mary E., 1869; and Ella, 1874. They reside at Genesee Fork, Pa. He is a farmer. His daughter Nettie married June 1st, 1887, Mr. Seymour Alexander, a merchant of Genesee Fork.

(554.) **WILLIAM ELLIS** was born in 1838. He married Anna Donaldson and they have three children: Violet, born 1870; Harry F., 1873; and William M., 1876. He was a merchant in Ellisburg.

(556.) **RICHARD ELLIS**, son of Harry Ellis, was born in Ellisburg, Pa., Jan. 11th, 1840. He married Maggie Locke Jan. 1st, 1861. She was born Feb. 23d, 1846. Mr. Ellis is in the mercantile business in Ellisburg. He has aided the writer greatly in procuring statistics and information for this work.

Their only child Nora, born July 29th, 1870, died of congestion of the brain Oct. 6th, 1886. She was a student at the time in the High school at Lewisville, and was one of the brightest and most accomplished scholars in the institution. She was both lovely in character and in person, and her untimely death was a sad blow to her fond parents. Truly, " Death loves a shining mark." For the bereaved parents the strongest sympathy is felt wherever their daughter was known. While this was of no avail to turn aside the blow, it will, in time, assist in softening their sorrow. The dear one is but gone on before. Death has embalmed her in all her youthful loveliness. Age can never blanch her cheeks nor sorrow dim her eyes, and her memory will remain the dearest treasure in the broken family circle, and the reunion will surely come.

> The dear departed gone before
> To that unseen and silent shore,
> Sure, we shall meet as heretofore,
> Some summer morning.

(**558.**) **ORSON ELLIS** was born in Ellisburg, Pa. He married Inez Pye and she died in 1882. He is a merchant at Ellisburg.

(**560.**) **MARION ELLIS** born about 1843 in Ellisburg. He died unmarried.

(**561.**) **AMASA ELLIS,** son of Harry, was born in Ellisburg, Pa., Nov. 4th, 1848. He married Allie Donaldson and they have three children, Elizabeth, Mary and Donaldson. Mr. Ellis is in a hardware store in Wellsboro.

(**562.**) **GENNET ELLIS,** daughter of Harry, was born in Ellisburg, Jan. 19th, 1846. She died in 1861.

(**563.**) **ELLA ELLIS,** youngest child of Harry, was born in Ellisburg, Jan. 18th, 1851. She married John Simons, March 14th, 1876. Mr. Simons was born March 12th, 1853. Their daughter Katie was born Aug. 25th, 1878. They live in Ellisburg, Pa.

(**566.**) **ELVIRA ELLIS,** only child of Reuben Ellis (172), of Ellisburg, Pa., was born Feb. 23d, 1833. She married Charles Coats, a thriving farmer of Ellisburg, Pa., Jan. 31st, 1850. Their children are Frances E., Catherine E., Harriet A., Reuben E. and William H. Coats, all born in Ellisburg. Miss Frances E. Coats married Benjamin F. Bishop, a farmer. They had one son, born 1874.

Catherine E. Coats married Ira Bishop, a brother of B. F. Bishop. He is also a farmer.

Harriet A. Coats married R. A. Bradley, her second

husband. They live in New Mexico, where Mr. Bradley is engaged in mining. They have three children : Bertha I. Coy, born 1879 ; Irvin R., 1882, and Rena Ethel, 1882.

William H. Coats, born 1866, died Nov. 8th, 1886. He was a young man of unusual brightness. His last sickness and death was supposed to have been caused by the rupture of a blood-vessel in his brain. When it became apparent that his end was near, the members of the family were called in and he bade good-bye to each, thanked the doctor for coming to see him, and sent his best respects to the doctor's wife, who had been his teacher. He spoke at intervals of the great beauty and brightness all about him, and once said, " The golden chariot is coming." " I would like to live if I could, but it is *all right*." His last words were, " Good-bye, mother, I'm going to Heaven," and a few minutes later the Angel of Death released him from suffering.

So passed away this noble boy, of whom every one says, " He was always so good." And no wonder, for rare indeed are they who possess so great a degree of amiability.

> His daily prayer, far better understood
> In acts than words, was simply doing good.
> So calm, so constant was his rectitude,
> That by his loss alone we know its worth,
> And feel how true a man has walked with us on earth.

Children of William Ellis, Sr. (176), of Springfield, Erie Co., Pa., and their Wives and Husbands, Grandchildren of David Ellis, Sr. (32), Great-Grandchildren of Reuben (4), and Great-Great-Grand-children of Richard Ellis, of Ash-field, From 570 to 587.

(570) WILLIAM ELLIS, JR., was born in Ashfield, Mass., May 17th, 1810. At eight years of age he went with his parents to Springfield, Pa., where he lived until his death, Nov. 29th, 1865. He married Sarah Geer in Springfield Nov. 12th, 1840. They had four children: David, born 1841, died 1870; Jesse, 1843; Rhoda, 1847, died 1855, and Martha, born 1851.

(572) **CHARLES PERKINS ELLIS**, was born in Ashfield March 20th, 1812. He died in LaGrange, Wis., Jan. 22nd, 1881. When a young man he settled on a farm of 120 acres, in LaGrange. This was in 1842. When six years of age his parents removed from Ashfield to Springfield, Pa.

When eight years old, Charles was accustomed to take the light axe provided for that purpose and go regularly to the woods with his father and grandfather, to assist in clearing up the farm. Springfield township was a heavily wooded region, and at that time only partially cleared up. The settlers were poor, and the educational advantages afforded the youth were very limited. The principal qualification of a teacher was the ability to flog the large boys. Greased paper in place of glass gave ingress to light in the log school houses, and slabs served for seats and desks. Three months study per year—reading, writing and arithmetic—constituted a liberal education in that day and region. On reaching manhood Charles found employment in the pinery on the upper waters of the Alleghany river, and continued for several winters to work at logging—going down the streams in the spring with the rafts. It was his custom, on reaching St. Louis with the lumber, to walk across the country to Michigan, where he worked at farming and building through the summer. On one of the latter trips he purchased eighty acres of fine prairie and timber land in Cass County, Michigan, which he afterward traded for a team of horses and wagon, when he moved to Wisconsin. December 15th, 1839, he was married to Sarah Harris. She was born in Henderson, Jefferson County, New York, May 11th, 1816. Jeremiah and Priscilla (Cole) Harris, parents of Mrs. Ellis, were also early settlers in Springfield, having located there six years after the Ellises.

The former was a grandson of Anthony Harris, who was born in Richmond, New Hampshire, in 1836; Jeremiah was also born in Richmond. When Mr. and Mrs. Ellis settled in LaGrange there were about a dozen families in the town, and people half a dozen miles away were considered near neighbors. Their residence was on the north-east corner of section 21, and was always a home for travelers. At first it consisted of a small log house of one room. In addition to the single room below there was a loft which served as a sleeping room.

Mr. Ellis was reared under strict Baptist teachings, but became a believer in the doctrines of Universalism, to which he steadfastly adhered from the time he was thirty years old. His family and friends were assured by him just before his death that he had nothing to regret in this regard, or any other. In this faith he was accompanied through a long life of Christian charity by his faithful helpmeet. In the days of the Whig party he was a supporter of its political creed, and afterward of its successor, the Republican party. He was an active worker in its town and county conventions nearly all his life, and often served as a town officer. He never sought nor accepted any higher positions. He was town Treasurer in 1844, and was four times subsequently elected to that position; in 1845 he was elected Supervisor, and filled that office for eight terms. He was an active supporter of religious services, and his house was always a home for ministers of every sect. For many years, the only churches in the township (which he had helped to build) were owned by the Methodists, and it was largely owing to his efforts and influence that the church near his house was finished jointly by the Methodists and Universalists and dedicated as free to all Christian denominations. The following testimonial to his character is taken from an obituary, written by one of his neighbors:

"The writer of these lines has known the deceased for nearly 35 years, and for the greater portion of that time was privileged to enjoy his friendship. With loving reverence for his memory, he testifies to his manly virtues. He was a man of stainless character, of strict integrity and solid worth. In his social relations he was genial and pleasant, being possessed of that personal magnetism which wins friends, and of those fine qualities of heart which retain them. He was

a kind neighbor and a good citizen; a faithful husband and
indulgent parent. He was a man who always took the
keenest interest in all questions affecting the public good,
and his opinions of men and measures were broad and liberal. In religious matters he had clear and well-defined
views. He believed in the infinite love and compassion of
God, in the universal brotherhood of mankind, and in the
ultimate salvation of all men. There was no doubt in his
mind touching these things; hence, in the hour of death, he
was

> 'Sustained and soothed
> By an unfaltering trust, and approached the grave
> Like one who wraps the drapery of his couch
> About him and lies down to pleasant dreams.' "

Mr. Ellis improved his farm in a high degree and erected
thereon excellent buildings, where his widow and daughter
now reside.

Priscilla Rumina, the daughter of Charles P. Ellis, was
born in La Grange Jan. 28th, 1845. She married Mr. John
E. Menzie April 15th, 1871, and lives on the homestead.

James Alfred, eldest son of Charles P. Ellis, was born in
La Grange, April 15th, 1852. He married Eva Lucretia
Williams Feb. 8th, 1873, at Hebron, Wis. They live at
Whitewater, Wis. They have seven children: Cicero Guy,
born Oct. 31st, 1873; Julia Maud, Aug. 6th, 1875; Priscilla
May, Jan. 7th, 1877; Minnie Madge, July 28th, 1879;
Charles Williams, July 2d, 1880; James Horace, Nov. 12th,
1882, and William David, Sept. 2nd, 1885.

Mr. James A. Ellis is a fine specimen of manhood, six
feet one and one-half inches high, and weighing 190 pounds.
He has been engaged in school-teaching, and more lately in
the book and map trade in various sections of the country.
He is a practical printer and was engaged in journalism for
a time, and is now a member of the publishing firm of
Beers, Ellis & Co., of New York City. In religious and
political convictions he follows the precepts of his father.
His wife was a daughter of Horace and Olive (Delano)
Williams, of Vermont. Mrs. Ellis was born in Cold Spring,
Jefferson Co., Wis., Oct. 24th, 1855.

Charles Elliott Ellis, youngest son of Charles P., was born in La Grange, March 16th, 1859, and was reared on the home farm. Beside the home school, he attended the city school in Delevan for several months. With the exception of four winter terms of teaching, the balance of his life has been spent on the farm, and, up to the spring of 1883, on the old homestead. At the latter date he purchased 120 acres in Geneva township, near Elkhorn, which he is now engaged in tilling. May 15th, 1883, he married Clarissa M., daughter of Alexander H. and Teressa A. Button, of Linn, where Mrs. Ellis was born May 1st, 1859. They have one child, Clara Inez, born June 7th, 1884.

(575.) **HARRIET ELLIS**, daughter of William Ellis, Sr., was born in Ashfield, Mass., May 14th, 1815. She married Mr. Amos Smith in Springfield, Pa., Dec. 24th, 1835. They have four children, Cyrus E., Cordelia L., John B. and William E. Mrs. Harriet E. Smith died at Springfield, Sept. 29th, 1858.

(577.) **LUCRETIA ELLIS** was born in Ashfield, Oct. 6th, 1817. She now resides with her brother, Joseph, on the homestead in Springfield, Pa. She was never of robust health, but is one of the best and most genial in nature and disposition.

(579.) **SAMUEL ELLIS**, son of William, Sr., was born in Springfield, Pa., Nov. 1st, 1821. In 1842 he removed to La Grange, Wis., where he worked as a carpenter and builder. He married Amanda Adams in La Grange, Wis., in 1849. Mrs. Ellis died July 24th, 1850, leaving one son, William Edwin Ellis, born April 2d, 1850, who now resides in San Angelo, Texas. William E. was married to Annie L. Black in Eau Claire, Wis., in 1871. They had two children: Mabel E., born at Eau Claire, Aug. 29th, 1872, and Samuel E., born at Chippewa Falls, March 10th, 1874. The latter died in infancy. In 1874 Mr. William E. Ellis moved to Texas. In 1884 he was married again to Mary B. McKenzie and they have one daughter, Cora Harriet, born June 1st, 1885.

Sept. 17th, 1854, Mr. Ellis married Harriet French, and they have three children: Cora Lucretia, born 1856; Frank Enrique, 1858; Verne Adrian, 1869, died 1870. Cora L. married Charles B. Walworth Aug. 15th, 1877. Frank E. married Maggie Cullen April 4th, 1880, at Chippewa Falls, Wis.

Mr. Samuel Ellis lived in Palmyra from 1852 to 1861, where he kept the Palmyra House, when he moved to Eau Claire, Wis., and went into the livery business, in which he is yet extensively engaged.

(581.) **JAMES F. ELLIS** was born in Springfield, Pa., Sept. 3d, 1824. He died, Oct. 3d, 1849, at La Grange, Wis.

(583.) **MARY L. ELLIS** was born in Springfield, Pa., Sept. 15, 1828. She married Jonathan Morrell in Springfield, Aug. 12th, 1847. They had five children, two of whom are now living. Mr. Morrell died in 1882. Mrs. Morrell now lives in East Springfield, Erie Co., Pa., where she has a beautiful home.

(585.) **JOSEPH ELLIS**, youngest son of William Ellis, Sr., was born in Springfield, Pa., Dec. 28th, 1831. He married Martha Weed, Feb. 26th, 1863, and lives on the farm where his father and grandfather settled soon after their removal from Ashfield to Springfield. This is an elegant farm with large and convenient buildings. Mr. Ellis is an ardent and influential Republican in politics. In religious faith he is a Universalist.

Mr. and Mrs. Ellis have had five children, three of whom are now living, Nevada A., George W. and Ralph G. Ellis. Nevada is married and lives with her parents.

(587.) **RUMINA ELLIS**, youngest daughter of William, Sr., was born in Springfield, Pa., Oct. 29th, 1834. She married Mr. John Potter in 1856, and they removed to Eyota, Minn., where Mr. Potter was a hardware merchant at the time of his death in 1859. Mrs. Potter has one son, Gilbert Ellis Potter, born Jan. 14th, 1858. Mr. G. E. Potter married Mary E. Fulkerson. She was born Dec. 9th, 1858, in Marion, Minn. They were married by Rev. John W. Fulkerson. They have one son, Ralph E., born 1885. In 1886 Mr. Potter settled in Ashton, Dakota.

In 1877 Mrs. Rumina E. Potter married Francis A. Owen, formerly of Allegan, Mich. Mr. and Mrs. Owen now live in Ashton, Dakota. They are Methodists.

Children of David Ellis, Jr. 180), of Springfield, Erie Co., Pa., Grandchildren of David, Sr. (32), Great-grandchildren of Reuben (4), and Great-great-grandchildren of Richard Ellis, of Ashfield. From 598 to 611.

(**598.**) LOUISA ELLIS, eldest child of David, Jr., was born in Ashfield, Mass., Feb. 6th, 1815. She was three years old when her parents settled in Springfield, Pa. In 1837 she married Robert Patterson, and they resided in Springfield several years, where they raised two children, William S., born 1838, and Joseph E., 1841. Mr. and Mrs. Patterson were Baptists and always active in church and Sunday school work. Mr. Patterson was born in McKean, Erie Co., Pa., in 1810. When a young man he settled in Springfield township, and lived on the same farm until 1866, when he removed with his family to Erie, Pa., where he died in 1868. His parents were Irish Protestants.

William S. Patterson was born in Springfield, Dec. 31st, 1837. He was a merchant in Springfield, and afterwards in Erie. He married Orrilla Spencer in 1860. They had one child, Ida E., born in 1862. Mr. Patterson died in Erie, Pa., in 1878.

Joseph Ellis Patterson was born in Springfield, Pa., July 25th, 1841. He lived on his father's farm until twenty-two years of age, then entered the store with his brother. He is still in the hardware trade in Erie, Pa., where he resides with his mother and family. In 1870 he married Martha M. Dyke, of North-East, Erie Co., Pa. They have two children, Georgia Louisa, born 1876, and J. Clyde, born 1881. Mr. Patterson and wife are Presbyterians and are very highly respected and upright people. Mr. Patterson has been a member of the City Council in Erie, and is a prominent and public spirited citizen.

(600.) MELINDA ELLIS was born in Ashfield, 1817. She has always resided in Springfield, Pa., with her parents, for whom she cared until their death, since which she has lived with her brother, Dr. George Ellis. She is a member of the Christian Church.

(601.) DR. GEORGE ELLIS, eldest son of David Ellis, Jr., was born in Ashfield, Mass., in 1818. He was six months of age when his parents removed to Springfield, Pa., where he has ever since resided. In early life he studied medicine and graduated at the medical department of Hudson University, at Cleveland, Ohio. He has a large practice in Springfield and surrounding towns. In 1865 he was appointed U. S. Examining Surgeon for pensions. He is a member of Cache Commandery of K. T., of Conneaut, Ohio. He is a Republican in politics, and a leading member of the Christian Church of East Springfield. Like most of the early Ellises, he is a thorough Bible student and quite a theologian. He has a large farm near where his father settled in 1818, which is operated mostly by his son, Orra M. Ellis.

In 1843 Dr. Ellis married Miss Eunice B. Lyon. She was born in Conway, Mass. (next town east of Ashfield), Oct. 25th, 1821. She was a daughter of Marshall and Chloe Lyon and grand-daughter of David and Betsey Lyon, old and influential residents of Ashfield. Her father, Marshall Lyon, was a cousin of the gifted MARY LYON,*

---

*Mary Lyon was the most famous woman of Ashfield, and one of the most justly noted of the age. She was born in the northeast corner of Ashfield, near the Conway and Buckland line Some years after her birth (about 1807) that part of the town, including her father's farm, was set off and joined to Buckland. Miss Lyon was a very ready scholar and had a most logical mind. She was a student in the Sanderson Academy on Ashfield Plain, and at Amherst College, and it is said that after studying a Latin grammar three days, she could recite in any class in the college. In learning, and as a debater, she was the peer of any man in that section of Massachusetts. In her early years she was a teacher for four terms in the district school of the Ellis neighborhood, and some are now living, including the writer's mother, who were her pupils in that schoolhouse. She afterwards was a pupil and teacher in the Academy on the Plain. In a late visit (May. 1887,) of the writer to those parts, he noticed at nearly every cross-roads for miles around, neatly painted signs directing the way and giving the distance "To Mary Lyon's birth-place," as a token of reverence for her memory, and to show the esteem in which she is held by all the people.

In 1836 Miss Lyon founded Mt. Holyoke seminary at South Hadley, Mass. She conducted this institution with the greatest success until her death, March 5th, 1849, in the 53rd year of her age.

Mary Lyon's parents were Aaron Lyon, Jr., and his wife Jemima Shepard, a daughter of Deacon Isaac Shepard a noted resident of Ashfield. Aaron Lyon was born about 1757, died Dec. 21, 1832, leaving seven children. His father, Aaron Lyon, Sr., was a noted patriot in Ashfield during the Revolution. All these Lyons were eminent for piety and general worth. In 1777 Aaron Lyon, Sr., was one of three persons what should be done with certain Tories then in Ashfield, who were jubilant at the progress made by the British under Burgoyne. The latter were expected to whose name is immortalized as the founder of Mt. Holyoke Seminary, the first institution for the higher education of woman known in the world.

In 1837 Miss Lyon, with her parents, settled in Girard, Erie Co., Pa. In 1838 she joined the Methodist Episcopal Church. She was a woman of uncommon piety, worth and intelligence. She died April 3d, 1862, leaving two children, Orra M. and Louella E. Ellis. Alonzo, a third child, had previously died in childhood.

September 5th, 1863, Dr. George Ellis married Miss Lizzie Flower, a daughter of Rev. Josiah Flower, of Poland, N. Y. She died Jan. 31st, 1873.

September 7th, 1876, Dr. Ellis married his present wife, Miss Sarah F. Mauck, daughter of Jacob and Lucy Mauck, a native of Virginia. She is a member of the Christian Church in Springfield, and is a woman of rare culture and refinement, wholly devoted to her husband and family.

Orra M. Ellis, eldest child of Dr. George Ellis, was born in Springfield in 1848. He married Miss Mahala M. Sherman, of Springfield, July 9th, 1873. She was born in East Springfield in 1854. They are farmers in Springfield and members of the Christian Church.

Louella E. Ellis was born in Springfield in 1858. She has been engaged for some years as a teacher, and at the present time in the high school at West Springfield. She is a young woman of superior education and talents. Miss Ellis is a devoted member of the Christian Church in Springfield, and takes a leading part in the Church choir and Sunday School.

(603.) **MARSHALL ELLIS** was born in Springfield, Pa., in 1820 ; is a farmer and carpenter in Springfield, Pa. He married Martha J. Wilson, of Springfield. She was a

---

march down to Fort Massachusetts at North Adams, cross the Hoosac mountain over to Heath, and down by Buckland and Ashfield right by Aaron Lyon's farm and home, to form a junction with other British forces in the eastern part of the colony. In the face of this, Aaron Lyon and the committee did their duty fearlessly, and reported the names of nine prominent and influential residents of Ashfield as "enemies of their country and that they should be brought to immediate trial." One of these was the father-in-law of one of the committeemen, which shows the trying situation in which these noble patriots were placed, and the fearless manner in which they performed their duty. Fortunately the surrender of Burgoyne near Saratoga before his plan of the invasion of Massachusetts was executed, gave to the patriots great rejoicing and strengthened their cause, while it greatly depressed the Tories, and even won some of them over to the cause of independence.

sister of Aaron, who married Mr. Ellis' sister Sarah. Mrs. Martha J. Ellis died in 1886, leaving one son, Harry W., born in 1868. They were members of the Christian Church.

(605.) **LEONARD ELLIS**, third son of David, Jr., was born in Springfield, Pa., in 1822. He married Rhoda A. Taylor March 5th, 1854. They were farmers in North Springfield, where Mr. Ellis now resides. Mrs. Ellis died in 1879, leaving four children, Elva C., born 1855; Dora S., 1858; Mina P., 1864, and Fred T., 1865. For his second wife Mr. Ellis married, Oct. 24th, 1883, Miss Adelia E. Mallory, a very refined and accomplished lady.

Dora S. Ellis married Curtis Crew July 19th, 1880. Their children are Carl Ellis, born 1881, and Claud Crew, 1885. They live in Ashtabula, Ohio, where Mr. Crew is an engineer. Mina P. Ellis is a very efficient school teacher.

(607.) **PETER ELLIS**, son of David, Jr., was born in Springfield, Pa., May 18th, 1824. He married Violet Davenport Feb. 11th, 1845. They are thriving farmers, living but a few rods from where David Ellis, Sr., settled in Springfield. They have three children living: George Wilbur, born 1852; Hazen W., 1854, and Orman F., 1858.

George W. married Louisa L. Kohler March 21st, 1877, in Erie, Pa.

Hazen W. lives on the farm with his parents.

Orman F. married Louisa C. Shetler May 24th, 1883, and they have two children, LeRoy F., born 1884, and Carrie, 1886.

Mrs. Violet Ellis was born Oct. 3d, 1826. She was a daughter of Paul Davenport, who was born in Colerain, Mass., May 12th, 1796. He died Oct. 15th, 1881. His wife, Rachel, was born in Colerain Nov. 25th, 1798, and died July 29th, 1884.

(609). **SARAH ELLIS**, youngest daughter of David Ellis, Jr., was born in Springfield, Pa., in 1827. She married Mr. Aaron Wilson and resided in Springfield, where Mr. Wilson is a farmer and painter by trade. They have one child living, Clara L., born 1866, who is engaged in teaching.

(611.) **ORMAN F. ELLIS** was born in Springfield, Pa., Feb. 5th, 1829. He was a farmer and lived in Springfield until his death, May 25th, 1870. He married Martha E. Nelson Sept. 23d, 1863. Mrs. Ellis was born Nov. 18th, 1840, in Cussewago, Crawford Co., Pa. Mrs. Ellis was the youngest daughter of James A. Nelson and his wife, Jane Patterson, daughter of James and Nancy (Holt) Patterson, early residents of Springfield, Pa. All these people were Baptists. Since her husband's death Mrs. Ellis has lived in Erie, Pa. She has two children, Frank H., born Nov. 25th, 1865, and Charles M., born March 6th, 1869. Frank H. is an engineer in Leavenworth, Kansas. Charles M. lives with his mother in Erie.

Mr. Orman Flower Ellis was a man of strict sobriety, uprightness and intelligence. He was over six feet high and well proportioned—a splendid specimen of physical development. He was a member of the Christian Church, and could ably defend its doctrines. He was a great reader and a well-informed man; in politics, an ardent Republican. He was a man who had the friendship and good will of all with whom he was acquainted.

Children of Azel Ellis (209), of Marseilles, Ohio, Grandchildren of John, Jr. (68), of Niles, N. Y., Great-grandchildren of Lieut. John, Sr. (15), and Great-greatgrandchildren of Richard, of Ashfield.
From 621 to 623.

(621.) **EDWARD ELLIS**, eldest son of Azel Ellis, was born in Cayuga Co., N. Y., November 7th, 1831. He was a carpenter and builder. He died August 17th, 1857, at Marseilles, Ohio. He was unmarried.

(622.) **PHEBE ELLIS**, eldest daughter of Azel, was born in Cayuga Co., N. Y., April 30th, 1834. She married Mr. John Winslow, March 3d, 1853, in Marseilles, Ohio. They had one child, Harriet Winslow. Mr. and Mrs. Winslow both died about two years after their marriage. Their daughter Harriet was raised by her aunt, Mrs. Lydia Terry in Canon City, Colorado, where she now lives.

(623.) **LYDIA ELLIS,** youngest child of Azel Ellis, was born November 30th, 1841. She was educated at Marseilles, Ohio, and at 16 years of age became a teacher, which occupation she followed several years. In 1865, she married Mr. John H. Terry, and they settled in Colorado. Mr. Terry was born in Marion County, Ohio, April 21st, 1838. He was engaged in mining and milling at Black Hawk, Col., until 1870, when he removed to Canon City, Col., where he now resides. He was elected County Judge in 1872, and again in 1880. He is now extensively engaged in farming and stock raising. They have three children, William L., born 1866; Nellie, 1872, and Joe, 1874.

Children of Hiram Ellis (214), of Niles, Cayuga Co., N. Y. 627 to 629.

(627.) **REV. ELISHA ELLIS** was born in Niles, N. Y., in 1837. In 1856, he married Miss Lovina Welden, and they have three children: Edwin, born 1858; Egbert, 1866, and Clark, 1874. Mr. Ellis was ordained as a minister in the Christian denomination in 1869, to which he gives his entire time and labor. He resides at Westbury, Cayuga Co., N. Y. Mr. Ellis was a soldier in the Union army three years.

(629.) **HANNAH ELLIS,** daughter of Hiram Ellis, was born in Niles, in 1834. She married William Cole, in 1856, and had three children: Clovy, Edwin and Ella. Mr. Cole was a soldier in the Union army, and died in the service. His wife died in 1873.

Children of Capt. Elisha Ellis (216), of Farmersville, Posey Co., Indiana. 630 to 638.

(630.) **NANCY ELLIS,** eldest child of Elisha, was born at Farmersville, Ind., in 1829. In 1848 she married H. W. Holleman, and had two children: Elizabeth, born 1849, and Elisha, 1850. The latter died in 1858. Mr. and Mrs. Holleman both died in 1852. Elizabeth Holleman married Richard Russell.

(632.) **ELIZABETH ELLIS,** born in 1831, married Felix Duckworth in 1849. She died in 1853, leaving two children, both of whom have since died. Mr. Duckworth was born about 1828, and died in 1872.

(636.) **ANN ELLIS,** born in 1836, married Sidney Allyn, of Farmersville, in 1854. Mr. Allyn died in 1884. They have five children, all born in Farmersville. Hannah Allyn, born 1855, married Lee Frothingham, and they have two children: Sylvia and Sidney.

Thena Allyn, born 1857, married Neal Reno, and they have two children.

Elisha Allyn married Laura Lewis, and they have one child.

·Indiana Allyn, born 1867, lives with her mother in Farmersville.

(638.) **JOHN DAVID ELLIS,** youngest son of Capt. Elisha Ellis, was born in Farmersville, Ind., in 1839. He married Harriet Russell in 1862, and resides in Farmersville. They have had six children: Elisha, born 1863; Samuel, a twin brother of Elisha, died the same year; Grant, 1865; John, 1870; Jay, 1872, and Birchard, 1876. All live in Farmersville.

Mr. John David Ellis is a farmer on the homestead of his parents.

————

Children of Richard Ellis (218), of Jackson, Hardin Co., Ohio, Grandchildren of John Ellis, Jr. (68), of Niles, Cayuga Co., N. Y. From 640 to 650.

(640.) **ISAAC NEWTON ELLIS,** son of Richard, was born in Niles, N. Y., January 22d, 1829, and now lives at Marseilles, Ohio. He owns the place which his mother purchased and lived on after the death of her husband, in 1853. He is unmarried and lives with his sister and her husband, Mrs. and Mr. Phillips.

(642.) CATHARINE ELLIS was born in Niles, N. Y., April 21st, 1833. She married Dr. C. J. Rodig, July 15th, 1854, in Toledo. He was a Lieutenant in the Union army, and was killed at the battle of Nashville, Tenn., October 16th, 1864, leaving two children: Johanna and Lena. Johanna married Robert Mouser.

Mrs. Rodig was again married to Richard Willard, September 5th, 1866. They had four children: Ines, Clara, Marion and Clyde.

Mr. Willard and family reside at Bellbrook, Green Co., Ohio. They are Presbyterians.

(644.) MARY ANN ELLIS, daughter of Richard Ellis, was born April 18th, 1837. She married Samuel Phillips in Marseilles, Ohio, October 11th, 1857. Mr. Phillips was born June 18th, 1835. They live in Marseilles. They have had ten children, of whom seven are now living. See page 62.

John W. Phillips, their eldest son, is travelling for a dry-goods house in Kansas City, Mo. Eva O. married J. L. Hastings, a farmer in Hardin Co., Ohio. James E. is in a dry-goods store in Marion, Ohio.

Mr. Samuel Phillips is a member of the Methodist church. He was a soldier in the Union army, 144th Ohio National Guards. Mrs. Phillips is a Presbyterian. Mr. Phillips carries on business in Marseilles.

(646.) WILLIAM M. ELLIS was born May 25th, 1845, in Jackson township, Hardin County, Ohio. He married Maggie A. Keyes, of Niles, N. Y., January 6th, 1869. She was born August 26th, 1843. They have had six children, of whom five are now living. See page 62.

Mr. Ellis was a soldier in the Union army three years, Company A, 123d Reg. Ohio Vol. He was in the battle of Winchester, Va., was wounded in the breast. the ball passing through a testament. He was a prisoner in Libby and Belle Isle prisons thirty-three days, when he was exchanged and joined his regiment, after which, he was in battles at New Market, Va., Opequon, Va., Round Top Mountain, Cedar

Creek, Hatcher's Run, High Bridge and at Appomattox Court House, when the rebels surrendered. Since returning from the army, he has been in the grocery and dry-goods business in Kenton, Ohio, where he now lives.

(648.) RICHARD S. ELLIS was born August 10th, 1831. He died September 23d, 1854, unmarried.

(649.) SYLVIA JANE ELLIS was born October 25th, 1835. She died in 1874. She married Mr. John Kishler, November 7th, 1852. They had five children. See page 63. Mrs. Kishler was a member of the Presbyterian Church. Mr. Kishler now lives in Marion, Ohio. He is a Presbyterian, as is also his present wife.

**Children of Hon. Pitts Ellis (220), of Genesee, Wisconsin.
From 652 to 657.**

(652.) HELEN MINERVA ELLIS, was born at North Prairie, Waukesha County, Wis., July 16th, 1842. She was married at Genesee, Wis., Nov. 6th, 1861, to Mr. Judson Shultis. They have no children. Their residence is at North Prairie, Waukesha Co., Wis. Mr. Shultis has been a merchant for many years, but is now engaged in farming.

(653.) LODOSKA S. ELLIS was born October 26th, 1845, at Genesee, Wis. She married Mr. Alexander R. Benzie, August 2d, 1866. Mr. and Mrs. Benzie are members of the Advent Christian Church. They live in Burns, La Crosse County, Wis., where Mr. Benzie is a farmer. They have five children. See page 63. Mr. Benzie was a soldier in the Union army three years. He is of Scotch parentage, and is a strictly temperance man.

(655.) PITTS B. ELLIS was born in Genesee, Wis., January 3d, 1851. He married Nellie Doane in 1875. They have one child, Richard Claude Ellis, born in March, 1882. They live at Eau Claire, Wis. Mr. Ellis is in the railroad employ at Eau Claire.

(657.) ANNIE A. ELLIS, youngest child of Hon. Pitts Ellis, was born at Genesee, Wis., November 20th, 1854. She married Mr. Lewis Barling, Feb. 14th, 1875, in Genesee. He was born in 1848, of English parents. They have no children. They reside in Milwaukee, Wis., where Mr. Barling is a salesman in a wholesale grocery house.

Children of John J. Ellis (222), of Sennett, Cayuga Co., N. Y. From 659 to 667.

(659.) JOHN R. ELLIS was born Oct. 13th, 1839, in Niles, N. Y. His first two wives were sisters named Dirgy. Married in Throop, Cayuga Co. By his first wife he had one son, Charles, born about 1863, in Throop. Mr. Ellis married his third wife in Cortland Co., N. Y.

(661.) MARTHA ELLIS was born March 16th, 1844, in Niles, Cayuga County, N. Y. She married William Wood and lived in Throop, N. Y., where her two children were born. Eva Wood, the eldest, about 1866. The youngest died in infancy.

(663.) MYRON ELLIS was born in Niles, Cayuga Co., N. Y., October 11th, 1845. He married in Ohio, and has two children. They reside at Marseilles, Ohio.

(667.) NEWTON S. ELLIS was born in Niles, Cayuga Co., N. Y., December 8th, 1855. He married Emma Amerman in December, 1885. Mr. Ellis is a book-keeper by occupation and now resides in Auburn, N. Y.

Children of Benjamin Ellis (225), of Marseilles, Ohio. 669 to 683. See page 35.

(671.) JOHN H. ELLIS was born April 18th, 1843, in Niles, N. Y. He married Jane McCleary, and they have two children: John and Elenora, both born in Marseilles, Ohio. Mr. Ellis and family now live in Kenton, Hardin Co., Ohio.

(675.) **CLARENCE L. ELLIS**, son of Benjamin, was born March 24th, 1848. He married Miss Alice Sweet, of Dunkirk, Ohio. Dec. 11th, 1884. Mr. Ellis is a farmer and resides at Marseilles, Ohio.

(677.) **MARY E. ELLIS**, daughter of Benjamin, was born in Ohio, December 25th, 1851. She married Mr. Vincent Long, March 27th, 1870. They reside at Marseilles, Ohio. They have three children: Arnold Vill Roy, Sylvester Hugh, and Charles Russell Long.

(683.) **MELINDA L. ELLIS** was born in Ohio, Dec. 11th, 1861. She lives at Marseilles, Ohio.

Children of Ebenezer Ellis (227), of Farmersville, Indiana. From 685 to 695.

(685.) **JULIA ELLIS** was born in Farmersville, Ind., March 18th, 1840. She married John H. Mockett in Genesee, Wis., March 14th, 1860. Mr. Mockett was born in Broadstairs, England, August 1st, 1840. They have four children: John H. Jr., Edwin R., Frederick E. and Ebenezer E. The two first were born in Genesee, and the two last in Stark, Vernon County, Wis. Mr. Mockett and family reside at Lincoln, Nebraska. Mr. M. and eldest son are engaged in Life and Fire Insurance business. Edwin R. is a stenographer for the Governor of Nebraska, with his office at the Capitol.

(687.) **SOPHRONIA ELLIS** was born in Farmersville, Indiana, Feb. 21st, 1842. She married Richard Hobbs Mockett in Genesee, Wis., April 24th, 1861. They now live in Lincoln, Nebraska, where Mr. M. is in Life Insurance business. He is a brother of John H. Mockett above, and was born in Broadstairs, England, February 13th, 1838. Mr. and Mrs. Mockett have two children, born in Genesee, Robert S. and Edith T., both students in the University of Nebraska.

(689.) EDWIN ELLIS was born in Farmersville, Indiana, February 27th, 1844. He married Eliza J. C. Mockett, sister of John H. and Richard H. Mockett above. Mrs. Ellis died in 1872, leaving one son, Willie E. Ellis, born February 17th, 1870, at Janesville, Wisconsin. He lives with his uncle and aunt, Richard and Sophronia Mockett. Mr. Edwin Ellis is a locomotive engineer on the Union Pacific Railway and resides at Jefferson, Col. He was a Union soldier, and served in the 28th Wis. Vol. Infantry over three years.

(691.) HARRIET ELLIS was born in Farmersville, Ind., September 15, 1847. She married Andrew Dean, at Stark, Wis., January 1st, 1869. They now live at Arkansas City, Kansas, and have five children. Mr. Dean was born in Medina, Ohio, July 18th, 1847. Of their children, Mabel was born in Wisconsin, Nov. 26th, 1869. Nellie in Wisconsin, June 13th, 1872. Asa, Dec. 7th, 1875. Ellis, Nov. 13th, 1877, and Mary, May 10th, 1880. The last three were born in Cuming County, Nebraska.

(693.) PITTS ELLIS, son of Ebenezer, was born at Farmersville, Indiana, on a farm three miles east of Mount Vernon, January 23d, 1852. He moved, in the spring of 1859 with his parents, to Genesee, Wis., and in 1866 to Viola, Richland County, Wis. In July, 1880, Mr. Ellis married Miss Olive L. Rose, at Scranton, Green County, Iowa. In 1881, Mr. Ellis' family settled in Arkansas City, Kansas, where he is engaged in buying and shipping grain. His parents, Ebenezer and wife, now reside with him.

(695.) MARY ELLIS, youngest child of Ebenezer Ellis, was born at Farmersville, Ind., Nov. 25th, 1854. She married Frank Clark, April 14th, 1876. Mrs. Clark died Dec. 22d, 1879; Mr. Clark died in Dec., 1880. They had two children, Clara and Samuel. The latter was born Dec. 14th, 1879, in Cuming County, Neb., and died in August, 1880. Clara E., the eldest, lives with her grand-parents in Dexter, Mich.

(708.) **ELIAS ELLIS** was born Nov. 10th, 1844, at Owasco, N. Y. He married Elizabeth Duryea in November, 1865. They are farmers in Owasco, on a farm adjoining Mr. Ellis' father, Anthony W. Ellis. Mrs. Ellis is a daughter of Benjamin Duryea, of Niles, Cayuga County, N. Y. Her mother was Huldah Forbush, half-sister to Cyrus and Edward D. Ellis. See page 112.

(710.) **ISAAC NEWTON ELLIS** was born at Owasco N. Y., April 7th, 1846. He is unmarried, and a farmer and lives with his parents in Owasco.

(713.) **DELLA JANE ELLIS,** youngest child of Anthony W. Ellis, was born at Owasco, Feb. 13th, 1864. She married Joseph W. Brinkerhoff, October 22d, 1884. They are farmers at Owasco, N. Y.

Children of Cyrus Ellis (233), of Niles, Cayuga County, N. Y., Grandchildren of Edward Ellis (70), of Niles, N. Y., Great-grandchildren of Lieut. John (15) and Great-great-grand-children of Richard Ellis of Ashfield. From 715 to 731.

(715.) **EDWARD D. ELLIS,** eldest son of Cyrus, was born in Niles, N. Y., about five miles north of Moravia, April 2d, 1826. He married Mary Camp in December, 1850. They had two children: Camp, born 1851, and Mary, 1858. Camp Ellis lives in Dennison, Iowa, is married and has two children. Mary Ellis married Mr. Stark; has two children, and lives at Sioux Falls, Dakota.

Mr. Edward D. Ellis was a soldier in the Union army, and died in the service while at Chattanooga, Tenn., March 22d, 1865. Mr. Ellis settled at Omro, Wis., in 1856, and was living at that place when he enlisted in the army.

(717.) **POLLY ELLIS** was born at Niles, N. Y., June 6th, 1828. She married Thomas W. Baker, Oct. 11, 1854. Mr. Baker died in 1877. Mr. Baker was a lumberman at Manitowac, Wis. They had three children: Clara, born 1855. Emma, 1856, and Ellis Baker, 1863. Clara Baker married, July 13th, 1874, Dr. W. H. Curtis, a homeopathic physician of Owasco, N. Y. Their children are: Lulu May, Nellie V., and Fred A. Curtis. Emma Baker married, Dec. 28th, 1875, Dorr Van Arsdale, a farmer in Moravia, N. Y. Mrs. Polly Baker now lives with and is house-keeper for her brother Birch Ellis.

(719.) **MINERVA ELLIS,** daughter of Cyrus, was born in Niles, Nov. 16th, 1829. She was married in Niles, February 5th, 1852, to Edward H. Deuel. Mrs. Deuel died Dec. 16th, 1872, leaving one child: Mary Jane, who married in 1880 George Conklin, a farmer, of Niles. They have one child: Eddy Conklin. Mr. Edward H. Deuel was born August 20th, 1819, in Stamford, Duchess County, N. Y.

(721.) **CLARISSA ELLIS** was born March 15th, 1832. She married Edgar Selover, of Niles, Dec. 29th, 1880. They are farmers and live in Owasco, N. Y.

(723.) **HIRAM ELLIS** was born in Niles, N. Y., March 28th, 1834. He married Margaret Van Etten, July 7th, 1859. They are farmers in Niles. They have two children: Levi L., born 1861, and Henry, 1863. Levi L. Ellis married Lura Bissell, of Owasco, N. Y., July 4th, 1882. They have one child: Hattie, born December 31st, 1884.

(725.) **CYRUS ELLIS, JR.,** was born in Niles, March 20th, 1836. He was a soldier of the Union army and died in the service at Brownsville, Arkansas, Sept. 5th, 1863. He enlisted at Manitowoc, Wis., in 1862, in the 27th Regiment, Wis. Volunteers.

(727.) **BIRCH ELLIS** was born at Niles, N. Y., July 3rd, 1838. He married Gertrude Selover, of Niles, Nov. 7th, 1866. His wife died August 19th, 1871, leaving one child: Gertie S. Ellis, born July 17th, 1871. Mrs. Ellis was born Dec. 28th, 1837. Mr. Ellis and daughter now live in Auburn, N. Y., where Mr. Ellis is engaged in the insurance business. He is a strong temperance man and is widely noted for his firm political and temperance principles. Mr. Ellis was a soldier in the Union army and was the only one of four sons of his father's family who returned alive. His three brothers gave their lives to the cause of liberty and Union. Mr. Birch Ellis enlisted Sept. 15th, 1863, in Battery C., 1st Wisconsin Heavy Artillery. He was in the battles of Chattanooga, Mission Ridge, and Lookout Mountain. He was mustered out at the close of the war, Oct. 17th, 1865.

(729.) HENRY F. ELLIS was born in Niles, N. Y., Feb. 9th, 1843. He was a Union soldier, and died in the service at New Orleans, Louisiana, April 20th, 1863. He enlisted at Auburn, N. Y., in the 75th Regiment, N. Y. Vol.

(731.) MILES M. ELLIS, youngest child of Cyrus Ellis, was born in Niles, N. Y., July 8th, 1846. He married Ellen M. Cleveland, of Sempronius, N. Y., Feb. 23d, 1870. He lived on the farm with his parents until their death. He moved to Hastings, Adams County, Nebraska, in April, 1886, where he is in the real estate and loan business. Mr. and Mrs. Ellis have five children: Arthur C., born in Niles, March 8th, 1872; Fred, Feb. 5th, 1875; Cyrus H., May 16th, 1876; Herbert L., Aug. 5th, 1880, and Frank, Sept. 14th, 1886, in Hastings, Nebraska. It is said that Mr. Ellis' father, Cyrus Ellis (233), was the first male child born in the town of Niles or Sempronius, in 1799.

Children of Hon. Edward D. Ellis (235), of Monroe, Mich.
From 733 to 740.

(733.) MARY MINERVA ELLIS was born at Monroe, Mich., Nov. 19th, 1831. She married Dr. E. R. Ellis, (751) of Detroit, Mich. For further sketch of her, see No. 751, pages 254 and 257.

(735.) **AMELIA ELLIS** was born in Monroe, Mich., Dec. 17th, 1833. After the death of her father in 1848, she lived with friends in central New York for several years, after which, she resided in Chicago, Ill., with her brother John for a time. She never married, and was never of robust health, being afflicted with rheumatism most of her life. She died in Detroit, Mich., Jan. 7th, 1887. She had lived for ten or twelve years past with her sister Minerva, and after the death of the latter, with her husband and family. She was a Presbyterian, and a woman of good character, generosity and unusual industry. Her great desire was to be just and do good to all.

(736.) **E. CHARLES ELLIS** was born in Monroe, Mich., June 23d, 1835. He never married. He was a Union soldier, and, after the war, went west, and no report of him has been had for many years.

(737.) **JOHN C. C. ELLIS** was born in Monroe, Mich., June 2d, 1837. Dec. 24th, 1863, he was married in Lansing, Mich., to Miss Lucy Jane Whitaker, and they went to Chicago, Ill., where they resided and raised their family of three children. About 1875, Mr. Ellis, being in feeble health, went to Florida and the south to spend a few months in travel. The last report of him was from Memphis at a time when an epidemic of yellow fever was raging. There was an extensive scattering of the people in all directions, and Mr. Ellis' name was reported soon after among the dead in Louisville, Ky. Mr. Ellis was a man of strict integrity and sobriety. Like his father, he was quite a politician and stump speaker in political campaigns. His wife was born in Detroit, Mich., in 1844. She is a woman of good sense, uncommon industry and devotion to her family. For her second husband, she married Mr. Charles Case, of Canon City, Colorado, where they now reside. Mr. Case is a prominent and highly respected man there, engaged in railroad business.

Mr. Ellis' children are: Harriet A., born Oct. 16th, 1864; Ada L., Nov. 3d, 1866, and Lewis T., October 26th, 1869.

Harriet A. Ellis married, in 1882, Mr. E. J. Reilly, and they reside at South Pueblo, Col. Ada L. Ellis was a school teacher, is now married and lives at South Pueblo.

Lewis T. Ellis lives with his mother, Mrs. Case and Mr. Case, in Canon City. He is said to be a very scholarly and promising young man.

(739.) **ELIZABETH T. ELLIS** was born in Monroe, Mich., October 7th, 1841. She lived in Chicago the later years of her life with her mother and brother John C. Ellis. About 1867 she married Mr. Louis Voyer, and they went to Louisville, Ky., where she died the following year. She was a very amiable and scholarly young woman.

(740.) **BENJAMIN F. ELLIS,** youngest child of Hon. Edward D. Ellis, was born in Detroit, Mich., Sept. 4th, 1844. When four years of age his father died and he went to Niles, N. Y., in care of his uncle Cyrus Ellis (233). Here he lived with Mr. Lloyd Slade, of Sempronius, until the breaking out of the rebellion, when he enlisted in the Union army, Company A. 75th Reg., N. Y. Vol. He was but 16 years of age, and as he was quite small, he was advised to go into the service as an officer's assistant, but he declined this, and insisted on carrying a gun and being a thorough soldier. He was a soldier about four years, and went through the entire war. · Just before the time for his discharge, from exposure and fatigue, he was attacked with mental derangement, and was transferred to the Government hospital for insane at Washington, D. C., of which institution he has been an inmate ever since. As a young man, he is said to have been remarkably bright, scholarly and promising, strictly sober, upright and conscientious. Patriotism and duty were strong with him. His company officers say of him that "he was steady, reliable, obedient in discipline, always in his place, and in every way a model soldier." It was said that he was the "literary man" of his company, so fond was he of reading, and in foraging parties books were the first thing which he sought to secure.

Children of Dea. Richard Ellis (239), of Belding, Mich.
Grandchildren of Dea. Dimick Ellis (72), Great-
grandchildren of Lieut. John Ellis (15), and
Great-great-grandchildren of Rich-
ard Ellis, all of Ashfield.
From 749 to 751.

(749.) C. DIMICK ELLIS was born in Pittstown,
(Boyntonville) Rensselaer County, N. Y., Sept. 24th, 1829.
In the spring of 1844 he removed with his parents to Belding, (Otisco township), Mich, where he now resides on the
farm on which his parents settled in 1844. This farm is on
the north side of Flat River, part of which is now included
in the thriving village of Belding. Besides farming, Mr.
Ellis deals in agricultural machines and implements of all
kinds. He is a prominent citizen, and has been town supervisor three years. April 30th, 1862, he married Miss Eliza
Antoinette Lockwood, of Grand Rapids, Mich. Mrs. Ellis
was born in Clinton, Mich., in 1842, but lived most of her
youth at Grand Rapids. She is a woman of unusual beauty,
purity and loveliness of character, beloved by all. For 20
years or more she has been a member of the New Jerusalem Church. Her father, Mr. Edward Lockwood, now 79
years old, lives with her. Her mother died in Boone, Iowa,
in 1884, and her sister, Mrs. Louisa Church, at the same
place, in May, 1887.

Mr. and Mrs. Ellis have two children, both born at Belding: Mae, 1863, and William E., 1867. Both reside
at home, where William E. works the farm. Mr. Dimick
Ellis' mother, Hannah Ranney Ellis (240), born in Ashfield
in 1805, still lives with him on the farm where she and her
husband, Dea. Richard Ellis (239), settled in 1844.

(751.) DR. ERASTUS R. ELLIS, youngest child of
Dea. Richard Ellis, was born at Pittstown, N. Y., March
3rd, 1832. At 12 years of age his parents settled in Otisco,
(now Belding) Ionia County, Mich., where he helped to clear
up a farm of wild land and erect the buildings thereon.
Mechanics being more to his taste than farming, he, from 16
to 19 years of age took jobs, a portion of the time to put up

buildings. In 1851 and '52 he attended St. Mark's College in Grand Rapids, and took courses in surveying and engineering. In August, 1853, his uncle, Dr. John Ellis, of Detroit, offered him special advantages for studying medicine, which he accepted. In 1854 and '55 he attended the medical department of the University of Michigan at Ann Arbor. In 1857 he graduated at the Cleveland Homeopathic College, and began practice at Owosso, Mich. At the end of one year he settled in Grand Rapids, where he practised until the fall of 1867, when he removed to Detroit, where he now resides.

April 22d, 1857, Dr. Ellis married Minerva Ellis (733), a second cousin, daughter of Hon. Edward D. Ellis (235), of Detroit. They were married in Belding by Elder Wilson Mosher, of the Christian Church. They have had five children: Elizabeth B., Helen M., Jessie R., Edward D., and Anna Belle.

Elizabeth Burpee Ellis, born in Owosso, Mich., May 18th, 1858, graduated at the Detroit High School and was a teacher for six or seven years. June 30th, 1887, she married Alexander Marcus Gunn, of Heppner, Oregon. Mr. Gunn carries on blacksmithing business in Heppner, and has a large ranch a few miles from that town. Himself and wife are members of the New Jerusalem Church. He was born in St. Thomas, Ontario, January 10th, 1851. His parents, Marcus and Catharine McPherson Gunn were born in Scotland. Mr. Marcus Gunn was born about 1800, and his second wife, Catharine, about 1824. Mr. Gunn died in London, Ontario, in 1878. He was a printer, and published the St. Thomas "Observer" for a number of years. His children were: Jessie M., married Thomas Truesdale, and they reside at Cedar Grove, N. J.; Emily J., married Giles Reed, and they live in Kingston, New Mexico; Isabel lives in Kingston, New Mexico; Alexander M. (and wife, above mentioned) in Heppner, Oregon; John C., Charlotte and Nellie. The last three live with their mother in London, Ontario.

Mr. A. M. Gunn left London, Canada, in 1879, for the West. He spent a short time in California, and then settled in Heppner, the county seat of Morrow County, Oregon.

Helen Minerva Ellis was born in Grand Rapids, Mich., Dec. 2d, 1860. She is a graduate of the Detroit High School and a member of the New Jerusalem Church in Detroit. She married Mr. J. Seward Andrews Sept. 11th, 1883, and they have one daughter: Marion E., born August 24th, 1885. Mr. and Mrs. Andrews have a fine residence at 950 Fourth Ave., Detroit. Mr. Andrews was born in Detroit Sept. 2d, 1851. His father, John L., was a Captain on the lakes for many years. His mother now lives on Fourth Avenue, near her son. Her children are: Josephine E., a teacher in Colorado; James Seward (above), Letta C., who married Dr. John J. Hood, and after his death in 1884, his brother, Peter M. Hood, of New Paltz, N. Y., in 1886, where they now reside, and Prudence E., born 1856, died 1883, in Detroit.

Captain John L. Andrews was born in Vermont April 7th, 1821. His father, Joel Andrews, sr., was born in Vermont Feb. 27th, 1785. He was a blacksmith, and settled in Michigan about 1823 or 24, at or near Newport, on the St. Clair river, where he died of cholera about 1832. Captain John L. Andrews' wife (mother of J. Seward Andrews above), was Miss Caroline Guedett, born in Walkerville, Canada (opposite Detroit), May 7th, 1827. Her father, Joseph Guedett, died when she was young. Her mother afterwards married a Mr. Crampton, and now lives at St. Clair, Mich., a very aged lady.

Jessie Ranney Ellis was born in Grand Rapids, Mich., February 17th, 1863. She attended the Detroit High School three years, after which she learned telegraphy, which she has since followed. She is a member of the New Jerusalem Church, of Detroit.

Edward Dimick Ellis (named from his maternal grandfather 235) was born in Grand Rapids, Mich., April 19th, 1867. He attended the Detroit High School three years, and at 18 years of age entered a wholesale hardware store. He is now living in Grand Rapids, Mich., and is salesman and purchasing agent for Belknap Brothers' wagon and iron works. He is a member of the Detroit Light Guard, and also of a company in Grand Rapids, and takes much interest in military affairs.

Anna Belle Ellis, youngest child of Dr. Erastus R. and Minerva Ellis, was born in Detroit, Dec. 11th, 1873. She died June 8th, 1874, a delicate but very bright child.

Mrs. Minerva Ellis, (see 733, page 251) wife of Dr. E. R. Ellis, was a woman of uncommon worth, purity and strength of mind and character. When quite young she learned type-setting in her father's printing office, which she followed after his death in 1848, and until about the time of her marriage in 1857. In early life, she joined the Detroit Society of the New Jerusalem Church, to which she was devotedly attached for over thirty-three years. She understood the doctrines of the church, it was said, more thoroughly than any other member, and that she lived them most conscientiously all agreed. While she entertained very decided opinions on morality and religious subjects, she was never obtrusive in presenting, although ever ready to defend them. In all respects Mrs. Ellis was a most devoted wife and mother, one whose memory is worthy of endurance forever. She died in Detroit Aug. 16th, 1884, of acute inflammation of the brain.

Children of Lewis Ellis (241), of Belding, Mich. 754 to 757.

(754.) **GEORGE B. ELLIS** was born in Ashfield, Mass., in 1837. When five years of age his parents moved to Otisco, Mich., and settled at what is now Belding, on the north side of Flat River, where they now live. George B. was a very bright and promising young man. He died in 1851. His parents had lost five other children, all sons, in infancy, one of whom, John, died before their removal to Michigan.

(755.) **GEORGE W. ELLIS,** youngest son of Lewis Ellis, was born in Belding, Mich., Sept. 26th, 1851. He attended the schools at home and afterwards the High School in Chicago, Ill. When about 21 years of age he entered the silk store of Belding Bros. & Co., Chicago branch. He also was traveling salesman for the same firm for several years, until 1881, when he was made manager of the Philadelphia house of the same company. This branch of the business, by skill and good management, he has built up and increased to a very flourishing condition. As his father is aged and in poor health, he carries on the farm at Belding, which he superintends and visits two or three times a year. He is a man of uncommon worth, talent, business capacity and integrity. Mr. Ellis married Miss Sophia Sheridan Belding, in Chicago, June 28th, 1877. Miss Sheridan was born near Brooklyn, N. Y., July 10th, 1852. At an early age she was adopted into the family of Mr. and Mrs. Hiram H. Belding, of Chicago. Mrs. Ellis is a very bright and highly respected woman. They live in Philadelphia, Pa. Their home is on the heights of Germantown Avenue, No. 5304, a beautiful and healthful locality, and historical as being the ground on which the battle of Germantown was fought between the American forces under Washington, and the British, during the Revolution. Although this is nine miles from Mr. Ellis' place of business, the cars take him back and forth in about twenty minutes' time, and from forty to fifty trains pass over the road each day.

(757.) **MARY L. ELLIS,** youngest child of Lewis Ellis, was born at Belding, Mich., 1854. She married Fred. E. Ranney, in 1875, and they have three children: Ellis W., born 1878; Carrie L., 1880, and Hattie B. Ranney, 1883.

Mr. Ranney was born in Ashfield, Mass., in 1853. His parents were Charles Ranney and Nancy Davis, his second wife. Mr. Charles Ranney was a brother of Hannah Ranny (240) and a son of Jesse Ranney, who purchased of David Ellis, in 1818, the old Reuben Ellis farm (see page 69). Mr. Fred. E. Ranney was born and reared on this place. When a young man he went to Belding, where he now lives. He is superintendent and general manager of the Belding Refrigerator Works, where, from 12 to 15 thousand elegant household refrigerators are made annually, and shipped to all parts of the world. This is one of the large manufacturing industries in Belding, established mainly by the Belding Brothers (see page 117). Mr. and Mrs. Ranney are very worthy, intelligent and highly respected citizens of Belding.

(759.) **ALFRED ELLIS** was born in Detroit, Mich., in May, 1847. He died in July, 1848.

(760.) **WILBUR DIXON ELLIS**, son and only child living of Dr. John Ellis, was born in Detroit, Mich., Sept. 13th, 1848. When about twelve years of age his father moved from Detroit to New York City, where they both now reside. Mr. W. D. Ellis attended the public schools of Detroit and New York, and also the High School in the latter city. When a young man he was employed for a time in the New York silk house of Belding Bros., until he was about twenty years of age, when he became interested with his father in the manufacture and sale of lubricating oils. Mr. Theo. M. Leonard became a partner, and through their united efforts a very large business has resulted. (See page 180.) Their New York store and depot is at 157 Chambers street, and their oil works or refinery at Edgewater, N. J., directly across the Hudson river from the tomb of Gen. Grant. Mr. Ellis is also extensively engaged in cattle and horse raising in Montana, where he has three extensive " ranches," or ranges. These are near Big Timber, on the Northern Pacific Railroad, and not far north from the famous Yellowstone National Park. Into this pursuit Mr. Ellis has put considerable money and a great deal of enthusiasm in breeding and raising superior and thoroughbred horses and cattle. He usually spends a few weeks or months of the hot season in that section for recreation, as well as business. Mr. Ellis is a man of unusual business capacity, talent and success. Himself and wife have traveled extensively in Europe, as well as all parts of this country. They have an elegant brown-stone residence at 13'6 West 72nd street, New York City, within one block of the elevated railroad and Central Park.

Seventy-second street, on which Mr. Ellis resides, runs from Central Park about sixty rods westerly to the bank of the Hudson river, where it joins the lower end of the great Riverside Boulevarde, the most elegant driveway on this continent. The latter winds along the bluffs of the river for about three miles, to its upper end, where it terminates in a wide plateau, on which is situated the tomb, and proposed monument of General Grant.   This locality overlooks the Hudson, and is one of the most sightly about New York.

Mr. Ellis married Miss Harriet Delta Chittenden, in Albany, N.Y., Sept. 1st, 1875. Mrs. Ellis was born in Nichols, Tioga Co., N. Y., Jan. 22d, 1853. Her parents were Curtis B. Chittenden, born in Durham, Greene Co., N. Y., June 30th, 1825, and his wife, Harriet Tutton, born in Westbury, Wiltshire, England, June 13th, 1838. She died in New York City, October 1st, 1881. Mr. Chittenden is now living in Montana. Mrs. H. Delta Ellis was reared mostly in Albany, where her parents resided. She is a woman of uncommon refinement, generosity and sociability.

MATTHEW ELLIS

AND HIS DESCENDANTS.

(13.) **MATTHEW ELLIS**, third son and sixth child of Richard Ellis, of Ashfield, was born in Easton, Mass., Dec. 19th, 1739. When the earlier pages of this book were printed but very little trace of him, and none of his descendants, had been found. (See pages 17 and 74.) Diligent inquiry since then has enabled the writer to give herewith some account of him and his posterity. His name and date of birth is found, with that of Richard Ellis' other children, in Easton. In the early records of Huntstown (now Ashfield), where Richard Ellis settled in about 1742, Matthew's name is found in several places. When Richard left Huntstown, and settled in Colerain, Mass., about 1764, Matthew went with him, and according to later reports remained there until his death, about the year 1800. About 1775 Matthew Ellis married Miss Hannah Clark, of Colerain. (Her name is given as Hannah and Anna Clark.)

As to Miss Clark's parentage, or to which family of Clarks she belonged, does not now appear. She may have been a daughter of the William Clark mentioned on page 75. The Clarks were numerous in Colerain.

As stated on page 13, Richard Ellis kept a country store

in Colerain from 1764 to about the close of the Revolutionary War. In his account book the writer finds the names of Clarks as follows, under dates from 1765 to 1768 : William Clark the First, William Clark the Second, James Clark, George Clark, John Clark, Alexander Clark, all of Colerain ; Samuel Clark, John Clark and James Clark, Jr., of Halifax, and Alexander Clark, of Deerfield. (Halifax is in Vermont, and is the first town on the north of Colerain. Deerfield is about ten miles southeast from Colerain.)

In Richard Ellis' account book is found these charges : "Jan., 1773.—William Clark, Dr., to cutting rail-cuts by Matthew, 15s." "May, 1769.—John Stewart, Cr., by paid Matthew, £1 : 15s."

Matthew Ellis had ten children—seven sons and three daughters, as follows : Jane, Noah, Seth, Levi, Lurena, Enos, Eliphalet, Reuben, Sally and David, all born in Colerain. The youngest, David, was born in 1798. When he was about two years of age his father died. Soon after his mother, Matthew's widow, married a Mr. Haskell, and removed with her children to Keene, N. H., about forty miles northeasterly from Colerain. Some years later she removed to Thetford, Vt., which is near the Connecticut river and about ninety miles north of Colerain. As her children grew up they scattered to various parts of the country, except Noah and Seth, who settled on farms in Thetford, where they raised families and lived to old age.

JANE ELLIS, eldest child of Matthew Ellis, was born in Colerain, Mass., about 1776. She married Caleb Brooks. They lived in Vermont, and had four children : Joseph, William, Caleb and Mary. William Brooks raised a large family. Joseph had none. Joseph, William and Mary Brooks lived and died in or near Antwerp, Jefferson Co., N. Y.: also their parents.

NOAH ELLIS, eldest son of Matthew, was born in Colerain Dec. 9th, 1777. He married Miss Nancy Dow, of Stratford, Vt., Aug. 28th, 1805. She was born Oct. 12th 1784, a daughter of William Dow and Rachel Chace, descendents of Aquilla Chace, who settled in Mass. in 1630. She died in Thetford, Vt., Sept. 16th, 1850. He died in Dunning Prairie, Wis., in the autumn of 1860. They were both members of the Methodist church many years. They were greatly respected and beloved people. They had ten children, all born in Thetford, Vt.: Rachel, Lydia, Warren, Sabra, Chace Dow, Dyer, Mary Ann, Sarah Ann, Adaline J. and Harriet. All are now dead except Dyer, who lives at Redfield, Dak.; Adaline J. Peck, in Hancock, Minn., and Harriet Miller, in Stanton, Minn.

Rachel, eldest child of Noah, was born May 16th, 1806.

Lydia Ellis was born Jan. 7th, 1808, married Dr. Solomon Warde July 18th, 1830, in Thetford. They lived in Ohio, Indiana and Morristown, Minn., where she died in 1869. Dr. Warde died there at about the age of 70 years. They had seven children : Mary, Finette, Amplias G., Curtis D., Lodema, Philena and Melvin Warde. Mary married C. Denman, a farmer near Northfield, Minn. They have four children. Finette married C. Eldred, and they live in Montevideo, Minn. Amplias G. and Curtis D. Warde are married and live in Minneapolis, and are real estate agents. They were both soldiers in the Union army. Lodema Warde is married and lives in Montana. Philena Warde married S. Wilder. They have two children, and live in Morristown, Minn. Melvin Warde lives in Minneapolis.

Warren Ellis, son of Noah, was born Dec. 29th, 1809 ; married Diaploma Eastman in Union Village, Vt. After living in Thetford many years, they moved to Beaver Dam, Wis., where he died. Mrs. Ellis married Mr. Woodward and now lives in Beaver Dam. Mr. and Mrs. Ellis had five children : James, Marvin, Amelia, Marshall and Warren, Jr. James Ellis died in Thetford, aged about 14 years. Marvin died in Beaver Dam, aged about 16 years. Amelia married Mr. Hood in Beaver Dam. He was a soldier and died in the service, leaving three children: Effie, the eldest, is a telegraph operator at Horicon, Wis.; Charles died in Beaver Dam in 1881, and Verne Hood now living in Beaver Dam. Mrs. Amelia Ellis Hood was married again to Mr. Livermore, a lawyer at Beaver Dam. They have three children. Marshal Ellis is married and lives in Wisconsin. Warren, Jr., lives in Hurley, Minn., and has three children.

Sabra Ellis, born 1812 ; Chace Dow, 1814, and Mary Ann, 1818, children of Noah Ellis, all died in Vermont.

Dyer Ellis, born May 9th, 1816, married Christiana Dawsey in Ohio, Jan. 24th, 1839. .They lived on his father's farm in Thetford about 12 years, when they all moved to Dunning Prairie, Wis., where his father died. He was a Union soldier. He now lives at Redfield, Dak. He had six children : Arlington C., Adaline J., Fred, May, Frank and Georgia Ann. Arlington C. was a Union soldier. He now lives in Shasta, Cal., unmarried and in poor health. Adaline J. married D. N. Hunt, a real estate agent and lawyer of Redfield, Dak. They have three children. Fred, May and Frank Ellis died in Wis. and Minn. Georgia Ann married in 1887 Albert Dikeman. They live in Redfield.

Sarah Ann Ellis, daughter of Noah, born June 21, 1822, married Halsey J. Yarrington in 1839, in Thetford. They lived at Norwich, Vt., where she died, leaving four children: Horace J., Jackson, Nelson and Merrill. Horace is married and lives at Stratford, Vt. He was a Union soldier. Jackson died at five years of age, and Nelson at 21. Merrill is married and lives in Thetford. He was a Union soldier.

Adaline J. Ellis, born Jan. 13th, 1829, married Ira Peck at Dunning Prairie, Wis., in 1857. They were farmers. Mr. Peck died in 1883. They had four children : Arthur D., Alice May, Alfred Chace and Arlie J. Peck. Arthur D. is married, is a farmer and lives on the old homestead in Stanton, Minn. Arlie J. Peck is married and lives at Hancock, Minn. His mother now lives with him.

Harriet Ellis, youngest child of Noah, was born Sept. 10th, 1830. She married H. D. Miller Jan. 4th, 1854, in Thetford. They went to Wis., where they lived four years; then to Stanton, Minn., where they now reside. They have four children : Alvin E., born 1856, is married and lives in Minneapolis ; Nelson, born 1861, is married and lives on the farm in Stanton. Cora E., born 1865, married and lives at Fergus Falls, Minn.; Fred C., born 1868, is in Minneapolis.

SETH ELLIS was born in Colerain, Mass., Oct. 14th, 1779. He was a farmer in Thetford, Orange Co., Vt., all his life, and died there May 22nd, 1869, aged 90 years. About

1805 he married Hannah Bartlett, of Norwich, Windsor Co., Vt., and after her death, Feb. 24th, 1835, he married Mary F. Burnap, of Norwich. The latter died Feb. 14th, 1868. Mr. and Mrs. Ellis were Presbyterians. Mr. Seth Ellis and his brother, Noah, after the death of their father, took charge of the family. They bought a farm in Thetford, and as their brothers and sisters grew up most of them went to New York or farther west. Besides farming Noah and Seth Ellis built two saw-mills in Vermont. They were in business together about twelve years, when each of them bought nice farms for that country. Seth Ellis had eleven children: Hannah, born 1806; William B., 1808; Stephen B., 1810; George C., 1813; John, 1815; Lucinda, 1817; Major E., 1819; Reuben H., 1822; Henry, 1825; Mary Jane, 1827, and Ellenor, 1838 —all born in or near Thetford, Vt.

Hannah Ellis lived with her father until his death in 1869, when she went to Mauston, Wis., where she lived with her sister, Lucinda E. Peck. She died in 1885.

William Burton Ellis married Louisa Dickinson, of Old Hadley, Mass., about 1835. She died June 1st, 1840. They had four children, three of whom died in infancy. A daughter, Hannah M., married Mr. Charles French, and they lived in Rumney, N. H. For his second wife Mr. William B. Ellis married Rosetta Bosworth, and they lived near Copenhagen, Jefferson Co., N. Y. They had two children, Louisa and William. The latter married and went to Kansas. His sister went with them to Kansas.

Mr. William B. Ellis died in Wattsburg, Erie Co., Pa., about 1879. He was a farmer and hotel-keeper.

Stephen Bartlett Ellis, son of Seth, of Thetford, Vt., born 1810, married Abigail Newcomb in Thetford, May 3d, 1832. They had four children: A. Elmina, Amanda P., Henry E. and Sarah O. The eldest, Abigail Elmina, born Feb. 14th, 1833, married Nathan Andrews June 3d, 1852, and they live in Meriden, N. H., where Mr. Andrews is a farmer. They have had twelve children: John S., Abbie O., Charles H., Addison W., Sarah A., Nathan R., Seth E., Emma G., Frank B., Minnie E., Lillian E. and Clarence

E. The eldest, John S. Andrews, born 1853, married Carrie L. Packard, and they have one child, Cora. Abbie O. Andrews, born 1854, married James A. Sloan, and they have four children : Ernest H., Arthur A., Herbert A. and Cleon N. Sloan. Charles H. Andrews, born 1856, married Verona Farnsworth October 10th, 1876. Sarah and Minnie Andrews died in childhood.

Amanda P. Ellis, second child of Stephen B., married Thomas Merrill Rugg Nov. 27th, 1856. Mr. Rugg was a farmer. He died in 1883, aged 51 years. They had four children : George E., born 1862 ; Luvina L., 1866, married Samuel E. Greeley; Hattie A., 1874, and Chester, 1878.

Henry E. Ellis, born Feb. 25th, 1841, son of Stephen B. Ellis, went into the army in 1862. He was wounded and died April 13th, 1865.

Sarah O. Ellis, youngest child of Stephen B., was born in Thetford May 7th, 1844. She married Henry C. Mace Dec. 26th, 1866. They have two children : Fred E., born 1869, and Henry O., 1871. Mr. Mace is a teamster.

Mr. Stephen B. Ellis' first wife, Abigail, died March 1st, 1848, aged 39 years. For his second wife he married a widow, Sarah Dewey, of Thetford. Mr. Ellis was a farmer and stone-cutter. He always lived in Thetford, where he died July 18th, 1877. He was an upright and highly respected man.

George C. Ellis, third son of Seth, was born in Thetford, Vt., Feb. 11th, 1813. He married and lives in Union village (Thetford township). He writes that "Robert Fulton (77) lived in this town. He was a cousin of my father. His children were, so far as I know, Stephen, Elijah, Henry, Jesse, James and Minerva. Robert Fulton came here from Colerain, Mass." He was the eldest son of James Fulton and his wife, Hannah Ellis (17), of Colerain. Mrs. Erastus Howard, of Thetford, is a granddaughter of Robert Fulton.

Mr. George C. Ellis married Julia A. Morse Dec. 28th, 1837. Mrs. Ellis was born Aug. 16th, 1816. They have had five children : Susan A. Ellis, born July 9th, 1839. She married Elias Foote May 10th, 1859. They have one child, Frank. Seth C. Ellis, born May 15th, 1841. He died Nov.

25th, 1854. Emma E. Ellis, born May 1st, 1843, died Sept. 5th, 1859. George Luman Ellis, born Aug. 27th, 1849, married Lizzie Waterman Nov. 25th, 1882. They have one child, Grace. Lilla G. Ellis, born Sept. 6th, 1855, died Oct. 7th, 1864. All born in Thetford, Vt.

John Ellis, son of Seth, was born in Thetford, Vt., March 11th, 1815. He was married March 11th, 1839, to Miss Abigail Peck, of New Hampshire. They moved to Harrisburg, N. Y., where they lived seven years ; thence to Beaver Dam, Wis., living there nineteen years. In 1868 they settled in Fremont, Iowa. Mr. Ellis now lives at Greene, Butler Co., Iowa. He is a farmer. He has been a member of the Christian church over 35 years. He had eight children : Abigail L., married C. S. Wheeler, reside at Calmar, Iowa.; Mary J., married W. B. Gilmore, live at Pipe Stone, Minn.; Carrie T., married W. Robinson, live at Fort Atkinson, Wis.; John M., lives in Greene, Iowa ; Daphna M., married G. J. Preston, live at Fort Atkinson, Wis.; Denzil N., marrried M. A. Pratt, live in Greene, Iowa, and Inez A., lives in Greene, Iowa.

Mrs. Abigail Peck Ellis was born in Wilmot, N. H., Jan. 19th, 1816. She died in Fremont, Iowa, Oct. 26th, 1879.

Lucinda Ellis, daughter of Seth, was born in Thetford in 1817. She married Mr. H. Peck. She is a widow, living in Mauston, Wis.

Major E. Ellis, son of Seth, was born in Thetford, where he now lives, a farmer. He married Roxana Clogston in 1840. She died in 1884. They had five children, three of whom died in infancy. Joseph Ellis, born in June, 1851, and Carrol, in March, 1861, are farmers in Thetford.

Reuben Hazen Ellis, son of Seth, was born in Thetford, Vt., March 21st, 1822. When 16 years of age he went to live with his uncle, Reuben Ellis, in Centerville, N. Y., where he was married to Martha A. Eddy, Nov. 21st, 1844. She died April 5th, 1849. In May, 1851, Mr. Ellis married Ruth Eddy, a sister of his first wife, and moved to Beaver Dam, Wis., where he now resides. His second wife died May 27th, 1870, in her 45th year. Jan. 23d, 1872, Mr. Ellis married Lydia Turner. She died Aug. 7th, 1885, at the age of 53. He was again married Jan. 19th, 1887, to Miss Anna L. Steptoe, of Beaver Dam. Mr. Ellis has been a farmer and cheese-maker most of his life. He moved to Beaver Dam in 1849, and has been several times elected a member of the Board of Supervisors, and to the Common Council of the city.

Mr. Ellis' children were: Shalon W., born 1847 in Centerville, died 1878 at Beaver Dam. He was a printer, and for two years a Union soldier. Amelia J., born 1852, married 1882 to E. S. Mason, of Beaver Dam. They have two children, Ruth and Edna Ellis Mason. Mr. Mason is a book-keeper. His wife had been a school teacher about 15 years before her marriage. Sarah E., born 1855, was married in 1877 to Maurice E. Henika, of Madison, Wis., a carpenter by trade. They have one child, Mabel C., born 1879. Mrs. Henika died in 1885 at Beaver Dam. Anna M., born 1857, died 1881. She was a school teacher. Dwight W. Ellis, youngest child of Reuben H., was born in Beaver Dam Dec. 27th, 1868. He is located at Schwartzburg, Wis., where he is station agent and telegraph operator for the Chicago, Milwaukee & St. Paul railroad, commencing there when 15 years of age.

Henry S. Ellis, youngest son of Seth, was born in Thetford, Vt., January 24th, 1825. At two years of age he became a mute from scarlet fever. He was well educated at Hartford, Conn., where he married a mute. They had three children, Elsie, Mary and John, all married and live in or near Boston, Mass.

Mary Ellis, daughter of Seth, was born in Thetford, Jan. 4th, 1827. She married William Morse. They lived in or near Union Village. She died young and childless.

Ellenor V. Ellis, youngest child of Seth, and only child by his second wife, was born in Thetford in 1838. She married a Mr. Pattrell, and resides in Norwich, Vt.

LEVI ELLIS was born in Colerain, Mass., about 1785. In early life he went to Centerville, N. Y., where his brother, Reuben, had settled. Soon after he went to Champion, Jefferson Co., N. Y., and settled on a farm. He was a clothier by trade. He was in the battle of Sackett's

Harbor in the war of 1812. He was married in Champion in 1816, and reared two sons : Ephraim C. and John E. Ellis. In 1836 Mr. Levi Ellis visited his brothers, Enos and Eliphalet, who were then in Vevay, Ind. Mr. Levi Ellis married Mrs. Anne Chamberlain, widow of Ephraim Chamberlain. Her maiden name was Coe, from Hartford, Conn.. She was born in 1775, and died in Beaver Dam, Wis., in 1853. She was one of the earliest settlers in Champion. Mr. Levi Ellis died in Beaver Dam, Wis., in 1849. It is said that he bore a strong resemblance to Dea. Dimick Ellis, whose likeness may be seen in the front of this book. Mr. and Mrs. Levi Ellis were Presbyterians.

His eldest son, Ephraim C. Ellis, was born in Champion in 1817. He married Melissa Wilcox, of Oneida Co., N. Y., in 1840. They had six children : Emma C., born 1841 ; Helen M., 1845 ; Edward L., 1849; Charles H., 1851; Fred E., 1857, and Frank O., in 1859. Mr. Fred E. Ellis died in Minneapolis in 1881. Emma C. married James Pettit. Their children were Lillie and Irving. They live at Cedar Springs, Mich. Helen M. Ellis lives at Somerset, N. Y. Edward L. Ellis married Nellie Hubbard. They have one son Dwight. They live at Somerset. Charles H. Ellis married Marietta H. Rice, of Grand Rapids, Mich. They have one child, Laura M. Mr. Ellis is a florist in Grand Rapids. Frank O. Ellis married Estella Webber and lives in Somerset.

Mr. Ephraim C. Ellis is a farmer in Somerset, Niagara Co., N. Y. Himself and family are Presbyterians.

John Everett Ellis, son of Levi, was born in Champion, N. Y., August 20th, 1820. Feb. 18th, 1847, he married Harriet M. Burke in Beaver Dam, Wis. Miss Burke was from Windsor, Vt. They now reside in Murray, Iowa. They are farmers. Mr. Ellis was a Union soldier in the Rebellion, Co. F. 1st Reg. Minn. Heavy Artillery. He was badly disabled and is now a pensioner. Their children were: Mary J., Frances E., Laura A. and George Washington Ellis. The first two are dead. Mr. John E. Ellis and family are Methodists. Of their children, Mary J., born April 13th, 1848, died in 1883. She married James V. Rice in 1864. Francis E., born May 31st, 1850, died 1852. Laura

A., born Feb. 21st, 1852 ; George W., Oct. 16th, 1856—all born in Beaver Dam, Wis. George W. Ellis married Anna E. Long. They live in Clark Co., near Murray, Iowa.

LURENA ELLIS, daughter of Matthew, was born in Colerain. She was unmarried and lived with her brother, Reuben in Centerville, N. Y., where she died in 1856.

ENOS ELLIS, son of Matthew, was born in Colerain, Mass. He went to Vevay, Ind., about 1814. But slight trace of him has been found by the writer. His nephew, Reuben (son of Eliphalet) writes that " Enos joined the Mormons at Nauvoo, Ill., in early times, left them, and died about 1842 at or near Warsaw, Ill. He married and had a family of six children, two sons and four daughters. Their names were Martin, Hezekiah, Electa, Sarah and Eliza."

Electa is said to have married Joel D. Clark, and lived at Warsaw, Ill. Eliza married a King, and lived at Warsaw.

ELIPHALET ELLIS, son of Matthew, was born in Colerain, Mass., about 1787. When a young man he went to Carthage, Jefferson Co., N. Y., and was engaged in the battle of Sackett's Harbor, N. Y., May 29th, 1813. He and his elder brother Enos went to Vevay, Ind., about 1814. He died in 1844 in Indiana. He was an upright and highly respected man. About the year 1815 he lived for a time, it is said, in Kentucky. He married for his first wife a Miss Haines. She died in 1823. Her children were : George, born 1815 ; Ann, 1817 ; William, 1819 ; Enos, 1821, and David, 1823. In 1829 Mr. Ellis married his second wife, Permelia Hardy. Her children were: Matthew, born 1830, died in infancy ; Reuben, 1834 ; Levi, 1836 ; Sally, 1838.

George Ellis, eldest son of Eliphalet, was born near Big Bone, Ky., in 1815. He died near Florence, Ind., in 1886. He had ten children : Ann, Catherine, Eliphalet, killed in the army, Jane, Caroline, James, Emeline and George. They live near Florence.

Ann Ellis married Andrew Given and died in 1859 near Florence, where her family now live.

William Ellis died of fever in Vicksburg, Miss., in 1842.

Enos Ellis, son of Eliphalet, lived near Osawatamie, Kas. He was a Methodist. He married Sarah Fuller in

1840. They had six children: Ann, Andrew, Mary, Emeline, Emma and William. They live in Kansas.

David Ellis was born in Switzerland Co., Ind., in 1823. He now lives near Moscow, Mo. He married Mercy Fuller in 1847, and has one child, Cynthia, who married a Chisholm and lives at Blue Eagle, Mo.

Reuben Ellis, son of Eliphalet, was born near Florence, Switzerland Co., Ind., in 1834. He married Nancy Skidmore in 1854, and now lives near Jackson, Tipton Co., Ind. Mrs. Ellis was born in Henry Co., Ky., in 1836. They have had ten children; five sons and one daughter are now living. Mr. Ellis and family are "Friends," or Quakers, in religious belief. Of their children—

W. D. Ellis, born in 1858, married Mary Hankens in 1880. She was born in Ripley Co., Ind., in 1863. They have four children: Estella May, Abilam, Nancy Ellen and Elizabeth, born 1886, died 1887.

Albert Ellis, second son of Reuben, was born in 1860; married in 1881 to Lydia Newhouse. Their children are: Drury V., born 1882; Louis. 1884, and Caly, 1886.

Sally Jane Ellis, daughter of Reuben, born in 1866, married Joseph McNew in 1883. They have two sons: Grimaldo Otto, born 1884, and Elmer, 1886.

Eliphalet Ellis, son of Reuben, born 1864, married Florence McCoy in 1887. She was born in Tipton Co. 1865.

Erodis, born 1868, and Marion 1872, are the younger children of Reuben Ellis, of Jackson, Ind. All his children were born in Switzerland Co., Ind.

Levi Ellis was born in Indiana in 1836. He married Rachel Jane Skidmore in 1859. She was a sister of Reuben Ellis' wife, Nancy. She was born in Henry Co., Ky., in 1840. They had ten children, four of whom are now living, Martha, Reuben, John and Levi, in Tipton Co. Mrs. Ellis has since married Thomas Ooten. Levi Ellis died in 1880. He was a Baptist.

Sally Ellis, youngest child of Eliphalet, was born in Indiana in 1838. She married Hiram Hunt in 1857, and had two children, Levi and Mary. Mr. Hunt died in 1860, and Mrs. Hunt married David L. Dunn, and had four children:

Marion, Reuben, Jenny and William. Reuben is dead. Mrs. Dunn died in 1886. They are Methodists. They live near Vincennes, Ind.

Of these sons of Eliphalet Ellis, of Indiana, Enos, David, Reuben and Levi were Union soldiers during most of the time of the Rebellion. All were in Co. D., 10th Ind. Cav.

REUBEN ELLIS, son of Matthew, was born in Colerain, Mass., about 1790. When a young man he settled in Centerville, Alleghany Co., N. Y., about 1811, where he was a farmer and a man widely noted for integrity and worth of character. He was a Presbyterian and a thorough Christian. He married Miss Annie Woodward, a daughter of P. B. Woodward, Esq., one of the earliest and most prominent settlers in Centerville. Mrs. Ellis died in 1858, and Mr. Ellis in 1868. They left no children. After the death of Mr. Ellis' brother, David, in 1847, two of the latter's children, Mary Ann and Henry, were reared by their uncle Reuben in Centerville.

SARAH M. ELLIS, daughter of Matthew, was born in Colerain. She was married in Vermont to John Tilden. They moved to Beaver Dam, Wis., where Mr. Tilden died. Mrs. Tilden moved to Kansas, where she died. They had six sons : Titus, Franklin, Daniel E., Crawford, Levi and Carlos. Several of them were living near Leavenworth at last report.

DAVID ELLIS, youngest child of Matthew Ellis, was born in Colerain, Mass., Aug. 3d, 1798. When a young man he settled in Centerville, Alleghany Co., N. Y., where he married Eliza Woodward and had four children : Andrew, Sarah M., Matthew Clark and Eliza. Eliza died in infancy. Mrs. Eliza Ellis died, and David Ellis married her sister, Polly Woodward. They had four children: Mary Ann, Darwin, Henry and Wayland.

In 1845 David Ellis moved with his family to Beaver Dam, Dodge Co., Wis., where he died Sept. 29th, 1846. Soon after Mrs. Ellis, with her four young children, returned to Centerville, N. Y., where she now resides. Mr. Ellis and wife were Presbyterians. He was a farmer. Mrs. Ellis was born in Ashford, Conn., in 1807. She was a sister of Annie Woodward, who married Reuben Ellis (David's elder brother), of Centerville. Mrs. Polly Ellis now lives with her daughter, Mrs. Allen, in Centerville.

Of David Ellis' children, Andrew died aged 19 years. Sarah Maria Ellis was born in Centerville, N. Y., June 11th, 1822. She was married to Peter Cole in September, 1841. They had four children : Mary A., Frank A., Elbert D. and Walter G., all living. In 1869 Mr. Cole and family removed to Omro, Wis., where Mrs. Cole and children now reside, engaged in mercantile business. Mr. Peter Cole died in 1880.

Of the children of Mr. and Mrs. Cole, Mary A. was born in Centerville, N. Y., in 1846, and was married in March, 1869, to Chauncey J. Fox, of Centerville. They are now living on a farm in Beatrice, Dak.

Frank A. was born in 1854 and married the third daughter of Rev. Jos. M. Walker, of Wis. M. E. Conference, in Sept., 1882.

Elbert D. was born in 1859, and Dec., 1880, married Miss Almeda Frost, of Vermont, and removed to Minnesota, afterwards to Nebraska, and finally to Beatrice, Dak., where they now live. They have one child, a daughter.

Walter G. was born in 1861. Was married Dec., 1884, to Clara C. Carpenter, of Dartford, Wis.

The Cole family are Presbyterians.

Matthew Clark Ellis, son of David, was born in Centerville, N. Y., Sept. 11th, 1827. In 1846 he went with his father to Beaver Dam, Wis., and later to Oshkosh, Wis., where he lived until about 1871, when he went to Minneapolis, Minn. Mr. Ellis' first wife was Adaline Gallant, of Milwaukee, Wis. They settled in Oshkosh, where Mr. Ellis was a farmer and subsequently engaged in the flour and feed business. They had five children, two of whom died in infancy. Mrs. Ellis died of consumption April 5th, 1862. She was of English descent, and a Presbyterian. Her children were: Frances A., Adelbert C. and Ida V. Ellis.

For his second wife Mr. Matthew Clark Ellis married Jane E. Morey, of Oshkosh. In 1871 Mr. Ellis moved to Minneapolis, where he was in the flour and feed business until his death, Aug. 12th, 1874. He was a Presbyterian, a kind and affectionate husband and father, and a highly respected man. Mrs. Ellis moved to Kansas City, Mo., where she lives with her three children, Nettie, Jessie and Amanda.

Frances A. Ellis, daughter of Matthew Clark Ellis, was born Jan 30th, 1851. She was married Sept. 20th, 1874, to Dr. Uriah D. Thomas. They have three children: Cora A., Ethel A. and Ernest C. Dr. Thomas and wife are Spiritualists. He practices medicine in Minneapolis.

Adelbert Clark Ellis was born July 1st, 1852. After his father's death in 1874 he remained with and cared for the family for several years. He is a clerk for a fuel company in Minneapolis. He was married Dec. 25th, 1884, to Ella V. Osborn, of Oshkosh, Wis. They have one son, Orison A. Ellis, born Aug 15th, 1886. Mr. and Mrs. Ellis are Methodists.

Ida Viola Ellis was born April 4th, 1860. She was married Dec. 24th, 1879, to Mr. M. P. Satterlee, eldest son of Rev. W. W. Satterlee. Mr. Satterlee is a printer. Himself and wife are Methodists.

Mary Ann Ellis, daughter of David Ellis and his second wife, Polly Woodward Ellis, was born in Centerville, N. Y., Feb. 27th, 1836. She married Amasa P. Allen in 1860. They have had five children: Alice D., born 1863; Darwin E., 1865; Lillian, 1868; Clarence, 1874, and Raymond, 1878. Mr. and Mrs. Allen live in Centerville, N. Y. All these people were farmers, and Presbyterians in religious belief.

Darwin Ellis, son of David, was born in Centerville, N. Y., in 1839. He enlisted at Centerville at the outbreak of the Rebellion, and died May 12th, 1864, from wounds received at the battle of the Wilderness, Va. He was unmarried.

Henry Ellis, born in Centerville, N. Y., in 1841, was a Union soldier. He was killed by the cars in Illinois in 1881.

Wayland Ellis, youngest child of David Ellis, was born in Centerville, N. Y. He died young.

APPENDIX

TO

Biographical Sketches of Richard Ellis

AND HIS DESCENDANTS.

Containing Sketches of Ashfield, Mass., where Richard Ellis was the first Settler, with brief mention of other localities where the Ellises have resided, and other Miscellaneous Matter of Interest.

The following paper, by Rev. Thomas Shepard, is now published for the first time. The manuscript has been in possession of Mr. Henry S. Ranney, of Ashfield, over fifty years, and is printed by his courtesy. Mr. Ranney has made some notes thereto, which are designated by his initials, H. S. R.

Rev. Mr. Shepard, during his residence in Ashfield, was highly esteemed by all the people, some of whom are yet living, and give his name and memory with honorable mention. His foresight and enterprise in writing these sketches should entitle him to the gratitude of all residents of Ashfield, as no other person, so far as is known, had, up to his time, written any connected history of the town.

SKETCHES

IN THE

HISTORY OF ASHFIELD, MASS., FROM ITS FIRST
SETTLEMENT TO THE YEAR 1833.

DEDICATION.

To the inhabitants of the First Parish in Ashfield over whom the writer was settled in the Gospel ministry for nearly fourteen years, and with whom he lived in uninterrupted harmony and mutual confidence, these sketches in the history of their town are most affectionately and respectfully dedicated, by their most obliged and obedient servant,

THE AUTHOR.

Amherst, March, 1834.

INTRODUCTION.

It cannot be expected that in a town comparatively of such recent origin, and so retired in its location as this, should afford, in the progress of its history, many events of general interest. To those, however, who were born and educated here, and to those who now live here, it must be a matter of considerable interest to know who were the pioneers of this town, and what are some of those principal events that have transpired here since the howl of the wild beast was alone heard through the forest, which spread unbroken over these hills and vales, now verdant under the cultivating hand of a numerous and thriving population. To the generations that may come after us, who may have little or no access to the facts connected with the early history of this place, which are familiar to us by tradition, a written history must be of increasing value. With a view of rescuing from oblivion many events connected with the early settlement of this town, and to hand them down for the information and amusement of those who may come after us, as well as to revive in the memory of many now living, the things of former years, I have, by conversation with the few surviving fathers of the town, and by a diligent examination of its ancient and modern records, drawn out the following imperfect sketch of the principal events in its history.

[275]

BOUNDARIES.

That portion of territory within the County of Franklin now called Ash-field was originally intended to embrace a tract of land six miles square; but, from some unknown cause, its present boundaries do not lie in this exact form. The town, if reduced to regular dimensions, would form a square whose sides would extend six miles and one-fifth, inclosing an area of 24,601½ acres.

SOIL—CLIMATE—DISEASES—POPULATION.

The surface of this town is broken into hills and valleys and contains but a comparatively small portion of arable land. Indian corn succeeds well, but English grain is of secondary quality compared with that raised on the lighter soils of Connecticut river. Wheat is seldom sown. Grazing may be said to be a principal object with the farming interest. Large dairies are kept here, and many tons of the finest wool are yearly furnished for the manufactories. The highest mountain in the town is that situated west of the pond. Its hight is estimated at about 800 feet.* There are no very considerable streams running through the town, inviting the manufacturing capitalist. The prin-cipal streams, however, furnish water power for all domestic purposes. Water from the springs and wells is generally of ready access and of the purest qual-ity. The winters are long and severe. The snow generally falls about the first of December and continues until the first of April. During February and March the ways are frequently blocked and passing difficult. The climate, though severe in winter, is nevertheless healthy. The prevailing disease with the middle-aged, upon these mountains, may be said to be con-sumption. This may be owing in part, perhaps, to the severe and variable winters. From the year 1819 to 1831, twelve years, one hundred and sixty-three persons died in this town over 12 years of age. Of these, nine died by casualties, or, as is commonly said, by accident; twenty-one of old age, and ten by diseases unknown to the writer; leaving one hundred and twenty-three persons over 12 years of age who have died in consequence of some definable disease. Of these 123 persons, fifty-four—nearly *one-half*—died with the con-sumption. Dysentery has frequently prevailed among children during the months of August and September. In 1825 twenty-one under five years died in this town, most of whom were carried off by the above complaint. During 1829 and 1830 the scarlet fever or canker rash prevailed very extensively, and in several instances proved mortal to children.

The average number of deaths during the fourteen years of the writer's connection with this people was a fraction over twenty-two a year, which would be one from every twenty-five of its inhabitants. The highest number of deaths in any one year during this period was *thirty seven;* the lowest number, *thirteen.*

The population of Ashfield in 1820 was 1,748; in 1830 it was 1,732. The town contains four houses for religious worship, one academy, thirteen school-

---

* Peter's Mountain, named from a colored man who lived there in early times. About 1885 Hon. James Russell Lowell, late U. S. Minister to England, purchased a site for a sum-mer residence on the east side of this mountain. Soon after, his wife died, and Mr. Lowell removed to England, and, it is said, has decided not to build thereon. It is a very sightly place, and from its top, on a clear day, points in New Hampshire, Vermont, Connecticut and New York are visible.

houses, two hundred and fifty dwelling-houses, three taverns, five stores, two gristmills, nine sawmills, three clothier shops and three carding machines. It also has two machines for turning broom handles, five blacksmith shops and two tanneries.

FIRST SETTLEMENT.

The original name of this place was *Huntstown;* a name given to it in honor of Capt. Ephraim Hunt, of Weymouth. In the year 1690 this gentleman was sent out, by order of Government, as commander of a company of men selected from Weymouth and vicinity, in an expedition against the Canadas, in a contest between the English and French, commonly called King William's war. This war commenced in the year 1690 and terminated in 1697. It was attended with many disastrous consequences to the American Colonies. An infuriated horde of savage warriors were let loose upon our scattered and defenceless population. The company under the command of Capt. Hunt composed a part of an expedition fitted out by the united colonies of New York, Connecticut and Massachusetts, for the reduction of Montreal and Quebec, then in the hands of the French. A combination of unfortunate circumstances, however, defeated the design, and the expedition, after encountering numerous hardships and disasters, returned without accomplishing their object. The success of the expedition had been so confidently anticipated that no express provision had been made for the payment of the troops. Massachusetts, in the low state of her finances, issued bills of credit as a substitute for money; and in the year 1736, after a delay of more than forty-six years, redeemed those bills; at least, so far as the aforesaid company was concerned, by granting them, their heirs or legal representatives, a tract of land within the limits of this town. In the conditions of the grant express provision was made for the early settlement of the town, the erection of a meeting-house, the settlement of a learned and orthodox minister, and the cause of common schools. By a Committee of General Court sixty-three lots, called Rights, containing from fifty to sixty-three acres each, according to the quality of the land, were set off and numbered, to be disposed of as follows: One right to be given to the first settled minister, one right for the use of the ministry, and one right for the use of common schools. The remaining sixty rights were to be divided by lot among the officers and privates of the aforesaid company, their heirs or legal representatives. The grantees—or Proprietors, as they were henceforth called—held their first meeting at Weymouth, where most of them resided, March 13, 1738, and on the 24th of July, 1739, they met again at the same place and drew lots for their respective rights, set off for them by government in this town.

The early settlement of the town being a desirable object with the proprietors, inasmuch as it would tend to enhance the value of the property they now owned in it, they passed a resolve, May 28, 1741, that a bounty of £5 should be paid to each of the first ten of their number who should take actual possession of their respective rights, build a house and bring under cultivation six acres of land individually. How many of those men who endured the toils and privations of the Canada expedition lived to receive their bounty of land, does not appear; but the lapse of forty-six years from the expiration of that expedition, very probably had carried the greater part of them to that "bourn from whence no traveler returns," and their heirs alone remained to realize the tardy remuneration which should have long before fallen to those who had sustained the burden and heat of that perilous day. Nor does it appear from the records that any of the original proprietors ever settled upon their lands in person. Their rights were sold to others of a more adventurous spirit, from time to time, as they had opportunity. In the meantime taxes began to accumulate upon them, and many of them were parted with for a little more than was sufficient to meet the demands of the collector.

The precise year when a permanent settlement was made in this town I have not been able to ascertain.* Soon after the lots were drawn, in 1739, it doubtless became the temporary abode of emigrants, as they came out from time to time to pioneer the wilderness From the best information I have been able to obtain, I have been led to fix the first permanent settlement of this town about the year 1745.† The first family that pitched their tent upon these hills as permanent residents was that of Mr. *Richard Ellis*, a native of Dublin, in Ireland. Respecting the immigration of this gentleman from that distant land to America, tradition has handed down in the family the following account, which, if true, is only in accordance with many of the like kind— the result of the cupidity and knavery of unprincipled shipmasters. The story is this: Mr. Ellis was the only son of a widow. A wealthy planter living in Virginia, a native of Ireland, having no children, made application to his friend in Dublin to send him out some youth of promise, to be adopted into his family and brought up under his care and patronage. Young Ellis was selected and sent out for this purpose. On his embarkation his passage was paid and an agreement made with the captain of the ship to land him safely on the coast of Virginia. Faithless to his trust, he brought the youth to Boston and there sold him for his passage money. After serving the time thus unjustly extorted from him he removed from Boston, and at length settled in Easton, where he was married. From Easton he came to this town. The first tree was felled by his hands, on White Brook, a small stream running a little to the west of the dwelling of Mr. Phineas Flower. He built for his family the first habitation in the northeastern section of the town—a log cabin, partly under ground, in the side of the hill, about fifty rods to the east of Mr. John Belding's, near the ancient burying yard, and where the new road runs. The next immigrant to this lonely wilderness was Mr. Thomas Phillips, with his family, from Easton, whose sister was the wife of Mr. Ellis. Mr. Phillips built for himself a log house about one-half of a mile to the north of the dwelling of his only fellow-townsman, Mr. Ellis. Soon a third family was added—that of Mr. Chileab Smith, from that part of Hadley now called South Hadley. Mr. Smith settled on the spot which the house of his son, Chileab Smith, now occupies. Mr. Smith, the present occupant, now in his 92d year,‡ was about 8 years old when his father removed to this town. To the retentive memory and free communication of this venerable father and pillar in the town I am indebted for many of the facts here recorded.

---

* A corn mill was built in the year 1743. It is believed that a permanent settlement was made in 1741.

† Preaching was had here as early as 1742. See Proprietors' Records, pp. 51, 54 and 55.

‡ He died in the year 1843, aged 100 years and 8 months.—H. S. R.

Among the earliest accessions to the settlement as it now consisted, of three families, was Dea. Ebenezer Belding, from Hatfield, and Samuel Belding, from Deerfield, with their families. Other settlers came in from time to time, from different quarters. A number of families joined them from the southern part of Connecticut, so that by the year 1754 they numbered from ten to fifteen families and nearly one hundred souls.

TRIALS OF THE SETTLERS-SETTLEMENT ABANDONED.

This little colony of immigrants, thus removed from their friends and from civilized society, in the midst of a mountainous wilderness, with scarcely any means of intercourse with those they had left behind, were permitted, under the watchful hand of Providence, to pursue their labors with comfortable success, subjected, of course, to a thousand self-denials incident to the pioneers of the forest, of which we, in these days of pampered indulgence, can form no adequate conception. For a number of years they had no other means of grinding their corn than by a mill turned by a horse. They had also to contend with bad roads, with rapid streams without the convenience of bridges, and with deep snows in the winter without the means of maintaining a beaten path. But all these inconveniences could be endured so long as they were secure from the attacks of the merciless savages, that still prowled around the infant settlements of our country, seeking whom they might devour. Such security and quietness, however, they were not long permitted to enjoy. The year 1754 was memorable for the breaking out of fresh hostilities between the French and the English. This war let loose again the Indians upon the defenceless frontier settlements of our colonies. During the month of June of this year a party of men at work near Rice's fort, in the upper part of Charlemont, was attacked by a body of Indians, and two of their number were killed and two taken prisoners. The tidings of this Indian massacre spread abroad and quickly reached the settlement in Huntstown and occasioned great alarm. Being few in number, and with small means of defense, they had no other alternative than to fly back to the older settlements, or to expose their wives and children to the tomahawk and scalping-knife of the savage foe. After a hasty deliberation the former course was resolved on. 'Accordingly, on the same afternoon in which they received the tidings from Charlemont, they abandoned their houses, improvements, stores, &c., except such as could be transported on horseback, and set off, one and all, for the older settlements on Connecticut River. A middle-aged woman, the mother of the present Chileab Smith, traveled ten miles on foot before they encamped for the night. What is now Conway was then a part of Deerfield and a howling wilderness, without an inhabitant or a shelter to protect the refugees. Their first halt was at Bloody Brook, where they spent the night. Early the next morning the few inhabitants of the latter place abandoned their dwellings and joined them in their various dispersions to places of greater security. This sudden abandonment of their possessions, after having just gotten into a condition of comfortable living, could not have been otherwise than a sore trial to the first settlers of this town. It must have involved them in very considerable loss of property, besides being a very serious disappointment to their plans and prospects. But it appears to have been submitted to by them with that patient endurance and undaunted fortitude for which the men of that perilous period were so eminently distinguished.

RETURN OF THE SETTLERS—MEANS OF PROTECTION.

According to the best information within my reach, the time during which the settlers were absent from their possessions was between two and three years. It is not unlikely, however, that during this period individuals might have visited this place; but they did not presume to return with their families until the time specified. After the return of the refugees to their possessions in Huntstown, the war still continuing, their first object was to erect a fort for their common defense. This was accomplished on the ground occupied by Mr. Smith, and principally at his own expense. The area inclosed by the fort was a square piece of ground containing 81 square rods. It was constructed of upright logs of sufficient thickness to be bullet proof, set three feet into the earth and rising twelve feet above. The inclosure had but one gate, open-ing to the south, which was always shut and strongly barred during the night. Within the fort stood the dwelling of Mr. Smith, which served as a garrison within which the settlers felt secure from attack during the night. On its roof was constructed, of logs, a tower of sufficient magnitude to contain six men with their arms. Port-holes were so arranged in its sides as to afford its inmates a fair aim at their assailants without, while secure from their balls within. This house stood in the center of the fort, and on the same ground now occupied by the dwelling of Chileab Smith.

After remaining in this state for about one year, standing on their own defense—keeping watch by night, and laboring by day with their arms by their side—they solicited and obtained from the authorities of the colony a company of nine soldiers, under the command of a sergeant by the name of Allen, for their greater security. This guard arrived, under the general order of Col. Israel Williams, June, 1757. This company continued in the settlement until the close of the war, which was about two years from the time of their arrival. Their duty was to go, under arms, with the people, to protect them in their labors during the day, and to return with them into the fort and, in their turn, stand sentinel during the night. In the process of time, and before the close of the war, another fort, six rods square, was built by the settlers, in the same manner as the first, about one mile and a half southwest of it, near the house now occupied by Mr. Sears. This fort was used for the same purposes as the other.

In the good providence of God the settlement was preserved safe from the attack of the enemy. Nor were any Indians discovered near it except in one instance. As a daughter of Mr. Smith was walking out one evening, just as the sun was setting, she discovered an Indian within about twenty rods of the fort, surveying it very attentively. With great haste and terror she flew back to the gate and gave the alarm: "The Indians are upon us!" The sol-diers immediately rallied and commenced pursuit; but darkness soon coming on, they returned without discovering the enemy. During the night they slept upon their arms and early next morning renewed their search through the woods, but saw nothing save the evident trail of a small hunting party, probably sent out to reconnoiter the settlement; but, finding it well garrisoned, they presumed not to molest them afterward. For about two years the first settlers of this town were destined to live in this state of constant agitation and alarm. Often were their sympathies deeply excited by the narration of savage barbarities committed upon their more unfortunate fellow-citizens in other places. They felt themselves in jeopardy every hour. As they retired to rest each night they knew not but that they should be aroused by the yell of the war whoop, to behold their dwellings in flames, and their wives and little ones in the merciless grasp of the wild men of the woods. The taking of Quebec by the enterprise and daring of the gallant Gen. Wolf, in 1759, restored peace to the colonies. The soldiers stationed here were disbanded, and the settlers, to their unspeakable satisfaction, were again permitted to pursue their daily avocations without fear of molestation.*

PROPRIETORS' ACTS.

The first meeting of the proprietors was held in Weymouth, or Braintree, as the town was originally called, March 13, 1738. They afterwards met at Hadley, then at Hatfield, and finally, in 1754, in Huntstown. The following gentlemen, in the order in which their names are here recorded, served as proprietors' clerks, viz : William Crane, Richard Faxon, Israel Williams. Esq., Ephraim Marble, Reuben Belding, Jacob Sherwin, Esq., Ephraim Williams, Esq.

The proprietors took early measures to supply the settlement with mills. They built, at their own expense, in the year 1743, the first grist mill on Pond Brook, about 100 rods northeasterly from the Episcopal Church, where the remains of a similar establishment may now be seen. Subsequently, in the year 1753, they erected a saw mill on Bear River, about half a mile east of the dwelling of Israel Phillips.

At the commencement of this sketch we noticed in the original grant express provision for the support of an orthodox ministry. The fathers of New England were the descendents of the Puritans. Although they sought no alliance between Church and State, they knew full well that no government could secure the morality and happiness of a people without the prevalence of pure and undefiled religion. Actuated by the same spirit, the proprietors took early measures to secure to the town the stated ministration of the Gospel. At a meeting held November, 1751, a sum of money was raised to supply the settlement with preaching. In 1763 they settled a Congregational minister, and in 1767 they erected and finished a convenient house for public worship. But more concerning these things will be related in its more appropriate place.

DOINGS OF THE TOWN—ACT OF INCORPORATION.

The records of the town previous to 1776 are very imperfectly preserved. There are remaining in the town clerk's office only a few separate scraps of paper bearing date prior to the aforesaid year. Of this early period I have been able to glean only the following items :

The first town meeting of which any record remains was held March 8, 1762, at the dwelling house of Jonathan Sprague. Ebenezer Belding was

---

*In 1761 there were 19 families residing here.

chosen Moderator, and Samuel Belding town clerk. The business was not of sufficient importance to be noticed here.

In June, 1765, by act of General Court, the town was incorporated by the name of *Ashfield*. The warrant to call the first meeting under the act of incorporation was issued by Thomas Williams, Esq., of Deerfield, and directed to Samuel Belding, clerk of this town. The first town officers under the incorporation were: Benjamin Phillips, Town Clerk; David Alden, Treasurer; Chileab Smith, Moses Fuller, Thomas Phillips, Selectmen.*

The subject of common schools began early to engage the attention of the fathers of this town. They seemed fully to understand the orthodox doctrine— that a free government can only be sustained by an intelligent population. Accordingly, they voted, in 1772, to divide the town into three school districts and to build a school house.†

According to the records, the first representative chosen for the purpose of acting in the affairs of the State was Capt. Elisha Cranston. In 1775 this gentleman was chosen to represent the town in the congress to be convened at Watertown, Boston then being in the possession of the British troops.

WAR OF THE REVOLUTION.

A period now approached fraught with the most trying scenes ever experienced by the citizens of these United States. It was the War of the Revolution. In the events which preceded and attended that trying period, the citizens of this town, although removed from the principal scene of action, were nevertheless deeply interested, and in them they took a decided part. As early as September, 1774, when events in and about Boston began to wear the aspect of hostilities, and the first Continental Congress had commenced its session in Philadelphia, the following covenant, previously drawn up by a committee chosen for the purpose, was signed by Benjamin Phillips and sixty-four others, citizens of this town:

"We, the subscribers, inhabitants of the town of Ashfield, from a principle of self-preservation, the dictate of natural conscience, and a sacred regard to the constitution and laws of our country, which were instituted for the security of our lives and property, do severally and mutually covenant, promise and engage, with each other and all of us:

" 1. That we profess ourselves subject to our Sovereign Lord the King, and hold ourselves in duty bound to yield obedience to all his good and wholesome laws.

" 2. That we bear testimony against all the oppressive and unconstitutional laws of the British Parliament, whereby the chartered privileges of this province are struck at and cashiered.

" 3. That we will not be aiding, nor in any way assisting, in any trade with the Island of Great Britain, until she withdraws her oppressive hand, or until a trade is come into by the several colonies.

" 4. That we will join with our neighboring towns in this province, and sister colonies in America, in contending for and defending our rights and

---

* See the Town Book of Records—copied in 1857—page 6.— H. S. R.

† In the year 1766, at the first annual meeting subsequent to its incorporation, they voted £1 for the school.

privileges, civil and religious, which we have a just right to do, both by nature and by charter.

"5. That we will make preparation, that we may be equipped with ammunition and other necessaries, at town cost, for the above purposes.

"6. That we will do all we can to suppress petty mobs, trifling and causeless."

That the signing of these articles of covenant was not a mere matter of unmeaning form appears evident from the fact that in the following August the town voted to send an agent to Albany for the purpose of purchasing guns and ammunition, at the expense of the town. At length affairs at headquarters came to a crisis. On the 19th of April, 1775, an attack was made by a column of the British army, under the command of Maj. Pitcairn, upon our unoffending yeomanry at Lexington; and thenceforth commenced that unequal conflict which, after eight years of toil, privation and blood, resulted, in the providence of God, in the independence of these United States.

Such was the poverty of our government, and such their inability to raise the necessary means of sustaining an army sufficient to face the hosts of Britain, that at the commencement of hostilities it, of necessity, devolved upon the patriotism of the towns from which the soldiers were drafted, to furnish them with supplies and, in many instances, to become responsible for their wages during service. The citizens of this town, as their records fully evince, did not remain idle spectators of this contest. They fell not behind the spirit of the times in their devotion to the cause of freedom, and their willingness to sacrifice almost any temporal comfort in securing it to themselves and their posterity.

It would extend altogether beyond the limits of this sketch to quote at length the patriotic doings of this town in lending their aid to encourage and carry forward the War of the Revolution. A few facts selected from their records is all that my limits will permit me to notice.

In fully estimating the sacrifices made by our fathers in coming forward with their voluntary contributions in sustaining the War of the Revolution, we must take into the account two important circumstances: first, the fact of their having just begun to subdue the wilderness, and the consequent state of dependence in which most of them were placed in regard to the necessary means of subsistence; and, secondly, the uncertain and changeable state of their monied currency. Notwithstanding these pressing embarrassments, we find the inhabitants of this town at one time voting, in open town meeting, to furnish the army with a lot of coats. At another time we find them offering a bounty to such as might enlist from among them to serve in the war; and at another, voting a sum of money to purchase provisions to be sent to the famishing army. In 1779 the town voted to pay the soldiers enlisted from among them, for nine months' service, forty shillings per month in addition to the bounty offered by General Court—the value of the money to be regulated by corn at 2s. 6d., rye at 3s. 4d., and wheat at 4s. 6d. per bushel. In 1780 the town voted to give, by way of encouragement, to each man who should enlist in the army for three years, "twenty calves." Said calves were to be procured in the following May and kept at the town's cost until the three years had expired. How many of these men returned to receive their bounty, then grown to be oxen and cows, does not appear. In 1781 the town voted to raise "ninety silver dollars" to purchase the amount of beef that fell to their share for the army. The same year eight men were enlisted from this town for three months' service who were to receive from the town treasury £4 per month, and $10 each before they marched. In 1777 Rev. Nehemiah Porter, in consequence of the enfeebled state of his people, and the consequent depreciation of his support, joined the army on the North River [Hudson] in the capacity of Chaplain, and continued with them until the capture of Burgoyne.

During this severe and protracted controversy with the mother country the people of this town, in common with their brethren in other parts of the provinces, suffered great embarrassments in consequence of the fluctuating state of their paper currency. The enormous depreciation of this currency in 1780 may be learned from the fact that during that year the town raised and expended upon the highways *three thousand pounds!* It was the custom of the town, at their annual meeting in March, to choose a "Committee of Safety, to do what in them lay to regulate the price of provisions and to ease the burdens of the people." A Committee of Correspondence was also appointed annually, to confer with similar committees in other places, in relation to the trying and critical state of public affairs.

One item of record in these troublous times—"times which" emphatically "tried men's souls"—I cannot omit to notice, although it is somewhat of a delicate nature ; but inasmuch as it evinces that ever vigilant and stern spirit which characterized the patriot of that generation, I shall be excused by omitting names in the narrative : At a legal meeting held July 18th, 1777, it was voted "that Aaron Lyon be a meet person to procure evidence against certain persons who are thought to be inimical to the American States." At a subsequent meeting, in August following, the Selectmen were requested to bring in a list of persons whom they viewed to be of the above description. This report contained the names of nine persons, among whom were some of the most respectable and leading men in the town. Whereupon it was voted that the persons thus reported "appear so unfriendly to the American States that they ought to be brought to proper trial." It was also voted at the same meeting, these suspected men "be committed to close confinement in this town." One of the prisoners, however, in consequence of the sickness of his family, was exempted from confinement on condition of delivering up his arms and ammunition. The others were forthwith dispatched to a private dwelling, under a strong guard selected and supported by the town. After continuing thus imprisoned for about seven days and nights the town met again and voted " to dismiss the guard and release the prisoners from close confinement." This transaction is but a faint specimen of what transpired in every section of the country between the resolute and the timid, the friends and the foes of war. Many an house was divided against itself; friends, neighbors, brethren, took different sides in the contest and were fiercely arrayed against each other. Nor can it be a matter of wonder that men of wisdom and foresight should have opposed resistance to the power of Britain; so unequal was the contest and, in human view, so very improbable the attainment of any permanent good on the part of our infant colonies. But the ways of Providence are not as our ways; the result exceeded the most sanguine expectations of the friends of the revolution; the God of Heaven went forth with our armies and the victory was on our side. Never was there a contest between nations in the decision and determination of which the overruling hand of God was more manifest; and the patriots of that day were led to feel that deliverance from the overwhelming power of Britain could alone proceed from the Power that ruleth the nations. Hence they looked to Heaven, and fasted, and prayed for help from above; nor did they pray in vain. In July, 1777, in legal town meeting, it was voted that "this town will do all that lies in their power to suppress vice, and especially that they will use their endeavors to prevent profane cursing and swearing, that the name of God be not blasphemed among them."

ADOPTION OF A STATE CONSTITUTION.

The question whether this Commonwealth should form for itself a constitution in consonance with the national compact already signed and adopted. became the subject of general discussion. In August, 1779, Capt. Benjamin Phillips and Capt. Samuel Bartlett were chosen delegates to attend a convention about to be held at Cambridge for the purpose of forming a constitution for the Commonwealth. These gentlemen were instructed by the town, among other things, to use their endeavors that an article be inserted in said constitution, "that each Representative, previous to his belonging to General Court, shall be solemnly sworn not to pass any acts or laws where his constituents shall be in any sense, name or nature, oppressed or forced in matters of religion." On this subject a portion of the people of this town felt peculiarly sensitive, for reasons which will hereafter be noticed.

In the following year came up the important question respecting the adoption of the constitution prepared by the aforesaid convention and sent out by them for the approval of the people. In open town meeting this constitution was taken up, debated and acted upon, article by article. The result was, that while many of its provisions were approved by a majority of the town, others were rejected. The *third article* in the Bill of Rights, which proposed that the preaching of the Gospel should be supported by taxation, was rejected, on the ground that it was "unconstitutional to human nature and nothing in the word of God to support it." The article specifying the appointment of the judges of the Supreme Court by the Executive was rejected, and a substitute proposed, viz : that they should be elected annually by the Legislature. The article constituting the Senate an essential part of the Legislature was rejected, on the ground that such a distinct body was unnecessary. Those articles specifying the pecuniary qualifications of the different officers of government, and of voters in town meeting, were rejected by a majority of the votes of this town. An amendment was proposed that Justices of the Peace, instead of being appointed by the Governor, should be elected by ballot annually, in legal town meeting, and commissioned by the Governor. It was also proposed that town clerks be the acknowledgers and registers of deeds, and that the Probate office be lodged in the hands of the Selectmen, and the Town Clerk be *ex officio* Clerk of Probate.

These transactions are referred to for the purpose of exhibiting the views of our fathers respecting the science of civil government. While it was happy for our Commonwealth that most of the alterations here proposed did not prevail, it is worthy of notice that the views expressed in relation to the Bill of Rights on the prevailing views of the Commonwealth at the present day, and after the lapse of half a century, have effected an essential alteration of this article in the constitution.

In the order of chronology it may be proper here to notice an incident which occurred here in 1781. During this year the north part of this town was infested with a company of vagrant religious fanatics called "Tremblers." Such extravagance and disorder and indecency were exhibited by them in their intercourse with the inhabitants, and especially in the acts of worship, that the people living in the vicinity where they located themselves became very seriously annoyed and presented them to the authorities of the town as a public nuisance. Whereupon it was voted in legal town meeting that "the Selectmen be requested to warn said straggling Tremblers now in town, and those that shall come in hereafter, to depart in twenty-four hours or expect trouble."

PECUNIARY EMBARRASSMENT—SHAY'S INSURRECTION.

In 1782 the pecuniary pressure became very severe upon the inhabitants of this town and the community in general. The enfeebled and partially organized condition of the General Government rendered it necessary for individual States to make great efforts to maintain their credit and meet the demands which the progress of the war was constantly bringing upon them. Massachusetts felt under the necessity of levying a heavy tax upon the people. The result was murmurings and insubordination from every quarter. The people of this town voted not to collect the portion of the State tax assigned to them, and to recommend to their militia officers to resign their commissions. They drew up and signed a covenant for their mutual defense and sent out a committee to inform the neighboring towns of their doings. Other towns were excited to similar measures of resistance from similar causes. Taxes were heavy and money scarce; county conventions began to be held, and one event after another transpired until Shay's rebellion broke out, in 1786. Such were the embarrassments of the times that the people not only resisted the taxes of government, but the demands of common creditors. The regular sittings of the courts at Northampton, Worcester and Taunton were obstructed by the people convening in tumultuous assemblies. Thousands of our citizens in different parts of the Commonwealth were arrayed in rebellion against a government which they had just established at the expense of great toil and much blood. A majority of the people of this town joined in the common panic and took sides with the insurgents. By consent of a majority of the Selectmen the magazine of the town was given into the hands of the rebels, and a militia officer and a company of soldiers volunteered their services and marched off to their assistance. But the same Almighty Hand that sustained our country during her contest with the hosts of England, carried her safely through these scenes of civil commotion, and caused them all to work together for good, to her future peace and permanency. With a few conflicts, and the loss of a few lives, the insurrection was quelled; the people, after further reflection, became satisfied that their embarrassments were occasioned rather by the necessary expenditures of the Revolution than by any defect in the government itself or the manner of its administration.

ADOPTION OF THE FEDERAL CONSTITUTION.

The commotions narrated above convinced the people of New England that some stronger bond of union between the States, for their mutual protection, was necessary. Accordingly, a convention was called at Boston in 1787 for the purpose of consulting upon the adoption of the confederated constitution proposed by the Congress of the United States. Accordingly, Ephraim Williams, Esq., was chosen to represent this town in said convention, and instructed "to use his influence that said constitution doth not take place." But, notwithstanding the views of the good people of this town, said constitution did take place, and for nearly fifty years the people of this town, in common with their fellow-citizens throughout the Union, have rejoiced in the many blessings which it has imparted.

ECCLESIASTICAL HISTORY.

It has been remarked that the original proprietors of this town took early measures to supply the first settlers with Gospel ordinances. In the original grant of the Soldiers' Rights two of them were reserved for the support of a learned and orthodox ministry; and in 1751 a sum of money was raised by the proprietors to supply the settlement with preaching. Rev. Mr. Dickinson, a Congregational minister from Hadley, was the first employed to preach in the settlement. Afterward they were favored with the labors of Rev. Mr. Streeter. Their meetings were held in the dwelling of Deacon Ebenezer Belding, which stood on the same ground now occupied by an house on the opposite side of the way from Dimick Ellis, Esq. [Now (1864) Mr. Bardwell's.—H. S. R.] Mr. Joshua Hall now (1887) owns and lives on this farm.

The first regular church formed in the town was of the Baptist denomination. It was constituted July, 1761, consisting of nine members. In the following August Rev. Ebenezer Smith, the eldest son of Chileab Smith, was ordained its pastor. In May, 1768, Nathan Chapin and seventeen others sent in a petition to General Court setting forth that they belonged to the persuasion called Anabaptists, and praying to be exempted from the taxation for the support of the Congregational ministry. This petition, after repeated and persevering efforts, during which the petitioners were subjected to many trying scenes, was at last granted. It is to be regretted that there should ever have been occasion, in this land of enlightened liberty, for such a petition as this. Nothing would seem to be more reasonable than that any religious denomination demeaning themselves as peaceable members of society, should enjoy free toleration in the exclusive maintenance of their own order. Our fathers fled hither that they might enjoy liberty of conscience in matters of religion. But it must be remembered, by way of apology for any seeming inconsistency in their legislative acts, that for a long while after the settlement of Plymouth the people of this land were very generally of one and the same denomination; hence their laws had respect to this particular denomination alone; and when in the process of events other sects sprang up, they were not so careful, perhaps, as enlightened Christian charity would have dictated, in so modifying their statutes as to give equal toleration to all who might conscientiously differ from them. Hence, in the tardy revision of the laws to meet the exigencies of the times, there were, without doubt, insulated cases of what would now be universally pronounced religious intolerance and oppression. But those were days when free toleration in the things of religion were but imperfectly understood. The progress of nearly a century has thrown much light on this subject; we have occasion to thank God that we have fallen on better times. Let not the errors of those years of comparative darkness, long since gone by, be revived and handed down as a matter of reproach or recrimination between Christian brethren differing only in modes, and all enjoying, to their full satisfaction, liberty of conscience and equal toleration. For a long number of years the kindest feelings have been entertained between the Baptist and Congregational churches in this town.

In 1798, after a ministry of thirty-seven years in this town, Elder Smith was dismissed from his pastoral charge in good standing. He soon after removed to the western part of New York, where he continued to labor in different places until he reached the age of 89. He died at Stockton, in the County of Chautauqua, N. Y. Mr. Smith, though not favored with early opportunities for a systematic education, is represented to have been a man of strong native powers of mind, thoroughly orthodox in sentiment, and an acceptable preacher. [See (10) page 71.]

January 14th, 1798, Elder Enos Smith, the youngest son of Chileab Smith, and brother of the former minister, was ordained pastor of this church, and still continues in this relation, having now reached the 85th year of his age and 36th of his ministry.

In 1800 this society, embracing a portion of the southeastern section of Buckland, obtained an act of incorporation. This church has, at different periods, experienced seasons of refreshing from the presence of the Lord. This was particularly the fact during the winter of 1831, when considerable additions were made to their communion. The exact number of communicants now belonging to this church I am not able to state. In the spring of 1831 it was *one hundred and six*. Their first house of worship stood about fifty rods north of Mr. Chileab Smith's. About two years since the society erected a new and convenient meeting-house, about one-half of a mile to the east of this spot.

This society, if not the oldest, is certainly among the oldest, of the Baptist denominations in the western section of Massachusetts. It has always occupied ground peculiarly its own, having never interfered with that preoccupied by others. Its church is venerable for its age; many in it have been raised up for the Kingdom of Heaven. It is entitled to and, I doubt not, it receives, the prayers of the people of God of every name around it, for its peace and prosperity.

December 22d, 1762, the Proprietors gave a call to Mr. *Jacob Sherwin* to settle with them in the work of the Gospel ministry. February 22d, 1763, a Congregational church consisting of fifteen members was formed by an ecclesiastical council convened for the purpose, and on the following day Mr. Sherwin was, by the same council, ordained its pastor. The Articles of Faith and Covenant prepared by this council were consented to and signed by the following persons: Jacob Sherwin, Thomas Phillips, Nathan Waite, Ebenezer Belding, Timothy Lewis and Joseph Mitchell.

Mr. Sherwin's ministry in this place continued a little more than eleven years and two months. Difficulties arising between him and his people, he was finally dismissed by an ecclesiastical council and recommended to the confidence of the churches. During the ministry of Mr. S. eighty persons were added to this church, including those who became members at the time of its constitution. *Forty-nine* of these were admitted by profession and *thirty-one* by letters of recommendation from sister churches. The ordinance of baptism was administered to one hundred and nineteen persons.

Mr. Sherwin was born in Hebron, Conn., and was graduated at Yale College in 1759. After his dismission from his pastoral charge he continued to reside in the town, became a Justice of the Peace, the first that was honored with this commission in the place, was elected clerk of the town for a number of years, and also clerk of the proprietors, and occasionally officiated as one of the Selectmen. Afterward he resumed the active duties of the ministry, removed to Shaftesbury, Vt., where he was installed and, as far as it appears, continued his labors until his decease.

December 22d, 1774, Rev. Nehemiah Porter was installed pastor of this church and continued in this relation until his decease, February 29th, 1820, aged 99 years and 11 months. During Mr. Porter's active labors, until the settlement of his first colleague, it being about thirty-five years and a half, 334 persons were admitted to the church—240 by profession and 94 by letter. Eight hundred and fifty received the ordinance of baptism. During Mr. Porter's ministry the church enjoyed several seasons of religious revival. In 1780 —a year distinguished in the annals of New England for the extraordinary outpouring of the Holy Spirit upon the churches— there were numbers gathered into the Church of Christ in this place; but more particularly in 1797-8, during which season of precious interest upwards of eighty were added to the Congregational Church.

Rev. Mr. Porter was born in Ipswich, in this State, in 1720, just about one century from the landing of the Pilgrims on Plymouth Rock, and lived to witness the mighty events that signalized the revolution of almost an entire century from that memorable period. He was graduated at Cambridge College in 1745, and studied divinity with Prof. Wigglesworth, of that institution. He was first settled at Chebosco, now Essex, in the County of Essex. After his dismission from that place he went with his family into the British Dominions, in New Brunswick, where he labored for a number of years in the character of a missionary. From thence he came into this region and was finally installed over this people in 1774.

Mr. Porter was a man of active, energetic and commanding powers of mind. He was favored with a vigorous constitution and an uncommon strength and fullness of voice. His religious sentiments were those of the Reformation, and his style of preaching, though somewhat redundant—a characteristic of the age—was, nevertheless, energetic and impressive. During the War of the Revolution, his support in a great measure failing, in consequence of the severe pressure of the times, he obtained permission to join the army on the Hudson River, in the capacity of chaplain.—He was there during the conflict with Burgoyne and the capture of the British army. That event, so propitious to the American arms, he was wont to say was not the result of human might or power, but by the arm of Jehovah of Hosts. During the heat of the battle which decided the fate of Burgoyne's army Mr. Porter, being with a reserve of men at a little distance from the scene of action, obtained permission of the officer to retire, with as many as were disposed, to a secluded spot at a little distance, for the purpose of prayer, and, while in the full hearing of the tremendous onset they were there calling upon the God of Armies to interpose with His mighty arm in behalf of the cause of liberty and religion, the noise of the battle died away and the victory of our arms was decisive. Perhaps there never was a contest since miraculous powers ceased, where the interposition of Heaven was more conspicuous, than in that which resulted in the independence of these United States.

Mr. Porter lived far beyond the common lot of men. He did not wholly cease from the labors of the ministry until he was over ninety years of age; and, indeed, until the last month of his life he was able to conduct the devotions of the family and to converse to the religious edification of his friends. With long life he was satisfied. He came to his grave in full age. He was gathered to his fathers like a shock of corn fully ripe in its season. [Rev. Mr. Porter entered the pulpit of his church, and took part in the service, when in the 100th year of his age. He was taken from his house and seated on a chair placed on a "stone boat," was conveyed to the meeting house. Mr. Porter, the present (1887) proprietor of the Ashfield Hotel, on the Plain, is a descendent of his].

Rev. Alvin Sanderson was installed colleague pastor with Rev. Mr. Porter June 22d, 1808, and was dismissed at his own request, on account of declining health January 3d, 1816, after an active and successful ministry of seven years and six months. During this period sixty were added to the church—forty-one by profession, nineteen by letter; number of baptisms, seventy-four. Mr. Sanderson was born in Deerfield and graduated at Williams College. Although his public ministry was short, yet it proved a rich blessing to the people of his charge. His talents were of the active kind, and, though he did not excel as a preacher, he was peculiarly qualified to do good as a pastor in his daily intercourse with all classes. His labors were, emphatically, in season and out of season. In the literary, moral and religious education of the young he took a lively interest, and to promote this he labored incessantly. The burden of duties which he took upon himself impaired his health, and the fatal blow was struck by an attempt to fill with his voice the illy-constructed house of worship recently erected by his congregation. The effort to be heard in its high pulpit, and from beneath elevated ceiling, produced an hemorrhage of the lungs and brought on a gradual decline. In the meridian of life his sun went down. By the last acts of his life Mr. Sanderson more fully developed the influence of that charity which seeketh not her own, over his own heart. Having no family of his own to provide for, the most of the property which he had acquired by his industry and habits of economy he bequeathed to purposes of public learning and religion. The cause of foreign and domestic missions shared each a distinct legacy in his will. To the society over which he had been settled he made a generous donation as a permanent fund for the support of the ministry; and, lastly, the academy which bears his name was originated and endowed, in his earnest desire to do all in his power to improve the minds and hearts of the rising generation in learning and piety. He fell asleep in Jesus June 22, 1817, in the thirty-seventh year of his age. The memory of the just is blessed. The name of Alvan Sanderson will long be held in grateful remembrance by many surviving members of his beloved flock.

After the dismission 'of Mr. Sanderson the society continued destitute of a pastor for more than three years. During this period it was greatly afflicted with dissensions—the trying question who should be its next minister had well nigh broken down its energies and prostrated its ability to sustain the ordinances of the Gospel. And yet, even in these troublous times, the Lord did not forget his covenant people. During this season of destitution a revival took place which brought twenty into the fold of the Redeemer.

The writer of these sketches was ordained colleague pastor with Rev. Mr. Porter, over this church and society, June 19, 1819, and continued in this relation witn mutual harmony and confidence until May, 1833, when, in consequence of feeble health and the hope of being more useful in a more active sphere of ministerial labor, he was, at his own request, and by the kind concurrence of his people, dismissed by a mutual council. He was born in Norton and graduated at Brown University in 1813. During his ministry in this place, which continued nearly fourteen years, three seasons of special revival were enjoyed. The first was during the winter of 1821-2, when upwards of eighty were added to the church; the second was in the winter of 1829 30, when about the same number was added; the third was in the autumn, when about thirty-five were gathered into the visible fold of Christ. During the whole of his ministry the number of admissions has been 274, all but thirty-two of which have been by profession. The number of baptisms during the same time were *three hundred and five*. From the origin of the Congregational Church until the time of the writer's dismission, it being a little more than seventy years, 766 have been admitted to its communion and the ordinance of baptism administered to 1,405 persons. The number of living members at the above date, in regular standing, was 290, of whom 104 were males and 186 females.

In May, 1833, Rev. Mason Grosvenor was installed pastor of this church and society. Mr. Grosvenor was born in Pomfret, Conn., and graduated at Yale College. Since the settlement of Mr. G. some additions have been made to the church. May the Holy Spirit continue to descend upon it as rain upon the mown grass, and many be added unto it from time to time, of such as shall be saved.

The following brethren have officiated as deacons in this church in the order in which their names are recorded, viz: Ebenezer Belding, Joshua Sherwin, John Bement, Jonathan Taylor, John Porter, Enos Smith, Elijah Paine, Samuel Bement, Daniel Williams, Jared Bement. Deacons Paine, Williams and Jared Bement are still in office.

The first Congregational house of worship was built by the Proprietors. The frame was set up on the hill west of the dwelling of Dimick Ellis, Esq., but before it was covered it was taken down and set up on the southwest corner of the old burying ground on the plain. The removal took place in 1767. The present house of worship was raised July, 1812, and occupied by the congregation in the autumn of 1813. May the glory of this latter house be greater than that of the former.

In 1814 a second Baptist society was formed in this town, and a meeting-house built on what is called the Flat, about one mile east of the Congregational

Church. For a number of years Elder Loummus officiated as the minister of this society. In 1820 Mr. L. removed into the State of New York. Since then they have had the occasional labors of Rev. Orra Martin, from Bristol, Conn., who resides in the town. This society shared in the revival of 1829-30, when a church was organized with twenty-seven members. Their present number, probably, does not vary much from what it was then.

In 1820 an Episcopal society was formed in this town, and in 1829 a neat and commodious house erected and consecrated by the Bishop, by the name of St. John's Church. The society has been supplied at different times by the labors of Rev. Titus Strong, Rev. Lot Jones, Rev. William Withington, Rev. Mr. Humphrey, and Rev. Silas Blaisdale, who now resides with them. Their number of communicants in 1831 was about thirty. Their number has probably increased since, but how many I have not the means of knowing.

During the four or five years past the Methodists have established a place of worship, near the southeast corner of the town, and their circuit preachers occasionally officiate in other parts of the town. They shared in the revival of 1830. Their number of regular communicants I have no means of ascertaining.

Each of these religious societies sustains a Sabbath school, through a part or all of the year, and has a library for the use of its scholars; that belonging to the Congregational Society contains rising of 500 bound volumes. Among these different denominations, mingled together throughout the town, a good degree of harmony prevails. May the language of Abraham and Lot ever be theirs: "Let there be no strife between me and thee, for we be brethren."

EDUCATION.

The General Court, as we have before noticed, in their original grant to the proprietors, made express provision for the maintenance of common schools by reserving one right for this object. In the wisdom of our fathers the cause of education—one of the main pillars of a republican government—was not to be overlooked in the early settlement of the country. The annual income of the school lands is a little rising of one hundred dollars. To this an annual tax of about six hundred dollars is added, and expended in thirteen districts, according to the number of scholars in each. The whole sum thus expended averages about one dollar annually to each scholar. The quantity of instruction in each district varies according to the number of scholars; taken together it will average about six months to each district. Although the standard of common education is not what it ought to be, and what it might be, in this town, yet it has much improved during the last ten years, and is not now inferior, it is believed, to what it is in other towns similarly situated in the Commonwealth. The occasional establishment of select schools in the vicinity, and particularly those sustained by Miss Mary Lyon, now of Ipswich, has done much to qualify teachers for the more successful management of district schools.

After Rev. Mr. Sanderson had resigned the duties of the ministry, his health remaining feeble, he prepared a building, one-half at his own expense, and in the spring of 1816 opened a school for the instruction of youth of both sexes in the higher branches of a useful education. Though soon interrupted in his personal labors, yet at his decease he laid the foundation for a continued seminary for the promotion of learning, morality and religion in the rising generation. In 1821 an act of incorporation was obtained under the name of *Sanderson Academy*, and in the autumn of the same year it went into permanent operation under the care of Mr. Abijah Cross, a graduate of Dartmouth College. After Mr. C., followed successively in the labor of instruction, Messrs. A. Converse and S. W. Clark, from Dartmouth College; Messrs. B. B. Edwards, H. Flagg and R. C. Coffin, of Amherst College, and Rev. Silas Blaisdale. For a number of years past, in consequence of the deficiency of its funds, but more especially the want of the united patronage of the inhabitants of the town, it has almost wholly ceased its operation. It is melancholy to contemplate an institution founded in the prayers and charities of a man of God, going to disuse and decay in the midst of a population greatly needing its advantages, merely for the want of a little harmonious fostering care.

A social library containing about 175 well selected volumes, and yearly increased by an annual tax of fifty cents upon each share, has been in operation since 1815. During the continuance of the academy a debating society, and afterwards a lyceum, were productive of much interest and profit to the young people of the village.

TEMPERANCE.

The inhabitants of this town, in common with their fellow-citizens located in a region of fruit and distilleries, have suffered much from the scourge of intemperance. For years the wave of liquid fire rolled over those hills and valleys, carrying disease and poverty and death in its trail, with scarcely an obstacle to withstand its course. Many of the distilleries, first set up for the distillation of mint, by a little additional expense of vats could be employed for a part of the year in distilling cider. It is believed that for a number of years there were as many as eight or ten of these magazines of destruction in operation in the town. It was almost as much a matter of course for the farmer to take his cider to the still and take home his stock of brandy for family use, as it was for him to carry his grain to the mill and furnish the staff of life for his household. But the times are changed—the Spirit of the Lord has lifted up a standard against the enemy of all righteousness. In the spring of —— a society was formed on the principle of total abstinence, consisting at first of twelve members. Many sober men were at first in doubt whether it was not pressing the cause too far; farmers were people that they could not hire their labor without the use of ardent spirits. But on further consideration their difficulties vanished one after another; the members of the society increased rapidly, until in the course of a few months rising of 600 names were found in the temperance constitution. The enemies of the cause were alarmed; they made every effort in their power to stay the work of reform; a strong union between the lovers of strong drink, the lovers of the gain of it, and the lovers of office, was formed, and showed itself at the polls and wherever any attack could be made upon the friends of temperance. But still the good cause could not be put down; opposition only served to strike its roots deeper into the hearts of its friends; an efficient society was formed in the north section of the town, whose fruits were soon manifest in the work of reform. The friends of temperance of different religious denominations go hand in hand in the cause; and, although one or two distilleries, and a few retailing stores and some temperate drinkers stand in the way, yet a purifying process is in progress which will not stop until the whole town and region is reclaimed from the cruel grasp of this common enemy of God and of man.

> " Fly swift around, ye wheels of time,
> And bring the welcome day."

PROFESSIONAL MEN.

The following persons, originally inhabitants of this town, have been educated at college, viz: Rev. Preserved Smith, graduated at Brown University and settled in the ministry in Rowe; Rev. Freeman Sears, Williams College, settled in Natick and deceased in 1812; Rev. Samuel Parker, Williams College, residing in the State of New York; Frederick Howes, Esq., Cambridge College, attorney at law in Salem; Francis Bassett, Esq., Cambridge College, attorney at law in Boston; Rev. Elijah Paine, Jr., Amherst College, formerly settled in Claremont, N. H.; Rev. William P. Paine, Amherst College, settled in Holden; Rev. Charles Porter, Amherst College, settled in Gloucester; Rev. Morris White, Dartmouth College, settled in Southampton; Rev. William Bement, Dartmouth College, settled in Easthampton; Leonard Bement, Esq.,[*] Union College, attorney at law, Albany, N. Y.; Francis Gillett, Yale College, attorney at law in Ohio; Rev. John Alden, Jr., Amherst College, principal of Franklin Manual Labor School in Shelburn; Mr. Adell Harvey, Amherst College, student in Divinity; Rev. Anson Dyer, not publicly educated, laboring as an evangelist. Several young men are now in the process of a public education.

Hon. Elijah Paine, a native of Hatfield, has been the only attorney at law which has settled in this town until very recently. Mr. Paine has been a member of the Senate of this Commonwealth and the Chief Justice of the Court of Session in this county until the time of its dissolution. David Aiken, Esq., has recently opened an office as attorney at law in this town.

The following regular authorized physicians have resided in this town in the order in which their names occur: Moses Hayden, Phineas Bartlet, Francis Mantor, David Dickinson, afterwards settled in the ministry in Plainfield, N. H.; Hon. Enos Smith, a graduate of Dartmouth College, once a member of the Senate from Franklin County, now living in Granby; Rivera Nash, Green Holloway, Lee, Atherton Clark, now living in Cummington; William Hamilton, now in Providence, R. I.; Jared Bement, a native of this town; Charles Knowlton. The last two are now practising physicians in the town.

COUNTY AND TOWN OFFICERS.

The following gentlemen have been commissioned Justices of the Peace while residing in this town, viz: Jacob Sherwin, Philip Phillips, Ephraim Williams, Elijah Paine, Enos Smith, Henry Bassett, Thomas White, Levi Cook, Dimick Ellis, James McFarland, Russell Bement, Chester Sanderson.

The following gentlemen have represented this town in the Legislature of the Commonwealth, viz: Capt. Elisha Cranston, Dea. Jonathan Taylor, Benja-

---

*Judge Bement removed to Grand Rapids, Mich., about 1850, where he died twenty to twenty-five years later. He was a highly respected man.

min Rogers, Chileab Smith, Wm. Williams, Esq., Philip Phillips, Esq., Ephraim Williams, Esq., Hon. Elijah Paine, Henry Bassett, Esq., Thomas White, Esq., Hon. Enos Smith, Capt. Bethuel Lilley, Levi Cook, Esq., Dimick Ellis, Esq., Capt. Roswell Ranney, Dea. Samuel Bement, Chester Sanderson, Esq., Jonathan Sears, Seth Church, Anson Bement.

The following persons have served as Town Clerks, viz: Samuel Belding, Benjamin Phillips, Jacob Sherwin, Esq., Dr. Phineas Bartlet, Dr. Francis Mautor, Levi Cook, Esq., Hon. E. Paine, Capt. Selah Norton, Henry Bassett, Esq., Lewis Williams, Hon. Enos Smith, Dimick Ellis, Esq., James McFarland, Esq., Russell Bement, Esq., Wait Bement.

The following gentlemen have served as Town Treasurers, viz: Benjamin Phillips, David Alden, Dr. Phineas Bartlet, Warren Green, Jr., Ephraim Williams, Esq., Levi Cook, Esq., Hon. E. Paine, Charles Williams, Henry Bassett, Esq., Chester Sanderson, Esq.

The following gentlemen have served as Selectmen, viz: Ebenezer Belding, Reuben Ellis, Nathan Chapin, Philip Phillips, Esq., Moses Fuller, Chileab Smith, Thomas Phillips, Samuel Belding, Dea. Jonathan Taylor, Aaron Lyon, Samuel Allen, Timothy Lewis, Isaac Shepard, Capt. Joshua Taylor, Peter Cross, Dr. Bartlet, Jacob Sherwin, Esq., Dea. John Bement, Rowland Sears, Warren Green, Jr., Uriah Goodwin, John Sherwin, Thomas Stocking, Benjamin Rogers, Chileab Smith, John Ellis, Ephraim Williams, Esq., William Flower, Philip Phillips, Esq., Capt. John Bennet, Lemuel Spurr, Abner Kelley, Joshua Howes, Abiezer Perkins, Hon. E. Paine, Samuel Guilford, Ebenezer Smith, John Alden, Thomas White, Esq., Capt. Bethuel Lilley, Josiah Drake, Chipman Smith, Nathaniel Holmes, Dimick Ellis, Esq., Capt. Roswell Ranney, Jonathan Sears, Samuel Eldredge, Simeon Phillips, Sanford Boies, Austin Lilley, Seth Church, George Hall, Capt. William Bassett.

CASUALTY.

In May, 1827, an event occurred near the center of this town of too signal importance in its history to be omitted in these sketches. I refer to the accidental drowning of five persons in the Pond west of the Plain. Their names were Dea. David Lyon, a worthy man, aged 63, and his son, Aaron, aged 18, Arnold Drake, aged 28, and two sons of Mr. Eli Gray, William and Robert, one 15, the other 13. These persons, attended by a few others, left their families and friends on a beautiful morning in May, to follow their flocks to the place of washing, under as fair a prospect of returning at evening as ever they went out with in any previous morning in their lives; but, alas! they were all borne home lifeless corpses. In a fit of merriment, excited by a poisonous stimulant which was then deemed a necessary appendage to the washing of sheep, six of the company seated themselves in a log canoe, with two sheep, for the purpose of a short sail. On reaching deep water, about eight or ten yards from the shore, the canoe dipped water, filled and went under. Two of the company—the eldest son of Deacon Lyon and a boy—with the sheep, sprung for the shore and reached it safely; Drake, Lyon and the young Grays immediately sunk and disappeared. Dea. Lyon, from the shore seeing his son in danger, sprang in to his assistance, but on stepping suddenly from shoal to deep water immediately disappeared. It is remarkable that not one of them, after sinking the first time, ever rose again until their bodies were raised by others. Alarm was immediately given by those from the bank, the people of the village were soon on the spot and measures immediately set in operation to raise their bodies. A young man dove and brought up Dea. Lyon, who had been under perhaps fifteen minutes. They next succeeded in bringing up Drake, after perhaps thirty minutes' immersion; next, the body of young Lyon; and last, after being under about an hour, were brought up the bodies of the young Grays locked in each other's arms. Measures for resuscitation were immediately commenced on the shore, and prosecuted after they were carried to the house of Mr. Asa Sanderson for several hours, but all in vain; the vital spark had fled, nor could it be recalled; not the least sign of reanimation appeared in either of them. They were ensnared in an evil hour. In an unexpected moment their souls were required of them. After all hope of recovering the drowned persons was given up messengers were dispatched to carry the sad tidings to the widows, children, parents, brothers and sisters of the deceased. Soon the messengers returned, bringing with them the widows of Dea. Lyon and Drake, and the daughter of Dea. L., who was the stepmother of the young Grays. The affecting scenes of that interview may in some faint measure be imagined, but not described. On the following day the funeral of these five corpses was attended in the presence of a large concourse of sympathizing friends and strangers, at the late dwelling of Dea. Lyon. An appropriate discourse was preached on the occasion by Rev. Mr. Martin, from Eccles. ix. 12, after which their remains were deposited in the graveyard by the Baptist meeting-house, in the north part of the town. Who that witnessed any part of that appalling scene can pass by the banks of that secluded pond without recalling fresh to mind the events of that melancholy day? And who that ponders upon the events of that day can think lightly of the Savior's exhortation: "Watch, therefore, for ye know not the hour when the Son of Man cometh."

CONCLUSION.

But it is time to bring these sketches—already, perhaps, too far protracted—to a close. Permit me then, my brethren and friends, with whom I have been permitted quietly to sojourn for a time, in conclusion to say:

It is now about *ninety years* since the voice of the civilized emigrant first broke upon the silence of this, then lonely, wilderness. Three generations of men have come up and passed off the stage since your fathers came hither. The lofty forests which then crowned these hills and valleys have bowed to the power and industry of man, and given place to cultivated fields and thriving villages. The haunts of wild beasts have been supplanted by the abodes of civilized society. You of this generation roam securely over your fields, and sleep quietly on your beds, where once lurked in ambush the merciless savage, and where your fathers toiled by day and lay down at night with their arms by their side. This goodly heritage, with all its civil, literary and religious blessings, purchased by their toils, privation and blood, you now enjoy. God forbid that you should prove so ungrateful as to despise such a birthright. Think not lightly, brethren and friends, of the talents committed to your care. Ninety years to come, and where will most of you be? Who will occupy your possessions? Who will dwell in your houses, roam over your hills and through your valleys, and sit in your sanctuaries? Who will break the bread of life to the generations who are to come after you, and point the dying sinner to the Lamb of God? And what will be the character of the history which will fill up the intervening years? These are questions of solemn import, and the practical answer must be given by you of this generation. God in mercy grant that you may so live, and train up your children, and so aid in laying broad and deep and strong the foundations of knowledge, morality, religion and good government, that future generations, as they come to reap the happy fruits of your labors, may rise up and call you blessed, as you are permitted to do the memory of your fathers, now no more.

THOMAS SHEPARD.

NAME OF ASHFIELD.

The original forests of Ashfield contained a large proportion of White and Black Ash trees, and it is thought that the name given the town, on its incorporation, was thus suggested.

EARLY SETTLEMENT IN ASHFIELD.

The following item is from Mr. H. S. Ranney, of Ashfield. In perusing the history of the township of Northfield I noticed the following statement: "In 1739 Richard Ellis and his son, Reuben, built a dwelling-house (log hut) and broke up five or six acres of land in township No. 1 (Westminster), on the west side of Connecticut river. Seth Tisdale and John Barney were with them."

At the time named Northfield was the first town above Deerfield, and Westminster about twenty miles above Northfield, in the State of Vermont. So Richard Ellis and son did not come here (Ashfield) without experience in roughing it." Richard Ellis' son Matthew was born in Easton in 1739, and soon after he took his family to Deerfield, where their next child, John, was born, in January, 1742. Most likely his family resided in Deerfield, while he and Reuben were engaged in Westminster, and also for the first year or two that they were making a start in Ashfield. This must have been about 1742, and it is well established that he was the first settler in that town. [See page 11.]

NOTE II.*

In the traditions of the Annable family, (Lieut. Edward Annable's wife, Jemima Smith, was a granddaughter of Richard Ellis. See No. 38, page 92,) it was related of Richard Ellis, of Ashfield, "that his parents were Welsh, his father being an officer under Cromwell, who overturned the English government, which at that time was strongly Catholic. After the downfall of Cromwell many of his adherents had to leave the country, among whom was Officer Ellis, who fled to Ireland, where the son Richard was born."

*See page 10.

It is hardly probable that such was the fact, so far as Richard's father being an officer under Cromwell.

Oliver Cromwell, one of the most noted personages in English history, was the son of a country gentleman, and was born in 1599. He was a strict Puritan, a sect or class of people who desired a wide departure from both the English and Roman Catholic churches. Charles I. was on the English throne from 1625 to 1649, and he attempted to crush the Puritans. This created civil war. Cromwell was a leader against Charles, and when the latter was dethroned and beheaded, in 1649, Cromwell was elected head of the government under the title of Lord Protector of the Commonwealth. Charles II., Prince of Wales, was the rightful heir to the crown, but did not succeed in establishing his cause until 1660, after Cromwell's death. The latter died in 1658, when his son, Richard Cromwell, was at the head of the Commonwealth about one year, when he abdicated.

Charles II. was then crowned and reigned until 1685. He died without heirs, when his brother, James II., was crowned, and reigned until 1689. James was a thorough Catholic, and through religious dissensions he was overthrown, and William of Orange, a Holland Prince, was invited to the English throne. Prince William was a leading Protestant, and he had married, in 1688, Mary, eldest daughter of King James II., just dethroned. They were jointly crowned, as William and Mary, in 1689. Very soon thereafter war arose between England and France, on account of the King of France, Louis XIV., espousing the cause of James II. of England. This was called King William's war, mentioned on page 277. The conflict extended to the American Colonies, and led to the expedition against the Canadas by those who were afterwards granted rights of land in Ashfield. In 1694 Mary died, and William was sole monarch of England. During the last quarter of the seventeenth century was the bloodiest era in English history. Protestants and Catholics were in constant strife. King William had many conflicts with James II. and his supporters, who were trying to recover the throne. James was driven into Ireland, whence he and many of his followers fled to France and never returned. Celebrated among their battles were Boyne and Aughrim, William died in 1702, and, as he had no heirs, Anne, sister of Mary and daughter of James II., became Queen.

In 1692 William and his army followed James into Ireland, and it is more reasonable to believe that Officer Ellis (Richard's father) was connected with him than that he was a soldier under Cromwell, whose career ended nearly forty years before.

The account of Richard Ellis' boyhood, as given by Rev. Mr. Shepard, in his Sketches of Ashfield (see page 278), does not differ materially from that above, nor that on page 10, which the writer derived from those closely related to Richard, and which may be taken as very nearly, if not exactly, the true account of him. While he was born in Dublin, there is no doubt that his father was Welsh.

COTEMPORARY EVENTS.

The history of the American Colonies was very closely related to that of England and France, as each had their possessions on this side of the Atlantic.

Hence when war arose between those great kingdoms it usually extended to these colonies.

After the death of King William (Prince of Orange) in 1702, Queen Anne reigned until her death, in 1714. Then came George I., who was on the throne until 1727, when he was succeeded by his son, George II., whose reign lasted until 1760. During his reign the settlements in America were greatly extended. Oglethorpe formed a colony in Georgia named in honor of the King. Detroit and most of the region west of the Alleghanies was claimed by the French. In 1755 Gen. Braddock, with an army of English regulars, joined by many colonists, marched against the French, who had established a fort at what is now Pittsburg, Pa. In this war the Indians joined the French and led Braddock into an ambush, and would have destroyed his forces had it not been for the aid rendered him by young Washington and his regiment of Virginians.

At the same time, war between the English and their colonists on one side, and the French and Indians on the other, was raging in New York and New England. The French were not always able to restrain their Indian allies, and many of the colonists were massacred. It was the imminent fear of this which led the early settlers in Ashfield to abandon their possessions and go to the older settlements, east of the Connecticut river, from 1755 to 1758. It is said that at the beginning of this war the French possessions in America exceeded the English twenty to one. In 1759 the English General, Wolfe, captured Quebec; and all of Canada, including Detroit, fell into the hands of the English. Peace followed, and quietness once more reigned over the colonists, greatly to their rejoicing.

George II. died in 1760, and his son, George III., ascended the throne, which he held until 1820, although for the last ten years of his life he became imbecile, and his son, George IV., was at the head of the government as Prince Regent. It was during the reign of George III. that the American colonists had the long and desperate struggle—for nearly eight years—in which they finally won their independence. It was during George III.'s time that the Irish Parliament was abolished; which now, under the leadership of Parnell and Gladstone, is so earnestly sought to be restored. George III. was said to have been pure, pious and honest, often mistaken in policy, but won the love of the English people. It was by his arbitrary and overbearing acts, mainly, which led his colonists in America to revolt in 1775 and declare their independence. This same unwise course, also, was the cause of the last war of the United States with England, in 1812. His son, George IV., was drunken and profligate, although denominated by his favorites "the first gentleman in Europe." The present Prince of Wales, according to reports, is his counterpart in most respects. His reign extended to 1830, when, on his death, having no heirs, his brother, William IV., became King, for seven years, up to 1837. During William's time negro slavery was abolished in all the British possessions. The first railroad was constructed—that from Liverpool to Manchester. King William and the four Georges who preceded him were of the Hanover family of Holland Princes. They were all more Dutch than English in their tastes and nature. On William's death, in 1837, having no male heirs, the crown fell to his niece, Victoria, the present (1887) Queen, who has just celebrated the fiftieth anniversary of her coronation. While Victoria is a woman of no marked talents, her reign has been a credit to her, and she commands the love and respect of the English people in a high degree.

Although England is a noted and historic country, her climate is not the most desirable, judging from telegraphic reports of the day on which this page is written (October 13, 1887): "Snow storms, accompanied by thunder and lightning, prevailed throughout England and Wales yesterday, and the country roads in Wales are blocked with snow." It is probable that nothing in New England equaled this at the date given.

---

*NOTE III.

As an illustration of the peculiar temper of Richard Ellis' master, during his early years in this country, he related the following incident: On a time, one of the daughters of his master accidentally broke her father's favorite cider mug, and it was agreed that for a shilling Richard was to assume the responsibility of the matter and take the expected flogging. When the discovery was made, and the parent savagely asked the daughter who did it, she silently pointed to Richard, who sat in the corner and who meekly nodded assent. The master looked towards the boy and in fierce language said: "Ah, you little Irish brat!" and then turned away. Richard missed the flogging, and, in consequence, was refused the promised shilling.

EARLY SETTLERS IN NEW ENGLAND.

The Pilgrims originated in Scrooby, England, and were called "Separatists," on account of their separating from the English church. In 1608, on account of persecution, they emigrated to Amsterdam, in Holland, where, from internal dissensions, there was another separation, and part of them went to Leyden, in 1609, twenty miles distant. The penalty in England for separation was banishment; and yet, when they attempted to leave England they were arrested and detained several months, as it was supposed that they intended to leave for the Colony of Virginia, where none could go without a royal license.

In 1620 the Separatists, then called "Pilgrims," had increased in Holland to about 300 persons, when they resolved to find a larger field for their operations. In 1620 one hundred and two set sail in the Mayflower for New England, where they landed at midwinter in Plymouth, after a passage of sixty-six days. The balance came over in the Fortune in 1621, the James and Anne in 1623, and the Handmaid in 1630.

The Mayflower landed at Plymouth, in Cape Cod harbor, in December, 1620, with 102 persons. During that month six died, and eight more in January, seventeen in February and thirteen in March. Within the first year fifty deaths had occurred. It was in the face of such discouragements that the Pilgrims made their home in the New World.

These noble men and women, exiles from their native land, braved the ocean's storms in winter on a small vessel of 250 tons. It was known that

---

they intended making their settlement at New Amsterdam, near what is now New York city. Historians have never been able to decide as to why they landed at Cape Cod, unless it was from an error in the calculations of the navigator. After resting here a few days they attempted to round the cape and go further south, towards New York—or Virginia, as the whole coast was then called; but the storm drove them back and they were glad to make a final landing.

From their settlement on the rock-bound shores of New England has grown out the greatest consequences ever recorded in the world's history. Before their time true liberty was unknown in the world. The name and fame of the "Pilgrims" will deservedly go down the ages as the brightest ever known to mankind.

MILES STANDISH, born about 1586, and his wife Rose, came over in the Mayflower in 1620. His wife died the next month, and he himself, in Duxbury, in 1656. Tradition says that he sought to marry Priscilla Mullens for a second wife, but was defeated in this by his rival, John Alden. However, he married Barbara, who came over in the Ann in 1623, and had Alexander, Miles, Josiah, Charles, Lorah and John.

ALEXANDER married Sarah, daughter of John and Priscilla *Mullens* Alden, and had Miles, Ebenezer (1672); Lorah, Lydia, Mercy, Sarah, Elizabeth, Thomas, Desire, Ichabod and David.

Descendants of both these Alden and Standish families settled in Ashfield and have intermarried with the descendents of Richard Ellis.

JOHN ALDEN, celebrated in the history of the Plymouth Colony, came over in the Mayflower in 1620. In 1623 he married Priscilla Mullens, and their children were John, Joseph, David, Jonathan, Elizabeth, Sarah, Ruth, and Mary.

He died in Duxbury in 1687, and his wife Priscilla about 1650. That John Alden and Miles Standish and their families were ever on pleasant terms, notwithstanding the episode of which Longfellow has made them immortal, may be presumed from the intermarriage of their chileren, Alexander Standish and Sarah Alden. Later generations of these families intermarried with several of the Ellises of Plymouth and Barnstable counties, and also with descendants of Richard Ellis, of Ashfield. (See pages 90 and 96.)

STORIES OF THE EARLY SETTLERS.

On one occasion a settler had the misfortune to cut his foot badly. His wife was alone with him, and it was not prudent to leave him to seek the assistance of neighbors, but her ingenuity was equal to the emergency, and help soon arrived. The ingenious expedient she adopted was to tie some bloody cloths around the neck of their horse and start him on the trail towards the nearest neighbor. The animal speedily went through to where he was well known. The gory emblem told the story of distress, and no time was lost in rendering the desired aid.

A settler, hearing his cowbell ring in a peculiar manner, suspected the presence of Indians. The bell would be rung violently for a few strokes and then all would be still. The settler took his gun, and by going out in a circuitous route he discovered an Indian watching in the direction of his home. As a matter of course, the settler got the first shot. The Indian escaped, but left a trail of blood for some distance, whence it was supposed he was helped away by his companions, as it was known that the Indians had a great dread of their dead falling into the hands of enemies.

OLD ROAD TO HUNTSTOWN.

Mr. F. G. Howes has copied from the records of Old Hampshire County the minutes of a road to Huntstown which reads thus: "Road to Huntstown laid out in 1754. We met at Deerfield, began at the east path, south from the top of Long Hill, which leadeth out to the old sawmill, and in said path until it comes to the path turning out northerly, commonly called Huntstown road, and on said road as it was marked by the town of Huntstown, and'now commonly traveled, until it comes unto the west side of Deerfield bounds, and from thence in the northern road unto Thomas Phillips' house in Huntstown, and from thence as the road now goes to the west side of said Phillips' lot, and from thence in a straight line to Richard Ellis' new house, from thence as the path now goes unto Meeting-House Hill [Bellows Hill], unto a beech tree with stones around it, near Heber's fence, the whole road to be ten rods wide."

LAND SOLD BY RICHARD ELLIS, 1751.

No. 1.—Warranty deed by which Richard Ellis conveyed fifty acres of land in Ashfield to his eldest son, Reuben, in 1751. The same being the 56th lot or "Right."

Know all men by these Presents, that I, Richard Ellis, of Hunts Town, so Call'd, in ye County of Hampshire, in his Majesty's Province of the Massachusetts Bay in New England, for and in consideration of Twenty pounds Lawful money, To me in hand before Sealing and Delivering hereof, well and truly Paid by Reuben Ellis of Sunderland in ye County and Province aforesaid, the Rec't w'rof I do hereby acknowledge, Have Given, Granted, Bargained, Sold and Confirmed, and by these Presents Do Give, Grant, Bargain, Sell, make over and Confirm unto him the s'd Reuben Ellis, his Heirs and Assigns, A Certain Lot of Land Lying and Being in ye Township of Hunts Town Afore S'd, and is the fifty-sixth Lot in Number known by the name of fifty acre Rights: To Have and To Hold the s'd Grante l and Bargained premises with the Privileges and Appurtenances Including, but Half of the after Draughts belonging or may hereafter be drawn upon S'd Lot and No more: and he the S'd Reuben Ellis Doth by these Presents Promise to pay to his Brethren when they come of age the Sum of Thirteen pound Six Shillings and Eight pence of Lawful money in Dollars* at Six Shillings apiece: and I the said Richard Ellis, for my Self, my Heirs, Executors and Administrators, Do hereby Promise and Covenant all and Every the S'd Granted and Bargained

*The Dollar was originally a German coin, which is said to have been first coined at a town called Dale.

premises unto him ye S'd Reuben Ellis his Heirs, Executors and Administrators Against the Lawful Claims and Demands of any Person or Persons Whatsoever for Ever hereafter to Warrant and Defend.

In Witness W'r of—I the S'd Richard Ellis have hereunto set my hand and affixed my Seal this Twenty-fifth Day of Decem'r, Anno Dom. 1751, and in ye Twenty-fourth year of the Reign of our Sovereign Lord George the Second of Great Britain, France and Ireland, King, Defender of the faith, &c.

RICHARD ELLIS. [SEAL.]

Signed, Sealed and Delivered
    in Presence of us,
        ISAAC HUBBARD,
        *SIMEON SCOTT.

HAMPSHIRE, ss., April ye 27, 1762. Then Richard Ellis appeared and acknowledged the above Instrument to be his free act and deed.

ELIJAH WILLIAMS,
Justice of the Peace.

HAMPSH'R, ss.

SPRINGFIELD, May 14, 1765.

Rec'd and Recorded in Libr. 6, folio 3. and Examin'd,

Per EDW'D PYNCHON, Reg'r.

LAND BOUGHT BY RICHARD ELLIS, 1753.

No. 2.—To All People to whom these Presents shall come, Greeting: Know ye that I Joseph Melton of Hull in the County of Suffolk in New England, yeoman, For and in Consideration of the sum of five pounds to him in hand before the ensealing hereof, well and truly paid by Richard Ellis of Huntstown in ye County of Hampshire and Province of ye Massachusetts Bay in New England, yeoman, the receipt whereof I do hereby acknowledge and myself therewith fully satisfied and contented, and thereof and of every part and parcel thereof, have given, granted, sold, conveyed and confirmed unto him the said Richard Ellis, his heirs and assigns forever, one single lot of land, excluding all other lands, lying and being in the Township of Huntstown in the County of Hampshire in the Province of the Massachusetts Bay aforesaid, being Number Seven containing fifty acres be it more or less, it being a house lot and no other lands or Rights but that only. * * * In witness hereof I now set my hand and seal ye first day of March in the year 1753 and in the twenty-sixth year of his Majesty's Reign George the Second.

JOSEPH MELTON.

CALEB LORING,
JOSEPH MELTON, JR.,
        Witnesses.

No. 3.—December 6th, 1782, Reuben Ellis deeded to John Ellis 50 acres, being the north half of lot No. 53, in the third division of house lot No. 9.

No. 4.—October 27th, 1790, Nathaniel Beale, of Braintree, sold to John Ellis and Edward Annable, lot No. 12, in the second division, containing 100

---

*This Simeon Scott was probably Reuben Ellis' brother-in-law.

acres by estimate, bounded south by George Ranney, northerly by Seth Waite and John Sherwin. Consideration, 200 pounds.

No. 5.—January 25th, 1798, Barnabas Annable sold to John Ellis about seven acres of Land, being a part of lots Nos. 12 and 13, lying on the north side of highway, by which it is bounded, the north side of the same piece of land is the land of Philip Phillips and John Ellis' bounds, excepting the dwelling-house now on it, which I engage to move off. Consideration, $200.

April 23d, 1763, Nathaniel Gunn, and Hannah Gunn, his wife, sold to John Ellis fifty acres. [This was probably the old Ellis homestead, where John, Jr., Edward and Dimick were born.]

REVOLUTIONARY INCIDENTS.

The following are extracts from a pamphlet entitled "Historical Sketches of the Times and Men in Ashfield, Mass., during the Revolutionary War;" by Barnabas Howes, Esq.[*]

"The year 1777 was a peculiarly dark and trying one to that part of the inhabitants of Ashfield who were patriotic. Prominent men did not disguise their sympathy with the British government, and the year before three men— soldiers from Ashfield—had fallen in the Battle of Long Island. The armies of Howe and Burgoyne were driving the Americans before them at almost every point. It is therefore an interesting inquiry: What did our fathers do? The historical account which has come to us gives the answer. They put forth vigorous efforts and offered earnest prayer to the God of Heaven for providential aid. I have often heard how, when a messenger came, on the 16th of August, to call for soldiers from that town he found men at the old meeting-house with their guns, ready to go promptly on to the army.

Mr. Stocking had nine men to guard in his house because of their Tory sympathy. Not only soldiers went on; their minister went as chaplain. The Rev. Nehemiah Porter left Ashfield soon after August 16th, and did not return until after the surrender of Burgoyne. His serving as chaplain in Gen. Gates' army is the great historical event of Ashfield. He was at the front at Saratoga, Fort Stanwix and Bennington.

Mr. Porter, in the darkest hours of our country, when men's hearts were failing them for fear, and when five Congregational clergymen in what is now Franklin county were Tories, went on to serve as chaplain in Gates' army. And, so far as we can learn, no other clergymen of any denomination offered to serve in that capacity in his army. The men of Ashfield were fully impressed with the doctrine that "all men were created free and equal." I have what I deem reliable information that the Rev. Jacob Sherwin, the Congregational minister in our town, owned a slave, and for his treatment of her he was dismissed from the ministerial office.

Of the other years, and of the other men who served in the Revolutionary war from our town, my space will require me to be brief and only relate the most interesting incidents. Their names were:

---

[*]A work of 22 pages, published in 1883; price twenty-five cents. Address the author, Ashfield, Mass.

Moses Smith, Sr., killed; Moses Smith, Jr., killed; Cornelius Warren, killed; Timothy Perkins, Jonathan Taylor, Jr., Zachariah Howes, Elisha Parker, John Ward, Samuel Guilford, Joseph Bishop, Samuel Burton, Jonathan Lyon, lost an arm; Elder Enos Smith (youngest son of Chileab Smith, Sr.), Jonathan Lilly, Spencer Phillips [see page 112], Sylvester Phillips, Timothy Warren, Bethuel Lilly, Caleb Ward, Lieut. Edward Annable [see page 92]. John Belding [father of Tiberias Belding, page 169], John Alden, died; Joel Cranston, died; Ebenezer Cranston, died; Henry Rogers, died; Josiah Fuller, Capt. Asa Cranston, Dea. John Bement, Phineas Bement, Robert Gray.

[To these may be added the names of Lieut. John Ellis (15), David Ellis, Sr. (32), Richard Ellis (29), Benjamin Ellis (22), and probably others.]

Twelve young men who served in the Revolutionary war settled in Ashfield, before it closed or soon after. Their names were as follows:

Lot Bassett, Stephen Warren, Solomon Hill, Caleb Church, Joseph Gurney, Laban Stetson, Caleb Packard, Ezekiel Taylor, David Vincent, Jonathan Sears, Calvin Maynard, Timothy Catlin, Zebina Leonard, Benjamin Shaw.

[Mr. Howes here follows with a short sketch of each of the above.]

ASHFIELD MOUNTAIN.

"There are many rare sights among the Green Mountains, one of which is Peter's Hill, the highest point on Ashfield Mountain. From this point an extensive view can be had, looking over into Vermont and New Hampshire, as well as a large extent of Massachusetts. The top of the mountain is a level plain for some distance. Old Peter had a lot of land and a home there, which gave the mountain its name. It is said that Peter was captured by slave traders in Africa, when he was a boy, and brought to New England. He was said to have been owned by Dr. Bartlett's father, and Dr. Bartlett called him a brother and said he seemed like a brother. He was liberated during the Revolution, and lived and died in peace, on the mountain which derived its name from him."

In 1887 Mr. Barnabas Howes published another work, of 20 pages, entitled "History of the Town of Ashfield;" same price as above—25 cents. The following is copied from Mr. Howes' pamphlet:

ASHFIELD, May 14th, 1777.

Received of the Selectmen of Ashfield, for mileages from Ashfield to Ticonderoga, the sum of twenty-six shillings and eight pence per man:

Lieut. John Ellis [see page 76], Ezekiel Taylor, Zebulon Bryant, Eliphalet Lindsay, Stephen Graves, Stephen Cross, Elisha Smith, Asa Wait, Daniel Mills, Barnabas Alden, Sr., Jasper Taylor, Abner Kelley, Elisha Howes, Zachariah Howes, Johnson Pelton, Bezar Benton, Nathan Cook, Preserved Smith [see page 90,] Lamrock Flower, [father of Mrs. David] Ellis, Jr.—see page 154].

On August 16th, the same year, five more men left Ashfield for the army, then at Saratoga—Dea. Jonathan Taylor; his son, Henry Taylor; Joseph Warren, Nathan Chapin and Elisha Parker."

LATER YEARS OF RICHARD ELLIS' LIFE.

About the close of the Revolution Richard Ellis returned from Colerain to Ashfield, where he lived the balance of his days, with his son, Lieut. John Ellis, and his grandchildren. The latter consisted of Richard and David Ellis (sons of Reuben), and Jemima Smith Annable, wife of Lieut. Edward Annable. Jemima was a daughter of Rev. Ebenezer Smith and his wife, Remember Ellis (Richard's daughter. See page 71).

It is probable that Richard's ashery and mercantile business in Colerain had not proven a success; at least, not sufficient to have given him a competency for the remaining years of his life. The disorder and instability of all business pursuits, consequent upon the prolonged war for independence, would account for this. Hence his return to his children and grandchildren in Ashfield, to pass his remaining years in quietude with them.

It is apparent that they formed an agreement among themselves to provide for him a home, and at the same time leave him in perfect freedom to pass his time among them or others, and come and go at his pleasure. According to this agreement each one rendered his account at stated times and was allowed by the others due compensation therefor. They associated together under the name of "The Brethren," evidence of which is found among their accounts of the time, one of which is as follows:

				£	s.	d.
July ye 6, 1790.		The Brethren Dr. to keeping Father Ellis four weeks		*1	4	0
Oct.	2, "	To 4 weeks' and 2 days' keeping........		*1	5	6
Feb.	26, 1791.	" 8 weeks' keeping by Edward Annable.		2	8	0
Aug.	10, "	" 8 " "		*2	8	0
Jan.	2, 1792.	" 8 " " by David Ellis...........		2	8	0
Jan.	27, "	" 8 " board		*2	8	0
Oct.	13, "	" 8 " " by Richard Ellis.............		1	16	0
Apr.	3, 1793.	" 8 " "		*2	8	0
Sept.	25, "	" 8 " " by Richard Ellis............				
Mar.	5, 1794.	" 8 " " by David Ellis				
		" Squire Phillips, for charges.....		†0	12	0

EARLY RESIDENTS OF COLERAIN.

Names of persons in Colerain, Mass., and adjoining towns, with whom Richard Ellis transacted business from 1764 up to the Revolutionary war, as taken from his journal or ledger:

Colerain, Mass.: William Sever, Nathan Smith, Samuel Ayres, John Hulburt, Charles Stewart, James Stewart, Samuel Stewart, Alexander Harroun, Thomas McGee, George Clark, Archibald Lawson, Daniel Donnelson, Sarah Fulton, Robert Fulton, James Lukes, Ann McCreles, John Harroun, Joseph

*These charges were evidently for times when Richard was at his son's, John Ellis.

†This was a charge for something which Squire Phillips had done for Richard. Squire Phillips (Lieut. Philip Phillips) was a son of Thomas Phillips, Sr., the second settler in Ashfield, and was a nephew of Richard's wife, Jane Phillips Ellis.

McClures, John Anderson, Curtis Clements, Nathan Oaks, Robert Willson, Hannah Murdock, James Wallace, John Sennate, Joseph Bell, Silas White, John Clark, Benjamin Henry, Mary McGlaughlen, James Kennady, Hezekiah Smith, Thomas Fox, Elizabeth Newman, Evan Evans (Hugh Smith, of Palmer, engaged to pay this account, before Wm. Stewart,, of Colerain), John Stewart, James Harkness, Abram Pennell, William ˙McCreles the 2nd, John Cochran, Jr., Dea. Cochran, Hugh Riddle, Thomas Morris, James Clark, Jr., William Wilson, John Mills, John Moore, Abner Newton, John Bolton, Robert Riddle, 1st, Robert Riddle, 2nd, Tennet Stewart, Andrew Lukes, William McCreles, 1st, Jonathan Wilson, Lydia Stewart, Deacon Riddle, Robert Pennell, Jacob Maquaid, Joseph Thompson, Hugh McClallen, Samuel Morrison, Alexander Thompson, John Morrison, John Stewart, 2nd, William Stewart the 1st, William Clark the 1st, Joseph McKown, John Workman, Hugh Bolton, Jr., Isaac Orr, Benjamin Mun, Thomas Anderson, Joseph Stewart, Nancy Wallace, John Wallace, Abraham Peck, Nathaniel Cornwell, Capt. Hugh Morrison, Samuel Stewart the 1st, William Clark the 2nd (son of Alexander Clark, of Colerain), Joseph McCluer, William Henry, Robert Cochran, Widow Sarah McCreles, John Sennate, John McCreels, Samuel Willson, James Clark, David Harroun [Charles S. D. Harroun, Esq., of Greenville, Mich., is a descendant of the Colerain Harrouns], Elisha Smalley, Robert Crosier, Ebenezer Fisk, Caleb Allen, Catharine Mills, Eunice Harroun, David Rich, Elisha Prat, Matthew Bolton, Martha Lukes, John Thompson, James Thompson, Thomas Crofoot, John Maywaters, Stephen Tones, David Smead, Abraham Shin, Nathan Davis, Nathan Williams, William Galt, James Bell, James Carr, Silas Herrington, Hugh McGill, David Mores, John Rugg, Robert Miller, Daniel Brace, Daniel Crace, William Stewart, Watson Freeman, Thomas Fox, Samuel Fisk, Thomas Mores.

Greenfield, Mass.: Samuel Hinsdale, Daniel Nash, Matthew Severance, Amos Allen, Matthew Clark, Ezekiel Brown.

Halifax, Vt.: John Crosier, Samuel Clark, William Henderson, Robert Pattison, Jeremiah Reed, Abner Rich, Dea. John Pennell, David Bartlett, Solomon Bartlett, James Hamilton, John Clark, James Taylor.

Deerfield, Mass.: John Henry, Samuel Hunter, Alexander Clark.

---

*CURRENCY AND PRICES OF COLONIAL TIMES.

Specimens of accounts taken from Richard Ellis' ledger while he kept a country store in Colerain. That the currency of those times was greatly depreciated is apparent from the high prices of all commodities.

* In 1743 Massachusetts proposed to the other New England colonies to appoint commissioners to agree on joint action for doing away with colonial bills. They refused to do so. Money was now scarce as ever again, the better kinds being hoarded, and only the worst paper of all the colonies circulating in any. The Governor of Massachusetts, in 1744, said that of £400,000 Rhode Island bills in circulation £380,000 were in Massachusetts. The people of the latter colony had lost £25,000 on this sum in nine months. The Governor now took it into his head to capture Louisbourg, on Cape Breton, from the French, and the New England colonies joined in the enterprise, issuing bills as they were needed to prepare for the expedition. The paper issues of Massachusetts alone amounted to £2,466,712. Louisbourg was captured and Parliament voted to ransom it from the colonies. The sum coming

AMOS ALLEN, OF GREENFIELD,

1765.	TO RICHARD ELLIS,	DR.
Jan. 24.	To 1 axe ....£2 12s. 6d.	
	" 1,000 of pins.. 0 14 0	
August, 1767.	Credit by 2 bushels of lime...........£1 6s. 0d.	
" "	" by cash.................................... 2 0 6	

	JAMES STEWART	DR.		
1765.		£	s.	d.
Jan.	To ½ lb. tea...	0	18	0
April.	" 1 broad hoe..	1	13	9
"	" 8 jacket buttons and 1 thimble	0	5	0
Aug.	" 1 cake of soap	0	6	6
Oct.	" 4 ounces of tea.......................................	0	16	3
Nov.	" 10 jack knife..	0	6	6
"	" 101 gals. and 1 quart of rum, at 20s per gal.	101	5	0

	CREDITS.	£	s.	d.
Feb. 1765.	By 3 days posting books	2	12	6
" 26,	" 3 bushels of ashes.............	0	13	6
April 2,	" 1 day posting books..........	0	15	0
Sept.	" 2 lbs. butter...................	2	0	0
Dec.	" 4 bushels of ashes............	0	18	0

	SILAS WHITE*	DR.		
1765.		£	s.	d.
May.	To 1 spelling book.......................................	0	10	0
"	" 1 ivory comb......................................	0	9	0
"	" 1 horn comb	0	3	9
"	" 1 paper of pins....................................	0	7	0

to Massachusetts was £188,649 sterling, and at the request of the colony this was shipped in silver dollars and copper coins. With this hard money the inflated paper currency of the colony was canceled at the rate of one pound of the former to eleven pounds of the latter—apparently the ruling exchange at that date. The silver remained in circulation for several years and trade revived steadily and rapidly. [Cape Breton, mentioned a᷉ ove, is an island between Nova Scotia and Newfoundland.]

In 1751 Parliament forbade any more legal tender paper issues, and allowed no issue save in the form of exchequer bills redeemable by taxes in a year, bearing interest; or, in case of war, similar issues redeemable in four years. The colonies set about retiring their old issues, but the war with France in 1756 involved them again in war expenses, and large amounts of bills of small denominations were issued. In 1762 gold was made a legal tender by weight at the rate of two and a half pence per grain. At this rate it was more profitable to pay in gold than in silver, and the latter was soon driven out of circulation, while paper money was depreciated five per cent. In 1767 the agitation was renewed for a new issue of paper money. The paper currency of Vermont appears to have been much more depreciated than that of Massachusetts, and this must have had its effect on prices in towns near the border. The colonial money was of all denominations. We have before us a bill issued at Hartford, Conn., in 1777. Its face value is fourpence, and it is about four times as large as a postage stamp. At the time of its issue the paper of Connecticut was inflated after the manner of the later Confederate scrip, worth, perhaps, ten per cent. in gold. At this rate it would take about thirty of these Hartford bills to pay for a dozen of eggs. Like the late Confederate, the old Connecticut patriot might carry his money to the store in a basket and carry his eggs home in his pocket.—[From *Prof. Sumner's "History of American Currency."*

* It is probable that Silas White was a shoemaker, as among his credits, Feb., 1767, is "one pair of shoes," and "mending a pair of shoes."

			£	s.	d.
Nov.		To 1 quart of rum	0 : 6 : 6
Oct.	1766.	" 2 quarts of rum	0 : 14 : 0
"		" 1 bushel of salt	2 : 8 . 0
March,	1769.	" Caleb going to Greenfield	0 : 7 : 6
"		" Caleb driving plow	0 : 7 : 6
"		" My cattle going to Sunderland	2 : 0 : 0

[This account was not settled until the following date:] "1785, Jan. ye 10. Then reckoned with Silas White and balanced accounts from the beginning of the world to this day, as witness my hand.—RICHARD ELLIS."

EUNICE HARROUN			DR.
1765.			£ s. d.
Jan.	To 4 china plates		1 : 14 : 6

CREDIT.

June, 1765. By sugar .... 1 : 8 : 6

JOHN WALLACE			DR.
1764.			£ s. d.
Dec.	To 1 paper of pins		0 : 7 : 6
"	" 1 pair of shears		0 : 7 : 6
April.	" 1 cake of soap		0 : 6 : 6
Nov.	" 1 axe		2 : 12 : 6
Apr. 1769.	" 3 days, Caleb and oxen		3 : 0 : 0

WILLIAM CLARK, THE FIRST,			DR.
1765.			£ s. d.
Jan.	To 1,000 pins		0 : 15 : 0
July.	" 300 nails*		1 : 13 : 9
Oct.	" 1 gallon of rum		1 : 6 : 0
Nov. 1767.	" stoning your well		1 : 10 : 0
Jan. 1768.	" Matthew,† one day at ye well		0 : 15 : 0
"	" 1 pair of garters		0 : 6 : 6
"	" cutting rail cuts by Matthew		0 : 15 : 0

HANNAH MURDOCK			DR.
1765.			£ s. d.
Feb.	To china cup and saucer		0 : 15 : 0
"	" 2 ditto		1 : 10 : 0
"	" 10 yards of plaid		10 : 0 : 0
"	" ¾ yard ribbon		0 : 9 : 0

CREDIT.

1765.		£ s. d.
Jan. 20.	By 2 pair of stockings	1 : 15 : 0
	" 5 yards of tow cloth	3 : 15 : 0

---

* Nails were made by hand and sold by the piece for fifty years after this date.
† Richard's son, Matthew Ellis. See (13) page 260.

JOHN STEWART, 2ND.   DR.

1765.		£	s.	d.
Oct.	To 2 doz. of coat buttons	1 :	2 :	6
"	" 2 sticks of mohair	0 :	9 :	0
"	" 100 shoe nails	0 :	3 :	9
"	" 1 yard of ribbon	0 :	12 :	0
Nov.	" 2 yards of check cloth	2 :	12 :	6
Mar. 1766.	" 1 hoe	1 :	12 :	6
Oct.	" 2 quarts rum	0 :	14 :	0
"	" 1 scythe	2 :	8 :	0

1764.	CREDITS.	£	s.	d.
	By 1 broom	0 :	4 :	6
	" 5 bushels of ashes	1 :	2 :	6
Feb. 1765.	" 800 of shingles	3 :	4 :	0
Oct.	" 1200 of shingles	4 :	12 :	0
Jan. 1766.	" 9 bushels of ashes	2 :	0 :	6
May.	" 1 shad fish	0 :	1 :	6
May, 1769.	" paid to Matthew	1 :	15 :	0

ALEXANDER CLARK, OF DEERFIELD,   DR.

1765.		£	s.	d.
Feb.	To 1 blanket	6 :	5 :	0
"	" sundries for Margaret Conkey	2 :	1 :	0
June.	" sundries—Day Book, page 4	0 :	11 :	3
"	" paid Isaac Orr's order	6 :	12 :	0
July, 1766.	" 3 lbs. 5 oz. potash	0 :	10 :	0
"	" a cider barrel	1 :	5 :	0
"	" ½ bushel of salt	1 :	3 :	0
"	" a mistake	0 :	1 :	3

1765.	CREDITS.	£	s.	d.
	By carting kettles and clay	5 :	12	6
	" 14 bushels of ashes	3 :	3 :	0
July, 1766.	" carting potash to Hadley	6 :	15 :	0
	" carting a load to Cheapside	2 :	5 :	0
	" carting salt from Greenfield	1 :	10 :	0
	" carting a barrel of rum from Deerfield	1 :	0 :	0
	" a draft chain	4 :	2 :	6

WIDOW SARAH McCRELES   DR.

1764.		£	s.	d.
Dec.	To 1 pair of gloves	0 :	18 :	0
Feb. 1765.	" 1 earthen pot	0 :	10 :	0
"	" 1 punch bowl	0 :	10 :	0
"	" lawn	2 :	1 :	7
"	" taffety	1 :	16 :	9
Jan. 1766.	" 1 tea kettle	3 :	15 :	0
"	" 500 nails	2 :	0 :	0

CREDITS.

		£	s.	d.
1765.	By 1 cheese	2 :	0 :	0
1766.	" 4 lbs. butter	0 :	16 :	0
	" Hannah	0 :	13 :	0
	" 8 bushels of ashes....................	1 :	10 :	0

FORM OF SPINSTER'S INDENTURE IN 1769.

This Indenture Witnesseth that Dinah Wood Daughter of Simeon Wood of Ashfield Jn the County of Hampshire and Province of the Massachusetts Bay in New England Husband Man Hath Put Herself and By These Presents Doth Voluntary and of Her Own free Will and accord and With the Consent of her Said Father Simeon Wood Put and Bind Herself aprentis to Amzi Childs of Deerfield in the County aforesaid Husband Man & To Submit His Wife To Learn their art Trade or Mystery and With them the s'd Amzi and Submit after the Maner of an aprentis To Serve from the Date of these Pres-ents for and During the Term of Eight Years Six Months Three Weeks and Three Days from thence Next Ensuing To Be Compleat and Ended During all which Term the s'd aprentice Her Said Master and Mistress faithfully Shall Serve, their Secrets Keep, and Lawfull Comands Every Where Gladly Obey. She Shall Do No Damage To Her S'd Master or Mistress Nor Suffer it to Be Done of others Without Letting or Giving Notice thereof to Her Said Master or Mistress. She Shall Not Waste the Goods of her S'd Master or Mistress Nor Lend them Unlawfully to Any. She Shall Not Comit fornication, Nor Matrimony Contract Within the S'd Term. She Shall Not absent herself By Day or By Night from the service of her S'd Master or Mistress Without their Leave, but in all things Behave Herself as a faithful aprentice ought to Do To-wards Her S'd Master and Mistress During the Said Term.

And the said Amzi Childs for Himself, and Submit His Wife, Doth Hereby Covenant and Promiss to Teach and Instruct, or Cause the S'd Aprentis To be Taught and Instructed, in the art Trade or Calling of a Spinster and House-oldry By the Best Way or Means She May or Can of the s'd aprentice Capa-ble to Learn and To find and Provide unto the S'd aprentis Good and Sufficient Meet Drink Washing and Lodging and aparrell Both in Sickness and Helth and To Learn Her To Read During the S'd Term and at the Expiration thereof To Give Unto the S'd aprentis Two Good Suits of aparell one for Sabbath Days and one for Week Days, in Testimony Whereof the Parties To these Presents have Hereunto interchangeably Set their Hands and Seals the 15th Day of February in the Ninth Year of the Reign of our Sovereign Lord George the Third of Great Britain &c anoghe Domini one thousand Seven Hundred and Sixty Nine.

Her

DINAH X WOOD.

Signed Sealed and Delivered

mark

In Presence of us,

AMZI CHILDS.

SAM'L CHILDS,

*SAM'L CHILDS, 2D.

*The handwriting would indicate that the above document, found among the Ellis papers, was written by Samuel Childs, 2d.

WALES AND THE WELSH PEOPLE.

The British Islands were first visited by the Phœnician and Carthagenian navigators, where they found tin in abundance. This was about 1,000 years before Christ. Greek navigators also visited these Islands later. They named the country Albion, from its numerous white chalk cliffs. But little, however, was known of these regions until the invasion by Julius Cæsar, Emperor of Rome, in the first century, A. D. The Romans found here a large population of brave and vigorous people.* Cæsar and his soldiers had many battles with them and finally subdued, for a time, most of what is now England, except that part which is known as Wales. The Welsh have always held a portion of England, and they are said to be descendents of the original Britons. Wales is a country in the western part of England, and is about 96 miles in width and 135 miles in length. The Welsh have a written language of their own, and in features and many personal traits they differ from any other people of Europe. They have ever been noted for their industry and independence. But few of them have ever become Catholics in religion. For centuries they defied the English Kings and maintained their independence. Through almost unceasing warfare they gallantly defended their liberties. Their last King was Llewellyn, who was slain in 1282 in a battle with the English under King Edward I. To conciliate the Welsh people, and gain their consent to union with England, Edward promised them a native born sovereign who could speak no English. In due time he had their barons assemble, when he presented them with his own son, born but a few days before in the Welsh castle of Cornowon. He was named Edward Prince of Wales. In 1307 he became King Edward the Second and reigned twenty years. Ever since that time the eldest son of the King or Queen of England has been called Prince of Wales, and the Welsh people have been a most conservative and loyal element in the kingdom.

Under the following date this note was given:

Jan. 24th, 1783. Dr. to Richard Ellice, for a pair of leather breeches, five bushels and a half of wheat. Witness my hand.

DAVID STEWART.

Also the following:

COLERAIN, Jan. 24th, 1777, for value received, I promise to pay Richard Elis or order the some of twenty Pound on demand, with intris till paid as witnis my hand.

JOHN NEWELL.

CALEB ELLIS,† witness.

---

*Some of these people were carried prisoners to Rome where they were called Angles by their captors, but St. Gregory when he observed their unusual beauty and symmetry of form said they were *Angels.*

†Son of Richard Ellis. See page 79 (19).

313

These sartifie that I, the subscriber, have reseved seven ew sheep from Richard Ellis, for which I promis to pay five pounds and one quarter of good clean wooll yerly and at the ende of three yeres return the same number.

Colerain, Feb. ye 20, 1777.

JOHN HARROUN.

LIEUT. JOHN ELLIS, OF ASHFIELD.

Commission of John Ellis (son of Richard), of Ashfield, as a Second Lieut. in the Revolutionary Army:

COLONY OF THE ⎰
MASSACHUSETTS BAY. ⎱

The Major Part of the COUNCIL *in the Massachusetts Bay in New England, To John Allis,* Gentleman, Greeting:*

You being appointed Second Lieutenant of the Sixth Company, whereof Benjamin Phillips is Captain, in the Fifth Regiment of Militia, in the County of Hampshire, whereof David Field, Esq., is Colonel, By Virtue of the Power vested in us, We do by these Presents (reposing special Trust and Confidence in your Loyalty, Courage and good Conduct) Commission you accordingly. You are therefore carefully and dilligently to discharge the Duty of a second Lieut. in leading, ordering and exercising said company in Arms, both inferior officers and soldiers, and to keep them in good Order and Discipline. And they are hereby commanded to obey you as their second Lieut, and you are yourself to observe and follow such Orders and Instructions as you shall from time to time receive from the major part of the Council and your Superior Officers.

Given under our Hands and Seal of the said Colony, at Watertown, the Third day of May, in the year of our Lord 1776.

By the Command of the Major Part of the Council.

JOHN LOWELL, Dep'y Sec'y.

[SEAL.] James Otis, W. Spooner, Caleb Cushing, J. Winthrop, B. Chadbourn, T. Cushing, John Whitcomb, James Prescott, D. Taylor, S. Hatten, Jabez Fisher, B. White, Moses Gill.

Lieut. John Ellis was, a portion of the time during the Revolution, on duty in Ashfield, where he was assigned to service ordered by the General Court, in session in Boston. Among his papers is a memorandum as follows: "Fines collected agreeable to an order of Court of Aug. 15th, 1777:"

£

Ashel Amsden 15
Eli Colton 15
Jedediah Sprague 15
Lieut. P. Phillips 15
Seth Waite 15
Reuben Ellis 15

*This name was a clerical error, afterwards corrected.

	£
Thomas Phillips	15
Joseph R. Paine	15
Ebenezer Belding	15
Daniel Belding	15
John Sherwin	15
Jeremiah Waite	15
Moses Smith	15
Samuel Belding	15
Des. Isaac Shepard	15
David Alden	15

" Fines paid agreeable to an order of Court of June 10th, 1778:"

	£
John Belding	10
Oliver Cook	10
Samuel Cranston	10
Lieut. Philip Phillips	10
Isaac Shepard	10
Philip Matigan	10
Abner Phillips	10
Daniel Bacon	10
Abel Smith	10
Vespatian Phillips	10
Johnson Pelton	10
Silas Lilly	10
John Ames	10
Samuel Truesdel	10
Abel Cook	10
Josiah Cook	10
Samuel Batchelder	10
Samuel Belding	10
Seth Waite	10
Jesse Edson	10

" Fines paid agreeable to an order of Court of June 20th, 1778:"

	£
Samuel Belding	20
Ebenezer Belding, jr	20
David Alden, jr	20
John H. Blackmer	20
Ashel Amsden	20
Chileab Smith	20

" Fines paid agreeable to an order of Court June 5th, 1780:"

	£
Johnson Pelton	150
Seth Waite	150

It is known that *some* of these men were stanch loyalists, or *tories* as they were called, and were opposed to the Revolution or revolt against the King of England. Such was the division of sentiment on the subject of the war at that time that many families were divided among their members. Many tory fathers had patriot sons who were fighting for the independence of the colonies. But in Ashfield, as elsewhere, there was a strong *home guard*, who did all they could to encourage the soldiers. At a town meeting held June 10th, 1777, it was voted "that Aaron Lyon was a suitable person to procure evidence against certain persons who were regarded as enemies of the American States."

About this time Burgoyne, who was at the head of the British army near Saratoga, N. Y., was expected to push his way through to join other British forces in Massachusetts and Rhode Island. It was supposed that his route would be to Fort Massachusetts (now North Adams), where he would cross the Hoosac Mountain over into the towns of Heath and Buckland, then ford the Deerfield river and pass through the north part of Ashfield, exactly by where Aaron Lyon lived.

This made the tories jubilant, but Aaron Lyon did his duty, and in August, 1777, he, with Peter Cross and Dr. Phineas Bartlett, Selectmen of the town, brought in a report "that * * * ought to be brought to a proper trial." (Nine tories. Their names are omitted here.)

CHARGES AND PRICES OF EARLY TIMES IN ASHFIELD.

Specimens of accounts taken from an old account book of Lieut. John Ellis, of Ashfield:

MAJ. LAMROCK FLOWER, SR.

TO JOHN ELLIS—DR.

1774.		£	s.	d.
Jan. ye 8.	To 1 bushel of rye and oats.....................	0	2	0
	" Cash by Bildad	0	5	0
Feb. 25.	" " " Ebenezer Belding...................	0	3	8
May 10.	" my oxen one day........................	0	1	4
Nov.	" my horse to Springfield..................	0	5	4
1784.				
Mar. ye 4.	" 1 pint of rum............................	0	0	6
Feb. 24, 1786.	" ¼ a pine tree...........................	0	2	6
Oct.	" 1 barrel	0	3	0
June 12, 1788.	" 2 days' work by Dimick.................	0	3	0
"	" 6 days' work by John	0	9	0
"	" 2 bushels of wheat	0	8	0
Feb. 28, 1791.	" 1 pound in grain for Thomas Phillips..........	1	0	0
May 3.	" my John one day...	0	2	6
Sept. 28.	" Dimick one day.........................	0	1	6
"	" Edward one day.........................	0	1	6
Aug. ye 20, 1792	" my horse to Conway....................	0	0	10
	" my cart to Buckland....................	0	1	0
	" my horse to Goshen	0	1	0
Dec. 10, 1794.	" Edward and Dimick one day...........	0	4	0

CAPT. LAMROCK FLOWER, JUN.   DR.

1799.   £   s.   d.
Mar. 21.   To ten hundred of hay.........................   1 : 0 : 0
            " 2 lbs. cheese............................   0 : 0 :10
                                                        $ c.   m.
May.*   " a plow 2 days and a half.................. 0 : 84 : 0
  "   " 1 bushel of parsnips.....................   0 : 33 : 0
  "   " 6 lbs. of iron...........................   0 : 24 : 0

                    CREDITS.   £ s. d.
1774, May 10. By 1 day with Phineas and your oxen... 0 : 3 : 6
    Oct. 29.   " ½ "   "   "   "   "   " __ 0 : 1 : 6

1774.   JOHN BELDING†   DR.
Jan. ye 24.   Then reckoned and settled all book accounts.
                                                JOHN BELDING.
                                                JOHN ELLIS.
                                                £   s.   d.
Apr. 28, 1785. To 1 bushel of corn...................... 0 : 3 : 0
            " my horse to New Providence .... 0 : 4 : 0
Mar.   " my horse and sleigh to Springfield....... 0 : 14 : 0
            " my two boys and one yoke of oxen and plow
                two days.............................. . 0 : 10 : 0
Mar. 6. 1788. " my sleigh to Deerfield..... .... 0 : 1 : 0
Jan. ye 6, 1789. Then reckoned all book account and settled the whole.
                                                JOHN BELDING.
                EBENEZER BELDING.‡   DR.
1774.   £ s. d.
Apr. 25.   To keeping of a heifer 8 weeks.............. 0 : 4 : 6
Jan. ye 30, 1775. "   "   " cow 15 " .... 0 : 13 : 4
            " 5 lbs. of cheese........................   0 : 2 : 4

                 SAMUEL BELDING §   DR.
1774.   £. s. d.
Sept. ye 24. To 2 baskets............................. 0 : 4 : 0
July 30, 1782. " cash paid Capt. Flower............... 0 : 7 : 6
   " 6, 1786. " 2 lbs. of tobacco.................... 0 : 1 : 0

1782.   CREDITS.   £ s. d.
Nov. 25.   By making 8 ropes to tie up cattle........ 0 : 2 : 8
  " 25.   " 1 bed rope.......................... 0 : 2 : 0
  " 13, 1785.   " making 3 small ropes................ 0 : 3 : 0
Dec. 12, 1791. " making one draw rope and leading line
                    and three small ropes............

---

*On and after this date the account was continued in dollars, cents and mills, which were written in the manner similar to that of pounds, shillings and pence.

†Grandfather of Belding Bros., silk manufacturers.

‡Father of Asher Belding. See page 117.

§ Great Grandfather of Belding Brothers.

DOCT. MOSES HAYDEN   DR.

1773.   £ s. d.
Dec. ye 15.   To 8 hundred of hay.... .... 0 : 8 : 0
Jan. 20, 1774. " cash .... 0 : 3 : 0
Mar. 18.   " keeping your horse 14 days... .... : 0 : 4 : 0
June 21.   " 16 hundred of hay.... .... 0 : 16 : 0

Conway, Aug. ye 6th, 1774.   Then reckoned and balanced all acct. with
Doct. Moses Hayden, as witness our hands.

MOSES HAYDEN.

DOCT. PHINEAS BARTLET   DR.

1773.   £ s. d.
Jan. ye 3.   To sleding two loads of boards from Abner Phillips'
                   mill.............................. .... 0 : 3 : 4
    "   " sleding one load from my mill.... .... 0 : 1 : 6
Feb. 1774.   " 4 lbs. butter .... 0 : 2 : 0
Jan. 1775.   " six hundred of hay..... .... 0 : 8 : 0
Oct. 1777.   " 13 lbs. of pork...... .... 0 : 6 : 9
Nov. 1779.   " ½ bushel of salt.................. .... 0 : 10 : 0
June 6, 1785.   " one quart of rum .... 0 : 1 : 0
Sept. 4, 1788. " 24 lbs. of flour .... 0 : 3 : 0
Mar. 24, 1792. Then reckoned and settled all book acct. with Lieut. John
                   Ellis in full.

PHINEAS BARTLET,

[Dr. Bartlet was a physician in Ashfield forty years.]

AARON LYON   DR.

1774.   £ s. d.
Nov. ye 23.   To keeping a colt 3 weeks.... .... 0 : 1 : 6
Aug. ye 19, 1776. " my horse to Charlemont .... 0 : 1 : 2
Aug. ye 10, 1785. " 1½ gallons of rum.......................... .... 0 : 6 : 0

CREDIT.

Dec. 8, 1785.   By 1 bushel and 10 quarts of wheat..... 0 : 5 : 6
June ye 20, 1785. Then reckoned all book acct. with Mr. Lyon and found due
                   to him six pence.   AARON LYON.
                                                   JOHN ELLIS.

KIMBEL HOWES   DR.

1776.   £ s. d.
July ye 18.   To cash .... 0 : 0 : 6
Jan. 21, 1777. " 8 bushels of corn............................. ...... 1 : 4 : 6

CREDIT.
                                                        £ s. d.
July, 1776.   By 8 days' work....................... 1 : 4 : 0
    "   "   " cash .... 0 : 0 : 6
Jan 21, 1777.   Then reckoned and balanced all book acct. between Kimbel
                   Howes and John Ellis, as witness our hands.

KIMBEL HOWES.

SAMUEL LINCOLN   DR.

1789.   £   s.   d.

Sept. 4.	To 1 bushel of wheat.................................... 0 : 4 : 6
	" one half a side of leather........................... 0 : 12 : 3
Apr. 1791.	" Edward two days' work.............................. 0 : 4 : 0
	" Dimick one " " .... 0 : 1 : 9
Oct.	" Dimick and the oxen 1 day...................... 0 : 3 : 0
" 1794.	" my horse to Hardwick*........................... 0 : 6 : 8

CREDIT.

£   s.   d.

Aug. 1791.	By weaving 29 yards of cloth .... 0 : 14 : 9
Feb. 1793.	" weaving........................... ....3 : 10 : 1
Apr.	" weaving a coverlid................... 0 : 7 : 6
Apr. 1793.	Then reckoned and settled all accounts, as witness our hands.

SAMUEL LINCOLN.

GEORGE RANNEY†   DR.

1785.   £   s.   d.

May 26.	To 1 quart of old rum............................ 0 : 1 : 6
	" 2 " " " " .... 0 : 1 : 11

CREDIT.

1785.   £   s.   d.

May 29,	By cash .... 0 : 1 : 6
	" flax................................ 0 : 1 : 11

LIEUT. EDWARD ANNABLE   DR.

1785.   £   s.   d.

Mar. ye 12.	To 1 quart of old rum............................ 0 : 1 : 6
	" more for rum.---................................. 0 : 1 : 4
	" 1 barrel of cider................................. 0 : 11 : 0
	" cash lent your father .... 0 : 3 : 10
Feb. 20, 1786.	" 38 feet of pine boards..... .... 0 : 1 : 3
Dec. 27, 1790.	" 3 bushels of rye................................. 0 : 10 : 0
May, 1791.	" 1 bushel of salt .... 0 : 6 : 0
Oct. 29, 1793.	" my Edward 1 day at work... .... 0 : 2 : 0
	" 2 days Edward, oxen and cart............... 0 : 8 : 0
Oct 24, 1794.	" Dimick and oxen one day...................... 0 : 3 : 6
Feb. 16, 1795.	This day reckoned and settled all acct. between Lt. Ellis and Lt. Annable. EDWARD ANNABLE.

June ye 19, 1785. Then received of John Ellis eight shillings and two pence, being the tax due on the Lot No. 53, on the north side of said lot.

PHILIP PHILLIPS, Col.

---

*Hardwick is in Worcester Co., Mass., about 40 miles southeast from Ashfield. As I find no other Lincolns in Ashfield, I think it probable that Samuel came from Hardwick. See page 107.

†Grandfather of Hannah Ranney Ellis (see page 175), and H. S. Ranney, of Ashfield.

ELDER EBENEZER SMITH   DR.

		£	s.	d.
1786.				
Jan. 3.	To my sleigh to Goshen............................	0 :	1 :	0
	" " " for a number of seasons............	0 :	1 :	4
	" butter......	0 :	2 :	6
May 11, 1789.	" grinding 2 bushels of wheat and 2 of rye........	0 :	1 :	5
	" 2 sheep that weighed 155 lbs.....	0 :	12 :	11
Mar. 11, 1790.	" 1 peck of wheat for father..................	0 :	1 :	4
May 11, 1789.	Then reckoned and settled all past accounts between Elder Smith and myself.			

JOHN ELLIS.
EBENEZER SMITH.

RICHARD ELLIS*   DR.

		£	s.	d.
1785.				
Apr. 18.	To 1 pint of old rum..............................	0 :	0 :	10
	" ½ " " "	0 :	0 :	4

CREDIT.

1786.				
Mar. 24.	By cash	0 :	1 :	0

BENJAMIN ELLIS, SR.†   CR.

		£	s.	d.
1789.				
July 15.	Credit by Boards, to be paid in Beef or grain at the market price...............................	1 :	9 :	10

DEBTOR

		£	s.	d.
1789.				
July 25.	To meat...............	0 :	4 :	2
Dec. 14.	" 98 lbs. of beef.	0 :	16 :	5
Nov. 20, 1790.	" 1 sheep...................	0 :	6 :	0

March 7th, 1791. This day reckoned with Edward Annable for keeping Father Ellis, and all other accounts, and found due him one shilling, as witness our hands.

JOHN ELLIS.
EDWARD ANNABLE.

Besides the foregoing the following are names of persons in Ashfield with whom Lieut. John Ellis did business between the years 1773 and 1800. It is probable that most of these persons lived in the Ellis neighborhood, or northeast part of the town:

Samuel Annable, Jr., Barnabas Annable, Edward Annable, John Amsden, James Andrews, Erastus Andrews, David Alden, Abel Allis, Isaac Alden, Ebenezer Belding, Jun., John Belding—was a soldier in the Revolutionary army, Daniel Belding, Samuel Belding, John Blackmore, Dr. Phineas Bartlet, Samuel

---

*Son of Reuben Ellis. See (29) page 83.   †See page 80 (22).

Bartlet, Davis Butler, Nathan Batchelder, Dea. John Bement, Rolin Blackmore, Samuel Bardwell, Bezer Benton, William Billings, Benjamin Crittenden, Jeremiah Center, Noah Cross, John Conley—a tailor, Nathan Chapin, Levi Cook, David Cobb, Benjamin Ellis, Richard Ellis, David Ellis, Samuel Elmer, Maj. Lamrock Flower, Sr., Capt. Lamrock Flower, Jr., Bildad Flower, William Flower, Phineas Flower, Oliver Field, Moses Frarey, Uriah Goodwin, Mr. Griswold, Mr. Gay, Dr. Moses Hayden, of Conway; Kimbel Howes, Aaron Hayden, Ephraim Jennings, Reuben Kendrick, John King, Caleb King, Jacob Kilburn—a shoemaker, Samuel Lincoln, Archibald Lindsey, Jonathan Lyon, Eliah Lindsey, Silas Lilly, Aaron Lyon, Dr. Francis Mantor, Samuel Moody, Capt. Norton, Jacob Orcutt, Richard Phillips, Abner Phillips, Philip Phillips, Timothy Perkins, Enos Pomeroy—clothier, of Buckland; Thos. Phillips, Jr., John Perry, John Porter, Samuel Porter, Rufus Perkins, Joseph Potter, Samuel Prince, Spencer Phillips—was a soldier in the Revolution, Daniel Phillips, Eliab Perkins, Elizabeth Potter, Samuel Rockwood, George Ranney, Abel Smith, Levi Steel, Jacob Sherwin—first minister of the Congregational Church, Elihu Smead, Ephraim Smith, Stephen Smith, Lemuel Spurr, John Sherwin, Nehemiah Sprague, Thomas Stocking, Rufus Sears, Mehitable Smith, Ezariah Selden, Chileab Smith, Jr., Ebenezer Sprague, Elder Ebenezer Smith, Jonathan Taylor, Capt. Thomas Warner, Seth Waite, Josiah Ward, William Ward, Samuel Washburn, Caleb Wood, John Wilke, Elijah Ward, Jonathan Yemans.

CELEBRATION AT THE ELLIS AND PHILLIPS FORT IN 1886.

September 8th, 1886, a celebration was held at the site of the old fort, near Thomas Phillips, Sr.'s, house, in Ashfield. This fort was situated about fifty rods north of Bear River, and twenty rods west of the north and south road which run from Richard Ellis' house to Baptist Corner. Rev. Mr. Shepard, in his sketches [see page 280], locates this fort at about one mile and a half southwest of Mr. Chileab Smith's residence, and near the house occupied in 1833 by Mr. Sears. The spot is really about one-half mile south of Mr. Smith's. This fort was the principal one in Ashfield, that at Mr. Smith's house being mostly of a private character and constructed mainly by the Smiths. Early residents of Ashfield say that the site of the Ellis and Phillips fort was the one, and only one, pointed out to them by their grandfathers, the first settlers, as being the site of their ancient refuge in the war of 1756. Mr. Lewis Ellis [241], of Belding, Mich., who was in Ashfield in May of the present year [1887], together with the writer, informed the latter that his father and grandfather had often pointed out this spot to him as the site of the old fort. His grandfather, Lieut. John Ellis [see page 76], was fourteen years of age at the time, and aided in building the fort. Mr. Lewis Ellis was thirty-one years of age when he removed from Ashfield to Belding. He was well acquainted with the Smiths and others at Baptist Corner, but never heard mention of the fort there.

The following is an extract from a letter from H. S. Ranney, Esq.:

"Respecting the meeting at the site of the old fort on the 8th inst. [September, 1886], I have to say: There was a very large attendance and a time of much enjoyment to all, a report of which, in the *Gazette and Courier*, I send you. The location is called 'Fort Ellis & Phillips.' The fort was not an earthwork, but was constructed of upright logs of sufficient thickness to be bullet proof, set three feet into the earth, and rising ten or twelve feet above.

"The location is at the spot where it is believed Thomas Phillips first settled, forty or fifty rods *north* of Bear river, about twenty rods west of the road and a little more than half a mile north of the first Richard Ellis' house, being on the south side of the discontinued road that led due east from the place where Obed Elmer lived fifty years ago.

"The stockade or fort that enclosed the dwelling-house of Chileab Smith was a half mile north from this."

But it is probable that Mr. Shepard was mainly right in what he states of the Chileab Smith fort, as he derived his information from Chileab Smith, Jr., who was fourteen years of age at the time the fort was built by his father and brother Ebenezer, and perhaps others.

The fact of the celebration of 1886 at the Ellis and Phillips site is confirmation that this was the historic fort of Ashfield—or Huntstown, as it was then called. By reference to the Map of that section of Ashfield, it will be seen that this locality is between the early residences of Richard Ellis and Thomas Phillips, and but a few rods south from where Mr. Sears lived in 1833.

The report of the celebration alluded to above is taken from the Greenfield *Gazette and Courier* of September, 1886:—

Away up in the town of Ashfield, three miles northeast of "The Plain," is a sort of basin formed by the hills, with a bottom nearly circular, a half mile or more in diameter. Upon this bottom, on a little rise not far from its center, the savants will show you a half-dozen hollows in the ground, the largest of which a half-dozen cartloads of earth would fill up, and a hole as big as a man's body and four feet deep. The hollows, they will tell you, were the cellars of buildings constructed within a stockade, and the hole was the well from which the water for the occupants was drawn. This stockade was the fort to whose protection the settlers would fly when danger menaced. From some of these early settlers it is supposed it took its name—Fort Ellis and Phillips. This was the spot of the celebration on Wednesday last, under the auspices of the Pocomtuck Valley Memorial Association [named from a locality near Deerfield, Mass.], an organization whose purpose it is to preserve ancient things, to mark with monuments historical spots, and gather up and preserve all fragments of local history.

The day was a fine one, and the thousand, more or less, of people who assembled in the fragrant pine grove, a few paces from the site of the fort, had a most enjoyable time. They feasted the inner man on the good things they had brought with them, or on the viands so bountifully provided at the table for the guests, and their eyes upon those worthies who occupy the seats of honor upon such occasions, and who by their labors and pre-eminence in this field are worthy to occupy them, of whom two good specimens are Hon. Geo. Sheldon and Jonathan Johnson. The committee of arrangements, of which F. G. Howes was chairman, had made every provision in way of platforms and seats for the comfort and convenience of audience and speakers.

In the forenoon at about 10:30 F. G. Howes, for the committee, made the address of welcome, and in the absence of Mr. Sheldon, who had not yet arrived, George William Curtis was designated to act as presiding officer. He happily introduced Prof. J. Stanley Hall, of John Hopkins University, and a native of Ashfield, to whom had been assigned the historical address. The following is a brief outline of what he said:

The history of Ashfield is preceded by a legend never written or printed, the elements of which are clearly of great antiquity; but which is only loosely allotted to these hills. I was first "let in" to it this summer by an aged man, known and revered by all, only after long persuasion, for fear lest I should regard it or him as ridiculous, and after a promise not to connect his name with it. It runs about as follows:

The world began in the vicinity of the "Tunnel Mountain," which first of all land in this part of the world rose out of the watery chaos. After many ages pale-faced men of great stature and sagacity appeared from the northeast and settled miles apart upon the best hills—one upon Indian Hill, one upon Catamount Hill, and others elsewhere, these two being the headquarters of all high hills and wild Indians. These two brothers were not satisfied with the world as they found it, and would make it better, and first sought to remould the great features of the landscape. What is now the Deerfield river was far larger than at present, and flowed south of these hills, making a broad and deep lake over Buckland Bay, the only outlet of which was by the Richmond or Hermon Howes place into the pond. Thence its majestic current covered all the plain and South Ashfield, with a dangerous rapid between them, down to Dug Way (the newer and narrower channels not being yet cut), and thence through Conway to the Connecticut. These two great squatter sovereigns agreed to employ large troops of Indians, working with sharpened sticks day and night for many years, first to drain Buckland lake toward the northeast, and finally to turn the river further up at Catamount Hill into its present and geologically new and unnatural course. The Indians followed the river for new fishing ground, as it washed over upon the barren wastes of Shelburne Falls and left Ashfield to the peace and solitude she still so devoutly cherishes, and with new and fertile acres. For several generations Ashfield flourished, till men grew idle, too comfortable, and therefore discontented, till the older families died out, public spirit languished, and reverence and love of truth had fled, and at length Indians and re-encroaching forests closed in and destroyed all trace of a period which, had it developed as nobly as it began, would have set an example in morals and industry that the world would not soon have lost.

*　　*　　*　　*　　"　　*　　*　　*　　*　　*

After the address came the intermission for dinner, and about two the seats were all occupied and the platform fringed by those desiring to hear the speaking. The Shelburne Falls band, which was in attendance during the day and frequently responded to the calls made upon it, opened the exercises, and then came an address of half an hour by Hon. George Sheldon, who had been felicitously introduced by Mr. Curtis*, as the master of ceremonies for the rest of the day. His address was in the historical line, and extracts are presented below:

Through the joint action of the committees having in charge the exercises of this day, I have been assigned a part in which it becomes my pleasant and

---

*Hon. George William Curtis, editor of Harper's Weekly of New York City. For twenty-two years Mr. Curtis has passed the summers in Ashfield.

grateful duty to thank the people of Ashfield for the cordial welcome which has been so gracefully offered, and especially to congratulate them on the possession of that spirit which alone made this gathering possible. * * As yet, I have found no sponsor for your name of Ashfield. It may have been named as, according to tradition, were the towns of Athol, Orange, Coleraine, Shelburne, Montague and Warwick, after some English, titled man, in consideration for a church bell which he was to present to the town honored by his name. * * Now, this is a pretty romance; but, to my knowledge, it has not been adopted by your people. I am sure, however, you have just as good a right to such a tradition as the towns named, provided you first catch the necessary Lord Ashfield. As I have not faith that you will succeed in that field, I will venture another theory to account for the name Ashfield—a theory, not a historical fact. But I give the facts on which the theory is founded:

The grant of Huntstown was to be laid out west of and adjoining Deerfield. When the settlers began their battle with the sylvan gods, it is recorded that it was "near the easterly bounds, so to be near our Deerfield neighbors," and consequently it must have been on the easterly tier of lots. The mighty oak, the towering pine, the dark, spreading hemlock, the fruitful chestnut—diadems in the glorious crown of a primeval age—bowed to the ground before their sturdy blows. The fierce flames assailed the prostrate giants, and in place of the green woodland nothing met the eye but charred stumps and a field strewn with ashes—an *ashfield* literally. It was this very clearing that Deerfield people claimed as being within their bounds, and while the process of cutting down and burning was going on, the Deerfield neighbors, near whom they were so anxious to live, would taunt them from the border woods, and cry out: "Clear away as fast as you can; we shall soon come and occupy it."

*　　*　　*　　*　　*　　*　　*　　"　　*

I wish here to acknowledge the lasting obligations which the valley towns lie under to Huntstown. But for her valor the river settlements might have been all swept away in the last French war. I speak now of her own estimate of her own prowess, given under her own hand, as found in history. It may be thought rather late in the day, but now, after 130 years have passed, as a representative of the valley, I tender grateful thanks to Ashfield; and no spot is so fitting on which to make this acknowledgment as that where we meet to-day. Here stood the bulwark of our safety. Here was shown—taking, as in common courtesy we are bound to do, Huntstown's view of it—the patriotism and self denial which assured our safe continuance in the land of the living. In a petition addressed by the people of Huntstown to the General Court, asking aid in holding the fort, one of the prime considerations set forth was its benefit to the settlements in the valley below. They say, from their own situation they are a "Spesil gard to Hatfield & dearfield, & thar viligses, to wit. a place cald roreing brook, a place cald Scras (?) and a place cald Moody brook, & the place cald the Bars & a place called wopin." This was in 1756. For the information of the General Court a map of this region was sent with the above. The Connecticut Valley—its base was represented by two circles with a dot in the center of each. One was marked: "Hear is hatfield;" thence ran a straight road marked: "Northwest about 18 miles is Hunts town." The other circle was labeled "Hear is Deerfield," and a similar road thence was marked "About 8 miles west is Hunts town." The acute angle where these roads meet must be at this very spot. This map was evidently home-made, and I assume it to be the work of Huntstown's first highway surveyor, William Curtis. * * *

Our Association comes here to-day, Mr. Chairman, to awaken a new public interest in one particular event in the life of Ashfield—the erection on this spot of that fortification which was the ark of safety to the settlers in 1756. We trust the interest so manifestly shown to-day will not die out until some appropriate monument marks the spot; to the end that coming generations may seek this place and take note of the patience and fortitude of their ancestors in battling against the forces of nature and a savage foe, and thence draw strength for their own warfare.

But from a different point of view this locality is worthy of another monument, to be dedicated to brave Chileab Smith, his faithful son Ebenezer and their compeers, who battled for long years to obtain what the Pilgrims sought afar—freedom to worship God after ways of their own choice; freedom to think for themselves. For this they struggled against the combined forces of church and State, which strove to stifle their thoughts and bend their consciences to one narrow creed. The men who planted themselves on this corner and on this principle were men of pluck, with iron wills and muscles of steel, with a tenacity which enabled them to hold their own against all comers—the Indian barbarian, the land-grabber from Deerfield, the exactions of civil and ecclesiastical oppression. They were persecuted, but not subdued. When their lands were sold and their cattle taken to support a doctrine to which they could not subscribe, they submitted, but with solemn protest and righteous indignation expressed in strong terms. What though their theological integuments were as tough as their own buckskin garments, it matters not. They stood up manfully for liberty. They fought a good fight for an inborn right—the right to think for themselves. They sowed good seed, but for them the harvest was scant. All honor, then, to Chileab, Ebenezer, the brave Remember, and their fellows, for their vigorous tugging at the cords with which the standing order essayed to bind the thoughts and emotions of men. Liberty stands to-day on a broader foundation; thought to-day is more free all over our wide land for the earnest and incessant protest that went up from Baptist Corner.

Mr. Sheldon also gave an account of what he called the first Fourth of July celebration in Huntstown, when Ebenezer Smith, with Remember Ellis [see page 71] on a pillion behind him, with his father riding in front as a body guard, rode through the wilderness to Deerfield, where the two former were united in marriage by Parson Ashley. It was during the hight of the last French War and a bold adventure. "Go back to the deeds of chivalry," said the speaker; "explore the whole circumference of the Round Table, and among all the heroes, clad in silken doublet and encased in burnished steel and gleaming silver, where will you find a more daring and romantic quest? Where a braver and more knightly heart than that which beat under the homespun butternut of your good Knight Chileab?"

At the close of Mr. Sheldon's address the St. Cecelia Club, of Shelburne Falls, composed of Mrs. Baker, Miss Bardwell and Messrs. Hawks and Hadley, sang most acceptably, repeating their success of the morning. Later they were called upon again, and made an excellent hit, proving once more that this is a musical combination of unusual merit.

J. Johnson, of Greenfield, gave a brief account of the organization of the P. V. M. A. and a brief review of some of the celebrations it has been instrumental in holding, and closed with an exhortation to the young to make collections of relics similar to that at Deerfield for every village. Prof. W. F. Sherwin, of the Boston Conservatory of Music, a native of Buckland, made a very felicitous speech, of which the main idea was that these gatherings are excellent for kindling anew the love for old-time things and the old-time virtues of the fathers. Hon. W. B. Davenport, of New York city, happening to be present, was presented, and he, too, dwelt upon the propriety of keeping green the memories of the early settlers, through whose pluck and endurance we have this fair heritage. Prof. Charles Eliot Norton, of Harvard University, the next speaker, warmly urged that in the public hall of each town mural tablets be put up, and, under the inscription: "These have done their part for Ashfield," or Charlemont, or Hawley, as the case may be, the names of the men who have been the leaders in the town's progress may be chiseled, that succeeding ages may have constantly before their eyes an inspiration to do their part in bearing public burdens. Judge Conant, of Greenfield, had a few words of the same general tenor, giving due credit to the P. V. M. A. for the unselfish work it is doing. The closing address was made by George William Curtis. Mr. Curtis spoke of the pride New England takes in these historical places, hallowed by the virtue, patriotism and persevering industry of the fathers, and thought that while this feeling of reverence for these consecrated things remains there need be no fear for the safety of the Republic; but when Concord and Trenton and Bunker Hill cease to warm the feelings and quicken the pulses, a decay in patriotic sentiment has begun that will end in the downfall of the nation. Mr. Curtis spoke on this theme with great eloquence, fascinating his hearers by a magic power of oratory possessed by few other Americans, if by any.

It was a little after 4 o'clock when the gathering broke up, and all went away feeling, as one man said, that "it was the most enjoyable picnic of his life."

SOLDIERS' GUARD AT HUNTSTOWN IN 1756.

The following is taken from a "History of Deerfield," by Hon. George Sheldon:

"March 27th, Col. Williams writes Shirley that 'Huntstown people quitted their place last summer for want of protection, but several families returned and lived there through the winter, & others will join them if they can have help. Encouraged by what they heard from you by their messenger they have begun to fortifie & in a few days will have a garrison completed. Before the war they had fitted a large area of land for tillage & raised considerable provisions. That is gone and they know not where to look for their bread, or what method to take for their support, & unless something can be done for them they must again leave the place—With a guard of 10 or 12 men they think they may work upon their land with tolerable safety.' Williams recommends putting part of the men under pay to guard the rest."

"July 8th, Col. Williams is directed to send a guard to Huntstown."

"Sept. 6th, Capt. John Catlin returns a list of men he had "impressed for his majesties Service," doubtless for the army under Lord London, near Albany. They were:

" 'Sergt. John Sheldon, Sergt. Joseph Smead, Sergt. David Hoyt, Corp. Nathan Frary; Centinals—Seth Catlin, Samuel Dickinson, Joseph Mitchell, John Hinsdale, John Hawks, Jr., David Childs, Caleb Allen, Eliakim Arms, Samuel Belden, Moses Nims, Augustus Wells, Jona: Catlin, Solomon Newton, Samuel Hinsdale, Justin Bull, Benjamin Munn, Jr.'

"These men were the real bone and muscle of Deerfield and could not well be spared in her straitened circumstances. Greenfield and Northfield were drained in the same manner of their best material for Loudon's army."

In the above extract Mr. Sheldon gives the names of two—Joseph Mitchell and Samuel Belding—who became, soon afterwards, residents of Huntstown.

COMMISSION OF LIEUT. DAVID ELLIS IN 1795.

By his Excellency, SAMUEL ADAMS, ESQ., Governor and Commander-in-Chief of the Commonwealth of Massachusetts, to David Ellis, Gentleman, of Ashfield, Greeting:

You being appointed Lieutenant of a Company in the Fifth Regiment of the Second Brigade, Fourth Division of the Militia of this Commonwealth, By Virtue of the Power vested in me, I do by these presents (reposing special Trust and Confidence in your Ability, Courage and good Conduct) Commision you accordingly. You are therefore carefully and dilligently to discharge the Duty of Lieutenant in leading, ordering and exercising said Company in Arms, both inferior officers and soldiers, and to keep them in good Order and Discipline. And they are hereby commanded to obey you as their Lieutenant. And you are yourself to observe and follow such Orders and Instructions as you shall from time to time receive from me or your Superior Officers.

Given under my Hand and the Seal of the said Commonwealth, the fourth day of September, in the year of our Lord 1795, and in the Twentieth year of the Independence of the United States of America.

By the Governor,

SAMUEL ADAMS.

JOHN AVERY, JUN.,
Sec'y.

May 1st, 1799, Lieut. David Ellis was honorably discharged, at his own request.

COMMISSION OF LIEUT. DIMICK ELLIS IN 1806.

On the 5th day of May, 1806, Mr. Dimick Ellis, of Ashfield, was commissioned a Lieutenant of a Company in the Fifth Regiment of the Second Brigade. The commission is in the same form as that above, but signed by CALEB STRONG, Governor, and John L. Austin, Secretary.

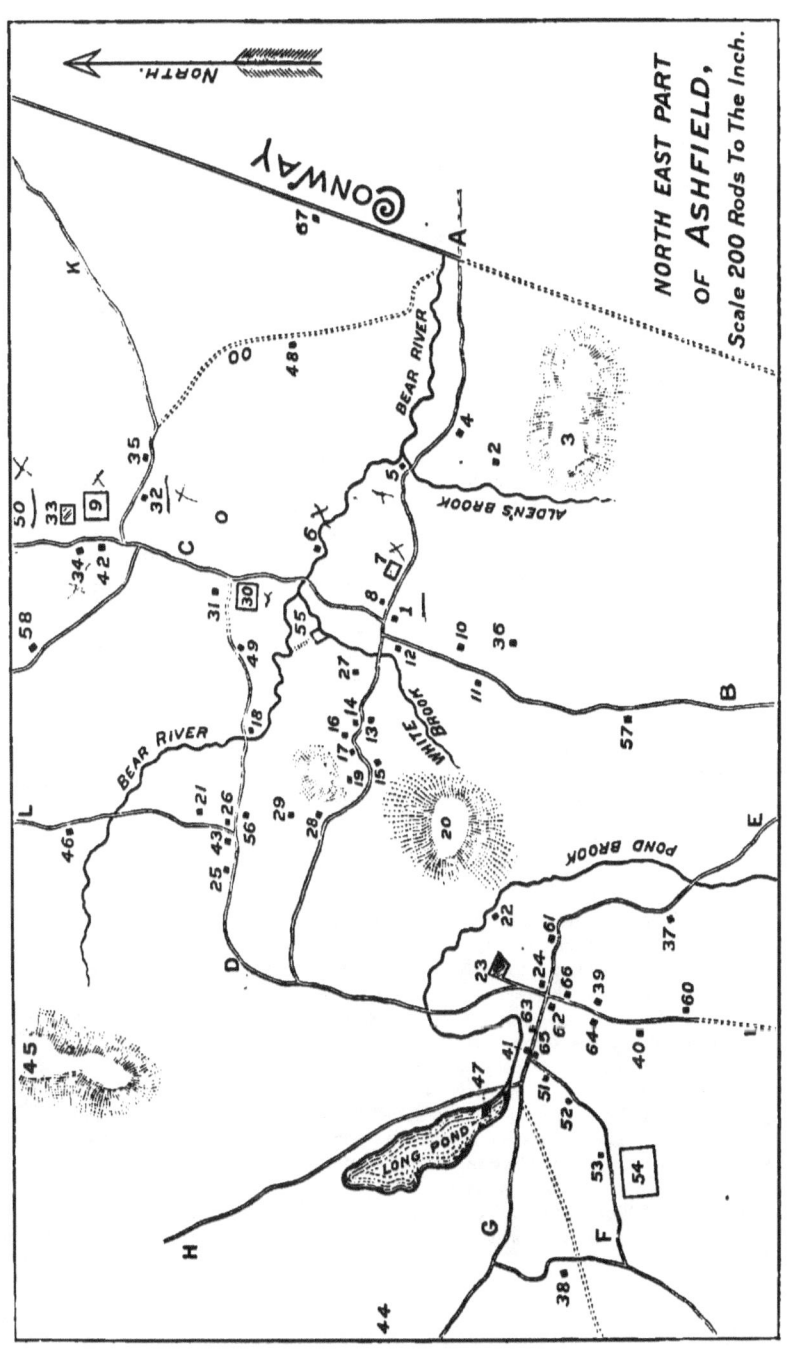

NORTH EAST PART
OF ASHFIELD,
Scale 200 Rods To The Inch.

EXPLANATION OF THE MAP OF THE NORTHEAST PART OF
ASHFIELD.

The Map is engraved from drawings kindly furnished by Messrs. Henry S. Ranney and Frederick G. Howes, of Ashfield. The reader is also indebted to the public spirit and generosity of these gentlemen for much of the descriptions following.

A. Is the roadway running from Conway westerly through the Ellis settlement up to the Plain or village near the center of the town—a distance of about three miles. Its many crooks and turns are to avoid impassable ledges of rocks. The whole face of country hereabouts is very uneven. Standing at the site of the old residence of Lieut. John Ellis (No. 14 on the map), is a plat of four or five acres nearly level. East and north is a steep descent of about 200 feet to White Brook and Bear River. South and southwest is Mill Hill, about 300 feet higher than the Ellis residence; directly west is Bellows Hill, about 100 feet lower than Mill Hill. Between these elevations is a depression, through which the roadway passes. North from the John Ellis home about three-fourths of a mile, and across Bear River, are high lands again, which, like all hereabouts, ar ecomposed of immense ledges of rocks, covered in places with thin soil. In early times these mountain sides were cleared, and made fair pasturage for cattle and sheep. Many of these places have been neglected, and are now covered with young pine and hemlock trees. Some of the valleys between these hills and along the streams are quite fertile, producing considerable grass and coarse grain.

B. Is the roadway to South Ashfield and Goshen township.

C. Road north to Baptist Corner (the Smith neighborhood) and Shelburne Falls. From Baptist Corner north to the Buckland town line is 352 rods.

D. Road from Baptist Corner, west and southerly, to the Plain (Ashfield village). This road now runs from No. 49 in a northerly direction to Baptist Corner. That part which originally ran from 49 *easterly* by the old fort at 30 to the north and south road is now discontinued.

E. Road from the Plain southeasterly to South Ashfield and Conway township.

F. Road from the Plain southwesterly to Plainfield township, and Peru. Hinsdale and Dalton in Berkshire County.

G. Road northwesterly to Hawley township.

H. Stage road northerly to Buckland township and Shelburne Falls.

OO. Road laid out in 1754 from Deerfield to Heber's fence, 29 (see page 302). What was then called "Deerfield bounds" included what is now the town of Conway, up to the line of Huntstown or Ashfield, marked A. on the map. Part of the road from A. to 35 is now discontinued.

The Streams of Ashfield are very unpretentious in size, except in times of freshets, and are of no importance as waterpowers. Bear River is the largest, and ordinarily is not more than twelve feet in width and eight to twelve inches in depth. It runs easterly through the eastern part of Ashfield, and then northeasterly through Conway to Deerfield River. There are now no mills on it within the limits of Ashfield.

Pond Brook is the outlet to Great Pond. It runs in the rear of the village on the Plain down through South Ashfield, where it becomes or is called

South River, then runs northeasterly and empties into Deerfield River, two or three miles east from Bear River outlet. At South Ashfield there were dams on this stream, with small mills. At the Pond there is a dam which raises the water about eight feet. In 1878 this dam was overflowed in a freshet and carried away. The waters of the Pond rushed down the narrow gorge, destroying a number of mills and other buildings in its course.

White Brook and Alden's Brook are small mountain streams about a mile in length.

1. Site of Richard Ellis' house in 1742. About 1764 Mr. Ellis removed to Colerain, and Mr. Samuel Belding then lived on this place. His son, John born 1756, succeeded his father on this homestead, where he lived until 1839. He raised a large family. His youngest son, Hiram, lived here until about 1855, when he removed to Otisco, (now Belding), Michigan. (See page 117.) This location is not the exact site of the "log cabin partly under ground, in the side of the hill," which Priest Shepard, in his Sketches (see page 278), says was about fifty rods further east, near the burying ground, and where the present road runs. In early times the road ran over the hill, in nearly a straight line from the Alden house (5) to the schoolhouse (8), and on the north side of the burying ground (7). Mr. Lewis Ellis, of Belding, Mich., born in Ashfield in 1811, says the location of his great grandfather's cabin was pointed out to him as being on the side hill near White Brook, where Richard felled the first tree, and not far from where Mr. Phineas Flower (12) lived in 1833. In 1754, when the "old road to Huntstown" (see page 302) was laid out, it ran from Thomas Phillips' south "to Richard Ellis' *new* house," which is the site marked 1 on the map. This makes it evident that Richard's first log cabin was not situated exactly at the corner, where the new house was built, and where the Beldings for four generations lived, and where Mr. Leonard D. Lanfair now resides. This farm, or "Right," where Richard Ellis first settled, was said to have been one of the best in that part of the town. It was lot 49, and was about 56 rods in width east and west, and 160 rods from Bear River on the north, to about 60 rods south of Richard's house at No. 1.

2. Is the house where Reuben Ellis (see page 68) lived and raised his family. He bought this farm—"the 56th Right "—of his father, in 1751. (See page 302.) This house, like all others in those days, was built of logs. It was occupied until about 1795.

3. Mount Owen, a rocky and almost inaccessible peak, about 100 rods in the rear of Reuben Ellis' house. It was named from a Mr. Owen, a surveyor, who became lost on the mountain when making the first surveys in the town. Its top is about 1,700 feet above the sea.

4. House built by David and Jonathan Ellis (sons of Reuben) about 1795. David Ellis, Sr., (page 86) lived here until 1818, when he sold the house and farm to Mr. Jesse Ranney, and moved to Springfield, Erie Co., Pa. Mr. Ranney lived on this place until his death, about 1859. He raised a large family, of whom five are yet living—Hannah (see page 175), Erastus, Edwin, Lucretia and Ruth—all living in Michigan except Ruth.

Mr. Charles W. Mann now lives on the old Ellis-Ranney homestead in Ashfield.

5. The Alden home. Dea. David Alden settled here in 1765. John

Alden, a very aged man, son of David, lived there as late as 1840. John, Jr., and Cyrus were his sons. A Mr. Kelley now lives on this place.

6. Old grist mill on Bear River, built about 1750 by Richard Ellis and Chileab Smith, Sr. It was on the north side of the stream and about 20 rods east of the present bridge and roadway. Remains of the mill were visible until recent times. In 1886 one of the old millstones was removed to the site of the ancient Ellis and Phillips fort, about 100 rods northwest. It is not quite certain whether this was the first grist mill built in Ashfield, or the one marked (22) near the Plain. Both have long since gone to decay.

7. Burying ground near Richard Ellis'. This was the second burying ground in Ashfield. It is small in extent—not over one acre—and only used for the immediate neighborhood. There lie the remains of Richard Ellis and wife. (See cut of monument on another page.)

On this ground are several tombstones bearing an early date. One marked "E. B., 1776," is a dark, rough granite, eight or ten inches across the face, and perhaps 15 inches high. It is presumed to mark the burial spot of Ebenezer Belding, Sr., the grandfather of Asher Belding. (See page 117.)

8. The Ellis neighborhood schoolhouse. District school where Mary Lyon taught three terms, about 1815-16.

9. Old Fort, built in 1756 around the house of Chileab Smith, Sr., at "Baptist Corner." (See page 280.)

10. House where Tiberius Belding (see page 169) lived from 1830 to 1840. Mr. Clarence Hall now lives on this place.

11. House where Dea. Ebenezer Belding lived at an early date, and where his son Asher (see page 117) lived and raised his family. Ebenezer died about 1820.

12. Site where Phineas Flower lived, from an early date up to about 1840. The house was built by his father, Maj. William Flower. The Major was a captain of militia, and aided to put down Shay's Rebellion or insurrection; just after the Revolution.

13. House where Maj. Lamrock Flower lived from the earliest times, in Ashfield, until his death in 1815. His son, Capt. Lamrock Flower, raised his family here. (See page 152.) Mr. Joshua Hall has lived here for about thirty years past. He has erected new buildings and reconstructed the old in a very handsome manner. This house stands opposite the Lieut. John Ellis house, where Dimick Ellis, Esq., lived in 1833, when Rev. Mr. Shepard wrote his sketches. Mr. Shepard (see page 287) states that Dea. Ebenezer Belding lived there in 1763. He may have done so for a short time.

14. House of Lieut. John Ellis, erected about 1795. His first house was built of logs, about 1763, and was some twenty rods west of the present house. Lieut. John Ellis raised his family on this place. (See page 76.) His youngest son, Dimick, lived on the homestead after the death of his parents, in 1827, and until about 1842, where he raised his family. Dimick's son, Lewis Ellis, now of Belding, Mich., was born in this house, in 1811, and lived on and worked the farm until his removal to Michigan, in 1842. Mr. Charles Rogers now owns and lives on this place. This house is on the southeast corner of lot 7, or the southwest corner of lot No. 8 according to the original survey of the proprietors.

15. Site where Samuel Annable, Jr., settled, about 1762, and where he lived until about 1802, when he removed to Cayuga Co., N. Y. He raised a large family here. One of his sons, Lieut. Edward Annable, was a prominent soldier in the Revolutionary army. (See page 92.) Rev. Jacob Sherwin, the first Congregational minister, lived at one time on this site, or very near it.

16. Nightingale's place. One of the first settlers was Samuel Nightingale. His cabin was on the north side of the road, the back of which was built up against the face of a large rock. This rock is one of the ancient landmarks. It has a perpendicular surface ten or twelve feet square, facing to the southeast, Nightingale was an emigrant from England, and was a man of uncommon learning but, withal, so queer in his ways that he was counted a "wizard."

17. Site of Joseph Mitchell's tavern, the first public house in the town. No remains of it are now seen.

18. Site of sawmill. Built by Lieut. John Ellis and Abner Phillips before the Revolution. It went to decay about 1790. About 1825 Luther Phillips built a carding mill, or works, on this site. No remains are now visible here except the mud-sill to the dam, at the lower edge of the bridge which crosses Bear River at this point. Before the Revolution Samuel Elmer settled about 100 rods east of this point, on the north side of the road.

19. Site, on Bellows Hill, of the first church (Congregational), built in the town. The frame was put up in 1767, and the following year it was taken down and re-erected, and the building completed in the cemetery on the Plain. (Marked 23 on the map.)

20. Mill Hill. Purchased by Dea. Dimick Ellis, about 1820, for a wood lot and sheep pasture. The top of this hill is about 1,700 feet above the sea.

21. Gray Brothers' house. About 1886 the Grays—two brothers—erected the largest and finest barn in the town, if not in the county. It is two stories high above the basement, and furnished with every convenience. The following year they erected an elegant and costly house on this farm, a few rods south of the barn.

22. Old Mill on Pond Brook. Erected by the Proprietors about 1743. After this went to decay another was built, which also disappeared many years ago, about 1831.

23. Cemetery, where stood the Congregational Church after its removal from Bellows Hill, in 1768. This is the principal cemetery in the town, and has many beautiful monuments in it.

24. Residence of Henry S. Ranney, Esq., town clerk for the past forty years. This is also the site of the ancient tavern of John Williams, built in 1792, by Zechariah Field. It is one of the finest locations on the Plain, or Ashfield village.

25. Residence and farm of Frederick G. Howes, Esq., an enterprising citizen of Ashfield.

26. Site of Philip Phillips, Esq.'s house. He was a son of Thomas Phillips, the second settler in the town, and was a very intelligent and influential man. He had thirteen children—eleven of whom were sons, each one over six feet tall. Esquire Phillips was an officer in the French and Indian war of 1756. He formed his sons into a company and took great pride in exhibiting them at military trainings.

27. Residence of Mr. Samuel A. Hall. Previous to 1860 this house-stood about 20 rods south of I, and was occupied by David, son of John Belding.

28. Site of a house on Bellows Hill, where Philip Phillips, Esq., once lived. Samuel Annable also lived there for a time. This is near the south-west corner of lot or Right No. 1. The old cellar-hole is yet visible.

29. Site of Heber's cabin, on the west side of Bellows Hill. Heber was a black man, said to have been brought a slave from Africa. He came to Ashfield with the Phillipses, from Easton, or the eastern part of the State. Lot or Right No. 1, where his cabin was built, was taken by him from the original Proprietors. Lots 2, 3 and 4 were on the west from this lot. Lots 7, 8 and 9 were on the east side of lot No. 1. That Heber was an honest and respected man is evident from the early records of the town, where he is mentioned in several places, when taxes were assessed to him, as "Heber honest-man," a compliment which any person might be proud of.

30. Site of the Ellis and Phillips Fort. (See pages 280 and 320.)

31. Site of house of Mr. Sears. This is the place to which Rev. Mr. Shepard referred as being near the fort. (See page 280).

32. Site of residence of Thomas Phillips, Sr., brother of Richard Ellis' wife. He was the second settler in the town. There is a tradition that his first house was about 80 rods south of 32, near the point marked O, and a few rods northeasterly from the fort, where there is yet to be seen a cellar hole. Nearly opposite (32) lived Thomas Phillips Jr., and after him his son, Russell Phillips, who married Rhoda, eldest daughter of Hannah Ellis Williams (see page 101). All of their children were born on this place.

33. Burying Ground at Baptist Corner.

34. First site of the Baptist Church, built about 1775.

35. Second site of the Baptist Church, about sixty rods east of the Corner. This church was built about 1830. A school-house now stands there. In early times Israel Standish lived about 60 rods east of No. 35.

36. House where John Sadler, an early settler, lived.

37. The farm where George Ranney settled, in 1780, and where he raised a large family. His son, George Ranney, Jr., and Henry S. Ranney, Esq., son of the latter, were born and reared on this farm.

38. Site of Capt. Samuel Bartlett's house, where the nine tories were confined, in August, 1777. This site should be marked about 60 rods nearer the Plain on the discontinued road. There is yet to be seen a cellar-hole at the site.

39. Seth Wait's tavern in 1783; now the Episcopal parsonage.

40. Capt. Moses Fuller's tavern in 1767. Moses Cook has built and now lives on this site.

41. Timothy Perkins' tavern in 1778. The Ashfield House, now kept by Lewis Porter, Esq., is on or near this site.

42. Chileab Smith, Jr.'s, tavern in 1786.

43. Jonathan Yeoman's house, 1767.

44. Peter's Hill, or Mountain, is about one-half mile west from this point. It is the highest elevation in Ashfield, being, according to U. S. survey, 1,800 feet above the sea and 600 feet above the Plain, or Ashfield village. It is now cleared of trees and affords some pasturage, and also grows the finest and largest wintergreen berries the writer has ever seen. The writer was misinformed, on page 276, about Hon. J. R. Lowell's having purchased a site on this mountain for a summer residence.

45. Ridge Hill, a mountain in the north part of the town.

46. Dea. David Lyon's residence, being the same where his father, Aaron Lyon, settled as early as 1765.

MARY LYON's birthplace was about one mile north from her uncle, Dea. David Lyon's. (See page 238).

47. That part of Great Pond where Dea. David Lyon and four others were drowned in 1827. (See page 295).

48. Site of residence of Dea. Samuel Washburn in 1764, and of his son, Samuel, Jr. David Ellis, Sr.'s wife, Sarah Washburn, was reared on this place. (See page 88.) John Pfersich now lives here.

49. Site of Capt. Benjamin Phillips' house in 1765. Capt. Phillips was the first town clerk of Ashfield, on its incorporation. The old cellar-hole is yet to be seen a few rods south of the figures 49.

50. The site of the residence where Elder Ebenezer Smith lived is about 80 rods north of this point. (See page 71). His younger brother, Elder Enos Smith, also lived on this place or very near it. From No. 50 north to the Buckland town line is about one-half mile.

51. Where Rev. Thos. Shepard lived in 1820, while pastor of the Congregational Church. See his Sketches of Ashfield, pages 275 to 297. Before Mr. Shepard settled in Ashfield he was a missionary and teacher in Georgia. After leaving Ashfield, in 1833, he was agent of the American Bible Society about two years, when he was installed as pastor in Bristol, R. I., in 1835, where he remained in active and successful service until his death, about 1875. This house is now the summer residence of Prof. C. E. Norton, of Cambridge.

52. Site of Dr. Phineas Bartlett's residence in 1765. Dr. Bartlett was a physician in Ashfield over 40 years. At his death, it is said, there was the largest attendance at the funeral ever known in the town. He was a great patriot in Revolutionary times. One of the seven tories whom he voted to confine in 1777 was a near relative of his. In 1792 Dr. B. built and lived in the house marked 51.

53. Residence of Rev. Nehemiah Porter in 1774. This spot is 100 rods southwest of where Dr. Bartlett lived.

54. Center Cemetery, in the geographical center of the town. In 1812 the Congregational Church was erected on this ground, the old church in the cemetery (at 23) having gone to disuse. About the year 1855 there was a division in the church, and a part of the congregation erected a new church building at the Plain, on the north side of the main street, the two societies of this church have united, and in 1857 moved the church building from the Center Cemetery to the south side of the main street on the Plain. This is a large and commodious building and is now the Town Hall,

55. Sawmill on White Brook, built about 1828 by Dimick Ellis, Asher Belding and Phineas Flower. Water to run it was brought from Bear River, in a race across the flat, shown by the dotted line. This went to decay and disappeared twenty years later.

56. Site where Israel Phillips lived in 1795.

57. Location where Dea. John Bement lived in 1759. On this place were raised Judge Leonard and Edmund Bement, who lived in Grand Rapids, Mich., in 1860.

58. Site where Dea. Isaac Shepard lived in 1764. His daughter Jemima was the wife of Aaron Lyon, Jr., and mother of Mary Lyon.

60. New summer house of Mrs. John W. Field, of Philadelphia.

61. Site of a Baptist church, built in 1870.

62. Episcopal church, built in 1827.

63. Site of old house where lived Thomas White, Esq., in 1794; father of Capt. Thomas White, who lived in Grand Haven and Grand Rapids, Mich., from about 1836 to 1880. His sister Amanda, who married Rev. Wm. M. Ferry, was born in this house. Mr. and Mrs. Ferry were Congregational missionaries among the Indians of Mackinaw and Grand Haven, Mich., in early times. They were the parents of Hon. Thomas White Ferry, U. S. senator from Michigan many years, and Vice-President *pro tem.* previous to the inauguration of Hayes and Wheeler in 1877. The old house was burned in February, 1820, and rebuilt in the same year. It is directly opposite the town hall, and is now owned by Mrs. Amanda Ferry Hall, a granddaughter of the original owner.

64. Site of residence of Levi Cook, Esq., an early resident of Ashfield. It is now the summer residence of Hon. George William Curtis, of New York city.

65. Town Hall, and Soldiers' Monument and Fountain nearly in front of it.

66. Residence of Hon. Enos Smith, M. D., in 1796. Present residence of Lemuel Cross, Esq.

67. House where James Ranney, Esq., eldest son of Jesse, lived from about 1825 to 1860.

REGARDING "ANGELS' VISITS"—NOTE TO PAGES 89 AND 90.

By request the following comments on the "Angels' visits," mentioned on pages 89 and 90, are given by Rev. A. F. Frost, pastor of the New Jerusalem Church, Detroit, Mich.:

The statements made about the visits of angels to certain members of the Ellis family seem to be well authenticated and are of an exceedingly interesting nature. That such visits are not only possible, but to those in their situation—cut off, as they were, from all other means of knowing of the exist- of a God and a life after death—it would appear as if the visits were wholly providential. All who read and believe in the Bible as a Divine revelation will not be slow to believe in the possibility or usefulness of such visitations, since the Bible is full of accounts of the people of all ages who have seen, heard and conversed with angels. Swedenborg, from actual experiences in the same direction, has very clearly explained what is said in the Bible about such visits, and the purpose of them. In his work entitled "*The Apocalypse Revealed,*" which is an explanation of the book of Revelation, commenting on the words: "I was in the spirit on the Lord's Day" (Rev. i. 10), Swedenborg says: "This signifies the spiritual state in which John was when he was in *visions.* Concerning the prophets, it is written that they were in the spirit or in vision; also, that the Word came to them from the Lord. When they were in the spirit or vision they saw with their spiritual eyes but not with their natural eyes. They were not in the body, but in their spirit, in which state they saw such things as are in heaven. In the state of vision the eyes of their spirit were opened, and the eyes of their body shut; and then they heard what the angels spake, or what the Lord spake by the angels, and also saw the things which were represented to them in heaven; and then they sometimes seemed to themselves to be carried from one place to another, the body still remaining in its place. In this state was John when he wrote the Apocalypse; and sometimes, also Ezekiel, Zechariah and Daniel; and then it is said that they were in vision, or in the spirit. Ezekiel says: "The spirit took me up and brought me in a vision by the Spirit of God into Chaldea; so the vision that I had seen went up from me"—xi. 1, 2, 4. It is also said that the spirit took him up, and that he heard behind him a voice of a great rushing, and other things—iii. 12, 24; also, that the spirit lifted him up between the earth and heaven and brought him, in the visions of God, to Jerusalem—viii. 3. The same was the case with Zechariah, with whom there was an angel at the time when he saw a man riding among the myrtle trees—i. 8; when he saw a man in whose hand was a measuring line—ii. 1, 5; when he saw Joshua the High Priest—iii. 1; when he saw the candlestick and the two olive trees—iv. 1. In a similar state was Daniel, when he saw four beasts coming up out of the sea—vii. 1; when he saw the battle of the ram and the he goat—viii. 1, which things he says he saw in visions. It was the same with John, as when he saw the Son of Man in the midst of the seven golden candlesticks, when he saw a throne, a book sealed with seven seals, four horses coming out of the book, when he heard the seven angels sound with the seven trumpets, when he saw the dragon, the two beasts, the great whore, the white horse, the new heaven and the new earth, and the New Jerusalem. All these things he says he saw in the spirit and in vision—i. 10; iv. 2; ix. 17. It appears, evidently, from these examples, that to be in the spirit is to be in vision; which is effected by the opening of the sight of a man's spirit, when the things in the spiritual world appear as clearly as the things in the natural world appear to bodily sight. I can testify that it is so from many years' experience. In this state the disciples were when they saw the Lord after his resurrection, wherefore it is said that their eyes were opened—Luke xxiv. 30, 31. Abraham was in a similar state when he saw the three angels and talked with them. So were Hagar, Gideon, Joshua and others, when they saw angels. In like manner the lad with Elisha, when he saw the chariots of fire and horses about Elisha; for Elisha prayed and said: "O Lord, I pray thee, open his eyes, that he may see; and the Lord opened the eyes of the young man, and he saw"—2 Kings, vi. 17.

This will easily explain the process of all genuine visions, where persons have seen, heard and talked with angels. Every man, as to his interiors, is a spirit, and is surrounded by and in association with spirits and angels in the spiritual world, although not ordinarily conscious of it. The spirit of man has eyes, ears, tongue, hands, feet, and all the other organs of the human frame, since the spirit is in a substantial human form. The eyes and ears of the spirit may be opened by the Lord whenever He sees that it is for some good and useful purpose. This frequently happens with those who are dying. They see those in the spiritual world with the eyes of the spirit, and are filled with rapture at the thought of soon joining them. The organs of the spirit of man are in a perfect state, however imperfect or deformed are the organs of the body. On their entrance into the spiritual world, those who had been blind, deaf, dumb or lame here, would at once see, hear, speak and walk. And if the spirit of those deaf and dumb should be opened while they were living in the body, they could perfectly hear and speak the language of the spiritual world, which is a universal language, is interiorly impressed upon the spirit of every one; and hence all understand all in the other life, whatever may have been their nationality or language in this world. It is perfectly reasonable to believe that the deaf and dumb persons of the Ellis family saw, heard and talked with the angels; and that deaf and dumb persons could speak with each other, provided both were in the spirit at the same time. The disciples talked with the Lord, and He with them, after the resurrection, when the Lord was in the spiritual world, and the interiors of the disciples must have been opened; for, otherwise, they could not have done this. Also in the mount of transfiguration, when Peter, James and John were in vision and saw the Lord in glory, they also saw and heard and spake with Moses and Elias, and likewise talked with each other. This would be just as perfectly the case with persons who were deaf, blind and dumb as to the body, since an impaired condition of the bodily senses does not extend to the spirit of man at all. As there was no sign language, or other means of instruction for the deaf and dumb, in the days when these members of the Ellis family lived, there was no other way for them to know anything about God, religion and the life after death, than by some such direct communication with angels as it is related took place. The Lord gave them these opportunities, which are denied men ordinarily, because most men can read the Bible and hear preaching and by these means learn spiritual truth. That Jonathan Ellis had both his speech and hearing when under angelic influence is easily explained, therefore, since both the tongue and ears would be controlled from an internal influence and power, and not by an external power, as is ordinarily the case. The angel that stood in the way of Balaam caused it to appear that even the dumb ass spake. This was only the appearance, however, as the angel himself, and not the ass, spake; but Balaam was so obstinate that he could not listen to the angel; he could be brought to consider his situation only when startled by the remarkable appearance that he was being reproved by his ass. Although at times, and for special reasons, men may see and speak with angels, yet the orderly way of receiving instruction in spiritual truth is by means of the Scriptures. It is disorderly, dangerous, and forbidden us in the Bible, to seek intercourse with the inhabitants of the spiritual world, or to come into communication with the dead. Under no circumstances of our seeking will any good spirit or angel appear to us. The spirits that operate by speaking, writing or other manifestations through modern mediums, are always evil spirits, of a low and sensual nature, who deceive and flatter, and lead men away from the Lord, heaven, the church and the Bible. As in the case of the members of the Ellis family there was no effort on their part to pry into spiritual mysteries, but a real need because of their inability to speak or hear, that they should learn about God, religion and the future outside of the ordinary means, it is reasonable to believe that what is related of their angelic visitants is true.

BRIEF ACCOUNT OF THE LIFE AND TRIALS OF ELDER EBENEZER SMITH, OF ASHFIELD, MASS.—WRITTEN BY HIMSELF.

[Elder Smith was a son-in-law of Richard Ellis, of Ashfield. For an account of him see page 71. The manuscript from which the following article is printed was sent the writer by Dr. A. P. Phillips, of Fredonia, N. Y., whose wife is a great granddaughter of Elder Smith. See page 98.]

"Come and hear, all ye that fear God, and I will declare what He hath done for my soul."

"One generation shall praise Thy works to another, and shall declare Thy mighty acts."
[DAVID.

Having been requested to write some of the experiences I have met with in my life, I did not conclude to do it until I received a letter from a much esteemed friend in which was the following: " I read your letter at the meeting of our Missionary Board, and the members expressed a wish that you would commit to writing the most remarkable circumstances of your life, and the observations you have made from time to time relative to the cause and church of Christ. You have outlived most of your cotemporaries; of course, you have more experience of the ways of God than many of your junior brethren; you have also experienced many trials which most of us have been exempted from. I hope, dear sir, while your health and powers of mind hold out, you will devote a little of your precious time to this labor of love, for the good of the cause and for the benefit of those who may follow after you."

Upon receiving this letter I thought it my duty to enter upon the work, concerning which, I would observe that I am now almost eighty-six years old, and I have nothing to write from but my memory, but I shall be careful not to write anything but what I am sure is the truth. Perhaps, in writing what was said many years ago, I shall not always use the same words, but I shall be very careful to give the true sense.—Stockton, Chautauqua Co., N. Y., Aug. 29, 1820.

I was born in South Hadley, Mass., October 4, 1734. There was but very little schooling for anyone in my young days. I went to a woman's school a little while and learned to read, and afterwards to a man's school and learned to write, which was all the teaching I had except what I received at my father's house. I could read pretty well, could write so as it might be read, and had a knowledge of arithmetic sufficient for the business of a common farmer, but never saw a grammar till I bought one for my own children.

In my seventeenth year my father removed to Ashfield. There were but two families in the town before him. I had serious impressions on my mind when very young and, by turns, throughout my youthful days; at times would be light and merry with my mates, but never went to what was then called a frolic. After we removed to Ashfield [then Huntstown] my father proposed to the neighbors to meet together on the Sabbath for religious worship; they assented, and my father took the lead in the worship. I was under deep concern of mind until in the month of March, 1753 (I do not remember the day of the month, but the place where and the time of the day—between sundown and dark), as I was looking to God alone, as a poor, guilty sinner, I was enabled to give myself into the hands of a just God, and a peace and joy followed which I never knew before.

I cannot tell of such views of the flames of hell, and of Christ hanging on the cross as I have heard others relate, but my *understanding* was led to see the holiness of God's law and my utter inability to do anything to recommend myself to Him; and I also saw the infinite fullness of the Savior's merits—that pardon could be had through His atoning blood, and justification through His spotless righteousness. And this is all my hope; whatever becomes of me at last, I can only plead: "God be merciful to me, a sinner;" and I believe it will be infinitely safe to be in this way.

I now began, as opportunity offered, to speak of the things of God. In the course of the summer my mind was led to particular texts of Scripture that would open to my view. This one often came to mind: "As every man hath received the gift, so let him minister the same;" but I am but a child; how can I speak to those who are so much older than I? To this self-questioning the answer would return: "As every man hath received the gift," followed by "Lo, I am with you." So I labored along under these trials until November. On the 29th day of that month I was called upon in such a manner that I could no longer refrain, and attempted to preach unto the people. From that day to this—sixty-seven years next November—I have endeavored to improve and to speak forth the truth according to my ability. I must now begin to relate some of the trials in my experience.

The next summer after this beginning I was requested to go and preach in another town. A great number assembled to hear; the minister of the town, and another scholarly man who had just begun to preach, were present, and they both remained seated during prayer. The minister several times interrupted my discourse, but the rest of the people behaved orderly. After the meeting the minister asked me what a butler was. I answered: a "cup-bearer." He said I used the word "butler" instead of "buckler," in my discourse. I cannot say but I might have made such a slip, and a few years afterwards my utterance at the time alluded to was ridiculed in the public prints by him. A further example of the minister's treatment of me was as follows: In praying for the ministers of Christ I used these words: "That they may stand in their lot." In his talk after the meeting he asked: "In what lot must ministers stand in—home lot or second division lot?" His whole conduct was in this line of mockery. I have ever been grateful that through the goodness of God I was enabled—young as I was, and among strangers—to go through with my discourse.

Soon after this the war of 1756 broke out, and for two summers we were forced to leave town from fear of the Indians. I was called to go into the army for about three months, and then we built a fort [at Ashfield or Hunts-town] and had some men sent to guard us. So we lived in the fort in the summer for three summers, and in our own houses in the winter. We were in a broken situation at that time, but I still continued to preach, when there was time for it.

I was brought up to believe that sprinkling infants was baptism, and never had much thought but such was right, until I was married and had a child of my own, then I thought more about it. I had never seen a Baptist nor a Baptist's writings. I heard there were Baptists, but they were spoken of as a deluded people, and my further inquiries about the ordinance of baptism led me to conclude that the subject was left in the dark—there was nothing certain about it, and I might accept what my father had done for me, and let that go for my baptism; but I could not get my own children baptised. O what blindness!

In April, 1761, a Baptist elder came into town on business. Inviting him to my house, I desired him to tell me how he came to be a Baptist, and I found that *he* was settled and unshaken in regard to that ordinance, whereas I had thought that *nobody* could be certain whether he was right or not. After discovering that one could be established in regard to that ordinance, I came to the determination to search carefully at once as to what was right, and I can truly say that I could not find, then nor since, that I had the least choice but to accept *the truth;* and this Scripture came to me with great solemnity: " Let God be true, and every man a liar." I went to my Bible; I read no other book; I said nothing to any man till I had become settled beyond doubt, that believers in Christ, and none other, had any right to that ordinance; and that to be buried in the water, and raised out of it, in the name of the Father, and of the Son, and of the Holy Ghost, is the only Gospel baptism.

And now I was brought to see the reason why I was so long in the dark about that ordinance. It was because I let the traditions of men be of weight in the balance with the word of God. And I am persuaded that every true believer in Christ that reads the Bible, if he has but a single eye, will let that doctrine of Antichrist—that sprinkling infants is baptism—go, and embrace the pure ordinance of Christ; delivered to the saints; for Christ saith: " If thine eye be single, thy whole body shall be full of light;" and He will fulfill His word.

Making my mind known to my friends I found some who had a desire to be baptised; and I knew of but one elder on earth that we could apply to, and he was sixty miles away; but I went to him with my errand, and he came, with one of his brethren, and baptised seven one day, and one the next day; and there was one of that elder's members who had moved into the town a little before; he joined us, making our number nine. We formed a church, the elder gave us the right hand of fellowship, and administered the Lord's supper.

It made a great tumult among the people. Such a thing was never heard of in that part of the country before. All manner of evil was said about us; and we a feeble band and no friends near us. But he that is a sanctuary to His people through His grace we were enabled to keep our ground, and the church gave me a call to be ordained and to become their pastor. We sent to the same elder (60 miles), and to another elder (90 miles), and to a church that had no elder (90 miles), they came, and I was ordained August 20, 1761.

From this time the Lord carried on His work, and additions were made to the church. One thing that took place a few months after my ordination I will mention, as perhaps it may do good: There came a young man from a distance of ninety miles, in order to be baptised. He went to meeting with me, but when it came time for him to tell his experience he was so dark in his mind that he could not do it. I pitied the young man, and took him with me to my house. After some conversation, I told the young man that I could tell what the difficulty was with him that kept him so in the dark: You live near one of the elders that attended my ordination; some of his church live in the same town with you, and you could not bear to take up the cross or be baptised among your old acquaintances, so you come up here into the woods to be baptised and shun the cross. He freely confessed that to be the very reason of his coming, and he soon had such light and comfort in his soul that he decided to return home and be baptised among his own people. The next I heard of him he was baptised and preaching the Gospel, and became a worthy minister of Christ.

If we mean to be Christ's friends we must deny ourselves and take up the cross.

When I was ordained above half the people that were then in the town were agreed in it and attended my ministry; but, the war being over, the Pedo-baptists [believers in infant baptism] came into the town, and in 1763 they settled a minister. There were 300 acres of land for the first minister who settled in the town. They took all that and did not let me have one foot of it. There were 300 more, the *use* of which was for the support of the minister, which was rented out to the utter exclusion of the Baptists. The General Court made a law that all the land in town might be taxed to pay the Pedo-baptist minister and build their meeting-house; and if any did not pay, the land could be sold to obtain the tax. We sent a petition to the Court for relief, and, not being heard, we all agreed that we would not pay the tax, let what would come of it. In the month of April, 1770 they came forward with a tax of £507 for their minister and meeting-house, and began selling our lands. They sold about 400 acres in all—ten acres of my home lot, that were worth ten dollars an acre. The man came with a surveyor and a band of men, to measure it off. My little son, about four years old, came crying to me, saying: "Father, has the man come to take away our land?" I saw the man next day, who told me to go and put up half the fence between us and he would put up the other half. I replied: no, there should be no fence put there; if he had a mind to sue me for the land I would stand trial, and see who had the best right to it; but come on it he should not—and I have never seen his face since. To be short about the matter, I went five times to Boston to try to get that law repealed, but failed in my errand. Other trials of those trying days are worth mention : One day, when Col. Dexter and some other members of the Court desired to see my ordination, the record was shown him; he read it over and said: "This looks like an ordination 'according to the pattern shown in the mount.'"

Once, when the matter was being debated in Court, Col. Bowers said he would "not call it highway robbery, but if such things were done on the high seas, he would call it piracy."

One morning I went to see Col. Tyler. He was unable to go to the Court that day, but he wrote a letter for me to carry to Dexter, to have him help me, and in the letter he said: "They are devilishly oppressed."

Discoursing with a number of the Court one day, one of them said: "Suppose eight or ten Baptists go into a new town and settle a minister, and then the other order are not able to settle a minister without the Baptists' help, must they do without a minister because there are eight or ten Baptists there?" I replied: "The Court allows sixty proprietors to every new town. Now ten Baptists go in and settle a minister, and the fifty cannot settle their minister without the ten support their own minister and help the fifty support theirs, too. Do look at it!"

While these things were going on there appeared an article in public print, said to have come from a minister residing near Ashfield, in which the writer says: "It is a common observation that the Baptists in Ashfield will not stick at any falsehood, to serve their purposes;" and to prove his charge, he says that we say in our petition to the Court: "there are £507 pounds raised for the minister and the meeting-house, whereas £100 were for highways." A·heavy charge; to come from a minister, too, and from one that lived near us. I thought it time to appear in my own and my brethren's defence. I sent to the Clerk and got a copy of the vote for raising money, and went right down to Boston and put an answer into the same paper, just four weeks after the other article appeared.

I said, in my answer: "We did in our petition say that the sum of £507 was raised for the minister and meeting-house; then, *he* adds that ' £100 was for highways,' which is a notorious falsehood. That £100 was raised for highways I well knew, but it was no part of the £507 for the minister and meeting-house; and, to satisfy the public, here follows a copy of the votes, attested by the clerk, that said £507 are for the minister and meeting-house and £100 for highways." I heard no more of that charge.

The last time that I went down to the Court at Boston, one of the men who sold our land also went down to meet me there. The Court chose a committee of five men, with Col. Brattle as their chairman. We pleaded our cause before them and left it for them to make their report. Col. Bowers told me that his affairs were such that he thought he must go home. I desired he would stay till the committee reported. He replied that if his going would be any damage to me, he would stay if it cost him £100. Accordingly he did stay. I cannot tell the very words of the report, but the substance of it was, that in the sale of our lands there was nothing unjust, but all was right and we had suffered no wrong; and, notwithstanding all my friends could say, the Court accepted the report. Thus were we left by an act of the Government in the hands of our neighbors, who might tax and sell just as much of our land as they pleased. This looked·like a dark day, but I had this for my support, that there is a ' God in heaven that governed the affairs of men.'

By the help of some friends the matter was sent over to the King. This was in April. The King's order came the same year, in October. I suppose there were but three men in the country who knew it had gone to the King, till his order came, by which order he overthrew the sale under our law, and put a stop to their taxing us any more. This was " good news from a far country," and rejoiced the hearts of my afflicted brethren.

Perhaps the reader will ask how I was exercised in mind by the trying circumstances of these times. I can say that I viewed them to be of the providence of God—that He cast my lot where it was, and that it was the cause of truth that I was called upon, according to my ability, to defend; and being in the path of duty I had God to go to; and, having His fear before my eyes, creatures vanished from sight; that I felt under obligations to speak my mind· plainly, before high and low. At that time there was much said about liberty, and the people in this land was complaining of Britain's oppression. One day, when I was discoursing·with a number of the members of the Court, they

pleaded for their right to tax the Baptists, and that they could not support
their ministers without the Baptists' help. I say the truth—I lie not; my
spirit was stirred within me; not with anger, but with an abhorence of such
tyranny; and with a zeal for the cause of truth, and to defend my oppressed,
brethren, I told them they were calling themselves the sons of liberty and were
erecting their liberty poles about the country, but they did not deserve the
name, for it was evident all they wanted was liberty from oppression that they
might have liberty to oppress !

I was told that the man who went down to meet me before the Court said
to his neighbors, after he came home, that "Elder Smith would speak the
truth, let the consequences be what they would."

In those days of trial I received many favors from my brethren in and
about Boston, which I have not forgotten. But they are now mostly all, if
not all, gone home to glory, I trust; while I, poor and unworthy, yet continue
in this vale of tears. O that I may be enabled to be faithful unto death. But
to return to my narrative:

The brethren in Newport sent a request to me to come and see them; and
a little after the King's order came into the town, and we had gained my
brethren's liberty, I went to see them.

As I was on my way home I met one of my acquaintances, in a town where
I intended to tarry over the Sabbath, and he told me that since I had left
home they had sent out a warrant to take me for counterfeiting money. I told
him I never was afraid to travel the King's highway, and I should not turn out
for that noise. He said they would take me as soon as I got home, or before.
I went on to where I intended to put up. When my friend saw me come in,
he said: "Are you here? I just now heard that you were in Springfield jail
for counterfeiting money!" I told him it was not worth while for me to say
anything about it, for people would reply that if I would counterfeit money I
would deny it; but you know that I am not in Springfield jail, because you see
me here.

He sent out to let the people know that I was come. I did not see but
there came as many to hear me preach as ever before when I had been there.
As I went on my way home there was a great stir about the affair, but I got
home the day I meant to, and they never showed me the warrant. May God
have the glory.

[It is astonishing to what indignities the Baptists were subjected during
these times, especially Mr. Chileab Smith, Sr., the father of Elder Ebenezer
Smith. Mr. Smith was the third settler in Ashfield, and was the most noted
resident of the town for thirty years or more. He was an ardent Baptist, and
was ordained into the ministry when 80 years of age. He died in 1800, in his
93d year. In the year 1771, in the midst of the persecutions mentioned above,
it was reported that he "had put off a bad dollar" upon a Mr. Pike, a resident;
and although Mr. Pike said that "there was no truth in the report," Mr.
Smith was arrested and taken before the Judge of the Court at Hatfield, twenty
miles away. Ten witnesses were summoned and no evidence was found against
him, yet the Judge was very insulting, and held him to bail in a sum so large
that he supposed Mr. Smith could not procure it, and hence could be kept in
jail a few months. The result was, as he himself stated, that "he was greatly
injured in his health and lost most of a winter's work." It turned out that

his arrest was mainly due to the fact that smoke was seen, by jealous persons, to issue from the chimney of his shop on Sundays, where he had built a fire to warm those who came to his house to attend meetings—Baptist meetings for several years being held at his house. Previous to this, his orchard had been torn up and twenty acres of his best land sold, to pay taxes to another minister and for building the meeting-house of another denomination. "His house was searched; and when he went abroad about his lawful business his track was pursued, to see if they could not find some evil thing done by him." His people were taunted with the saying: "When the negroes get free, then the Baptists may," &c. In all the trials to which these people were subjected they were fully vindicated; and the verdict, finally, of all who ever knew Chileab Smith, Sr., the champion of the Baptists, was: "that he was as honest a man as ever lived." He never wavered in his faith or purposes, and could have gone to the stake with as much heroism as any martyr of old. He was the human embodiment of that inspiration which at Baptist Corner gained for religious freedom one of the greatest victories in the world's history. Yet, for one of the present time who looks over these "rock-ribbed and sterile hills," now mostly deserted, the wonder is, how these hardy pioneers gained a bodily subsistence, even. The name and fame of CHILEAB SMITH, SR., should be perpetuated forever among men, and a monument erected to his memory on the sanctified ground of Baptist Corner. Some future generation will do this.—It may be said that the odium which was sought to be cast upon the Baptist people by other denominations continued for thirty years later, until the time when that great missionary, Adoniram Judson, was sent out from Massachusetts to India in 1812 to convert the heathen. On his passage to that country he investigated Baptist doctrines, and soon after his arrival announced his conversion thereto. This was the end of the persecution of the Baptists in this country, the humiliation of their opponents being complete. See page 324.]

And now they took another method to annoy me: They put me into the civil tax three years going; made up the tax and put the collection thereof into the hands of three collectors. One of them called on me to pay. I told him I should not pay, and forbade his taking anything of mine; I agreed not to go out of his way, so that he might take me if he would, but meddle with my property he must not. Before he distrained on me another Elder in the county was taxed in the same manner, who sued the town for his right, in the Supreme Court at Northampton, and gained his case. These three collectors were present at that trial, and never again called on me to pay the tax.

Concerning this affair I would make the following remark: The assessors who made up the tax were under oath to proceed according to law. The law forbade taxing a minister of the Gospel, and the only way they could tax me without violating their oaths, as they thought, was by denying that I was a minister. Had I paid the tax when it was demanded I would seem thereby to have acknowledged that I was not a minister, and thus have brought reproach upon my calling, my people and the cause of God. These considerations moved me to refuse to pay the tax; the money was only a trifle, but the honor of God required that I should not wound His cause or give occasion to the adversary to rejoice. I fully expected when I refused payment that my property would be levied upon, and my escape from loss or annoyance was due to the judgment of the court in the case of the other elder. It appeared to me a providence of

God in my behalf that the case was tried just at this time, and that the three collectors should have been present at the trial and have been convinced that they had no right to collect a tax from me. Such things do not come by chance. To God be the glory!

But I turn to relate things of a different nature: Though our adversaries had lost the power to oppress us, they yet manifested their spite by all manner of reproaches and evil-speaking, and the ministers would try to prejudice the people against the Baptists. One instance I mention: A man belonging to the Pedobaptist Society desired me to go and preach at his house. I passed the house of the minister on the way to my appointment, and the minister, seeing me, set out to follow me, keeping a distance behind, so as to avoid speaking with me. He came into the house a little after my arrival and began to reprove the man for inviting me to preach at his house without leave from him. The minister displayed much heat of spirit, but I thought it prudent not to interfere between them, and sat silently by. When, however, the people had assembled, I spoke to the minister and told him the time for worship had arrived. He arose and said: "If you will go on, I charge all my people not to stay to hear you," and went out. As he was going these words came to my mind, which I repeated so that he might hear:

> ' Why should the nations angry be?
> What noise is this we hear?
> The Gospel takes away their gods,
> And that they cannot bear."

One man followed the minister; all the rest remained throughout the service.

But Jesus is King upon the holy hill of Zion, and notwithstanding all the rage of the devil and antichrist, He carried on His own work and the church increased; another church was formed in New Salem, and I was sent for to baptize a number in Chesterfield—I suppose the first ever baptized in that town—and soon there were enough to form a church. I was soon after called to baptize in Colerain, and a church was gathered there; another church ormed in Montague; another in Leyden; a second church was formedin Cole rain; another rose up in Charlemont, and I had the happiness of assisting in ordaining elders in five of these churches. O what hath God wrought in my day! Glory to His holy name!

When the Pedobaptists found they could not stop the work of God by oppression nor reproaches, they turned to flattering. "Come, let us all be one; we allow your baptism to be good; we can commune with you, why will you not commune with us?" And a number of their ministers invited me into their pulpits to preach for them on the Sabbath; and it so happened that I went into my own county town, where I was born and brought up—South Hadley—and their minister being away they requested me to preach for them. That was a good occasion for me to preach the Gospel of Christ to my kinsmen according to the flesh, and to those who had been my neighbors from my infancy. What will be the fruit of that day's labor I must leave till the Lord brings it to light.

In these times of flattery there came three persons to me from a town adjoining, where they had no minister—men who had been acquainted with me a number of years and had often been to my meetings—to see if I would not go and be their town's minister. They offered me a good salary and consented to my baptizing in my own way all that so desired; but also to sprinkle infants for them who requested it, and so to commune with them. I suppose these men were really honest in their own minds, and thought that baptism was such a nonessential thing that we might compromise. I thought that if they had ever felt the power of that word: "Let God be true, and every man a liar," they would not have made such a proposal to me. I told them I could not sell the truth. I pitied them, for they were men for whom I had a high regard, and they appeared to be really grieved that I could not grant their request.

This brings me down to the year 1795. And now, to look back and see what the Lord has done in thirty-four years, when we were but nine in number, surrounded by enemies that would gladly have rooted us out of the world if they could, and the nearest of our Baptist brethren sixty miles from us, but now with churches all around us, but a few miles away, and elders ordained with whom I could take sweet counsel; verily, it is all of the Lord, who hath said: "A little one shall become a thousand and a small one a strong nation; and the Lord will hasten it in his time."

In this year I was called to part with the dear companion of my youth, who had been a partner with me in many joys and sorrows, through more than thirty-seven years; and now, being left alone in the world, I took a journey into the new country, starting the first of November, and being absent six months, traveling and preaching in the new settlements where there were no churches nor ministers of any order. From the middle of December to the middle of March I preached as many sermons as there were days, and was so favored, "through the good hand of my God upon me," as never to have missed an appointment in all my journey, and I trust "my labor was not altogether in vain in the Lord." I reached home the last day in April. After a while, in 1796, I was married again, to one who was truly a helpmeet to me, with whom I lived over twelve years. In the year 1798, the church having another elder ordained, I requested a dismission, which the church granted in January, and thereafter I preached where Providence opened a door. There was a Church newly organized in a town then called Partridgefield, containing two parishes—the first is now called Peru, and the second Hinsdale; they will be called by these names in what I have further to say. The Baptists lived in both these towns. In June they sent two brethren to request me to come and see them. In response I preached to them and administered the Lord's supper. They were a church of eighteen members, and desired me to visit them again with a view of settling among them, and in the course of the summer I baptized a number there—one a man about 80 years old. Some of the townpeople had said they thought Elder Smith would not baptize children, but I baptized one child, though he was not so young but that while he lived —which was a number of years—he was an honor to religion, and his wife as well, who had been baptized before. They brought forth fruit in old age, to show that "the Lord is upright, and there is no unrighteousness in Him."

In November I removed into that town, joined the church and became their pastor. Here new trials awaited me that I had not thought of. The people in Hinsdale were building a costly meeting-house, which was about half completed at the time of my settlement. They had sold the pews in advance, and were paying the costs of erection from the proceeds of these sales. Very soon one of the building committee came to me saying many who had engaged pews had moved away without paying therefor and the cost of the building was to be met by a tax upon the town, and suggested that the Baptists should thus help to build it and have the use of the house part of the time. We considered the matter and replied that such measures would not accommodate us and we declined to accede to them; they might build and enjoy the full fruits of their work, which was the same privilege that we asked for ourselves.

Upon this they voted to lay a tax upon the town—Baptists and all—and made up the tax roll. To give an idea of the burden upon the Baptists it may be mentioned that one poor man who had no land, but supported a large family by his daily labor and had only one cow, was taxed ten dollars in one tax, besides other small taxes; and others were taxed in like proportion to their means. When the money was called for the General Court was sitting in Boston; it was in the month of February, in the year 1800. The brethren desired me to go down to Boston and see if I could get any help for them. Setting out on Thursday morning, when the weather was so cold that some travelers I met would not encounter it, I made thirty miles that day. The next day at about 9 o'clock it began to snow, and a northeast wind as severe as any I ever experienced blew directly in my face, yet I pursued my way for another thirty miles before putting up for the night. The third day I made six miles over an unbeaten track before breakfasting. As the people began to break the road I went on and passed out of the town of Worcester as the clock struck twelve. I rode until nine o'clock. The next morning I came to a guide-board, a few rods from where I had tarried for the night, which said: "38 miles to Worcester." I write this that others may know what I have gone through to help my brethren when in distress. I went into Boston on Monday, put in a petition to the Court setting forth our distress and praying for help, and they chose a committee of both houses to look into the affair. When they came to meet and consult upon the matter they said we were free by the law of the State, and there was no right to tax us, though they did not see as that Court could help us; our remedy for such oppression should be sought in the civil courts.

I became acquainted with a number of dear friends in Boston from whom I received no little kindness, for which I here record my thanks and wish them the best of Heaven's blessings.

When I came home they began to seize my brethren's property and sell it at vendue. One man whom they carried to jail desired me to go with him, and take advice of a lawyer, which I did. The advice was to pay the tax and sue for its recovery, as there would be no advantage in remaining in jail. I assisted that man in counting out upwards of sixty dollars for one tax, to enable him to get out of jail. Then one of the brethren sued the town for his money. I was called upon to attend the court. As an incident I may relate that the lawyer for the town, during his plea began to disparage me. He had spoken but a few words in that vein before he was interrupted by the first judge of the court, who said: "Gould (his name was Gould), you had better let Elder Smith alone; he is a man of as good credit among his own people as Dr. Stilman, of Boston. Don't let me hear you run on against Elder Smith here." I could not but rejoice at the goodness of God, that He should move the heart of such a man, at such a time, to defend me from reproach, for the court-house was very full of people.

The Court gave judgment in favor of the Baptist, and the town appealed to the Superior Court. When it came to trial at that court the judges said the case had not been brought in the lower court according to the forms of law, which ruling turned the case against the Baptist and involved him in $100 costs. This was a distressing day for my poor brethren, left, as they were, in the hands of their oppressors by the highest tribunal of the State.

At their desire I went down to Boston again, to see if I could get any information as to how to proceed for relief. I found that by taking the matter up in my own name there was a prospect of gaining the case. When the town learned that I was going to take it up they offered to pay back half the tax, and the Baptist agreed to that and so settled the matter; thus they got half the tax and $100 court charges of the Baptist, as unjustly as if by highway robbery; and this to build a house for the worship of that God who says: "I hate robbery for burnt offering;" aye, by those who call themselves the church of Him who said to His followers: "All things whatsoever ye would that men should do unto you, do ye even so to them, for this is the law and the prophets." "Be astonished, O ye Heavens! and amazed, O Earth!" Inasmuch as the town, by paying back half the tax, plainly confessed that they had been unjust, and restored the half only from fear that otherwise they might lose the whole.

But my labors in defense of my brethren did not end here; I had still another trying scene to go through. Part of my brethren lived in Dalton, where a minister was about to be settled. A farm was bought for him for $1,300, and for this sum and the minister's salary the Baptists were sought to be taxed. I went there and requested that my brethren should be let alone. "No," they said; "if they can escape by law they may, otherwise we shall tax them." I put a short account of our persecutions in the public print. A writer undertook to answer it, and charged me with falsehood. By town records attested by the clerk, and writings received from inhabitants of the town of the Pedobaptist, I proved his article to be a complete libel. I never heard more of my alleged falsehood, nor did the writer attempt to reply. Who he was I never knew.

He said: "If the Baptists in Dalton think they are exempt from paying taxes to the minister, let them try it in the courts; but they dare not try it." As the judges of the Supreme Court had said that the minister must sue for the money because those who paid the tax could not recover it, I thought I would venture to "try," notwithstanding that writer had said I dare not.

The town authorities said I had better sue for one man's tax; that if I got the case for one they would pay the whole, and such a course would diminish the costs. Accordingly, I sued before a single justice, who gave me the case. They then appealed to the County Court, where I also won the suit and the bill of costs against them, which was $30. The town's agent advised me to let the costs lie over, for they intended to carry the case to the Supreme Court, and if the decision went against me I would have to refund to him. I replied that I knew that as well as he, but as the town had had the use of the money, I believed it right for me to have it now, and so the bill must be paid.

They took it to the Supreme Court by what was called a writ of error. It came up for trial on Tuesday. The court met in the afternoon, discussed the matter till sundown, when the judges said they would consider it until morning. But what an afternoon it was to me! The court-house crowded with people, and no faces known to me except those of the members of the court; and by all that the judges said, it looked as if they intended to turn the case against me. I went to my quarters with the sole consoling thought that there was a God in heaven that disposed of all events on earth. But little sleep visited me that night. In the morning I went to the court-house to see my attorneys, one of whom said it looked as though the decision would be against me. The other said he had talked with the judges after the court broke up, and was inclined to believe that I should win the case. This was all my encouragement till the afternoon of Saturday, when the Court gave their judgment—and gave it full in my favor, which put a stop to taxing the Baptists in that part of the State.

After I was ordained parties came to me to be married and I married them, whereupon a great outcry was raised. Some said they would complain of me, and there was £50 fine. It went on a few years; I married when applied to, and the threatenings continued. At length I was told that they had carried a complaint to the grand jury at Springfield, but could get nothing done. During my residence in Ashfield nothing more was heard on this subject, but after my removal to Hinsdale, going to court one day I met a neighbor who said he should enter a complaint against me for marrying people. I replied: "Very well, you may complain of me and I shall continue to marry, and we will see who holds out the longest." After further conversation, I remarked that it was my intention to act up to my profession before all mankind; it was well known that a settled minister had a right to marry and I professed to be one; should I refuse to perform the ceremony when called on it would be a virtual denial of my profession; so you may complain, and I will marry.

I saw one of the grand jury after they had completed their business, who said that the man had entered his complaint to them, but that they would not entertain it. This ended the whole matter.

Let me here remark, that I have lived in the world and dealt with my fellow-men almost seventy years, and never had so much difficulty with any man in my own private concerns but that it could be settled quietly without a mediator. But, in defending the liberties of the Baptists in the State of Massachusetts I have had as much law, and perhaps more, than any man in my day. It seemed to be laid upon me in the course of God's holy providence, and through the good hand of God upon me I have always obtained the right. Sometimes matters would look exceedingly dark, yet it was so overruled that the enemy did not triumph over me. O the marvelous goodness of God!

And now, that through the good hand of God my brethren were free from oppression, I thought it best to leave them, and they gave me a dismission from the pastoral care of the church and a recommendation, but a request to continue my relation with them as a member. In November, 1807, I moved back to Ashfield, and in the course of the seven following years met with nothing in my religious life uncommon to Christians generally. I continued to preach where Providence opened the door, made one journey up to the new country of eight weeks' duration, buried my second wife, married again, and buried my third wife in October, 1814. Being now left alone in the world, in 1815 I et out on a journey, spending sixteen weeks in the new settlements in New

York State, traveling and preaching. And the land was not a wilderness, nor a laud of darkness to me; I enjoyed much of the Divine Presence, and have reason to think my labors were not in vain in the Lord. Though I had not the care of any particular people, I was called to preach somewhere the chief part of the time.

In 1816 my son desired me to accompany him to a permanent residence in the new country. I therefore spent the summer making farewell visits to the churches and people with which I had formerly been associated, preaching and endeavoring to confirm the souls of the disciples, and exhorting them to continue in the faith. The visiting finished, I set out on my journey the 10th day of September, having many calls to preach during my progress, insomuch that my destination was not reached until May 27th, when I found I had traveled 1,600 miles, preached 149 times, assisted in one ordination, attended one council where a church was under some trials, attended the Lord's supper three times, and about twenty other religious meetings.

When arrived at my new home I found a small church had formed just previous to my arrival, which I joined; and there has been a number added to it, and four new churches raised up a few miles distant. There is a large field for labor in this wilderness, and though I am old and feeble, truth appears at precious as ever. There are many errors and false doctrines in the world, yes I am at rest, because I believe truth will finally prevail over every error; and it is a comfort to me that God is raising up witnesses for the truth that may stand when I am laid in the grave. Oh, in looking back through the years since I was called to be a witness for the cause of God, and against the doctrines of Antichrist in the face of a frowning world, I cannot but rejoice at the overwhelming goodness of God, who has carried me through so many trials; that He should so care for a poor unworthy worm, and suffer me to live to see the churches of Christ on the right hand and on the left. I exhort all to keep on the side of truth and trust in God; we have nothing to fear; let us bear a faithful testimony against the mother of harlots and all her daughters, and never cherish the thought of a confederacy with Popish errors. Oh, that all the world would come out of Babylon, that they be not partakers of her sins and receive not of her plagues. The day will come when every plant which our Heavenly Father has not planted shall be rooted up. May the Lord hasten it in its time.

> Still has my life new wonders seen
> Repeated every year;
> Behold, my days that yet remain,
> I trust them to Thy care.
> The land of silence and of death
> Attends my next remove;
> O may these poor remains of breath
> Teach the wide world Thy love!
>
> By long experience have I known
> Thy sovereign power to save;
> At Thy command I venture down
> Securely to the grave.
> When I lie buried deep in dust
> My flesh shall be Thy care—
> These withered limbs with Thee I trust
> To raise them strong and fair.

When the above was written I thought of concluding, but on further consideration a little more will be added.

I never gave much weight to dreams, but about the time of beginning the
land suit with Dalton I had a dream that I will venture to relate: It was that
the Lord ordered me to lead the tribes of Israel out of Egypt to the land of
Canaan; I thought the Lord spoke to me plainly, as we read he spoke to Moses.
I got the tribes together and we set out on our march, but had not gone far
before Pharaoh met us with a mighty army. The people were in great distress, but I told them to be quiet, we should be relieved, though I knew not
how; I had a calm and assuring faith in our deliverance. The Lord spoke and
bade me go to Pharaoh and demand a free passage for the chosen tribes through
his host, also saying: "If he does not grant it, I will smite him and all his
host." I was not bidden to make the threat, but only to demand the passage.
Telling my people to halt, I went up to the army and called for Pharaoh.
Some of the leading men came forward and inquired what was wanted. My
reply was: I must see Pharaoh and deal directly with him. At length he
came, I demanded a quiet passage for the chosen tribes through his host—that
we must go through unmolested. The request was granted, so that I led the
tribes safely through, got them clear of danger—and awoke, and behold it
was a dream.

Having related my dream I now give a more particular account of the lawsuit with Dalton. There were but few Baptists in that town, they were not
very forehanded, and the town had taken about forty dollars from them for
the first tax, and the case could not be prosecuted unless they could let me
have what money was needed for the purpose. They said they did not see as
they could do it, so they must submit to the oppression, for the town said the
tax must be paid unless they could get clear by law. And they sank down,
having no hope of deliverance, apparently as much distressed as the tribes
were in my dream. Then one of my hearers who lived in Peru heard how the
matter stood, and the Lord opened his heart, so that he offered to assist me
with what money I should want to carry on the suit, provided those who
paid the tax should make a free gift of it to me in case I recovered it; he said,
moreover, that he could spend $1,300 without breaking in upon his estate.
Having reported this offer to the brethren concerned, I further added that I
would prosecute the case without cost or trouble to them—would take it all
on myself. In other words, as in my dream, I called to the tribes to halt
while I went to seek a way for them. Without repeating what has before
been written, some other circumstances of this trial may be mentioned: The
case was continued through several terms of the courts to await its turn, so
that three years elapsed before a final judgment was obtained, which made
it necessary for me to be present at every session of the courts during this
time, because of not knowing when the case would be called. Twice had I to
leave Lenox on Saturday night after sundown—and once in January, when the
cold was as severe as we have in winter—and ride home 20 miles, and on the next
morning go eight miles the other way to preach. But the Lord carried me
through, so that I never disappointed a religious meeting by attending courts.
After three years' labor and toil, through "the good hand of my God upon
me," I brought the chosen tribes through the Egyptian host in safety, to where
they were out of all danger.

And now, looking back over these times, it brings to my mind what the prophet Micah said: "Remember, O my people, what Balak, King of Moab, consulted, and what Balaam the son of Beor answered, that ye may know the righteousness of the Lord. Balak built his altars three times to have Israel cursed, and Balaam was no better friend to Israel than Balak, yet he had to bless Israel every time." So in this case, Dalton consulted to have the Baptists cursed, and built their altars three times; and the judges, and the attorneys that had the management of the case against us, were none of them Baptists, and yet they blessed them altogether. It was not my wisdom, nor any power of mine; no, it was the Lord who did it, and may all the glory be given to His holy name.

While this case was in the law three years they kept taxing the Baptists and getting their money, and it took me another year to get those taxes back. Once while the men were talking to me who were to see that the taxes were refunded, their minister came in remarked: "You must wait for your money; I have to wait for mine; I can't get it so soon as I should." "There is a great difference," I rejoined, "between your waiting and mine; you wait on your own people; my people have paid their money and you have had it, and now tell me I must wait; no, you ought to pay me that money *now*." Some things were trying to the old nature within me. I found there was much need of watching and praying, that I might not say or do anything that would dishonor God, or bring reproach on the Redeemer's precious cause.

There was one thing that I passed over when writing about my ordination and, on further thought, I will give it here: We appointed the ordination to be on Thursday, and the elders we invited sent word that I must preach a sermon on Wednesday in the afternoon, that they might hear me before my ordination. On the week before an inflamed sore came upon my foot. I made out to attend the Sabbath meeting and preach, though in much pain. After returning home from meeting my foot grew more painful and distressed me exceedingly all night. The cause of God lay near my heart, and how would our enemies triumph if I were unable to keep my appointment. This thought caused me an anxiety less endurable even than my physical pain. I tried to carry the case to God, and finally was enabled to leave it with Him; then was my spirit comforted by the promise of the prophet to King Hezekiah when he was sick, that the King should "go up to the house of the Lord the third day." The passage was presented to me with such power and sweetness as to bring entire relief to both body and mind, and I was enabled to rest under the most complete assurance that I should perform my duties for the week, as usual. This peace was given to me on Monday morning, and Wednesday afternoon would be the "third day." I said to wife that however dark matters might appear at the present, I should certainly go to the house of the Lord on the third day. The boil broke that day, the pain abated, and when the third day arrived I performed my preaching and all my work with comfort and satisfaction. How marvelous hath been Thy goodness, O God, to such a poor, unworthy worm as I. Oh, that all might trust in God, keep His commandments, deny themselves and take up the cross.

I have experienced many trials, also, among my own brethren, that for the honor of God should not enter into this narrative. I dismiss them in silence. Let them be forgotten. Amen.

EBENEZER SMITH.

THE ORIGINAL PROPRIETORS OF ASHFIELD,

The proprietors of Ashfield, or Huntstown (see page 277), lived in the eastern part of the State. They mostly sold their claims or " Rights" to others, and but few of them ever settled in the town. The following are the names of the original proprietors in 1739: John Hunt, Thomas White, Nathaniel Wales, Benjamin Ludden, Gideon Turrel, Richard Foxon, William Crane, Ebenezer Hunt, Rev. Joseph Belcher, Jonathan Webb, Seth Chapen, Capt. John Phillips, John Herrick, Zechariah Briggs, Job Otis, Jonathan Dawes, Hebr. Pratt, Richard Davenport, Ezra Whitman, Solomon Leonard, James Meares, Joseph Good, Thomas Bolter, Ephraim Emerson, Benjamin Beal, Barnabas Daily, John Miller, Josiah Owen, Samuel Thayer, Ephraim Copeland, James Hayward, Samuel Gay, Ebenezer Staples, Samuel Staples, John King, Samuel Niles, Jr., Joseph Penniman, Joshua Phillips, William Linfield, Ebenezer Owen, Samuel Darby, Jonathan Webb, John Bass, —— Keith, J. French, Amos Stetson, Joseph Drake, Thomas Wells, Samuel Andrews, John White, Benjamin Stuart, Joseph Veckery, Joseph Lobdle, Joseph Melton, and John Bartlet.

EXTRACTS FROM PROPRIETORS' RECORDS.

A few notes from the " Proprietors' Records" will indicate the measures taken by the proprietors to induce settlement and make it permanent. For several years their meetings were held in the eastern towns.

May 28, 1741.—"Voted that William Curtis be employed in mending The Way to said Township, the Labour done on said way by him not to Exceed ten pounds."

By the following votes it seems the proprietors had a good deal of trouble in getting a saw mill or corn mill that was satisfactory:

June 28, 1739.—"Voted that One Hundred and twenty pounds be assessed on ye Proprietors, as an Incouragement to him or them yt shall build a saw mill in some convenient place & Convenient to ye Lots allready Laid out; Provided, The Owner or Owners of said mill saw for the Proprietors for the first seven years For twenty shillings per Thousand; Provided, also, that the said miller or milleres, viz't, Owner or Owners, do keep said mill in order for business for seven years, and as he or they shall have water; and if said Proprietors do bring logs, that he or they saw them as aforesaid. Passed in ye affirmative."

Sept. 16, 1741.—"Voted that those who build a saw mill do not have liberty to draw the money from the Treasury."

Feb. 12, 1742.—"Voted to do nothing further in the matter of a saw mill."

Sept. 21, 1742.—"Voted, That a good Whip Saw be procured at the expense of the Proprietors, and that Samuel White and Job Porter have said saw delivered to them for sawing boards for the Proprietors, provided that they saw sd boards for said Proprietors for £4 Old Tenor per Thousand, for the sd Proprietors; and Chileab Smith, Nathaniel Kellogg and Richard Ellis be a committee to procure saw and files, and take bond from said White and Porter in behalf of the Proprietors; also that 18 pence per pound be paid Richard Ellis for a crank and gudgeon for saw mill, to be delivered to Ichabod Smith." A committee was appointed at the same meeting "to take Care that no White pine timber be Cut and Convey'd out of the Town, and to Prosecute all such offenders."

July 1, 1743—(At Hadley, the previous meetings being held at Braintree.) "Voted, That we will proceed the present year to build a corn mill in said Huntstown, on the Pond Brook, so called, where a committee for that purpose shall think proper. Voted that this com. agree with some person or persons to build it; also to lay out a mill lot; also, to give opportunity for ponding, shall serve the people with grinding, as they shall have occasion, for lawful or customary toll."

At Braintree, Feb. 1, 1744.—"Voted to take the accounts of work done on the corn mill." And Apr. 4, "Voted that Caleb Phillips [probably a son of Capt. John Phillips, of Easton] be intrusted the care of the corn mill lately built in Huntstown, and be tender thereof."

Dec., 1751.—"Voted to raise five pounds six shillings and eight pence to repair the corn mill— Mr. Chileab Smith and Mr. Thomas Phillips to be paid the money." And in May, the next year, Chileab Smith directed to put the gristmill in order at once, and have charge of it for one year. Committee chosen to see if they can find some one to build a saw mill.

July 6, 1752—"Voted that Chileab Smith, Samuel Smith and Charles Phelps be a committee to see about a new corn mill; meanwhile to see if they can't agree with some person to keep the present grist mill in good repair and run it."

Apr. 12, 1753.—Granted the corn mill to John Blackmer, also 50 acres of land on Mill Brook and 50 more near it; Provided he will put the mill in good repair, live near it and do grinding for the inhabitants: must bind himself and heirs to do this; failing to fulfil, the property reverts back to the proprietors. At the same meeting: "Voted to grant William and Nathaniel Church sixteen acres of land at the [north] end of Ri'd Ellis' lot, also the right of Bear River, if they will set up a saw mill within six months.

Voted, May 29, 1754, the mill and its appurtenances, ½ to Chileab Smith, ¼ to Eliphalet Cary, of Bridgewater, and ¼ to David and Barnabas Alden, of Stafford.

May 20, 1761.—Voted to leave it to indifferent men what Chileab Smith should have for sawing, and accordingly made choice of Col. John Hawks, Lieut. David Field and Mr. Zadoc Hawks, all of Deerfield, to settle that affair. And, Dec. 9, voted to choose a committee, viz: Ebenezer Belding, Samuel Belding and Reuben Belding, to confer with Mr. Chileab Smith as to why he does not perform, as he is obliged to do, the sawing of boards for the Proprietors.

1763.—Voted, That complaint now being bro't to this meeting that Mr. Chileab Smith has a corn mill at some place which is said to be detrimental to the saw mill, and to boards being sawed for the proprietors, it is therefore Voted, That said Chileab Smith be ordered and directed forthwith to remove his corn mill, which he has erected at the saw mill dam, as he would avoid what may ensue upon his failure hereof. Voted, That Ebenezer Belding, Samuel Belding and Philip Phillips be a committee to warn said Smith to remove his corn mill as aforesaid.

(It looks as if the corn mill on Pond Brook was not well built, and failed to give satisfaction, therefore the corn mill on Bear River was built [at **6.** See Map, page 328.] Tradition says that Blackmer failed to repair the mill in a satisfactory manner, under his lease.—F. G. H.)

August 22, 1777.—"Voted yt * * * [nine tories] be committed to close confinement in this Town."

"Voted that Capt. Bartlet's house be the place of their confinement."

"Voted yt the Selectmen make Provision for the support of those who are put under confinement; as also for the Guard which shall have the care of them, upon the Town's cost."

May 24, 1781.—"Voted to allow Elisha Bartlet £7 for going to Surrotoga to Carry Packs to the Soldiers."

"Voted to allow £14 as Rations for fourteen Men from Ashfield to Ticonderoga, in Feb., A. D. 1776, &c."

PARTIAL LIST OF VOTERS IN 1798.

In the records of Ashfield for 1798 the list of voters is given. In this list of names are the following (there being then a property qualification, this list does not include the names of all the men of the proper age for voting): David Alden, David Alden, Jr., Samuel Annable, Samuel Annable, Jr., Barnabas Annable, Samuel Belding, John Belding, Ebenezer Belding, Daniel Belding, Bezer Benton, Dr. Phineas Bartlet, Lieut. John Ellis, Lieut. David Ellis, Capt. Lamrock Flower, Maj. William Flower, Jonathan Lyon, Lieut. David Lyon, Aaron Lyon, Philip Phillips, Esq.; David, Simeon, Thomas, Elijah, Abner, Lemuel, Philip, Jr., Israel, Vespasian, Spencer, Caleb, Sylvester, Daniel and Joshua Phillips; George Ranney, Thomas Ranney, Francis Ranney; Chipman Smith, David, Chileab, Jr., Chileab, 3d, Jeduthan, Elijah, Martin, Abner, Jonathan and Ebenezer Smith, Jr.; Israel Standish, Apollos Williams.

SELECTMEN OF ASHFIELD.

On the list are the following names:

1762. Ebenezer Belding, Chileab Smith, Thomas Phillips.
1763. Nathan Wait, Reuben Ellis, Samuel Belding.
1764. Reuben Ellis, Jonathan Edson, Nathan Chapin.
1768. Moses Fuller, Reuben Ellis, Philip Phillips.
1774. Samuel Belding, Reuben Ellis, Jonathan Taylor.
1784. Thomas Stocking. Chileab Smith, Jr., John Ellis.
1816-19. Nathaniel Holmes, Dimick Ellis, Bethuel Lilly.
1820. Bethuel Lilly, Roswell Ranney, Jonathan Sears.
1854. Aivan Hall, Henry S. Ranney, Addison Graves.
1865. Alvan Hall, Frederick G. Howes, Josiah Cross.

REPRESENTATIVES IN THE LEGISLATURE OF MASSACHUSETTS.

Among the Representatives from Ashfield are the following: 1775, Capt. Elisha Cranston; 1787, Chileab Smith, Jr.; 1789, Capt. Philip Phillips; 1809, Thomas White; 1814, Dr. Enos Smith; 1823, Dimick Ellis; 1829, Capt. Roswell Ranney; 1851 and 1867, Henry S. Ranney; 1874, Frederick G. Howes.

TOWN CLERKS.

The first Clerk was Samuel Belding, from 1762 until the incorporation of the town, in 1765. Then followed Benjamin Phillips, up to 1775; Phineas Bartlett, in 1776; Dimick Ellis, in 1823; Henry S. Ranney, from 1839 to 1847, and again from 1873 up to the present time.

INDUSTRIAL PURSUITS IN ASHFIELD.

As has already been remarked, the leading industrial interest of the town is that of agriculture. The want of ample water-power has prevented capital of much amount from being invested in manufacturing enterprises. Saw mills are erected on the streams, and considerable timber is sawed during the season of high water and carried to other places for sale. Gristmills have also always existed in the town. The first was built in 1743, to supply the first settlers in the town with meal, and stood about one hundred rods northeasterly of the present Episcopal Church (22 on Map), and was in use until about the year 1831. In 1753 a saw mill stood upon Bear River, one-fourth of a mile east of the dwelling-house of Solomon H. Deming. At the present time A. D. Flower has a gristmill at Ashfield Plain, and Walter Guilford another at South Ashfield; L. & J. S. Gardner a saw mill at South Ashfield; Nelson Gardner a saw mill at Spruce Corner, and William E. Ford one in the west part of the town. Besides these, different varieties of wooden-ware are manufactured in the town by Nelson Gardner, Marcus T. Parker, Walter Guilford and Charles H. Day.

Many considerable fortunes were made in earlier portions of the present century in the traffic of various essences and oils. There were several distilleries where all kinds of herbs and plants that could find a market were made to contribute of their peculiarities. Ashfield essence-peddlers could be found all over Massachusetts and neighboring States, and many even sought the West and South.

About the year 1814 Samuel Ranney introduced here, upon his farm, the culture and distillation of the peppermint herb, which was found to be for many years quite a profitable pursuit. For a number of years the price of oil of peppermint was from $6 to $16 per pound. Its production was continued to a considerable extent until about the year 1833, many acres being raised each year. At that time and before, its cultivation had been commenced in Phelps, N. Y., where the soil and the climate were better suited to its growth, and where it was produced at much less expense. Of late years the crop is largely raised in Wayne and St. Joseph Counties, Mich.

ASHFIELD FOR SUMMER RESIDENCE.

The writer learns, with much satisfaction, that quite recently there has been "a boom" in the price of desirable sites for summer residences in Ashfield. The salubrious mountain air in the warm season, with its inland quietude, commends that town to those who seek relief from overcrowded cities in hot weather. A mile or so southwest from the Plain are a number of very elegant building sites, looking down a valley between the mountains, which by a little imagination some consider to be the "Switzerland of America,"

The streams and hills of Ashfield also are quite a resort for sportsmen. It is said that there is no game there, but this makes all the more "hunting." Several acquaintances of the writer go there periodically for this amusement, which they find quite invigorating.

MONUMENT TO RICHARD ELLIS AND WIFE.

The above cut is a *fac simile* of a monument erected in 1887 to the memory of Richard Ellis, and Jane Phillips his wife, in the Ellis burying ground (marked 7 on the map on page 328). The monument is of highly polished Quincy granite. The upright part is two feet square [and three feet two inches high. The base, also of Quincy granite, is two feet six inches square and twelve inches in hight. The sub-base, of sandstone, is three feet two inches square and sixteen inches high. Total hight, five feet six inches.

In May, 1887, a party of Ellis' relatives were visiting in Ashfield, composed of the following, Mr. Lewis Ellis and wife, of Belding, Mich., and their son, Geo. W. Ellis and his wife, of Philadelphia; Dr. John Ellis and his son, W. D. Ellis, and wife, of New York City, and the writer. While the party were looking over the old burial pláce, Mr. George W. Ellis proposed that a monument be erected to the memory of their first progenitor in this country, and offered to contribute $100, or more if necessary, towards the same. Dr. John Ellis and W. D. Ellis cheerfully responded, and the next day the contract was made with the Shelburne Falls Marble Co. for the erection of the monument for the sum of $350.

It is further proposed to have engraved on the monument, at some convenient time, the inscription that "Richard Ellis' first cabin was located about ten rods south of this spot." See page 278.

BURIAL PLACES IN ASHFIELD.

The oldest burying ground is in the northeast corner of the town, and was probably laid out at the time of the organization of the Baptist Church in that locality, in 1761. It comprises about half an acre of land. Some of the earliest settlers of the town are buried there. Three Chileab Smiths are buried there, but with no inscriptions on the stones at the head of the graves. The following inscription to Mary Lyon's father is found:

"Aaron Lyon, died Dec 21, 1802. Aged 45 years."

"A loving husband, kind and true,
A tender father was, also;
A faithful son, a brother dear,
A peaceful neighbor was while here.
Though now his body here doth rest,
We trust his soul's among the blest."

The next burying place in point of age is a mile and a quarter south of the first named. Richard Ellis, the first settler of the town, and others of that name were interred there; also the Beldings and Ranneys, and other settlers of the town. It was laid out about the same time as the other, comprises about an acre and is still in use.

The burying ground near the "Plain" was in use as early as 1767, though not formally devoted to public use until 1770, in accordance with the following vote of the town:

"Dec. 17. 1769.—Voted to purchase a piece of Land by the Meeting-House for a Burying-Place; also, voted and Chose Mr. Nathan Waite and Capt. Moses Fuller and Timothy Perkins a Committee to purchase and lay out a burial place.

There are other local burial places at Spruce Corner, Northwest, South Ashfield and Brier Hill.

Some of these grounds have been sadly neglected, but last summer (1887) the "Ashfield Burial Ground Association" was formed, having for its object the improvement of these old places, and the work in some of them has already been commenced.

CENTENNIAL CELEBRATION IN ASHFIELD.

June 21st, 1865, just one hundred years from the incorporation of the town, a Centennial Celebration was held in Ashfield. A large assembly gathered, many of which were from abroad and had been former residents, or were descendants of those who once lived in the town.

Rev. Dr. William P. Paine, of Holden, delivered the address.

Rev. Charles S. Porter wrote the following poem for the occasion:

ONE HUNDRED YEARS AGO.

One hundred years ago
  The sun walked in the sky,
Stars in their far-off homes
  Blinked bright and silently,
And savage beasts and savage men
Were monarchs sole of hill and glen.

The hardy pioneer
  Rose mid the sylvan scene,
The woodman's sturdy stroke
  Rang loud o'er hill and plain ;
From hillside and from mountain nook
Curled slow to heaven the cabin's smoke.

Since then the scroll of time
  Hath record of vast change ;
Harvests have graced the fields,
  Flocks, herds, the mountain range,
And human life hath been ablaze
With bridal and with burial days.

We stand where others stood ;
  Where others sowed, we reap ;
Transmit the garnered good,
  Then with them fall asleep.
God over all does thus fulfill
His purpose vast, His sovereign will.

One hundred years to come,
  Fled hour by hour away,
Who then will here find home
  And celebrate the day ?
That history of joy or woe
Nor man nor angel can foreknow.

God of our Fathers, hear ;
  Command Thy grace to rest
On coming thousands here,
  All blessing and all blest.
A grand succession here arise.
Be called and garnered for the skies.

An incident of the celebration was a toast by Hon. Henry L. Dawes, U. S. Senator in Congress from Massachusetts, who presided at the table, and given in honor of Mrs. Eunice Forbes, then living at 104 years of age, as "the only living bridge then spanning the century of time." Mrs. Forbes was mother of Daniel Forbes and Bliss Forbes (or Forbush), who married Mabel Phillips, daughter of Elijah, the eldest son of Philip Phillips, Sr., Esq.

INCIDENTS.

On December 10th, 1878, a great freshet swept over the Green Mountain region of this State, caused by a powerful rain falling upon fifteen inches of newly-fallen snow. As evening came on the temperature rapidly grew warm, the thermometer rose twenty-five degrees in two hours, and the melting snow, filled by the accumulated rainfall of the day, came down the hillsides in torrents. At 9 o'clock in the evening the Great Pond reservoir in this town, on South River, gave way, immediately draining off the 75 acres of water that had there been held in check, thus precipitating a great flood into the valley below. The gristmill of A. D. Flower and the tannery of L. C. Sanderson, at the center village, were destroyed. At South Ashfield, three dwelling-houses, two barns and a blacksmith shop were swept away on the instant that the flood reached them. In the southwest part of the town Darius Williams' reservoir broke away, carrying his large saw mill to destruction. The roads and bridges here and throughout the region were greatly damaged. Through the valley, in the course of South River, the fields, fences and bridges suffered almost total destruction. This saw mill was originally built in 1771, by Darius Williams' grandfather, Ephraim Williams, Esq., who came from Easton to Ashfield, a journey of 120 miles, on foot, with a hired man, carrying on their backs what tools would be necessary to build a saw mill.

In June, 1830, a full-sized bear was captured and killed. He was discovered when crossing the road near the present residence of L. W. Goodwin, chased into a tree near by where Stephen Jackson lives, and soon made to smell powder.

ITEMS FROM COLERAIN.

About 1764 Richard Ellis moved from Ashfield to Colerain, where he lived until about the close of the Revolution. During the war of 1756 the settlers in Colerain had a similar experience with Indian incursions as had the settlers in Ashfield. They were driven to the eastern settlements for two or three years. After the war they returned, and "by 1767 ninety farms were occupied and nearly 1,000 acres cleared."

In 1765 Richard Ellis, William Henry, John McCreles and Matthew Bolton were selectmen of the town.

During the Revolutionary war there was great patriotism manifested by the people of Colerain. In 1779 the town resolved that:

"No person belonging to any other town shall purchase cattle or any other provisions in this town, unless such person shall produce a certificate from the town to which he belongs that he is not a monopolizer or forestaller, and that he is a friend to the United States."

At the close of the war, in 1783, it was voted that "the people called refugees that have gone to the British shall not return to live among us."

In 1753, on April 12th, the members of the settlement observed a day of fasting and prayer, and a record relates that Mr. Abercrombie and Mr. Ashley, ministers of Deerfield, were invited "to come and keep the fast."

Hugh Morrison kept a house of entertainment very soon after the earliest settlement, and he presented a bill in 1753 "for bording the ministers and some likyure spent at the ordenation."

A bridge was built over North River, a stream in the town, in 1752, and for the "Rhumb," furnished by him on the occasion of the raising of the bridge-frame, Hugh McLellan presented a bill.

It should be borne in mind that the use of liquor was universal in those days. The writer's great-grandfather, one of the earliest residents of Ashfield, and a pious man, regarded it as "one of the good gifts of God to man, when used with discretion." Even Scriptural arguments were used then to sustain this custom, as it was, one hundred years later, to defend human slavery, by its mistaken advocates. But times change; the world does move, even if slowly, and the best-loved customs of one generation are often overturned by the innovations of the next. Physicians have taught, and mankind have believed, for ages, that alcohol "strengthened" the system. This is the greatest falsehood ever invented. Its first action is that of an irritant or excitant, followed, if taken in large doses, by congestion and partial, if not complete, paralysis. If used continually it *always* disorders the system, corrupts the morals and *shortens life*. The sooner its use as a beverage, or as a medicine, is forever abolished, the better will it be for mankind.

THE "TREMBLERS" OR SHAKERS, OF ASHFIELD.

The "Tremblers," spoken of by Rev. Mr. Shepard (p. 286), lived and held their meetings on the old road, about eighty rods east of where Mrs. Samuel Hale (near 35) now lives, where the old cellar is still visible. They were presided over by a woman called the "Eleck Lady," and she had the reputation of being "a witch." The old people remember hearing them spoken of as "Shakers," oftener than "Tremblers." The meetings were attended by people from other parts of the town, and created much excitement. Many who came into their meetings out of mere curiosity, in a short time "shook" or "trembled" with the rest. In the churches the members were warned to beware of the "Tremblers," and finally the action taken by the town cleared them out.

VALUATIONS AND ASSESSMENTS IN ASHFIELD IN 1766.

The assessors of taxable property in Ashfield in 1766 were Richard Phillips, Aaron Lyon and Nathan Chapin. The number of persons assessed was 71. The total number of acres assessed was 735; of houses, 49; oxen, 37; cows, 86; horses, 19; swine, 76; sheep, 185; goats, 4; mills, 3. Total amount of assessment, £1,633. It does not seem possible that this comprised all the property in the town; and if not, the balance may have been exempt from taxation.

Those who were assessed for mills were: Reuben Ellis, 1; Thomas Phillips, ⅔; Philip Phillips, ⅓; Jonathan Sprague, 1. In another valuation, in 1771, the following were assessed as noted: Benjamin Phillips, £65; David Alden, £61; Aaron Lyon, £30; Ebenezer Belding, £37; Ebenezer Belding, Jr., £28; Chileab Smith, £25; Reuben Ellis, £63; John Ellis, £57; Capt. Moses Fuller, £74; Samuel Belding, £113; Isaac Shepard, £36; Joseph Mitchell, £97; Philip Phillips, £90; Thomas Phillips, £54; Zebulon Bryant, £25; Timothy Perkins, £34; Samuel Allen, £49; Jonathan Lilly, £29.

was Mother Ann Lee The founder sect of Shakers who came to ed and lived at This place. for a

FIRST DIVISION OF LANDS IN ASHFIELD.

The original survey comprised but one division; a small portion of Hunts-town, or Ashfield.

To carry out the conditions of the grant, a meeting at Braintree, March 13, 1738, was held. The Proprietors voted: "That the first lots laid out in said Township shall, at the least, be Fifty acres; and, on account of badness of land, the said lots should extend to the number of 65 acres, according to the Goodness or Meanness of the land in the opinion of the Committee." These lots were accordingly laid out in 1738, lot No. 1 being described as follows: "The N. W. corner is a stack and stones which stands about 23 rods south of Bear River, where there is a Beaver Meadow, so called, on said River, from which it runs south 20 degrees west 160 rods, thence east, 20 degrees south, 50 rods; thence north, 20 degrees east, 160 rods, thence west, 20 degrees north, 50 rods, and closed at point of beginning." This includes just 50 acres.

This beaver meadow is now a part of the mowing lot of L. F. & W. H. Gray, of the "Beaver Meadow Farm." The west line of the lot runs a few rods east of their buildings, now south about 22 degrees west, instead of 20 degrees, and the S. W. corner is near the old cellar hole (28 on the map), at the south end of Solomon Demming's pasture, close by the highway; then the line runs over the hill to a point about 12 rods north of the green level spot in Mr. Rogers' pasture (site of Mitchell's tavern, 17), thence north, 22 degrees east, through the west part of the locust grove, crossing the highway just west of the "Factory" bridge, near 18; then continuing to the northeast corner, on the line between the Gray farm and land now owned by George Church. Lot No. 2 is directly west of lot 1, and extends to the corner where the highway goes north past the Gray Bros.; Nos. 3, 4 and 5 being west of that. No. 7 was east of lot 1, the southeast corner being near the old cellar hole near 14. This is the lot sold by Joseph Melton to Richard Ellis (page 303). Nos. 8 and 9 are east of this, the east boundary of 9 being a little west of the highway leading north to Baptist Corner. The first division of lots extended north to "No Town" (afterwards Buckland), east to what was supposed to be Deerfield line, south to land now owned by Job Lilly and Hiram Warren. Richard Ellis settled on lot No. 49 (I on map), Thomas Phillips probably on No. 24 or 25 (at 30 or 32 on map); he also paid taxes on the north end of No. 9, where the Phillips & Ellis Fort was, and might have first located there (at 30 on map). In 1739 it was voted "That the Twenty-fourth Lot be for the Minister, that the Fifty-fifth be for the Ministry, and the Fifty-fourth Lot be for the School." The minister's lot was where E. D. Church and J. Yeomans now live, extending north to the road east past Houg'.ton Smith's (35 on map). The school lot included the top of the hill southwest of the village or Plain, a large portion of the Flat and old cemetery, extending south to Job Lilly's and H. Warren's land. In 1742 Chileab Smith, Richard Ellis and Nathaniel Kellogg were chosen a committee to lay out more lots, but for some reason they were not laid out, probably because the first division was not sold and settled upon as soon as the proprietors anticipated. In 1754 it was again voted to lay out a second division of lots, and additions were made to this committee, but the lots were not laid out until 1761. A large portion of these lots were laid out in South Ashfield, and contained 100 acres each, instead of 50; the rest were scattered.

Between this time and 1800 three more divisions were laid out—the third
of 100, and fourth and fifth of 50 acres each. The third division was mainly
in the south and southwest part of the town, the fourth mostly in the northwest part, and the fifth over the town, to fill up some vacant spaces that were
left. These irregular gores, and the four rod roads left between the lots, have
made many disputes over lines between landholders, and some serious neighborhood quarrels.[1] Most of the large swamps—some now being valuable
meadow land—were not laid out at all, being called worthless. Some of these
old lots were laid over into other towns; at least Deerfield claimed about two
tiers of the lots through the whole length of the east part of the town, causing
the proprietors and settlers much trouble. The dispute was finally settled by
a committee appointed by the General Court, who reported June 18, 1765, giving the disputed territory to Huntstown. See *Province Laws, Vol. IV., p.
865.* Differences also arose afterwards between the towns of Buckland and
Plainfield in regard to the lines. Nathaniel Kellogg was the surveyor employed in laying out the early lots, and Ephraim Williams, Esq., those later.

About twelve years ago a map was made of these old lots from the Proprietor's records, and in 1880 all the school lots in town were surveyed, located,
and a map made of them by a committee chosen for that purpose. These maps
are deposited in the Clerk's office.

EARLY FAMILIES OF ASHFIELD.

THE ALDENS.

The Aldens (page 90) were conspicuous actors in the early history of the
town. Elder Noah Alden, of Stafford, Conn., was the minister who ordained
Elder Ebenezer Smith over the Baptist Church, in 1761. In 1753 Daniel
Alden, of Stafford, deeds lots Nos. 22 and 28, also 100 acres to be laid out, to
his son Barnabas. In 1754 Daniel Alden is Moderator of a Proprietors' meeting held in Huntstown. In 1761 he sells to Israel Standish, of Stafford, lots
35 and 28.

May 5, 1764, David Alden and his wife, Lucy, joined the Congregational
Church, by recommendation, from Stafford. He settled on the place now
owned by T. & C. Kelley (No. 5 on map, page 328). His house was a few
rods to the west of the present building, a part of which he built in 1791. He
had Isaac, David, John, Enoch and Lydia. In 1766, on the first town valuation, he is taxed for 30 acres of improved land, showing that dilligent work
had been done on the settlement. Isaac (page 90) was the oldest son of David.
He was of the sixth generation in descent from John Alden, who came over in
the *Mayflower* in 1620. The descendants of the Aldens tell this story in connection with Isaac's marriage to Irene Smith, daughter of Elder Ebenezer and
Remember Ellis Smith: David, whenever a question was asked him, had an
inveterate habit of rolling up his eyes before answering. In those good old
days of filial respect it was the custom of the son to ask the father's consent
before marrying. When Isaac asked the consent of his father to marry Irene

he told him he need not reply, but signify his assent by rolling up his eyes; which, it is said, David did. Their children were Philander, Joshua, Pliny, Hiram, Enoch, Richard, Philo, and Isaac, Jr. Philander was drowned in Lake Erie. Joshua went to sea when a lad, was pressed into the British service, escaped off the coast of Spain near Cadiz, went to South America, came home, married, and died about 1850. Pliny, Hiram and Enoch are dead. Richard settled in Warren, Pa., and Philo and Isaac, Jr., settled in Louisiana. Isaac, Sr., died in Pennsylvania, aged 65 years. John, the second son of David, remained on the old farm in Ashfield and married Nancy Gray; while her brother, Jonathan Gray, married Lydia Alden, John's sister.

John left a numerous posterity in the vicinity, and Lydia was the grandmother of the Gray brothers, now living on the Beaver Meadow farm (21 on the map). Rev. John Alden, now living in Providence, R. I., was formerly principal of the Shelburne Falls Academy, and was the second son of John; Betsey married William Ranney; Armilla married Aaron Lyon, a brother of Mary Lyon; Lucy married Dr. Charles Puffer, of Colerain; Eunice married Luther Ranney; Nancy, Capt. William Bassett, and Cyrus, who died about 1842 His widow now lives at Shelburne Falls. William Ranney and Aaron Lyon moved into the State of New York. The wife of John Alden, Sr., died in her 42d year, and was buried with her fifteenth child on her arm. He afterwards married a Mrs. Gillett, who had a son, Francis, attending school at Sanderson Academy while his mother was living here. He was afterwards United States Senator from Connecticut.

Barnabas Alden, Jr., a relative of David, came to town later, and settled near where Elisha Wing now lives.

In February, 1814, the Baptist Church voted to give Bro. John Alden a ",Letter of Recommendation, as having a Gift of Publick Improvement by way of Doctrine."

THE ANNABLES,

The first of the Annables who settled in Ashfield was Mr. Samuel Annable, Jr. He came from Windham, Conn., where he had resided but a short time; Barnstable County, or "The Cape," as it was more generally called in those days, being the place of his nativity, as well as that of his wife's family, the Dimicks. Freeman's "History of Cape Cod" states that Anthony Annable came over in the ship Anne, in 1623, with his wife Jane, and daughter Sarah. His wife died in 1643 and he married Anne Clarke in 1645. He was a prominent man, much in public affairs. In September, 1642, he formed a company, of which Miles Standish was captain, to guard against the Indians. He died in 1674. His children were: Sarah, born in England, married Henry Ewell in 1638; Hannah, born in Plymouth in 1625, married Thomas Freeman in 1645; Susanna, born 1630, married William Hatch, Jr., in 1652; Deborah, born 1637; Samuel, born 1646; Desire, born 1653, married John Barker in 1677.

Samuel Annable, born in 1646, married Mehitable Allyn in 1667, and died in 1678. His children were Samuel, Jr., born 1669; Hannah, 1672; John, 1673, and Anne, 1676.

Samuel Annable, Jr., born 1669, married Patience Dogget in 1695. He died in 1744, and his wife in 1760, aged 90 years. Their children were: Desire, born 1696; Anne, 1697; Jane, 1699; Samuel, 1702; Patience, 1705, and Thomas, 1708.

John Annable, born 1673, married Experience Taylor, daughter of Edward Taylor, in 1692, and had Mehitable, born 1694; Samuel, 1697; John, 1699, Cornelius, 1704, and Abigail, 1710.

Samuel Annable, Sr., born 1697, was a farmer at Cape Cod. He died in 1794, aged 97 years. His son, Samuel Annable, Jr., was born in 1717. He married Desire Dimmick and settled in Ashfield about 1762, as above noted, where he raised his family of eight children. Mr. Annable, Jr., was a prominent man in Ashfield many years. He resided at No. 15 on the map, a little west of the residence of Lieut. John Ellis, whose wife was Mrs. Annable's sister. About 1802 Mr. and Mrs. Annable removed to Sempronius, Cayuga Co., N. Y., where some of their children had settled before them, and where Mr. Annable died, in 1806, aged 89 years. Mrs. Annable lived with her son Barnabas until her death in 1818.

Samuel Annable, Jr.'s children were Mehitable, Thomas, Edward, born 1753; Barnabas, Samuel 3d, David, born 1771; Mary or Polly, born 1774, and Bethiah.

Sept. 14, 1768, Mehitable Annable married Dr. Phineas Bartlett, of Ashfield, where they lived, and where both died—Mrs. Bartlett about 1785 and Dr. Bartlett in 1800. Their children were Moses, Mabel, Phineas, Jr. and Hannah. The last named married a Hall. Moses Bartlett married, had four children, and lived in Saline, Michigan.

Thomas Annable never married. He was a school teacher in Ashfield, where he lived and died. He was a peculiar character, and said to have been very odd in his ways, but a man of talent and worth.

Lieut. Edward Annable, son of Samuel, Jr., was born in Windham, Conn., June 22, 1753. He married Jemima, a daughter of Elder Ebenezer Smith, of Ashfield, and lived about 50 rods northeast of where Mr. Nelson Drake now lives, just north of the present Ashfield line, in the town of Buckland. The lot is called the "Annable Lot;" the cellar hole is still pointed out, and the house he occupied was moved off and is now occupied by Mrs. Samuel Hale. The lot is about one-half mile from where his wife's father, Elder Ebenezer Smith, lived, and the houses in sight of each other.

About 1802 Lieut. Annable and family removed to Aurelius, Onondaga Co., N. Y., where he died in 1836. The youngest and last survivor of his children, Mr. Fernando C. Annable, of Almena, Mich, died in 1886. For further account of Lieut. Edward Annable and his descendants, see page 92.

Barnabas Annable, son of Samuel, Jr., married Ruth Moon, of Ashfield. About 1802 they moved to Sempronius, Cayuga Co., N. Y. Mr. Barnabas Annable was a very worthy and extremely pious man. He was a great Bible student and religious enthusiast—and preacher, a portion of his time. His father and mother lived with him in their later years, and he and his wife were greatly devoted to them. After the death of his mother, in 1818, he removed, the next year, with his family, to Mt. Vernon, Indiana, in the extreme southwestern part of the State. From Sempronius they went overland to Olean, Cattaraugus Co., N. Y., on the Alleghany River, where they went on rafts and flatboats down that river and the Ohio, to their new home in Indiana.

There they lived the remainder of their lives. Barnabas Annable died in 1835, and his wife Ruth in 1827. Their children were Electa, Nancy, Samuel, Fanny, Bromley, Bartlett, David, Daniel and Enos. Electa Annable married. Elisha Phillips, a son of Vespasian Phillips, of Ashfield, and brother of Abilena Phillips, the wife of John Ellis, Jr., of Sempronius (see page 111). Elisha Phillips and wife settled in Farmersville, Indiana, in 1818, where they raised. their family. Two of their sons, Ransom and Moses Phillips, yet live near Farmersville, Ind. Each of them has several sons.

Elisha Phillips was born in Ashfield. His parents were Vespasian Phillips and Abilena Belding. Vespasian was a cousin of Joshua Phillips, of Ashfield. Elisha Ellis, and Enos and Bromley Annable, went with them to Indiana. They all went down the Alleghany and Ohio rivers on boats and rafts. Capt. Elisha Ellis, then but 13 years of age, is yet living there (see page 156).

Samuel Annable, son of Barnabas, went to Mt. Vernon soon after his parents left Sempronius, N. Y. In early life he was a school teacher. He was an unusually bright and scholarly man. He was born in Ashfield July 7, 1794, married M. W. Davis September 13, 1832, and had one child, David D. Annable, born October 12, 1840, and now living in Grayville, Ill. Mrs. Samuel Annable died January 29, 1861, and Mr. Annable married Hannah Kirby June 10, 1862. Mr. Samuel Annable died April 4, 1870, in Grayville, where he had lived many years.

Fannie, fourth daughter of Barnabas and Ruth Annable, born 1812, married in 1836, in Mt. Vernon, Ind., Mr. J. C. Wellborn. In 1849 they removed to Lafayette Co., Mo., and in 1854 to Sherman, Tex.; and to Pilot Point, Denton Co., Texas, in 1868, where they now live. She had two sons and three daughters. Her eldest son, D. A. Wellborn, was a strong Union man, and is now a thorough Republican. When the rebellion broke out, in 1861, he came north and enlisted as a private soldier. Before and at the close of the war he was a captain in a regiment of which Gen. George Spalding, of Monroe, Mich, was the colonel. He is a man of unusual intelligence and worth. Mr. Wellborn, Sr., and the balance of the family, were Democrats. The other son, Samuel N. Wellborn, went into the Southern army. He is now dead. Mrs. Fanny Annable Wellborn is in her 77th year, and in vigorous health for that age. Pilot Point, where they live, is a thriving place on the Missouri Pacific Railway.

Bartlett Annable, son of Barnabas, went to Texas in 1838. About 1848 he started for the City of Mexico with a drove of cattle. It is supposed that he was murdered by the Mexicans, as he has never been heard from since.

Bromley and Enos Annable, sons of Barnabas, went to Indiana in 1818 with Elisha Phillips, their brother-in-law. They lived and died in Farmerville, Ind. Bromley had a daughter Rhoda, who married a Mr. Sessions and moved to Texas in 1858. She died in 1861.

Daniel, David and Nancy Annable, children of Barnabas, removed to Farmersville with their parents in 1819, where they all died, leaving no children. Enos had no children.

Samuel Annable, 3d, was a son of Samuel, Jr., of Ashfield. He married Rebecca Standish, a daughter of Israel Standish, of Ashfield, a lineal descendant of Miles Standish, one of the pilgrims who came over in the Mayflower in 1620. They were married in Ashfield, Feb. 4, 1790. Mrs. Rebecca Standish

Annable was a sister of Mr. Peleg Standish, a prominent man, in his day, of Sempronius, N. Y. Mr. Annable and his wife Rebecca removed from Ashfield about 1800 and settled in Sempronius, where Mr. Annable died, about 1810. He had no children.

Dr. David Annable was born in Ashfield, February 23d, 1771. He married Lucy Whiting, who was born in Groten, Conn., May 25th, 1774. They were married in 1800 and settled in Moravia, near Sempronius, N. Y. Dr. Annable was a physician and surgeon, and practiced extensively in Scipio, Moravia and Sempronius. He died November 23d, 1829. His wife died June 2d, 1851, at Ann Arbor, Mich. Their children, all born in Cayuga Co., N. Y., were Minerva, Whiting, Lucretia, Lucy, and Wealthy Ann. Minerva, born Nov. 13th, 1801, died May 7th, 1851. She married Dwight Kellogg, in Moravia. Their children were Charles, Calvin, Julia, William Henry, Daniel W. and George D. Julia Kellogg married Richard Merritt and lives at Battle Creek, Mich. Whiting, born October 3d, 1802, died at Dubuque, Iowa., August 31st, 1834, leaving no children.

Lucretia, born November 20th, 1803, died at Ann Arbor, Mich., in 1862. She married Dorr Kellogg, and they settled in Ann Arbor, Mich., in 1836. He came from Cayuga County, N. Y., on horseback, in 1825, and remained a few weeks, buying some land. He returned in 1836 and, in company with his brother, built a mill about 1½ miles up the river from the city, known as the McMahon mill, which was burned a few years ago. Since 1874 he had been living a retired life at the University city. In 1835 he went with a brother to Buenos Ayres, South America, being on the water 47 days, the time being the shortest that had been made. He had held many responsible offices, having been Justice of the Peace, City Collector and City Treasurer. He died in Battle Creek, Mich., March 15th, 1884. They had no children.

Lucy Annable, born March 25th, 1807, lives at Iowa City, Iowa. She married Oliver Reynolds, in Geneva, Cayuga County, N. Y. Their children were Julia, Mary and Augusta. Julia Reynolds married L. S. Saunders, and they live at Iowa City, Iowa.

Wealthy Ann Annable, youngest daughter of Dr. David Annable, was born December 25th, 1808. She married Matthew N. Tillotson October 11th, 1832. Mr. Tillotson was born February 1st, 1800. They settled in Owosso, Mich., about 1842, where Mr. Tillotson died, March 23d, 1851. Their children were Whiting A., William K., Seth H., Dorr, Lucy A., and Charles N. Tillotson. Whiting Annable Tillotson was born in Sodus, Wayne Co., N. Y., September 3d, 1833. He lives in Detroit, Mich., and is in the fur trade. William K., born November 13th, 1835, in Sodus, N. Y., married Miss Beach and lives in Owosso, Mich. They have two sons and two daughters. Mr. T. was a Union soldier. Mr. and Mrs. Tillotson are prominent and highly respected people in Owosso, where they have lived many years.

Dorr Tillotson was born in Owosso, where he now lives, September 20th, 1844.

Charles N. Tillotson was born in Owosso, September 24th, 1848. He is married and lives in New York city, and is employed in the office of the *Scientific American*.

Seth H. and Lucy A. Tillotson died in infancy.

Mrs. Wealthy Ann Annable Tillotson was a widow thirty-four years.

She lived most of the time with her son, William K., in Owosso, where she died. The writer was acquainted with her for nearly twenty-five years, and can truthfully say that she was a woman of uncommon intelligence and worth. Of her a friend, in the local paper (*Owosso Press*), comments as follows:

"After a protracted illness, Mrs. Wealthy Ann Tillotson died, at the residence of her son, Mr. William K. Tillotson, Saturday, September 5th, 1885. She was the widow of Matthew N. Tillotson, one of the early settlers of Owosso, and one of its first merchants. He maintained also for years a prominent trading post for Indians. Mrs. Tillotson was a very useful, active and popular woman in society in her vigorous days—one of the old pioneer stock that "pushed things" in the early times of Owosso, and her nfluence and work were felt in the community. She was a true Christian woman, an early member of the M. E. Church in this city, and also a hearty co-operator with other denominations in Christian and benevolent work. The esteem in which she was held by our older citizens, who knew her in her days of vigor and public usefulness, was manifested by the large attendance of prominent citizens at the funeral services, which took place at the residence Monday afternoon. Rev. Mr. Wilson, of the Congregational Church, of which church, we understand, she was of late years a member, officiated. There were beautiful flowers and floral designs placed upon the casket—tributes of love to this excellent woman.

"Wealthy Ann Annable began to teach school at the early age of fifteen. Later she finished her education at a young ladies' seminary, after which she continued to teach until her marriage with Mr. Matthew Norton Tillotson. Mr. Tillotson was a merchant at Sodus, N. Y. In 1836, with the tide of emigration setting westward, Mr. Tillotson and his little family came into the Territory of Michigan and settled at Ann Arbor. A few years later they came, pioneers, into Owosso, then only a trading post. Mr. Tillotson opened a store where Mr. McBain's clothing store now stands, and became famous among the Indians of this region as "Bekanoga," the cheap trader. Mr. Tillotson died in 1851. The eldest sons, William and Whiting, continued in business and cared for their mother and younger brothers, Dorr and Charles, till the breaking out of the war, when William and Dorr enlisted in the army and Whiting moved to Detroit. This separation of the family and anxiety for her soldier boys, though she with true Christian patriotism bade them obey their country's call, so wore upon their mother that she never again recovered her health or former exuberance of spirits. Mrs. Tillotson's rare social qualities, tempered by a most lovely Christian character, endeared her to a large circle of friends in the church and community. She was keenly alive to every plan for doing good; in her home she was ever mild, gentle, and loving; her presence has been a benefaction upon the grandchildren, and in the years to come how often will her sons, with their children, 'rise up and call her blessed.'"

Polly Annable (also called Mary and Molly) was a daughter of Samuel Annable, Jr., of Ashfield. She was born in 1774 and married Dea. Dimick Ellis. They lived at 14 on the map, page 328. For further account of her see page 116.

Bethiah, youngest child of Samuel Annable, Jr., was born in Ashfield about 1776. She never married. She lived with her brother Barnabas, and went to Indiana with him and his family, where she died.

According to the records of Ashfield Anna Annable was married December 9th, 1778, to Pelatiah Phillips. No other account of her is found, and it is not known whether she was a daughter of Samuel Annable, jr., of Ashfield, or not.

(In an old letter, written in 1804, by Mrs. Desire Annable, wife of Samuel Annable, Jr., then living in Sempronius, N. Y., and directed to her daughter Polly, wife of Deacon Dimick Ellis, of Ashfield, she mentions Thomas Annable as an *uncle* of Mrs. Ellis. Hence it is an error on page 366, where Thomas is given as a *son* of Samuel Annable, Jr. It seems that he was his *brother*.)

--- -- -- --

THE BARTLETTS.

Dr. Phineas Bartlett, a son of Rev. Moses Bartlett, was born in 1745, at Chatham, now Portland, Conn., on the place now occupied by Wm. H Bartlett, Esq.

He settled at Ashfield in 1766, and at the age of 21 began the practice of his profession, which after a few years became extensive and lucrative; and he earned and enjoyed the esteem of the community which he served.

He was quite active and prominent in the public affairs of the township; was for many years its clerk and treasurer, and was permitted to witness a rapid and large increase in its population, which increase was from about 300 at the time of his arrival, to nearly 1,800 at the date of his death, Oct. 20, 1799, at the age of 54 years. The manner of his death was by falling from his horse in a fit, while on a visit to patients in a distant part of the town, after which he lived but an hour. ·

He married, Sept. 14, 1768, Mehitable, daughter of Samuel Annable, Jr. She died Oct. 31, 1780, aged 30. He married (second) March 20, 1781, Sarah Ballard. She died Jan. 9, 1832, aged 81. His children were Mehitable, born Nov. 14, 1769; Moses, born May 22, 1772. He married, Feb. 1, 1801, Persia, daughter of Thos. Ranney, of Ashfield. Hannah, born Aug. 13, 1778; Lydia, born Jan. 17, 1782. She died June 14, 1807. Phineas, born Aug. 8, 1783, harness maker; settled at Conway, where he became a leading and influential citizen; held various offices; had a family and died in old age. Jerusha, born April 31, 1785; Horatio, born Oct. 8, 1786; remained in Ashfield and died Feb. 23, 1836; unmarried. William, born Jan. 7, 1793; went to central New York, where he became a leading man; was member of State Assembly and Senator, and one of the Court Judges.

About 1770, and later, three of Dr. Bartlett's brothers came to Ashfield to reside, one of whom, Capt. Samuel, was a leading citizen here, and represented the town in the General Court in Boston.

It is probable that Moses, son of Dr. Phineas Bartlett, soon after his marriage in 1801, lived for a time in Sempronius, N. Y., and afterwards in Saline, Mich., where he raised a large family and died at an advanced age.

The Bartletts were an influential people in Ashfield, and took an active part during the Revolution in aid of the independence of the Colonies.

THE BELDINGS.

Two of the early families in Ashfield were those of Samuel Belding, of Deerfield, and Ebenezer Belding, Sr., of Hatfield. It is not known whether they were relatives, but probably they were cousins, or if not, then more remotely connected.

1. William Belding, of Wethersfield, Conn., in 1646 removed to Norwalk; married a Thomasine.

Children: Samuel, July 20, 1647 of Norwalk, 1734; Daniel, Nov. 20, 1648 (2); John, Jan. 9, 1650; Susanna, Nov. 5, 1651; Mary, Feb. 20, 1653; Nathaniel, Nov. 14, 1654.

2. Daniel Belding, son of William. (1) b. 1648; of Hartford, 1671; of Deerfield, 1686; lived on No. 10. Sept. 17, 1696, a great part of his family was killed or captured by Indians. He was a leading man in town, and d. Aug. 14, 1731. M., Nov. 10, 1670, Elizabeth dau. of Nath'l Foot, of Weth.; she was k. Sept. 16, 1696; (2) Feb. 17, 1699, Hepzibah (Buel), wid. of Lieut. Thomas Wells; she was cap. Feb. 29, 1704, and k. on the route to Canada, aged 54; (3) Sarah, dau. John Hawks, wid. of Philip Mattoon; she d. Sept. 17, 1751, a. 94.

Children: William, Dec. 26, 1671, (3), Richard, Mar. 29, 1672; Elizbeth, Oct. 8, 1673; m. Ebenezer Brooks; Nathaniel, Jan. 26, 1675; cap. Sept. 15, 1696; d. Aug. 21, 1714; Mary, Nov. 17, 1677; m. 1698, James Trowbridge; Daniel, Sept. 1, 1680; k. Sept. 16, 1696; Sarah, Mar. 15, 1682; m. Mar. 27, 1702, Benj. Burt; cap. 1704; Hester, Sept. 29. 1683; cap. Sept. 16, 1696, not after heard from; Abigail, Mar. 10, 1686; d. June 25, 1696; Samuel, Apr. 10, 1687; wounded 1696, (4); John, June 24, 1689; d. the next day; Abigail, Aug. 18, 1690; wounded 1696; d. before 1732; John, Feb. 28, 1693; k. 1696; Thankful, Dec. 31, 1695; k. 1696.

3. William Belding, son of Daniel. (2) b. 1671; rem. to Norwalk, 1725; m. May 2, 1700, Margaret, dau. Wm. Arms.

Children: Margaret, Feb. 10, 1701; m. Dec. 17, 1719, Nathaniel Stoffon, of Norwalk; Daniel, Sept. 14, 1702, (5); Elizabeth, Nov. 10, 1704; Thankful, Feb. 9, 1707; d. Aug. 26, 1717; Mary, June 25, 1709; Abigail, Jan. 4, 1711; Ruth; Jan. 18, 1713; Miriam, Nov. 11, 1714; Esther, Oct. 11, 1716; Thankful, Oct. 5, 1718; Sarah, Aug. 20, 1721; Azor, Dec. 10, 1723.

4. Samuel Belding, son of Daniel, (2) b. 1687; d. Dec. 14, 1750; m. Feb. 26, 1724, Anna Thomas; she d. Dec. 13, 1724; (2) Sept. 26, 1726, Elizabeth, dau. Nathaniel Ingram, of Had.; alive in Hatfield in 1761.

Children: Samuel, Apr. 1, 1729, (6); Elizabeth, Nov. 1, 1731, m. Jan. 24, 1751, Seth Hawks; John, Aug. 15, 1734; Daniel, June 17, 1737; d. Aug. 27, 1743, and Prob. Lydia, who m. Joseph Mitchell.

5. Daniel Belding, son of William, (3) b. 1702. In the spring of 1744, "his brethren, with six horses, came up after him," from Norwalk, and that is the last heard of him here; m. Feb. 22. 1727, Esther, dau. Samuel Smith, of Hatfield.

Children: Esther, Nov. 1, 1727; Daniel, July 10, 1729, d. Jan. 1, 1730; Daniel, Dec. 18, 1730; d. Jan. 21, 1731; Sarah, Jan. 27, 1732; Eunice, Dec. 5, 1734; Abigail, Dec. 12, 1736; Margaret, Feb. 16, 1739; William, Jan. 22, 1741; Miriam, May 14, 1743.

(The above account of the Belding's is taken from Hon. Geo. Sheldon's genealogical reports in the Greenfield *Gazette and Courier* for July, 1887.)

6. Samuel Belding, son of Samuel (4), born 1729, was a resident of Deerfield previous to his locating in Ashfield, or Huntstown, as it was then called. He was the first town clerk in 1765, when the town was incorporated as Ashfield. He settled at the four corners—marked 1 on the map, page 328 — where Richard Ellis made the first settlement in the town. It is probable that Mr. Belding purchased this farm of Richard Ellis. From records given on page 316, it is probable that Mr. Belding was a manufacturer of ropes as well as a farmer. He married, June 28, 1753, Mary, daughter of Joseph Mitchel, of Deerfield, who afterwards kept tavern in Ashfield, at 17 on the map.

Children of Samuel and Mary Belding: Daniel, born June 17, 1754; John, Dec. 17, 1756; Mary, March 3, 1758; Mercy, Nov. 29, 1759; married Sept. 6, 1781, Azariah Cooley; Esther, April 18, 1761; Samuel, Jr., Nov. 26, 1762, (died young); Aseneth, Feb. 29, 1764; Louisa, June 6, 1765; Samuel, Jr., Nov. 10, 1767; Elizabeth, Jan. 7, 1770, and Aaron, July 21, 1774. Daniel Belding born 1754; settled in Shelburn, Mass.

John Belding, born 1756, married, July 15, 1784, Priscilla Waite, and lived on the old farm of his father's at No. 1 on the map, page 328, where he raised a large family. He died in 1839, and his wife near the same time, very aged and respected people. Their children were: Aaron, Moses, Reuben, Esther, Submit, David, Tiberius (see page 169) and Hiram.

Hiram Belding, youngest son of John, married Mary Wilson, step-daughter of Deacon Dimick Ellis, of Ashfield. They remained on the old place at No. 1, where they raised their family of six children. About 1855, Mr. Hiram Belding removed to Otisco, Mich., and purchased what is now the site of Belding in that township. He died there some years later. Mrs. Mary Belding is still living, at an advanced age, most of the time with her son Hiram H., in Chicago. Her four sons (see page 117) constitute the firm of extensive manufacturers of silk thread and cloths. One of their large factories is located at Belding, besides which they have recently erected a large brick and stone hotel building and opera house. The Belding Bros. have other large manufacturing interests in Belding, as well as an extensive farm adjoining the village. They reside as follows: David Wilson Belding, in Cincinnati, Ohio; Milo M., in New York city; Hiram H., in Chicago, Ill., and Alvah N., Rockville, Conn. Their youngest brother, Frank, died in New York city in the fall of 1887, and was buried at Belding, Mich. Their only sister, Jennie, married Mr. Jerome Vincent, a farmer near Belding. She died about 1875, leaving two sons. The Messrs. Belding often visit Ashfield, their native town, and take much interest in its prosperity. Some of them, with their families, usually pass the hot season on the Plain.

Mr. Hiram H. Belding usually spends the summers in Belding with his family, where he has a large farm and commodious buildings. Of the other sons and daughters of Mr. Samuel Belding the writer has no further account.

Of Mr. John Belding's children, David married and lived on the old farm in a house situated about 20 rods south of No. 1, where his father lived. One of his daughters, Jennie, married a Baptist clergyman, and they now reside at Shelburne Falls.

Submit Belding, daughter of John, married Elder John Liscomb. In their old age they lived with his son, Horace Liscomb, one of the earliest settlers in Otisco. They died about 1855. Mr. Horace Liscomb has a farm two miles west of Belding, where he lives a hale and hearty old gentleman of 80 years or over.

One of Mr. John Belding's daughters married a Mr. Putney, of Ashfield. Of their children, Mr. Charles Putney has lived at Belding, Mich., about 30 years past. He is a prominent man there, and an ardent supporter of the Christian church in Belding, of which himself and wife are members.

Another son (brother of Charles), Norman Putney, has lived in Ionia, Mich., for many years.

Deacon Ebenezer Belding, Sr., was an early settler in Ashfield. He was from Hatfield, a town about 20 miles southeast of Ashfield. The writer gets but little account of him, except what is given in Rev. Mr. Shepard's sketches, page 279. He lived at the site marked 11 on the map. In the old burying ground at 7, there is an ancient looking headstone marked "E. B., 1776." It is presumed that this stone marks his grave.

Ebenezer Belding, Jr., (son of the above) married Jenezer Ingram. They lived at No. 11, where they raised children as follows: Ebenezer, born Aug. 23, 1769; Abigail, Sept. 2, 1771; Nathaniel, June 22, 1774, and Asher, born Jan. 20, 1777. Asher married Sylvia Ellis (see page 117). Of the others no further account is found. In the early settlement of Ashfield, and up to about 1840, the Beldings were numerous there, but the writer is informed that none of that name now live in the town. Most of them went "west" as they reached manhood.

THE ELMERS AND LILLIES.

Samuel Elmer, before the Revolution, settled where Geo. B. Church now lives. Most of the Elmers in this vicinity are his descendants. One of his daughters, Keziah, married Ebenezer Smith, Jr., son of Elder Ebenezer. She and her husband settled at Stockton, N. Y., in 1815 (see page 96).

Of the Lillies, David, Silas, Samuel and Jonathan, all Stafford people, mentioned in the old records, only Jonathan left descendants. David and Silas owned land on the Plain, and Jonathan, in 1764, bought of Jonathan Sprague, of Huntstown, for £100, lot No. 61, with a dwelling house thereon standing; also all rights belonging to No. 32, of undivided land. Lot No. 61 was west of where Henry Lilly now lives, and was where Jonathan settled. All rights belonging to No. 32, meant one sixty-third part of the then unsurveyed part of the township.

Jonathan Lillie served four years in the French war, and was in the Revolutionary war. He had seven children, and left numerous descendants in this vicinity.

Alonzo Lilly, of Newton, a grand-son of Jonathan, has been a liberal benefactor to the public institutions of this, his native town.

THE FLOWERS.

Major Lamrock Flower was an early settler in Ashfield. He was born in Connecticut in 1720. His wife was a Goodwin, of West Hartford, sister of Uriah Goodwin, of Ashfield. The first of the Flower family in New England was Lamrock Flower, born in England about 1660. The "American College of Genealogical Registry" states that he was probably a son of Capt. William Flower and grandson of Sir William Flower, of Whitwell, England.

Lamrock Flower, born 1660, emigrated to America, and was in Hartford, Conn., where he married in 1686. He had eight children, four sons: Lamrock; born 1689; John, 1695; Francis, 1700, and Joseph, 1706. Lamrock, born 1689, had two children: Elijah, born 1717, and Dinah, born 1714. John Flower, born 1695, was probably the father of Major Lamrock Flower, of Ashfield. Major Flower lived across the road from Deacon Dimick Ellis, at No. 13 on the map, in the gambrel-roofed house where Mr. Joshua Hall now lives. He was a prominent man in Ashfield, and raised several children. He died Jan 8, 1815, aged 95 years. His children were Hannah, Bildad, Lamrock, Jr., and others.

Hannah Flower married, it was said, Major William Flower, of Ashfield, and their son Phineas resided there until about 1840, when he removed to Phelps, N. Y., where he died many years ago. "Uncle Phin's" sons, James B. and Chester, now live in Greeley, Colorado. Mr. Chester Flower, born in Ashfield about 1812, always lived there until in the autumn of 1887, when he went to Colorado. Calvin was also a son of Phineas.

Bildad Flower, son of Major Lamrock, was born about 1750. He married and had two daughters, Ruth, who married Jesse Ranney, of Ashfield, and Amanda (see page 111), who married Edward Ellis, and second, Rev. Lyman Forbush, of Sempronius, N. Y.

Capt. Lamrock Flower, son of Major Lamrock, was born in Ashfield, where he raised a family of several children: Rhoda, Rumina (see pages 152 and 154), Horace and others. Mr. Horace or Horatio Flower removed to Otisco, Mich., about 1850, and later to Muir, where he died. One of his sons now lives at Muir, in the jewelry trade. Louisa, a daughter of Horace, married Mr. Volney Belding (see page 186).

The Flowers, of Connecticut, and their posterity were numerous.

Hon. Roswell P. Flower, of New York city, a Democratic politician of note and prospective candidate for the Presidency, is a descendant of the Connecticut branch. He is said to be one of the most charitable of New York millionaires. He was born in Theresa, N. Y, in 1835. His father was Nathan Munroe Flower, of Oak Hill, N. Y., born in 1796, a son of Elijah Flower, of New Hartford, Conn., born 1750, who was a son of Elijah Flower, born in Hartford, Conn., in 1717, a son of Lamrock Flower, of Hartford, born 1689, who was a son of Lamrock Flower, of Whitwell, England, born about 1660, and who settled in Hartford, Conn., previous to 1686, as above.

THE CHAPINS.

Nathan Chapin was a descendant of Samuel, who settled in Springfield in 1642, and whose statue has recently been erected on one of the parks of that city.

There is a legend current among Nathan's posterity here that he was one of the guard sent to Huntstown, and that while here he fell in love with Chileab Smith's oldest daughter, Mary, and married her in 1757. After living here a number of years he moved back to Springfield, where several of his

375

children were born. Afterwards he returned to 'Ashfield, where he spent the rest of his life. He lived at one time at or near 32 [see map, page 328], owning quite a tract of land to the northeast of this, on which he probably lived for many years. He was a Revolutionary soldier, and was taken prisoner at the battle of Ticonderoga, but escaped in a short time with nine others. He was one of the selectmen as early as 1764 and '68. One of his daughters married Samuel Elmer, 2d, father of Erastus Elmer, now living in this town at the age of 90 years. Nathan's son, Japhet, was a justice of the peace for many years, and in the southeast part of Buckland. He was the father of Luther, now living in this town, who has in his possession a diary kept by his father, from which this extract is made from the year 1831:

"May 4.—Raised the Baptist meeting-house in Buckland.

May 5.—Raised the Baptist meeting-house in Ashfield, moved down from the hill." Moved from 34 to 35, see page 333.

THE DIMICKS.

Lieut. John Ellis and Samuel Annable, Jr., residents of Ashfield, married sisters—Mary (or Molly) and Desire Dimick (see pages 78 and 366). They were from "the Cape," or Barnstable Co., Mass., where the Dimicks were numerous.

The first of this family in New England was Elder Thomas Dymock, as the name was then spelled. He died in 1658, leaving a wife, Annie, and several children: Eliza, John, Mehitable and Shubael. The latter, Shubael, born 1644, married Joanna Bursley in 1663, and had Thomas, John, Timothy, Shubael, Joseph, Mehitable, Benjamin, Joanna and Thankful. Shubael, born 1673, married Tabitha Lothrop, and had five children: David, Samuel, Shubael, Joanna and Mehitable.

Joseph Dimick, born 1675, married Lydia Fuller in 1699, and had Thomas, Bethiah, Mehitable, Ensign, Ichabod, Abigail, Pharaoh and David.

General Joseph Dimick, a lineal descendant of Elder Thomas Dimick, was born in 1734, and died in 1822. At the opening of the Revolution he took a decided stand on the side of liberty. He was early a professor of religion, and ever maintained a consistent Christian life. He married Mary Meiggs in 1759. Their children were Braddock, Prince, Martha, Temperance, Mary, Joseph, Anselm, William and Tabitha. Hon. Braddock Dimick, born 1761, was many years a member of the State Legislature, and a deacon in the Congregational Church for 35 years. He died in 1845. His son, William F., now lives in Falmouth, Mass.

Lieut. Lot Dimick, brother of Gen. Joseph Dimick, was a most daring soldier during the Revolution. He was of a party who captured a British brig, a valuable prize, in Nantucket harbor. It is said that "he handled his gun so as to make sure to get two Britishers in range." On his tombstone is written: "He merited the noblest of mottoes—An Honest Man." He died in 1816, aged 80 years.

Charles, Edward and Constant Dimick, of Barnstable, were probably brothers of Desire and Molly, of Ashfield.

THE LYONS.

Aaron Lyon, Sr., and Mary, his wife, probably came to town in 1764. They settled on Lot 44, and there is little doubt that he built the house where Arnold Smith now lives, 46. They joined the Congregational church by letters from Sturbridge, Nov. 17, 1764, but in 1767 joined the Baptist church under Elder Ebenezer Smith. They had five sons and five daughters. Of these, Nathan settled in Baptist Corner, Aaron 2d, located just over the line in Buckland, and David continued on the home farm until his death by drowning (page 295). In 1784, Aaron, Jr., married Jemima Shepard, daughter of Deacon Isaac Shepard, who lived at 58, just over the hill from where Aaron, Jr., lived. Her mother was Jemima Smith, daughter of Chileab, Sr.

The young couple moved into their little house about half a mile north of Ashfield line into Buckland. Here several children were born previous to 1797 when Mary Lyon was born. Aaron, Jr., died in 1802, when Mary was five years old. Mary attended the district schools in Buckland and Ashfield, and the Sanderson Academy on the Plain. The story of the life of this wonderful woman has been told by several authors,* and is familiar to most people. The little house where she was born has gone to decay; the cellar and chimney foundation, partially grassed over, remain. There is a very large boulder just west of the old cellar, and into the side of this rock is cemented a bronze tablet, bearing this inscription:

MARY LYON,
THE FOUNDER OF THE
MOUNT HOLYOKE SEMINARY,
WAS BORN HERE,
FEB. 28, 1797.

Hundreds of people every year visit this secluded spot, and at the road corners, within several miles, are placed guide boards, giving the direction and distance to the "Birthplace of Mary Lyon."—[See page 238.]

Her brother, Aaron Lyon, 3d, moved to Stockton, N. Y. Two of her sisters married Elisha Wing, of Ashfield; Lavina married Daniel Putnam, of Buckland. Electa, who is remembered by some of our oldest people as an excellent schoolteacher, went to Stockton. None of the Lyon posterity bearing that name are now in town, but are found in the Wing and Elmer families. Mary's mother, for her second husband, married Deacon Jonathan Taylor, of Ashfield.

Deacon David Lyon, who was drowned in 1827, had seven children. One of his sons, Marshall Lyon, married a Sherman and removed to Girard, Erie Co., Penn., about 1834, where they raised a family. Eunice, one of their daughters, married Dr. George Ellis, of North Springfield, Pa. (see page 238). Other children of Marshall Lyon were Elvira, married Marshall Pengra, and lived at Juda, Wis. Washburn lives at Union City, Erie Co., Pa.; David at Platea, Erie Co., Pa.; Sophia, Betsey, Josiah and Minerva, who married Henry Howard, of Irving, Barry Co., Mich. Marshall Lyon died in Girard in Jan. 1880, and his wife Aug. 15, 1875. Children of David and Betsey (Washburn)

---

* See "Life of Mary Lyon," by Dr. Edward Hitchcock; "Recollections of Mary Lyon," by Miss Fiske, also "Life of Mary Lyon," published by American Tract Society.

Lyon: Betsey, Achsah, David, Marshall, Sally, Hepzibeth and Aaron. Betsey married Eli Gray; Achsah m. Aruna Hall; Sally m. Constant Dimick; Marshall m. Chloe Sherman, daughter of Caleb and Eunice (Bacon) Sherman, of Conway, Mass. Their children were: Joseph, John, William, Caleb, Orra, Chloe, Lydia and Eunice Sherman. Marshall Lyon and Chloe Sherman were married in Conway, Apr. 20, 1818. They were the parents of twelve children, five of whom are now living.

THE PHILLIPSES.

Of all the families of Ashfield, whether in early or later times, the Phillipses were the most numerous.

In the settlement of the town in 1745, Thomas Phillips, son of Captain John Phillips, of Easton, Mass., was the second settler, his brother-in-law, Richard Ellis, being the first. Thomas married in or near Easton. He and his wife, Katharine, lived at Deerfield a time previous to settling in Ashfield. He was born in Easton, Jan. 25, 1712. He located in Ashfield at No. 32 on the map (page 328), or possibly his first cabin, as many of the dwellings were then called, was about 80 rods further south, and at or near the Ellis and Phillips fort, No. 30.

Capt. John Phillips, of Easton, father of Thomas, was a soldier in 1690 in an expedition undertaken by the Colonies for the reduction of Quebec, Canada. For this service he became entitled, about 40 years afterwards, to "Rights" of land in what is now Ashfield. Undoubtedly this fact is what led Thomas Phillips and Richard Ellis, a son-in-law of Capt. John Phillips, to seek homes in this then wilderness region.

Of Capt. John Phillips, of Easton, it is said that he was a man of unusual ability and integrity of character. He was one of the earliest settlers in Easton in 1694. He removed from Weymouth, Mass., to Easton, with his wife, Elizabeth Drake, daughter of Thomas and sister of Benjamin Drake, residents of Weymouth, who settled in Easton about 1700. Capt. Phillips was a prominent man in the early town history, and was the first town clerk, serving for twelve years. In his bold handwriting is found on the records of Easton the marriage of his daughter, Jean, to Richard Ellis in 1728, and the names and date of birth of seven of their children. The writer is greatly indebted to Rev. Wm. L. Chaffin, of Easton, for these reports, without which he could have made little or no progress in tracing the descendants of Richard Ellis. (Mr. Chaffin has searched the records of Easton thoroughly, and has lately published a volume of over 800 pages of the history of that town).

Capt. John Phillips is noted as the first person in Easton who held a commission as captain. He was a son of Richard and Elizabeth (Packer) Phillips, and grandson of Nicholas Phillips.

Capt. John Phillips' children were John, Jr., William, Experience, Samuel, Joshua, Caleb, Jean (or Jane), Thomas and Richard (see page 16).

John, Jr., was born at Weymouth in 1692. He died in Easton in 1758. His son, Deacon Ebenezer Phillips, lived there after him. Samuel, son of Capt. John, was born 1702. He married Damaris Smith, of Taunton. He lived and died in Easton, and his son, Samuel, also.

William Phillips, son of Capt. John, was born about 1695. He was a carpenter, and built and owned a saw mill in Easton.

A few years after the settlement of Ashfield there were Joshua, Caleb and Richard Phillips's names on the town records. It is not now certain whether these were all sons of Capt. John, of Easton, or not. However, such is probably the fact, as Thomas and Jane (Richard Ellis's wife), children of Capt. John, had become permanent residents there, which would naturally lead others of their kin to the same locality. Jean or Jane, daughter of Capt. John Phillips, of Easton, married Richard Ellis, the first settler in Ashfield (see page 16).

Thomas Phillips, Sr., son of Capt. John, was born in Easton, Jan. 25, 1712. He lived in Deerfield for a time, and then followed Mr. Ellis to Ashfield about 1745, where he remained the rest of his life. His children were: Philip, born Feb. 3, 1739 (one account gives the year as 1738); Simeon, April 15, 1742; Charity, Oct. 10, 1744; Thomas, Jr., June 7, 1747; Elizabeth, Oct. 31, 1749; Sarah, 1752, and Caleb?

Of Thomas Phillips, Sr's, children, Capt. Philip Phillips was the eldest, and in his time one of the most prominent men of Ashfield. It is said that his mother died when he was a babe, but it seems that his father married again, for the Congregational Church records say that Thomas Phillips and his wife, Catharine, were among the fifteen members that first formed that church in 1763, and that she died in 1775. When Thomas, Sr., settled in Ashfield, there came with him a colored man, Heber (Honestman), by name, and his wife. It is said that this colored woman was a nurse for the children, and in return for her and her husband's kindness, they were taken care of by Capt. Philip Phillips in their old age. Heber occupied a cabin at 29, just north of Capt. Phillips, a short distance above the spring. According to the old Congregational records, Heber joined that body at its formation in 1763, and died in 1768, aged 67 years.

Capt. Philip Phillips lived at 28 on the map, on the southwest corner of lot No. 1. He afterwards moved 100 rods north and located on the corner at 26, where he built a large frame house. He was a Justice of the Peace, Selectman, and represented the town in the State Legislature. He married Mercy, daughter of Joshua Phillips, of Dighton, Mass., a town about 15 miles south of Easton. She was born in 1737, and died Oct. 15, 1815. She was a sister of Richard Phillips, a resident of Ashfield, and of Abiather, Samuel and Joshua Phillips, of Dighton. One of her sisters married a Truesdale, and the other a Dwelly.

Capt. Phillips died in Ashfield Aug. 10, 1800. He had 13 children, 11 sons and two daughters. Each of his sons were over six feet tall, and formed a platoon or military company, in which the father took great pride in exhibiting at trainings and on other public occasions. The names of Capt. Phillips's children were Elijah, born 1759; Abner, 1760; Lemuel, 1762; Philip, Jr., 1764; David, 1766; Simeon, 1768; Israel, 1770, Joshua, 1771; Abiather, 1773; Samuel, 1775; Liscomb, 1777; Hannah, 1779, and Anna, 1782.

Elijah Phillips, born Feb. 14, 1759, married Cynthia Goodwin, of Ashfield, and removed to West Virginia, where he died in 1840. They had 17 children. Elijah, Jr., married Fannie Rude, and had a family of 10 children, some of whom live in Buckland, Mass., with their descendants. Mabel married Bliss Forbes, or Forbush, of Ashfield. Ansel, Abiezer, Mercy, Eusebia, Lyman, Cynthia, Samantha, Delia married Elias Perry, and once lived in Fredonia, N. Y. Edwin, Lydia, Jonathan and others died young, all children of Elijah, Sr. His descendants in West Virginia took an active part in the Union army in the great Rebellion. They were noted for daring bravery. One of Mercy's sons was a captain, and had 14 Phillips' relatives in his company. They lived at French Creek, and did noble service during the war.

Abner Phillips, born March 25, 1760, died in Ashfield, Nov. 26, 1829. He married Molly Cranson, and had five children.

Lemuel Phillips, born Nov. 26, 1762, married Sarah Cranson, or Cranston, and had 11 children. He died April 28, 1843, in Ashfield. It is stated that he had 11 children. Many of the descendants of Lemuel Phillips and his brothers, Israel, Simeon and Samuel, are now in the vicinity of Ashfield.

Philip Phillips, Jr., was born July 29, 1764. He married Elizabeth Smith, only daughter of Chileab Smith, Jr., of Ashfield. In 1816 they removed to Cassadaga, Chautauqua Co., N. Y., where they located on a farm and remained until their death. They had five children: Sawyer, born 1791; Elizabeth married John Robinson and died about 1828. Esther married Israel Smith, Jr., and died about 1830. Philip died about 1808, aged eight years, and Joshua, who died in Cassadaga, unmarried, aged 28. Sawyer, born 1791, married, in Cassadaga, Jane Parker, a daughter of Benjamin Parker, and granddaughter of Thomas Parker, of Washington Co., N. Y. They had 15 children, all born in Cassadaga.

Alonzo, born 1821, died 1826. Thomas D., 1822, resides in Cassadaga, and has three children; Williston, 1824, lives in Cassadaga; Rosina, 1825, died 1836; Dr. Alonzo P., Dec. 28, 1826, resides in Fredonia, Chautauqua Co., N. Y., where he has an elegant home on a high bluff, about 100 rods from the center of the village, surrounded with several acres of the choicest gardens, grape vines, fruit and ornamental trees, etc. Dr. Phillips has been a practicing physician in Chautauqua County for many years. He has mostly retired late years, and is enjoying the well earned luxuries of a long and active professional life. His wife was Miss Fidelia Wood, a daughter of Elijah Wood, and his wife, Fidelia Smith, daughter of Ebenezer Smith, jr. Mrs. Dr. Phillips is thus a great granddaughter of Elder Ebenezer Smith, a celebrated Baptist minister in the early history of Ashfield (see pages 71 and 98), and Dr. Phillips is a great-grandson of Chileab Smith, jr. (he of 100 years of age), a brother of Elder Ebenezer. Dr. and Mrs. Phillips have had three children, none of whom are now living. From personal acquaintance the writer can say that they are most genial and worthy people. They have aided him greatly in furnishing material for this part of the work.

William W., sixth child of Sawyer Phillips, was born Oct. 8, 1828, and now resides at Cassadaga. He has two sons.

Charles, born 1830, lives at Cassadaga. Sawyer, jr., born 1831, died 1854; Joshua, 1833, died 1850; Philip, born 1834, is noted as the "Singing Pilgrim," in 1880 he published a volume of nearly 500 pages, giving an account of a "Song Pilgrimage Around the World," which he had made, a most interesting work, giving an account of his trip with numerous incidents connected therewith.

Rosina, eleventh child of Sawyer Phillips, was born in 1836. She married M. E. Beebe, and resides in Fredonia. She has one son.

Benjamin C. and Alphonso R., children of Sawyer, died young.

George H., born 1841, resides in Springfield, Ohio, and has two children.

Zerah Barney, youngest child of Sawyer, born 1843, died in 1879, leaving four children. Mr. Sawyer Phillips, father of this large and very intelligent family, died in 1872, in Cassadaga; his wife a few years previously.

David, son of Capt. Philip Phillips, of Ashfield, was born Feb. 2, 1766. He married Anna Goodwin, of Ashfield. They had nine children. David moved to West Virginia with his oldest brother, Elijah. They went overland with teams and wagons, containing their families and goods.

Simeon, sixth child of Capt. Phillips, was born in Ashfield, June 1, 1768. He married Ruth Andrews, of Ashfield, a very superior woman, and had five children. He lived in Conway, Mass., and died about 1855. Their children were: James, Phillip M., Simeon, jr., and others, who died young.

Capt. James Phillips, eldest son of Simeon, was a farmer all his life in Ashfield and Conway. He married Mary Ann Wheeler, and had two children. Joseph, a farmer, who lives in Conway, and has two sons: Charles, in Hatfield, Mass., a fine piano tuner, and James, living with his father in Conway. Capt. James Phillips had a daughter, Harriet, now Mrs. A. P. Eldred, residing in Springfield, Mass. She has two sons: Willis and Fred, now living in the same city. Capt James Phillips died in Conway about 1873, at an advanced age, a few weeks after the death of his wife.

Philip M., second son of Simeon, was a farmer, and spent his life in Ashfield and Conway. He married Dollie Carrier, a woman dearly beloved by all. He died about 1879, and his wife two years later. They had four children, the first dying in infancy. The second, Ruth, now Mrs. Lee, a widow, living in Conway. She has four children. George married and living in Conway; in trade there. Frank, unmarried. Capt. Eber, unmarried, a carpenter in W. T., and Nettie, now Mrs. Eddy, living with her mother in Conway.

Philip M.'s second daughter, Mary, now Mrs. Emerson Markham, lives at Hoosac Falls, N. Y., where her husband is in trade. They have three children.

Philip M.'s third daughter, Julia, now Mrs. R. M Tucker, lives at Orange City, Florida, where they have orange groves.

Simeon Phillips, jr., was born in Ashfield, Feb. 22, 1815, at a house situated on the road from the Plain to Buckland four corners, and about half way down the long hill. He first married in Plymouth, Conn., Emily Wolten. She died four years later childless. He then moved back to Conway, where he engaged in farming, and married Louisa Carrier, of Hawley, Mass. After four years he moved to Greenfield, Mass., where he now lives; he is a machinist. They had three children; Jennie E., now Mrs. Frank E. Wood. Mr. Wood is a brick mason and plasterer. They have no children, and live with her father, Simeon. Mr. Simeon Phillips had two other children, who died young. His wife, Louisa, lived 18 years, after which he was married 14 years ago to Lucy Wade—a young widow—had two children: Raymond, now eight years, a very bright child, and Harold M., who died in infancy. Mrs. Lucy Phillips died in 1884.

Israel Phillips was born May 23, 1770. Although not a doctor, he was, on account of his being the seventh son, called "Doc" Phillips, from a superstition then popular that the seventh son had necessarily some mysterious or curative virtues as a physician. He married Mabel, or Mehitable Belding, and had one child, Israel, jr., who married Sabrina Ward, and had nine children: Emeline married Henry Barrows, of Ashfield; John W. married D. D. Reniff, of Buckland; Alonzo married Eliza Green, of Ashfield; Winsor, unmarried, accidentally shot and killed, aged 37; Louis married Henry Green, of Ashfield; Mabel married Alonzo Paine, of Ashfield; Edwin married Eliza Ann Phillips, of Ashfield; Ann Eliza married Henry Bassett, of Ashfield, and Ralph, who married Mrs. E. M. Wilder. Israel Phillips, Sr. and Jr., lived all their lives at No. 56 on the map.

Joshua, son of Capt. Philip Phillips, born Nov. 30, 1771, died unmarried, May 9, 1826, in Ashfield.

Abiather Phillips, born Oct. 27, 1773, married Hannah Ranney. They moved about 1816 to Orleans Co., N. Y., where they lived for a time, and from there to Allegany, Cattaraugus Co., about 1830, where they died about 1858. They had 11 children: Esther married a Leach, and lived and died in Michigan; Ann married Elias Fish, and died in Minnesota; Eliza married Robert Wilbur, had three children, and lived in Cattaraugus Co.; Abiather, jr., married Amanda Ellis (one of Barzillia Ellis' descendants of Chautauqua Co.) had one child, and lived in Hillsdale. Mich; George married M. Andrus, had four children; lived and died in Wattsbury, Penn.; Samuel Ranney Phillips married Safronia Smith, had three children, and lived and died in Cattaraugus Co.; William H. married Elmira McClure, and lives in Clearwater, Minn.; Charles married Elmira Blackman, and lived in Cerro Gordo, Iowa; John married Mrs. Safrona Hughes, and lived in Allegany, Cattaraugus Co., N. Y. Alonzo died in Michigan, unmarried. Harriet, youngest child of Abiather and Hannah Ranney Phillips, lives with her brother, William H., in Minn.

Samuel, tenth son of Capt. Philip Phillips, of Ashfield, was born Aug. 14, 1775. He married Sally Ranney, and had six children: Sally, born 1794, married a Mansfield, and died in 1853; Rachel married Ansel Elmer; Emily married a Bassett; Francis married, and his son, Francis R. Phillips, now lives at or near 58 on the map of Ashfield; Ann E., born 1803, and Anson.

Liscom, youngest son of Captain Philip Phillips, was born March 23, 1777. He married Nancy Padelford, and had nine children. He was a physician, and lived in South Adams, Mass. He died Oct. 10, 1821. His children were: Henry P., born 1807, was a physician in North Adams. He died in 1880. Sarah, born in Savoy, Mass., in 1808, married William Smith; Erasmus D., born 1810, resides in Geneva Wis.; Charles F. lives in Blackwater, Wis.; William, born in South Adams, died at 11 years of age; Julia Ann married S. E. Dean, of South Adams; Benjamin F. married Miss Moran, and second, O'Neil; Albert Liscom, youngest child of Dr. Liscom Phillips, was born in 1821; he married a Miss Green, and resides in Racine, Wis.

Hannah, daughter of Capt. Philip Phillips, was born Feb. 5, 1779. She married Mr. Henry Bassett, one of the principal citizens of Ashfield. She died Feb. 14, 1849. It is said she had nine children. Many of her descendants are now living in Ashfield and vicinity. Esquire Bassett's children have often heard their mother relate how the family used to go from their cabin down to the Ellis and Phillips fort to stay nights from fear of the Indians.

Anna, youngest child of Capt. Phillips, was born Oct. 27, 1782. She married Ebenezer Porter, of Ashfield, a grandson of Rev. Nehemiah Porter, a celebrated Congregational minister of Ashfield. She is also grandmother of Mr. Lewis Porter, the present landlord of the "Ashfield House," on the Plain. She died Dec. 26, 1820, leaving six children.

Of Thomas Phillips, sr's, other children: Simeon, born 1742; Charity, 1744, and Elizabeth, 1749; the writer gets no further report. They probably left Ashfield in an early day. The Congregational church records say that in 1770 Simeon Phillips was killed by the falling of a tree, but his age is not given. There was a Simeon Phillips on the valuation list for 1766, but his name does not appear on the list for 1771. Hence, he may have been this second son of Thomas Phillips, sr., and brother of Capt. Philip Phillips. There were other Simeons, but they came on later.

Sarah, daughter of Thomas, sr., was born 1752, and died Dec. 22, 1822, aged 70. She married Elisha Cranson, jr. He died May 27, 1813, aged 62. She married (second) Zachariah Howes. One grandchild and later generations of hers are now in Ashfield.

Caleb, supposed to be a son of Thomas, sr., married about 1780, Sally Green, of Ashfield. They had six or more children baptized at the Congregational church. Early in this century they moved on to a farm in Phelps, N. Y., and died there, where they have descendants.

Thomas Phillips, jr., son of Thomas Phillips, sr., born June 7, 1747, married Elizabeth Noyes, and resided in Ashfield until his death, July 9, 1829. They were married in Easton, Nov. 7, 1771. Their children were: Rhoda married Enoch King; Molly (or Mary) married Zenas Elmer; Betsey married Roger Bronson; Rachel married Samuel Bronson; Dorcas married Rev. Ibri Cannon, and Russel, born 1785, married Rhoda Williams, eldest daughter of Apollos Williams and Hannah Ellis, his wife (see page 101).

Dorcas Phillips, daughter and youngest child of Thomas, jr., was a woman of remarkable piety and loveliness of character. Aged residents of Ashfield remember her as "the most gifted person [in prayer] in all that section." At 30 years of age she married Rev. Ibri Cannon, a Methodist minister, and lived in Troy, N. Y. She had several children. One of her daughters, Achsah, now Mrs. Thomas M. Dunham, lives at Ocean Grove, N. J. She is a highly educated and accomplished lady, and has a family of four daughters. Her parents are both dead. Mr. Cannon, her father, died in Troy many years ago.

Thomas Phillips, jr., had another son (brother of "Uncle Russ"), who left home when young, of whom no trace has since been had by his relatives. This may have been Caleb. Many of Thomas Phillips, sr's, descendants are still in town, but they are descendants of Capt. Philip Phillips. Thomas, jr., lived with his son, Russell, in a gambrel-roofed house, nearly opposite No. 32, on the map, where he died in 1829. This place was just west of where Mr. Houghton Smith now lives. It is said that none of his descendants are now in Ashfield.

Of the other Phillipses, of Ashfield, the writer gets but little information. Vespasian, Richard, John, Spencer, Pelatiah, Benjamin, Caleb and others lived there in an early day, 100 years and more ago. Vespasian Phillips married Abilena Belding, May 7, 1772. Their names were on the Baptist Church records in 1798, and were dismissed in 1803. Their daughter, Abilena, married John Ellis, jr., and settled in Sempronius, N. Y., (see page 110).

Richard is said to have been a brother of Mercy, wife of Captain Philip. He·joined the Baptist Church in 1766. His house was a·little east of O on the map. He is said to have had several children, and Spencer, Vespasian, Petetiah and John may have been his sons. John joined the Baptist church in 1773, and died in 1776. Pelatiah married Cynthia Wait in 1789.

Caleb Phillips was early spoken of as tender of the corn mill. It is sup·posed that he was either a brother of Thomas, sr., or Richard. He disappeared soon, and about 1780 another Caleb joins the Congregational church; also Daniel. Caleb has first child baptized in 1787, and a number more up to 1800. About this time he went to Phelps, N. Y. There was a general exodus from Ashfield about this time to central and western New York.

Spencer Phillips married, Nov. 28, 1783, Dorcas, the widow of Bildad Flower, who died in the Revolutionary army (see page 112). One of his sons, Spencer, jr., lived in Ohio, near Sandusky, about 1850. Another son, Bildad, settled at Clarkston, Mich., About 1835. He died there about 1862. His widow and several sons live there now—Theodore and Sylvester, and two daughters, Mrs. Jane Vliet and Mrs. Ruth West, and a grandson, Clarence Phillips.

Hon. S. W. Smith, of Pontiac, Mich., is another grandson of Bildad's. Mr. Bildad Phillips was born in Ashfield in 1797, and his wife about 1808.

Samuel and Daphne (Butler) Phillips lived in Deerfield. It is not known whether they were of the Ashfield Phillipses or not. Their daughter Theo·docia married Ebenezer Ellis (see page 159).

THE RANNEYS.

Thomas Ranney, believed to be the progenitor of all of the name in America, was born in Scotland in the year 1616, the year of Shakspeare's death. He migrated, when young, to this country, and was one of the original settlers in Middletown, Conn., being one of the 15 or 20 who first struck the axe into the forest at that place. In May, 1659, at the age of 43 years, he married Mary, aged 17, daughter of George Hubbard, also an early settler there.

He subsequently purchased the homestead and other lands of George Graves, situated in the south part of that part of Middletown called "Upper Houses," since 1850 known as the town of Cromwell, beside the Connecticut river. It is the location on which the Meriden Railroad Company have built their depot. The house which stood on the street at the west end of the land was the home of the adventurer and the birth-place of four generations of his descendants. The deed of sale to Mr. Ranney was made Nov. 17, 1663.

He was energetic and thrifty, and was rated second in amount on the township tax list of 1670, and was identified with the settlement and growth of the town. He lived 54 years with the bride of 17, and died June 25, 1713, aged 97, being the first one buried in the second cemetery consecrated for burial purposes in Middletown. As the snows of almost a century of winters had silvered his locks, he was doubtless one of the very last of that patriarchal band of pioneers who first settled in the town.

His wife survived him some eight years; the record of her death being Dec. 18, 1721, aged 79. The inscription on his headstone is nearly illegible, and there is no other stone of the shape of that which marks the grave of this first American Ranney. At times he wrote his name Rheny.

This has been a highly respectable and moral family for more than two centuries; many of their posterity have helped the new States, and a few remain in the land of their fathers. And it has been a prolific race, embracing several thousands who have lived in this country, the names of several hundreds of whom are in possession of the writer.

1. Thomas Ranney, farmer, born in the year 1616, in Scotland; settled at Middletown, Conn.; d. June 25, 1713, aged 97; m. in 1659, Mary Hubbard; she died Dec. 18, 1721, aged 79. They had 10 children.

Their children: Thomas, jr., born March 14, 1661 (2).

John, born Nov. 16, 1662; married, in 1693, Hannah Turner. Had eight children.

Joseph, born Sept., 1663; m. in 1693, Mary Starr; had eight children; he died in 1745.

Mary, born Oct., 1665; m. John Savage, jr.; had 11 children; she died in 1734.

Elizabeth, born April 12, 1668; m. in 1698, Jonathan Warner; had two children; she died Feb. 11, 1737.

Esther, born in 1674; m. 1696, Lieut. Nathaniel Savage; had nine children; died April 1, 1750.

Ebenezer, born 1678; m. 1698, Sarah Warner; had five children; died 1754, aged 76.

Hannah, born ——; m. Samuel Wilcox; died Nov. 29, 1713.

Margaret, born ——; m. Stephen Clark, of New Haven.

Abigail (twin of Margaret), born ——; m. Walter Harris, of Glastonbury; had one child, and died Dec. 15, 1714.

2. Thomas Ranney, son of Thomas, (1); born Aug. 14, 1661, farmer; removed in 1710 across the river and settled in Chatham; died Feb. 6, 1727; he married, May, 1690, Rebecca Willet, of Hartford; she married, second, Dec. 16, 1729, Jacob White; they had seven children.

Children: Thomas, born Aug. 14, 1692, (3); Willet, born March 30, 1694; m. April 20, 1720, Anna Johnson; she died March 29, 1731; he m., second, Dec. 23, 1732, Deborah White, and had six children; George, born Oct. 28, 1695 (4); Rebecca, born Dec. 10, 1700; Nathaniel, born June 17, 1702; died Sept. 25, 1766; m. Jan. 16, 1734, Rebecca Sage; had eight children; Ann, born July 23, 1706; Margaret, born Aug. 21, 1708.

3. Thomas Ranney, son of Thomas (2); born Aug. 14, 1692; died 1764; m. Feb. 26, 1720, Esther, daughter of Ephraim and Silence Wilcox.

Children: Jeremiah, born July 13, 1721; m. Martha Stow, and have children; he removed to Woodford, Conn.; Thomas, born Feb. 13, 1723; m. Mary Little, and removed to Westminster, Vt.; had two children; Ephraim, born April 10, 1725; died 1762; m. Nov. 26, 1747, Silence Wilcox; had seven sons and four daughters. He accumulated for those days much wealth, giving each child at their marriage $1,000, and leaving a large dividend at death. In 1760 they removed to Westminster, Vt. He was prominent, and an active, influential Christian; for many years a deacon of the Congregational church. With but few exceptions, his descendants have followed him in his religious faith, many of whom have been professional men, and among whom were Dr. W. R. Ranney, late Lieut. Governor of Vermont, and Ambrose A. Ranney, late Representative in Congress from Massachusetts.

4. George Ranney, son of Thomas (2); born Oct. 28, 1695; died March 26, 1725, aged 29; his wife, Mary, died Nov. 26, 1749.

Children: George, born 1723 (5); a daughter, born 1725; died young.

5. George Ranney, son of George (4); born 1723; lived in Chatham, now Portland, Conn.; died Feb. 23, 1804, aged 81; he m. Jan. 23, 1746, Hannah Sage; she died June 9, 1797; had nine children.

Children: George, born Jan. 9, 1747 (6); Thomas, born July 6, 1749 (7); Francis, born April 19, 1753 (8); Hannah, born May 9, 1755; m. Joel Hall; her sons were Capt. Joel, Samuel, Joseph and Jesse Hall; Molly, born June 9, 1757; m. a Bosworth; Esther, born Jan. 8, 1761; m. a Parks; Lucy, born Sept. 6, 1763; m. Seth Knowles; Jonathan, born Sept. 3, 1765; died in 1831; m. Sally Parsons; she died in 1851; they had nine children; Nabby, born about 1767; m. Capt. Ithamar Pelton.

6. George Ranney, son of George (5); born Jan. 9, 1747, at Chatham, Ct.; was in early life in the West India trade; he died in Ashfield, Jan. 14, 1822, aged 75 years; he m. in 1770, Esther, daughter of Capt. Samuel Hall; she died March 3, 1807, aged 56; m., second, Aug. 8, 1809, to Alithea, widow of Oliver Patch; she died Aug. 6, 1827, aged 76. In the spring of the year 1780 he removed with his family to Ashfield, where he had purchased from Lamberton Allen the 100 acre farm now owned by Charles Howes. Only a small portion of the original forest had been cleared from his land, and a house of logs was the only dwelling place ready for their reception. That house was on the hillside, some 35 or 40 rods westerly from the residence of Charles Howes, where the site is yet visible. He was a man of industry and perseverance. To clear and bring his land into proper condition for crops, a great outlay of strength and vigor was required, but with the ultimate help of his rugged boys growing up around him, he accomplished the task, and the farm became one of the best in the township, and here he brought up his large family of children. Upon the location, in 1798, of the new county road through this farm, leading from South Ashfield to the Plain village, Mr. Ranney erected the substantial two story house where Mr. Howe resides (37 on map, page 328.) Mr. Ranney was for more than 40 years identified with the growth and prosperity of the town; a man of retiring disposition; an exemplary character, and much esteemed. His religious associations were with the Society of Congregationalists. His children were:

Samuel, born March 6, 1772 (9); Sarah, born Dec. 20, 1773; died Jan. 11, 1774; Jesse, born Oct. 13, 1775 (10); Joseph, born July, 1777 (11); Hannah, born Oct. 3, 1781; m. Dec. 4, 1800; Abiather, son of Philip Phillips, Esq.; they had 12 children; she died July 28, 1857; Esther, born March 5, 1784; m. May 3, 1804, Benjamin Jones, jr.; he died Sept. 20, 1804; she married, second, July 27, 1809, Forest Jepson; they had 12 children; he d. Sept. 20,

1844; she d. Aug. 23, 1862; Anna, born June 20, 1786; m. Nov. 27, 1806, James McFarland, Esq.; had four children: George, born May 12, 1789 (12).

7. Thomas Ranney, son of George (5); born July 6, 1749; settled in Ashfield about 1792, on the farm now owned by Chauncey Boice; died April 20, 1823, aged 72, m. widow Mary Miles; she died Oct. 5, 1819, aged 72.

Children: Persis, born ——; m. Feb. 1, 1801, Moses, son of Dr. Phineas Bartlett; Catherine, born ——; m. Jan. 1, 1799, Wm. Belding; Roswell, born Nov. 22, 1782 (13); William, born June 30, 1785 (14).

8. Francis Ranney, son of George (5); born April 19, 1753; settled in Ashfield, Feb., 1786, in south part of the town, where Charles F. Howes lives; died April 7, 1804, aged 51; m. Rachel, daughter of Capt. Samuel Hall; she d. 1827. He was a Revolutionary soldier.

Children: Sally, m. Samuel, son of Philip Phillips, Esq.; Giles, born Aug. 15, 1773; Daniel (16), born 1776; moved to LeRoy, N. Y.; m. Anna Bittern; Dr. Geo. E. Ranney, now or formerly Sec. of State Medical Society, at Lansing, Mich., is a grandson of Daniel. His children: Charlotte, Joel, Hezekiah, Ozias, Julia and Laura Ann; Betsey, m. Feb. 17, 1802, had five children; Ruth, m. Josiah Wells; Luther, born Sept. 6, 1785; Rachel, m. an Eastman; Lucy m. Enos Bush.

9. Samuel Ranney, son of George (6); born March 6, 1772; settled in Ashfield on the farm next south of his father's. In 1821 he built the two-story brick house that is yet standing there. In 1836 he removed to Phelps, N. Y., where he died June 27, 1837; m. 1795, Polly Stewart, of Branford, Conn.; she died in Michigan about 1850.

Children: Lucretia, born June 17, 1796; she d. May 17, 1879 at Schoolcraft, Mich.; she m., 1816, Lemuel Sears; he d. May 28, 1819; she m., second, 1820, Col. Nehemiah Hathaway, blacksmith; he died 1844, at Grand Rapids, Mich.; she had five children; Charles W. and his son, Charles S., both living in Detroit, Mich.; Emily, who married James D. Lyon, of Grand Rapids, and another daughter who married Dr. Freeman, of Schoolcraft. [Mrs. Lucretia Ranney Hathaway was a woman of unusual intelligence and worth. She lived many years at Grand Rapids after the death of her husband; the last few years with her daughter in Schoolcraft.] Braddock, born May 20, 1800; d. Sept. 6, 1803; Harriet, born March 12, 1802; d. Aug. 22, 1803; William, born Oct. 23, 1805; he moved to Michigan about 1838; was, in 1860, living in Iowa; postmaster and deacon; m., 1828, (?) Eliza Ann Smith; she died April 16, 1832; he again m., and had several children; is now living in Potawotamie, Kansas; Dexter, born June 5, 1808; was drowned Aug. 22, 1850, in Grand River, Mich.; m. Laura Robinson; Lucius, born June 17, 1812; d. Feb. 1, 1815; Julia, born Nov. 7, 1815; d. Sept., 1838, unmarried; Emily, born Jan. 9, 1818; died April 22, 1837; she m., April 12, 1837, at Phelps, N. Y., Dr. James Davis; Frederick T. was born March 12, 1820; he married and settled in Grand Haven, Mich. where he was in the lumber business many years. After the death of his first wife he married, in 1857, Miss Fannie A. Bates, a very estimable lady, by whom he had two sons and three daughters. Mr. Ranney lived in Petoskey, Mich., 10 or 12 of his last years, where he died about 1885. His eldest son, Frederick T., m. Jan. 26, 1887, Miss Mary E. Balch, dau. of Geo. W. Balch, Esq., of Detroit, Mich. Mr. R. lives in Detroit, where he is doing a large and successful business in real estate. He graduated at Williams College, Mass, in 1884. His mother and her three younger 'children now live in Olivet, Mich., where the children are being educated in Olivet College. Mr. Ranney was a very active business man, and highly respected by all who knew him, and his children give promise of great usefulness. Samuel H. is a son by his first wife; m. and lives at Grand Rapids, Mich. (a lumberman); and a dau. Mary, who married Albert D. Reed, of Batavia, Ill.

Of Mr. Ranney's children, by his second marriage, Fred T. was born Apr. 19, 1859; Florence, 1862—living in Detroit; Lewis J., 1872; Elizabeth, 1875; Francis A., 1877.

10. Jesse Ranney, son of George (6); born Oct. 13, 1775, at Chatham, Conn.; settled on the farm in Ashfield next north of his father's; built a house on that farm, which he sold to his brother Joseph, and in 1818 removed to the large farm in Ashfield that he purchased of David Ellis [see page 86], where he died July 18, 1861, aged 86 years. For many years he had been a consistent and worthy member of the Baptist church; was a man of sterling good sense; of retiring disposition; of exemplary life, and most esteemed by those who knew him best. He m., Dec. 5, 1798, Ruth, dau. of Bildad Flower.

Children: James, born Sept. 15, 1799; Bildad, born Feb. 27, 1802; d. Aug. 4, 1815; Charles, born Dec. 4, 1803; Hannah, born Dec. 16, 1805; m. Nov., 1827, Richard, son of Dimick Ellis, Esq.; Erastus, born Oct. 8, 1807; Amanda, born Aug. 17, 1809; died Oct. 19, 1884; m., March, 1829, Elijah Richmond; m. (2) Wilson Elmer; she had three children; Edwin, born July 25, 1811; Polly, born Feb. 16, 1815; m. Augustus F. Daniels; Lucretia, born Feb. 7, 1819; m. Darius Cross; Ruth-Ann, born June 23, 1821; m. Sylvester W. Hall.

[Of these children of Jesse and Ruth Ranney, the following may further be said: James m. Sally Andrews, and lived at 67 on the map, where he raised a large family of children. About 1878 he and his wife came to Belding, Mich., where they lived three or four years with their daughter, Mrs. Field, a widow, and their son, Charles. Mrs. Field married Mr. Wheeler, and moved upon a farm in Augusta, Mich. (near Kalamazoo), where Mr. and Mrs. James Ranney died about 1883, at advanced ages. They were very worthy and highly respected people. Their children were: Jane (dead) m. a Woodbridge; Caroline (dead) ,m. Alden and Young; William, Charles, James H. (dead); has a widow and several children in Hartford, Conn.; Elizabeth m. Field and Wheeler; has two children: Edgar Field and a daughter, in Hartford, Conn.; Austin in Concord, N. H., and Silvador O. Ranney, in Hartford, Conn.

Charles Ranney, son of Jesse, m. Sarah Hall, and had two children. He remained on the farm in Ashfield and took care of his parents. He died about 1870. Mrs. Sarah R. died about 1847, and he again m. Mrs. Nancy Davis, and had two sons. Mrs. Nancy Ranney died many years ago in Ashfield. Mr. Charles Ranney's children are all living. Martha, wife of Theodore Wood, lives in Shelburne Falls, Mass.; George in Portland, Mich., unmarried; Thomas and Frederick E., in Belding, Mich.; Fred. E. m. Mary L. Ellis (see page 258).

Hannah Ranney, mother of the writer (751), m. Richard Ellis. She now lives at Belding, Mich., in her 83d year (see page 175).

Erastus Ranney, son of Jesse, left Ashfield when a young man and settled on a farm four miles east of Eaton Rapids, Mich., where he and his wife now live in comfort, with their only son, Charles. Their only daughter, Climena, died in 1887. They are most worthy people, and enjoy the esteem of all in that region of country, where they have lived nearly 60 years.

Amanda Ranney m. Elijah Richmond, and lived for a few years in the north part of Ashfield, about 20 rods north of the Ellis and Phillips fort, where their children were born—Alanson, Diadema and Lucretia. Alanson now lives on a farm near Shelburne Falls. Diadema, now dead, m. Mr. Whiting, and lived in Shelburne Falls many years, where her sister Lucretia, now Mrs. Ware, lives, with her husband and married daughter. Mr. Elijah Richmond was a man of unusual enterprise and capacity. He died about 1850. His widow, Amanda, m. Wilson Elmer, about 1870, and lived in Ashfield, a few rods east of No. 35, where she and Mr. Elmer both died, about 1885.

Edwin Ranney, son of Jesse, was a cooper, lived in Pittstown, N. Y., when a young man, where he m. Eliza Button, a very superior young woman. After a few years they removed to Belding and purchased a farm, one-half mile north of the village, where Mr. Jerome Vincent now lives. Their children were Edwin J., Marcia (m. a Smith), Alvor, Franklin, Loudon, Cora and Charles. Mrs. Eliza Ranney died about 1870. Mr. Edwin Ranney lives most of the time with his son, E. J., on the latter's farm, near Hungerford, Mich. Alvor, Franklin and Loudon are in Colorado, on a ranch near Bear river.

Polly Ranney m. Augustus Frederick Daniels and settled on a farm six miles south of Adrian, Mich., about 1840, where they had three children. Mrs. Polly Daniels died about 1870, and Mr. Daniels married again and still lives on his farm.

Lucretia Ranney m. Darius Cross in Ashfield. They settled on a farm four miles south of Adrian, Mich., about 1840, where they now live, on a large and valuable farm. They have one son, Edwin, and two daughters.

Ruth Ann Ranney, youngest daughter of Jesse, m. Sylvester Woodbridge Hall in Ashfield. They have lived in Greenfield, Mass., many years, as do also their children.]

11. Joseph Ranney, son of George (6), born July, 1777. He died January 15, 1838. Early in life he worked for many years as a stonecutter, at the Chatham quarry, for his uncle. In 1818 he settled in Ashfield, upon the place he bought of his brother Jesse. He m. Sarah Allen. She d. Sept. 9, 1825; m. (second) Feb., 1826, Tempey Eldredge; he m. (third) May 17, 1831, Lucy Selden, widow of Lemuel Eldredge. Mr. Ranney was killed in his wood lot, in Ashfield, by a blow from a falling tree. He was a member of the Episcopal Church.

Children: Clarissa, b. 1803; d. before 1830; unmarried. Harriet, b. Sept., 1805; m. Lyman Williams. Emily, born Dec., 1808; died April 5, 1811. Samuel A., born Sept., 1811; lives in Ashfield; m. Sept., 1836, Flora, dau. of Jesse Selden; had six children. Edward, born Nov. 9, 1814; d. Dec. 15, 1839; m. Nov. 1837; Marvilla Selden, she m. (second) Levi Gardner; no children. Sarah Amelia, born Nov., 1817; m. Levi C. Kingman. Eliza Ann, b. Sept. 9, 1820; m. Samuel Kingman. Sabra, b. Dec. 25, 1828; m. May, 1848, Oscar Richardson; has two children. Clarissa, b. 1832; m. C. Thos. Parker.

12. George, son of George (6), b. May 12, 1789. He succeedod to his father's old homestead in Ashfield, where nearly all his children were born and reared. With his family, in Oct., 1833, he removed to Phelps, N. Y., where he died, Sept. 9, 1842, aged 53 years. In the years 1836-37 he spent about a year on Grand River, Mich., with two of his sons and Col. Hathaway, on a contract which they took for getting lumber down the river to Grand Haven. Mr. Ranney much resembled his father in personal appearance—was short in stature, thick-set, with a compact, vigorous frame. Of a mild and retiring disposition, he was kind, unobtrusive and exemplary in his conduct, and highly respected. Near the close of life he became a professor of the religion of Christ, and died in that faith. He m., Nov. 11, 1811, Achsah, dau. of Paul Sears, of Ashfield. She d. Aug. 7, 1869, aged 80; a woman of unusual worth. She united with the Congregational Church at Ashfield, in 1830.

Children: Alonzo Franklin, b. Sept. 13, 1812. George Lewis, b. Mar. 10, 1815; d. Apr., 1881 at Hillsdale, Mich.; m. Sarah McConnell; had no children. Henry Sears, born Mar. 5, 1817 (15). Lucius, born Apr. 12, 1819; lives at Allen, Mich; farmer; town treasurer; m. Clarissa A. Wilcox. Their daughter, Caroline E., d. Feb. 2, 1858, aged 8 years. Priscilla M., b. Jan. 19, 1822; lives at Allen, Mich.; m. Randolph Densmore. He died in Michigan. Had a dau. that died young. Harrison J., b. Mar. 4, 1824; merchant; lives at Clearwater, Minn.; m. Helen McConnell; has three children, that are married. Lyman A., b. Aug. 1, 1828; d. Mar. 7, 1854, at Van Buren, Ark.; was a merchant's clerk; unmarried. Lemuel S., born Jan. 7. 1831; lives at Hillsdale, Mich; alderman; supervisor, former member of Legislature of Michigan; m., May 24, 1882, Maggie, dau. of Samuel Gilmore; has one son, Samuel Owen. Anson B., b. May 31, 1833; d. Mar. 24, 1886, near Hillsdale, Mich.; farmer; m. Caroline Baggerly; had one son, Everett B.

13. Capt. Roswell Ranney, son of Thomas (7), born Nov. 22, 1782, at Chatham, Conn.; became prominent in public affairs; Captain of Militia twice; twice Representative in Massachusetts Legislature; held various town offices in Ashfield. With special qualifications as a presiding officer, he was often called to serve as moderator in town meetings. He was an enterprising and honorable business man; was a farmer and speculator, dealing largely in peppermint and other essential oils. His sagacity and integrity were crowned with such a degree of success that he accumulated and left a large estate. He succeeded his father in possession of the farm in Ashfield, and in Sept. 1839, removed to Phelps, N. Y., where he died Sept. 7, 1848, aged 66. On his farm in Phelps he had built a large house and barn, both of cobble stone. He m. Feb. 17, 1903, Irvinda, daughter of Dea. John Bement, of Ashfield. She died Apr. 18, 1844.

Children: Horace, b. May 22, 1803. He removed, about 1832, to Phelps, N. Y., and thence to Penfield, where he died. He m. Sept. 24, 1834, Waity Phillips. Had three children. Willis, b. Sept. 24, 1805; became a lawyer; has been for many years a merchant, at Louisville, Ky. He m. Nov. 8, 1837, Sophia A. Leight; has four children. Clarissa, b. Oct. 3, 1807; d. Mar. 15, 1849; m. Sept. 4, 1834, Wait Bement, Esq.; had one daughter. Madison, b. Oct. 9, 1809. He was long connected with railroad business at Framingham, Mass., where he died. He m. Sept. 9, 1840, Adeline M. Cary. Mary, b. Oct.

9, 1814. She m. Apr. 23, 1839, Doctor Milo Wilson. She had three children. Dr. Milo Wilson was a brother of Louisa, who m. Lewis Ellis (see page 177). Dr. W. practiced medicine in Ashfield several years. He lived on the Plain, and about 1850 removed to Shelburne Falls, where he continued in practice until his death, about 1870. He left two children—a son and daughter. The son, Charles, is a physician, practicing in Kansas. His mother lives with him. Amanda, b. Mar. 23, 1817; m. Oct. 7, 1841, Jacob Jenkins. She d. June 14, 1847. Hiram, b. Aug. 7, 1819; m. Jan. 7, 1841, Sarah, dau. of Lucius Smith. He lives in Monroe Co., N. Y.; has three children. Thomas, b. Aug. 7, 1825; was for many years chief clerk in the office of collector of United States revenue, at Boise City, Idaho Territory, where he d., about 1881. He m., Sept. 6, 1848, Cordelia Butler; had a daughter.

14. William Ranney, son of Thomas (7), b. June 30, 1786. He removed from Ashfield in 1823, to Aurelius, N. Y.; from thence, in 1835, to Elbridge, N. Y., where he died Sept. 9, 1857; a farmer. He is represented as having been a leading man, of good judgment, and large influence in the communities where he resided, and was honored with their confidence. He m., Dec.. 1807, Betsey, a daughter of John Alden. She d. May 9, 1870, aged 81.

The Aldens trace their lineage directly back to John Alden, who landed from the Mayflower, on Plymouth Rock, 1620—the same John who asked Miss Priscilla Mullens if she would have Capt. Miles Standish, and she hinted to him to ask for himself, and he knew enough to take the hint. The Aldens have been noted for their great longevity and strong Puritanic religious character, many of them having been clergymen.

Children: Betsey, m. Fernando C. Annable. They removed to Almena, Mich., and died there (see page 96). John, b. 1811; settled at Almena; unmarried. Luke, b. Nov. 8, 1815; is a resident of Elbridge, Onondaga Co., N. Y.; a farmer and surveyor; formerly a teacher; member of State Assembly. A man of sterling qualities; he has frequently been called by his fellow-citizens to positions of honor and trust. He m., May, 1844, Rebecca, daughter of Dea. Cyrus Lyon; they have children. Martha, ——. Mary, m. Edwin Whitney.

When in the legislature of New York, Hon. Luke Ranney's speeches gave him a State reputation as one of the best debaters in the assembly. Mr. Ranney says that the greatest good he ever accomplished for his country was in the organization of the opposition to the increase of the way fare on the New York Central Railroad, and continuing the contest until its final defeat by the veto of Gov. Fenton. By this defeat the way passengers are saved from paying into the treasury of that mammoth corporation from five hundred thousand to one million dollars annually.

He has been extensively employed as a surveyor, and often on disputed lines has harmonized parties and saved litigation. He has had many estates to settle, as executor, administrator and assignee, in Onondaga and Cayuga counties, and in Michigan. He is president of the board of trustees of Munro Collegiate Institute, an institute of learning hardly second to any in the county.

15. Henry Sears Ranney, third son of George (12), was born in Ashfield March 5, 1817. In early life he was a merchant on the Plain, and in Boston for four years. Of all the Ranneys, who were so numerous in Ashfield from

50 to 100 years ago, he is one of the few now remaining there. He has been town clerk for most of the time since 1839, and has been Justice of the Peace since 1851. He has been also twice a member of the State legislature, and one of the most useful as well as noted men in the history of Ashfield. He is thoroughly informed regarding every item of value in the history of the town, from the earliest times to the present, and has aided the writer greatly in compiling this work. For the great amount of time and labor he has thus expended he is entitled to the thanks of every reader of this book. Mr. Ranney married, June 20, 1844, Maria Jane, daughter of Anson Goodwin, of Ashfield. She died Jan. 14, 1855, aged 33 years. He married (second) June 26, 1856, Julia A., daughter of Francis Bassett, Esq., of Ashfield. They reside on the Plain, at 24.

Of Mr. Ranney's four children none are now living. Ralph Henry was born in Ashfield, March 16, 1845; he died in Boston, Oct. 30, 1876. He m., 1868, Rosa Bassett. His children: Clara M. was born Jan. 8, 1869; Raymond R., born July 29, 1871.

Ella L., born in Charlestown, Mass., Sept. 24. 1847; she died in Ashfield, Dec. 21, 1874. She m , Jan. 21, 1869, Albert W. Packard. Her children: Austin G. was born in Brooklyn, N. Y., Jan, 24, 1870; Ella M. born Dec. 15, 1874.

Clara Maria, born Aug. 2, 1851; died Sept. 28, 1855.

George G., born May 22, 1853; died Sept. 8, 1853.

16. Daniel Ranney, son of Francis (8), was born in Springfield, Mass., about 1776. He lived in Ashfield until 1821, when he went to LeRoy, Genesee Co., N. Y. He had four daughters and three sons: Charlotte, who m. Lorrin Havens, of LeRoy; she died leaving several children, one of whom is Mrs. Susan Dodge, of Downer's Grove, Ill. Hezekiah Bartlett Ranney, son of Daniel, b. 1808, d. 1832. Julia, dau. of Daniel, m., about 1836, Asiel Crittenden, of Pavilion, N. Y.; they both died about five years later, leaving one son, Edward, who has since lived with his aunt, at Downer's Grove. Ozias Ranney, son of Daniel, m. Abbie Northrup. He died in LeRoy in 1845, aged 28, leaving one daughter, Marian. Laura Ann, m. Alphens Wilsey, and they now live at Dell Rapids, Dakota. They have one child married and living near them.

Mr. Daniel Ranney died in 1857, in Dupage Co., Ill., being at the time with his daughter, Mrs. Havens. He was aged 86 and very smart for his years.

Joel Ranney, son of Daniel (16), was born in Massachusetts in 1807, d. in 1851. He m. Elizabeth Peck Champlain in 1830. She was a dau. of Isaac and Sarah (Peck) Champlain, who came to West Bloomfield, Ont. Co., N. Y., in 1803. Isaac died in 1815, at 33 years of age, from injuries received in the war of 1812. He was a lineal descendant of Samuel Champlain, a celebrated French naval officer who, in 1609, discovered Lake Champlain, and founded Quebec in 1608, and to whose courage and enterprise France owed much for the establishment of her colony of Canada. Mrs. Elizabeth P. Ranney was born in 1811. They had four children: Hezekiah B., b. 1833, d. at the age of 49. He was a physician, m. Martha Barnett. Elizabeth Jane, b. 1835, m. John Morris, ex-warden of the Michigan prison, at Jackson. Dr. George E., b. at Batavia, N. Y., in 1839, m. in 1861, lives in Lansing, Mich., is a noted physician and surgeon; and John S. Ranney, b. 1842, youngest child of Joel, is a pine land and real estate dealer in Chicago, Ill. Mrs. Joel Ranney now lives with her son, Dr. George E., in Lansing. Dr. Ranney entered the Union army in 1861 as a private soldier, and was soon made hospital steward of the Second Michigan Cavalry. In 1863 he was made assistant surgeon, and soon after brigade surgeon and placed in charge of Corps Hospital of Cavalry of the Division of the Mississippi. Since Feb., 1866, he has practiced in Lansing, Mich., and has acquired a wide celebrity. He is a member of several American and European medical societies, and consulting surgeon for several railroads in this State. Dr. Ranney m. in 1869 Isabella E. Sparrow, d. of the late Bartholomew Sparrow, of "Kellebeq," Enniscarthy, Ireland. They have one son, Ralph S., aged 15; and a dau. Florence, 7 years of age.

Other Ranneys of the same descent as the above are Judge Rufus P., of Cleveland, O.; also three sisters living in Howell, Mich., wives of Dr. Wells, Philo Gay, Esq., and Mr. McPherson, and Hon. Peyton Ranney, of Kalamazoo, Mich.

HON. ELIJAH PAINE.

Conspicuous among the prominent men of the town was Elijah Paine, Esq., a lawyer, who settled in this village near the close of the last century, and spent the remainder of his days here. He was a son of Dr. Elijah Paine, of Hatfield and Williamsburg; was born in Hatfield, Nov. 29, 1760, graduated at Yale in 1790, and died Aug. 3, 1846, aged 85. He m., July 1, 1795, Patty Pomeroy, of Northfield. She d. Jan. 28, 1842, aged 69. Esquire Paine became a man of much usefulness and influence in the community; of sterling character, with dignified bearing, and manners of a gentleman of the old school; a ruffle on his bosom was always a part of his attire. He served as a member of each branch of the legislature; and, on the division of the old county, in 1811, was appointed Chief Justice of the Court of Sessions, and held the office some fifteen years, until it was abolished by law. For his dwelling he built, in 1794, the house where Mrs. Pease now resides, and which, with land adjoining, is yet owned by his grandchildren. For many years he was a deacon of the Congregational Church, and three of his sons—Elijah, William P. and John C.—became clergymen.

His children were: Louisa, born Nov. 21, 1795; Elijah, Dec. 9, 1797; Henry, Mar. 20, 1799; William P., Aug. 1, 1802; Mary, June 15, 1804; John C., Jan. 29, 1806; Lucius H., Jan. 7, 1809; Martha was baptised Oct., 1811, and Frederick baptised Nov., 1815.

THE TAYLORS, SEARS, PARKERS, HALLS AND HOWES.

Dea. Jonathan Taylor, mentioned in several places in these pages, was one of the three brothers settled near each other in the northerly part of Cape street. Jonathan settled about half a mile south of where Harrington Kelley now lives, and built a sawmill near there. He was in town as early as 1769, coming here, with his wife, from Hardwick, although originally from Yarmouth. He and his wife, Thankful, joined the Congregational Church, but, having some trouble with Mr. Sherwin, the minister, he left and joined Elder Smith's church, at Baptist Corner, and he and his descendants were ever after strong supporters of the Baptist denomination. Quite a number of his children went West. His son Jonathan remained on the old place for many years, and was the father of Mrs. Epaphroditus Williams and Miss Sally Taylor, later, wife of Elder Pease.

Isaac and Jasher Taylor came to town later, from Yarmouth; probably in 1771. Isaac settled on the farm where his great grandson, Henry, now lives. He had four sons, of whom Ezekiel and Stephen staid in Ashfield, on the old farm. Ezekiel was the grandfather of Daniel and Henry, now living in town, and Stephen was the father of Ansel, who went to Buckland and left numerous descendants. Isaiah, the third son, settled in the northwest part of the town and was the grandfather of Alvah Taylor, of Buckland. Jeremiah moved to Hawley, and from his family have come a large number of ministers. Jasher, the third original Taylor settler, moved to Buckland. Geo. Taylor, of Buckland, also Wells and Darius, of this town, are his descendants.

Rowland, Jonathan, Paul and Enos Sears were also early settlers in Cape street, Rowland being in town as early as 1772 He and Paul, although only distantly related, bought and worked a tract of land together. They built two frame houses and then cast lots for the occupancy. Rowland drew for the north house, where Mr. Cowan now lives, and Paul about thirty rods south, the house afterwards occupied by the Kelley family. Rowland, when asked how they could live together so peaceably, said that Paul wouldn't quarrel, anyway. They both died in town. Rowland had eight children; of the sons, only Abira staid in town. He lived and died on the old place. Paul had 11 children; and of the daughters Clarissa married Sanford Boice, Achsah m. George Ranney and was the mother of H. S. Ranney, Esq., Betsey m. Ansel Taylor, and Priscilla m. Mr. Pratt, of Buckland. Enos was a brother of Paul, and lived where his grandson, Nathan, lived for many years.

Jonathan Sears settled on the farm where Benjamin Sears now lives, and was his great grandfather. He had Jonathan, Jr., who settled on the old place; Freeman, a minister, located in the east part of the State, and Asarelah, who settled on the south part of the old farm. Other settlers, about the time of the Revolution, were Elisha Parker, grandfather of Marcus, and a Revolutionary soldier; Levi and Eli Eldredge, Abner Kelley, Asa Selden and Samuel Hall.

All the settlers through that street came from Yarmouth, on the Cape; hence, "Cape street." Elisha Parker settled on the hill, about 50 rods south of the schoolhouse; Levi Eldredge, south of Enos Sears, building the house now standing where Levi's son Samuel lived; Abner Kelley settled just opposite him, and Asa Selden 50 rods farther south; Samuel Hall settled about 100 rods south of the Taylor Corners, and was the ancestor of Samuel W. Hall, Atherton, of Savoy, and Daniel and Joshua. Nearly all of these settlers had large families, seventy-five scholars attending the school in that district in the winter. "Cape Street" is in the south part of the town. It was so named because all the settlers who came to that locality and settled, near the close of the last century, were emigrants from Cape Cod. It is simply a school district, nearly all the inhabitants of which are on one road a mile and a half in length.

Mr. Marcus Parker says that the settlers of Cape street came up one year and cleared their land and built their log houses, and the next year brought up their families. While here the first season they boarded a portion of the time at Aaron Fuller's tavern, where Hiram Warren now lives.

Besides the Samuel Hall who settled in Cape street, there were Joseph and Reuben Hall. Joseph came from Yarmouth in 1797, and bought of Jonathan Taylor lot No. 2, 2d division, being the farm where his grandson, A. G. Hall, now lives. He married in Yarmouth Lucy Sears, sister of Jonathan, who married Joseph's sister. Of Joseph's children, Joseph, George and Seth lived and died in Ashfield. The others emigrated to the State of New York. Joseph Hall, of Hartford, Conn., son of Seth, has been for twenty five years principal of the Hartford High School.

David Hall, brother of Samuel, came here previous to 1780, with his son Reuben, and settled about 100 rods west of where Allen Hall now lives. Reuben was an officer on the ship from which the tea was thrown overboard in Boston Harbor. Reuben was the father of Thomas, who left a large posterity in this town, and great grandfather of Dr. G. Stanley Hall, professor in the Johns Hopkin University, of Baltimore, and a noted writer on educational topics.

Of the Howes families there were seven different men by that name who settled and died in town. Kimbal and Zachariah came to town in 1775 or 1776, and settled on land now occupied by Ephraim Williams, Kimbal living where Ephraim now lives, and Zachariah 100 rods farther south. Afterwards Kimbal moved to New Boston, where he died. He was the father of Capt. Kimbal and Barnabas, and grandfather of Barnabas, late author of the two books of Ashfield history before alluded to.

Zachariah moved to Briar Hill, on the farm now occupied by his grandson, Otis Howes. He was also the father of Nathan, and grandfather of Mrs. Moses Cook.

Samuel came to town about the same time and settled on the farm north of Great Pond, now occupied by his great grandson, Charles Richmond. His son Heman married Eliakem Lilly's sister, and the same year Eliakem married Heman's sister. Heman lived and died on the old place, raising a large family, most of which settled in Ashfield and vicinity.

Ezekiel and Mark, sons of "Sailor Thomas," settled a few years later in the northwest part of the town. They both raised large families. David S., son of Ezekiel, now lives on the farm his father occupied, and Henry A., grandson of Mark, now tills the farm his grandfather cleared up.

Dea. Anthony Howes and Joshua, his brother, distant relatives of the other Howes, settled on the hill, about 100 rods south of Mrs. John Field's new house (60 on map), on the old road to South Ashfield. They came previous to 1788. Anthony was the father of the late Frederick Howes, Esq., of Salem (see page 294), also of David, who was the father of Mrs. Wait Bement. Joshua had one son, Joshua, who married a sister of Seth Hall and emigrated to the Mohawk Valley. None of the descendants of Anthony or Joshua are now in town. All these families were descendants of Thomas Howes, of Yarmouth, who, with John Crowell, bought of the Indians, in 1636, what now comprises the towns of Dennis and Yarmouth.

One of the best known and highly respected men of Ashfield at the present time is Frederick G. Howes, Esq. He is a farmer and resides at 26 (see map, page 328), a member of the Massachusetts State Horticultural Society, and a surveyor by profession. An old resident of Ashfield says of him: " I wish you should not fail to know that he has for many years been a leading and

influential citizen here; has had most of the town offices; was for a long time
school teacher; has done valuable and long continued service on school committees; was member of State legislature, and is in service as Justice of the
Peace." Mr. Howes has kindly given much time and labor to preparing
matter for this part of the book.

THE WILLIAMSES.

The following is an extract from an address delivered by Rev. Francis
Williams, of Chaplin, Conn., at the Williams family gathering, in Ashfield,
Sept 4, 1878:

Our grandfather, Ephraim Williams, Esq., was descended on the maternal
side from Capt. Hunt, who had command of a company of men who did such
good service in the early conflicts of the colony, that Ashfield, first called
Huntstown, was granted to that company. His mother was a Hunt, and it
was from his connection with this grant that he came to settle in Huntstown.
He was a skillful surveyor, and his services were called in constant requisition
among the first settlers of the town. He bought out many of the soldiers'
claims and owned more than 1,500 acres, most of which he afterwards gave to
his children. He was for a time reckoned one of the wealthiest men west of
the Connecticut river. He came to Ashfield in 1771, a journey of 120 miles,
on foot, with a hired man, carrying on their backs what tools would be necessary to build a sawmill, and a few necessary pieces of sawed lumber. They
fixed upon a place for the mill where the mill of Darius Williams now stands.
The first night he slept between two hemlock barks, on his great coat, keeping
up his camp-fires as a protection against wild animals; and during the night
the howling wolves appeared near enough for him to see their eyes glisten
from the light of his fire. By the second night they had a cabin built, where
they could sleep with a sense of safety. The millwright, who came from
Easton to do the work, finished the job, and his bill is now in the hands of one
of your number present to-day, and it was $13.33, when computed in our cur-
rency. Wages were really low then, and yet strikes for higher wages were
not even dreamed of. The boards for covering the mill were sawed in it as
soon as they could put it in running order.

When he could establish a home, like a good domestic man, as he was, he
went to Mendon and took his bride elect, Miss Mercy Daniels, who was born
Aug. 7, 1757. They were married Sept. 14, 1775, and set out immediately for
their wilderness home. Both were of good families, but their wedding trip
differed essentially from that of persons in like position in modern times. An
ox wagon was constructed, the wheels from two carts of the same size were
put upon it, two yoke of good stout oxen were yoked to it, some necessary
household furniture loaded on, a seat prepared for the bride, and they left the
old homestead, with many good wishes for their success and happiness in life.
The roads were rough, but the young bridegroom, cartwhip in hand, started
his gentle team with the precious freight, all carefully cared for by joyous,
youthful love. He walked by the side of his team where the roads were rough,
and when they came to the smooth plains she gladly gave him a seat by her
side, and they talked of the new home, anticipated with so much interest.
When hunger told its story—as it will, even to loving couples—the oxen were

fed, the bride set out the frugal lunch from the boxes and baskets, the blessing was asked, and a feast, better than a stalled ox without love, was enjoyed.

When they come within a little more than three miles of their new home, nothing but a bridle path lies before them; they can go no further. At a house on or near the place of the late Mr. Fuller, on the opposite side of the road from the old Williams home, where grandfather died, and where Mr. Orville Hall now resides, she remained for about a week, until her young husband, and kind friends from near and far, could cut through a road for an ox team to pass. Then the young bride, amid the congratulations of most persons in the vicinity, was conveyed to her new home, of which she became the light and joy.

When winter came no corn could be ground nearer than Williamsburg, southeast nine miles. Snow fell to the depth of four feet on the level. He pounded corn in his 5-pail iron kettle, with his mill-bar, and was happy in the thought that he was so conveniently situated, with so good implements for obtaining his meal. Before he went back for his bride he went to what is now New Boston, bought half a steer, bound it upon his saddle before him and started around through the center near by, as there was no bridle path nearer. Night drew on, and the wolves began to call and answer each other. He knew they scented meat and were gathering the pack for pursuit. His horse was good, and anxious, like himself, to reach safety and home. His plan was quickly formed—to hasten as fast as possible, and if they overtook him to cut the cord, drop the side of beef, with which he thought they would be fully occupied until he reached home. But his good steed bore him safely through, and his new bride found the beef in good order for her winter cooking. Others, however, were not so well provided. It was thought the road must be opened to the mill in Williamsburg, and the scattered inhabitants of Ashfield started with their teams and shovels to break out roads. After a few days of earnest work they met, in Goshen, a party from Williamsburg who were breaking through to relieve those they feared were suffering form hunger. That was a joyful meeting for the tired men and teams from Ashfield. They realized the good of having kind neighbors, if they were nine miles from them.

By hunting and fishing the early settlers helped out the winter's provisions. The bears, raccoons, rabbits, partridges, squirrels and other game often made a well filled larder and a cheerful fireside. Grandfather, with his gun and traps, often came from the forest a successful hunter. The home circle was also enlarging, and a numerous family cheered the hearts of father and mother with their joyful, loving greetings.

Grandfather had ten children—nine by his first wife and one by his second. David, born Dec. 6, 1776, died in Ashfield, in the house where we are now assembled, at a good old age. Daniel, b. Mar. 2, 1778, was a most consistent Christian, deacon in the Congregational church, and lived and died on the old homestead of his father, where his son Darius now lives. The old place where grandfather commenced domestic life has always remained in the family, and the sawmill has always been a place of busy activity in the lumber business since this town was a wilderness. Rebecca Mantor, b. Nov. 28, 1779, d. in Hawley in 1807; Abigail Warren, b. May 7, 1781; d. in Conway; Ephraim, b. June 22, 1783; d. while a member of Williams College preparing for the ministry, and his room-mate, Gordon Hall, afterwards a missionary, pronounced his college eulogy. Apollos, b. May 24, 1785, died in Ashfield; Ezra, b. May 21, 1787, d. in Ashfield; Israel (my father), b. Sept. 4, 1789, d. in Geneva, Wis., Oct. 14, 1846, at the age of 57; Moses, b. April 6, 1793, d. at the age of 14; Abel, b. Sept. 26, 1794, son of grandfather's second wife, resided with his father upon the new homestead until after grandfather's death, and some years afterwards sold his place and removed to Windsor, where he died after a few years' residence.

[Feb. 14, 1763, Joseph Belcher of Stoughton, conveyed to Daniel Williams, Esq., of Easton (Ephraim's father), "so much of that share of the common and undivided lands in Huntstown, that belonged to my honored father, Joseph Belcher, as to make up and entitle him to 250 acres;" consideration, £30. Squire Williams bought the place now occupied by Orville Hall in 1793.]

Apollos Williams, who married Hannah Ellis, (see page 101), was a grandson of Daniel Williams, of Easton. Daniel married a Hunt, probably a daughter of Ebenezer, the head petitioner for the grant. Daniel owned lands in different parts of the town. Apollos was a nephew of Ephraim Williams, Esq., and lived on or near the James Ranney place, about 150 rods north of 48.

THE SHEPARDS.

Dea. Isaac Shepard was in Huntstown as early as 1763, and was then 31 years of age. He married Jemima, the fifth child of Chileab Smith, Sr. It is not known that he lived at any other place than 58, on the farm now occupied by Francis R. Phillips, where he is supposed to have settled, and upon which he died. In 1770, by the Springfield records, he bought of John Blackmar lot No. 22, which was the lot adjoining his on the west. Not long after, Isaac's brother, Samuel, settled on this lot. The house upon the lot was already built when Samuel settled there, and is now occupied by Chapin Elmer, a great great grandson of Samuel Elmer, 1st, and Nathan Chapin. The house must be 120 years old, and was probably built by John Blackmer.

Dea. Isaac had Isaac, Jr., who married Jerusha Phillips and moved to Stockton; Stillman, who died on the old place; Jemima, who married Aaron Lyon, Jr., and was the mother of Mary Lyon; Almena, who married Deacon Harris Wight, of Buckland, and Lura, who married Deacon William Putnam, of Buckland. Isaac was chosen deacon in Chileab Smith's church, just after the division in 1788, and continued in the office until his death. He was a man highly esteemed in the town and served on the Board of Selectmen and in other offices. He was buried in the Baptist Corner burial ground, and on his headstone is inscribed:

"In memory of Deacon Isaac Shepard, who departed this life May 13, 1802, aged 69 years.

A husband dear, a father kind,
A pious heart, a patient mind;
He's left all things below in peace,
And gone, we trust, where sorrows cease.
His body rests beneath this bed
Till Gabriel's trump shall raise the dead."

Samuel, with his five children, went to Stockton. Pamelia, his eldest daughter, married Quartus Smith, grandson of Elder Ebenezer. Mr. Smith and his wife celebrated their golden wedding a few years since, and both died soon after. Not many years before their death they visited Ashfield, and were greatly interested in looking over the places familiar to them in their youthful days. They were much affected when they bade a final good bye to the old birth places, and looked upon them, as they said, for the last time. (See page 98.)

THE SMITHS.

Chileab Smith, Sr., moved with his family to Huntstown, from Hadley, in 1750. It is probable that he was there before that time, and held some interest, as he was chosen, at a meeting in Hadley in 1742, a committee, with Richard Ellis and Nathaniel Kellogg, to lay out lots. The next year he was chosen on a committee to "provide and agree with a minister to preach to such as Inhabit at Huntstown." Between this time and 1750 he was on a committee to build the corn mill, and for other purposes. He settled on lot 27, and built his house at the southerly end of the lot, about a dozen rods southeast of the house occupied by his great grandson, the late Ziba Smith.

A history of the Baptist Church in this part of the town is a history of the Smith family at this period, and their peculiar traits of character can be shown no better than by giving extracts from the early records of this church, now in the hands of private parties.

"RECORD OF THE PLANTING, GATHERING AND PROCEEDINGS OF THE BAPTIST CHURCH OF CHRIST IN ASHFIELD:

"In the spring of the year 1753 Chileab Smith moved it to his Neighbors to set up Religious Meetings, which they did, and a Blessing followed; and a Number (in the Judgment of Charity) were brought savingly home to Christ.

"Oct. 25, 1753. A number met to Gather for solemn fasting and prayer, and Chileab Smith and Sarah his wife, Ebenezer Smith, Mary Smith and Jemima Smith entered into a written covenant together to keep up the Worship of God, and to walk up to farther light as they should require it.

"Nov. 29, 1753. Ebenezer Smith, being desired, began to improve among them by way of Doctrine."

At this time Chileab Smith was 45 years old; his son, Ebenezer, just named, 19; the daughter Mary older than Ebenezer, and Jemima younger. The records continue:

"In the years 1754 and 1755 they were Forced to leave the Town for some months, for fear of the Indians.

"1756. They continued in the Town and kept up the Publick Worship of God on the first day of the week continually, Refreshing all that Came to Hear and Attend the Worship with them."

July 2, 1761, they were embodied as a church of ten members, of whom six were members of Mr. Smith's family. Chileab, Enos and Eunice, three more of his children, a short time after united with the church. The records, after giving the formation of the church, articles of faith and the covenant, with a list of those baptised and joining the covenant, continue thus:

"Feb., 1763. The people of another Persuasion settled a Minister in the Town, and obliged the Baptists to pay their proportion of his Settlement and Salary till 1768. Then the Church sent Chileab Smith to the General Court, at Boston, with a petition for Help; but Got None.

"In 1769 the Church made their ease known to the Baptist Association at Warren [Worcester Co.] and Received from them a Letter of Admittance into that Body.

"In April, 1770, the other Society sold 400 acres of the Baptist Lands for the support of their Minister and Meeting-House.

"Under our Oppression we sent eight times to the General Court at Boston for help; but Got None.

"In Oct., 1771, We were set at Liberty by an Order from the King of Great Britain, and our Lands Restored."

Between 1771 and 1785 the records are meager and incomplete, eight pages being missing during this time. The church seems to have flourished and received large accessions under Elder Ebenezer Smith's ministrations. The church on the hill [34 on map] was built during this time, about twenty rods north of Chileab Smith's house.

In the year 1785, with Enos Smith as clerk, the records give a minute account of a difficulty which arose between Elder Ebenezer Smith and his father Chileab, respecting the salary of a minister, the Elder contending that he should have a fixed salary, and his father that ministers should not be hirelings, but should preach for a love of the work, and be content with what the church sees fit to give him. The church and Mr. Chileab Smith's family were divided on the question. Meeting after meeting was held, the advice of neighboring churches sought without avail; the breech grew wider. Finally, (resuming the record):

"Oct. 25, 1786. The Church Concluded that any further Labour with the Elder amongst ourselves would be fruitless, agreed once more to send to sister Churches for help."

The Council, being convened Dec. 27, after hearing both sides, decided:

"That the Elder was justifiable in his conduct; and advised the church, after they had concluded their acts were invalidated, to receive the Elder into his office in the church again, and to let him know that we have made him a Reasonable Compensation for his Labours amongst us, and then to Continue the Relation as Church and Pastor, or Dismiss him in Peace."

"Jan. 24, 1787. The Church considered the Result of the Council before mentioned, and found that it wanted the Testimony of Scripture for its support, by which we desired to be tried; and that if we followed their Result and advice we must leave God's word as to our understandings. Therefore, Voted, That we cannot agree with their Result, for many obvious and Scriptural Reasons, which may be seen at Large in the original Records.

"Aug. 29, 1788. Friday the Church met for solemn fasting and Prayer to Almighty God, it being a dark time with us, we being Despised by men, Elder Smith and his party having taken from us our meeting-house, and we turned out to meet where we could find a place, and the Association, on hearing his story, having dropped us from that body."

But Chileab Smith did not despair. He immediately set about organizing a church again, without the aid of ministers or other churches, and, Jan. 14, 1789, Chileab Smith, Sr., then over 80 years of age, and Enos Smith, his son, were ordained as elders and leaders in the church, and Isaac Shepard and Moses Smith, deacons. They united with Baptists from Buckland and built a church building just opposite where the house of Nelson Drake now stands.

It was a one-story building, with a four-sided, pointed roof. There is good evidence that they built this house in 1789. (It was a little over one mile north of the church then at 34.) The church seemed to gain in numbers, and was by degrees received into fellowship with the other churches. Jan. 23, 1798: Voted to receive back Elder Ebenezer Smith, with such members as are willing to tell their experience. Eighteen members are recorded as received into full communion. Among them were John Alden, Mehitable Ellis [widow of Reuben Ellis], Elisha Smith, Japhet Chapin, Thomas Phillips and Nancy Alden.

Chileab Smith, Sr., died in 1800. Elder Enos Smith continued to preach for many years. He lived up to his belief, charged nothing for preaching, but was supported by voluntary contributions. Erastus Elmer, now 90 years of age, well remembers the neighbors and his father carrying in their gifts. Elder Enos lived on the opposite corner from Nelson Drake's house. Elder Ebenezer lived nearly opposite where Mr. Temple now lives. Both were good men, highly respected by all who knew them. Elder Enos died in his old house, and Elder Ebenezer moved to Stockton, N. Y., in 1816.

One of Elder Enos' daughters married Hiram Richmond. Several of her sons are now living in this vicinity. Nathan Elmer married the other daughter, Julia. Enos' son Calvin moved to Stockton, Emory to Wisconsin; Enos, Jr., died in Tully, N. Y.

Chileab Smith, 2d, died on the old place in 1843, aged 100 years and 7 months. He had two sons, Chileab, 3d, and Jeduthan. Chileab lived where Mr. March now does, and Jeduthan on the old place. When Jeduthan went to Stockton, N. Y., Chileab, 3d, moved to the old place, where he died, leaving Ziba, Elias, Daniel and Russell. Ziba lived with his father, and died on the old place; Elias lived and died on a farm one-third of a mile south; Daniel was deaf and dumb, and Russell went West, to a locality unknown by his relatives here. Chileab, 3d, had six daughters, four of whom married in adjoining towns; Sybil, a Fairbanks, of Adrian, Mich., and Louisa, a Fisk, of Brattleboro, Vt. Elias left no issue. Three of Ziba's children are now living; one son, Houghton, now lives on a portion of the original farm, with three boys and one girl, and these members of Houghton's family are the only descendants of the Chileab Smith family in Ashfield bearing his name.

The houses built by the Chileabs 1st and 2d are torn down; the house built by Jeduthan, and occupied by Chileab, 3d, and Ziba, is deserted. The meeting-house on the hill just above, was taken down and moved 60 rods east, in 1831. Very soon desertions to the Free Will Baptists made havoc in their already enfeebled ranks, and between 1840 and 1850 Millerism and the Second Adventists so diminished their numbers that meetings ceased to be held. The building soon went to ruins, and now a modest schoolhouse stands upon the spot.

Not only the building, but the church itself, which Chileab Smith and his sons planted and gathered with so much labor, has ceased to exist.

The following document was written by Elder Ebenezer Smith the year before his death:

"STOCKTON, CHAUTAUQUA Co., N. Y., May 1st, 1823.

"For the information of 'my children I write the following account of my grandfather's posterity. My grandfather's name was Preserved Smith; his wife, Mary Smith, by whom he had one daughter and six sons. He died when they were all small. His daughter, Mary, and oldest son, Preserved, died young, and were not married; his second son, Ebenezer, married, had a son, Preserved, and a daughter, Hannah; he was killed at raising my Grandfather Moody's house; his son went into the army and died with sickness; his daughter married, had a family, and died in old age. My grandfather's third son, Samuel, married Sarah Morton, and had 12 children. My grandfather's fourth son, Chileab Smith, who was my father, married Sarah Moody, and had 13 children. My grandfather's fifth son, James, married Sara Smith; had only two daughters that lived to grow up. Samuel, Chileab, James, three brothers, all lived to be upwards of 90 years of age, and died one after another—as they were born. My grandfather's sixth son, Moses, died when a child.

"My father's children were Mary, who lived to have a family, and died Aug. 4, 1787; then myself, Ebenezer, then Moses. Sarah, Jemima and Chileab, who are all living; then Enos and Mariam, who died little children; then Mariam and Enos, who are yet living; then a son who died an infant; then a daughter, Eunice, who is yet living. Of my father's twelve children, four sons and four daughters are yet living, April 30, 1823. I am the oldest, in my 80th year. Eunice, the youngest, in her 67th year. My grandmother, Mary Smith, died in 1763, aged 82 years. My mother died on her birthday, Dec. 23, 1789. My father died Aug. 19, 1800, aged 92 years. I married Remember Ellis July 1, 1756, and she died Sept. 15, 1795, aged 60. She was a daughter of Richard Ellis, who was born in Ireland Aug. 16, 1704, and died in Ashfield Oct. 7, 1797, aged 93 years. He came to America at the age of 13 years, and lived in Easton, then moved to Deerfield, then to Huntstown, now Ashfield, in the year 1750. He was the first settler of that town, and cut down the first tree in the town. I married Lucy Shepardson June 14, 1796, and she died Oct. 5, 1808, aged 68. I married Esther Harvey Jan. 4, 1809, and she died Oct. 14, 1814, aged 78, since which time I have lived alone; that is, without any companion, and spent my time chiefly in preaching the Gospel. My children are so scattered about the world that I cannot tell how many there are of them, but, by the best information that I can get, I suppose that there is not much odds of one hundred of my posterity now living. I never expect to see but few of them in this world, but if we may all meet in that world of JOY, how happy it will be; but, oh! how awful the thought that any of my offspring should hear that dreadful sound: Depart! O thou God of grace, display Thy saving power and bring them home to Thyself. And oh, my dear children, my prayer for you is that you might be saved. You must deny yourselves and follow the Lamb, or lie down in sorrow for eternity. "Strait is the gate and narrow the way that leadeth to life, and few there be that find it." Oh, to be born again, and become new creatures in Christ Jesus, is of infinite importance to every one. So I leave this as the token of my regard for my dear children, praying the Lord to bless them all."

P. S.—My son, Ebenezer: I commit this to your care to show to as many of my children and grandchildren as you have opportunity. E. S.

Letter from Dea. Aaron Smith, of Stockton, N. Y., to his second cousin, Dea. Ziba Smith, of Ashfield, dated Mar. 30, 1851. Aaron was a son of Ebenezer, Jr., and grandson of Elder Ebenezer Smith. Ziba was a son of Chileab, 3d, and grandson of Chileab, Jr. The latter was a brother of Elder Ebenezer.

"DEAR COUSIN: I sit down to inform you of our welfare. We are all well as usual. It is a general time of health here. I have had a good deal of sickness in my family since I have begun to keep house. I have had ten children; have buried five of them, all daughters; have three sons and two daughters living; the oldest a daughter of 22, the youngest a son 7 years of age. As to religion, it is quite a low time here. Ziba, I want to see you and your family, and brothers and sisters, very much, once more, in the land of the living. Have not forgotten the comfort taken in your company at school, and at the old Baptist meeting-house, in singing, in our younger days. I want to go to New England, the land of my birth, once more; think some of going this season, if my life is spared and my family are well. The last time I saw you was thirty-one years ago this month, at your father's. I want to go with you once more on to the ground where the old meeting-house used to stand; also to the burying ground; think I could pick out Jeduthan's grave; also our great grandfather's, Chileab Smith's; and the first one who was buried there, who was a sister of your father. My father and mother are quite old and feeble. Father doesn't labor any; his memory is very good for so old a man; he lives with his youngest daughter; he will be 85 next month. My brother Quartus and his wife are well, also Gerry and my sisters. Your cousin, Nathan Smith, and family are all well; his four older sons are great stout giants. your aunt Naomi is well, and lives with Lyman, on the Fox river, in Illinois; he has married his second wife. Your cousin Sawyer Phillips is well; he has sold his farm and gone to Latarany; it is 70 miles from here. His oldest son is a widower; his second son married Asa Ellis' daughter, is a doctor, and lives near his father. Your cousin Hiram Lazelle and family are all well; he pays the highest tax in town—that is $30; he has a dairy of sixty cows, the income of which last season was $1,800. Your cousin Philip Lazelle and family are well. He and Royal Carter are in the mercantile trade; are doing well. Royal's mother is well. Your cousin Alvrary Lazelle is well. I will give you a sketch of the Smith family which we belong to: It is to be traced to Rev. Henry Smith, of Wethersfield, Conn., who came from Old England. All such information is important to be collected for the benefit of our posterity, that the branch of Smiths that we belong to may not be lost. Henry Smith is as far back as I can trace our ancestors.

The first of our ancestors that came from England were Henry Smith and his wife, Dorithy Smith. On his passage to this country he had a son born, and from the unusual circumstances of his birth he called his name Preserved, which is the origin of this name, which has since been retained in several branches of the families of his posterity. The first notice of Henry Smith is on the records of the First Congregational Church in Charlestown, Mass. He and his wife Dorithy were admitted to the full communion of the church the 5th of October, 1637. It is believed he came to America in the year 1637, which was seventeen years after the Plymouth company. He was the first minister of the first Congregational church in Wethersfield, Conn., as near as can be ascertained. He was installed in the spring of 1641, at which time the church was gathered. He died in 1648, and very little is known of his ministry. Dorithy, his widow, married a Mr. Russell, father of Rev. John Russell, who succeeded Henry Smith in the ministry at Wethersfield. Mr. Russell and his son, the minister, went to Hadley with a colony, comprising the larger body of the church, in 1659, and some of Henry Smith's children went with the colony to Hadley and settled there. Rev. Henry Smith was great grandfather to our great grandfather, Chileab Smith. We are the seventh generation from the Rev. Henry Smith The Preserved born on the passage to this country was grandfather to our great grandfather, Chileab Smith. Our great grandfather's father's name was Preserved, jr. Our great grandfather, Chileab Smith, was born in South Hadley, June 1, 1708, and died Aug. 19, 1800, in the 93d year of his age. He left when he died, living, 8 children, 46 grandchildren and 91 great grandchildren; total, 145. He was ordained in the Gospel ministry when he was 80 years of age. He had a family of 12 children. He was one of the first settlers of Huntstown, now Ashfield. He settled in the town in the year 1751. My grandfather, Elder Ebenezer Smith, was born in South Hadley Oct. 4, 1734. He began to preach Nov. 29, 1753; ordained Aug. 20, 1761. He died July 6, 1824, aged 89 years. He had a family of seven children. He was a preacher of the Gospel ministry 72 years, and preached nine thousand and twenty sermons, rode one horse 19 years, and traveled in that time 23,000 miles. Our great aunt, Jemima Shepard, was born in South Hadley March 26, 1740, and died Sept. 29, 1828, aged 88 years. She had a family of seven children. I will give you a sketch of what my grandfather left on record before he died. [See above.] Twelve of our great grandfather Chileab Smith's posterity are and have been ministers; all living but three; two settled in this county, and five of the females married ministers; two of them and their husbands are missionaries, one in China and the other in India. There is not much odds of one hundred and thirty of his posterity living in this county; the sixth generation from him lives in this town, and the tenth from Rev. Henry Smith lives in the county. If you conclude to come here this season, send me a letter the time you are going to start on your journey, that I may not miss of you if I go down, for I want to visit you more than any one in Ashfield. Give my respects to your brothers and sisters, especially to Betsey and her husband. Read this to your brother Elias and your sisters.

Believe me your affectionate relative,

AARON SMITH.

To Dea. Ziba Smith, of Ashfield.

Of Ebenezer Smith, Jr., second son of Elder Ebenezer, and Remember (Ellis) Smith, and his descendants, an acquaintance writes as follows:

"They all lived in my native town of Stockton. Ebenzer, Jr., was a self-educated man, could calculate an eclipse with accuracy. He was a natural mathematician [like his sister Jemima, see page 92], and able to solve any problem, that the inquisitive pedagogue had the inclination to offer. Venerable Doctors of Divinity would visit him, for his opinion on Bible expositions. He was greatly afflicted with rheumatism, for more than twenty of his last years. He was a small man in stature, but very active, never requiring more than four or five hours sleep in the twenty-four. The young and old sought his counsel, as well as to share the richly stored knowledge he possessed. He was a great reader, and it was said he never forgot a thing worth remembering. When he began to converse, he would always say how limited was our knowledge to what the human intellect was capable of, and would speak often of the attainments we should make in the future life. He was thoroughly orthodox and often spoke of the masterly love of God, in the redemption of the world. His daughter, Keziah, tenderly cared for the aged couple. He died in 1855 and was buried in the Cassadaga Cemetery, by the side of his son, Ebenezer, who died a young man, about twenty years previous. See page 96.

"Of his children: Dea. Aaron Smith married Laura Harrison, who was born in Conn., May 29, 1802, and is now living on the old homestead—next to the lands of his father, Ebenezer, which was bought of the Holland Land Company, in 1816. Aaron Smith was a very peculiar man, perfectly unostentatious, possessing a memory of history and events that is rarely equaled; self-sacrificing and willing to deny himself, that he might add to the happiness of others. He, like all the others, was a zealous Baptist of the old type, but it seldom expressed itself in other than noble, honest and benevolent acts. He possessed great fondness for relics and archeological specimens, and his collection of such, and manuscripts, was quite extended. He had in his collection spikes and hinges, from the door of the fort at Deerfield, Mass., where the settlers defended themselves before the Bloody Brook massacre at that place, by the Indians. He was a historian of quite enviable attainments, and often his countenance would brighten in describing events in the reign of the Cesars. He died in 1876, aged upwards of 80 years. He quietly passed away, conscious to the last, cheerfully welcoming the change. He was buried in the old Stockton Cemetery by the side of several of his children. He had ten children; only three of whom are living, two sons and a daughter. The two sons live upon the old homestead and are highly prosperous and worthy citizens. The only daughter living (Pomilla), married August Sornberger, a worthy farmer, and lives in the adjoining town of Charlotte. The sons, (living) names are William, who married Minerva Guest, and they have one child, named Aaron, the other son (living), Aaron Jr., is unmarried and lives with his mother on the farm.

"An older brother, Cyrus, who died soon after the close of the war, was with Sherman in his grand campaign through the South, and was a brave and loyal soldier. He died in Iowa. He left two daughters; one, named Laura, has lived here with her uncle Aaron, Jr., since her father's death, and in December, 1887, was married to Edson Phillips, a son of Wm. W. Phillips. See page 379.

"Quartus, the second son of Ebenezer, married Pomilla Shepard, a daughter of Dea. Samuel Shepard and grand-daughter of Jemima (Smith) Shepard. They had no children. Both lived to be upwards of eighty years of age. They were industrious and frugal in their habits, accumulated a competence and were liberal in charitable objects and strongly attached to the religious faith of their ancestors. As they were childless, the last few years of their lives were spent with her sister Polly, (Mrs. Isaac Miller), and their son, Phineas M. Miller, who gladdened their last years with all the kindness and affection of an own child. Mrs. Smith died January 14, 1885. They were buried in the Stockton Cemetery and the highest granite monument of the ground marks their last resting place.

"Fidelia Smith, dau. of Ebenezer, Jr., married Elijah Woods, who was a native of Keene, N. H. She was a woman who possessed the usual family traits in a marked degree, which rendered her a devoted mother to her children, and a worthy help and aid to her companion in early pioneer life. They had a family of six children, three sons and three daughters; two of the sons died in boyhood The oldest, Fidelia Woods, married Dr. A. P. Phillips, a native of her own town. See page 379. They had three children, Jenny, Burton and Frank Hamilton Phillips. Frank died in 1875, and Jenny in 1878. Burton m. Nellie Baker; had one son, named Frank B., who died in 1882 aged three years. The father had died in 1880.

"Gerry Smith was the fourth of Ebenezer Jr.'s children. He suffered early from physical infirmities. He m. Louisa, daughter of Barzillai Ellis, of Sheriden, Chaut. County, and had a family of six children. Three were soldiers in the Union Army, and two (William and Hiram) sacrificed their lives. Three are now living. Flora, a daughter, married Alson Tambling, a thriving farmer, and resides in Pomfret, where her father was so tenderly cared for and died about 1882. His wife, Louisa, died about 1870.

"Rebecca, dau. of Ebenezer, Jr., married Freeman Richardson. They had eight children, all born in Stockton. They emigrated to North La Crosse, Wis., about 1855. The husband died there, about 1865, and she in 1887. Most of her family are settled in that vicinity. She was a noble woman, partaking freely of the 'Smith' blood, and was a devoted Christian of the Baptist faith."

1. Rev. Henry Smith and his wife, Dorithy, came from England in 1637. (See above). Their children were: Mary, John, Preserved (2), Samuel (3), Dorithy, Joanna, Noah and Elijah.

2. Preserved Smith was born in 1637, on board of ship coming to America. Of his children we have an account of but one, Preserved (4).

3. Samuel Smith, son of Rev. Henry (1), had a large family of children: Samuel, Sarah, Dorithy, Ebenezer, Ichabod, Mary, James and Preserved.

4. Preserved Smith, son of Preserved (2), married and had seven children. He died when his children were young. His wife, Mary, was born in 1681 and died in 1763. Their children were Preserved, Mary, Ebenezer, Samuel, Chileab (5), James and Moses. Preserved, Mary and Moses died young. Ebenezer was killed at the raising of Mr. Moody's barn; he had two children —Preserved, who died in the army, and Hannah, who married and had a family. Samuel m. Sarah Morton and had 12 children. He lived to be over 90 years of age. He settled in Northfield, Mass. James m. Sarah Smith, and lived to be over 90. He had two daughters.

5. Chileab Smith, son of Preserved (4), was born in South Hadley in 1708. He m. Sarah Moody and became the third settler in Ashfield, in 1751. He was, in his time, the most noted man in Ashfield, and was the champion of the Baptists for many years in that town. In 1774 he printed a pamphlet of 18 pages, entitled " An Answer to the many Slanderous Reports Cast on the Baptists at Ashfield, wherein is Shown the First Rise and Growth of the Baptist Church there, together with the Sufferings they Passed Through." This work was in the possession of one of his descendants, Mrs. Rebecca Smith Richardson, of North LaCrosse, Wis. Mr. Smith died in 1800. His children were: Mary, Ebenezer (6), Moses, Sarah, Jemima, Chileab (7), Mariam, Enos (8), Eunice, and three others who died young. Mary m. Nathan Chapin. They lived and died in Ashfield, where some of their posterity are yet to be found. They had seven children. Moses m. Diathena Briggs and had 11 children. He died March, 1828, aged 94 years. Sarah m. three times—Nathaniel Harvey, Israel Standish and Samuel Elmer. She died aged 92. Jemima m. Dea. Isaac Shepard, of Ashfield. She died in Stockton Oct. 29, 1828. Mariam m. Ephraim Jennings and had 5 children. Eunice m. Benjamin Randall.

6. Elder Ebenezer Smith, son of Chileab, Sr. (5), m. Remember Ellis. The last few years of his life was spent with his son, Dea. Ebenezer, Jr., in Stockton, N. Y. He was buried in the cemetery in the village of Delanti—which is in the town of Stockton—by the side of his grandson, Quartus, and his sister, Jemima, widow of Dea. Isaac Shepard. A neat monument marks his grave. For further account of him and his descendants see p. 71.

7. Chileab Smith, Jr., son of Chileab (5), was born in Hadley, Mass., Oct. 16, 1742; died in Ashfield May 25, 1843. He married for his first wife Elizabeth Sawyer, of Montague, and raised three children, two sons (twins) and a daughter—Chileab, 3d (9), Jeduthan (10), and Elizabeth (11). Chileab, Jr. (7), had four wives. He married the last when he was 96 years of age, and it is recorded that "the fifth generation of his posterity were present at the nuptials." His last wife outlived him. Long accustomed to the good old ways, he at first opposed, it is said, the use of stoves and instrumental music in churches. He was a rigid Baptist, a sincere and pious man, and believed in the Divine ordinance of marriage, claiming that, as to his wives, "the Lord provided them," and each time that "the last was the best." Good philosophy, whether based on religious motives or not. He outlived all his children. The writer saw him a year or two before his death. He retained much of his mental and physical vigor to the last. Ashfield produced many aged men, but Chileab Smith, Jr., was noted as the only one who reached the full period of a century.

8. Elder Enos Smith, youngest son of Chileab, Sr. (5), was a Baptist minister over 40 years in Ashfield. He m. Hannah. Drake, of Buckland. He died at 87 years of age. Their children were Zebina, m. Hannah Smith; Calvin, m. Eunice Cobb; Emery, m. a Johnson; Uriah, m. Hatura Smith; Laurilla, m. Ozee Munson;*Enos, m. Cynthia Chapin; Theressa, m. Hiram Richmond, brother of Elijah; Julia m. Nathan Elmer.

9. Chileab Smith, 3d son of Chileab, Jr. (7), was born in Ashfield Aug. 4, 1765; d. 1839. He m. Lydia Briggs. Their children were: *Daniel, Lucy, Betsey, Patty, Huldah, Russell, Sybil, Louisa, Ziba (12), and Elias (13).

10. Jeduthan Smith, twin brother of the above, d. 1835; m. Naomi Bryant. Of their children: Nathan, born Sept. 15, 1788, m. Sally Putnam; Polly died at the age of 56; Benajah, Eunice, Jeremiah, Lydia, Amerancy, Andrew, Ezra, Lyman, Jeduthan, d. aged 19; William d. aged 21.

Jeduthan came to Chaut. Co. in 1816, but afterwards went west, where he died. His son, Nathan, came with him from Ashfield and settled in Cassadaga, N. Y., and had a family as follows: Dexter, now in Stockton; Pliny and Jason in Fredonia; Sidney in Boston, Mass.; Newell and Lydia in Stockton; Naomi, who died in 1847, and Charlotte, who m. Ami Richardson, and has several children in Chaut. Co.

11. Elizabeth Smith, dau. of Chileab (7), m. Philip Phillips, Jr., and moved to Cassadaga, N. Y. (See page 379).

---

*The star indicates that the births of these children were not in the order named.

12. Ziba Smith, son of Chileab, 3d (9), was born April 9, 1797; he lived and died in Ashfield. He was a deacon in the Baptist church. He died June 5, 1881, aged 84; married December, 1821, Rebecca Thayer; she died 1830; married (second) June, 1832, Hannah Holoway; she died July 18, 1887. Their children were: Edward T., born December 26, 1823, died 1851; Lucius F., born May 25, 1826, died 1855; Hassadiah, b. April 17, 1830, m. Austin Drake; Josiah Holoway, b. March 24, 1835, d. about 1870; Lydia M., b. June 6, 1839, m. Drake; has one daughter; Sarah S., b. May 2, 1842, (died), married November, 1873; John L. Newell; had one son; Houghton Z., b. February 22, 1846, (14).

13. Elias Smith, son of Chileab 3d, (9) was born October 10, 1799, died July 4, 1879; married Lydia Holoway. She died July 25, 1875; no children.

14. Houghton Z. Smith, son of Ziba, (12) b. February 22, 1846; is a farmer; resides in Ashfield, and owns the land where his forefather, Chileab Smith, Sr., settled in 1751. His is the only Smith family in that township representing that ancestry. He m. April 20, 1870, Sarah M., dau. of Samuel Howes, and their childen are: Charles Ziba, born April 5, 1871; Anna May, b. September 9, 1872; George Holton, b. February 22, 1877; Frank Holoway, b. September 16, 1878. Mr. Houghton Z. Smith lives at or near 35. See map page 328.

THE BASSETTS.

Toward the close of the last century, among the many immigrants from Cape Cod, were two sons of Capt. Elisha Bassett, of Dennis, Elisha, and Lot.

1. Elisha Bassett, with Susanna, his wife, settled on the farm now owned by Ezra Packard, near the great pond. He was born in 1745; died December 31, 1832. His wife d. July 27, 1831; had four children, Mary, Henry, Abigail and William.

Mary Bassett, born in 1774; died in Ashfield, February 15, 1855. She married Alvan Clark, and had nine children. Her fourth child, Alvan Clark, Jr., was born in Ashfield, March 8, 1804. He was a successful portrait painter, and later became noted and distinguished as an astronomer, and as a manufacturer of telescopes. The one in the Lick Observatory, on Mount Hamilton, California—the largest one in the world—was made by him and his sons. He died at Cambridge, Mass., Aug. 19, 1887, aged 83 years.

Henry Bassett, Esq., born August 9, 1775; died in Ashfield, October 4, 1851; farmer; a respected and honored citizen; was for several years town clerk, selectman, treasurer and member of State Legislature. He married Hannah, dau. of Capt. Philip Phillips. She d. February 7, 1840. See page 381. Their children were: Susanna, born 1801; m. J. F. Upton, no children; George, born April 2, 1803, d. April 11, 1885, unmarried; Mercy, born June 4, 1805, died February 21, 1874; m. Lorenzo Lilly, and had four children; Phillip, born September 19, 1807, d. June 17, 1874; was selectman and member of legislature; m. Sarah Vincent, she d. June 1, 1862; he m. (second) Jerusha S., dau. of Sanford Boice, has one daughter; Henry, born April 22, 1810, lives in Charlemont; m. Hannah Chapman; has children; William, born November 1, 1819, d. November 9, 1869; m. Lucretia Crittenden; no child; Hannah, Anna and Mary Bassett died, unmarried.

Abigail Bassett, born 1782; d. 1867. She m. Barnabas Howes, and had nine children, born in Ashfield. Her son, Barnabas Howes, Jr., has published historical sketches of Ashfield. See page 304.

Capt. William Bassett, born in 1787. An estimable citizen. About the year 1825, settled on the Capt. Philip Phillips' farm, where he d. September 22, 1857. He m. in 1823, Nancy, dau. of John Alden; she died April 8, 1840. He m. (second) November 1841, Lydia Gray. Their children are Wm. F., b. July 11, 1825, and Nancy, b. August 22, 1828.

2. Lot Bassett, (son of Capt. Elisha,) was born in 1755. Settled on a farm, in the Spruce corner district, about 1784; farmer and land surveyor; had served some years in the Revolutionary war. He died July 23, 1835; m. Deborah Howes. She d. June 6. 1846. They had ten children.

William, born December 17, 1782; lived in Hawley, and died there in old age; had two children.

Elisha, Deborah and Mary Bassett died young.

Thomas, born April 10, 1789, d. about 1862; m. Fanny Sears; had nine children; oldest son, Elisha Bassett, born in Ashfield, is a lawyer in Boston, and Clerk of the United States District Court.

Lydia, born February 10, 1794, d. July 7, 1880; m. Lucius Smith, and had seven children.

Francis, born May 4, 1796, in Ashfield; d. May 18, 1876. He m. Mehitabel Ford, and had three sons, who are in business in New York, and six daughters, of whom, Julia A., the eldest, is wife of Henry S. Ranney. See page 391.

Abigail, born May 27, 1799; d. May 5, 1881.

Samuel, born July 26, 1802; d. April 11, 1876. He was member of School Committee many years, and teacher for over twenty terms.

Lot, born March 13, 1805; d. March 15, 1881. Had served as selectman, and justice of the peace. The three last-named remained in possession of the old homestead farm, and were unmarried. The inventory of their estate was nearly $100,000.

EXTRACTS FROM RECORDS OF FIRST BAPTIST CHURCH IN ASHFIELD.

December 24, 1800. At this meeting, after solemn labor with Bro. Elisha Smith* for joining the Freemasons. After choosing a committee to confer with him, and after solemn labor with him, the Church voted that they could not commune with him in his present condition.

May 27, 1801. After considerable labor with Zadok King, for his joining the Methodists. Voted that this Church cannot commune with him. —[Zadok wanted a letter giving Scriptural reasons for their course.]

1803. Elisha Smith wished to be restored to the Church. After much labor with him the matter was postponed to some future opportunity.

June 24, 1818. Voted to give Bro. David Ellis and his wife, Bro. William Ellis and his wife, a letter of recommendation where God in his Providence may cast their lot. [See page 87.]

---

*From Buckland; father of Hoyt Smith.

April 25, 1827. After consulting about the Freemasons, voted that it is a burden to the Church that any of its members should be of that order.

June 18, 1828. At a Church meeting: voted that it is a grief to the Church for any member of the Church to belong to the Freemasons, but, voted that the grief is not so great as to expel a member from the communion; by thirteen members to five against it, including the Elder for one.

At a Church meeting, June 25. Voted again, that it is a grief for any member to belong to the Freemasons. Five members, including the Elder, voted that they have no fellowship with the Freemasons. Voted to put by the communion next Lord's day, by reasons of the difficulty attending those five members as mentioned above.

Lord's day, June 29. By reason of so general attendance of the Church and the materials for the communion provided, the Church voted to reconsider the above vote for putting by the communion. Voted, by a great majority, to attend upon the communion this day.

August 27. Taking into consideration, concerning the Freemasons who belong to the Church, the following was voted:

"Viewing the imperfections of mankind which causes various minds in the Church, we view it reasonable and agreeable to the word of God, that we should use great condescension one towards the other in church discipline, and not hastily expel a member from the Church who thinks different from us, who are the majority. We find that many things creep into the Church hurtful to the minds of some; one in particular concerning the Freemasons, which causes uneasiness for a member to join that order; and, as there is some of that order who are members of our Church, we view it as a duty, as a body, to let it be known throughout the Church, that we think it will be for the union of the Church and for the honor of religion, for those members of the Masonic order not to meet with the lodge, to the grief of their brethren, which if they do, they may expect it will cause a labour if not a discipline with them. And, if any member hereafter should join the Freemasons, knowing that it is a grief to the Church, it should be considered just grounds for the Church to excommunicate them."

NAMES OF SOLDIERS WHO BECAME ENTITLED TO "RIGHTS" OF LAND IN ASHFIELD.

The following list of soldiers, in the Canada expedition in 1690, by sea and by land, is copied verbatim from the manuscript record, that was evidently made by the clerk or some member of the company. His remark that "several dyed" accounts for the remainder of the company.

Capt. Hunt was Colonel in the expedition at Groton, Mass., against Indians in 1706-7, &c. He died at Weymouth in 1713, aged 63. He had twelve children.

The sacrifice of toil and blood, which was the price of the territory of this township, should at least be recognized in the preservation of the names of those by whom it was accomplished. [H. S. R.]

"A list of the trained soldiers under the command of Capt. Ephraim Hunt, Left., Ebenezer White, Ensigne, Nath'l Wales; Sergeants: Ben. Ludin, Henry Prane, Gideon Tirrel, Thomas Fackson; Corporals: Nash, Palmer,

Bailey, Chapin; Soldiers: Richard Phillips, Sam'l King, John Harricks, John Phillips, Clement Briggs, James Otis, Sam'l Dawes, Sam'l Pratt, Richard Davinport, John Whitmarsh, Jacob Leonard, Thomas Hollis, Joseph Gooding, Thomas Bolter, Ephraim Emerson, Moses Guest, Barnabas Douglas, John Miller, Josiah Owen, Samuel Thaire, Ephraim Coupland, Jehosaphat Crabtree, Will Black, William Howard, John Pooll, Isaac Staple, John Staple, Cornelius Campbell, Caleb Littlefield, John China, Samuel Nightingale, Joseph Penniman, Joshua Phillips, William Linfield, Joseph Drake, Ebenezer Owen, Edward Darbie, Nath'l Blancher, Samuel Bass, Joseph Pratt, John Wild, Isaack Thaire, William Drake, William Wells, John Joans.

"Wee arrived in Cape pann, November the 22; Several dyed."

One of the early proprietors of this township—Col. Israel Williams, of Hathfield, an active leader in military affairs—was, in 1746, chosen Proprietor's Clerk, and held the office fourteen years until 1760. Fourteen of the quarto pages of the book of records of doings and proceedings at their meetings, stand written in his clear and firm hand. And doubtless the families of this little border hamlet were to him much indebted for their military protection against the relentless savages during the last Indian wars.

The tradition, that the settlers were absent from their homes here between two and three years* from the date of their flight, June 11, 1755,— the day of the Charlemont massacre—is not confirmed by further investigation, as will appear in the following recital.

In August, 1754:—hostilities with the French having again broken out— Gov. Shirley placed Col. Israel Williams in command of all the forces raised, and to be raised, for the the the defense of Hampshire County.

Col. Williams writes to Shirley, September 12: "It is open war with us, and a dark and distressing scene opening. A merciless and miscreant enemy invading us from every quarter."

On the first scent of blood the border Indians put on the war-paint, and the whole frontier was in danger from their incursions. The neighboring forts were garrisoned, and Corporal Preserved Clapp, of Amherst, was sent with ten men, as a guard, to Huntstown, but there was no fort there. The corporal reports that they "garded the inHabitance until we had a Desmishon from them."

1755. This was a year of great activity, and of disaster in the colonies. On the 9th of July, Gen. Braddock was defeated at Fort Du Quesne, from from which Col. Geo. Washington conducted the retreat.

June 11. Moses Rice and others were killed at Charlemont—and hostilities continued throughout the year.

In March, 1756, garrisons were established in the neighboring forts, and towns. July 1, occurred the notable wedding trip of Ebenezer Smith and Remember Ellis. July 8, Col. Williams stationed a guard to the families there.

The spirit actuating the French commander, in conducting the war, is indicated by the following extract from Montcalm's despatches home, September 22: "I will, as much as lies in my power, keep up small parties to scatter consternation and the miseries of the war throughout the enemy's

---

*Rev. Dr. Shepard; page 280.

country," and with the help of his Indian allies well did he succeed in that purpose.

"The man of thought, and even he of the dullest imagination, can picture the daily life of the pioneer far better from such notes than it can be painted by the readiest pen. The parting each morning—which may be the last—as the husbandman goes forth to sow or reap, that those dependent on him may have bread. A slow death for them by starvation, or the risk of a swift one by the bullet or tomahawk for him, was the only alternative. We picture the slow hours of torturing anxiety to the wife and mother, 'til night brought the loved ones home."

During this year, many were the alarms, conflicts, deaths and captivities suffered throughout the valley and the colonies.

1757. This spring the various garrisons were renewed; that at Huntstown with nine men, under Sergt. Ebenezer Belding, and for a portion of the time, under Sergt. Allen. There was an active campaign during the season, throughout the colonies. The British arms suffered general disaster, and the greatest was the surrender of Fort Wm. Henry, on Lake George, which occurred August 9, with loss of great numbers of men and munitions of war. The season closed with a great degree of gloom among the colonists.

1758. This year opened with improved prospects regarding the war, in consequence of the accession of the able and intrepid William Pitt to the head of affairs in the British government, and the campaign was conducted with much greater success.

Colerain was twice invaded by Indians, by whom one or two of its inhabitants were killed, and several taken prisoners. Huntstown was this year garrisoned by Sergt. Moses Wright with nine men.

The enemy suffered many repulses, which paved the way to the reduction of Quebec in the following year, and soon after to the conquest of Canada, and the final close of all Indian hostilities in New England.

The so-called "bars fight" occurred on the Deerfield Meadows, June 25, 1746. Several persons while haying there were attacked by a large party of Indians, and made a stubborn defence with their guns, which they had taken along. Five of the men were killed, a few escaped, and some were taken prisoners; among the latter was the boy, Samuel Allen, who was for three years held a captive in Canada. He and John Sadler, who escaped, were afterwards among the most honored citizens of Ashfield.

The following, residents of Huntstown, or who afterwards became such, were active participants in those old French and Indian wars: Richard Ellis, Lieut. John Ellis, Reuben Ellis, Moses Nims, Asabel Amsden, Dea. John Bement, Robert Gray, Nathan Frary, Joseph Mitchell, Samuel Belding and Jonathan Lillie.

In March, 1758, the Indians attacked and wounded John Morrison and John Henry, burnt a barn, and killed several cattle, in Coleraine. On the 21st of March, 1759, Indians again appeared in Coleraine, and captured John McCown and his wife, and the latter was murdered on the second day's march.

The population of Ashfield increased rapidly upon cessation of hostilities. In 1776 it was 628, in 1790 it was 1,460, and in the year 1810 it had risen to the number of 1809, the largest census it has had. The homes of the original proprietors were near Boston, but by removals and sales of rights, by the time this town was settled, many persons in Hadley, Deerfield, and vicinity held titles in the township lands.

The first recorded meeting of the proprietors of Huntstown was held at Weymouth, March 13, 1738, when Capt. John Phillips was chosen moderator, and a Clerk and Treasurer were also chosen. Measures were taken to have the granted lands surveyed, divided, and settlements thereon made, and ways constructed. A committee for that purpose was appointed, consisting of Capt. Phillips, Capt. Cushing, and three others. Their report was made in the month of July, 1739, at a meeting held in Braintree, and the first division of lands there made Capt. John Phillips drew lot No. 6 for himself. He drew No. 13 for Richard Phillips, and Joshua Phillips drew No. 56 for himself. The Proprietors' Records are in my possession and in pretty good condition. The manuscript covers over two hundred large pages, made by successive clerks, of good intelligence and capacity. At the time of their services as soldiers, Capt. Hunt and his men were residents of Weymouth, Braintree, Stoughton and Easton, towns situated near Boston, and contiguous to each other.   H. S. R.

THE ELLISES OF GREAT BRITAIN.

The name of ELLIS is common in English literature for several centuries past. In early times it was written in various ways thus: Allis, Allice, Elis, Ellis, Elles, Elys, Ellys, Ellice, &c. In our branch in this country, so far as I can learn, it has uniformly been written *Ellis* by themselves, but in several old letters written a century and more ago, and addressed to Richard and John Ellis by others, they were sometimes addressed as Elis, Allis and Allice.

Wm. Smith Ellis, an attorney, of London, England, has given much attention to the origin of the Ellis families of Great Britain from the earliest times. His investigations extended over many years, and have been published under the title of "Notices of the Ellises of England, Ireland and Scotland."

The earliest date at which the name is found is A. D. 815, in Wales, where Griffin, a brother of the Ellises, was slain. In 843, Roderick the Great, King of Wales, had a grandson named Elis, who, it is thought, was the progenitor of the numerous family of Ellises in that country.*

A descendant of Roderick, by name of Gwynedd, who was king of North Wales in the twelfth century, is said to have been the progenitor of the Ellises of that section. The name of Ellis in Wales during several centuries was not common, at least the record of the same is very imperfect, down to the beginning of the seventeenth century. Since that time, as I am informed, there have been many of them there. Of these it is probable that most of the early representatives came from England.

Rev. John Ellis was born in Wales, in 1638. He was an Episcopal minister in Dublin, where he died.

Rev. James Ellis, rector of Lelanduroy, died about 1596.

Anthony Ellis died in Wales about 1763.

In the later generations of Ellises, in Wales, the names of Richard, Edward, John and Benjamin are common.

---

*In the tenth century the Christian names of the fathers were taken by the sons as surnames.

Wm. Smith Ellis estimates that there are about 40,000 Ellises in Great Britain, of which about 2,500 are in Wales. His "Notices" contains the names of probably 5,000 altogether, but a careful inspection does not enable the writer to trace Richard Ellis, of Ashfield, Mass., back to any definite family there. In Alrey, Wern and Pickhill there are Ellis families of great antiquity. Common names among them were: Richard, John, David, Ralph, Edward and Thomas.

Hugh, Thomas, Richard, Andrew and Edward Ellis lived in Northope, Wales, from 1580 to 1724.

Richard, David (a clergyman), Owen, and other Ellises, lived in Bodychan, Wales from 1649 to 1788.

At Overleigh, Wales, was a large family of Ellises, extending from 1500 to 1689. There were one or more in each generation named Matthew.

In 1884, John Ellis lived at Machynlleth, Wales, and Richard Ellis resides there now. The latter is a grocer and in commercial business. His father, John, was born in 1806 and is yet a strong and hearty man. Evan, a brother of John, is now over 80 years of age. The father of these aged men was Richard Ellis, and his father was Evan, who lived in 1720, and his grandfather Rees Ellis, who was born previous to 1700. This branch of Ellises was from Talyllyn and Mallwyd, in the County of Montgomery, Wales, in early times. Rees had seven sons and two daughters. Two of his sons went abroad and never returned.

In 1683 to 1711, Edward, George, James, Ralph, Matthew, and other Ellises, are found in Yorkshire, in 1689.

In Leinstead, England, John Ellis and Mary Venns were married in 1673. Also William Ellis in 1683. Peter and Elizabeth Ellis lived at the same place in 1694.

In 1689, John and Mary Ellis lived in Boughton, England.

William and Stephen Ellis lived at Lydd in 1449.

John Ellis and Mary Palmer were married in Wadhurst, England, in 1685.

Benjamin Ellis was a churchwarden in Lewes, England, in 1720.

In 1697, Thomas Ellis and Mary Ayres were married in Chailley.

In 1689, John Ellis and Mary Culpepper were married in Wadhurst.

In 1727, James Agar, son of Henry, married Lucia Martin, and their only surviving son, Henry Welbore Agar, assumed the name of Ellis, since which time that family have retained the name of Ellis.

Benjamin Ellis, of Somerset, died in 1758. His son, John, born 1754, died in 1803. The latter's son, Benjamin, born 1784, died in 1844; leaving seven sons: Octavius, Septimus, George, Gerard, Henry, William and Benjamin.

In 1734, John, Anthony and Richard Ellis lived in Sussex, England. Richard Ellis and Elizabeth Young were married in Leeds, England, in 1663.

Henry and Annie Ellis lived in Lydd, England, in 1701.

In 1701, Edward Ellis and Elizabeth Gawen were married in Otham. John Ellis, Jr., and Elizabeth, his wife, lived in Otham.

THE ELLISES OF IRELAND.

Thomas Ellis was Dean of Kildare in 1508.   He had one son, Alson.

John Ellis, of Londonderry, died in 1754, leaving a son, Joseph.

Robert Ellis, of Dublin, died in 1746.

Thomas Elllis died in Cavan in 1758.   He had two sons, Thomas and Humphrey.

Henry Ellis was sheriff of Galway in 1731.

William Ellis was a scholar in Trinity College, Dublin, in 1711, and Edward Ellis also, in 1713.

Thomas Ellis, of Athlone, made his will in 1637.   He was from Wales. He mentions his son, Thomas, Jr., and his brothers, Hugh, Robert, Oliver and Richard.

Richard Ellis, of Ireland, about 1750, was ancestor of Richard Ellis, M. D., of Newcastle-on-Tyne in 1867.

THE ELLISES OF ENGLAND.

Thomas, Simon and Adam Ellis are mentioned as early as 1270 to 1300, in Yorkshire.

John, Ralph and Richard Ellis are found there in 1480.

Rev. John Ellis died there in 1493.

Richard Ellis was married there in 1640.

Matthew Ellis was sheriff in that county in 1787.

An old and numerous family of Ellises lived at Kiddall Hall, in Yorkshire county.   Sir John Elys, of Kiddall, died in 1398.   Robert Elys was his heir. Successive members of this family were: Thomas, Henry and William Elys. Then followed Richard Ellys, Rev. John Ellis and Welbore Ellis, who was a Bishop in the Episcopal church in 1705.   The latter had a son, Welbore, who married Anne Stanley, and they had a daughter, Anna Ellis, born 1707.

Wm. Smith Ellis, in the last number of his "Notices of the Ellises of Great Britain," issued in 1881, states that the Ellis family of Kiddall endured upwards of five centuries, and the Ellises of Stoneacre nearly four centuries. His inquiries have been widely extended and he arrives at the consoling conclusion, "that many of the Ellises of the present day may feel that—

> They are not of those whose ignoble blood
> Has crept through scoundrels ever since the flood."

OTHER ELLISES.

The name of Ellis is at this day common in England, Ireland and Wales. The first mention of this family that the writer finds is at Kiddall Hall, in the West Riding of Yorkshire, England, and it dates back to the time of the Norman Conquest, (A. D., 1055).   In 1503, John Ellis was sheriff of Yorkshire.   One of this family, Sir Thomas Ellis, was six times mayor of Doncaster.   He died in 1562.

In 1617, Bernard Ellis, Esq., was recorder of York, and in 1709 William Ellis, Esq., was high-sheriff of Yorkshire.

In 1606, John Ellis was born at Kiddall Hall. He became an Episcopal clergyman. He had six sons, one of whom, John, born 1645, was collector of revenue for King James second, in Dublin Ireland, during the years 1686, 7 and 8. His brother, Phillip, known at Westminister School as "Jolly Phil," was when a boy kidnapped, it was said, by the Jesuits, while in school, and became a priest. In the "Gentlemen's Magazine," for 1769, is an article, headed "Anecdotes of the Ellis Family," in which the writer says: "that about the year 1730, there lived in Piccadilly a Mr. Ellis, [the above-named John Ellis born 1645 and died in 1738] the history of whose family, as related by himself, is very remarkable. Of his brother Philip, of whom he had not heard for many years, he says: that being in a coffee-house one day, he overheard an officer, who had been in Flanders, mention the great civilities he had received there from a catholic priest, who was commonly known as 'Jolly Phil.' This excited Mr. Ellis' curiosity, and, on further inquiry, he was induced to write to the Bishop of Flanders, when he soon found that the priest was his brother, Philip Ellis. He invited him over to England, where he remained for some time, and was Confessor and in high favor with James second, until the Revolution of 1688, when King James was overthrown, and the penal laws against Catholics being strictly enforced he went to Rome, where he was made a bishop."

Welbore Ellis (Episcopal) was Bishop of Meath. He died in 1734. None of these brothers left children, and the family is believed to be extinct, unless Samuel, who was Marshall of the King's Bench in 1688, or Charles, who became a clergyman, left children.

OTHER ELLISES WHO WERE EARLY IN MASSACHUSETTS.

The first Ellis of whom we find mention in Massachusetts was Dr. Edward Ellis, a native of Wales. The year of his arrival is not given, but in 1652 he married Sarah Blott, a daughter of Robert and Susan Blott, of Boston. Dr. Edward Ellis lived on the corner of Winder and Washington streets. He died 1695, aged 74; his wife in 1711. They had ten children: Sarah, born 1654; Anna, 1658, died 1678; Lydia, 1661; Edward, 1663; Mary, 1666; Lydia, 1669; Robert, 1671; James, 1674.

In the settlement of this country, Ellis is a name early found among the pioneers. Soon after the first landing of pilgrims, John Ellis located in Barnstable county, Massachusetts, and his descendants were very numerous in the seventeenth and eighteenth centuries. About 1690, Samuel, John and Ebenezer Ellis, three brothers, came to Boston from Chester, England.

Samuel settled in Dedham, Massachusetts, and had four sons: John, Samuel, Noah and Ebenezer. Dr. L. S. Ellis, of Manistee, Michigan, is a descendant of Samuel, Jr. Dr. Edward Ellis, of Meadville, Pennsylvania, 82 years of age and in the active practice of his profession, is a son of Ebenezer. This Ebenezer, about one hundred years ago, had an interview with Richard Ellis, of Ashfield, but they could trace no relationship. Doctors Rufus, George, and Calvin Ellis, noted men in Boston and Cambridge are descendants of the Ellises of Dedham.

According to the records of Middleborough, Plymouth county, Massachusetts, Joel Ellis and Elizabeth, his wife, lived in that town in 1716. Their children were: Samuel, Matthias, Rebecca, Charles and Thomas. Of these: Matthias, born 1720, had ten children: Joseph, George, Cornelius, Ebenezer, Gamaliel, Daniel, etc. Ebenezer married Hannah Wood in 1777 and they had ten children, Zephaniah, Daniel, Orren, Cyrus, Ebenezer, Jr., etc. Ebenezer, Jr., born in 1797, married Mary D. Wheeler and they had four children, two sons, James H. and Wm. W. Ellis, etc. The last was born in 1838, and now resides in Detroit, Michigan.

About 1700, an Ellis family from Wales settled in Montgomery county, Pennsylvania, and a numerous posterity are found in that and in adjoining counties now. Mrs. W. H. Holstein, of Bridgeport, Pennsylvania, and J. Alder Ellis, of Chicago, Illinois, are of that family.

About the time of the Revolution, Barzillai Ellis and two brothers came from England and settled in Massachusetts. Barzillai removed to Conway, Massachusetts, and afterwards to Chautauqua county, New York, where he died about 1830. He had seven sons, all now dead, but they have numerous descendants in western New York. Dr. David E. Ellis of Belvidere, Illinois, and Dr. Samuel G. Ellis, of Syracuse, New York, now 72 years of age, are grandsons of Barzillai Ellis.

Early in the history of the colonies, John, Amos and William Ellis came from Wales to this country; it is said that they were shoe and leather dealers. John settled at Boston, Amos in Quebec, and William in Jamestown, Virginia. Rev. Dr. F. M. Ellis, now of Tremont Temple, Boston, is a descendant of William, who settled in Virginia. It is probable that this last is the family which it was intended Richard Ellis, of Ashfield, should find, when he emigrated to this country, an orphan boy, in 1717. See page 9.

Thomas Ellis came from England soon after the landing of the pilgrims. He settled in Medfield, Massachusetts. His son, Samuel, had two sons, named Samuel and Timothy. The latter, Timothy, settled in Medway in 1725. His son, Oliver, lived on the homestead, where he died in 1848, aged 81 years. His son, Simeon, died there in 1872, aged 83 years. The latter's son, Chester Ellis, now lives in Medway, and Chester's sister, Mrs. Mary Ellis Jones, in Milford, Massachusetts.

Judge Caleb Ellis, born at Walpole, Massachusetts, 1767, died 1816; graduated at Harvard 1793, and practiced law at Claremont, New Hampshire, was in Congress in 1804.

Rev. Rufus Ellis was ordained in Northhampton, Massachusetts, in 1843, where he preached ten years, afterwards in Boston.

In 1762, Mercy Ellis, of Plymouth, married John Bartlett, and had Ellis in 1770, who m. Anna Bartlett in 1796, and had Ellis, born 1817, who m. Sophia Ashmead, of Philadelphia, and had Wm. Ashmead Ellis Bartlett, in 1846, who married Baroness Burdett Coutts, of England.

In the town of Orange, Franklin county, in 1791, the town was divided into five school districts or wards. In ward five were the names of John, Nathan, Moses and Seth Ellis.

Rev. Harmon Ellis preached to the Baptist church in Hancock, Berkshire county, Massachusetts, in 1849.

Rev. Robert F. Ellis, Baptist, preached in Chicope, Hampden county, Massachusetts, in 1845.

Rev. Geo. E. Ellis, of Boston, is author of "Massachusetts and its Early History."

Dr. Ellis was a physician in Ludlow Massachusetts, many years ago.

Children of Jonathan Ellis, of Vermout: Hiram Ellis, born about 1800, now dead; Loren Ellis lives in Ohio; Thomas Ellis, dead; Daniel Ellis, born 1806, died in Rawsonville, Michigan, in 1871; Elijah Ellis lives in Cleveland, Ohio; David Ellis, dead; lived in Ypsilanti, Michigan; John Ellis, born about 1812, now dead; and Mary Ellis.

Daniel was father of Hon. Myron H. Ellis, aged 45, of New Boston, Michigan, late member of the Michigan Legislature.

Mrs. J. S. Jenness, of Ypsilanti, is a daughter of Elijah Ellis, of Cleveland.

Barzillai Ellis lived in Conway, Massachusetts, next town east of Ashfield, a century ago. He removed with his large family to Chautauqua county, New York, where he died in 1827. His children were: Barzillai, Jr., died 1854; Asa, d. 1857; Freeman, d. 1842; Benjamin, d. 1855; Joel, d. 1852; Elnathan, d. 1854; Samuel, d. 1856, in Chicago.

Barzillai Ellis, Jr.'s children: Louisa, m. Gerry Smith; Samuel, was a physician in Syracuse, New York; David, a physician in Belvidere, near Chicago, and Elisha.

Asa Ellis' children: Mary, m. Williston Phillips; Asa, Jr.; Levi; Clarissa, m. a Goulding; Lucy, m. a Bailey; Franklin, m. a Smith; and Sally, m. a Crawford.

Freeman Ellis' children: Barzillai, Freeman, Lyman, Lucius, Livenus, lives at Laoni, New York; Lewis, Polly, Lydia and Rachel.

Benjamin Ellis' children: Permelia, Eleanor, Jane, Sophia, Mason, Datus, Joel and Ensign.

Asa Ellis, born 1804, in Smyrna, Chenango county, New York, now lives in DeRuyter, New York. His father, Joel, was born in Conway, Massachusetts, in 1775. Joel was a son of Barzillai and Sarah (Tobey) Ellis. Barzilliai was born June 9, 1747, and his wife June 5, 1755; married March 6, 1773. This family lived in Conway, Massachusetts, and later in Chautauqua Co., New York. Joel Ellis died in Madison Co., New York, about 1852.

Thomas, Samuel and Timothy Ellis lived in Medway, Massachusetts, in the middle and later part of the last century. Chester Ellis died there in 1872, aged 83 years. His father, Oliver, died there in 1848 aged 81 years. He was a son of Timothy, Jr., son of Samuel, and great grandson of Thomas. All the Ellises are now gone from that town, except Chester Ellis. John and Caleb Ellis, aged men, now live in Medfield, Massachusetts. Mrs. Mary Ellis Jones, sister of Chester Ellis, now lives at Milford, Massachusetts.

John W. Ellis, a leading capitalist and banker of New York city, resides at 20 W. 57th street. His wife is a lady of unusual intelligence. She has given much attention to the genealogy of some of the New England Ellises, as well of those of Great Britian, and has favored the writer with several volumes mentioning these families. Mr. Ellis is a lineal descendant of John Ellis, Jr., who m. Elizabeth Freeman in 1644. He was a surveyor in Sandwich, Barnstable county, Massachusetts. Their children were: Bennet,

Mordecai, Joel, Matthias, and John, Jr. Mordecai, born 1650, m. 1671, d. 1715. His children were: John, Samuel, Josiah, William, Mordecai, Jr., Benjamin, Sarah, Eleanor, Mary and Rebecca. Josiah m., 1712, Sarah Blackwell; children: Josiah, Jr., Deborah, Stephen, Elizabeth, Benjamin, Philip, Micah and Sarah. Benjamin, son of Josiah, born 1721, d. 1806, m. Elizabeth Tupper in 1745. Their children: Susan, born 1746; Philip, 1750; Sally, 1752; Micah, 1754, Mordecai, 1759; Jesse, Elizabeth and Polly. Philip, b. 1750, m. an Alden; Micah, b. 1754, m. Mary T. Copeland in 1780; she was b. 1762 and died 1812. Their children: Tryphena, b. 1781; Benjamin, b. 1786; d. in Brooklyn, New York, 1862; m. Sallie Tweed in Ohio, February, 1815; she died in 1826. Their children: Mary, b. December, 1815; John Washington, b. August 15, 1817, and Townsend, 1821. Mr. John W. Ellis has one son, Ralph N., b. March 12, 1858.

Henry D. Ellis, of Cambridge, Massachusetts, has devoted 'much time and labor to collecting Ellis genealogies. He is of the Alden-Ellises, a grandson of Josiah, above. It is hoped that he will have his researches in the Ellis' genealogy published.

John French Ellis, of the Stoneacre family of Ellises, was born in England in 1776; came to America in 1795; m. Maria, dau. of Wm. Willcocks, field officer in the Continental army. He had four sons: William, d. in infancy; Henry A., d. unmarried; John French, d., leaving no male issue; and Samuel Corp. The latter m. Elizabeth, dau. of Aug. C. Van Horn and Margaret Livingston, of the Livingston Manor, and had five sons: Gen. Aug. V. H. Ellis, who died without issue; John Stoneacre, having one son; Col. Henry A., of the U. S. Army, died without male issue; Maj. Julius Livingston, died unmarried; and Samuel Claudius Ellis, unmarried. The latter lives at 121 Madison Avenue, New York city.

Their were several Ellises in Dedham, Massachusetts; settled as early as 1643. Richard Ellis, a fine penman, whose signature is on record. Also a John Ellis, at about the same date, lived near Richard, could not write—makes his "mark" when signing documents. R. Ellis married Elizabeth French, 1650; he was born 1621, or 2. She was also born in England. John Ellis, of Dedham, married, in 1641, Susan Lombard or Lambart.

Ann Ellis, of Dedham, married Edwin Colver, 1638.

An early settler of Salem was named Thos. Ellis. Another was Christopher Ellis.

Mary Ellis, of Boston, Massachusetts, nearly related to Edward Giblons, who married Samuel Scarlett, in the town of Kersey, County Suffold, England, previous to 1657.

Freeman Ellis' will, St. James Clerkenwell, proved at Doctor's Commons, October 2, 1664.

E. R. Ellis, a young man, with his brother, Richard A., and another brother, a sister and mother, have recently located 2,000 acres of land on Big Sandy creek, about twelve miles north-east of Lamar, Bent county, Colorado. They were from Georgia. Wm. A. Ellis, (455) late of Ashtabula, Ohio, has settled on a farm near these Ellises.

William J. Ellis, born in Wales, 1837, now lives in Auburn, New York.

There are many Ellises along the Ohio river, of Welsh stock. Ellis Ellis came to this country about the middle of the last century. His son, William, left the homestead, near Hagerstown, Maryland, and went to Kentucky.

William Ellis had three sons: Elias, Amos and Isaac, who were then young men—Elias having a wife and two children. Slavery was repugnant to the family, and as soon as it was safe to risk the Indians, they crossed from Maysville, Kentucky, to Ohio. William and his sons, Amos and Isaac, settling in 1795, in Brown county, and Elias, in Muskingum county. There was another large family, also of Welsh descent, who settled in Adams and Brown, about the same time; and still another who settled in the river counties, on the Kentucky side of the Ohio. The family names were: Abram, James, John, Nathan, Samuel, Noah, etc. Col. Elias Ellis, who for many years represented Muskingum county, and Amos Ellis, of Woodford county, Illinois, are the only living children of the pioneers, and they are now very old men.

Mr. E. C. Ellis, grandson of Isaac, above, lives at Elliston Station, Ohio, on the C., H. & D. Railroad. The place was named for John W. Ellis, Esq., of New York City, a Vice-President of the road.

Orville N. Ellis, of Kankakee, Illinois, and Anderson N. Ellis, of Hamilton, Ohio, are both physicians of note.

Seth Ellis, a farmer of prominence, residing near Springboro, Warren county, Ohio. He was for four years Master of the State Grange of Ohio, and is something of a local preacher in the M. E. Church.

A few years ago, there was also a family of the name living at Cedarville, Green county, Ohio, who were Methodists. One or two of the young men became preachers.

There was a John Ellis, a preacher in the Christian Church, who resided several years in Dayton, Ohio. He was a New Yorker—now preaching in California.

There is an Ellis family in Cincinnati, from Massachusetts. They are mostly bankers, and Unitarians in religion.

W. R. Ellis, Esq., is a prominent lawyer at Heppner, Oregon. His father, James, born in Kentucky, about 1823, died in Montgomery county, Indiana, 1851. His grandfather, Thomas, lived near Shelbyville, Kentucky, and was formerly from Virginia. H. C. Ellis, son of Thomas, lives at Rossville, Illinois.

Mr. W. D. Ellis, inventor of an automatic gate, lives at Blaine, Illinois. His father, William, was born in Yorkshire, England, in 1812, and a brother, James, lives at Marinette, Wisconsin. Jackson Ellis lives in Beloit, Wisconsin, and a Dr. Ellis at Rockport, Illinois.

Gideon Ellis, born in Massachusetts, died in Randolph, Vermont, about fifty years ago, aged nearly 100 years. His children were: Calvin, Elijah, Josiah, Bethuel, Asa and Gideon. The last-named died in 1861, aged 90 years; had nine children. H. G. Ellis, of Roxbury, Vermont, and B. W. Ellis, a lawyer, of Chicago, are his grandsons.

Rev. Luther Ellis is an aged clergyman, of Waterloo, Iowa.

James Fulton Ellis lives at Marinette, Wisconsin. He has brothers, William A., at Peshtigo; Robert and Oakman A., at Oconto; and Charles J., at Marinette. Their father, William, was a son of Rev. Jonathan Ellis, born in Franklin, Connecticut, 1762; m. Mary, dau. of Robert Fulton, of Topsham, Maine. She died in 1860, aged 91 years. Jonathan was a son of Rev. John Ellis, born in Cambridge, Massachusetts, in 1727—Chaplain in the Revolutionary army—died at Norwich, Connecticut, 1805. He was a son of Caleb Ellis, who came from England, and lived in Cambridge, Massachusetts.

Samuel Ellis was an early settler in Dedham, Massachusetts. His children were John, Noah, Ebenezer and Amelia. He went to Norwich, Hampshire Co., Mass., in early times, and where he died about 1825, a very aged man. He had three brothers, two of whom died in the French and Indian war. His son, Ebenezer, lived in Chester and Norwich, Massachusetts, where his children, Samuel, Edward, Hylas, Ebenezer H., Harriet and Christa, were born. Samuel, born in 1802, died in Cummington, Mass., In 1875. Dr. Edward Ellis, of Meadville, Pennsylvania, born 1804, d. 1886, was the second son of Ebenezer. Samuel, born 1802, was the father of Dr. L. Stiles Ellis, of Manistee, Michigan, and Miss Elvira Ruth Ellis, of 324 E. 27th st., New York City. Miss Ellis is a noted teacher. Dr. E., of Manistee, is a prominent physician and widely noted temperance advocate.

Moses Ellis, born about 1766, came to East Barnard, Vermont, from Walpole, Massachusetts. His brothers were: Joseph, Daniel, Aaron and Jesse. Moses had two sons, Clark and Enoch. Clark was born 1795, died 1862. Enoch, born 1804, died 1879, leaving four sons. Joel C., only son of Clark, was born 1816 and now lives in East Barnard. Aaron lived in Walpole, and had five sons: James, Charles, Oliver, Caleb and Albert. Jesse had two sons, Joseph and Jesse, Jr.

Thomas J. Ellis, of Covington, Ky., was born 1836; his father, James, born 1802, in Virginia; his grandfather, William, was born in Virginia about 1764, died in Kentucky, at 81 years of age. Russell B. Ellis, son of William, now lives in Kokomo, Ind., over 70 years of age; the last of eight children.

Amos Ellis lives in Williamsburg, and his brothers, Nelson and Alonzo, in Ripley, Ohio.

Hon. Lorenzo Ellis lives at Elliston, Ohio; he is in the stave and store business; he was born in Walpole, Mass., in 1834; has a son, William D., b. 1860. Billings Ellis, elder brother of Lorenzo, lives at Walpole, Mass. Lorenzo Ellis has been a member of the Ohio legislature two terms.

Mr. A. D. Ellis is a prominent resident of Owego, N. Y.

N. J. Ellis is a farmer, lives near Springfield, Mich. His father, Benj. A., lived in Ontario Co., N. Y. Harry, a cousin of Benj. A., a very aged man, lives in Victor, N. Y., as does his son, Bolivar Ellis.

Benj. Ellis, son of John, lives in Freeville, N. Y. His grandfather, John, Sr., had brothers, Peleg, Arnold and Oliver.

Rev. Charles D. Ellis is a Presbyterian clergyman at Saginaw, Mich.

Hon. J. V. Ellis, of St. John, N. B., member of the Canadian parliament 1887, declared himself in favor of the annexation of Canada to the United States.

Richard Allis, or Ellis, was a passenger in the ship Lion, June 22, 1632, for New England. (New England, at an early date, was often designated as Virginia.)

Mrs. Mary Ellis Durkee, born 1798, lives with her son-in-law, T. J. Potter, at Fort Edward, N. Y. Her father, John, born 1759, died 1826. Her grandfather, John, Sr., died in Montreal, in 1770, aged 79 years. James

Ellis, of Plymouth, Ohio, is a nephew of Mrs. Durkee. Benson Ellis lives at Greenwich, Ohio.

David F. Ellis, born in Wales in 1841, a printer, lives at Utica, N. Y. His father, Ellis Ellis, lives at Deerfield, Oneida Co., N. Y., on a farm, with his son, Hugh M. They all came from Wales, about 1848. Hugh was four years in the Union army.

Mr. J. W. Ellis, of New Castle, Ind., is of the Carolina Ellises. His grandfather, John, and two brothers were from Scotland.

James M. Ellis, born 1810, lives at Syracuse, N. Y.; a banker. His father, Gen. John Ellis, was born in Hebron, Conn., 1764. His parents were John, Sr., and Elizabeth (Sawyer) Ellis.

M. E. Ellis, of Pittsburg, Pa., was born 1852. His father, Geo. Riley Ellis, was born in Henrietta, Monroe Co., N. Y.; grandfather Guerdon and great-grandfather William Ellis were from Norwich, Conn.

Mr. William P. Ellis lives in Washington City, Ind., of which he is mayor. His father, William, born 1802, died 1883; was from North Carolina, and was the youngest of his father's family; his brothers were John and David, all sons of William, Sr.

Mr. H. Z. Ellis, of Philadelphia, Pa., is agent for the Ellis Family of Professional Vocalists. He was born 1824, at Plymouth, Vt. He has Ellis uncles, Caleb, Ebenezer and Warren, at Newton Center, Mass. His children —the vocalists—are Misses Romie M., Fanny May, Gracie Marie, and Messrs. Frank H. and Fred. S. Ellis. Their summer residence is at York Beach, Maine.

Dr. Edwin Ellis has a drug store at Ashland, Wis. He was born in Maine in 1824. His father, John, born 1798, died in California in 1871, had brothers, Ebenezer, Gideon, Jonathan and Scott.

Elias Ellis, born 1805, in Ohio; lives at Ellis, Muskingum Co., Ohio. He is a farmer. His great-grandfather, Ellis Ellis, was a Welshman; came to America early in 1700; his grandfather, William, died 1813, in Ohio; his father, Elias, died 1833.

Mr. A. N. Ellis, of Austin, Minn., was born at Potsdam, N. Y., 1834. He is in the farming and cattle business. His father, Freeman Ellis, was born at Yarmouth, Mass., in 1790. His grandfather, Isaac, lived in Yarmouth, and afterwards in Springfield, Vt. Great-grandfather, Joseph, and the latter's father, Joshua Ellis, were from Cape Cod, Mass.

Dr. Richard W. Ellis is a druggist at Los Angeles, Cal.

John Green Ellis lives at Auburn. N. Y. His father, Richard, is English, born 1830; died 1872.

Ernest Spencer Ellis, born 1858, in Vermontville, Mich., is a lawyer at Kalkaska, Mich. His father, Elmer Eugene was born in Genesee Co., N. Y. Grandfather, Harvey, and great grandfather, Gideon Ellis, all resided in Genesee Co., N. Y. Elmer Eugene Ellis now lives in Charlotte, Mich.

Mr. W. C. Ellis lives at North's Landing, Ind. His father was John, of Calhoun, Ga., a son of Stephen Ellis, of South Carolina, of Scotch descent.

Burwell P., Carlos W., Charles, Geo. W., Luther P., Mortimer M. and Caroline S. Ellis live in Richmond, Va.

Dr. C. F. Ellis is a physician at Ligonier, Ind.

Noah, John, James and Joseph Ellis were coopers, and lived near

Newburg, and later near Goshen, N. Y. Noah m. Hannah Carpenter; born
1786; had seven children: Lydia, Samuel, Lewis, Susan, Harriet, William
and Ira. James Ellis had four children: John, William, Walter and Eliza.
Noah Ellis died about 1840. Ira, son of Noah, had several children; one of
whom, George A. Ellis, lives in Brooklyn, N. Y., and has been book-keeper
and local manager for Leonard & Ellis—see page 259—for twelve to fifteen
years. He has a younger brother in the same office.

J. M. Ellis, Esq., is a lawyer, of Denver, Col. His father was a native of
North Carolina, and was of Welsh descent, and a brother of Geo. R. Ellis,
of Pontotoc, Miss.

Robert Ellis is a resident of Pompey, N. Y. His grandfather, Robert,
had six sons: Clark, Samuel, Hiram, Elias, John and Pierce; born in or near
Amsterdam, N. Y. William B. Ellis, son of Clark, lives at Greenwich, Ohio.

Mr. W. R. Ellis lives at Goshen, Ind. His father was Erastus W. H.,
born 1815, and grandfather, William R., born in Windham, Conn., in 1784;
great-grandfather, Ezekiel Ellis, an officer in the Revolutionary war.

Daniel Ellis, from North Carolina, settled in Indiana about 1810. His
children were: Levi, Jesse, James, Marvin, John, Willam, Mary Elizabeth,
Margaret and Sarah. Marvin, born 1821, has a son, O. W. Ellis, born 1845,
at Dubois, Ind.

J. A. Ellis. Chicago, Ill., is a commission merchant. He has a sister,
Mrs. William H. Holstein, Bridgeport, Pa. Their grandfather, Wm. Ellis,
lived in Muncie, Penn. His son, William Cox Ellis, father of J. A., was a
lawyer and Congressman and widely noted for talent and benevolence.

The Ellises of this country number many thousands, some of whom
descended from Welsh, English and Scotch ancestors, who came here soon
after the landing of the Pilgrims in 1620.

In 1883, Wm. T. Davis, of Plymouth, Mass., published a volume entitled
"Genealogical Register of Plymouth Families and Ancient Landmarks of
Plymouth." Mr. Davis had made extensive researches and his book contains
the names of nearly three hundred Ellises.

PERSONAL LETTERS AND DOCUMENTS.

It is usual in books of the nature of this to include some family letters
and documents, for the purpose of revealing to the later generations somewhat of the trials and experiences of those who have gone before. With
those here given is revealed much of the personal traits of the writers and
the motives by which they were actuated, as well as the struggles which
they cheerfully and nobly made to overcome the obstacles of their often
unpropitious surroundings. Considerable of historical interest is also to be
found in these communications. Many of these people were pioneers in the
then wilderness regions of country which, in order to develop and make for
themselves and their posterity desirable homes, required a degree of heroism
which we now can scarcely appreciate. So far as we can ascertain they were
all people of integrity and virtue, with just and pure ambitions and filled
well the duties of their station. Few of them attained much of worldly
wealth, the standard of success which is now so generally recognized, and yet

we, in this day, have an instinctive feeling that no one makes a failure of life, if in all his life-work he keeps his affections pure and tender, his head clear and his heart right. In this respect our progenitors have given us examples worthy of imitation and are entitled to our gratitude and veneration.

The following letter was written in June, 1804, by Mrs. Samuel Annable to her daughter Polly (or Molly) Ellis, wife of Dea. Dimick Ellis, of Ashfield. Bethiah, whose name is found at the close of the letter was Mrs. Annable's youngest daughter. See page 366. The numbers in brackets thus [ ] refer to corrresponding numbers in the main part of the book.

SEMPRONIUS, N. Y.

To MOLLY ELLIS, Ashfield, Mass.:

These lines come to let you know that we are all well. I think I am better than when I lived in Ashfield. Your father also has his health I think very remarkably. David [see page 368] and family are well. We heard you were coming up this fall. I suppose you and your child are well, but, oh! remember, we are liable every day to sickness and death; and do, Molly, let us strive to be prepared to change worlds, it will soon come; and do let us strive to live in love with God and set our affections on things above, so that we may live happy and die happy. When you see Hannah H., tell her that Irene [probably 34] does not forget her—wants her to live so that she may be happy with Christ to all eternity. Your uncle, Thomas, [see page 366] seemed to live this world purely. He told me, often, he prayed all the time. I take much satisfaction in Moses [probably her grandson, Moses Bartlet] and his wife. I bid you all farewell.

DESIRE ANNABLE.

Remember my love to all my neighbors, one and all, and all my friends. Give our love to Mr. Lyon and wife.

To SAMUEL AND REBECCA : [See page 367.]

We heard from you by Mr. Belding. You were all well then and I hope these lines will find you well. I heard you had three children to take care of; do teach them the fear of the Lord as well as to take care of their bodies. I want you to write to us about Edward [probably 39] and his family. Rufus Johnson's wife has got a son. Mrs. Forbush [71] has a daughter. She names it Elizabeth Mindwell, [born June 13, 1804.] Jonathan Ellis [26] and his family are well. I want you to write concerning Abigail Belding, whether she was willing to die. Give my love to Sylvia [75.] I went to quarterly meeting last winter. A solemn assembly met together. Mr. Savage has bought about a mile and a half from our house. Give my love to Hannah Williams [63.]

BETHIAH.

Letter from Edward Ellis [70] to his father, Lieut. John Ellis, of Ashfield. No date is given, but it must have been written probably in June, 1799 or 1800.

HONORED PARENTS :

SEMPRONIUS, N. Y.

I now take my pen in hand to inform you of the welfare of my family. Amanda is sick and has been under the doctor's care for some time. Although she is some better, the doctor thinks she will not be able to do much this summer. It is a general time of health here: our friends are all well. My cousin, Benjamin Ellis, has bought him a farm, about a mile from here. Peleg Standish lives with me this summer, and has bought land adjoining Mr. Ellis and Mr. Stafford, and now there is a lot to be sold a mile west of him. I think it is as handsome land as ever I saw. There is a great deal of valuable timber on it and is well watered by a number of very fine springs. It is number 33 and is owned by one, Major Newkirk. I have been informed, by men who have seen him, that it may be had very reasonably—for two dollars if paid down or twenty shillings if paid one-third down. Major Ledyard says it is as good a title as any in the country. Maj. Newkirk lives on the Mohawk river, at Palatine Church, and if there is anyone coming from Ashfield into this country they can call and see Newkirk. That land is worth four dollars an acre, and I should be glad to buy one hundred acres myself. Crops look promising. The distance is so great that we can seldom see each other, but I mean to come to Ashfield as soon as I can, but I get little time and I do not know what will happen. I am haying and in a hurry and must close my letter, hoping these lines will find you all enjoying the blessing of health. Give my love to all inquiring friends.

From your son,   EDWARD ELLIS.

Letter from Dimick Ellis, of Ashfield, to Barnabas Annable of Sempronius, N. Y.

DEAR SIR: ASHFIELD, MASS., May 12, 1802.

The note that you left in my care, against Ezra Williams, I have received the contents of, except seventy-three dollars. I have taken up the orders as you directed and have paid Dr. Dickinson, Dr. Smith and Thomas White some money, in settlement of their accounts. I did not take my pay for my note that I hold against you, as I did not stand in need of it, but will send you the note and take my pay of Williams, when he pays the balance due you. I am well at present and Polly also. Our child is sick, but I think he is getting some better now. I hope these lines will find you well. Give our love to father and mother Annable and to all inquiring friends, etc.

DIMICK ELLIS.

P. S. Please write to me by the bearer of this and send receipt for the money I send you.

SEMPRONIUS, June 2, 1802.

This day received by the hand of Lieut. John Ellis, $309.45 in full of this bill.   BARNABAS ANNABLE.

Letter from Barnabas and his wife, Ruth (Moon) Annable, to Dea. Dimick Ellis and wife.

SEMPRONIUS, N. Y., Aug. 26, 1806.

DEAR SISTER: I am now quite sick. I have not been so well the last two years as I was the two first years after we came into this country. Dear Sister: The Lord, in his providence, has been pleased to visit this family with the stroke of death. Our brother Samuel is gone and left us here to mourn, but not as those without hope. [See page 367.] You desired us to write the particulars of his death. He was sick about two months, he got better twice when he had the third relapse. David [his brother, see page 368] told him he must certainly die. He said they must send for his brother Barnabas, to pray with him, for, said he, I must certainly go to —— if I die in my present situation. Barnabas went and stayed with him until the day of his death, all the time of which he appeared in bitter agony of soul, pleading for salvation, until about three days before he died, when he revived and said he had been in perfect readiness for three days.

Ruth failing, I take the pen to finish her letter. He readily confessed that he had many hard thoughts of me for spending so much time in preaching, but now, said he, I see that souls are of some consequence and you have done much good in preaching; therefore, go and do all the good you can. Respecting his property, he left it in will to his wife, or widow, during her life, directed after her decease to Hiram Dennison, provided he serves the widow faithfully his time out, and in case he should die, leaving no heir, then what may be left is directed unto us, as heirs, the brothers and sisters of the deceased. Peleg Standish is administrator with the widow. It was supposed that she was soon to have married had not the Lord have taken the young man's life. She is now going to live with her brother Peleg.

Respecting religion here Electa has written. Brother Ellis, if you have collected the Crapo notes, I wish you would send the money due unto daddy Moon to him, then take your own pay for your pains and send the remainder to me the first good opportunity and by Daniel Ellis, [125] if he returns soon. * * I have many trials in life which would make me weary of the world did not the Lord often happify my soul with showers of divine blessings. May the blessings of heaven rest on you and yours.

From your feeling brother,
BARNABAS ANNABLE.

P. S. We hear that Capt. Lincoln [67] is at Lake Erie.

Letter from Lucretia Smith to Miss Polly Annable. See page 116.

SHELBURNE, MASS., April 23, 1797.

To MISS POLLY ANNABLE:

Please to read these lines with patience. Well, Polly, I did not begin my school until the third day after I arrived at Shelburne, and those days should have been glad to have spent with you in Ashfield. I have kept school three days and tedious long days they were. I shall not tell you that I am homesick, but will venture to say that I feel very low-spirited, though my school is very agreeable, yet the people are all strangers to me in this town and it seems as if they always would be. Mary, [or Polly] if you had any idea of my feelings you would come and see me. I saw Mr. Norton that evening, after I parted with your dear self, and earnestly requested him to wait on you to Shelburne. He said that would be a very great pleasure, but he expected to go out of town next week. Hark! Somebody knocks. I must bid you good bye for a moment, but shall disturb you again directly.

Mary, I have a short story to tell you. While I was engaged in writing to you, I was interrupted by a gentleman and lady, who came to see if I would walk down town with them. So accordingly I went, and there I saw a number of your acquaintances, which afforded me but little satisfaction. What I should call satisfaction would be to see or here something from all my good friends at Ashfield. If I do not get a letter (if not two) from you soon I shall ever cease to subscribe myself your affectionate friend and admirer. I shall come home in about three weeks if I can have a horse.

LUCRETIA SMITH.

Letter from Ira Butler, husband of Phebe Lincoln, to his wife's uncle, Dimick Ellis. In 1812, Capt. Samuel Lincoln and his wife, Jane Ellis, suddenly died leaving a large family of children. See pages 107 to 110.

MURRAY, [Orleans Co.] N. Y., May 16, 1813.

DEAR UNCLE: With a favorable opportunity we inform you that we are all well now, and hope these few lines will find you enjoying the same great blessing. Last week we heard from the children and they are all well and feel contented with their situations. Your nieces, Polly and Phebe, lost each an heir. March 27, I, Polly, lost my child, aged ten months about; died with quick consumption. Phebe's died the 24th of March, with camp distemper. We have enjoyed a good state of health since. The letters that you sent me we never received. They came to a neighbor's house, Mr. Wilber's, and were burned. He had everything burnt up. We think it is very hard times, for we are afraid of the Indians. Betsey has Benjamin, the baby, with her and he has been very sick all winter, but he has grown hearty again and grows smart, and weighs eighteen pounds.

This from your loving nieces, in the town of Murray, Phebe, Polly, Betsey.   IRA BUTLER.

From Mrs. Ruth (Moon) Annable—see page 366—to Mrs. Polly (Annable) Ellis, of Ashfield. No date is given, but it must have been written previous to 1818.

SEMPRONIUS, N. Y.

DEAR SISTER: I take this opportunity to inform you that we are all well at present. Mother and Bethiah are very well. Mother has been able to visit the Doctor, Moses and Lecta. [Dr. David Annable, Moses Bartlett, her grandson, and Mrs. Electa Phillips, her granddaughter.] I have the sorrowful news to write that we have heard of the death of father and brother Daniel Moon. I think my poor mother must be in trouble. I wish you would come and see your mother and sister once more, if I never can mine. Your mother grows childish, but not troublesome. Edward and Mima [Lieut. Edward and Jemima Annable] were here on a visit last week. Mima was ill. She said the doctor said she was going into consumption. Alcemena [see page 94] has been very sick. Samuel and Nancy [her children] are teaching schools. The Doctor [David Annable] talks of going to see you. We all send love to uncle and aunt, [Lieut. John and Molly Ellis] likewise to Hannah Hale.

MRS. RUTH ANNABLE.

Letter from Edward D. Ellis to his mother and step-father, in Sempronius. Young Edward had gone out to learn the printer's art. [235].

WATERLOO, N. Y., Aug. 24, 1819.

DEAR PARENTS: I have succeeded in making as advantageous a bargain with my employer as we had anticipated. He is to allow me one hundred dollars in cash and twenty in whatever I may wish, payable quarterly.

I am of opinion that cash can procure whatever you may think best, at better advantage than trade. One quarter will end about the middle of January next, when $25 in money and $5 in something else will be due. I shall probably be in want of many articles, however, I have been thinking that it might be a good plan at the end of the first quarter to take a quantity of garden seeds, that is if you can turn them to advantage at any of the stores where you trade. Mr. Leavenworth is to receive them for printing, and if you can let them go to merchants for articles of trade, it may not be amiss to take them. I merely mention this that you might make inquiries, in which case let me know the kinds wanted. * * The sickness which has prevailed all over the United States is gradually subsiding. In New York the inhabitants are gradually returning to their dwellings, where several weeks since the yellow fever raged to an alarming extent. * * I have sent two papers for you by the mail. I expect to procure me a decent chest for $1.25, if so, I shall not be obliged to send for my basket.

From your obedient son,
E. D. ELLIS.

Letter from Minerva Ellis [733] to her uncle, Cyrus Ellis, regarding the death of her father, Edward D. Ellis [235], brother of Cyrus.

DETROIT, MICH., June 3, 1848.

* DEAR UNCLE: I received your letter, of the 24th of May, written to my dear father, but it came too late for his perusal. He died on the 15th of May, Monday morning, at 8 o'clock, after being confined to his bed only one day. The cause of his death was over-exertion at a large fire, which took place a few weeks ago. He died very happy, rejoicing in his Saviour. He was beloved and respected by all who knew him. He has been a worthy citizen, and a kind affectionate father and husband, but it pleased God to take him to himself, and I hope one day to join him in that land of bliss.

There let his spirit rest secure
In the arms of angels blest and pure.

There are six children of us. I am the oldest, and was 16 last November; Benjamin F. is the youngest, aged 4 years. You mention in your letter visiting us next year. We shall be happy to see you out here. Mother is in very poor health at present. The children are all well. Aunt Mindwell Potter father's half-sister is out in Hillsdale, Michigan. Cousin John Ellis [243] lives here, and his family. Mother sends her love to you and your family.

Your affectionate niece,
MARY MINERVA ELLIS.

From Hannah Dimick to her aunt, Mrs. Lieut. John Ellis [16], of Ashfield:

BARNSTABLE, Oct. 17, 1806.

DEAR AUNT—These lines are to inform you of the death of my father. He died four weeks ago last Friday, after being sick about ten months. He was so as to be able to go out till four weeks before he died. We are all well now and hope this will find you and family the same. We have not had letters from Sandwich since my uncle Edward died, but hear that they are all well. My mother sends love to you and family, and wishes you to write to uncle Annable.

From your friend and niece,

· HANNAH DIMOCK.

To Mrs. Mary Ealis.

Letter from John Agry, of Hallowell, Maine, to his cousin, Dimick Ellis. Mr. Agry's mother was a Dimick, from "The Cape." She was a sister of Mrs. Samuel Annable, Jr., and Mrs. Lieut. John Ellis. See pages 78 and 366.

HALLOWELL, MAINE, March 23d, 1818.

MR. DIMICK ELLIS, ASHFIELD:

DEAR SIR—Your letter of the 15th December last came safe to Hallowell, but my brother, Thomas, and myself being in Boston the most part of the winter, will account for this late answer. It was with pleasure we received information from relations known to us only by the affectionate regards of my mother, who never ceased to cherish an anxious desire for their welfare while she lived. I will now proceed to give you the information requested, with a short account of our family since they left Barnstable; occurrences prior to this, I presume, are familiar to your mother. My father and mother removed to Gardinerston, now called Pittston, in 1763; the family consisted of one daughter and three sons: Hannah, Thomas, David and John. My father died in 1783; my sister married Samuel Oakman, and died, much respected and lamented, in 1787, leaving two sons and four daughters, both sons are since dead, one of which has left three children (the oldest, a daughter about 13), and are now under my guardianship, the daughters are married and well settled in life. My mother died in 1807. The oldest son, Thomas Agry, has seven children, two sons and five daughters. The two eldest daughters are well married and live in the neighborhood; one son is settled at Bath, about 30 miles off, the rest are young and at home. David Agry died in Petersburg, Virginia, August, 1813; he followed the sea in a ship of which he was master and owner, and left no family. John Agry, the third son and writer of this, has seven children, four sons and three daughters, the oldest 24 years 2d day of August last. I have been thus particular, thinking it might be interesting to your mother, as I think I have heard my mother say that my aunts made a visit to Barnstable before she left there, and your mother may recollect some of the children, although young at the time, and wish to know something particularly about them. The business of myself and brothers has been commercial, and we have suffered greatly with the war, having lost between thirty and forty thousand dollars, but fortunately saved enough to continue our business, though it is now dull and nets but little profit.

Betsy Lewis married Reuben Colburn, and they are now both living in Pittston; they have one son and six daughters living. Her husband's mind, for two or three years past, has been slightly deranged, but not so far as to require confinement. They subsist comfortably with the assistance of their children. Hannah Dimick I have heard nothing from for two years past, she then lived by herself in one part of a house occupied by her brother, Charles Dimick. My uncle, Edward Dimick, died in 1803. He was in perfect health one hour before his death.

Pray write us; it will be a great satisfaction to hear from you often. Please present my regards to your mother and all relations, and accept my sincere wishes for your and their health and happiness.

I am, dear sir, yours affectionately,

JOHN AGRY.

Letter from Samuel, son of Elder Barnabas Annable, to his aunt, Mrs. Polly Annable Ellis. See page 367.

SEMPRONIUS, N. Y., Sept. 27th, 1818.

DEAR AUNT—In compliance with your request, and my own feelings do I gladly embrace the opportunity of writing to one for whom I ever have and ever shall cherish the highest sentiments of respect and esteem. I cannot but reflect for a moment on the happiness your presence afforded in the early hours of my life. Nothing could then afford more pleasure than the company of those to whom I was allied by the ties of natural affections. Fondly imag‧ ing them to be the best of human beings, I really enjoyed‧ in their presence cousummate bliss.

But in the dispensations of Providence, it was ordained that I should part with some of them and move to the new country [from Ashfield to Sempro‧ nius.] This was trying, though I was hardly large enough to realize it. Nothing caused greater sorrow and made deeper impressions on my mind than the thought of leaving Aunt Polly—perhaps never to see her again—never did the impressions of sorrow fully wear away; and it was long before, in sweet remembrances of past scenes, I could hail your arrival in Sempronius. Your visits were gladdening to my feelings, and I only regretted that you must return again.

But those scenes are past, and I have now one still more trying to relate. Last Thursday, Electa and Nancy, Bartlet and Enos, two ever dear and affec‧ tionate sisters, with two beloved brothers, took their leave at Sempronius for the long contemplated journey to the wilds of Indiana. The rest of the family remain till next spring. You will, no doubt, be curious to know the feelings that were manifested on this trying event. In the morning the neighbors flocked in to pay their respects and render them what assistance they could about loading and getting them ready for a start. Notwithstanding all seemed to be filled with the deepest regret at the thought of separating, each one assumed as much of an air of merriment as they could, in order to repress in some measure the anguish of those who were about to leave us. Each cor‧ dially bestowed their best wishes for their future comfort and prosperity. Sister Nancy, with a firm resolution, if possible, to restrain her feelings so as to refrain from tears, braved it till she got as far as Elisha's, where we accompanied her. We went in; I shook hands with sister Electa, and she burst into tears. Sister Nancy could no longer restrain her feelings—she wept, and most of the women present gave vent to their feelings in the same way. For my own part the scene was truly heartrending. The boys braved it. To think that fourteen hundred miles should separate me from those with whom the happy, though transient, morning of my life had been spent, was truly painful. I could hardly refrain from giving vent to my own feelings in a flow of tears. Yet I did. Not that I was ashamed to cry. Ah, no! Reason forbade that I should add fuel to the fire of anguish already kindled in the breasts of those who were about to leave us. The struggle was hard indeed. With many a deep drawn sigh did I resist the anguish of my soul.

They are gone, and how shall I be reconciled? Reason dictates flattering with a hope that all is for the best. Considering it providential, already begins to calm the anguish of my soul. How good, how comforting is the power of reflection. Were it not for this, the passions would overcome the other faculties of the mind, the soul would sink into a state of dejectedness which would render life miserable.

I am sorry to inform you that Nancy, through extreme hurry of business in preparing to get away, was obliged to neglect copying that writing which she promised you. Having to go away myself in search of employment, I could not attend to it.

I have not yet engaged a school, but I expect to soon. Bromley has engaged to work for uncle David this winter in the brewery. We are all in tolerable health. Mrs. Fuller being present, wishes me to write her compliments [Rhoda Annable Fuller, see page 94.]

Grandmother wishes me to remember her; says she is still alive, but does not expect to be a great while. She is nearly as comfortable as she was when you was here. Aunt Bethiah wishes me to write her respects to you and the family. She wishes Desiah [237] would write to her. She sends her compliments to Mr. Belding's people [John Belding's, see page 372.]

Father and mother wish me to write for them. They feel anxious to have you write to them. It is a general time of health with us. Give my respects to uncle Dimick, to great-uncle and aunt, and likewise to the rest of the family, your children, and to all enquiring friends. I wish you or uncle would write me.

I am, dear aunt, your sincere friend and affectionate nephew,

To Mrs. Polly Ellis.   SAMUEL ANNABLE.

Letters from Elder Barnabas Annable and wife to Dea. Dimick Ellis and other relatives in Ashfield.

SEMPRONIUS, N. Y. February 14th, 1819.

May God prepare the hearts of my dear sister and brother, aunt and uncle to receive the particulars of the death of mother Annable. She continued to decline from the time you left here until some of the first days of February, when she grew worse, having her senses to the last minute, and exercising, as her prayer was perfect patience, until her Lord should come. She lived from midnight, after being sensible that she was struck with death, until the next night, sun half an hour high, when faltering a few minutes, her struggles being over, she apparently breathed her life sweetly out. This was on the 9th day of the month. Another exemplary life and peaceable death stimulated us all to fear God and keep his commands that we may have right to the tree of life, and enter into the city where we trust she is gone. The text was: "Be ye also ready, for in such an," etc. We, our friends and yours in this quarter are well. John is well [68].

We have received a letter from our children in Indiana. They inform us that they are well and pleased with the country, and have bought four miles from Mount Vernon, a village on the Ohio river, and fifteen from the Wabash river. Probably in about three weeks we shall start. We now expect that Bethiah will go with us. However, Edward [39] appears anxious to have her stay and make her home at his house. We shall make it a point to write from that place when we get there, hoping thereby to perpetuate a remembrance of each other. With warm affections to you all whom I cannot see, and strong attachment to all my old acquaintances,

I subscribe myself yours,

BARNABAS ANNABLE.

DEAR SISTER—The reason that I did not write according to my agreement is, my health has been very poor, my two little ones very cross, my care other ways very great, which renders me unfit for writing. O Polly, my trials have been great since I saw you last fall. Four of my children fourteen hundred miles from me, and the trial of parting with mother and Bethiah, together with my own mother and the neighbors, has been as much as I could bear.

We received three letters from our children after they left this town before they got to Indiana. The water was very low, for which reason they had to buy a small boat, and then taking some boards and forming a small raft, they put a part of the goods on it, and set Enos and Elisha Ellis to stearing it. Then they had to hire two robust men to help them lift the boat over the shoals and stones until they got almost 100 miles below Pittsburg. They were from the 22d of September until the 5th of December before they landed at their home. They in their letters have expressed good health and good courage. I leave this subject.

Perhaps you would wish to know something more concerning Bethiah. She bears the death of her mother better than any of us had expected. She inclines to go with us, though her trials seem to be great about leaving friends behind.

I went to the Nine Mile Creek to Eleazar Smith's last fall. Had a very agreeable visit. Likewise to Edward's. I can think of nothing more at present but to give my love to your family and connections and your neighbors. Bethiah is not at home, or she would send a great deal of love.

I remain your affectionate sister,

To POLLY ELLIS.   RUTH ANNABLE.

Letter from Cyrus Ellis—page 160—to Dea. Dimick Ellis, written soon after he left Ashfield and settled on the homestead where he was born, in 1799, and where he lived until his death in 1885.

SEMPRONIUS, N. Y., May, 1820.

RESPECTED SIR: I now have the satisfaction to sit down to write a few lines and to inform you, agreeable to your request, that I am in perfect health, and have been so almost without exception ever since I left Ashfield. It is a tolerable healthy time here now, but it has been rather sickly in several towns adjoining the Cayuga lake,—that is many are laid up with the fever and ague. The position of those places, in the spring season of the year, is calculated to bring it on. Sempronius is not much distinguished for this disorder, yet there are some in our own neighborhood that have had it.

As a disease, chills has never as yet attacked me, and I humbly hope never will. I received the letter which you wrote, in ten days after date, and hastened to know what was contained in your very brief letter, but I have made no haste to send back another. You write that it was a healthy time in Ashfield, yet there had been several deaths since I left there, the mention of those (especially S. Bement's) came quite unexpected to me. You would have favored me much if you had given more particulars of their deaths and the time when they occurred. Two persons have died since I came here; they were neither young nor old, and there was no funeral ceremonies, only but a few neighbors collecting to inter the dead, having no prayers, attendance, nor address to the mourners. I think it as being a singular thing. The old farm, seventy acres, which my father left at his death, I have the whole charge of it given up to me. My step-father not having lived upon said farm for four years past, in which time different families have lived upon it, it has been rather badly conducted. I have reasons to blame somebody as to the management of it, yet I think I have succeeded in making as advantageous a change of residence as I could have anticipated; that is, my earnings and employment are more satisfactory, and at present there is a probability of its being much better for me than I could possibly have done, if I had stayed at Ashfield.

The suffrages for governor were taken on the last Tuesday in April, the last month, throughout this State, and a hot election too. The parties with us are not Federals and Republicans, but Clintonians and Bucktails. The one upheld Mr. Clinton, as candidate for Governor, and the other Mr. Tompkins, the Vice-President. These men, previous to the late election, have been reproachfully abused and degraded by their enemies, and cried up and magnified by their friends, by every newspaper in the State. Indeed, where there is a great strain of party zeal for statesmen, the fittest and best are, and will be scandalized when there is no cause for it, and in fact it is curious and intelligible to read the papers, at the present time, if nothing more than to see what genius and ideas are displayed by electioneering; time has not sufficed yet to ascertain the number of votes given in the whole State, but from the counties, as far as we have heard, there is a very small majority for Clinton, so it is impossible to tell at this time of whom the choice for Governor is in favor of.

From your obedient,

C. ELLIS.

P. S. You will remember me to all the family, etc. Inform Desiah that I saw Emma and Climena Rhodes last month.

Letter from Ruth Annable, wife of Barnabas, to Dr. David Annable and Moses Bartlett, of Sempronius, N. Y. See page 370. The letter was received February, 1820.

BLACK TOWNSHIP, POSEY COUNTY, INDIANA.

DEAR FRIENDS: I expect it is with anxiety you have waited to see some of my scribblings. I will assure you that it has not been for want of affection towards you, but, having much trial and suffering, I have felt unwilling to fill your ears with the same. Surely, dear friend, I never shall forget you, neither the favor you bestowed on me before I left you. I often sleep a short nap, then awake, can sleep no more till the day breaks, thinking of my neighbors and friends I have left behind. I one night began my meditations thinking of you all. I could not close my eyes to sleep that night. I remember my promise, that I would write to you my journal and how I liked the country, after I should get here, and how we fared.

I expect Mr. Belding* gave you my journal by land. We took water about two weeks after our teamsters left us. We began with pleasant sailing, for a few hours, then we met with sudden turns in the river, and, the current being swift, we were hurried on shore, or driven upon an island or sand-bar. The boat struck so hard against the root of a tree, the first day, that every child was sent upon its head, and the one who commanded our boat crying out, "we are gone for it," gave me such a shock, together with the cold, set me into such ague fits as I hardly ever experienced; for we had two families aboard, which made nineteen souls of us, all inexperienced hands. So I lived the first week, having sudden shocks. It got my stomach so weak that I could not receive any food, but once in four and twenty hours, for about ten days. My fatigue was likewise very hard, my little ones being sick. I had them both to wait on and to hold in my lap, till I could hardly stand when I rose up. When we entered the Ohio river my trials were some less by day, but then we sailed at night too; which filled me with fear that we should run on to a sawyer, [fallen trees.] I had but little rest. We had no pilot and strove to follow a boatman, that was used to the river, by this means was deprived of the privilege of visiting Stephen Ellis' family, [119] for which I was very sorry. We found where they were and an opportunity to send the gown and letter directed to them.

We stopped at Cincinnati; there we saw Levi Fuller and John Wood. They both appeared to be very glad to see us. John Wood has since been to see us; he said that Stephen Ellis was doing tolerably well, but his wife was weakly; likewise, that they had received the gown and letter. At Gallipolis, about 100 miles down the river, we got rid of a very disagreeable family; for which I was never more glad. I would warn every one that takes passage to keep everything they can under lock and key; for I lost, by not having this care, Eliza's gingham frock, three pair of stockings, one run of stocking yarn, one sheet, one shirt, a pair of pillows, and mother's old long loose gown.

I have been sick and unable to write. The last of October now begins. I now again begin to write. My sickness was the same as when Doctor White doctored me, though not so severe. I suffered considerable for nourishment that could not be had. I am now in tolerable health. I shall not strive to give you much more of my journal. On the Ohio we had some pleasant sailing, some pleasing prospects—such as steamboats, floating-mills, together with villages. We landed at Mount Vernon the 22d of April, all in good health, excepting myself and babe. We found our children all in good health, but Nancy. She grew more ill, and was not able to do her own work for as much as one month. I went into the house with Nancy. We suffered for provisions, for we could not get anything but hoe-cake, but I think it no disparagement to the country, but a neglectful people; but, being unwell, this kind of fare went very hard, but harder yet when we could not get our bacon.

---

*Probably Wm. Belding, who m. Catherine, dau. of Thomas Ranney. See page 386.

Meat was very scarce, by reason of its being sent off in boat-loads to New Orleans, so the people did not save enough for themselves, so we have had to do without meat, sometimes two and three weeks. We bought two cows. Three quarts of milk were the most that ever we had from them both, besides suckling their calves, and were as good as cows commonly here that run in the woods. We could not get any sauce, if it had been to save our lives. I have not room enough to finish my letter. I will conclude on another sheet.

The people of this place care for nothing but to raise corn and hogs. They raise a few beans, which they call snaps, only. There are men here who have lived here twelve years, and have not a spear of grass growing; but I think grass will do well here. I saw a small piece of meadow; I think I never saw so much hay come off so small a piece of ground in my life. Wheat does well here; is a very sure crop. Potatoes can be raised largely to the acre; the sweet potato in greater abundance; they are the best potato that ever I ate; could live on them alone. The season has been too dry for potatoes to do well. The people say it never was so dry since the country has been settled. We have not raised much sauce, by reason of the same, but we have a few bushels of potatoes, some small turnips and French turnips, some cabbage, about three hundred pumpkins, and three hundred and fifty bushels of corn. We have sowed thirteen acres of wheat and some expect to sow three acres more. We have two cows and four calves, one five-year old mare, seven yearling hogs and eight shoats. We fared hard this year, but no reason to complain, for my family was never so healthy as they have been this season.

I am not discouraged about getting a living, but the people do not seem natural. We have not received a visit from any woman since we have been here, excepting two of our own country people. Tell her that was the Widow Foster, that she has a brother living near neighbor to me. He came here this summer; likes the country well. I think he will get rich. I do not look for riches for my own part, but I think that we could have done well, if we had only brought $200 with us. We have bought two cows, one to give milk, the other one to fatten for beef; one at thirteen and the other at nineteen dollars.

I like our farm very well; it lies handsome, and tolerably well watered. There are two living springs upon it, and plenty fencing timber. We have a house built, with a good cellar under it, and a corn house, seventeen feet square, set on blocks, made very convenient. We have a well close to the house. The snakes, that were so much dreaded, have not been seen on our farm. I think the hogs have thinned them off. The water in this place will not wash without cleansing, but the pleasant showers affords us water enough to wash, in the fore part of the season, but we have been very much pestered for water to wash with for two months past. My life has been made very uncomfortable by reason of inconveniences, but we have a hope of having things better.

I have no wheels, but can borrow one. My flax and wool are not yet spun. I have to patch comfortably, and I keep my family comfortable and decent. I could advise a family that comes here to be well clothed, for flax and wool can hardly be gotten till you raise it. Flax does well here, with those who know how to raise it. I have seen but few sheep; they were large;

they shear them twice a year. I have written many irregular mistakes; you must patch as well as you can. I have but little time to write. I have my bread all to bake by the fire, and get but little time to do anything else but get victuals. I have not seen an oven since I have been in this town. The people are very ignorant of house-wifery. They have a very different way of cooking, in almost every respect. They make a pie that suits my taste very well. They make a crust, put it into a bake kettle, fill it up with peaches, put in a little water; then put on a crust and bake it. We have gotten brick for an oven and a hearth. We have bought a fraction of land, consisting of about twenty acres, adjoining our farm. Our boys all have good courage; like the place well. I never saw fellows work so well as they have this summer, in my life.

My husband flies around like a boy; better than since he was a child. They say that I have written concerning the corn, instead of three hundred and fifty I must write four hundred and fifty bushels, and they have got it all harvested; they raised part of it on shares. On the whole they reckon they have raised six hundred. Our wheat, on the ground looks like a pink-bed. You need not be afraid that you will have to eat all Indian bread, for wheat does better here than in York State. I think there is no danger but what a man can get a good living, if he can have money enough to buy a horse and cow or two, and other provisions to give him a start. It is far better for fruit in this place than in York State. Some of our grafts have grown a yard and half in length, this summer. The longer I stay here the better I like the place.

We understood, before we came here, that it was difficult to preserve meat, but it can be here, as well as in York State. Flies are not so very troublesome. If you wish to know about other insects, I must tell you that musketoes are very troublesome, a few weeks in the spring season; fleas, there scarcely ever are any seen in the hottest of summer. By this time you think it strange that I say nothing about Bethiah. She has not shed one tear to where she did ten thousand before she left Sempronius. She never will own that she is sorry that she came with us. She sends her love to you all. Says I must tell you that she likes here well, and, likewise, to tell you that blackberries are plenty, and the people give us plenty of peaches; that we have muskmelons and watermelons in abundance; and that we have a nursery of two thousands apple trees, growing. It has been very healthy in this place. There has been no need of a doctor in this place this summer.

Samuel lives at Evansville, has just made us a visit; is in good health. He earned for himself $70 in three months. Now for you to know the particular advantages and disadvantages of our country. Salt, at present, is scarce and dear; it is not to be obtained for less than three or four dollars a bushel, but the people think it will be found more plenty. Sugar is scarce and dear; the price is thirty-two and a half cents a pound. There are some of our neighbors who have maple trees, and make three or four hundred weight of sugar in a season. I think the difficulty about milling is not great, for we have horse and water mills a plenty; the latter does not grind, only in a time of high water. The horse mills will grind thirty bushels a day; but it is somewhat bad for a poor man, for he must find his own team, or pay twelve cents for every bushel, besides the toll. Corn whisky is generally seventy-five cents per gallon; wheat whisky, one dollar.

It is now the tenth of December. It begins to be cold weather. We have a very pleasant season. I shall advise no one to come here; for I know not how they will like it, but I have wished many times that I had my old neighbors and friends around me. The great distance does not hinder my feeling for you whenever you are in trouble. When I heard of the death of Mr. Whitewood, I can truly say, my feelings were very much affected. Peleg Allen came into our neighborhood, yesterday. Abigail has gone to live in a house close to Nancy; he has not purchased yet, but thinks he shall in this place I have enough more to write, but have not room on my paper. You may wish to know about the privilege of meetings. There are Methodist and Baptist preachers in this place, but the people are not so fond of meetings as I wish they were.

I conclude, subscribing myself your friend and well-wisher until death,

RUTH ANNABLE.

(Moses Bartlett, mentioned at the head of this letter, and on pages 366, 370 and 386, settled in Sempronius about 1800, where he lived until the spring of 1837, when he removed to Saline, Mich., where he died in 1846, aged 74 years. His wife died there in 1843, aged 60. They had nine children: Mary, Mabel, Hannah, Kate, Phineas, Jerusha, William, Moses, Jr., and Horace. Mary m. a Hull, and both lived and died in Saline. Mabel m. Abraham Bodine and lived in Clarence, Erie Co., N. Y. Hannah m. Cooper Snyder and lives in Moravia, N. Y., aged about 82. Mr. Snyder is dead. Kate m. Amos Miller, moved to Saline in 1837, where both died. Jerusha m. Austin Convers, of Saline; both are dead. The four sons, Phineas, William, Moses and Horace are farmers—all living in Clinton, Lenawee Co., Mich.)

Letter from Dea. David Lyon (see pages 295 and 376) and wife, of Ashfield, to Dea. David Ellis and wife (see pages 86 and 88), of Springfield, Eric Co., Penn. Mrs. Lyon and Mrs. Ellis were sisters.

ASHFIELD, MASS., June 8th, 1824.

BELOVED BROTHER AND SISTER: These lines are to inform you that through a merciful God I and my family are enjoying a measure of health, thanks to His name, and hoping these lines may find you and yours enjoying health and prosperity. As to particular news, I have nothing worthy of remark. It is a general time of health in this place, although there has been several deaths. Abraham Jones and daughter died a few weeks past; Dr. Clark's wife, Col. Banister, and a number of others. As respects religion, it is now much as it was when you left these parts. I understand she, that was Chloe Drake, now Zenos Field's wife, has of late experienced religion. I hope she will follow on to know the Lord. Oh, brother and sister, pray for us in this place that the Lord would visit us in mercy. Almorean Hayward came here the fore part of December. He stayed about a fortnight. His health improved much while he was here. I received a letter from brother Hayward last March; they were all well. We heard from Norwich last winter; they are all well there. We heard from Hawley; Brother Brackett's folks were well. Last week brother Cobb's family were all well as common. Please to write me by Jonathan Taylor [see 182], the bearer of this letter. He can tell you much more than I can write. No more at present.

We remain your friends in love,

DAVID LYON,
BETSEY LYON.

To Dea. David Ellis, Springfield, Pa.

Letter from Mrs. and Mr. Barnabas Annable to Mr. and Mrs. Dimick and Lieut. John and Molly Ellis, of Ashfield, written in 1820, after they reached their new home in the extreme southwestern part of Indiana:

My Loving Sister, Brother, Uncle and Aunt Ellis:

My neglect of duty to you unto the present, has been owing to much care and a disposition to have a fair opportunity to judge of the health of the country. Proceeding, I inform you that we took water at Olean, N. Y., on the Allegheny river, Mch. 28; 1819, and landed the 23d of April at Mount Vernon, on the Ohio river, a distance of more than twelve hundred miles by water. Four miles from this place I found my children on a pleasant and good piece of land, entered for me. After the fatigue of the journey was over with us. Myself and family have spent a year in animating hopes of prosperity; the country being by far the best, in my opinion, that the good Lord ever made. We are now, and have for the most part of the time, enjoyed a far better state of health than ever before in the course of our lives. We have had only one five dollar doctor's charge, and that was for setting a broken leg of David's, my little boy, occasioned by his improving the uncommon snow of six inches deep in sliding down hill.

Wheat, in common, is worth seventy-five cents per bushel; corn, fifty in the spring season, but twenty-five in the field. Mast, or shack pork, is worth from three to four dollars per hundred, and is raised in vast quantities. Common farmers have for stock from fifty to one and two hundred hogs, the best article of trade in this country.

We have about twenty acres of new land that I expect to plant. I have fifteen acres of good looking wheat on the ground, and have sowed three or four acres of oats, flax and barley. The corn of this country makes better bread than corn in your country, and likewise wheat, as it never smuts; but from the long season of hot weather, after harvest, it is liable to breed the weevel, as the peas do bugs in your country, which affects the taste of the wheat bread. I have reason to hope that of all kinds of grain, with a common blessing, to raise twelve hundred bushels the present season. We expect to reap our wheat by the middle of June; it is full in the milk; looks the best I ever saw.

Dear Sister and Brother, by this time you begin to think that we do not care to write to let you know how we do. Surely, dear sister, the long absence, neither the great distance which separates us from each other, can ever erase you from my memory. I often wish Dimick and Polly here, were but it may be that you would not like it here as I do. I am well suited with the country, but the ways and manners of the people are not so agreeable as they were in New England or York State, although they are friendly to me and my family. The place is very beautiful; there are peaches in abundance; apples do well here. One of our neighbors gathered one hundred bushels of apples from twenty-five trees, only eleven years from the seed. We have a nursery of two thousand apple trees. We have thirty grafts that we brought with us from our old orchard. We have pear, cherry and plum trees—red and damson—quinces, currants and grapes. Every thing looks well. We live on a big road. Electa lives about a quarter of a mile from us. Nancy, on the same road, a half-mile. Electa has a babe one week old, and Nancy has one four months' old. Samuel lives at Evansville, about twenty miles from here; he keeps school; he has been sick, but is regaining his health. The rest of the family never enjoyed such good health as they have since we have been here. As to my own part, I have been so unreconciled to leaving friends and relations, together with hard fare and inconveniences, that it has taken off my flesh more than any fit of sickness that ever I had. In about ten months I lost forty-four pounds of flesh. The reason of hard fare was not because provisions were not raised, but they had been sent down the river to Orleans for market. We were put to to get meat, but we got enough bread. The inhabitants are a singular people; their living is chiefly corn bread and bacon. They raise but little sauce, if any; if they have any flour they know not how to use it as our country people do; they use it without raising it. I expect you want to know more than I can think to write. I agreed to write my journal, but it would be quite a volume, so I will give it to you in short terms: Such trials and frights I never experienced in my life as I did coming down the Allegheny river. I could not take any food only when we landed at night so long as we were on the Allegheny river, but this was all by reason of inexperienced hands. There was aboard of our boat no one that knew anything about the water, but thanks be to God, we were all landed safe. The whole family is well pleased with the country. Your brother acts ten years younger than ever he has since I knew him. They work as if they hurried; they all live at home but Samuel. The rattlesnakes that were so much dreaded have become very scarce. It's now the first of May; the wheat is heading out and looks wonderfully well. Some are hoeing their corn. My garden seeds are all up and growing well. Bethiah wished me to write all that I had to and then write for her; her health is as good as it has ever been, considering her age. She says I must tell you she is contented and likes this place, but feels anxious to hear from you and your children. She sends her love to uncle and aunt and all their children. We wish you to write as quick as you can. We want to hear from you all. Give my love both to friends and relations. I remain,

Your affectionate sister,

RUTH ANNABLE.

Ruth, being a little unwell, closes, leaving room for a few lines, charging me to write her love to Hannah Hale.

Direct your letter to Mount Vernon Postoffice, Posey County, Indiana.

It is now the 28th of May. We are all in good health. Perhaps you wish to know something more concerning Bethiah; although we have fared hard the season past, she never has appeared to be sorry she came with us. I have asked if she was not sorry; she would always say, No; could not have contented herself from the children. She seldom sheds tears, but she mourns the loss of her mother.

It is now July 12th that I have come to finish my letter. As to religion in this quarter, the Sectarians are numerous, but luke-warmness greatly prevails. I still believe in *Apollion's coming from his place of perdition, Saint Helena.

BARNABAS ANNABLE.

P. S.—Give my love to all; hoping these lines will find you well, with all inquiring friends of my old acquaintances, paper and time fails me. B. A.

From Dea. Ebenezer Smith [42] to his cousin, Dea Dimick Ellis, of Ashfield. (Ebenezer Smith's mother, Remember (Ellis) Smith and Dimick Ellis's father, Lieut. John, were sister and brother.)

CHAUTAUQUA, N. Y., Feb. 10, 1820.

MOST RESPECTED AND DEAR FRIEND:

Through the goodness of God I am enabled to take my pen in hand to write to one whom I sincerely respect and long to converse with, but as I am somewhat troubled with rheumatic complaint, I must convey my desire in writing. My family enjoys good health, and I hope this will find yours with the same blessing. The bearer of this letter will inform you of matters of news better than I can.

I understand that my affairs at Ashfield are very precarious, which causes me to write you. I sent letters to brother Gad Elmer, in August, desiring him to get security by a mortgage, or some other way as he should think proper, on some notes due me. I conclude that he never received them, and now I must desire one in whom I can put the greatest trust and confidence, to accept of my request. I have two notes against Ebenezer A——, one of $400, and another of $351, and some other money to be paid by Mr. Mallory. The $400 note was out, I think, a year ago last May. The other is out, I think, next May. I cannot travel as well as my son, and I send him to Ashfield. I wish the debts to be secured, if possible, and I send you the power of attorney in case there is need of it. * * I shall leave it entirely with you to act your judgment, as you are acquainted with Mr. A's circumstances, and as you are one of the selectmen, and have lately been called upon to prize brother Gad Elmer's estate, near him. I do not wish to hunt

---

*Mr. Annable regarded Napoleon Bonaparte as the APOLLION predicted in Revelations IX, 11. He was a very pious man and a devoted student of the bible. About 1812 he wrote and printed a book, in which he presented scripture texts and prophecies, which convinced him that the "end of the world" was near. He believed that he had solved the meaning of all those texts referring to "golden candlesticks," "seven seals," "falling stars," "bottomless pit," "ten horns," etc., etc. His ardor and sincerity is evident, from the fact that he invested most of his property in this work. But he failed, as all religious enthusiasts, before and since his time, have and *ever will*, who attempt to predict or explain natural events from the literal sense of the bible. The world, or globe, on which we live, is *round*, and has no "*end*", and will continue for millions of years in the future, as it has for ages past. The "coming of the Lord" is evidently to individuals, spiritually, "like a thief in the night," in which "one is taken and another left," and is not attended with any worldly change or commotion of Nature. As the first Christian era had been inaugurated nearly three hundred years before it was recognized, so, probably, we will be two or three centuries into the New Jerusalem before the world at large is aware of it. The "second advent," in the manner generally looked for, is one of the most enormous follies which pious, but deluded man has ever invented. It would seem as if 1800 years of continual disappointment would suffice to cure him of it.

any man, but I think it right that I should have my just due. * * Could I see you, and your family, and your parents, one hour, it would be of such satisfaction that it is not possible for me to dissemble, but I hope through the tender mercies of God, that we shall yet see each other face to face. * * . There has been considerable of an awakening in these parts. Last Sunday Elder Wilson baptized nine persons.

I will satisfy you for whatever trouble you are at on my account.

Very truly yours,
EBEN'R SMITH, JR.

From Dr. David Annable, to his brother-in-law, Dimick Ellis. See p. 368.

SEMPRONIUS, N. Y., April 7, 1824.

DEAR BROTHER : It has been a few days since I received your letter. I was at that time unable to write. I have now so far recovered as to be able to do some business. My complaint was vertigo, or dizziness in the head; objects appeared to turn around. The vertigo continued until I was bled largely, three pints from my arm and three pints from the temporal arteries. I am at present recovering slowly, but my head does not feel well, and I think there is danger of another attack and that it will be likely to terminate in appoplexy or palsy. But I mean to be as prudent as I can well be, but it is hard to govern my appetite, agreeable to the dictates of my judgment, as that is very keen. I was very glad to receive your letter. I have received a letter from Samuel Annable, [his nephew] in Indiana. He informs me that our friends there are well, and doing well in that country. He said he had just returned from a tour of service in the legislature. He says the legislature are for Adams for President. He remains a bachelor. My family are well. Whiting was again elected constable. * * It is a healthy time here, but there are many sudden deaths. I never saw the time before when death seemed so near as it does now. I am in some hope of completely recovering and enjoying my usual health, which hope, I suppose, generally continues to the end of life. All our friends are well in this quarter. It is cold weather here now, but some people are plowing.

Our two daughters, Lucy and Welthyann, think of engaging in school teaching. I have not seen your brother [John, 68] since you left here. My wife and children were very much gratified with your visit and send their best respects to you and your family. I hope you will write again soon. I shall want more than ever to hear from you.

Your affectionate brother,
DAVID ANNABLE.

Letter from Elder Barnabas Annable to his relatives in Ashfield.

MOUNT VERNON, Ind., Oct. 11, 1825.

DEAR BROTHER AND SISTER, DIMICK AND POLLY ELLIS: With my uncle and aunt, if in the land of the living. Although it is a long time since I have written to you, yet I have often thought of you with due affection. Not having much news to write, my neglect has been great. Two years ago my son Enos died in his one and twentieth year, at a time when I was very low myself with the fever and ague. This year, in July, our sister Bethiah died after lingering a few months with consumption. Samuel is apparently recovering from a liver complaint that has afflicted him nearly a year. The rest of us are now in tolerable health, God be thanked. We are in a country abounding with plenteousness of provisions, and a land delightsome to till, and our fruit trees begin to bear, so we should be happy if we were but well on it for religion, which at this time is at a low ebb, yet we despair not. I recollect you wished me to write concerning the price of Congress lands. The price is one dollar and a quarter per acre paid down, and there is a considerable wild land in this county not bought up.

The season here has been the dryest perhaps ever known here, but our land bears the drought exceedingly well.

The topic of conversation here in these days is Mr. Robert Owen's Social System,* now going into operation about twelve miles from this place. Perhaps you may have formed some idea of the system by reading his speeches to Congress last March, that is, if you have had them in your papers. There is a flocking to his standard of rich and poor from all parts of the United States and many from Europe. I have been out to see them; went through the rotations of their schools, of about one hundred and fifty scholars, and looked at the laboriousness of teachers who were not allowed to chastise them, and I likewise visited the Committe Room and made rather a favorable estimate of their community, to which the best enlightened part of the western world or States are rapidly becoming converted. We have a very favorable site in this neighborhood. If we can obtain it, I think we shall soon go into operation, and as it is but a few miles from the Ohio river it will be favorable for emigration. Should you, or anybody else, become converted, please direct them to Posey County, Indiana. From the landing at Mount Vernon to Mr. Owen's New Jerusalem, so called, to be completed in three or four years, is but fourteen miles from the Ohio river. Perhaps you may come to see, as you can come eleven hundred miles by the way of the Ohio river. The projected institution is not a patent right one, if it was your State would doubtless go into it. The range of buildings for dwellings are to be on four lines of seventy rods; the space way in the middle to be for play-grounds—except a few public buildings. On this space all the male scholars are learned to march and perform some military evolutions. Here note. Mr. Owen says, "That as wars come through delirium, it is therefore necessary for the enlightened to learn to defend themselves when nations become crazy." However, he is sanguine in the opinion that the nation will receive the light which surrounding circumstances lead him in the way of, and when they do, wars will cease. As for religion, his

* Robert Owen, a social reformer, was born in North Wales in 1771. He died in 1858. He married a daughter of David Dale, of Glasgow, Scotland. In 1823 he came to the United States and bought 20,000 acres of land at New Harmony, Indiana, on the Wabash river, where he started a communistic scheme which was quite novel and popular for a time, but soon failed. In 1828 he tried the same system in Mexico, by invitation of the government of that country, but this also failed. His son, Robert Dale Owen, born in Glasgow in 1801, lived at New Harmony for a long time, and was a member of Congress from that district in 1843 to 1847. He was a ready writer and published many pamphlets and books, the most noted one was a spiritualistic work called "The Debatable Land." His brother, David Dale Owen, born 1807, died in New Harmony in 1860. He was a noted geologist and employed by the government in 1837 to make a geological survey of Iowa, Minnesota and Wisconsin.

worship-house doors are open for all denominations, Brahmins, Mohammedans, or even Deists not excepted. He urges, in the most vehement manner, the necessity of charity, and thus shames the Christian world. His love for mankind is apparently great, although taken to be a Deist. As his pamphlets will be scattered through the country, you may soon know more about him and his institution; so of this no more at present.

Brother and sister: I have not heard from you for five long years. Do write me soon, pardoning my long neglect in writing to you. Ruth often speaks of Polly with great feelings of heart. May they one day meet where tears will be no more.

Give our love to all of our friends and acquaintances who may not have forgotten us. Our children would be remembered to you and your children. Nancy and her husband are calculating in a few months to join the New Harmonian Community, of which I have written. I was drawing to a close, but as it is long since I have written you doubtless will read with patience what the present quarter sheet will contain, whether of more or less importance.

I have latterly attached myself to a people in this quarter, known by the name of Christian Body, who take the bible, as it stands, for a rule of faith and practice, discarding all other disciplines, creeds and confessions of faith pretended to be drawn from it. They are Unitarians in general, at least of one kind. I therefore preach more constantly than when in an independent state.

Perhaps you would know as to the productions of our country. We raise cotton for our own use, and the last two seasons as good crops of flax as ever in Massachusetts, and if the frost should hold off, as we expect it, two weeks longer, we shall raise something better than four hundred bushels of Irish potatoes, which are a good article for Orleans market. We have likewise a good crop of sweet potatoes. The wheat in this country is generally good for some months, when it is affected by the weavel and sometimes wholly devoured, unless kept in some cold state by threshing it out and putting it in underground rooms or immediately flouring it. Wheat is worth fifty cents, corn commonly twenty-five cents per bushel.

The inhabitants may be said to be from the four winds or quarters of the world, but we insensibly shape to each other's manners, and the God of peace is helping us to love one another. Finally, everything considered, I think we are in a very good portion of the country for beauty, fertility and accommodations as to market, as the steamboat business is increasing and carried on reasonably, which is a dollar and a quarter per hundred, and often less. So I can freely invite those who are of an emigrating spirit to inquire for Mount Vernon, Posey County, Indiana, which is four miles from my cabin, in the township of Black.

I am, with all due respects, yours,

BARNABAS ANNABLE.

Letter from Elder Barnabas Annable to Des. Dimick Ellis, of Ashfield, in reply to one announcing the death of his wife, Mrs. Polly Annable Ellis. See page 116.

BLACK TOWNSHIP, POSEY CO., IND., June 17, 1826.

DEAR BROTHER: I received your letter the 20th of May, stating the sorrowful news of the death of my sister. It is a great consolation to me to expect that after her many painful hours in a short life she changed worlds for a glorious resting place in heaven, where, I hope, it will be the anxious care of us all who survive, so to live as that we may meet in the paradise of our God when our time on earth shall be out. By your letter my uncle and aunt are yet alive; may their last days be their best days, by reason of a redoubled life of holiness. My sister's children I should be glad to see in this life, but cannot expect to. I hope their fond mother may be permitted to have a guardian angel's charge of them, at least to lead in visions of the night, convincing them when they awake of the great propriety of remembering their Creator in the days of their youth.

Brother, the influenza has been severe the winter past with my family, yet, through mercy unexpectedly, we are all alive till the present. It affected all in the family but myself. I was taken about the first of March with a complaint that I had been accustomed to in York State, called dry colic, operating in the bowels like the gout pains in the limbs. For about a month I did not expect to get well, and have not been able to work until two or three weeks past, and although I have suffered greatly by the complaint a number of years by spells, at present I have no symptoms of it, God be praised !

The season of the year has been highly favorable for crops. You doubtless would wish to know how I like the country by this time. I know no reason why I should dislike it, for it is feasible, there being no stone, and it is very fertile. The only reason why produce is low in this country is, and ever will be, the great abundance of it raised, for steamboat charges are but from seventy-five cents to one dollar per hundred for freight from New Orleans to this place.

My wife would have written, but her nerves have failed for several years, so that she has excused herself from writing to any of her friends, but wishes to be remembered with the rest of our family to you and yours that may be yet living, and Hannah Lincoln, together with all who may remember us. I expect you would wish to have the paper filled out, and am at a loss to know what news might entertain you. The Owen System, of which I wrote last, is still progressing, and but for the old corrupt doctrine of man's not being blamable or praiseworthy, he being a creature of circumstances, being connected with it, I could wish it great success. The first, or old community, like a beehive, has swarmed twice this season, and others are forming upon the same plan, except doctrines.

Mr. Owen professes great love for the poor of mankind, and sacrifices great pains, or gives himself to great laboriousness for his people, yet is prudent with his money or fortune. With me, he is a paradox, as in some of his written addresses there is language so arranged as to answer the description of St. Paul's man of sin, mentioned in Paul's second epistle to the Thessalonians, and second chapter. He has about as much to say about Jesus Christ as Mahomed had, but applies those Scriptures which the prophets wrote of Christ, to himself. I read his newspaper weekly. He has capable writers. His papers are quite entertaining, and there is something appertaining to his system to be found in almost all his newspapers. I think his system will revolutionize Europe before it will America, therefore, it will be a long time before I may expect to see you here on a pilgrimage visit, as the Mahomedans to Mecca or Medina; yet I hope as long as we all live that I shall have the prayers of all my relations and friends that we may steer our course so as to meet with approbation in heaven at last to solace our souls in seas of heavenly bliss.

I remain your faithful brother,

BARNABAS ANNABLE.

SEMPRONIUS, N. Y., July 29, 1827.

DEAR UNCLE: This letter is to inform you that Azel Ellis' [209] wife died one day after Independence, and her child a week before. This was a great loss to all her acquaintances, and especially to Azel, who appears to mourn above measure in parting from his family. Her illness was short, being a little over a week, and previously she openly manifested her reconciliation to God. All the powers of men could not make her to live, I suppose. I attended the funeral; the sermon on the occasion was by dominie Becrow.

I think your land may be sold for ten dollars per acre, one half ready pay. There was such a chance a while ago; probably a fair price as lands around about it are selling. We have heard of the extraordinary casualty on Ashfield pond [page 295.] It was a great shock to us all. We want to hear the particulars. We are hoping and expecting you to visit us in Sempronius next fall or winter.

To Dimick Ellis, Ashfield. CYRUS ELLIS.

Memorandum of a trip in 1828, by Dea. Dimick Ellis, from Ashfield to Sempronius, N. Y., and return.

ASHFIELD, Jan. 2, 1828.

At three o'clock in the afternoon took the stage for Sempronius, New York, arrived at Smith's Tavern, in Cheshire, in the evening, and started from there at two o'clock in the morning. Arrived at Troy in the afternoon. Crossed the Hudson River on the ice, on foot, and arrived at Albany the same night, and put up at Milliken's Inn for the night, and paid four dollars for a passage in the stage to Utica. Left Albany at ten o'clock the next day for Utica; arrived there at seven o'clock the next morning, and went from there to New Hartford. The 6th, set out in the stage for Marcellus Village; arrived there the 7th, at one o'clock in the morning. Found the traveling very bad, snow all gone, and the frost all out of the ground. Visited Benjamin Rhoades. The 8th, left Mr. Rhoades and went to Auburn. The 9th, left Auburn and travelled to Sempronius on foot, and found my friends in health; and went from Sempronius to Mentz and visited Lieut. Edward Annable and wife. Saw them at their daughter's, Mrs. Wheaton. [See page 94.] From there went to Sennet and visited Elder Twiss and family. [Page 94.] Returned to Auburn and went into the State Prison. Saw the prisoners at work, in their different departments, numbering five hundred and thirty-one males and seventeen females, and returned again to Sempronius. February, the 21st, left Sempronius and came to Mr. Rhoades, in Marcellus. The 22d, took the stage at Marcellus Village for New Hartford; found the travelling very bad, and arrived at New Hartford the 23d; at four o'clock P. M. left New Hartford for Paris, and stayed at Daniel Lanterman's the 24th. The 25th, left Paris and took the stage at Utica for Albany. Arrived at Albany the 26th at five o'clock, P. M. The 27th, left Albany for Pittstown; arrived there in the afternoon and stayed over night at my son's, Richard Ellis. The 28th, left Pittstown and arrived at North Adams. The 29th, left Adams in the stage and crossed Hoosack Mountain, found the traveling very bad; arrived at Charlemont in the evening. March 1st, left Charlemont and arrived at home at five o'clock P. M., and found my family all well.

Letters from Thomas Lincoln, of Springville, Erie Co., N. Y., to his uncle, Dea. Dimick Ellis, and his youngest sister, Annie, of Ashfield. Mr. Lincoln's mother, Jane Ellis, was a sister of Dea. Ellis, and when she suddenly died in 1812, in western New York, the latter went there and took two of the children, Thomas and Annie, to his home in Ashfield. In 1825 young Thomas, not being pleased with his prospects in that rather forbidding country, somewhat unceremoniously, it is said, departed. See pages 107 to 110.

SPRINGVILLE, N. Y., Sept. 10, 1831.

DEAR UNCLE: Once more, by the leave of Divine Providence, I take my pen in hand to inform your honor of my present situation. I am in pretty good health, and hope this will find you and my friends in Ashfield enjoying the same. I am still a single man and living in the village of Springville. I make my home at a public house where I have lived for about two years. I give $1.75 per week for my board, and the proprietor is a great friend of mine. But this is not living much as when I lived with you. Oh, what a kind parent you was, and you have done all for me that a parent could for his own children, but I cannot express my feelings on this paper as I would if I could come and see you. I work at my trade, and work by the job. I have just commenced to build a meeting-house which will take me until next spring to complete it. Give my respects to your children and all who inquire for me. When I look back upon the days I spent with you and your children, it seems but a few weeks ago. Time rolls swiftly on. Please write as soon as you get my letter.

THOMAS LINCOLN.

P. S.—Please convey these few lines to my sister. Dear sister: I long to see you very much and all my relatives. If I have my health I will come and see you within one year. I have been sick some, and have had many troubles and trials. * * * Write as soon as you can, and give my respects to all. T. L.

SPRINGVILLE, N. Y., Jan. 12, 1833.

DEAR SISTER: I have written to uncle Dimick several times, and have addressed a few lines to you in each of them, and have not had but one letter from you and one from him. Eight years have passed and gone since I left your town, dear sister. Do you remember the last time I saw you I told you that I should not see you again in one year. You did not seem to believe it, but the year has come and gone and gone again, and the hour of meeting has not yet come, and perhaps it never will whilst we live on earth. * * * Dear sister, I cannot give any encouragement as to when I can come to see you, as my business is such that I cannot leave at present. I have taken another meeting-house to build, and have to finish it by the first day of August next. I hope these few lines will find you well and enjoying the

sweet comforts of life, and that you may receive them as a token of friendship. I am still a single man. Give my respects to uncle Asher's folks and
Jane, and all others of my cousins, and all who ever know me.

Yours with respect,

THOMAS LINCOLN.

P. S.—A few lines to my uncle Dimick Ellis. Dear sir: I have written
one or two letters to you and got no answer. I hope you have not forgotten
me, and especially when you call your little family around you to offer up
your prayers to Almighty God. I am not a professor of religion, but I am a
well-wisher of the cause and help to support the Gospel here. Last spring
there was a protracted meeting here for 18 days, and a great reformation followed.   *   *   *   Dear uncle, while you are reading these lines over
think of the days that have passed and gone when I was one in your family,
and whether you did your duty or not in offering your prayers for me. I can say
for one that I do think you did, and that you gave your best advice to me.
But I was young then, and did not always know what was best. I shall not
be able to come and see you till next fall.   *   *   *   I have built me
a shop and got a good stock of tools. I send my warmest love and best
respects to you and your family, and to all who ever knew me. Please send
me a letter as soon as you receive this, with all the deaths, marriages, etc.

Yours with much respect,

THOMAS LINCOLN.

From Fernando C. Annable, youngest child of Lieut. Edward Annable, to
Dea. Dimick Ellis, of Ashfield. See pages 96 and 390. Mr. Annable settled in
Almena, Mich., one year after the date of this letter, where he died in 1886.

MENTZ, CAYUGA Co., N. Y., June 24, 1835.

HIGHLY RESPECTED UNCLE: Through the kindness of Mr. Cyrus Alden,
who condescends to be the bearer of this letter, I have an opportunity of writing to you. The most important news which I have to communicate is the
death of my mother. She died on the first of February of an inflammatory
complaint which was quite prevalent through this country last winter, and
generally fatal to old people. The first alarming symptom of her disease was
a severe ague chill nine days before her death, and when the chill subsided the
succeeding fever deprived her of her senses, and she remained delirious except
at short intervals, during the remainder of her sickness. Her sufferings were
rather more than is generally experienced by old people in their last illness. Her
hope in the Redeemer of souls was unusually lively, and at intervals of sanity
was always expressed. Father lives in Marcellus, enjoying good health, but
has lost almost all his faculties. I have recently heard from Anna and that
she is in a dangerous situation as to health, with small prospects of recovery.
The rest of the friends are well, as far as I know. I have commenced keeping
house in the neighborhood in which I was brought up, and have postponed
my intended removal to Michigan for the present. Betsey's health has been
very discouraging most of the time since we were at Ashfield—the cause of my
settling here—but is something more encouraging now. Let me hope, sir,
that the opportunity may yet occur when I shall have the pleasure of seeing
you here, when I shall have a better opportunity of expressing my feelings

towards you for the kind reception you gave me when I was in Ashfield. I perceive, as I am more and more deprived of the society of my parents, my affections increase towards those with whom they were familiar and esteemed. The evening is far spent, and I believe that I have communicated the news of importance. I wish you to give my respects to aunt and each member of your family, and believe me,

Your obedient servant,

F. C. ANNABLE.

From Samuel Annable, son of Barnabas, to Dea. Dimick Ellis, of Ashfield.

YANKEE SETTLEMENT, POSEY COUNTY, IND., Dec, 15, 1839.

DEAR UNCLE: Agreeable to brother Elisha Phillips' wish, I cheerfully undertake to answer your letter to him, bearing date September 14th, and would have written sooner, but at the date of your letter I was on an expedition to Iowa, Wisconsin and the northern part of Illinois, under Mr. David Dale Owen, who was employed by the government as principal agent to explore those regions for the purpose of ascertaining the localities of the mineral lands, from which expedition I have but just returned. It affords me great satisfaction to see a letter from under your hand. I have often thought of you in connection with the scenes of my childhood, and thought it would afford me great satisfaction to pay a visit to the place of my nativity, and to my esteemed uncle, but I am afraid that circumstances will never favor such an undertaking. I have often thought about writing, but the uncertainty of your being in the land of the living would deter me. It appears by your letter that you have never been fully informed with regard to the mortality in. my father's family, and I am now unable to give you the precise date, having had a house burned in which the records were consumed, and I am not able to recollect them.

It was eleven years ago last summer that an unusual fever for this country broke out in our family in the month of June. My mother was the first who fell a victim to it, sister Nancy next, then brother David and Bromley, then sisters Eliza and Rhoda—all in the space of six weeks. I had the same fever, but through the mercy of God, recovered after a long and severe illness. Three others of the family had it and recovered. It was confined principally to our family, but few of our neighbors having it. As to the cause, there was a diversity of opinion. Some thought the disease was brought from New Orleans in some articles of clothing which my brother Bartlet (who had been trading down the river the winter previous) had brought with him. Various other causes were assigned. Suffice it to say, it was a very unusual occurrence for this country, and you may be sure a very trying season.

My father died the ninth of May, 1835, after suffering for something more than a year with pulmonary consumption. My brother David died in October 1836 of bilious fever. Brother Bartlet has gone to Texas. I have had no letter from him since last winter. He was much pleased with the country, had obtained 2,750 acres of land, was unmarried. This is about all the information I could get from him. [See page 367]. I have but one brother left in the country. That is Russel, the youngest. He is a young man, about twenty-three, rather an odd fellow, something like old uncle Thomas Annable.

Sister Electa, Elisha Phillips' wife, is still living; her eldest son and daughter are married and have children. She has four other children living, two sons and two daughters. Sister Fanny is married to a man by the name of Wilbourn, and has two children, a son and daughter. [See page 367]. I have been married only seven years; have a very agreeable companion; we have had but one child, which we lost. My wife's maiden name was Davis. I am proprietor of the farm on which father settled; have 160 acres of land, about half under good improvement; an orchard of bearing fruit trees; have built me a comfortable framed house and barn, and we are generally blessed with plenty of the good things of this world, though we have had to labor under considerable embarrassments.

With regard to religion, I would like to say something, feeling a deep interest in the cause. There is a great proportion of the population who are religious, and a considerable degree of religious excitement prevails at times, but the people are so cut up into different denominations and manifest, at times, so much of party spirit, as I fear, seriously to affect the prosperity of Zion. The denominations are Methodists, what are called Regular Baptists, General Baptists, Cumberland Presbyterians, a few Congregationalists, and those who style their church by no other name than that of Christian. Of the latter, I, my wife, brother E. Phillips and wife, and brother John Wilbourn and his wife are members. As a religious society, we seem to be every where evil spoken of ; by some called heretics, unitarians, Campbellites, reformers, and by some disorganizers, etc. But we wish to take the bible for the man of our counsel, and trust in God that if we live agreeable to its dictate it will go well with us; without so doing, we feel assured that it would go ill with us, no matter to what church we may have attached ourselves.

I would remark, in relation to health, that it is a general time of good health in this section of country, though it was very sickly in parts of the country I traveled over in the fall, particulerly Iowa. I had always heard Iowa spoken of as a very healthy country, but I think it has been much overrated. Fever, I think, must prevail to a great extent, owing to the swamps with which the country abounds.

I wish you to write and let us know that you have received this. Give what information you can about such things as you think most interesting, and should we never meet in life, pray God that we have the happiness to meet and enjoy each other's society in a happier state of existence.

Your affectionate nephew,
SAMUEL ANNABLE.

Letter from Dea. Richard Ellis [239] to his brother, Lewis Ellis, of Otisco —now Belding, Mich.

PITTSTOWN, RENSSELAER Co., N. Y., March 2d, 1844.

DEAR BROTHER : I take my pen to answer your letter. I have delayed writing to hear from Ashfield. Edwin [Ranney] and wife have been to A., and returned yesterday. He was married to Miss Eliza Button, January 29. [See page 388.] We are all well here and father and mother, in A., also. Tell Abner Wright and Hiram Green that their friends here are well. [Messrs. W. and G. removed, in 1843, from Pittstown to Otisco, and settled on farms adjoining Lewis and Richard Ellis.] Kingsley Slade and Miss Martin were married January 30; also Michael Weters and Emeline Gibbs last Tuesday. [Mr. and Mrs. W. settled in Otisco, in 1845, where they now live.] You want to know if we are coming to Michigan this spring. I will give you a direct answer. We shall come. We have had a cold winter and the most sleighing I ever knew. Abner's brother, Norman, was married to Miss Maria Hydorn in January. He and Elder Mosher intend to go out to Michigan in the spring. [They both settled in Otisco the next year.] Job Gibbs, I think, will come. He talks of taking a thrashing machine along. It works by horse-power, and it is said that with it three hands can thrash one hundred bushels a day. I should have started last fall with John, but could not then get father and mother started. [Dr. John Ellis located in Grand Rapids, Mich., in the fall of 1843.] I have sold my place here and turned myself, so as to be ready to go this spring. I will bring the nails you wrote for. I have had built a very stout wagon. I think it will carry one hundred bushels of wheat anywhere. Volney Belding is in Ashfield. We expect him here soon. Give my respects to all our friends. We want to see them all.

I remain your brother,
RICHARD ELLIS.

Letters from Dea. Dimick Ellis to Cyrus Ellis, of West Niles, N. Y., near Moravia.

OTISCO, MICH., March 9. 1850.

DEAR NEPHEW: I received your letter of 2d of January, and meant to have answered it before this time. I was much pleased on receiving it, being the first information that I had received from you since you left this place. Was glad to hear of your safe arrival at your home, and that you found your family in health. In regard to my own health, it is very good and has been, with but little exception, ever since you left here. My wife's health has been poor. She has been much troubled with rheumatism. She is more comfortable now. Lewis' health is good; his wife has been sick with the ague and fever, but is better now. The rest of the family are well. Richard and family are well; he and sons are at work in the pinery; has bought him a span of horses and has paid for them in drawing saw mill logs; gave $230 for the horses and harness. Tiberius Belding and family are well and doing well. Deacon John Shaw [247] and family are well. Stephen Wilson is married again; is well and family. The wheat crop last season fell short almost one-half of a full crop. Corn and potato crops good. Lewis and Richard sowed nearly 60 acres of wheat last fall; it looked very well in the fall. The winter past has been very moderate; snow not over two or three inches deep. I will now proceed to write you a copy of the record of your grandfather Ellis' family, agreeable to your request.   *   *   [See page 19, Nos. 15 and 16].

You will perceive by this family record that I am the only surviving person of your grandfather's family, and, no doubt, before many years are past away that I shall go the way of all the earth. Solemn thought; and when I cast my thoughts back to the years of my childhood and youth and middle age life, it fills my mind with solemnity. I can truly say that one generation hath passed away and another come, and the generation that I belonged to has mostly passed away and another hath come. I hope that when it shall be ours to die that we shall be prepared to meet in another and better world, where there is no sin and, of course, no sorrow. There has been quite a gold excitement here of late. There has been a man [Michael O'Connell] from this place to California and returned home the winter past, and brought home something like $18,000, and there has been a number of other men started from this place of late for California. Thomas and Chandler Belding [251 and 253] have both gone. I wish you, as soon as convenient after you receive this letter, to write to me about your mother's health, and what you know about brother John Ellis' widow and children, and likewise, what you know about your uncle Lincoln's children, and be pleased to receive for yourself and family my best wishes. Your aunt sends her respects to you and family, likewise Lewis and wife send theirs. DIMICK ELLIS.

Otisco, Mich., February 19th, 1853.

DEAR NEPHEW: After a long delay I take pen in hand to answer your letter of December last, in which you informed me of the death of Hannah Lincoln [see page 180] and of the ill health of Marilla Lincoln. It seems that the greatest part of the Lincoln family are dead. There were ten of them, and I believe there are but three or four of them now living, two sons, Thomas and Benjamin. Thomas is married, has eight children and lives in Springville, Erie Co., N. Y. Benjamin is now in Otisco, an unfortunate man, forty years old; has been out of health five or six years with the rheumatism. You wrote that you, together with many others in New York State, were engaged to get the Maine liquor law passed. I hope you will see it become a law in your State, for I am well assured that it would be a great benefit to the inhabitants thereof. There are many people in Michigan engaged in the temperance cause. I have been engaged in that cause twenty-two years past, and feel now the same anxiety to see it prosper that I ever have. I have ever considered it to be one of the best of causes. I have learned of late that the legislature of Michigan has enacted a law similar to the Maine law, and I understand it is to be submitted to the people whether it shall become a law or not. It is believed that the people will vote in favor of it. My own health is good. I have entered my 77th year. My wife's health is very poor. Lewis and the rest of the family are well. Richard and family are well. Tiberius Belding and family are well. Jane Shaw and family are well, and it is a very healthy time at present in this part of the country. Mr. Moseman, who lived in Ionia, and who formerly lived in your town of West Niles, N. Y., died a few weeks past. We have had a very moderate winter so far, had but little snow. Wheat sells at Grand Rapids for 75 cents, corn at home for 50 cents, oats for 37½ cents. Lewis sowed last fall 37 acres of wheat. He is getting lumber to build him a new house. I wish you to write a letter to me as soon as convenient after receiving this, more particulars about your family. Have any of them settled in the world, and if so, where do they live? And write how your mother does [71] and how her children do and where they live, and likewise how your uncle John's widow does [69] and where she lives and what you know about her children. Give my respects to your wife and family, and like wise to your mother, and to your aunt Ellis, and to all inquiring friends, and be pleased to accept for yourself and family my best regards. DIMICK ELLIS.

To Cyrus Ellis, Esq.

Letter from Russel Phillips' daughter [see page 102] to Dea. Dimick Ellis, of Otisco, (now Belding) Mich. Her mother, Rhoda (Williams) Phillips, was a niece of Dimick Ellis. Rhoda's mother, Mrs. Hannah Ellis Williams, was Dimick Ellis' eldest sister.

RACINE, WIS., March 24th, 1853.

DEAR UNCLE: By the request of my parents and from the remembrance of you, I am induced to perform the agreeable task of writing to you. Allow me first to introduce myself as Elizabeth, the youngest of Russel and Rhoda Phillips' family. The memory of myself has probably passed from your mind, but that of my parents must still remain fresh. You have probably before this heard of our removal to this State. We came here in the summer of 1848. From that time until last summer my parents made their home with my brother John, who lives about a hundred miles from here in a farming place. Last summer they removed to this city where they have since remained. Since my parents' residence in this State their health has been very good. My father has had several attacks of the fever and ague, which has affected him very much, but mother's health has been better since she came west than it was east.

While I have been writing, your letter has been brought in. It was joyfully received, I can assure you. I should have written ere this had I known where you lived. And the knowledge that we have obtained came from Mr. McDonald; and now that we know that you are alive and well, and also where you live, I can finish it with all pleasure, and tell you about the situation of my parents' family. Of the family of eight, they are all still living and well. Hannah Phillips [see page 102] and husband live in the county where my brother John lives. They have a family of four. John's wife is unknown to you. He has a family of three. Both John and Flowers are farming, and possess very valuable farms apiece. Monroe is married and has one child. Himself and family reside in Lockport, N. Y. He is in the mercantile business. Galusha is also married and lives in Rochester, N. Y. Allan and wife still remain in Ashfield, Mass. Mary is married to a Mr. Yout. They reside in this city, have a family of three. Sarah is also married to a Mr. Hill; herself and only child are now staying with me, her husband having gone south. Our family and our families family have not only been blessed with life and good health, but prosperity, which, taking all things into consideration, is uncommon for so large a family as ours. We are very pleasantly situated in this place, and like living here very well. Mother and father send their love to you and would like to see one and all of you at any time. We would like to know about the death of uncle Asher Belding. I wish you would visit us, uncle Dimick; I remember you very distinctly. I remember you as being a large, corpulent man, with a round, smiling face, hair that was white with the frosts of age, and a stiff white beard, which you said was good to make childrens' cheeks red; consequently, when I was a child you used to put it to the test, and many a time my cheeks have smarted keenly from its brushing. Sometime ago we received a letter from uncle Apollos Williams [see page 104], stating the death of grandfather and uncle Edward. I answered it and received in return one from his son, which I enclose, that you may peruse it. Please return it when you write. My love to all.

Your niece,

ELIZABETH A. PHILLIPS.

Letter from Dea. Dimick Ellis, of Otisco, now Belding, Mich., to Cyrus Ellis [233].

OTISCO, IONIA Co., MICH., Jan. 7, 1856.

DEAR NEPHEW: I now take pen in hand to inform you of my present health, which is as good as it was when I left you last spring on my way to Massachusetts; likewise, all your friends in this part of Michigan are as well as usual. I will next proceed to write you about my journey to Massachusetts, and of my safe return home to Michigan. You recollect, no doubt, carrying and leaving me and the young man that was with me to the railroad, near Benjamin's Rhoades. I took the cars and arrived at Springfield, Mass., at 9 o'clock p. m. The young man left me at Albany. I stayed at Springfield over night. Next morning I took the cars for Greenfield, then the stage for Shelburne Falls; arrived here at about 2 o'clock p. m. I called on Dr. Milo Wilson; found him and family well. I stayed at Shelburne several days, then went to Ashfield to your uncle Jesse Ranney's; found them comfortable for people of their age. I then visited about among old friends. There are but few persons living in the school district where I used to live when you lived with me. Your uncle Jesse Ranney and family, David Belding and widow Perry and one son, I believe, are all that live in the district now. The rest have died or have moved away. Surely, one generation passeth away and another cometh. There are not so many inhabitants in Ashfield now as there were when you lived there. I went to South Hadley and saw the Mt. Holyoke Female Institution, founded by Miss Mary Lyon; saw the monument raised to her memory by her pupils. The institution is in a flourishing condition. The pupils frequently go to Buckland to see the place where she was born. Truly, she was an extraordinary woman, and her name will go down to posterity as such. Shelburne Falls has become quite a village; there are three meeting houses there; one Baptist, one Congregationalist, and one Methodist. There is a large knife factory on the Buckland side of the Falls. There is a flourishing academy on the Shelburn side, and it has become a place of considerable business. Lewis [241] and wife came to Massachusetts about the middle of October and stayed until the 3rd day of December, when they returned, together with myself, to Michigan. We stopped at Detroit and stayed at John's one day and two nights. Found him well and doing well. We returned home the 9th day of December all well. I wish you, on receiving this letter, to write an answer immediately. Give my respects to your mother and to your uncle John's children [68], and receive for yourself and family my best wishes for your and their present and future health and happiness.

From your affectionate uncle,

To Cyrus Ellis, Esq.   DIMICK ELLIS.

Letter from Dr. John Ellis (243) on the death of his brother, Dea. Richard Ellis, (239) of Belding, Mich.

NEW YORK CITY, March 27, 1878.

DEAR NEPHEW: Your telegram came at one o'clock this morning announcing the death of my dear brother, your father. It was not unexpected, for the symptoms you have written of in cases like his denote approaching dissolution of the material body. Allow me to sympathize and console with you in this, our affliction. A kind husband, father and grandfather has departed and left your little circle; a dear brother from our older circle; a good citizen, au earnest and sincere Christian in the good providence of the Lord has moved on and entered the real, the living world. His past life—useful, earnest and true—is an assurance to us that what is our loss is his gain. He has simply gone before us, for death in this world is but birth into the next, for as the material body dies, the spiritual body is raised. As the material eyes close on friends in this world the spiritual eyes open amid friends in the spiritual world. In a very short time—a few years at most—we must all follow him. How short is life.

After receiving your dispatch I lay awake three or four hours, dwelling in thought, amid the days of my childhood, youth and adult life; amid scenes of joy and gladness, and sorrow and sadness. Such is life in this world. Let us all strive to do our duty faithfully and honestly, trusting in the Lord, for His providence is around us ever. May the Lord preserve and keep you in this hour of trouble, is my earnest prayer. A little circle of four—one sister and three brothers—which has existed from childhood to old age has now been broken in this world, to be re-united, ere many years, in the spiritual world, for we are all advancing step by step, and one by one we shall lay aside our mantle of flesh and join our brother. God grant that we who remain may strive earnestly to be as well prepared to depart as was he who has now gone before us.

Affectionately yours,

To C. D. ELLIS, Belding, Mich.   JOHN ELLIS.

Extracts from No. 20, "Vol. 2," of the "*Michigan Sentinel*," published by Edward D. Ellis. See page 165.

MICHIGAN SENTINEL.

MONROE, MICHIGAN TERRITORY, Nov. 4, 1826.
Monroe on the River Raisin. Published every Saturday, by Edward D. Ellis.
Terms, $2.50 per annum.

Sample articles—"A proclamation by John Quincy Adams, president of the United States, by H. Clay, Secretary of State, of a General Convention of Friendship, Commerce and Navigation between the United States of America and His Majesty, the King of Denmark. Done at Washington Oct. 4, 1826."

Market reports—Butter, 10 to 15 cents. Wheat, 62 cents. Oats, 25 cents. Flour, $3.50 to $4.00. Pork, 12 to 14 cents. Salt, $4.50 to $4.75 per bbl. Sugar, 10 to 12. Whiskey, 37. Apples, 38 to 50.

Lewis Cass was governor of the territory. The territory was governed by a legislative council appointed for two years. Those from the 9th of March, 1826, were Abraham Edwards, Harry Connor, Andrew G. Whitney (deceased) and Robert Forsythe, from Wayne and Washtenaw; Walcott Lawrence, Hubert Leacroix and Laurent Durocher from Monroe and Lenawee; Sidney Dole, Wm. F. Mosely, from Oakland; John Stockton, Wm. A. Burt, Macomb; Zephaniah W. Bunce, St. Clair Co.; Robert Irwin, jr., Mackinaw and Crawford counties. June 9th, 1826, Gen. Cass made proclamation calling together the council for Nov. 2, 1826.

"Marriage enlarges the scene of our happiness and miseries. A marriage of love is pleasant; a marriage of interest easy, and a marriage where both meet happy. A happy marriage has in it all the pleasures of friendship and all the enjoyments of sense and reason, and indeed all the comforts and sweets of this life. Good nature and evenness of temper will give you an easy companion for life; virtue and good sense an agreeable friend ; LOVE and CONSTANCY a good wife or husband."

"Printer's Call, June 9th, 1826. The undersigned finding it hard to live entirely upon *air*, earnestly requests that those indebted on account of Vol. 1, will make payments on or before Jan. 1st, 1827, and those who are unable to pay are requested to call and *promise*."

Luther Tucker & Co.. of Rochester, N. Y., propose to publish the *Telegraph*, a daily paper, for six dollars a year.

There is an account of the proposed Welland Canal in Canada, and the formation of a company with a capital of $1,000,000 to construct it.

The *Sentinel* is a five column folio. Over one-half is devoted to publishing United States and Territorial laws.

In a subsequent number of the *Sentinel* is the following: "We should never despair, for we may be assured that there is a Pilot at the helm of all earthly concerns who is guiding the great ship of human affairs in the best possible way to a haven of peace and prosperity."

THE OLD DELMAR CHURCH.

The following extract from the *Wellsboro Agitator*, (Tioga Co., Penn.) for March 21, 1876, was written by Elder O. N. Worden, of New Milford, Penn. It relates mostly to Dea. Richard Ellis and his descendants, who were among the first settlers in that portion of Pennsylvania in the early part of the present century. See pages 83, 86.

"Perhaps the first church in Delmar, when this township comprised nearly one-fourth of the west part of the county of Tioga, was on Big Pine Creek, west of Wellsboro and the Big Marsh or Meadow. The meetings were principally at the first school house and at the house of the Ellis family. There had been no preaching or special efforts recently, if ever, and yet a work of grace on the hearts of the people was evident.

In June, 1819, Elder Oviatt preached at the house of Richard Ellis to most of the people of the settlement.

Eleven were baptised on the 27th day of June, 1819. They were Reuben Ellis, Richard Ellis, sr., and jr., Asaph, John, Consider, Chloe,(Richard's wife), Amanda and Lucretia Ellis, Martha Herrington and Eunice Bacon.

June 29th, Elder S. Bigelow, from New York State, baptised four—David Dimick, Anna Phœnix, Eunice Herrington and Patience Ellis.

In September of the same year, Elder John Stone visited the settlement and baptised Polly Ellis and Nancy Bacon. On Dec. .22d, 1819, the above and a few others were organized into a regular Baptist church. The next day David Ellis was baptised.

More than half of the early members of this church were of the Ellis name or relations of the family. Reuben, the oldest, was a deaf mute, who had long waited to follow Him he loved in His holy ordinance of baptism. "Asaph Run" is named after Dea. Asaph Ellis. Ellisburg, Potter County, is named after this family there located. One Ellis was a deacon in Tioga Church. John, Richard and Consider were licensed preachers or exhorters, and the last named was ordained in Potter County, March 19th, 1835. In 182—[the exact year is not given] there was what was known as the "great sickness," in which there was great mortality among these people."

Localities where numbers of the Ellises have located, or where they now reside.

OTISCO AND BELDING, MICH.

The township of Otisco is the northwest corner town of Ionia County, Mich. It began to be settled about 1836 and 1837, principally by emigrants from Central New York and Ashfield, Mass. The first township election was held April 2d, 1838, at the shanty of Mr. Robert W. Davis, who, with several others from Oakland County, Mich., had settled there. Mr. Davis' home was a little northwest of the house and farm of Mr. Volney Belding, whose place was one mile north of the town center and was on the northwest corner of the cross roads at that point.

The officers elected were as follows: Supervisor, John L. Morse; Clerk, R. W. Davis; Assessors, Amos H. Russell, George W. Dickerson and Ambrose Spencer; Highway Commissioners, Geo. W. Dickerson, Ambrose Spencer and Rufus R. Cook; Directors of the Poor, William M. Springer and Volney Belding; Justices of the Peace, R. W. Davis, G. W. Dickerson, Rufus R. Cook and Nathaniel E. Horton; School Inspectors, Robert W. Davis, Geo. W. Dickerson and N. E. Horton; Constable and Collector, Ambrose Spencer.

There are but three men now living (1888) who cast their votes at that time: John L. Morse, C. S. D. Harroun and Volney Belding; the others have been rowed across the river by the silent boatman. Fourteen votes were cast. Those who did not aspire for office were Wm. Russel, C. S. D. Harroun, Daniel Horton, Munson Seeley, Asa Palmer and Patrick Kelly.

There are but two persons now residing in the town who were there then, Mrs. James Moon and Gilbert Russell. This year (1838) was born the first white child in the town, Eliza Russell, daughter of Amos Russell, now the wife of L. C. Fales, of Orleans. The first white boy born in the town the following February, was A. B. Morse, son of John L. Morse, now Supreme Judge of Michigan. (See page 171.) In fifty years the town has grown, by birth and immigration, from fourteen votes to about six hundred.

Otisco was a town of remarkable fertility, and settled almost exclusively by men and women of uncommon intelligence and worth. Among the agricultural towns of Michigan it has for many years stood next to one the highest in the state for wealth, enterprise and moral and intellectual advancement. Among the early settlers were the following from Ashfield, Mass.: Volney and Thomas Belding and their sister, Mrs. Jane Shaw. (See page 186,) Joseph and Nathaniel Fisk,(the latter has just died, March, 1888), Frederick and Silas Kimberley, with several sisters and their father, Sterns Kimberly, Geo. Cooley, Dexter Cutler, Mr. Coombs. Most of the above had families and located there previous to 1840. In the forties there arrived Mr. Tiberius Belding, Lewis Ellis, Dea. Dimick Ellis, Horace Liscomb, Orpheus Nelson, Chandler

Belding, Charles and Norman Putney, all of whom, except Mr. Nelson, had families. Nearly all of these Ashfield people located on farms in the north part of the town and were neighbors and steadfast friends during all their lives. But few of these people are now living, but they have all left names worthy of lasting remembrance.

In the township of Otisco are several villages—Smyrna, in the south part of the town; "the corners" or Otisco Center; Kiddville, in the extreme northeast, and Belding about one mile and a half southwesterly from Kiddville. The latter place is a station on the Detroit, Lansing & Northern railroad, from which point a branch road runs over to Belding. Freight trains go out and in from Belding every day, but passengers are conveyed by a horse car which connects with all trains. Belding is a flourishing village of about 1,000 population and rapidly growing.

At this locality is what was known in early times as Broas' Rapids, so-called from Mr. Charles Broas, one of the early settlers, whose house was one-half mile south, and whose farm included the lands where Belding now stands. In 1855 Mr. Hiram Belding, from Ashfield, purchased this site, and a few years after improvements of the water-power and the erection of a large saw mill by the Wilsons, Luther and Belding Bros., and a first-class flouring mill by Knott & Co., led to the quite rapid growth of the village. In 1886, the Belding Bros. erected a large mill there for the manufacture of sewing silks, and at the present time have nearly completed one of the largest and finest brick and stone hotel and opera house buildings in that part of the State. The same parties also have a factory employing 100 workmen engaged in making refrigerators, and are about to enlarge the same works four fold.

The churches of Belding are the Christian, built about 1875, and the Methodist, erected in 1887. Belding also has a flourishing union school with a large and costly brick building. At Otisco Center there is a Baptist church, erected about 1855. Belding is one of the largest shipping stations on the D., L. & N. railroad. The Belding Bros. have here nearly 1000 acres of land, mostly under cultivation and well stocked with superior cattle and sheep.

On the north bank of the Flat river, opposite the main part of the village, are the farms of Messrs. Lewis and Richard Ellis, who located there in 1842 and 1844, and where they and some of their descendants now reside—except Dea. Richard Ellis, (239) who died in 1878.

PITTSTOWN, N. Y.

Pittstown, Rensselaer County, N. Y., is an agricultural town situated on the Macadam or stone road half way between Troy, N. Y., and Bennington, Vt. It is a large township and near the southeast corner is the hamlet of Boyntonville, named for Mr. Wm. Boynton, who was born there about 1830, and still lives there. At this place, Dea. Richard Ellis, (239) eldest son of Dimick of Ashfield, settled when a young man. When he was about 21 years of age, he started out, as did most of Ashfield young men, (see page 118), on a prospecting tour through Vermont and New York. In a year or so he located at Pittstown and began the coopering business—manufacturing barrels for the market at Troy, 15 miles distant. This was about 1826 or 1827. Here he remained until the spring of 1844, when he removed to Otisco, Mich.

In 1842, his brother Lewis and brother-in-law Tiberius Belding having settled in Otisco, he made a trip out there and bought 200 acres of land. At this time the emigration to the west was beginning to set in quite strong, and within a few years several families and many young men left Pittstown for Otisco. In 1843, Messrs. Hiram Green, John Penny, Abner Wright and James Tallman were among these. In 1844, were Dea. Richard Ellis, Job Gibbs, Wm. Stokes, Aaron Weaver and Erastus Jencks. Within the next year or two, these were followed by Elder Wilson Mosher, Charles Spicer, John Gibbs, Michael Weter, Allen Thompson, Edwin Ranney, Alex. Tallman, Daniel Green and his father and mother, James, Norman and Charles Wright, (brothers of Abner above) Joseph Boynton, Joseph Felshaw, John and his son, Matthew Hydorn, Nicholas Demory and Andrus Phillips. The last four were from Grafton, about one mile south of Boyntonville. Several more of Pittstown people settled in other parts of Michigan in the forties, and soon after Loudon, Darius and Demetrius Button, with their mother and the latter's brother, Allen Thurber, in Grand Rapids, Mich., and Mary Wadsworth, who married a Lawrence who owned and kept the Lawrence hotel, in Adrian, Mich., for many years up to the spring of 1888. The writer left Boyntonville, his native place, when but a lad. Forty-three years later, (in 1887), he made a short visit there. It is a bright spot with many cheerful happy faces to be seen, but few who were known to him. The Gibbs, Warren, Haskins and Wadsworth families, once numerous and influential, have mostly "gone west" or that other "way of all the world." Some of the Campbells and Richmonds, elegant people, hold to the old homesteads yet, each of which have strong attachments—near relatives—in Otisco now.

SPRINGFIELD, PENN.

Springfield, the northwestern township of Erie County, Pa., lies on the southern shore of Lake Erie, and is where Dea. David Ellis, with his sons William and David, jr., with their families from Ashfield, settled in 1818. See pages 86 to 88.

The lake shore plain is about three miles wide. In the eastern part of the plain and along the ridge road are excellent farms. When the first settler, Capt. Samuel Holliday* came here to locate in 1796, he found an unbroken forest. Other settlers soon followed, and when in 1818 the Ellis families came, Springfield contained about 700 inhabitants. East Springfield, situated on the Ridge Road, three miles from the lake, was then Springfield Four Corners, and contained two hotels, a store, a school-house and a few houses, mostly built of logs. On the beach of the lake was a road which extended west as far as Conneaut, Ohio, along which many of the new comers settled. All trace of the road has now disappeared, the water having washed away the bank, in some places, over 100 feet since then. Some buildings have been moved over one-half a mile for safety from the waves. The first Methodist-Episcopal church was erected a mile south of West Springfield in 1804. There are now two M. E. churches, one at East and one at West Springfield. The first Presbyterian church building was a small log structure standing on the older

*Mrs. Richardson, wife of Hon. D. M. Richardson, of Detroit, Mich., was a Holliday, born and reared in Springfield.

portion of the cemetery grounds. It was built in 1804. The Christian church at East Springfield was organized in 1826, with twelve members, one of whom was Mrs. Rumina Ellis, (181.) A church was built in 1839, and the present building was erected on the same site in 1885. The Baptist congregation was organized in 1826, at West Springfield, a village on the Ridge Road four miles from East Springfield. David Ellis, sr., (32) was a charter member and deacon in the Church. At West Springfield a Universalist church was built in 1850.

Of the three villages, East, West and North Springfield, the East village is the largest. There are several handsome residences with beautiful lawns and gardens, several places of business, an academy used as high and public school. A large, well kept cemetery in which are many beautiful and costly monuments, is situated one half mile north of East Springfield. There are two lines of railroads, Lake Shore & Michigan Southern and New York Central & St. Louis. (The latter road is popularly called the nickle plate from the fact or impression that its builders spared no expense of money in its construction.) This road has a depot at East and West Springfield, the former a depot at North Springfield. A short distance east of the depot at North Springfield, is the most solid and costly piece of work in the township, the L. S & M. S. culvert and embankment over Crooked Creek. The embankment is 90 feet above the water and between 700 and 800 feet in length. About 200 men were employed in its construction, and it required two years to complete it. About one mile south of this structure, where the "nickle plate" road crosses the same stream and gulch, there is a long and high tressle-work of iron and steel for the roadway—an elegant and costly structure. The depot of this latter road is only about twenty rods from Dr. George Ellis' residence, and is in the immediate neighborhood where the Ellises settled in 1818.

The following will illustrate the courage, resolution and sound principles of some of the early settlers in that new country:

"Many stories are told of the courage of the women of that early generation which first broke the ground in the forests of Pennsylvania. They were in constant peril from wild beasts and hostile Indians, but with heroic patience endured hardships, labor and disease. An example of another kind of courage is preserved of Christina Dickson, the wife of one of the first settlers of Erie County, Pennsylvania.

She was a small, low voiced woman, extremely timid by nature; but upon one subject she was resolute; she had a horror of drunkenness. She lived in the days when the use of liquor was universal. Whisky was as common as a drink of water among these hardy, hardworking pioneers. A temperance or abstinence society was unheard of. But when her sons were born, she resolved, as far as she could, to put a stop to whisky drinking in her home.

Her husband being absent, her brothers called for the help of the neighbors, according to the custom of the time, to put up a barn needed on her farm. They all assembled and went to work, while she prepared a great dinner. After an hour or two whisky was asked for. One of the brothers came to the house for it; she refused to provide it to make her friends drunk. Her other brothers, and at last an elder in the church, came to reason with her, to tell her she would be accused of meanness. Without a word the little woman went out to the barn, and baring her head stepped upon a log and spoke to them in a faltering voice. "My neighbors," said she, "this is a strange

459

thing. Three of you are my brothers, three of you are elders in the church; all of you are my friends. I have prepared for you the best dinner in my power. If you refuse to raise the barn without liquor so be it. But before I will provide whisky to give you, these timbers shall rot where they lie." The men angrily left the work and went home; the little woman returned to the house, and for hours cried as though her heart would break. But the next day every man came back, went heartily to work, enjoyed her good dinner, and said not a word about whisky.

Afterwards, whisky at barn raisings was discontinued in the county. Her sons grew up strong, vigorous men, who did good work in helping to civilize and Christianize the world; and their descendants are all of high-standing, intellectual, moral men and women. If she had yielded this little point, they might have degenerated, like many of their neighbors, into drunkards and spendthrifts.

There are still vices and maligant customs to be conquered, and for the work we need women of high souls and gentle spirit like Christina Dickson."

EASTON. MASS.

Easton, Mass., is in the northeast corner of Bristol county. About 1690 to 1700 many settlements were made here from families near Boston and Cape Cod. Probably the most numerous familly was the Phillipses—Capt. John Phillips and his brothers and their descendants. The first two families who settled in Ashfield, Richard Ellis and his wife's brother, Thomas Phillips, and their families were from Easton. It is now a flourishing manufacturing town and has long been noted for the immense Ames Shovel Factories. Oakes and Oliver Ames, men of great industry and enterprise, began this business here nearly sixty years ago. One of their descendants, Hon. Oliver Ames, a native of Easton, is now governor of Massachusetts. In 1886 Rev. William L. Chaffin, pastor of the Unitarian church of Easton, wrote and printed a large volume of over 800 pages of the history of Easton. It is a work of great merit and a credit to the town.

CONNERSVILLE, IND.

Connersville, Ind., on Whitewater river, is the county seat of Fayette county, Indiana. The town was organized in 1819. The first settlements were made about 1804 to 1808. John Conner and his family lived here among the Indians in those days. About 1825 Stephen and Moses Ellis (see pages 130 to 132) settled near here, where several of their descendants now live. It is a thriving city of about 4000 population.

CHARACTERISTICS OF THE ELLISES.

In concluding his work, the writer would be glad to give somewhat of the personal traits, or characteristics, of his branch of Ellises, but inasmuch as they probably differ but little, if any, from most of those of their times and localities, and as his acquaintance with them is somewhat limited, whatever is said in this respect need not be greatly extended.

It can, he believes, be said in truth of a great majority, if not all of these people, that they have, in a commendable degree, a strong desire to be and become moral, intelligent and respected citizens of the localities wherever they may chance to live. Industry and persistence in whatever they undertake are also traits worthy of mention. In these respects failure to obtain great results suddenly, gives no disappointment and leads to no relaxation of steady, consistent effort and patient toil. With them, more than with many others, if the expectations of youth and mature years are not fully realized, no discouragement follows, nor is old age soured thereby and rendered complaining; and with some, their most successful efforts and best work comes late in life.

Firmness is also a leading trait of the Ellises. With all there is a becoming desire to be right, to be grounded in correct principles and in truth, and in this will they maintain their position with an unalterable determination and firmness even to obstinacy.

They are, too, a religious people. With the earlier generations the religious sentiment predominated. One hundred years ago books and newspapers were not common, and the literary propensities of the average New Englander had a limited range. The bible was the great book and often the only one in the family. With this all the members became, in time, familiar, and many were devoted students of the sacred volume. The head of the family often became a decided theologian and was not loth to meet in bible argument any adversary. He had very positive and fixed opinions regarding salvation, damnation, infant "sprinkling," immersion, predestination, foreordination, the trinity, or unity, of the Godhead, the co-equality of "God the Son with God the Father," etc., etc. No day was too long, or fair, or business too urgent to interfere with the periodical discussion of these questions. The casual visit of a stranger was soon followed by the usual salutation, or inquiry, "What are your *views?*" meaning his opinions on all the various theological tenets—and often he found one as fully informed and determined as himself, with whom he quickly "locked horns" for, perhaps, a day's discussion, the result of which was only to end where it began, if, indeed, each was not the more fully confirmed in the truth and importance of his own opinions. They were withal a practical people, free from the follies and dissipations which impairs, if not destroys the usefulness of so many in these later times.

In political sentiments all with whom the writer is acquainted, or of whom he has heard, are Republicans, and during the late great rebellion not one was disloyal to the Union.

While the present generation of Ellises is noted for sobriety, it is doubted by some if they, as a whole, maintain the standard of piety, devotion, perseverance and all the general excellencies of their New England ancestors. Without examples of vaulting ambition or astonishing brilliancy, they seem content generally to follow the even tenor of a life of virtue and usefulness, and evidently in the great economy of God and nature they fill well their sphere. Of such it is a credit to be one.

INDEX.

SPECIAL INDEX.

[In the back part of some of these books the binder will insert blank pages in which every family may keep their Family Records. It is hoped that this will be done with completeness and accuracy for generations to come.]

Descendants of Irene Smith (34) and Isaac Alden.

1- **Irene Smith** (34), Sixth Generation from Rev. Henry Smith; and eldest child of Rev. Ebenezer Smith and Remember Ellis, was born at Ashfield, Mass. July 4, 1757. She married, May 18, 1780, Isaac Alden, Eldest Son of David Alden, of Ashfield, and of the Sixth Generation from Pilgrim Alden. Six children were born to them in Ashfield, two of whom, Fanny and Jacob, died there.

In 1794 they removed to Oneida Co, New York, where five children were born. Isaac Alden built and operated mills at Williamstown until 1811, when he was captured by British Soldiers while on a lumbering expedition on the St. Lawrence River, and because of his refusal to swear allegiance to the King, was deported to England, from which exile he did not return to America until 1820. He died at the home of his son, Richard, at Warren, Pa., March 5, 1822. During his absence and for some years after, Irene, his wife, resided with Richard Alden. In 1830-31, she went to the home of her son Isaac, in Claiborne Parish, La., where she died March 14, 1834. The old family Bible of Irene Smith-Alden and her husband is now in the possession of their grandson, Philo Alden, who resides at Osage Mills, Ark., from which is obtained the following record of their Eleven children (a full history of same being contained in the Alden-Smith-Genealogy, published by the writer in 1903):

Seventh Generation.

2. **Philander Alden**, born at Ashfield, Mass., Jan'y. 31, 1782; was drowned in Lake Ontario, July 28, 1810. Married, Dec. 10, 1804, Betsey Hall, of Pownal, Vt. who was born Oct. 8, 1779.

Children:

(13) Harriet Hall
(14) Philander Do.
(15) Philomela.

3.. **Philomela**, born at Ashfield, Dec. 10, 1783; died June (or July) 1861. She married, Aug. 22, 1802, Dr. Joel Rathbun, of Camden, N. Y., born Aug. 20, 1779; died Aug. 23, 1820. She removed to Madison Parish, La., in 1835-40 and resided with her son Joel at whose home she died.

Children:

(20.) Lysander.
(21) Dorliska.
(22) Philomela.
(23) Joshua.
(24) Joel.

4. Joshua Alden, was born at Ashfield, June 10, 1785. He married, Nov. 15, 1827, Louisa Fletcher, of Worcester, Mass, born Nov. 15, 1798; died May 24, 1860. Joshua ran away to sea and was impressed into the British Service. He escaped and went to Chili where he became Captain of a vessel. Resided at Valparaiso until about 1825; when he returned to Asheville, N.Y. He died at Bristol, Ill., Nov. 2, 1846.

    Children:
    (25) Mary Jane.
    (26) Emma Frances.
    (27) Isaac Fletcher.
    (28) Lucy Ann.
    (29) Ellen Cornelia.

5. Pliny Alden. was born at Ashfield, Mar. 28, 1787; married May 27, 1812, Anna Upson, of Litchfield, Ct., born Feby. 26, 1787; died April 2, 1862. He was a farmer and resided at Floyd, N.Y. Died Nov. 14, 1834.

    Children:
    (30) Isaac. (31) Fanny. (32) Henry. (33) Nancy Irene.
    (34) Mary Alma. (35) Philomela & Joshua. (37) Lyman Pliny.

6. Isaac Alden, was born at Ashfield, Feby. 19, 1789. Removed to Claiborne Parish, La. where he married, April 27, 1834, Sallie Henderson, of Tennessee, born —; died Aug. 24, 1848.

    Children:
    (38) John. (39) Infant Son. (40) Isaac.

7. Fanny Alden, born at Ashfield April 2, 1792: died Apr. 4, 1792.

8. Jacob Alden, born Jany 27, 1792; died same date.

9. Hiram Alden. born at Ashfield, Oct. 28, 1792. Removed to N.Y. with his parents; was educated as a physician. Began practice at Asheville, N.Y. Married, Jany. 28, 1816, Melita Huntley, of Rome N. born Oct. 26, 1798; died Sept. 5, 1849. Removed to Michigan in 1834. Member Territorial Legislature 1835–37; died, Detroit, Nov. 26, 1858.

    Children:
    (41) Matilda. (42) Hiram Rathbun. (43) Maria. (44) Irene.
    (45) Eliza Mary. (46) Alma. (47) Isaac Reuben. (48) Philander.
    (49) Willis. (50) Elizabeth. (51) Harriet.

10. Richard Alden. born at Western, N.Y. May 19, 1795. Removed to Russellburg, Pa. in 1826. Married, Jany. 1, 1827, Betsey Newman, of Otsego, N.Y. born Sept. 26, 1801; died April 11, 1894. Removed to Warren, Pa. Served as a magistrate for many years. Died May 2, 1883.

    Children:
    (52) Elizabeth Irene. (53) Isaac Simeon. (54) Lucinda Amelia. (55) Bishop Richard.

to Claiborne Parish, La., married, Jany. 18, 1819, & died June 30, 1833, of yellow fever. Enoch Alde disease June 27, 1855.

Children.

(56) Joshua E. (57) William. (58) Philomel

12. Philo Alden. born at Williamstown, N.J., Ju a Carpenter. Removed to New York City, where 15, 1827, Margaret Ellen Riemer, born July 23, 1805, Removed to Claiborne Parish, La., engaged in on business. Was Depty Sheriff of C— Co.— accide his home, Bellevue, La., Nov. 6, 1866.

Children:

(59) Elizabeth Ellen. (60) Margaret Emeline. (61, (62) Rinaldo. (63) Mary Jane. (64) Irene. (65) ((66) Pauline 2nd. (67) Philo.

Eighth Generation:

13. Harriet Nail Alden, born at Williamstown, & married, Feby, 15, 1837, to John Bell Dinomon, a born Aug. 15, 1792; died ... 1871, Resided & died at Ripley, N.J., July 14, 1876.

Children:

(68) John Bell (69) Henry. (70) Geo. Wash (71) Elizabeth Alden. (72) Susan Bell. (73)

14. Philander L. Alden, born at Williamstown Ran away to sea, Engaged in mining in Calif Mexico, was Col. Comdg. of meurgeuts(?), & fall of 1859. He married a Spanish lad — and had three children — possibly & information can be obtained regarding the here are given as (74), (75), (76),

15. Philomela Alden, was born at Rome, married, at Ripley, N.J., May 6, 1832, to (a Baptist Clergyman of considerable repute, at Pittsfield, Mass., April 2, 1787; died at Rock 1886. She died at Buffalo, N.J. Feby. 10, 1898.

Children:

(77) Adrian Van Horn. (78) Elizabeth Isabella Harriet. (80) Marietta. (81) Minerva Gabrie

16. Rev. Levant Rathbun, was born at Camde He was a Baptist Clergyman of great usefulness ;

18.- Alden Rathbun, was born at Camden, N.Y. Oct. 24, 1808: Where he resided, at the old homestead there, until his death June 10, 1888. He married Sept. 14, 1831, Rosanna Dunbar, of Camden, born Dec. 13, 1809; died Dec. 23, 1877.
Children:
(92) Frances Maria. (93) Edwin Dunbar. (94) Joel E.
(95) D. Henry. (96) Dorliska Hernando. (97) Henry A.
(98) Theodore Frelinghuysen. (99) Matilda.

19. Philander Rathbun, was born at Camden, N.Y., Dec. 10, 1810 and died, unmarried, about 1842.

20. Lysander Rathbun, was born at Camden, N.Y., June 11, 1813. Removed to Miss. about 1840. Married 1st, Ruth Ann Lowther, born in N.Y., May 23, 1826; died Sept. 23, 1851; 2nd, Mary M. King born in 1832; died Apr. 12, 1860. He died at Holly Springs, Miss. Nov. 2, 1862.
Children:
(100) Philander Alden. (101) Morris. (102) Frank.

21.- Dorliska Rathbun, was born at Camden, N.Y. Aug. 22, 1815. Removed to La. Where she married Luther Easton Pratt, born in Vt., in 1815: She died at New Orleans, La., Jany. 23, 1887.
Children:
(103) Edward Eugene. (104) Frances Almedia. (105) Clarence Byron.
(106) Daniel Webster. (107) William Curtis. (108) Helen Ophelia. (109) Sara Belle. (110) Alice Amanutha.

22. Philomela Rathbun, was born in Camden N.Y., Dec. 15, 1817. Removed to La., where she married, 1853, S.P. Day. She died at Minden, La., Sept. 8, 1903. - No Children.

23.- Joshua Rathbun, born at Camden, N.Y., Oct. 5, 1819. Died in infancy.

24.- Joel Rathbun, was born at Camden, N.Y. Jany. 21, 1821. Removed to Madison Parish, La. Died at Poplar Grove, Ark., Jany. 15, 1879. Name of wife not known. Only child known:
(111) Son, born about Oct. 1, 1856.-

25.- Mary Jane Alden born at Ashville, N.Y., Aug. 24, 1848; died in Louisiana, July 15, 1846.

26.- Emma Frances Alden was born at Ashville, N.Y., July 11, 1830. Married, Oct. 13, 1883, Abel Russel Proctor born Methn, Mass., July 29, 1821; died Arlington, Mass. July 7, 1889. - She resides at Fredonia, N.Y. Only surviving descendant of Joshua Alden (4).

27.- Isaac Fletcher Alden, born at Ashville, N.Y., Apr. 14, 1832; died in La., July 21, 1840.

28.- Lucy Ann Alden. born in La., Sept. 2, 1837; died July 18, 1843.

29.- Ellen Cornelia Alden, born in La. June 6, 1839; died June 1, 1840.

30.- Isaac Alden, was born Williamstown, N.Y., Jany. 8, 1813. Married, Mar. 18, 1845, Mary Hopkins, born at Goshen, N.Y. Nov. 11, 1819. He removed to Michigan and located at Coldwater where he engaged in flour milling business. Died there, Feby. 7, 1892. -
Children:
(112) Marian. (113) Willis. (114) Anna.

31.- Fanny Alden, born at Williamstown Feby. 8, 1815; died in infancy.

32.- Henry Alden, born at Williamstown, N.Y., Aug. 16, 1817; died

33. - Nancy Irene Alden, was born at Ahilia
22, 1822. Married, Oct. 16, 1856, Horace
at Marcy, N.Y., May 13, 1820; They reside nea
She is the eldest living descendant of Irene Smith

34. - Mary Alma Alden, was born at Williamst.
1825. Married, May 7, 1846, Horace French, b.
died Mar. 29, 1896. - She resides at Rome, N.
Children:
(115) Anna, (116) Mary E., (117) Lyman Agdi.
(119) Charles (120) Mary Genevieve.

35. Philomela Alden, born at Williamstown, N.Y.,
Cook, farmer, of Coldwater, Mich., born at Jonku
1808; died July 30, 1888. - She died Dec. 11, 18

36. - Joshua Alden, died in infancy.

37. - Lyman Pliny Alden, born at Floyd, N.Y., Sep
Apr. 20, 1863, Lena P. Kidder, born Stratton
For many years engaged in work of Charity - a
Supt of Rose Home, Terre Haute, Ind., when he
Children;
(121) Lena Eva (122) Ernest Gallaher. (12.

38. - — Alden, infant son, born about 1838.

38 - John Alden, born —— died June 4,

40. Isaac Alden, born in Claiborne Parish, Lo

41. - Matilda Alden, born Ashville, N.Y. Dec
Alonzo Waterman, of Coldwater, Mich., Ma
born in 1809; died July 29, 1877. She died
Children,
(124) Mary. (125) Martha. (126) Al
twin daughters.

42. Hiram Rathbun Alden, born at Ashville, N.
Removed to Coldwater, Mich. 1834. Married, Dec. 2
born Aug. 26, 1823; died May 17, 1893. He died S.
May 13, 1863. Children:
(129) Hiram Rathbun, (130) Byron W.

43. Maria Alden, born at Ashville, N.Y. Dec. 28, 18

44. - Irene Alden, born at Ashville, N.Y. June 26.
Jany, 14, 1841. Roland Root; of Coldwater,
1813, died Aug. 11, 1885; She resides at Cold.
Children;
(131) Aurelia Melita, (132) Martha Matilda
(134) Edward, (135) Edward Roland, (136) Flora (137),

2nd to David B. Dennis, Feb. 17, 1890, who was born June 12, 1818, died Apr. 11, 1902. She died May 8, 1895. No Children.

47.– Isaac Reuben Alden, born at Ripley, N.Y., Feb. 22, 1828. Removed to Montana in 1863. Married, Feb. 14, 1864, Frances Jan thaume, born Jany. 5, 1851. Resides Oakland Calif.

Children:
(149) Alma Priscilla. (150) Daniel Webster.

48. Philander Alden, born at Ripley, N.Y., Oct. 15, 1830, Married, Apr. 6, 1856. Jane Mason, born Nov. 15, 1833. Resides Coldwater, Mich.

Children:
(151) Shelby S. (152) Prescott. –

49.– Rev. Willis Alden, born at Ripley, N.Y., Oct. 22, 1832. Removed to Oregon in 1851. Married, Aug. 4, 1894, Alice Bennett, born May 24, 1860; died July 1, 1895. Resides Holland, Oregon. –

50.– Elizabeth Alden, born at Coldwater, Mich., died in infancy.

51. Harriet Alden, born at Coldwater, Mich., Jany. 28, 1835. Married, Dec. 10, 1851. John Sedgwick Lewis, born at Farm= ington, Conn., Sept. 28, 1826. Reside at Jonesville, Mich.

Children:
(153) Annie. (154) Herbert Alden. (155) Belle. (156) Fred Huntley. (157) John Sedgwick.

52.– Elizabeth Irene Alden, born at Russellburg, Pa., Oct. 16, 1831, died Nov. 10, 1833. –